Praise for *Our Child of t...*

'This strong and generous first novel w...
sleeve and embeds all the thrills and chills...
and non-human, emotion...
*Daily Mail*

'Part *ET*, part *Wonder*, part *Snow Child*, it...
combination of science fiction and heart-tugg...
that Stephen King does so well'
*Grazia*

'A pleasing, big-hearted read, its late-1960s setting...
*Financial Times*

'Wholly fresh and intensely gripping. A tightly personal story'
Juliet McKenna, author of the
No.1 bestselling *The Green Man's Heir*

'Sympathetic characterisation and fine storytelling . . .
an optimistic take on the *ET* theme, done without
the schmaltz of the film'
*Guardian*

'An endearing story well told and I would recommend it as
an uplifting tale to read on a dark and stormy winter night'
*My Weekly*

# Our Child of the Stars

## Stephen Cox

Jo Fletcher

BOOKS

First published in Great Britain in 2018
This edition published in 2019 by

Jo Fletcher Books
an imprint of
Quercus Editions Ltd
Carmelite House
50 Victoria Embankment
London EC4Y 0DZ

An Hachette UK company

A CIP catalogue record for this book is available
from the British Library

PB ISBN 978 1 78648 996 8
EB ISBN 978 1 78648 994 4

10 9 8 7 6 5 4 3 2 1

Typeset by CC Book Production

Printed and bound in Great Britain by Clays Ltd, Elcograf S.p.A.

MIX
Paper from
responsible sources
FSC® C104740

Papers used by Quercus Editions Ltd are from well-managed forests and other responsible sources.

To my awesome parents, Peter and Jenny, for everything

# CHAPTER I

# Fall, Year Two

Molly sat by her bedroom window, sewing Cory's Halloween costume. Looking out, Crooked Street was warm in the soft sunlight. Soon the old porches would shine with pumpkin lanterns, heads of orange fire with their savage grins. Long ragged witches and skeletons hung from the gutters and swayed as the wind ruffled the leaves of yellow, red and brown. She loved the sad beauty of fall, the possibilities as summer left and winter came.

The Myers house had been full of Halloween for days. The three of them carved pumpkins while sugar girls wooed their candy boys on the radio. Cory rescued his first brave attempt and now it sat in his bedroom with its quirky, jagged smile. The second magnificent globe would be shown off tonight. Gene and Molly had enjoyed days of Cory's endless chatter, and making things from painted leaves, and Molly's attempts to bake new things from her old *Joy of Cooking* book. Cory couldn't decide between a pirate and a sorcerer, so Molly said at last, 'Be both.' He flailed his arms in excitement. Then he saw how much gold braid she brought back from the shop – two double fistfuls – and he 'want it all-all Mom'. Red and gold – Cory never did half-measures. There was so much small print in being a mother, like racing to finish the costume because not disappointing him mattered.

Molly's stitches were firm, rather than neat. Cory got so antsy and up close, she couldn't sew straight around him. She retreated to the bedroom, with the chair propped under the handle. Gene thought that when he found time he'd mend the lock, but it never quite happened. She smiled, remembering last night, the signal that passed between husband and wife, the chair jamming the door in case Cory came wandering in, as he still did now and then. Last night he'd slept, and it was just Gene and Molly. They made the old moves under the patchwork quilt, with its wild pattern like leaves in fall.

As a child, the jack-o'-lantern was a familiar friend, and yet it still brought a shiver as night fell. Little Molly had loved dressing up as someone else, staying up late to hear scary stories, eating more candy than was good for her and running through the back streets at dusk, kicking up dry papery leaves. She could pretend twisting shadows were real horrors. The years passed and for a while it became more knowing, a game between friends who were hovering at the doors of adulthood. Then Molly put Halloween away, like a favourite toy in an attic box, though she still loved fall when the year ran downhill to the dark. In time, adult joys and adult fears came instead: her first job, a wedding song, the house. And a death.

She shook off a cold shudder. There were things to do.

Childhood was a lost country, something well known but now too distant — but then Cory came: their son, their miracle, and Gene and Molly had found so many things again. Snow angels and Christmas stockings, birthday surprises and fireworks on the Fourth of July. Cory would squat to look at some tiny green flower or stand entranced by the song of a single bird. He adored the day of disguises; he was made for Halloween and it was made for him.

As she sewed, Molly heard him outside in the hallway. That eerie creak could only be Cory swinging from the fold-down attic ladder and the little *pad pad pad* was him running along the corridor and back. You could never mistake that tread for anyone else. Sometimes all went quiet, which might mean Cory was hanging off the stair rail, upside down, to see how long he could do it. Or he might just be rearranging his treasure table in his neat little room. He might be out of the attic window and up onto the roof with his telescope, like some pirate up the mast. Cory often looked out across Amber Grove, official population 18,053 and proud of it, gazing north to the forest with its strange scar.

'Safe Mom, look. Cory too clever to fall.'

But she didn't think he'd fall. It wasn't falling that frightened her.

*Stitch stitch stitch*, the red cloth against her dark slacks. Only a truly formal occasion or the most burning summer could get her in a skirt nowadays.

Their doorbell rang.

At once Molly put down the sewing and moved the chair from the door. She heard Cory scurry up the ladder into the attic and as she entered the corridor, the hatch shut. Cory had heard the bell; he would stay out of sight.

She walked down the stairs, taking care to look for any signs: a left-behind toy, a roller skate. On the walls hung her best photo of Gene's parents, her nursing qualifications, the poster *War is not good for children and other living things* and the smiling portrait of Dr King. What would the Reverend have thought of Cory?

The door had a peephole now, and a thick chain. A lanky werewolf lurked on the porch with his sister, a teenage witch, and a friend, an Egyptian princess . . . These older kids were from down the zig-zag road, good kids, and they did not know Cory existed.

Molly adopted her public face: polite, not unfriendly, but not welcoming either. She picked up the bowl of candy and opened the door. 'You're a little old for this,' she said, a little tarter than she'd intended.

The werewolf looked hungry, but the girls frowned at his outstretched paw.

The princess spoke. 'Oh no, Mrs Myers. We're going to a party. It's just . . . Isaac has run off again. He's a mutt, kind of brown and white, about so big.' She held her hand about two feet off the ground. 'Have you seen him?'

'Sorry, I haven't,' Molly said, pleasant but distant. She knew the dog; she'd seen them walking it.

'He keeps running off,' the witch tried to explain, 'and someone must find him 'cos they keep taking his collar off – do you think any of the kids around here might be doing it?'

'No kids in this house,' Molly said. 'I'll keep an eye out, though.'

The teenagers looked at each other. Far from here, boys and girls not much older than these were marching against the war, protesting the horrors of Vietnam, and dancing in the sun.

Molly's stomach twisted in knots. She'd bet it was Cory 'helping' the dog, and that could expose him. The last thing she wanted was these teens hunting around the back of these houses. This was how it might start, like a spark on dry leaves.

Soft as milk, she said, 'Oh, maybe it's the ghost. Years back, there were three trick-or-treaters who came to a strange old house at the end of the road . . .'

They looked at her, too well brought up to be rude, but still teenagers enough not to laugh.

'Hope you find him soon,' she said, proffering the bowl. The werewolf took a big paw of candies. She shut the door, half hearing a low joke, and some protest from one of the girls.

Up the stairs, back to her bedroom, to finish the job. Cory was nowhere to be seen, and that gave her a moment to shut the door and finish her work.

*Stitch stitch stitch.* Molly shook out the Space-Admiral-Wizard ballgown or whatever it was. You could spot it wasn't even, with bits finished too fast, like it was a race. She needed to check the supper, and this'd have to do.

*Pad pad pad.* When she opened her door, Cory squatted there. He sprang up from the floor like an unfolding frog to his full height. Violet eyes widened as he saw the red sack with arms. He made the *tick-tick-tick* of excitement. His ears went up to ten to two. That was full marks enthusiasm.

'Best costume EVER Mom! Thank-you-thank-you-thank-you!' and he grabbed her in a skinny hug. She put her face down to his and he stroked her cheek with his outer face tentacles, seven-inch fingers the colour of red plums. He popped a sweet little kiss with the inner feelers. 'Very special,' he said. By the end of the day his scent was crushed lemon balm, horses and rain. 'Try-on-now-now-now.'

'Cory, you need to stop bothering the Robertsons' dog. And *don't* take his collar off – that tells them someone with hands is involved.'

He met her gaze and said, 'Playing not-bothering. Poor dog hate collar, Cory only helping . . .'

'Do we have a deal?' as she held out the costume like a prize.

Cory nodded and grabbed it, his rope-like tail swishing. Molly smiled. He didn't care one sleeve was too long, and he must-must find the toy sword, although he'd never hit anyone, it was just for waving. He must practise his casting-spells game, all fierce frowns and nonsense words and fluting noises. She remembered little Molly dressing up in a sheet, her joy at running between dark trees, and the taste of strange candy. Since Cory fell into her life, he'd opened Molly up to live the fun of it all over again. His joy made all that time sewing worth it.

'Where is big pirate hat? When-when we light Pumpkin Jack? Do Russians have Halloweeen? Do Russians have pumpkins? What China people do Halloweeen? Different from us?'

Gene would hate the risk, but she would take a Polaroid, just one, and hide it in their secret place. You couldn't expect a keen photographer not to want snaps of her son.

She walked towards the stairs – but there was Gene's brisk

6

knock on the front door: *shave and a haircut, two bits*. Her tall, dark, bearded librarian was home early, as promised.

'Dad-Dad-Dad!' cried Cory, and holding up his robe with both hands, he was round Molly and down the stairs two at a time. Cory's skin was the colour of lavender milk, the colour of vigour and health. How Molly loved to stroke his long, hairless skull.

On Halloween, he could be hidden. With the gigantic fake beard and the hooded costume and the robes a bit too big . . . he could pass. He'd go out with his only two friends and no one would pay any attention to the child at the back. This was his second Halloween; how special that felt for him, to be out in it, to be part of it this time.

The family embraced, Molly standing on tiptoe to kiss Gene.

*Farewell Angelina* went on the record-player, the LP worn from years of enjoyment. Joan Baez filled the house with music, that extraordinary voice making mournful love to the air so the whole house became sad and beautiful. There were many great singers but she was a family favourite; every time Molly played her records, Cory would sit and sway in time, cooing along, and, maybe later, Gene would reach for his guitar.

Gene pulled on his faded Yankees sweatshirt and grinning, slipping on his glasses, he wove one of his tall tales about a borrower in the library and what sinister thing was under his hat. The story only ended when Cory jumped in his seat and went, 'Ooo ooo Dad teeesing. Dad big liar.'

They ate soup and hot sandwiches, Cory in the costume; he'd probably wear it for days now, even sleep in it. From time to time, Gene rubbed Cory behind one ear, purple with lighter stripes. In shape, his ears were half a piglet's and half some strange shell.

'Light lantern now-now,' Cory pleaded as Gene finished his soup.

Pretend-serious, Gene said, 'Not yet. The sun needs to be further down, so we can see.'

Every family inherits odd rules. Gene, who would listen to some arguments so easily, even change his mind when necessary, insisted that the pumpkin carved with such love could not be lit until today, *the* day.

Cory hopped up and down, flapping long arms and saying, 'Can't-wait-can't-wait!' Molly raised her eyebrows and Gene made a show of checking first his watch, then the window. When these passed some mysterious male test, Gene opened the front door and looked both ways to check the coast was clear. Mr Forster's flag flew across the road; it wouldn't tell. Only a bird or two looked on.

The strange shelf in the porch was perfect for Pumpkin Jack. The adults went first, looking and listening, and then Gene gestured for Cory to come. He helped him stand on a chair, a little stooped, with his hood up, Gene close, in case Cory fell – Cory, their son, who went over rain-slicked roofs and up high trees without fear. They were the last house in the last turn of six, but from habit, Molly kept her eyes fixed on the road, in case someone came.

'Cory big-big, can do it, Dad,' he said with his funny little crease of a frown. Gene lit the foot-long match and handed it over, and solemnly, carefully, Cory did the duty. The candle flickered, and then the pumpkin glowed orange from within.

*Cory must have grown two inches since the Fourth of July*, Molly thought; she should mark the doorway in the hall, with him craning to stand as upright as he could.

There were moments you could live in for ever, too full to speak. Molly rested her head against Gene's shoulder and remembered how they had brought Cory home from the hospital, a secret in the night, without a clue if it would even work.

Cory was a secret. So few people knew and those friends held his life in their hands.

The attic window and the roof looked to the north. You could still see where the Meteor fell, the flaming stone from space that had turned miles of State Forest to flame and smoke, and then to mud and ash. The Meteor brought destruction, it brought Cory, and it changed everything.

## CHAPTER 2

## *Some years earlier*

Winter held Amber Grove in talons of ice, sketching fairy-wings on every tree. Molly and Gene came out of the cinema, where she'd sniggered throughout the space film he'd chosen, his feelings be damned. He'd snorted and sighed.

Cold air burned her throat now, but his familiar arm was warm around her shoulders. 'I've seen kids in the road make up a better story than that,' she said, smiling.

'Okay, sorry, that was garbage. Let's go skating,' Gene said. They walked the length of Main Street, past City Hall, past shops closed for the evening and one heaving bar, until they came to the park. The pond had frozen deep and solid and many people had thought of skating too. They lined up to hire the skates from the wooden hut that sold ice-creams in summer.

They'd been Gene-and-Molly for six months. They'd first met in a basement, painting signs for the demonstration. Gene, walking into a room of people, moved like he'd just rented his body and didn't quite have the hang of it. He was handsome,

11

though the faded clothes were behind the times, and he looked away when their eyes met. But throughout that afternoon, she'd often caught him gazing at her. Maybe he thought that her mouth was too wide. Maybe he'd spotted her only vanity: the popular bottle which kept her hair the golden blonde she had been at five.

She'd discovered Gene was quiet, never the first to speak in the group's discussions, but what he said struck a chord with her. *Imagine the impossible, but keep your feet on the ground.* She contrived to sit near him.

They lived under the shadow of the Bomb, but they believed that the times they were a-changing. Gene and Molly hitched across the state to hear the singers and bands they both loved, whose music was not just beautiful but meant something profound. They'd marched against unjust laws, against the vicious, stupid war and the draft that fed it, against the horrendous weapons which threatened all life on land and sea and sky.

But Gene and Molly argued endlessly too. A trip to New York City revealed his indifference to real art like painting and sculpture; he hated having to be in the endless photos she took of everything. Meanwhile, he couldn't believe she was so quick to sneer at the bands taking risks and breaking new ground. Sometimes, with a few old friends he trusted not to mock, Gene would pick up his guitar and play their favourites, love songs and protest songs, singing in his light, ordinary tenor.

They had been on other dates, but this one felt special. On the pond people swooped, trailing the white memory of their breath, laughing and shouting as they bumped into each other. Some walked on the ice like new-born foals. Molly saw a teenager take a tumble and heard a so-called friend cheer. Gene was all legs and arms, so skating might be embarrassing.

'I haven't done this for years,' Molly said, taking a few hobbled steps to the edge. He held her hand so she could step safely onto the ice.

Like riding a bike, you couldn't forget – then he zigged and zagged away, competent and picking up speed, and she accepted the dare, beginning the chase and gaining confidence as her body remembered. How different his movements were now; even when he was showing off she forgave him.

He grinned as she caught up. 'The creek behind the farm froze every year.'

She thought, *A man who can skate can learn to dance.*

Above them the Moon was almost full, haloed with ice. Soon she'd taste his mouth and he'd taste hers, familiar and exciting all at once.

Out on the pond, a dark-haired mother was helping a little girl of perhaps six. The woman held the girl's hands in hers, her face shining with encouragement. The girl looked down at her feet and up at her mother, fear and hope balanced. Molly wished she'd brought her camera to capture the moment.

Gene smiled; he often smiled at children. He wanted a family too. Already, something burned in her heart. *Please, please, please.*

They sat very close on a cold bench, making clouds with each breath. Her face burned with cold as she sipped hot chocolate, admiring the Moon. It made her remember her years in the bustle of Brooklyn. Out here in Amber Grove, she could get away from electric light and wonder at the stars blazing, filling the night with glory.

She went back to their old argument. 'Put a man in a tin can and whizz him around the Earth, what good does that do?' she asked. 'They'll send soldiers to the Moon, with bombs, so every time we look up we'll see the threat of war. We'll spread death through the stars like a disease.'

He took her hand, as he did at any excuse. 'Humans got here by being willing to look over the next hill, to risk crossing the next sea. Space is the next place to go.'

'People down here need real help now: clean water and safe births and a hundred vile diseases to conquer,' she said. She was glad to be there right then, with him.

He looked up at the sky. 'We'll live to see people living on the Moon. There'll be a city run by the United Nations, for science and peace and exploration. Weapons will be banned, it'll be a place of kindness, so when we gaze up at it, we'll see hope. In fact, maybe they'll get a woman to run it.'

'You idiot,' she said, touched by his vision. If he didn't kiss her soon, she'd make the move herself.

'You know, the film was okay. As a metaphor, the flying lizard people worked,' he said, his eyes sparkling behind the glasses.

She gave him a little punch on the shoulder. She didn't want to talk disintegrator rays and whether those trashy books he read could ever be art, so she shut him up with her eager mouth. That kiss told her. She decided beyond all doubt: this man who believed in spaceships and aliens and justice and world peace was the one for her.

Molly waited, barely patient, for him to propose. It took Gene until that long hot summer when President Johnson stepped up the bombing in Vietnam. There in his tiny apartment which smelled of the laundry below, he did it with his guitar and a song, 'Molly Skating on the Moon'. With tears in her eyes she said of course she would marry him, what took him so long? She didn't know he wrote his own songs, the most beautiful thing anyone had ever done for her. He pulled faces and said none of his stuff was any good.

The first person she told about the wedding was sharp-nosed, brown-eyed Janice Henderson, her best friend from nursing school; she had a dirty laugh and a spine of steel. Janice's neighbour Diane came over to share the celebration. She taught in middle school, Amber Grove's first black teacher, and you just knew no mean boy would dare pull braids in her class. She'd lost her husband the year before, a lean, healthy man whose heart just stopped, leaving her and three kids; one of those tragedies that made so little sense.

The women saw a future bright and just and full of hope. They shared fierce books and articles about how things had to change for women and the world; they drank and they argued. Sometimes, Molly remembered, the three friends danced, just them, drunk in the kitchen at midnight. Gene liked her friends, but a couple of times he'd commented, 'Hey, you and Janice can really put the booze away. Jeez, I couldn't drink like that.'

Molly thought marriage mattered – not what they spent or whether they had a honeymoon, but the *act* of it; their promises before the people who mattered to them.

It was the second winter they'd been together. Her wedding day dawned very cold, the sky the bright blue of the brooch Gene's mother had lent her. Molly's cream dress was too tight.

She was so nervous she had nothing but Scotch for breakfast. Gene's father walked her into City Hall – her own parents had taken their frigid judgements to sunny Florida years ago, and good riddance.

Gene stood grinning in his best suit, with the flower in his lapel crooked. He was the one for her. The people they loved had come to support them and neither of them tripped over the words. Then off to dance, to his choices and hers: 'Stop in the Name of Love', the Temptations and the Supremes. Peter, Paul and Mary, the Byrds, the Beatles and the Stones.

Hours later, it was Janice who said, 'They'll have to put the old Baker place up for sale soon. It's a ruin, so it should be cheap. We could be neighbours.'

The first warm day of spring. Crooked Street ran right up to the drop, that sharp slope of trees too steep to build on. Down there was the disused railroad line and then the meadows, a square mile of scrub, old walls and little creeks. Number forty-seven was the last house in the last turn, six houses half surrounded by the woods. With those gables and that porch, it should have been made of gingerbread.

Gene chuckled. 'Looks a tad Addams Family. This place hasn't seen any love for years.' Creepers swamped the fences, two windows were boarded up and paint peeled on the front door.

The portly lady realtor in bright blue could spot newlyweds at a hundred paces. She chatted away as she stepped onto the porch and they heard the boards groan. When she opened the door, something scurried away.

16

Stairs creaked and they fought to open doors. The whole place smelled damp; mould had left green messages across the wall. Its last makeover was probably in Roosevelt's time. But as Molly explored, she recognised her home-in-waiting; it was Cinderella by the fire.

'I smell rot,' Gene said. 'What's wrong with the roof?'

The realtor's bright smile got brighter. 'The kitchen has real potential. And the woods make it lovely and quiet.'

Molly signalled Gene with five fingers behind her back. Five was 'adore'. Gene gave her a three, with that twist of the eyebrows she knew well.

Gene played the hard cop, but the realtor knew you always sold to the wife. 'Look, wouldn't this make the most darling nursery ever?' she said, opening a door with a flourish. Yes, it would, with the view over the overgrown yard, then through big old trees; she'd paint it blue for a boy, pink for a girl.

Molly hugged Gene, full of wild baby-making thoughts.

'I'll be honest,' the realtor said, 'the place is a fixer-upper. Yes, it needs work. But the executors want a brisk sale, so that's in the price.'

'You're kidding,' Gene said. 'I mean, it's got a certain ruined grandeur and it's not a bad size. But it's a three-legged horse – it's what's missing that matters. That roof worries me . . .'

That evening, Gene drove them to one of their secluded places to talk over the cost. He had bought an old mud-green Ford, which already bore a new scar. Sober and on a fine day, he had misjudged a turn and scraped a wall.

Molly touched his home repair and felt a tiny whining mosquito of anger. *Don't spoil the mood.*

They sat on the hood of the wounded car, looked up at the heavens and talked for twenty minutes or more as they tried to decide.

Then Molly pointed. 'Look! A shooting star!' A rock burned in the sky, just a bright hairline streak of falling silver.

'Make a wish,' Gene said, joking, 'but don't tell me, or it won't come true.'

She kissed him and thought it already had. Everything was possible.

Gene and Molly told themselves it was a bargain if they did the repairs themselves. For months, they lived among crates and ladders and dustsheets and when they went to work, they smelled of fresh paint and old dust, no matter how much they showered. Gene slogged away at it every evening and all weekend, his dark hair dripping with sweat, while Molly worked extra shifts at the hospital to keep ahead of the bills.

Their first evening, Molly, Diane and Janice had sat on boxes and toasted Molly's new home. Janice drank soda, pulling a face; she was pregnant again and alcohol made her ill. It had taken them years to conceive again after Chuck was born.

Friends helped when they could: Gene's dad came down and the men fixed the roof with few words between them and no beer until afterwards. Molly stripped paper at midnight and, half-asleep, rolled paint onto everything. Sometimes Molly and Gene, exhausted, quarrelled about nothing, but they solved every problem under their old patchwork quilt.

Soon after moving in, one breakfast in that old-fashioned

kitchen when she was tired and queasy and had a long shift ahead, she snapped, 'If you want bacon, cook it yourself.'

'Are you okay?' he asked, and after a moment's fear, she took the plunge.

'I'm, you know, late.' She wanted to conceive so much, but there had been a false alarm before which had brought disappointment so deep it shook her.

Gene held her and the seconds rolled on and on. 'See the doctor,' he said at last. 'If it's not this time, well, it's fun to keep trying. It'll happen.'

Soon, even a whiff of alcohol made Molly ill. Every morning the sun came up with a song and she'd be bent over a basin in a horrible and joyful sort of way. Gene wanted to touch her belly all the time.

*It's a girl*, Molly said, she just knew, and they argued about names. She'd feed the baby the natural way; the baby would drink love from her own body.

Gene's blue eyes, her hazel – the baby might have either.

The busy weeks passed, she felt the baby move and the whole world changed after that. The leaves out back started to colour, one or two canary or scarlet. Molly dreamed of a bright birthday with the trees in bloom, her daughter blowing out her candles under the flowers. What a strange new world the girl would inherit.

There were no portents of doom, no croaking crows or sinister shadows. Gene was working, bleary-eyed, and Molly was up a step-ladder, half-asleep, finishing the nursery – sunshine yellow, in case it turned out to be a boy, but she'd filled a drawer with pretty things for when she was proved right.

Someone ran a sword into her side, a burning sword, and she thought she'd faint. She swayed on the ladder but didn't fall. No pain would let her risk that. Clinging to the steps, then the banister, while the beast gnawed at her guts, she made the long march to the phone downstairs.

By the time the ambulance came Molly was on the floor, coming around from the faint, sobbing with pain. Her baggy overalls were smeared with yellow paint, but Molly's hand was daubed with red.

'Call Gene,' she sobbed, 'call Gene.'

## CHAPTER 3

# *Two cursed years*

Someone folded up the sunshine and put it away. Dark clouds rolled down from the north and filled the marriage bed. The joy drained out of the music Molly and Gene had so loved, through the cracks between the boards and down into the earth.

When they came home from the hospital, Molly stood in front of their house, the place where it happened, with Gene's strong arm around her shoulder.

She hadn't given her lost girl a name. In her grief, she hadn't been able to decide, so the child was cremated without one. That failure ached.

'I'll get the door,' Gene said, and Molly felt more tears bubble up. Would they ever stop?

In the weeks that followed, even waking up felt like a betrayal. Molly walked away from the work she loved because she couldn't face the sick and dying. Worse was seeing a healthy baby in its mother's arms: that was a wound.

The doctor wrote her a prescription for pills that stopped her feeling anything at all, except empty-headed and dry-mouthed. She existed, that was all, too dead to rise before Gene left the house or to stay awake for his return. She couldn't choose which book to read, or between two cans of beans in the supermarket. Trees, sunsets and pretty girls' dresses all turned to washed-out grey.

After three weeks, she flushed the pills down the toilet and reached for a bottle of Scotch, making a different choice to dull the pain. So days ran into nights and then into months.

One blurry day among many, she woke in their bedroom, confused by the dim evening light. Gene stood by the bed with a tray. The acid taste of vomit clung to her mouth and nose, but she didn't remember being sick. She must've passed out and he'd washed her and got her to bed. Tomato soup steamed in one of their best china bowls, buttered toast beside it on the matching side plate. Her stomach revolted and her head rang. She smelled of sick people and she was thirsty.

'You've got to stop drinking,' he said, red-eyed. 'Coming home to find you like that? I'm worried half to death.'

'I'm a grown-up,' she snapped. 'You're not my mother. Leave me alone.'

'Eat something and we'll talk,' Gene said. 'I thought this'd be good for your stomach . . .'

'I need a proper drink. I don't want to talk.'

He sighed. She hated the conversation he'd start – she knew it by heart now. Janice and Diane said the same things: none of the doctors thought it hopeless. There was a famous specialist in New York City. They'd find the money. He'd always thought adoption was a cool, loving thing to do. He held a childlike faith that she could do it, that she could be a mother.

Molly seethed with rage because *he did not understand.* She might feel a new life stir inside her and then have to live through another death. She couldn't dare to hope again.

'I'm not a damn car to be fixed.' She shoved the tray away and the bowl toppled over the edge of the bed and smashed. Red soup sloshed over the carpet.

'Hell. I'll sort that.' Frowning, Gene went off.

Molly rolled out of bed and knelt. She felt disgusting; the hand tremor was back and she thought she might throw up again, even though her guts were empty. A small drink would settle her.

The half-full bottle of Scotch wasn't under the bed. She looked again. She was forgetting things nowadays, but she knew she'd left it there. It was the last of six she'd bought in Bradleyburg, hoping she'd be less conspicuous in the bigger town.

Gene stood in the doorway holding a wet towel.

'Where in hell did you put it?' she said, levering herself up.

'I poured it down the sink, and the bottle downstairs too. Don't move, you'll cut your feet.'

'Good,' Molly said, shoving past him.

A few days later, it was raining. She'd screamed and shouted at him, at death and at the sky, and now Gene shouted back, and slammed doors. She just wanted to sleep and not wake up, or be so drunk she couldn't tell the difference.

They stood at the back door, looking out at the tangled garden and the tall fences. Rain ran off the piebald leaves, like the trees had lost their child too. Molly felt washed out with crying, empty and hollow. Without Gene's strong arms around her she could've dissolved herself in Scotch and poured herself away.

She needed him, always, but he had to leave her wounds alone.

Gene grieved like a dying animal, out of sight. Sometimes she heard a groan, or choking gasps, but if she dared mention it, he would walk away. He played the radio loud to shut her out, or he retreated to the attic. There were nights he left the house. He started smoking again; she loathed the smell that permeated the house. Gene's parents came and John took him away to do whatever men do about grief – fishing, maybe, long silences by quiet water – while Eva sat for hours at the kitchen table, holding Molly's hands. Janice and Diane came too, and listened and talked, holding her head above water, for a while. They had both known grief and understood it, although not the death of a child.

The nights grew longer and her heart grew bleaker. And it didn't stop.

She wanted to work – at least, part of her did – but the wards now raised such dread in her. Fall turned to winter and many people faded from their lives. The phone rang less often, so staggering down the cold stairs, Molly wondered, *Who calls at five in the morning?* But it was Roy, Janice's husband, calling from the hospital: their twins had decided to arrive a few weeks early.

Molly said the right things, hung up the phone and wiped away tears.

Later, she stood in the flower shop, trying to decide. Janice liked her flowers loud and colourful. She raised an explosive bunch of red and orange blooms to her nose, but they smelled of nothing. What had she expected?

She parked in the hospital lot, determined to be on time. Janice would be glad of a visit, because hospitals reeked of boredom as much as disinfectant. She was so pleased for her friend, but just looking at the building brought everything back. The cold north wind blew straight into Molly's heart. She sat in the car and just breathed, in and out, in and out, for twenty minutes, until the chill air got too much to bear.

Janice had argued herself a corner bed with a little more privacy than the rest. She looked exhausted, but she and the girls were fine. Above her head hung a vast picture, a loving scrawl which showed Chuck had already been in to see his new sisters.

'I love these flowers!' Janice said, then, 'It's such nonsense to keep the babies and mothers apart.' They had read books together that wanted women back in charge of birth. 'They could stick them in a little crib right here. Male doctors have turned pregnancy and having babies into an illness . . .'

Molly felt a prickle of tears come, *how stupid*.

Janice's face turned to one of horror. 'Molly, I'm sorry . . .'

'I'm fine,' she said, biting the inside of her cheek, just a little, enough to help her keep it together. 'I agree, it's ridiculous.'

Janice used her mix of force and sweetness to get the nurse to bring her the twins, Alice and Tammy. They slept on as Molly cuddled one, wrapped in white, and stared at that unmade look of a brand-new baby: the little pouty mouth, eyes shut like kittens. Both were perfect pink, with tiny tufts of their father's copper hair. She found more bright things to say, more obvious questions, while she ached inside. She understood, deep in her guts, how that crazy lady had walked into the hospital three years back and tried to steal a baby.

Janice looked at her. 'How've you been?' Janice's friends didn't keep their secrets long.

'Well, no one's burned down my house. I think Gene's finding it tough. Roy should take him out for a beer.' Recently the thought would not go away, that Gene would be happier married to someone else.

'He did, last week. Gene's worried sick about you. About the drinking. He said you've said some crazy things.'

'Gene worries too much.' She should be angry with Gene, telling tales outside the marriage, but she felt nothing, just more tears threatening. She fought to keep them in, determined not to spoil the moment or wake the babies. Janice looked tired and Molly didn't want to burden her. 'This isn't your problem,' she added. 'Roy and Chuck and these great girls, that's enough to deal with. We'll survive, Gene and I.'

Janice's eyes were moist too as Molly stroked one little Henderson forehead with a finger.

Molly added, 'I'll bounce back, you'll see. Gene and I will fight through.' And as she said, 'We're pretty tough, you know!' the thought swam up, as it had too many times: *Why fight?* Why not just let the darkness rise and take her away?

'Let me show you what I found for them – here, can you hold both girls at once? I wouldn't want to drop one.' She'd bought toys and clothes from the department store in Bradleyburg, not the stuff she'd so carefully collected for her own child. She'd never give that away.

When visiting hours were over, Molly drove back the long

way through cold fields, remembering that perfect velvet evening when she and Gene decided to buy the house, that shooting star and the naïve wish she'd made. That Molly felt like a different person, the Molly who thought life was just beginning: so young, such a fool to hope.

Those thoughts came. Take the hose-pipe from out back and run the exhaust into the car, in a sealed space like a garage. It would be like going to sleep. Or she could go back to work and steal drugs. She hated incompetence; there'd be no half measures if she decided to end it.

Bleak months passed before Molly told Gene about those dangerous thoughts. Holding him, she knew she needed to find purpose, to turn herself outwards. Bit by bit, this came.

Now she longed for her work, her passion, and she fought to persuade them she was well. She put on the starched white dress and stiff white hat and returned to the wards. There was comfort in efficiency and routine, and in the certainty of a job well done. It wasn't easy, and there were days when even looking at the hospital entrance still brought a savage catch to her throat, but she took strength and pride in what she did. She couldn't fix the world, but she could help those people in front of her. When things went badly, when medicine could do no more, at least she could wait with the families in the dark. Her church-going days were long past but she thought sometimes of those grieving women waiting at the foot of the cross.

She planted an ornamental cherry tree in her garden, cosseting it with straw against the worst winter could do. It flowered each spring, pink for a girl, and its survival gave her hope.

Seasons came and went and came again. Across the country strange winds blew, whipping away old certainties and blowing in peacock clothes and rainbow words. People spoke up who'd long been silenced, although some were answered with billy-clubs and teargas. Dr Martin Luther King, Molly's great prophet of peace and hope and justice, was gunned down, then someone shot Bobby Kennedy, the younger brother, who had turned against the war. In tears, she watched the cities burn in retribution and heard the new voices that said change must come in fire and blood. It was the best of times, it was the worst of times and no one knew where the country was headed.

She watched Gene grow colder, until the evening a bitter wind stripped the last leaves from the trees, he came to her and confessed about *that woman*: what he had done, and almost done. Molly screamed and slapped him and raged at him until even she was frightened to be so out of control. He took the punishment, not trying to defend himself, until she ordered him from the house.

Gene told her he had changed his mind at the motel room door. She always knew when he was lying and even in her fury, she believed him. He had betrayed her, but only in heart and soul and not in body.

It was a fragile straw, but she clung to it. Gene had confessed and made no excuses. He swore he wanted to save their marriage – he had not actually screwed that scheming woman. Nine days later, still barely able to speak, Molly let Gene return, but to the spare bedroom. It was a month before she would let him touch her.

In January, a new President took the oath: a grey man who'd come back from the political dead. That jowly politician gave his dishonest smile and claimed he had a special plan to end the war — yet still the young men were sent out to drop fire on villages and to kill and to die in the mud.

The world was full of news, the year they said America would put men on the Moon.

That morning, a cold Tuesday in April, she finished her long, tiring shift on the hospital's fifth floor. The work drained her, but it was still a good shift, of sorts.

She walked across Founders Green to the red-brick diner. Francine's smelled of coffee and bacon and toast. It was the unofficial centre of the town; more business was done there than anywhere in City Hall. Francine herself grew greyer and wider each year, although she was never seen to eat. On the wall hung the black-framed picture of her only son, in uniform, with his Purple Heart. They had brought him back from Korea in a box.

She was looking forward to seeing Gene. This meal would be his breakfast and her supper. Gene needed his sleep — she'd never met a man so desperate for eight uninterrupted hours — but here he was, rising from behind their usual table.

Gene kissed her on the cheek. Together, they sat and he put an awkward hand on hers. Just months ago, she'd have found some excuse to brush him off.

He made his old joke about her nurse's hat, then, hopeful, said, 'It's been like a shipwreck. I don't believe how tough it's been. But since New Year, I feel we've reached some kind of land. Don't you?'

She took his hand and squeezed it. 'I think so.' Life would never be great again, so why should she expect to feel as she did before? But this was okay. All you could do was take it a day at a time.

'Sixty-four days sober,' she said, to encourage him. She was twenty pounds heavier than on her wedding day, but nothing comes free. *Stay sober, stay working, stay married.*

'That's great,' he said, smiling just a little bit more. 'Do the meetings still help?'

Molly shrugged. Perhaps those AA meetings in the damp church hall made a difference, although she struggled with the piety she didn't feel around a Higher Power she didn't believe in. She thought what helped was just the people: they had a raw human need, they stared into the abyss together and somehow, they helped each other, one day at a time. Molly's sponsor was a strange woman, but she had written a beautiful, impossible letter. 'You can't help stop war in the world unless you end the war inside yourself.'

After Gene's betrayal, she'd moved to night shifts, to punish him and to banish him from her bed. It was time to make it right.

'Working nights is too hard on both of us. I'll talk to Sister tomorrow, although it might take a while to move back to a day shift.'

'Great.' He grinned, as he used to do. 'Maybe "Better Times" after all.'

He had written that song at New Year, how he still wanted

her, how sorry he was and how he still had hope for the future. He had played on his guitar, all thumbs from nerves, and it had made her cry. Taking him back had been the right thing.

'Baby steps, Gene. Don't let's pretend it will all be the same.'

'Things will be better,' he said. 'I know they will.'

'Everyday People' played on the radio.

## CHAPTER 4

# *Meteor Day*

No one in Amber County would ever forget that cold spring day, clear, but with cloud due from the north. Everyone had their Meteor Day story, but Molly believed hers was the strangest of all.

She ate an afternoon breakfast in the kitchen. When Gene left that morning, without waking her, he'd left a children's book on the kitchen table, about a talking walrus. He'd added a note with a badly drawn lady walrus that had made her laugh.

She smiled at the memory of how they'd made love on Sunday, gentle forgiveness. Then she went outside to fix the porch light. She'd been asking Gene to do it for weeks. Now she wanted it done.

It was a day, an hour, a minute like any other. Then, in a heartbeat, the light changed behind her. Molly glanced up and saw the Meteor rip open the sky like a flaming sword. Of course she had no idea what it was: this strange blazing moon falling to the north, trailing fire and smoke and smaller fragments across the blue . . .

*I'm going to die.* Her heart went wild and the light bulb dropped from her fingers to shatter on the porch. *It's the end of the world. They've gone crazy and launched the Bomb. It's the end — the end for everyone.*

A few moments later noise slammed into her and the sky became thunder. She fell to her knees.

Then came the impact and the world shook like a bucking horse. Molly grabbed the porch pillar and held on.

A second roar — a second gale. She should've taken cover, stupid not to; she should've covered her face so as not to be blinded, but the sheer impossibility of whatever it was had stopped her thinking. Her head ringing from the noise, she tasted blood.

A giant tree of black smoke rose in the north.

Whatever it was must have missed the town, but she had to check. She ran up the road, past those few houses before the road dipped down and she could look out at a picture-postcard view of Amber Grove. Yes, the big strike was north, but smaller things, like half a dozen comets, had struck right in the guts of the town and now plumes of smoke were rising from somewhere on the Green, near Gene's library. Her skin crawled.

A siren wailed.

Molly ran back inside, dialled the library and hung onto the phone. It rang and rang, for ten minutes or more, but she didn't give up, even as she wondered if she should drive in to look for Gene or report to the hospital. There'd been the chaos of the derailment when she was in high school . . . She had been a volunteer in the hospital, a candy-striper; the memory told her the hospital would need everyone they could get – but first aid would be needed in the middle of town too.

If that was the Bomb, fallout was coming. Man's towering achievement was invisible poison in the air to destroy children yet unborn. Perhaps she should hide away.

At last, a young woman's voice buzzed down the telephone line. 'L-library . . .'

It was the new assistant. Evie? Emmie? 'It's Molly Myers – where's Gene? Is he hurt—'

'He went out to help,' the girl gabbled. 'There's a big fire on Main Street – I can see it – and more, there're fires all over town . . . There's only me here—'

'Listen, I need you to get him a message, okay? Tell him not to be stupid. Let the damn place burn down.'

'But people are hurt,' the girl said, suddenly showing a hint of backbone, 'and they need to stop the fires spreading.'

Molly breathed. Of course Gene wouldn't stop, not if someone was in danger. And anyway, how could she argue with him third-hand?

'Tell him I'm going to the hospital – tell him I love him, will you? And don't take any risks.'

'I'm scared,' the woman said. *Evelyn.*

'Here's the secret.' Molly tried to keep her voice calm. 'We're all scared. Breathe, take one step at a time. You're doing a good job.'

She felt good, saying that. Almost as soon as she hung up, the phone rang.

'Nurse Myers, are you coming in?'

'On my way.'

She grabbed her first-aid kit and a clean uniform; it always reassured patients, knowing who was who. She slammed the car door, gunned the engine and took the back roads, skirting the town. To the north that vast threatening column of smoke hung like their own volcano, or a spreading black funeral tree. The impact site must be in the woods where Gene took her walking, near Two Mile Lake.

Horns honked and sirens wailed, an angry chorus of metal voices. *Gene will be all right*, she told herself. *Gene won't take any risks.*

This was going to be worse than the derailment ten years back, when the train had hit a car, some three miles from town. All those fires and rocks falling from the sky – how could the firefighters battle on so many fronts at once?

She still remembered the man who'd lost a leg, bleeding out five feet from her while the professionals sought to save him. Although she'd been frightened and sick to her stomach, she had truly understood her calling. In that moment, the younger Molly had stepped forward, pretending a calm she did not feel, to act.

She almost missed the old man standing shaking by the road-side, his toothless mouth gaping, his bleeding hands held out in entreaty. He was just standing there barefoot in a dressing gown. She couldn't see any house, but he must've come from somewhere. She braked, and her work began.

Out of the car, the wind brought the stench of smoke: the end of the world stank of petrol and burning tyres, like a hundred junkyards in flames. And still the great tower of darkness grew where the blazing thing had fallen. Her mother always said the world would end with a falling star.

★

Meteor Day slipped into endless night. Cold rain streaked every hospital window black with ash. Molly worked alongside many others, setting up a casualty station in the hospital coffee shop; there were cheery plastic daisies everywhere, but it was the smells of smoke and disinfectant that fought for dominance. Every chair was taken; there was nowhere else to put people who'd crashed their cars or who'd been hit by debris and who weren't going to get worse for a while. Outside she could see yet another damn fool sheep wandering loose. A farmer had brought in an injured neighbour on their truck – but who'd been stupid enough to let his livestock out?

As her grandma had always said, *It's only help if it's helpful*. Molly's team was a long-retired doctor, half blind but still reassuring; some Girl Scout den mother, half an adequate first-aider as long as Molly checked her work, and a peroxide teenage candy-striper straight off a bubble-gum poster. The girl wiped her eyes and set her little girl's chin. 'Just tell me what to do, Mrs Myers.' They looked at each other and the girl grew four years and a couple of inches in that moment. *God bless the women who have it*, thought Molly, *for they'll save the world*.

Burst eardrums, cuts and burns, broken bones . . . the County Treasurer, bleeding from the mouth, went into cardiac failure. Molly gave him CPR and brought him back.

She washed her hands, readying herself for the next round. And Gene walked in, ragged and dirty and smiling. The trousers of his best work suit were torn beyond repair and his hands were bandaged, not very well. Her heart gave a little leap, like old times.

'You're busy, Molly-moo,' he said.

She wiped a smudge of soot from below his hairline. 'Not too busy to see you.' It wasn't private, but they found a corner where they hugged, reassuring each other without words. Their bodies had long memories and forgave more easily.

'You idiot. You should've stayed out of it.'

Gene frowned. 'It's madness out there. They think it was a massive meteor, not a Russian attack. Empire State Gas went up in flames, there was a tanker . . . Molly, there are fires *everywhere* . . . and this giant rock ploughed up the Green.' He paused for a moment, then dropped his voice. 'Sol Rosenthal died, getting some kid out of a burning car. What a guy.'

The chief firefighter, a likeable guy: the first of the named dead. Then Molly shuddered as she took in Gene's words: a few hundred yards closer and that space rock would have destroyed the library. For a moment, she froze in the thought of Gene's death.

She stroked the back of his neck. 'I'm needed here, darling. Take the car. Don't drive through town, okay?'

Their hands touched as she passed the keys. *Don't say, drive safely. Don't think of his mishaps driving.*

'Get some sleep when you can,' he said. 'I guess I won't see you for a bit, but look after yourself too.'

Back to her duties: save the world one nosebleed at a time. She kissed him properly, the audience be damned.


Midnight in the casualty station and Sister Pearce strode in, short, grey-haired and sour. Their feud was old and fierce. Molly called her Sister Barracuda behind her back.

Pearce handed over cow-eyed, sulking Nurse Hooton, who

was looking sick and sullen. There was always one student in every class who disgraced herself throwing up in the operating theatre.

Sister rubbed tired eyes. 'Doctor, if you have any trouble with Hooton, send her home. You'd think people would make some sort of an effort in an emergency. Nurse Myers, we have a problem on the isolation unit. You're tough, you're smart and you'll keep your mouth shut.' That was an order.

They went to the fifth floor. Outside the door, Pearce said, from nowhere, 'I was going to fire you.'

Molly blinked; the only surprise was that Sister had said it out loud.

'You got sloppy.' Molly had never seen the stern leader of the fifth floor look so anxious and uncertain. 'But I knew . . . I *hoped* . . . That's why I gave you another chance.' She went on, 'I think I was right, but now I need you at your best. It's unbelievable – and a secret. I mean it: you cannot talk to *anyone*. Do you understand me?' Almost under her breath, she added, 'We're stretched so thin . . . Hooton is weak, but I had no one else.'

Molly wasn't sure if she was more curious than worried. 'What is it, Sister?'

'I'll have to show you.'

Pearce led the way to the end isolation room, like all of them with an outer space for staff to robe up and prepare, the inner room for the patient. The blind was down. As they went through the rigorous counter-infection procedures, Molly noted a child-sized shape on the bed. It was only when she entered the inner room and drew closer that she saw, and her mind stumbled. The thing on the bed, whatever it was, wasn't right. The face had two fistfuls of tentacles, a rich reddish-purple colour. Molly's mouth opened, then clamped shut in disgust and shock, with curiosity bringing up the rear. Those thick worms longer than fingers were obscuring where a mouth might be. Did it even have a mouth?

For a moment, Molly wondered if this was some sick joke, a puppet to make a fool of her. Then it coughed, and the tentacles writhed for long seconds before falling still. The skin was an unhealthy grey colour and covered with a light oily sheen. She took two steps closer. The creature twisted. Its eyes had white films, like inner eyelids. Somehow, it reminded her of a child on the edge of fevered sleep. But it was *very* strange . . .

The thing gave a low moan. '*Cor-cor-cor* . . .' Was that speech? There was a silver device on its wrist, but even a monkey could wear a watch.

Those tentacles were the biggest shock. She came another step closer, wanting to see if they were really part of it. She couldn't know then that they were like fingers, so dextrous he could use them to put in cufflinks, and part of the wonderful openness of his expression.

She started when Sister Pearce broke into her thoughts, saying, 'Yes, it's real and, yes, it comes from space. We've treated the wounds, but there's something else wrong and we don't know what. The mother's in the next room.' Molly had never heard Sister Pearce's voice so strained. 'Her breathing is very weak now . . . She's going to die.'

Far away, a bell rang. Molly forced her attention back to the thing on the bed.

'This one's sweating, so we're guessing it's too hot, but that is just a guess. Now, infection control.' Pearce ran through procedure like Molly was a raw student. She must've been wearing her 'dumb insolence' face because Pearce suddenly snapped, 'It came from another planet. It may not have immunity to Earth diseases.'

*Ah.*

'Yes, Sister, good point.'

'The fever's been getting worse since Sheriff Olsen and Dr Jarman found them. Who knows if we're immune to what they carry? It might be like Indians and smallpox – we might be putting the lives of millions at risk of a space plague.'

'Yes, Sister.' *Be professional.* 'So how will we know what medications we can give it? Or what to feed it? Or how much?'

'Boiled water is safe and we've got a few alien drugs, pain relief and the like, and some food. Dr Jarman's still trying to save the adult. Administration don't know and they're not to be told. I guess we've got until tomorrow morning before they figure it out. Lord knows what'll happen then.'

*Rocks and fire and thunder from the sky!* Unlike Gene, Molly had never wasted time worrying about aliens. They didn't exist or they weren't here, so either way they weren't a problem. Like God really. But here was a creature who was breathing and moaning and it needed her care.

Sister Pearce looked down at the creature, then left.

*A patient is a patient,* Molly told herself, just like any one of the dozens of others she'd helped tonight. She began by sponge-bathing the alien and brought her masked face down to see if the diaper needed changing. Nursing was so glamorous!

It smelled rank, sharp and musky. That first day, she couldn't quite figure out how to fit a diaper around the thick rope of a tail. She'd learn the healthy smell of the child's skin in time, like a pony, or herbs; she'd understand that pale purple was a good colour. The neat little slit in front made her think it was a girl. It was hairless everywhere, with ridges where eyebrows might be. The outer eyelids were back, but the inner white ones made it look blind.

Their ignorance would kill it – how can you help a creature if you don't know what *normal* is? How would you intubate it, or put a line in a vein? Could you give it human saline? Surely this strange thing was going to die . . . but she'd never given up on a patient yet.

Nurse Fell, the new nurse with dark eyes and a tangled love-life, came in. *Good*, Molly thought, *she's calm and competent.*

'The mother looks the same,' Fell said, rolling her eyes. 'Dr Jarman wants an update.'

They exchanged glances, colluding on this extraordinary secret, before she took the report and left Molly alone with it. For a while the alien lay very still, but then it jerked like a hooked, dying fish, crying out and thrashing, as if it were having a fit. Molly noted the time: 1.27 a.m. She put a gloved hand to its chest and rang the bell. In the turmoil, who knew if anyone would come?

'You're not allowed to die on my watch,' she whispered. 'I'm here, I'm here. You're safe. We'll do our best. Heavens above, you're a strange one, but I'm not giving up yet.'

She felt so helpless, but who was here to help it except her? 'I'm here to look after you,' she said softly. 'Pearce is a sour old cow but she knows her job. She'd arm-wrestle the Grim Reaper. I could tell you stories . . . Come on, be strong. We've Earth to show you.'

Slowly, a webbed paw came up to touch her hand. It was frightened and sick and in need of comfort.

Something opened inside her.

She began to sing, old lullabies, through the mask. Gene told her often enough she could hold a tune but she'd always hated an audience. Yet sometimes, in the dark of a hospital night, she would sing to a child who needed it.

The strange ears moved: maybe it heard? But when she moved her hand a little, its four-fingered paw fell away. No, *hand* – it had a thumb. Skinny ribs rose and fell like breathing was hard labour, and it gave that weird little cough.

*It's a child.*

She rang the bell again, keeping her finger down, until Dr Jarman, the man who led the doctors and knew it, walked in, already masked. That tall, stooping shambles of a man came to work each morning looking like he'd been up all night in his clothes; he moved like someone had taught a bear to walk. His hands were enormous, but Molly once saw him draw a shard of glass from a child's cheek, fingers as delicate as a lace-maker. People forgave him a lot.

Dr Jarman walked with shoulders down, his head forward and his eyes low. 'The mother died at 1.30 a.m.,' he said. 'Nothing we could do. We've lots of questions, but we need to focus on the child. Report, please, Nurse.'

Molly said what she knew, which wasn't a lot.

'We're flying through thick cloud. His mother did give me

their first-aid box and some food packs. Let's hope he gets better before we run out. Let's hope he can eat our stuff.'

*He?* 'It appears to be female.'

'His mother was clear he's male,' he said, attempting a smile. 'I'll try another one of their shots.'

She must have missed something. 'The mother spoke English?'

'A box on her suit spoke for her – translated, I guess. She managed to tell us what the drugs were. It was like . . . *Masterpiece Theatre*.'

Molly had so many questions: *Where had it come from? And how? Had they been watching the Earth? Were there more of them?*

Jarman broke the silence. 'There were two dead when we found them, an adult and a child. Now the mother's gone too, leaving just the smallest.'

'Do we know his name?' she asked.

'Oh, nothing I could pronounce. Boy Alien. If we save him, we can ask.' He pulled out what looked like a plastic pen and started searching on the child's arm for a vein.

*You need to give the patient a name*, thought Molly, *something to call him. Little cor-cor-cor. If nothing else, you need a name to bury him under.*

## CHAPTER 5

# The day after Meteor Day

At the nurses' home, Molly managed three hours' sleep. When she came to, muggy-headed, it was afternoon and Amber Grove was sulking under weird black cloud. She phoned the library and left Gene a message, then went to find a sandwich.

In the crowded canteen, two firefighters in unfamiliar uniforms slumped over their coffee. Were the fires still burning, even after that rain? Beyond them stood Mayor Rourke, deep in conversation. She thought the other man was the Mayor of Bradleyburg. All around, tired-looking people wearing makeshift armbands with *Volunteer* written on them sat silently in front of uneaten food.

She thought, *I could stand on a chair and tell them about the alien.* What would happen? Maybe they'd all jump up and rush upstairs to see, pushing over chairs and tables in their excitement. Maybe someone would lead her away to one of those wards or hospitals where they took people who saw things. She shuddered a little; that wasn't a place she wanted to be, as a nurse or as one of the dead-eyed patients.

Ahead of her in the line were two bright-eyed nurses burning with other news. Rumour always travels fast round a hospital.

'There's troops everywhere,' one was saying, 'and helicopters buzzing all last night and trucks parked anyhow. They're saying they won't let anyone near the impact site.'

'And if you do try, they just bring you back under armed guard.'

Molly bolted her sandwich and walked to the foot of the stairs, past two teenage boys helping an old woman limp down the corridor and a man with a bandaged head arguing with two nurses and a doctor. There must be hundreds injured, and no word yet on how many dead.

She climbed to the fifth floor, wondering if the boy was awake, to find Jarman had put an even more strident notice on the boy's door:

### CONTAGIOUS AND DANGEROUS
### FULL INFECTION PRECAUTIONS
### AUTHORISED PERSONNEL ONLY

Jarman's flamboyant signature at the bottom gave it added weight.

She went into the outer cubicle to scrub up before donning gloves and mask and apron. The larger inner room was sealed behind two glass doors; the airlock system had air filtered to cut the risk of infection. A tiny risk remained.

Peggy Fell was standing by the bed, thank goodness. She quickly ran down the details before making her excuses; she was due elsewhere in this busy hospital with so many needy people.

Soon, Molly was alone with little Cor-cor-cor, pale and still; what could be done? No normal mask would fit that face, so last night they'd lashed something together to give him oxygen. She touched one ear with a gloved finger and wondered how it might feel to be so alone. The child's eyes were still covered with those white inner lids, seeing nothing, and the tentacles were still. Only the rise and fall of his skinny chest and the machine recording his pulse showed that he was alive.

His temperature was back up and he didn't respond to the straw. Boiled water was sterile and safe, fed from a plastic bottle designed to sip from. Did they dare a drip?

She put the bottle down to help the child sit up, mindful of the gash in his side, and noticed the silver wrist device was gone.

'Cory,' she said out loud, testing the name. Well, she had to call him something. 'Are you thirsty, Cory? We've got lots of time together now. You'll be all right.'

An ear twitched and the child's body moved a little into hers. It was bony, but not that unlike a human child to hold. When she slipped the straw into his mouth, the tentacles twitched.

*Come on, little one, remember what to do.*

She glanced at the clock and realised it was twenty-four hours since the Meteor had fallen. Just one day, and this was another world.

Holding a child who needed her, nothing else existed. After a while, there came a feeble little movement. His eyes stayed closed, but he began to suck.

In the staff lounge, Molly sat with her shoes off, each foot massaging the other under the table. Dr Jarman looked like he'd been awake for a week and Sister Pearce looked like she wanted to punch someone.

'I promised his mother we'd keep him safe,' Jarman said, pouring coffee. Molly watched as he began to spoon sugar, one, two, three, four. 'She'd heard of the Hippocratic Oath, although Lord knows how. So, the boy's need-to-know only. I'm in no hurry to tell anyone official. Who knows what they'd do? Sheriff Olsen tells me they've got hundreds of soldiers at the impact site.'

Molly imagined the nightmare: the boy might disappear into some government laboratory and never come out. He'd be cut up like the frogs in biology class; she'd hated that part. Who'd stand up for him then? 'Won't the Sheriff tell the authorities?' she asked.

Olsen was popular, re-elected twice, always to be seen swaggering along the sidewalks or spinning a yarn in front of the station. Dark rumours surrounded him, though: how he swore in his brothers and cousins as deputies; that prisoner who'd somehow broken his own arm, lawsuits . . .

'Sheriff Olsen will keep his mouth shut. He promised the mother, he promised me. Trust me,' Jarman said.

Pearce was boiling over. 'We need to be *serious* – we're stretched to breaking point. The child is very sick and we haven't the first idea what to do for him. We need the best minds in the country. The government can throw money and people at the problem, they can nurse him in isolation for weeks, months, even a year, whatever is needed. Everyone wins.'

Molly was reeling at the idea that they might hand Cory over. The boy was her patient – *hers*; how dare Sister suggest they give him away?

'The Governor's coming for some media circus or other. Let's hope the President stays away.' Jarman sipped, grimaced, and added another two spoons of sugar. He said firmly, 'We must keep the boy a secret.'

'Why?' Pearce demanded.

Jarman swigged the coffee down. 'The moment we tell them, he'll be whisked away. We've got to keep him secret until I've got a better plan. That means only the staff who already know, Sister.'

'A secret?' said Pearce, quivering. 'The entire *floor* knows we have a mystery patient – by tomorrow, the whole hospital—'

'Nobody has any idea *who*, though. I've told the Director we're treating a burns case with some virulent unknown infection – that's so we can cover the face if we need to.'

Pearce gave her trademark sigh and tried one last time. 'Why not call in some of the real specialists, in confidence?'

'Most of the top people do defence work,' Jarman said, with a slight frown, 'and the more people who know, the more likely it'll get out. Then we'll have the army camped on our doorstep.'

'I can't stop people talking.'

Jarman smiled. 'Sister, you could teach the Navy a thing or two about discipline. Your staff will take your word for it – and if you have problems, just send them to me.'

Molly's cautious inner voice said, *We mean well but a country hospital mightn't be good enough.* Then she thought of the four-star generals and their body-counts and body-bags and the sharp-suited politicians with their smart words and their excuses.

'I think we should keep him quiet for now,' Molly said. 'I need to go back. Uh, Dr Jarman, what did his mother tell you? Why are they here? What happened?'

'Well, she was dying and she was pretty confused, but she did keep saying she'd sent a message to their people and they'll be coming to find him, in large numbers. She said they'll judge us by how we treat him.' His face was grim. 'I don't blame the mother. We must look like violent savages from the outside.'

'We can't let him die through sheer pride,' Pearce said, rubbing her eyes. 'You *must* call in other people – people you can trust.' She looked to heaven as she said, 'This puts him in danger, it puts other patients in danger, maybe the staff. Lord, we might be putting the whole planet in danger.'

'That's my decision,' said Jarman, who wrote beautiful angry letters to the *Hermes* about the war and every type of injustice. Who played poker with Sheriff Olsen. Who expected to get his way.

Sister Pearce got up and stalked out of the lounge, all but slamming the door behind her.

'I'm going to get back to Cory,' Molly said.

Jarman looked amused. 'Oh, he has a name now?'

It was late morning, but they kept the blind down in Cory's room, even though it was absurd, because no one could look in, unless they had wings. Molly read in her chair, trusting to the machines to warn her if he stopped breathing. After a while, she looked up and saw two purple eyes gazing at her. With the inner eyelids back, the eyes were compelling. The extraordinary tentacles twitched and moved.

'Hello,' she said, keeping it cheery. 'Would you like water? Are you hungry?' Of course he wouldn't understand. During his mother's fevered last hour, the translator box had stopped working. Maybe Cory knew how to restart it.

She brought over the bottle and shook it a little so he could see the water in it. After a while, a hand pointed at it. Cautiously, the tentacles danced over it and then the straw disappeared into his mouth.

'Water,' she said.

Cory drank most of it, then curled back up on the bed with his back to her.

Molly walked to the refrigerator humming in the corner of the room. She'd stacked his food-packs here, sealed plastic pouches with alien writing. The elaborate swirls and strokes, curves and lines made her think of music on a stave, or maybe Arabic. If they couldn't feed him, it'd all be for nothing.

She opened the first and the thick, creamy alien liquid filled the air with the smell of ageing fish. *Hot or cold?* She warmed it up on the single electric ring perched on the fridge. Another pack held dark brown slices like rye bread or cookies. She cracked the pack open just to sniff; it smelled of damp and onions.

She took samples; lab tests were needed to figure out if the aliens' bodies used the same basic building blocks as Earth life. If his chemistry was too different . . . Earth food would poison him, or he would starve.

He wasn't moving, but she walked around to his front side, the bowl and spoon on a breakfast tray. 'Here's food,' she said, as cheerfully as she could. 'My name's Molly. Hard to tell one from another with the masks, I know – I bet we all look the same to you. But I'm Molly.'

He lay there, very still, with his eyes closed. Then his tentacles twitched and his ears moved up a little. The bigger outer tentacles were drier than the damp inner ones which he could draw into his mouth. He opened his eyes, beautiful and inhuman.

*How can we know what he thinks, what he feels?* It was an unreadable face.

'Just like home. I hope this smells nice to you,' she said. 'I'm not sure I like it, but it's not meant for me, is it?'

He turned over, hiding from her, and she put the tray down, determined not to give up. Opening a precious pack of food and wasting it . . . In her mind, she saw the child starving himself to death. Would they need to spoon in the food against his wishes?

'Hoo . . . hoo . . . hoo.'

She sat on the bed and put her hand on his shoulder. How could she do the right thing for him, not knowing what that might be? The room felt full of sadness.

She sang silly songs she remembered from her childhood, the one about the farmer's goat and the sneezing mouse, and stuff from the radio, and he made the heartbreaking noise less and then, after a while, it stopped.

*He knows his mom died*, thought Molly. *He's sick and doesn't feel like eating.* Children have a natural zeal for life, but sometimes they just give up. But he'd asked for water and she'd given it to him: communication had begun.

He turned and tried to sit up, but the coughing got worse. She held him until he made fluting noises, then looked for the tray.

Molly brought it across his legs and he bent his head down to the cooling bowl. He spent a good couple of minutes, smelling it, she guessed, then dipped in a tentacle to try the temperature. He looked at her as if there was some question. Then he broke off a piece of what she thought of as alien bread and dipped it in.

He didn't bother with the spoon but used his tentacles, making efficient little slurping noises. It looked bizarre, but it worked. A slice of the bread-stuff and maybe a third of the soup and he was done. Each tentacle went into the mouth for a clean, then he curled back up and shut his eyes.

Later, she would find those inner tentacles helped him smell and taste; the world was as much a web of smell as pictures and noise for him.

It was a little victory, although the road ahead was still dark and foreboding.

He said something very quiet and she brought her head down to listen. 'Moh-lleee,' he said.

She touched his back, too full to say anything.

Molly hunted in the storeroom for more clothes they could sterilise for Cory. Nurse Hooton came in and shut the door. She had that horrible high-school cheerleader-conspirator look. Pearce had her working at the other end of the building, nowhere near Cory.

'It's weird and creepy, isn't it? It scares me.' Hooton gave a little theatrical shiver.

Molly stared, as cold as she could. '*He*. Not it. He's a sick child in our care.' She hoped her voice would freeze Hooton solid.

Hooton flushed. That look, freckles and brown hair and

quivering lip, heaven knows why it dragged in men. Too much make-up, although to be fair, probably to cover tired eyes.

'Oh, we should treat it—'

'*Him*. It's a him,' Molly said. 'He keeps his penis tucked away.' It was fuchsia, like his bifurcated tongue, and she longed to tease Gene about the practicality of the arrangement. But Jarman had ordered them to tell no one and Molly had obeyed.

Hooton frowned. 'I'm not saying we shouldn't look after . . . him . . . it's just . . . he's *horrible*. Frightening. I took a blood sample and I was shivers all over – like a graveyard, you know? Like he called up a cold gust of wind.'

Molly felt a surge of rage and dislike. She needed to keep herself under control. 'That's ridiculous.' She took a breath, then tried to be encouraging. 'It's been very hard for all of us. And he looks odd, of course – he does take some getting used to.'

Hooton glared at her. 'I know what I felt.'

Molly remembered how angry she'd got in training when some nurses had gossiped about a poor boy with a deformed skull. And for the first time in years, she remembered Annie at school, the silent girl with the twisted lip. Molly had become her defender, at the price of her own popularity.

'Maybe we should only save the pretty children,' Molly said, when she wanted to say, *What a disgrace you are*.

'Of course we should help,' Hooton snapped. 'It's our patient. You're twisting my words.'

Molly felt the ripped-out sadness of Cory's loss and that called up her own heartache. Cory deserved commitment. She'd go to Sister Pearce and get Hooton sent somewhere else. Geriatrics or Community Clinics. Alaska.

Cory's fluting noises must be speech. Sometimes he cocked his head to one side, listening to her babble on. She touched things and named them – bed, mask, glass, hand, floor – and he watched and said nothing.

Hooton was scared, she knew that. The boy was different and strange, but it hadn't occurred to Molly that people might be frightened of him. Frightened people are dangerous. She would need to protect him.

'I know what I felt,' Hooton repeated, standing between Molly and the door. 'And I don't like your tone. I know my job.'

'Get out of my way,' Molly said. 'If you gossip about him, I'll break your neck. Then Sister Pearce will fire you. Get it?'

'We ought to hand it over to the government,' said Hooton, standing aside. 'That's the right thing to do.'

*Everyone is stretched thin*, Molly thought, *everyone's on edge.* Dr Bradshaw, the promising young doctor, had gone to pieces when the mother died and Jarman had sent him home. Molly had liked him; he was pretty tough for a young one.

She needed serenity, courage and wisdom. They all did.

## CHAPTER 6

# Dr Pfeiffer

The days and nights began to blur. Gene called and she drove home to Crooked Street that evening. She needed him, and fresh supplies, and perspective.

Gene had mended the porch light and here he was, standing underneath it, looking for her. They embraced, a long and welcome hug, and she smelled pork for supper.

'I'll have to leave first thing,' she said. 'Things are crazy.'

'Do they not have any other nurses?' Gene frowned. 'Molly, that place treats people like dirt. You must be owed a day off.'

'It's an emergency – everything's up in the air.'

'You've always told me a good nurse looks after herself. You'll get exhausted . . . If you get sick, that doesn't help anyone.' And he knew the dark road tiredness might take her down.

She changed the subject. 'That smells delicious,' she said with a smile for the chef.

As they ate, Gene talked the most, which was not how their

meals usually were, but how could she discuss what was really going on?

'I know the sky fell in last week, Molly-moo. They're really lucky to have you. Just look after yourself, okay? There're journalists and TV everywhere, taking photos and sticking microphones under people's noses. They've got no compassion. It's like they're treading on our graves.'

Eleven dead that they knew of, and corpses they couldn't identify, and a dozen people still missing. People who'd managed to patch themselves up on Meteor Day were coming out of the woodwork too, needing proper treatment. And life went on: Maternity was always busy. One woman had gone into labour when the Meteor fell; they'd called the baby Stella.

But all Molly could think about was Cory. Just think, if the press got even a sniff of the boy. It would be out of their hands.

'They're building a fence out there in the woods,' Gene said, 'the places we used to go. It's covered in signs saying "Danger, keep out" – you won't believe how many soldiers there are up there. Who knows what they think they'll find . . .'

'What I need is a bath and a back-rub,' Molly said firmly. No more talk, just holding each other under the old quilt, in gladness they still had each other.

Back on the fifth floor, Sister Pearce said, 'There're some army bigwigs meeting in the boardroom. We're wanted, but you'll have to go for me. I'll watch the child.'

Molly trotted down the stairs, and along the corridor, almost bumping into Dr Jarman, who was standing by the boardroom door. A much shorter, bald man stood beside him, holding forth, his hands cutting the air for emphasis, as Jarman, stooping a little, listened with an insincere half-smile.

Molly prided herself on her memory for faces; she knew the sour-faced man from somewhere . . . He was in his fifties, with heavy dark-rimmed glasses, a scar on the forehead . . . That flabbiness under his throat suggested he had once been fatter. She wondered why he stirred up some hostile reaction in her . . . then she remembered a television debate on the evening news: the man had been spearing the air with a finger, arrogant and aggressive, exulting in the war as he constantly interrupted the presenter and the other guests.

*Dr Pfeiffer, the President's pet scientist. The germ warfare man.*

Pfeiffer, ignoring Molly, said, 'We need to go in, Dr Jarman. This community looks up to you and it's your responsibility to keep them calm.'

'Give people the facts and they'll decide for themselves,' Jarman said mildly. A meek man in even thicker glasses stood to one side, watching Pfeiffer like a dog would its master.

Molly waited, trying to work out what to do, whether to walk between the men. What was the most frozen of Cold Warriors doing here?

'Shall we go in, Dr Pfeiffer, Dr Tyler?' Dr Jarman opened the door.

Now Pfeiffer looked at Molly, a determined set to his mouth. He spent a second looking her up and down, his eyes bright, but with no more reaction than if she'd been a telegraph pole. He looked back at Jarman, then they went in.

Most people in the long room were standing. She saw medical staff, the hospital director, some of the senior nurses, as well as two State Troopers, a grey-haired soldier and some men in suits she didn't recognise. The Mayor was chatting to three Councillors. And there was Diane, who looked surprised and pleased to see her.

Molly made her way to her friend, who raised a notebook. 'The Principal sent me. Who's he?' Diane whispered, looking at Pfeiffer striding to the end of the long table as if he owned it.

'Dr Pfeiffer – remember? He wanted to destroy the rice harvest in North Vietnam to starve their women and children until there was peace.' She shivered: a man who took the power to heal and perverted it to a weapon of war. Pfeiffer had advised the last President and, without blinking, had moved to do the same for the new.

'Oh, *him*. The students loathe him, don't they!'

Pfeiffer pulled the empty chair away and stayed standing. 'I'm Dr Pfeiffer, Chief Scientific Counsel to the President,' he started brusquely. 'He has sent me to take charge of the scientific team looking into the Meteor. You'll have heard lots of wild rumours, so I'm here to explain why our army colleagues are fencing off the site. As leaders in your community, I'd like you to encourage cooperation with the army – they're handling a difficult job very well – and prevent loose talk.'

Someone held up a hand, but he waved them away. 'I'll take relevant questions at the end. The matter's simple. There's radioactive debris out there, dangerous stuff with rare isotopes. We've already had local people wandering in – they'll poison themselves and spread contamination to others if we're not careful. And not just locals: people are coming to rubberneck, if you can believe it. That fence is for everyone's safety. Now, as rational people, you'll be wondering if there's any danger to you here in town. Dr Jarman?'

Dr Jarman spoke with care. 'We've looked for radiation in the soot that fell on the hospital and Meteor fragments and the army has done their own tests and I can assure you neither we nor they have found anything.'

Pfeiffer's smile was not reassuring. 'Radiation is within normal range. You'd be in more danger in my lab.'

If that was a joke, no one smiled.

'If anything does change, we'll know at once. We're drawing up plans to evacuate the town if the radiation spreads, no expense spared. In Amber Grove, as Dr Jarman has said, there's no evidence of the slightest danger. Out in the woods, though, it's a different story.'

He looked around the room. 'I'll take one or two questions.'

Up went a forest of hands, but a younger man in a suit had pushed forward and started shouting, 'Baby-killer! Monster!' There was something in his raised hand.

Pfeiffer's face turned to pure, ugly rage. 'Jarman. *Control your people*,' he snarled.

The soldiers pushed through the crowd to the man, but the Sheriff had already got him in an armlock and was slamming his clenched hand against the table. The metal thing he was holding bounced and fell to the ground. A can of spray paint.

Dr Jarman rose, coughed, and became the centre of attention. 'Easy, Lars,' he said calmly, then, 'Everyone, drawing up an evacuation plan is sensible, as I've advised both the hospital and the Mayor.' His eyes met Molly's.

Pfeiffer glared at everyone: the man, the Mayor pushing forward, the crowd, the cursing protester.

Getting away from Diane took a while, but Molly didn't hurry; she needed to keep her nosy friends away from what she was up to. It was a couple of hours later before she finally got back to Cory's room. As she opened the outer door, she could hear Jarman and Pearce arguing, their voices low. The alien boy slept; at least, she hoped it was sleep.

'. . . ridiculous charade,' Pearce was saying. 'I must protest . . .' Then she saw Molly through the glass.

'We're coming out,' Jarman said, although three people made the outer room cramped. An odd feeling told Molly something big was coming.

'Well, now we know who'll be in charge if we talk,' Jarman said. 'That *skunk* – that *warmonger*. He's a disgrace to medicine.'

'I'd have thought a world-renowned expert on the immune system is just what we need,' Pearce said, her mouth turned down.

Jarman frowned. 'Pfeiffer's a nasty piece of work. He stabbed old Lippincott in the back . . . he'd have been no one without him. Then he sold out to the military. No, we must keep the child hidden at all costs.'

'You can't be serious,' Pearce said, looking shocked.

Jarman held Molly's gaze. 'Pfeiffer is as nosy as hell and our mystery infection story has just become a liability. Cheese to a rat, he'll demand to see the patient – to identify the bug. He always was a show-off. Or he'll be thinking it's an alien microbe. So we need to close this down, now. It must stay secret, as few as possible knowing.'

'How?' Molly said.

Jarman took a deep breath. 'We'll fake his death tonight and stage a cremation. We'll hide the boy until we figure out what to do. There's a sealed observation suite in the annex; it's not been used in years and I doubt anyone even remembers it's there. He'll be safe.'

Molly certainly hadn't heard of it. The annex was an unloved after-thought to the west wing: it held no wards.

'Only the people we absolutely need will know,' he repeated.

It was wild, but he was right: the mystery patient needed to disappear. She had no doubt Pfeiffer would tear the building down if he got even a hint of what was happening.

'I trust Nurse Fell,' Molly said. 'I don't trust Hooton. Tell her he died.'

'I thought Bradshaw had more stomach for the job,' Jarman said, 'but he's still getting flashbacks from the mother's death. We'd better keep him out of it too.'

Pearce tutted. 'This is absurd. We can't possibly make it work. And if the boy gets better, what then?'

'We'll cross that bridge when we come to it,' Jarman said.

Molly felt a hope wriggling inside her, not yet ready to be born.

Pearce drew herself up to her full five foot three inches. 'You've both taken leave of your senses. We need more staff and a proper scientific team. If you don't trust the government, Dr Jarman, at least bring in people you can trust.'

'No,' Molly said, surprising herself, 'he's fine here with us. I'll need to see this place in the annex.'

Jarman looked at Pearce as if willing her consent. 'Pfeiffer's lying,' he said, from nowhere, with loathing. He got a map out of his white coat pocket, folded any old how, and thrust it at the nurses. A big finger tapped a streak of blue. 'That fence they're building? It goes around Two Mile Lake as well. It's not for keeping people out of the crater – or not just that. They must want the mother's spaceship. She told me it was so badly damaged, it might explode at any minute. *That's* why they want an evacuation plan.'

'What's the lake got to do with it?' Molly said.

Jarman grimaced, a tough, humourless smile. 'I heard Pfeiffer talking to his flunky about diving, so I guess Cory's mother hid their spaceship in the lake, maybe even booby-trapped it. What do you think Pfeiffer will do with an alien vessel? He'll try to make a weapon out of it. Would you trust a man like that with Cory?'

Even Pearce hesitated.

'We're running out of time; Pfeiffer's going to hear about the fifth floor sooner rather than later, so we need to stage his death and hide him,' Jarman said. 'Us three and the new nurse, Fell. That's all.'

'What about Sheriff Olsen?' Molly said suddenly. He'd been brutal, the way he'd nearly broken that protester's wrist, and the boy had turned out to be the Mayor's nephew, brought along to take notes.

'We don't need Lars,' Jarman said. 'I'll tell him the boy died.'

That night they moved Cory to the observation suite. Molly, thinking of the boy's mother, wept real tears for her colleagues, lying fluently to keep her little patient safe.

Now she read by Cory's bedside, a broken-backed novel she'd found in the storeroom. Cory was sleeping at last, after a difficult day of fever coming and going. She'd promised Gene she would come home, but her eyes grew heavy. Sleeping on duty was unforgiveable, but she could rest her eyes, just for a moment . . .

Molly dreamed the dream she'd had in the worst of times, when Grandma, all yellow and etched thin as a skeleton, had died in the drab clinical room in the crowded hospital. For a week, young Molly had watched the person she'd loved so dearly ebb away, confused from the drugs and eaten up by the thing inside her. Sometimes Grandma dying turned into the pain on the ladder, when her hand was yellow with paint and red with blood.

The dream was so familiar and yet nothing could strip it of its horror. This time it became Meteor Day. Black rain was falling and Gene's hands had been burned off. She needed to find him, because no one else could tie the bandages right . . . Gene had no arms left to hold her . . . how could he play his guitar for her? And this test would be her final nursing exam and she didn't have the right uniform. Old Sister King would fail her.

And there was Cory: wide-eyed and reaching out his hands. Molly never remembered dreaming smells before, but the air was thick with his unmistakeable scent, and disinfectant, and human sweat, even the tang of the disgusting cigars that clung to Dr Jarman's clothing.

She took Cory's hand and walked out onto a warm beach of sharp green sand towards sunset and a dark sea. The sun

65

went down in impossible colours on a little lagoon; there were translucent sails out on the water, green forested mountains rising steep from the sea and the air was thick with salt and spice and musk.

Aliens just like Cory played by the dozen, adults and children running and chasing and splashing in the shallows, proper purple people without furry heads. Cory ran off to those he knew. Against that unbelievable sky, silver craft like birds rose into the heavens and were gone. That evening star was a city in space. His mother flew those little ships, but today, she wasn't flying; she and Cory were playing.

There were no words, but none were needed. Cory's bright love for his mother filled Molly, along with less familiar feelings and images and sensations. Later there would be fires and ring-dancing and juicy hot food: four types of shellfish, baked in their shells, all good, but Cory liked the rough-shelled green ones like fists best of all.

A wind blew and the images became confused; now she was in a fever-dream, a boy's-eye view of the hospital room and the strange giants who stank. Cory was terrified and in pain, his chest and head hurt and he wanted his mother, but she was dying. He could feel her even through the wall, and soon the screaming would return, a tearing pain beyond imagining. The images changed, like a hand brushed through a reflection, and Molly was floating in a maze of green corridors . . . a burning light . . . the pain in her chest tightened, stabbing over and over . . .

Molly jerked awake in the chair by Cory's bedside, her heart thundering, sweating and afraid. The boy was twisting and turning, moaning.

'There, there, Cory, Molly's here,' she said, laying her hand on him, ashamed to have slept. She ran a basin of cool water and wiped his face and chest. Somehow, she had entered his dream, feeling his memories as vividly as if she'd been there herself – but that was impossible, wasn't it? How could she have *been* there, seen memories she couldn't possibly know?

*Water*, she thought. *He'd be reassured by water.* When he was a little better, she'd bathe him.

Cory became a little cooler, a little calmer. Acting on instinct, Molly got onto the bed beside him – it was unprofessional, she knew, a breach of procedure, but like any human child, being held calmed him . . . How strange she looked to him, and how odd she smelled.

'Where have you come from, sweetie-pie?' she said aloud. 'What terrors have you seen?'

# CHAPTER 7

## *May*

After he was moved, Cory was better for a few days, although he tired quickly. He learned their names, and useful words: *food drink yes no bedpan. No-no diaper. Too hot, too cold, going-to-throw-up. Sing, stay, hug, pleeese.*

Then his fever returned with a vengeance, as if it had learned to overcome the alien drugs.

That evening, when Peggy Fell arrived, she told Molly, 'Go to the canteen, get some hot food.'

Molly picked up that Peggy was trying not to smirk, but she was too tired to process it. 'It's okay, I'll stay. Couldn't you bring the food up?' Even as she spoke, she recognised how selfish that sounded.

'Molly, go, for heaven's sake! I'll cover.'

She walked through the deserted annex and down the corridor to the canteen, which was closed, and half-dark, and there was Gene, in his second suit. She needed to persuade him to buy another, one not so out of fashion. He'd covered a Formica table with their second-best tablecloth and set a candle in the middle, next to some sprigs of blossom in a little vase. Her favourite soda had been poured into a crystal glass.

Molly was flooded with guilt. She'd cried off a rock-solid date with him yesterday.

Behind him stood Janice in an apron, grinning.

'The best table in town,' Gene said, getting up.

'Idiot,' she said, glad, kissing him. He wore the bright green plaid tie she'd bought him as a joke, and a badly ironed shirt. 'Hi, Janice.'

'I thought I'd come to you,' he said. 'We're dining on the famous Henderson meatloaf.'

Janice brought two plates piled with meat and gravy and greens. 'Careful, it's hot. And there's cheesecake and fruit for dessert. I'm off. You lovebirds have fun. Although if I don't get a long coffee soon, Molly, I am going to report Dr Jarman for abduction.'

'Thanks,' Molly said, meaning it, but worried; her friends were getting pushier too.

Now they were just Gene and Molly and she took his hands gently, to see how they were healing. She guessed they'd always be scarred: marks of courage.

'Sorry,' she started. 'I was looking forward to it, so much, but something came up.'

'Well, again . . . I was pretty hacked off,' Gene said. 'But you know, our heroine, saving lives, et cetera, et cetera. As long as you're okay.'

She said something banal and took a mouthful. She found she was hungry.

'Boy or girl?' Gene said.

She blinked.

'You only get like this when there's a kid involved,' he said. 'Some tragic case. I bet you're the only nurse working these crippling hours. It's not fair.'

She was frightened to say it was a child, because other questions would follow. He might find out she was on special duties, not on the fifth floor. With her drinking and his infidelity, honesty mattered in their marriage more than ever.

Last time she got over-involved with a patient, Gene had said some tough things. 'I'm not adopting a dying one,' he'd told her, and at first she'd raged, until she realised he wasn't being callous; he was worried about her, about what might happen if things went wrong.

How did Gene and Cory fit together?

'Gene, I love you. You know I can't talk about some things at the hospital.'

He looked at her for a long, long time. 'You're working with Dr Jarman, right?'

She nodded and moved a potato onto his plate. Gene was always scrawny, no matter how much he ate.

'Something doesn't add up with the official "radiation" story.' He plucked a thick grey book from his case.

*Oh heavens, he's going to give me a lecture.*

'Dr Jarman says the evacuation plan is just common sense,' she tried.

'Not like Jarman to be tied up with the military.'

'You know I can't talk about these things . . .'

There was so much she could say, and so little she was sure

about. Molly opened her mouth to say something, she wasn't sure what, but she heard the creak of the canteen door, and footsteps behind her. She turned and looked over her shoulder and there, coming towards them, was Pfeiffer's go-for – Tyler, she thought – and a soldier. *Why?* Her stomach roiled, like on a fairground ride. Were they looking for Cory?

'Uh . . .' the scientist said.

'This is private,' she said, as coldly as she could. She needed to call Peggy, in case this was a search. Or maybe they'd been betrayed. Maybe the army already had him.

Pfeiffer's flunky blinked as if baffled.

Gene said, 'The canteen's closed. We're just using a table. Francine's might be open, or O'Reilly's on Second.'

'I'm looking for Dr Pfeiffer.'

Molly had seen the odious man an hour back, lambasting the hospital's director, although she had no idea about what.

Gene kept chewing, and Molly tried the smile she used on difficult patients. 'I'm so sorry, I've no idea.'

Gene picked up another roll as their interrogators left. 'Jeez, those two really spooked you,' he said once the door had banged shut. She thought she'd hidden it better. 'Is that *the* Dr Pfeiffer? There's a story in the *New York Times* today on this radioactivity nonsense.'

'Oh, he's been here once or twice, showing off. Horrible man – a real nuisance.' She wanted an afternoon in bed with Gene, him playing her a new song – but what she needed was to go back to Cory, to check that he wasn't worse.

'Jarman's got you working on the plan,' he said, 'and for some stupid government reason, it's secret.'

Molly looked at him and felt her heart sink. They owed each other honesty, but she'd promised she wouldn't tell Gene. And if she said it was a sick child, he would ask a thousand questions; last time she'd got fixated, he'd wanted to see the child himself.

Knowing he would leap to the wrong conclusion, she said, 'I can't tell you everything I do at work, Gene.' She felt so guilty.

'I trust you not to do something stupid. Well, come home.'

'Not tonight – no one can cover. We'll see each other tomorrow.' Although how she would make that happen, she didn't know.

Disappointment reigned on Gene's face. 'The next time, I'm going to walk into Jarman's office and complain,' he said. 'You'll make yourself ill at this rate.'

An image haunted her, blazing like a fire in the night: the little boy had lost his mother. Cory needed what every child did, someone who would put him first. The idea kept returning, unbidden: why couldn't *she* adopt him, strange smell and odd face and all?

Cory tired easily, but he soaked up words. Molly thought she could pick out expressions from the way he used his ears and his eyes and those tentacles. He liked being bed-bathed. And he could flute the opening chords to eight Earth songs now. 'Mollee sing, Mollee sing.'

She tried to imagine telling Gene . . . but how would she do it? Where would she start? Her stomach turned. What if her asking something so monstrous, so absurd, was the last straw? He'd leave her, find someone else. He often talked about cities on the Moon and mankind's future in space, but to hide Cory from the world . . . She feared the practical, write-a-list-and-make-a-budget side of his brain would over-whelm the part that gazed up at the stars.

'Dessert looks great,' she said. 'I'm just too tired to talk. I need to sort my hours.'

They needed another nurse on the team.

The stoical set to his jaw meant: no row, not tonight.

Gene kissed her, and she held him a little longer than she'd planned. 'I love you,' she said, then she turned away and walked briskly back to the hidden rooms. The little gang dare not leave Cory unattended. They all agreed Cory liked them all, but Molly was his favourite.

Beyond the door, Cory lay on the bed, hot and unseeing. She remembered a spaceship coverlet she'd seen in the Sears catalogue; maybe he'd like that.

'I want to be your mom,' she said into thin air. It felt crazy, saying it out loud, but good. 'You need one and I want it to be me. I want you to eat again, sweetie-pie, use those weird little teeth. I want you to run and climb and swim.'

She dipped a cloth in cold water. Thanks to Jarman's tests, they knew Cory's proteins were similar to Earth ones. That didn't prove he could eat Earth food, mind, so maybe this was all a waste of time.

She'd lied to Gene, but she couldn't rebuild her marriage on lies. Gene or Cory? She did not want to choose.

Sister Pearce took a shift with Cory so Molly could have a day off, as much to placate Gene as anything. A hot bath followed by a delicious long sleep with Gene's arms round her, then 'just an hour, girls' with Janice and Diane. Gene was brewing a big talk; she knew the signs. She wanted to put it off, just to be with him and not worry about Cory. She'd hoped she'd be clearer about what to do after some decent sleep.

Gene showed her the sight she had been avoiding. On Meteor Day, a massive fragment had ploughed up Founders Green, burning the grass and throwing up a crater wall as high as a man. That scorched chunk of iron was as big as two houses and their yard, its surface dark and rippled like some black frozen brain. The army had erected a wire mesh fence round the fragment and stationed a bored soldier on guard duty.

The sight of the fallen rock brought back the chaos and fear of Meteor Day. Molly looked from the rock to the library and back; compared with the countless miles of space, those few hundred yards were a hair's breadth.

'I know,' Gene said, although she hadn't spoken.

Then they walked to the park where they had courted to see how the trees and the flowers were flourishing, turning their backs on the chaos of rocks from space. New scaffolding had sprung up along Main Street, the first signs that Amber Grove was healing. She tried not to react as a truckload of soldiers passed. All around them were strangers, tourists, lots of them, and cars parked illegally, displaying number plates from all over. Hippies were busking in the park and doing Tarot readings to pay for beer or drugs.

These people had come from all corners of the country and far beyond to catch a glimpse of the destruction Meteor Day had wrought. To them it was a wonder, but to Molly it was morbid and cruel, wandering around looking at the blackened fronts of buildings, the For Sale signs. Children played and people gawked: *Look kids, you can see up north where the forests burned. That's Main Street, where people died!*

In the afternoon, Gene had on his 'this isn't going to be pleasant' face.

*Not now, Gene*, thought Molly. *Not today . . . Don't spoil it.*

'It's been good to see you,' he started. 'So, the day before Meteor Day, we agreed you would move back to normal shifts. But things have got worse, not better' – as she opened her mouth, he held up a hand to stop her, determined to have his say – 'and yes, I know it's been terrible, but the hospital's got those extra staff now, and Federal money coming. You *know* what happens when you overdo it, Molly.'

When her mood was up, she knew she could live with the grief. It was the darkness and the drink that could overwhelm her. 'I'm doing the best I can—'

'Molly, you can't solve everything. You're nailing yourself to the cross again. Don't let Jarman work you to death . . . I'm going to go over his head and complain.'

Fear turned her stomach. The last thing she needed was Gene poking the overwhelmed hospital administration into paying attention, asking questions.

He took her hand. 'Molly, you need to look after yourself.'

Her face grew warm with rising anger. 'Other people need me too, Gene. I'm sorry I can't be there for you all the time.'

But something more was coming, she could feel it. 'Molly, I spoke to one of your colleagues yesterday – she came into the library. Betty says you're not even on the ward.'

She had a moment of sheer panic then, like the times she had promised and then he had still found the bottles. For a moment she had no idea what to say.

'Jeez, Molly. I'm *worried*, don't you get it? I know there's something you're not telling me.' He was trying to look her in her eyes. 'Are you ill, or drinking again?'

'No!' She sounded as indignant as she felt. 'You know I can't discuss the work I'm doing – I've told you that.'

But he wouldn't let it go. 'You can't be working for the army – you wouldn't. And nor would Jarman.'

If in doubt, attack. 'You're spoiling my day off, the time off *you* wanted me to have. You're being unreasonable and selfish . . . Books don't die if you leave them. My work is *my* business.'

He snapped, 'I don't believe there is a patient. I'm fed up with being sold a line. Don't dump your garbage on me.'

That phrase goaded her, it always did, and he knew it. She exploded. 'It's work that keeps me alive – you've never under-stood that. There've been times when it was the only thing keeping me going.' As she threw some of the old arguments at him, a tiny, calm voice inside her was horrified.

Gene was shaking his head. 'I notice you haven't denied lying. How long must we pretend this is okay, Molly?'

People were watching. This was no place to have this discus-sion, but Gene would not be stopped. 'You're hiding something – I *won't* be lied to, Molly. We can't do that anymore.'

'You're a fine one to talk,' she said, and all the while a part of her screamed, *No, no, no!* but her rage carried her on. 'I didn't have to take you back. You knew I was sick and you still screwed around.'

His face burned. A woman walking her dog stopped. 'Don't change the subject.'

'When *that woman* threw herself at you, you could have said no.'

'I *did* say no,' Gene said. 'I've said it a hundred thousand times: I was stupid – I risked our marriage and I had no excuse. I nearly lost you, Molly, but I stopped at the edge, and I came back. You gave me another chance. And now you're lying to me.'

'How dare you!' Through her rage and shame, she thought, *Take it back, take it back, now.* In the dark years, Gene had learned to fight back.

'I know you're hiding something.'

'So go find some stupid housewife who doesn't want to work,' she said.

'You said you'd try, Molly. You said you'd make space for us. You said it would be different now—'

'—and then real life happened. Live with it.'

At that, Gene got up from the bench and strode off. Molly didn't follow. He'd walk for an hour, calm down and come back. She sat there and cried and wished she had a better grip on her temper, and when she'd stopped, she dried her eyes and composed an apology. *For bringing up that scheming woman, anyway. You're right. That's the past.* She would make firm commitments, somehow: a day, even a weekend off. But the conspirators were too few.

Gene just needed to be patient . . . But he'd ask, for how long, and what could she say? What if Cory never left isolation? How could she abandon him . . . even for Gene?

*I want a Scotch*, the little voice said. *Scotch makes this go away.*

Schoolchildren came and went, high-school students threw a football, a young man read a book, oblivious to the pretty girls passing by. Molly watched and waited, but two hours later, Gene still wasn't back.

And again, she thought: *I want a Scotch.*

How Cory would love to run and smell the Earth flowers . . . Maybe the pollen would kill him, or the bugs on the grass. Their latest fear was that he might be allergic to everything. Jarman was doing what experiments he could.

Yesterday she'd cried in the storeroom and snapped at the colleague who found her there. All children in danger brought up the nameless child she'd lost, who'd never had a chance. Well, crazy or not, Cory still stood a chance.

She sat on the bench as the sun sank, re-running the argument in her head. He was right. Before their child had died, there had been no secrets between her and Gene.

Darkness came, a dark night with no Moon, and at last, she drove back to Crooked Street. The lights in the house were off, just the porch light left on so she could see to slip in the key. Her stomach tensed. If Gene were awake, she might not have the courage to face him.

On the side, he'd left the little copper saucepan full of casserole. She lit the blue flame under it and made toast. She still had a bottle of Scotch hidden in the one place he'd never found. *Just one drink, just one*, her body cried.

Cory didn't need a drunk. He needed a mother. He found the toothbrush astonishing, but he quite liked the taste of baby toothpaste. He'd try to sneak a lick at the tube when he thought Molly wasn't looking. She had to hope it wasn't bad for him.

She ate the casserole half warm. *Not every husband would have done that*, she thought, even though she could tell Diane had made it. And she looked at the reproachful note in his cramped writing, not daring to open it, but knowing she'd need to.

Molly,
I thought we agreed, no secrets. When I screwed up, I told you. I don't know what the deal is, but it's eating you up. You've got to decide, because I can't live with someone who doesn't trust me.

That hieroglyph meant, *Love you, Gene.*

She lay in her cold single bed. On the other side of the wall, Gene snored in the double. Doubtless he'd spent hours wondering what'd gone wrong.

She'd keep this strange little boy alive, but it was driving her and Gene further apart. He knew she was lying – he knew she was not on the ward. He would expose her, even unintentionally, and Cory would be taken from her.

And yet, somehow, Molly's fear faded. She had decided Gene was the one; she had taken him back and the two of them had sworn to each other that there would be no lies.

Gene deserved to know. Gene *needed* to know.

Her oath as a professional was a wall, but brick by brick, it was crumbling.

She slipped out of the spare room and back into the double bed, under the warm quilt. Gene still slept neatly on the far side, his body always leaving the old space for her.

'Gene, are you awake? I've something important to tell you.'

He didn't stir, so she just held him close.

## CHAPTER 8

# *The day she told him*

Gene came into the kitchen in the grey light of dawn, vaguely conscious that Molly had been in his bed and was now gone. Molly was crying over pancake mix and a hot griddle. Without words, he took her in his arms. Sometimes tears were her fullest apology. He guessed that there had been a child and it had died. Any death was a tragedy, but maybe it would make their life simpler.

'It's fine,' she said, wiping her eyes with a hand. She sounded brisk and determined, like the old Molly he used to know. 'I just needed a clear-out. I've decided to tell you the story. You were right, I've hidden stuff, and I had a good reason, but it was still wrong, even though it wasn't my decision.'

They sat and he listened while she told him the story, rich in detail. She held his hands and he listened, unbelieving, but seeing the life in her face. How the tone of her words jarred with the shadows under her eyes . . .

When she had finished, she looked at him for a response, but his mind was whirling.

He repeated the story back, without comment. 'Sheriff Olsen and Dr Jarman found aliens on Meteor Day. Aliens from space. The mother died, but the boy survived.'

'Jarman told Olsen he died,' she said. 'Keep the thug out of it.'

Gene felt mocked – or maybe it was far worse; maybe she really was ill. Maybe she'd lost the ability to tell the real from the imagined . . .

'Cory's so sweet and smart and brave. You'll love him,' she said, sweeping back a stray lock of hair.

'You need to prove this,' Gene said.

'Of course. I'll tell the others I've told you, then you need to see him.'

Struggling to understand, Gene's voice was quiet as a breath. 'You don't even know if you can take him outside isolation. And you want to hide him from the government?'

'We *must* hide him, don't you see? If they find out, he'll disappear into some lab, for ever. He needs real parents, Gene, like us. Think about it: that monster Pfeiffer and that butcher in the White House?'

She looked like that time on borrowed bicycles, out by the lake, when he'd handed her the necklace, still unsure, and she'd loved it. The rain had caught them and even Molly thought being soaked and cold was a joke then. Her eyes were shining and he'd wanted to be in that moment for ever.

Now, here in their kitchen, his heart skipped a beat: she could still look like that. But for what?

*She's so stubborn, she'd drag a mountain behind her if she needed to,* he thought. Of all the Moon-touched nonsense . . . He realised

82

he wasn't ready, not for Molly to be ill again. Not for aliens to be real, here, today.

He was angry, he guessed, but more frightened that she was ill. 'This has to be true, Molly. I can't take another lie. I can't do it. It will bust our marriage apart if this isn't true.'

'You don't believe me. So come and see him.'

He'd nearly lost her into unimaginable darkness, so maybe her mind had gone. And if by some chance it was true, what a risk! What kind of people could take it on?

There must be more; she was nervous.

'Now, he looks a little unusual, but I bet we look really weird to him.'

'What do you mean, *unusual*?'

She ducked and weaved and in the end, she tried to draw this Cory with coloured crayons. Her attempts confused him more than explained anything; it looked like a creature from a nightmare.

'I just can't get it right.' She flicked the page. 'Oh, those things are just like fingers and tongues – honestly, you barely notice after a while. But they help you understand how he's feeling, his ears too: ears up means cheerful. He's very affectionate – and he's musical, he likes me singing. Bring the guitar, he'll love that. And Gene, he's so smart. Yesterday we ran through the words he's learned . . . eighty of them already!' She opened her eyes wide, pointed here and there and said 'What-called? What-called?' in a high, strange voice.

Words failed him. He couldn't think what to say.

'His language is unbelievable, it's all burbling and hoots and

whistles,' she went on. 'None of us can manage his real name.'
*Please*, her eyes were saying, *please*.

Every time Gene looked up at the stars, he knew there were
wonders there. Since he was a kid, he'd known the future would
bring a flood of great things, as certainly as he knew a thrown
ball must fall. Some would be bright and some terrible; some
would be both. But Gene knew he was no one special. He'd
hoped to meet the right person and have kids and maybe do
some good in a small way. But this? This was too big for him.

'What does he say . . . about where he came from?' he asked
at last. 'About what happened?'

Her eyes saddened. 'Not much. It's painful, he gets so distressed. We all figure he'll talk when he's ready.'

Perhaps someone had slipped her LSD? Once, she'd been as
Puritan about the new drugs as he was, but that . . . that *creature*
certainly looked like a hallucination.

But if the kid was real, what if he couldn't love it, with its
bizarre face? It was just like Molly to bet the farm on this one,
this strangest of all the sick children. If it died or didn't work
out, could they soak up another death?

He asked the next question as tenderly as he could. 'Suppose
the kid doesn't like me?'

'He's such a little bundle of love, he will,' Molly said, but
she looked away.

Gene wasn't ready to be a father. He wasn't sure he would
ever be ready. But how could he say that?

Gene watched Molly dress in her white uniform. Four months
without smoking and as he watched her go, suddenly Gene

hungered for a cigarette. Nerves like mice scampered in his gut. He'd agreed that at seven that evening he'd come to a side entrance of the hospital, one no patients ever used, and then he'd know the truth. But now he had to work.

The radio sang of *the Age of Aquarius*. He loved the idealism of the times but he loathed the mumbo-jumbo the New Age had brought with it.

Locking the front door, he saw Roy Henderson waiting in his truck.

'Want a ride?' Roy said. Gene preferred to walk, but he nodded; he liked Roy. He might be square and unimaginative as a brick outhouse, but he was a decent guy to have a beer with, as long as you stayed off politics. Roy never ran late by chance; if he'd parked outside, he had something to say.

In the truck, there was a solid, friendly silence. Two military trucks sat on the road, but that was nothing unusual nowadays. In the past few weeks, the traffic had changed in Amber Grove. A big Volkswagen camper, yellow with pink and blue flowers, made a clumsy turn; Roy braked and frowned.

'Jokers.' Then, he said, 'Diane was over last night. Janice and Diane, you know how those two talk.'

'Uh-huh,' Gene said.

'Yak about anything.'

'I guess.' Many times, Roy would drop over to take Gene out for a beer while Molly, Janice and Diane were putting the world to rights. It would be a long conversation, and men would be largely to blame.

'You and Molly should come over,' Roy said, glancing from

Gene to the road, to the mirror, then Gene again. 'We owe you supper, I'm sure.'

'She's working crazy hours,' Gene said. 'The Meteor shot everything to hell.'

'Yeah, tell me about it!' Life was now reckoned in two eras: Before the Meteor and After.

'When things quieten down,' Gene said. Did he believe Molly or not? If he did, the Myers wouldn't be chatting to anyone about the boy. Janice and Diane were like the FBI when it came to questions. Then you'd have to trust them not to tell their children, their relatives, their co-workers . . . Raising a kid completely on your own? But he'd have to tell his own parents at some point.

'How's business?'

'Nose above water,' said Roy, parking adeptly in sight of the library. 'Drop you here?'

Gene liked that men didn't need to spell things out. But he'd an odd question he needed to ask. He remembered all those bright afternoons playing ball with Roy and Chuck out on the meadow. The two red-heads, one big, one small, with the same smile and the same frown and, after a few days' sun, the same freckles. Chuck the Scout, the Little League slugger, the patient guardian of his little sisters. Any father would be proud of Chuck. 'Kind of a strange question . . . Molly wanted to know. When they hand you your kid in the hospital . . . for the first time . . . what's it like?'

*Does a father's love switch on like a light bulb, or is it like learning a musical instrument, all work and false starts and practice? Do you know when it works? Do you know when you're ready?*

The truck engine purred for almost a minute while Roy looked at him as if he had fallen from space. Then he sighed. 'It takes ages. You just stand there. Chuck looked at me with big eyes like, *This wasn't my idea. Your move, big guy.* But I guessed I was the father and I had to get on with it. I figured sometime, something would happen inside, and it did. Longest seven minutes of my life.'

Roy laughed, and Gene laughed too and got out of the truck.

That strangely endless day, Gene walked around his beloved library thinking, *If this is true, this is the biggest story in the world.*

Nowadays visitors streamed into the library to ask the same questions, over and over. Was it true the army built a fence in the woods? They'd heard someone found shards of strange metal and the government paid a bounty, no questions asked. Was that true? Intense men brandishing maps with red trajectories drawn on them explained their theories about why the Meteor should've fallen much faster from space. Ghouls wanted to see the damage. No one knew who first coined the phrase 'the Meteornauts', but it stuck.

Gene stayed polite, of course; he was a public servant – but people died on Meteor Day and seven people were still missing, one a fourteen-year-old girl. This wasn't some Disneyland spectacle to be gloated over. People here were tough, but sometimes he knew they were holding back tears. Amber Grove had scars, visible and invisible; it was far worse than the derailment, which still haunted the town all these years later.

He picked out some picture books and tucked them in his

attaché case. He had asked what the kid was interested in, and Molly had smiled widely and said, 'Everything!'

The library was there for everyone, respectable or not. They'd always had the odd hobo, pretending to read the newspapers to keep out of the cold, but now Amber Grove had all sorts. Some, with their shaggy hair and bright-coloured, stale-smelling clothes smelling of pot, clearly marched to a different drum. Sometimes they brought a child or two and Gene gladly steered them to the kids' library at the back, his particular pride and joy.

Sheriff Olsen would come like a wolf, looking for drugs or any other excuse to harass them. Amber Grove had its own long-hairs, but by and large they went to school or had jobs and parents who voted, so he sneered, but did no more. Outsiders who fell into his hands didn't get off so lightly. The Sheriff kept electric clippers at the station specially.

The library closed, his colleagues left, and Gene occupied himself with a back issue of *Witness*, skipping the editorials, admiring the photography and skimming the articles that took his interest. He planned to walk, although he hated carrying his guitar in its scuffed case; people always joshed him, asking for a song. He always joked that he'd learned it to attract girls, but then he found Molly before he'd got any good. You could stick him in front of a stranger and he could give a fulsome book report or talk about the town history without fear. But play or sing to someone he didn't know? It made his chest tighten and his pulse race.

Gene sat looking out of the window. Founders Green was once kept as neat as a golf course. He remembered his ears ringing on Meteor Day and how the solid stone library had bucked and the windows cracked. Now Meteornauts took photos of the giant fragment buried in the ground, ignoring the drizzle. In the solid pages of the *Hermes* and around the tables in Francine's, the town argued about what to do with this rock and who should pay. Mayor Rourke wanted a memorial to the dead and a museum for the tourists, something to bring more jobs, so no one would be digging up the rock without his say-so.

Gene bit a fingernail. He had two big fears: that he'd turn up to the hospital and Molly would say, 'Surprise!' and the others would come out laughing – or they'd show him the child, the unbelievable bomb that had dropped into their lives. Molly needed him to fall in love with the child so badly it hurt. If the child wasn't true . . . well, he didn't know where that left him, or his marriage. They'd made it through the dark years so far, but now he was scared. He thought they'd turned the corner these last few months. The war against the drink – well, they were surviving that, not winning, but at least they were fighting it together. There were small, tender wonders in Amber Grove: the return of her smile, the return to making love, the return to her jokes.

Now it was time for the truth.

Gene locked the library door, picked up his guitar and set out into the early evening dark and drizzle.

At the hospital side door, he put on the *Volunteer* armband as if it conveyed some sort of magical protection. His pulse was up, his stomach unsettled. He walked up the stairs and there was Sister Pearce, the short, ferocious one.

'She was specifically ordered not to tell you,' she said.

He shrugged. 'Try being married to her.'

The woman gave a cold smile, then turned and led him along a corridor.

He noticed a sign on a door:

LABORATORY.
NO UNAUTHORISED ADMITTANCE.
USE GROUND FLOOR LABS, EAST WING.
DR JARMAN

Sister Pearce stopped and said, 'Mice, guinea pigs, frogs and goldfish – none of them hurt by any of his bugs. So far at least.' She harrumphed. 'Doesn't mean his bugs can't wipe out the human race.'

They walked through a storeroom; she unlocked a door and ushered him into what turned out to be an outer room with an inner glass door to a much larger room beyond. All he could see was his wife, uniformed and masked.

Molly had already explained the anti-infection procedures, but Sister Pearce ran through it all again while Gene stripped off his rain-speckled outer clothes.

'You can watch his blood kill human bacteria in real time, but we can't test every possible danger. Jarman is worried about viruses. The boy's DNA seems similar to ours.'

She looked at the guitar case like it was a rattlesnake, then opened it and wiped the instrument down with a sharp-smelling cloth.

'Surgical gloves,' she said, holding out a pair.

'I can't wear gloves and play,' he protested.

She waved them. 'Surgeons remove brain tumours from children wearing these gloves.'

He decided not to mention the books.

No amount of words, no crayoned sketches or breathless descriptions had prepared him for what was waiting in the inner room. The creature sat cross-legged on the bed; he coughed and his tail twitched. Those big violet eyes focused on the guitar and the purplish-red tentacles danced like some exotic seaweed from *National Geographic*. Gene tried to hide his shudder. The eyes were beautiful, but not in a human way, and that face gave him the same unease in his gut as seeing his grandfather dead and made up in the open casket.

Of course it was an alien. The disturbing child in T-shirt and shorts had wires sticking everywhere. Molly went to sit by his side and even from that distance he could see her eyes above the mask were looking worried – but she had to realise how strange this was for him, how difficult. This creature belonged under alien skies unspeakable distances away.

*I'm not ready*.

He took a breath. 'Hi, little guy. I'm Gene.' He sat down and showed the boy the guitar.

The boy started to rock a little. 'Pleese-pleese-pleese,' he said, clapping with each word. He seemed all nerves too.

*Ridiculous*, thought Gene. *How can you tell what an alien with no real face is thinking?* He fumbled a note or two and launched into – *what an idiot!* – 'We Shall Overcome'.

Molly sang along and the alien swayed in time, and after a bit he joined in with fluting noises, wordless notes in harmony. He sure had good pitch.

'Good-good-more-pleeese.'

No one had ever written a book about this. In that tucked-away corner of the hospital, Gene invented three new choruses, singing, '*Humans and aliens together . . . some daaay-ay-ay-ay-ay . . .*'

Then he tried 'Puff the Magic Dragon', thinking he should've brought that kids' song-book they'd never used.

'What-meeen?' asked the boy.

*Lord knows how people argued over that.*

Those big eyes gripped him with their weird beauty. That odd skull. The tentacles weren't like worms really, much more like fronds of a sea anemone. Molly insisted they were neither cold nor slimy.

He pulled himself together and flashed Molly a sign with one hand: three fingers. Three meant, not bad.

She growled.

Gene said, 'We can explain his looks. We'll say he takes after your mother.'

Molly cuffed him. 'You monster, this is serious.' *She's all nerves*, he realised; *that stiffness is her hiding it.* She'd been living with this all those weeks without telling him, frightened of his response, just bluffing away.

He launched into 'Better Times' and the alien – *Cory* – clapped along with those strange paws – hands. They got two verses in before he realised that Molly was wiping her eyes.

'I'm ridiculous. Crying doesn't mean anything to them,' she said to Gene, then, 'It means I'm happy, Cory.'

'Yes-yes. Cory-home-with-Molly-and-Geeene. Sooooon.'

'When we can, sweetie-pie.'

Gene looked at her.

'Jarman's building an isolation unit in his house. I'd have to live in, like a housekeeper — maybe we could rent our place and live at his, free, of course. He's even got a car to lend us.'

But Gene knew Molly had another plan; he'd found rolls of thick plastic sheeting and hospital disinfectant. Medical equipment catalogues. Two unexplained tins of blue paint, enough to redo the back bedroom with the sunshine-yellow walls. They kept that door locked, as if to keep the memories trapped inside it. She'd always said blue for a boy.

Where else would Molly want her son to live?

Gene wasn't going to talk about that now, not here.

Cory was staring at the guitar like he might lick it. He moved those odd hands and after a burst of his language, a flurry of clicks, said, 'Cory-do?'

Gene vowed to take Molly through every rational objection. Yes, the kid was an orphan, yes, it needed love like any child, yes, it talked and could sing in tune — but this was *crazy*! Just the three of them, maybe for years, maybe for ever, against the whole world? Every man's hand would be raised against them if it got out. And this was not a healthy child, but one who might die at the first mistake they made. The child was so very different — a child he might not learn to love. Molly *must* see sense. It was down to him to be the realist, to be firm. This wasn't their problem. And he wasn't ready to be a father.

Inside, a little voice said, *But she loves him, and she needs you too. Yeah yeah yeah . . .*

# CHAPTER 9

## *Making plans*

They had to find things to feed Cory, as the alien meal pouches were running low. They had been trialling one human item at a time, the alien drug for anaphylactic shock at the ready, smelling his rations and trying to recreate smells and textures. Rice, eggs, bread and applesauce were all acceptable. Sardines mashed with peas had gone down well; he'd asked for that again. Molly, thinking of his dreams, had tried canned clams; they'd worked too. He liked cheese, but it gave him diarrhoea.

That lunchtime she'd made Cory an honest-to-goodness chicken sandwich; he'd sniffed it solemnly, looking at her, before slowly chewing a corner. Then he'd eaten the whole thing and four hours after, he still hadn't thrown up, so they added chicken to the list. He got odd purple rashes, but they went in hours, not days. The humans around him dared to hope he might be able to live safely on Earth. His colour was consistent now, and he wanted to exercise, which he did in strange jerky moves. And he wanted to *talk, talk, talk.*

'He's getting well,' Molly said.

Dr Jarman looked edgy, like a boy wanting to ask her on a date. 'Molly, did you take the old air-pump?'

Molly froze. 'What makes you think that?'

Jarman sighed.

*He doesn't want to confront me*, she thought, holding his gaze until his eyes dropped. She saw the flicker of knowledge on his face.

He said, 'You're building your own isolation unit. You want to take him to your house.' That curious smile hid anger. 'I have plenty of space, and research facilities – a little palace. And you're working behind my back.'

'Cory needs a home,' Molly said serenely. She hadn't felt like this for years. 'You're only offering him a nicer, more comfortable lab.'

'Molly, he'll expect you to be there. You'll have a key, and your own room. You'll be his main carer . . .'

Not a carer; she would be his mother. The word fitted, and it made her powerful. With another smile, she said, 'We'll give him a family, not a rota. Bless you for all you've done for him, but he's coming home.'

He stared. 'I won't allow it. We don't know it's safe—'

'Let's ask him,' Molly said. 'Let him decide. It's Cory's life.'

'You're being absurd.' He fell silent.

From inside the room came the sounds of hooting joy. Molly and Jarman turned to look through the glass door. Cory rolled the dice and moved his piece around the game-board in big exaggerated hops, counting in English. Pearce looked different when she was playing with him. Cory waved his hands over the board and Pearce laughed, trying the same odd motion.

Yesterday Molly had found herself chatting to Sister, who was very private outside the fierce discipline of her work.

'You could come to Mass with me on Sunday,' Pearce had said.

Molly judged Pearce's expression and decided it was a diplomatic opening of some sort. 'It's been a long time,' she said, politely.

Pearce shrugged. 'I bring my aunt. She's very frail, and confused by the changes in the church. Then we go for a little walk, or a coffee or something. You're probably busy.'

'Well, maybe we could meet afterwards?' Molly knew she needed Pearce on her side.

'Call me Rosa. Off-duty.'

Now, looking at the laughing child, she knew she hadn't yet won, but she was looking forward to the battle.

The following evening, when Gene came to the hidden rooms, Molly watched Cory hurl himself into Gene's arms, and how natural the embrace looked. The man and the boy had been so awkward together that first week, so uncertain, and it had worried her.

'Hello-hello Geeeeen. Read and sing and wash. Why no geetar now? Why sixty minutes hour . . . why twenty-four hours day? What banjo meeen?'

Molly needed to go scavenging. Jarman could disapprove all he wanted but she needed supplies and she knew how to get them. She told Cory she'd be back in a bit and went a-roving through the hospital she knew like her own home.

It always felt very different when visitors and day-cases were gone. Her route took her through the west wing, then along the main corridor on the ground floor, where just a few people were dawdling ahead of her. It was safe, familiar—

—when suddenly men started shouting and somewhere up ahead a high voice shrieked – and into the hall trotted soldiers, rifles held across their chests.

Molly's heart jumped. *No no no!* Weapons in the hospital felt so very wrong. A male voice barked, 'Secure the building!' and men in dark suits followed the soldiers towards the stairs and the elevators.

She wanted to flee, but she needed to understand the danger. In front of her, two orderlies and their grey patients in wheelchairs stared at the spectacle. Molly moved to the side of the corridor, hoping to see but somehow not be seen.

And there was the grim truth: in the centre of the hall stood Dr Jarman, stiff-backed and defiant. His arms were awkwardly positioned behind him and she realised he was handcuffed. Dr Pfeiffer, in a raincoat, had his back to Molly, but she could see he was waving his fists. And a few steps behind Pfeiffer, a tissue to her eyes, was Nurse Hooton. A stern woman beside her wore a uniform Molly didn't recognise.

She was finding it hard to take it all in. Pfeiffer's ugly voice, raised almost to a shout, was unmistakable. 'This is *obstruction*, this is *theft*, this is *treason*,' he repeated. 'What did you hide? Where are your notes? Tell us *everything*—'

'I'd like a lawyer,' Jarman said, calm and forceful, projecting his voice. His eyes caught Molly's just for a second. He showed no recognition, but his head twitched a little: *Go! Take Cory!*

Only one thing mattered now: she needed to keep Cory safe.

Pfeiffer snapped, 'Major, stop these people staring. Disperse them.'

Her heart thundered but she needed not to show it. She turned and walked away, busy, but not too busy. Running would look suspicious. There were dozens of soldiers swarming the hall. She had to find a phone – she had to warn Gene . . .

Had they been betrayed? Were more troops on the way? Did they know exactly where to look? She wouldn't think of Jarman, who'd saved Cory's life; she couldn't help him now.

Her heart skipped a beat: there were soldiers ahead of her too, guarding the ambulance entrance. Were there enough of them to guard every exit? Out in the parking lot, she saw camouflaged trucks and yet more uniformed men. She stilled her face and walked into a deserted clinic. Her hand trembling just a little, she picked up the phone and dialled the extension number that was listed nowhere but rang in the outer room of Cory's hiding place. Ring four times, pause and call again. Four, pause, four meant safe to answer. *Stay calm*, she told herself, *keep breathing and get on with it*.

Time was passing and Gene didn't answer. There were a dozen reasons he mightn't pick up. Two rings, pause, two rings, stop. That was the alarm.

For a moment, sheer fright held her: so many of them – what could she and Gene do? There was no time to lose.

The hospital grounds were surrounded by a wall. The southwest gate was for patients and visitors; the east gate for staff and deliveries. It was a trivial matter to block and guard both exits; there wasn't any way to get Cory to their car without being seen. Surely they'd search every vehicle trying to leave?

That left the long-disused, locked north gate. She got to the foot of the stairs and took them two at a time.

She turned on no lights, closed all doors quietly behind her and wherever she could, she ran. It felt like an age, but at last she reached the door to the hidden rooms. When she opened the outer door, she saw Gene hurling books and Cory's clothes into his hiker's backpack while Cory shuffled his drawings into a neat pile. His ears were right down.

'Soldiers and trucks,' Gene said. 'We saw them through the window. Molly, we have to take everything – we can't let them guess he was here.'

Molly put on her gloves, mask, apron. 'Jarman's been arrested. I'll get Cory's medicine box and the notes.'

'What-mean-bad-men?' said Cory. 'Molleee what-mean arrr-rest-ed? What sowl-jers?'

'Don't worry, sweetie-pie, it'll be fine,' Molly said, opening the inner door. 'We're going on an adventure: a drive outside.'

'Where's the car?' Gene said.

'It's in the staff parking lot. We can't take him out there, there'll be soldiers. We'll have to use the maintenance truck.'

'Go-out?' Cory asked, outer tentacles waving. The little inner tentacles slipped into his mouth, a bad sign, but those huge violet eyes looked hopeful. Going outside was Cory's dream. 'Driiive in truck?'

'It's a surprise,' she said. 'A lovely surprise.'

So far, all their lab tests had been largely reassuring, but they didn't know if letting him out was safe – for him, or for the world. His little room at home wasn't ready. And yet . . . what else could they do?

She took a deep breath. 'Let's take him home,' she said to Gene, her voice firm, brooking no argument.

Gene continued ramming things into pillowcases while they talked. 'They'll figure out who might be involved – they'll soon be after us.'

'Well, we can't stay here, can we?' She glared at him, then went back to checking items off her list on the wall. Did he expect to hide the boy in a tent in the woods?

They'd planned for this, of course. She bundled Cory into the sterile carrier they'd concocted, a plastic-lined wicker laundry basket on wheels. After weeks of fiddling, they'd got the fish-bowl helmet working again and attached to an oxygen tank.

Molly felt sick, her chest tight. *Soldiers with guns.* She hated guns, but if she had one now, she would be tempted to use it. *Get on with it*, she told herself. *Time is passing.*

How would you arrange a search? From the top down, with special attention on the fifth. *How much does Pfeiffer know?* If they had any clue about the annex, they'd be here already. She needed to rein in her fear and anger and focus on getting Cory out.

'What are we going to do?' Gene said.

The plan had assumed a little notice: load the laundry basket into their car or the hospital laundry truck and then drive away. But the main gates were guarded now. They would never get out that way.

'What about the roof?' He reached into the hamper and stroked Cory's hand.

She'd thought about hiding Cory in that strange kingdom of odd nooks and crannies, but it was too risky. The soldiers would be thorough.

101

'We use the north gate,' she said at last. The north grounds had been planted with flowering trees and bushes, allowed to flourish and hide the paths. And somehow, Jarman had tracked down the key, which was now safely in her pocket, along with a couple more she wasn't supposed to have.

'Okay . . .'

She tucked the folder of notes, the sacred papers of her profession, into the basket with Cory and told him, 'Remember, it's a keep quiet game, just like we played before, okay? It'll be fine.'

She dropped their aprons and masks into the bag of laundry and tagged it for full disinfection. 'Okay, once this goes in the chute, everything will disappear into the system. I'll just need to dive out on the first floor.'

Gene pulled a face. Molly looked at him, his face determined, and felt love despite the terror.

'What if the truck isn't there?' he said.

All she said was, 'Time to go.'

It was getting darker, but the Moon was almost full. The Myers pulled the wheeled basket, awkward with the heavy bags, out into the corridor. Around them was only the silence of the empty annexe, but the soldiers would surely come soon. They hurried for the back stairs. What would they say if soldiers found them? Molly would try something about clinical waste, but the truth was, if they were seen at all, it was over. The basket would be searched.

'Where's the truck kept?' Gene said.

The tricky part. Well, one of the tricky parts.

'The garage is behind the bushes. The quick way, we'll have to get Cory across a bit of yard and a footpath into those big bushes. After that, we'll be in the clear.'

He looked at her and said nothing.

The laundry basket was stubborn on the stairs but between them, somehow, they made it down the first flight.

'Okay, this is where I need to dump the laundry,' said Molly. 'I'll be quick. Hide in the storeroom.' She opened the door slightly and listened before walking, fast but not suspiciously, and Cory's laundry went down the chute.

Back with Gene, and Molly went a little ahead at the end to check the way was clear. The wheeled basket was easier on the flat. Round the next corner was the toolroom, a cubby-hole where the maintenance staff drank coffee and sometimes, at night, other things.

Molly listened, dreamed up a story and breezed into the room as if she belonged, but to her eternal relief, the room was dark and empty. She turned on the light, went to the rack of keys, each in its own place—

The truck key wasn't there. She paused, biting her lip. Had someone borrowed it? People did borrow hospital vehicles from time to time. She had no idea where else they could get a ride. Their own car was out of the question: even the stupidest soldier wouldn't let anyone out of the staff parking lot.

She reached out and touched each labelled key-hook, just to be sure she'd not missed it, but she hadn't. There was no truck key. Did Gene know how to hotwire a truck? He was good with vehicles. She should have stolen it and made a copy.

*A place for everything and everything in its place.* She always kept tools and medicines and important papers where she knew she could find them, but Gene . . . not so much.

She heard the door behind her. 'What's up?' Gene hissed.

'I can't find the key. Wait for me – I'm still looking.'

So maybe a man would think putting the key on the side, or maybe on top of the key board, was smarter. Her heart fluttering, she ran her fingers along the top of the wood. It was rough and dirty – and there was a key there, although heaven knew what for; it wasn't a vehicle.

Beneath the rack was a narrow bench. She swept her hand over it, then knelt down and peered underneath it. There was a glint of silver and green: the crucial key must have fallen. She scooped it up and ran back to Gene.

Somewhere far away she heard a shout and her heart skipped a beat, but they kept moving, pushing the basket to the side door. Thinking a calming prayer to a deity she did not believe in, Molly pulled out the copied key, pushed it into the lock, turned it – it didn't move easily, but at last she heard it click – and peeped out. Through the cool night air she could hear voices on the other side of the building; somewhere, a child was crying. A helicopter flew overhead, its searchlight illuminating the grounds. *Wait, wait*. No one was visible. They just needed to check no one was on the footpath.

'Behind us,' Gene hissed. 'People at the windows might see—'

But there weren't any ways out hidden from high windows; there was nothing they could do. Some risks had to be taken.

They had to cross the footpath and a strip of grass to get into the rhododendrons. Glossy leaves laden with flowers of red and pink and Cory-purple grew higher than she was. They would soon be hidden from view. But they had to get there.

'We'll be a sitting target,' whispered Gene, looking in every direction, judging the distance.

'Well, let's sit here until you have a better plan,' she snapped. *There's no innocent explanation if we're caught.* Heart pounding, she took her end of the basket and they started off, until they heard the helicopter again. Molly badly wanted to pee; she wanted to look back at the building and see who was looking down at them – but instead, she just kept ploughing forward, one step after another, until the glossy leaves closed around them.

Now even the hospital disappeared as the trail curved and the shielding undergrowth closed around them. Up ahead of them was the back of the garage, shrouded in trees. Molly walked round to the front. The key turned easily and there was the dark green pickup. If it had been moved, they'd be stealing a car, or walking Cory home.

Gene's mouth was at her ear. 'This might even work,' he said.

She sketched out the route in the air. 'This trail, they drive the truck on it all the time, so it'll be fine, and there's no reason for any soldiers to be there. I think we'd better drive without headlights . . .' She paused, all the things that could go wrong raising their ugly heads. But at least they had a chance.

Without any more discussion, they loaded Cory's basket into the pickup, locked the little wheels, then tied it in for safety.

Gene went around to the driver's side as Molly shut the tailgate. She took a few steps towards him, about to argue – she knew the way; she was the better driver – when she felt a cold wave of fear wash over her. Gene turned and stared at her, as if he was feeling it too. Somehow, she knew it was coming from Cory.

She went back and put her hand on the basket. 'Cory, we're here,' she whispered. 'I'm not going away, I promise. I'm here – we're both here, okay?'

And the feeling faded.

Gene was still staring. 'What the—'

'I don't know.' But they had no time to discuss what she didn't understand. 'Cory, sweetie-pie, we're going to drive in the truck now. Do you understand?'

He made some noise she took as assent.

Gene was in the driver's seat, but she had no patience for his unbending male pride behind the wheel. 'I know the way,' she said. 'I checked it out two days ago, when I was oiling the lock.'

He ignored her. 'Open the door, Molly, let's get going.'

*His ridiculous stubbornness! But don't lose your temper, now of all times . . .*

So she opened the garage door and Gene, frowning, started the truck and edged forward at a learner's pace. The rumbling truck engine sounded like a herd of elephants to her, but surely it wasn't that loud? There was plenty of noise coming from all over, so maybe one more engine would be ignored.

She closed the garage door and locked it. *Leave no clues.*

White stones along the edges of the track helped, and the foliage on either side was enough to hide them from the hospital, so long as the helicopter didn't fly right overhead – so long as no one was actively after them. Molly heard an owl, disturbed by the unnatural activity around it, but there were no soldiers barking orders behind them, no spotlights arcing around to capture them in their glare. Whatever chaos was engulfing the hospital, it wasn't following them, not yet . . .

Now Gene saw the north wall, eight feet high, stretching left and right in front of them.

'Up to the right,' Molly said softly. They were nearly at the gate. Nerves prickled, as if even the hairs on her skin could listen for danger.

'Stop!' she hissed, but he already had; he too had seen the flashlights moving up near the gate.

Was it just a couple of people, or were there more? Two, she guessed, two lights anyway. In the darkness, she couldn't be sure. But now the flashlight waved towards them and her heart started to pound again.

One of the men shouted, 'Armed police – halt!'

She touched Gene's shoulder. Surely he wouldn't try to drive through them? Shots would bring more people. 'Back up, Gene,' she said urgently, 'back up!'

Another little breath of fear came off Cory, picking their mood.

'Police! Stop right there!'

Gene backed up, not something you could do quickly, even if you wanted to. He had once broken a tail-light, backing up in a temper. 'Which way?' he snapped.

'Uh . . . keep going back into the woods.' *Concentrate on directions, remember the route.* She was sure it was just two men, but they might have radios. Where could they drive to? 'Turn around,' she said suddenly.

'No space. Where're we going?'

The truck lurched, tipping to the left, and there was a

sickening crunch. Gene hit the accelerator; the wheels spun and the engine ground, but the truck wasn't moving.

Gene cursed. 'I ran over something.'

The men would surround them soon, her wonderful Cory would fall into the hands of Dr Pfeiffer and his cronies and they would be put in jail.

Gene was fighting a tree to get the door open. 'Maybe the axle broke?'

Molly took deep breaths, counted slowly to three. *A nurse never panics; she figures out a plan.*

'We'll take him into the trees and hide him,' she said. *What else can we do?*

She leaped out, lowered the tailgate and took hold of the basket, wanting to croon to it. *The ropes, I have to undo the ropes.* She fumbled at the knots. This was taking too long.

She looked back to see the flashlights heading closer, moving slowly and steadily into the woods. They weren't running. Maybe they knew help was coming? Or perhaps they didn't want to run into a trap.

Gene was behind her now. Her breathing started to feel tight, but murmuring reassuring nonsense, she readied Cory's basket so they could slide it to the ground.

Then she heard a twig crack: someone was coming the other way. There was at least one person ahead and two behind. They were trapped, out of time and ideas.

'Cory,' she whispered. She felt him, somehow, fear coming off him in waves, strong, cold and vivid, but she couldn't open the basket to soothe him. Then something was happening: the world around her went away a little. The light was less light, the dark less dark. Sounds were muted and the sensation of fresh air on her skin faded just a touch. The only thing that remained was the fear; a little animal in the dark thinking *hide-hide-hide* . . .

Gene had hold of her arm. He was in this with her, whatever *this* was.

Molly turned her head to see a State Trooper walking round the truck, flashlight in one hand, something in the other. The light blinded her, full on her face . . .

He called out, 'They've gone.' He was looking in the front of the truck, searching for keys, she guessed, or anything left behind.

The other two were behind them now. Surely they must see them? Again, a torch shone right on her.

Scared, baffled, bewildered, she hugged the basket. How strange the night was. The woods around her were like a picture of woods; the men sounded suddenly so far away.

One was looking all around the pickup while another paced the ground a little further away. The third was still searching the cabin.

'This place is real creepy,' someone said.

'Where do you think they bury the corpses?' another asked. 'I hate hospitals, full of ghosts.' He walked around, lightly brushing against Molly, but still he didn't react.

'The truck didn't drive by itself,' said the one leaning through the driver's window.

The third spoke for the first time. 'If you think I'm telling anyone this truck is haunted, you've got a damn screw lose. They can't have got past us, so we keep going.'

And with that, they all walked away from the truck, away from the gate.

She sat in the strangeness, Gene's hand in hers. Cory pushed the basket-lid up and climbed out into her arms. He took the helmet off and for the first time, she touched her unmasked lips to his ear; for the first time, his cool tentacles stroked her bare skin.

'Cory,' she whispered, 'it's fine. Mom is here.'

Cory had hidden them both from the world. Somewhere a quiet, rational mind screamed, *Infection, disaster, death!* But she would be his mother and keep him safe for ever.

Was it minutes or hours? The night deepened around her, smells and sounds and shadows returning as Cory's fear and anxiety evaporated away. The sliver of Moon hanging above suggested little real time had passed. She smelled Cory properly: crushed herbs and some animal scent she remembered from childhood. A nightjar sang and his ears twitched. A big white moth fluttered here, some small thing scurried in the bushes there and his eyes darted to and fro. In his dreams, Cory never feared the dark. It was as if his tentacles were tasting the air of Earth, of *outside*, and found it good.

More police would be coming, so whatever had just happened, they had to move.

'You need to put on the helmet and get back in the basket, sweetie-pie,' Molly said, wondering when she had sat down. Cory's hand was stroking the wet grass that might have a million diseases on it, ticks and parasites.

His tail twitched against her. 'Tired-now,' he said. 'Earth so-good.'

She ought to disinfect him, but she needed to get away. Wiping his hands with alcohol was the best she could do right now. He gave her another strange, tentacled kiss. Gene was already up and looking under the truck to see if it could move.

'Back in the basket,' she ordered, but Cory's ears were up; he was listening to the owl.

'You drive, give it all we've got, I'll push from behind,' Gene said. 'Come on, Cory, in the basket and we'll take you home.'

'Home,' Cory said. He looked fit to drop. They packed him in the basket and heaved it back on the truck and, praise be, Molly took the driver's seat. They could hear shouting, but it was far away now; all they could do was hope some other drama was distracting the searchers.

Molly turned the key and jammed her foot down on the pedal. Gene grunted, the engine strained – and finally there was a clang from underneath the truck and it lurched forward.

Gene got in the back, panting. 'Let's go . . .'

Molly imagined Cory dozing in the basket, curled up like a puppy. Her world was full of wonders.

## CHAPTER 10

# *The escape*

The gate was unguarded, as they'd hoped, and the locks and hinges Molly had been oiling worked effortlessly. They took Cory home in joy and fear, desperately worried someone would notice them driving the hospital truck, or miss the vehicle, or that Dr Pfeiffer would find evidence of Cory.

Damnation! The lights in Mrs Hardesty's place were on, which meant her daughter-in-law was there, keeping an eye on the property. She was far more likely to snoop than old Mrs Hardesty. Well, there was nothing to be done but to move fast. Molly brought the truck to a stop outside their house, Gene clambered out of the back, looking up and down the little twisted end of the street to make sure no one was looking.

'I'll help you get him in, then I'll get rid of the pickup,' Gene said.

Together they lifted the basket out of the truck and walked up to the porch of their house. As soon as the front door was shut, Cory had the lid open, his eyes darting here and there.

'Home-now look-look everything.'

Molly put out a hand to stop him taking the helmet off. Just because he'd been exposed once didn't mean they should throw caution to the wind.

*Pad pad pad* as he raced off, twice around every room, a crazy purple cannonball, then up the stairs, *pad pad pad*, like a dog or their own little running ghost. She'd sketched him maps in those long evenings before going to sleep.

'Why room-only-Cory?' he'd kept asking.

*Pad pad pad* and here he came down the stairs, too many at a time; he skidded three from the bottom and grabbed the rail.

'You-show now-now-now. Everyplace. What little-door? What-that? What-for?'

'In a bit, I'll show you the attic. That's an exciting place.' That's where they'd hide him if anyone came; there was a crawlspace no grown person could get into.

His bedroom was blue, of course, with silver stars glued to the ceiling. Inside, they had constructed an inner room of plastic sheets with the air pump and filtration system spatchcocked so he could live in a clean bubble. It wasn't right; it needed more love to be a bedroom and more equipment to be a proper isolation unit, but they hadn't expected to need it so soon.

Cory rolled on the bed while they tried to figure out their next steps.

'Maybe we should leave town?' Gene suggested. They'd have to use the pickup with *Amber County Hospital* on the side as their car was still at the hospital, guarded by soldiers. Maybe they could borrow Janice's car?

'If Hooton is their source, they don't know he's alive.' Molly was clinging to that. 'We'll just have to bluff. Stow the truck somewhere out of the way.'

Cory was tired; his eyes were drifting shut and his head bobbing, beyond eating. 'Get him to bed,' Gene said. 'I'll put the truck in the garage for now.' Halfway through the first lullaby, she felt him slip into sleep. She wanted to join him, exhausted, but they needed to plan.

When Gene eventually rapped on the door – *shave and a haircut, two bits* – Molly was almost frantic. 'What took you so long?' she whispered, pulling him inside.

'Young Mrs Hardesty caught me. When will we tidy up the yard? Yak yak yak . . . But I've been thinking: we need to get on the road while we still can.' He rubbed his forehead. 'They'll come, tonight or tomorrow. It won't take them long to figure out which staff were involved . . . The truck is a smoking gun.'

Running away would be a blazing cross of guilt, of course. It would mean losing their friends, the house, everything they'd worked for . . . and with Dr Jarman in jail, the only doctor who knew anything about keeping Cory alive . . .

'Where would we even go?' she said, as if they'd not had the discussion before, dozens of times.

'Oh, it's a big country,' he said, waving his hands. 'The West Coast, maybe? Some little town in the redwoods, near the ocean . . . Or Canada, like the draft-dodgers.' They had talked of travelling, years ago, before the death. They could try Molly's sister in Indiana, but they'd grown apart. If Molly turned up as a fugitive, of course her sister would take her in, for a night, or even a couple of days, but her brother-in-law was painfully square and, rightly, she wouldn't want to put her nephews at risk.

'Or we could go to my parents',' Gene suggested. 'Grandpa was always telling us stories about how easy it was to hide around the farm in Prohibition days.'

They were home at last. Would it be any safer to flee? 'Or we just brazen it out,' Molly said. 'They all think he's dead, after all.'

At midnight, Gene went out and hid the truck in the scrubland. They couldn't decide whether to burn it or keep it as a getaway until they had their own vehicle readied.

Cory sat by the window looking out at the trees, his tentacles rippling a little. That was his *wanting something* expression.

'Outsiiide,' he said when Molly asked. 'Hide-from Bad Men outside. Birds-and-flowers.'

'Cory, it would really help if you explained how this hiding works. The soldiers couldn't see you – or us.'

He looked at her, head on one side. 'Hiiide. Cory not understand. Not work on adults. Are Bad Men children?'

'No, humans can't do that. None of us can.'

'Good. Cory hiiide from Bad Men.'

'Yes, good. If they come.' She felt like tearing her hair out. Gene had walked to the truck and found it gone, so someone knew how to hotwire a truck for sure.

'Go outsiiide.'

'Cory, you'll get sick.'

'Outside smell fiiine.'

Molly remembered the feeling that had come off him in

those first days, when Nurse Hooton had said, 'I was shivers all over . . . like he called up a cold gust of wind.' Cory was so likeable, but these things showed he *wasn't* human.

Gene offered to distract him so she could make lunch. A few minutes later, as she got out the makings for a tuna salad, she heard 'California Dreaming' coming from their bedroom while Cory crooned along, something unworldly.

There was an imperious rap on the door.

It'd begun.

As a teenager, Molly had realised that her mother couldn't see the truth in her face, no matter what she said. And a drunk is always a good liar; they get so much practice lying to themselves. She had prepared her story for this moment with the same care she'd taken with her nursing exam.

Wiping her hands, taking her time, she went to the door.

The banging got louder. 'Open up, Mrs Myers,' someone shouted. 'We have a warrant.'

She opened the door to Dr Pfeiffer and a tall man in FBI black.

'Special Agent Anderson, FBI,' said the tall man. 'I think you know why we're here, ma'am.' Black hair touched with grey; fearless eyes. Polite and tough.

Behind them was another FBI agent and two young soldiers, one carrying a holdall. Pfeiffer had cut himself shaving; he looked ragged and red-eyed. Behind them she could see a military truck and two more FBI waiting in a black town car.

'You'd better come in,' Molly said, her eyes lowered. 'I'm not going to deny anything.' Inside, she was burning, but she had a role to play. Men with guns were coming into her house,

but that wasn't what made her scared. They all knew the plan:
Cory would go into the attic crawlspace, which had been lined
with clean plastic. It was just she wanted to be holding him,
reassuring him, keeping him safe.

'Do you want coffee?' she asked. Her voice sounded dull,
defeated.

'This isn't a social call,' Pfeiffer said, looking to see that the
front door was shut. 'You hid the alien.'

'Yes, and he died.' She turned away from him and called,
'Gene, we have visitors.' She was playing for high stakes: Cory's
freedom, or even his life.

The intruders sat in the front room and Pfeiffer looked at the
bookshelves, a sour expression on his face. Gene came down
the stairs, very sombre, and said, 'Dr Jarman should be locked
up. My wife's *sick* and he took advantage of her. She told me
everything, after the creature died.'

'You're in serious trouble,' Pfeiffer said. 'This is a matter of
National Security, do you understand that? *Serious*. Let's get
the facts straight.'

'I'd better start,' Anderson said, butting in. The two men
were clearly at odds, which reassured Molly a tiny bit. 'Tell us
what happened, Mrs Myers.'

She got out a tissue, to illustrate her grief, but really, she
was using it to hide her nerves. It felt as if a quivering bird was
hiding in her stomach.

'We called him Cory. He was a child, a real person.' She told
the unvarnished truth about those first few days, not sparing
her feelings. To her surprise, one of the soldiers took down her
words in confident shorthand.

118

Anderson wanted to know who knew – surely everyone on the fifth floor must have known? Who had she told? Family, friends . . . Molly was still shaking her head when the doctor interrupted.

Making a face, Pfeiffer growled, 'What *possessed* you? You took such a risk, with the child, with *infection* . . .'

She gave him chapter and verse on their precautions, how professional they had been. Then she gave them Cory's death, complete with tears that were heartrendingly easy to summon. Pfeiffer looked embarrassed and the shorthand soldier sympathetic, but the FBI man was the one she feared: he was a cipher, a machine who watched her face, spat out polite sentences and gave nothing away.

The conspirators had play-acted the death to make sure they got the story exactly right. They'd even walked the route to the incinerator.

Pfeiffer began throwing questions: *When did you know? Who did Jarman tell? Was he working with anyone outside the hospital? Was there any discussion with a foreign power? Did you talk about selling the alien?*

'Don't bully her,' Gene snapped at last. 'She'll answer your questions, but you haven't even let her speak.'

Looking grim, Anderson took control again. 'Perhaps one point at a time. Mrs Myers, did Dr Jarman ever discuss telling a foreign power?'

'We just wanted to keep him alive,' Molly said, 'so that I could bring him home.'

And on it went.

'Why didn't you tell us when the child died?'

Gene simmered and sometimes snapped, visibly angry at Jarman's arrogance and how he'd dragged Molly into the affair, but other than that, he said as little as possible; after all, he had never been on the fifth floor.

Pfeiffer and the FBI agent looked at each other. Pfeiffer opened his holdall and spread folders out on her table. One was a Xerox of notes, the fake set that ended with his death. There were photos of the dead adults. Another folder had *Myers, M* on the cover: her employee file. She was angry, but she could use what her file said against them.

'This was dangerous and unprofessional. You were unbelievably reckless,' Pfeiffer repeated. 'You could have released some alien epidemic – it could have been worse than the Black Death. You ought to go to jail for stupidity alone!'

Pfeiffer was clearly obsessed with Cory. He kept asking for her observations and challenged things they had written in the notes.

Molly talked freely, because she was cooperating, wasn't she? 'He was like a human child, really,' she said for the third or fourth time. 'I mean, he looked bizarre, but in time, we could have learned to understand him. He already knew my name . . .'

Pfeiffer sighed. 'Well, of course he died. If you people had only told me, I'd have been able to save him – and not just the child, but everything he could have told us: their science, their culture, their intentions towards Earth, how to use their machines—'

'The nurses all thought we should tell the authorities.' She was as pious as little Molly had been, going to school Mass in her plaid skirt.

The FBI man said, 'Please don't sell me that line, Mrs Myers.'

Molly kept her face still as a new fear washed over her. What would happen if the FBI took them away? Cory had enough food and water in the attic to last for a few days, but how frightened he would be . . . Could he even use a can-opener? How would he cope? The men would search the house, of course. There were so many things they hadn't thought through . . . She felt the power and the reach of the government all around her.

'You're right,' she said, humble now. 'We got carried away. It was stupid, really.'

'If you don't mind, Dr Pfeiffer.' The FBI man returned to the peace groups Gene and Molly used to be involved with. Had they discussed Cory with any of them?

'All that feels such a long time ago,' she said honestly.

Gene insisted on getting Molly a soda, and a soldier went with him. As soon as they stepped out of the room, the conversation turned.

'What about the alien machines?' Pfeiffer asked.

'We had some medicines and their spacesuits, but I never had anything to do with them,' Molly told him.

Pfeiffer opened the holdall and produced a clear plastic bag. Inside was the black and silver box, about the size of two cartons of cigarettes.

'That's the voice translation machine,' Molly said, remembering how Cory, frustrated, had thrown it across the room. *How much easier things would have been — would be now — if we fully understood him.*

Pfeiffer produced a second clear bag from the holdall. Inside was the slim watch-thing that had disappeared from Cory's wrist in those first hours.

'Oh! Yes, he was wearing that on the first night,' she said, 'but it disappeared.' Cory asked for it, much later, by drawing it; he said it played music.

'Nurse Hooton took a little souvenir,' Pfeiffer said, like he was enjoying revealing human weakness. He put the device back into the holdall. 'When she tried to sell it, we realised she had something much bigger. One night under armed guard and she told us *everything*. Don't worry; we'll be searching the house for any souvenirs you might have taken too.'

The soldier who had escorted Gene went out to the street and reappeared moments later with two dogs, German shepherds, not a breed Molly liked. She gave Gene a look, her heart in her mouth: they should've thought of dogs. Would they bother taking them up the ladder to the attic? Would the dogs find Cory's scent over the disinfectant?

'What do you want dogs for?' Gene said. 'I'm allergic.' She could have kicked him for the stupid, unnecessary lie.

The FBI man showed the first sign of being human. 'Go in the garden if you need to.'

Molly took control. 'I'll come upstairs to open things up for you. I don't mind the dogs, so long as they don't make a mess.'

Cory's bedroom made the FBI guy stare at her. 'You planned to bring him here?'

'We wanted to give him a home,' Molly said, and now the tears flowed for real. 'His mother had died . . . he didn't have anyone . . .'

There were clothes and books and toys bought for him. At midnight, the Myers had decided it to leave it all out, like some perverse shrine, rather than try to hide it all. Right now, it felt like a big mistake.

Dr Pfeiffer looked at her oddly as the men searched Cory's things. They got to the drawer of clothes, the things she'd kept from years ago.

'My baby died,' she said simply, the tears still flowing. She turned away so she didn't have to see them violate her memories.

The other FBI men had joined the search. One climbed the attic ladder and was feeling for the light-switch.

She closed her eyes and silently said the drunkard's prayer, sending it up for all she was confident there was no one to hear it. *Was that a muffled sneeze?* She tried to control her breathing, not give anything away.

'Guess we could get a dog up here,' he called down at last. 'Mind you, it'll be fun getting her down again.'

'There's something going on down here,' the handler said as the dogs went running in and out of the bedrooms, their tails wagging, eager and a little perplexed. They rolled on the carpet in Molly and Gene's bedroom like puppies.

'Bess, Marcie, work time! Quit playing!' said the handler. He had rather a sweet face, Molly thought; she liked the way he jollied the dogs along rather than snapping at them.

'What've they found?' asked Pfeiffer eagerly.

'A bird flew in a few nights back and bashed its brains out,' Molly said. That had happened once. 'Can't you smell the disinfectant? And we have mice – I keep thinking we really should get a cat.'

'Take up the carpet in case there's something under it.' Anderson turned to her. 'You can go downstairs, ma'am.' It wasn't a suggestion.

'I'll take that coffee, Mrs Myers,' said Pfeiffer as she left.

*You invade my home and expect me to cater?* she thought, furious.

Downstairs, Gene was standing by the open back door, smoking; he flicked the cigarette away as soon as he saw Molly. She was so tense herself that she easily forgave him the lapse. Outside, two soldiers were searching the overgrown tangle that was their garden.

She mustn't look upwards, although she could hear the FBI men and their dogs trampling through the bedrooms . . . Only Cory's strange power could save them.

'How did you know he understood you?' Pfeiffer said, appearing suddenly at her shoulder. She hadn't even heard him come down the stairs. 'We pretend we know what dogs and cats are thinking, but we're just anthropomorphising them.'

She thought about his question. 'Well, even though we were always masked up, he could tell me from Nurse Fell. He understood names . . .'

*Pfeiffer must be able to hear my heartbeat. Keep breathing*, she told herself, *breathing as slow as you can. Keep talking about how smart he was, not how smart he is.*

Oh Lord, the neighbours – the whole street would know they were in some sort of trouble. Not that she talked to many of them . . .

Gene and Molly, holding hands, went to sit in their kitchen while the clock hands ticked round. The dogs came down the stairs, followed by the handler and the FBI man, and Pfeiffer went over to confer with them.

Molly could hear the dog handler praising the dogs. 'Marcie was just playing . . . yes-she-was. Bess too . . . yes-she-was.'

'Mr Myers, Mrs Myers, let's talk,' said Anderson, coming into the kitchen. 'Your politics are none of my business. I just care about my country. A word of this and you'll go to a Federal prison. You will be locked up for life, alongside the spies and the traitors who have put our country at risk. Do you understand what I am saying?'

Gene, bristling, demanded, 'Which *actual* laws did Molly break?' but Molly started to shush him.

'Don't be hostile, Gene,' she said, putting a hand on his arm. 'You were right: it was a mistake and I know that. I'm not going to tell the world about it.'

'Word gets around in small towns,' Anderson said. 'We're going with the radioactivity story. There'll be more questions, and we'll need you to sign an agreement. If you keep your mouths shut, then we can just let this ride. If it gets out, we'll know who talked.' He produced papers. 'The Executive Order, and the Acts that authorise it.'

Molly nodded. 'We won't make any trouble,' she said, pinning Gene with a glare. 'We'll sign anything. Come back if you have more questions. We'll try to help.'

'It's a weird house,' someone in the hall said. 'Did you feel it? Like we were being watched . . .'

'What about Dr Jarman?' Molly said. 'Will he go to prison?'

There was a pause. *The authorities have a problem.* Everyone knew Dr Jarman. He'd cared for their sick children and

125

grandchildren, delivered their babies in thunderstorms and on holidays, he'd offered trusted advice to the adults and he'd given his energy to serving the people. As if that wasn't enough, his father-in-law was rich, a Bradley, no less, who knew people in State politics. Dr Jarman was not someone you could lock up without causing an enormous fuss.

'I can't discuss that,' Anderson said at last, ignoring Pfeiffer's glowering.

Maybe it was a trap: the FBI would let them all go and be on the watch for them to incriminate themselves.

Pfeiffer was looking at Molly, rather oddly.

'Let me show you out,' Gene said.

Without any word, Pfeiffer turned and left.

Molly counted to ten, and then did it again, and again. *Had they left anyone?* She checked the ground floor, then went up the stairs two at a time. *Is the house really empty? We must* never *talk about Cory on the phone.* Three steps up that stupid attic ladder it suddenly struck her: Cory hadn't been hiding there at all.

She hurried to their bedroom, where the dogs had been acting up, and stood in the doorway. *Where was he?* 'Cory, it's me,' she whispered, and the next second, Cory appeared in the closet. To her alarm, the helmet was in his lap. She took him in her arms and carried him to the bed, hugging him.

'Clever to hide,' she said. 'The bad men have gone. But we need to be careful: always keep watching for them, okay?'

'Bad Men gone,' he agreed. 'Cory hiiiiide. What-called?' He made an excellent little bark.

'Dogs, Cory. The bad men had dogs. Like the ones in the book.'

'Dogs like Cory. Dogs freeennds.'

That hug lasted for ever and he showed no signs of wanting it to end.

She'd never again hear a knock at the door without wondering if it was someone come to take Cory away.

Footsteps sounded in the hall and Gene appeared at the bedroom door. 'That Pfeiffer is an odd guy,' he said.

'You're telling me. What a reptile.'

'What rep-tile?' asked Cory.

'You won't guess what he said to me,' Gene went on. 'He told me he guessed male doctors don't get what it's like for a woman to lose a baby! Honestly! He said you should find a female doctor – a psychiatrist.'

'Oh, he'd love to find someone to spy on me,' she said, feeling heat in her cheeks. 'That little skunk.' He couldn't have been genuine, surely. But purple ears were listening; she had to be careful.

'Well, maybe.' Gene didn't look convinced. 'You do crazy very well, Molly: cold, quiet and nuts.'

'Nuts enough to marry you,' she said.

Cory sneezed. It was quite a show, tentacles writhing all over the place, and Molly jumped up. 'Come on you: let's get you washed up, shall we?' She got him disinfected and back in the clean room, but it looked like Earth wasn't going to kill Cory just yet.

Later that day, in the kitchen, Molly started plotting. Lying to the authorities didn't trouble her one bit, but lying to her friends did – but what choice did she have? Off work again, and soldiers at the house for hours? Janice and Diane would need a story. Since the Meteor, there'd been endless notes and calls, but she'd played tired, managing a quick coffee here and there to keep things more or less under control. Now she was home, though, Janice would be popping over, expecting to stay all afternoon, searching the refrigerator or the cupboards for snacks, generally treating the place as her own, just like normal. She'd likely bring the twins, who'd be halfway around the house before you'd finished turning your back.

Diane's steely gaze could tell almost instantly if Gene was smoking or if Molly was drinking; Molly sometimes thought her friend even knew when the Myers weren't sharing the double bed.

'Put them off – go to theirs,' Gene suggested. 'I like your friends, I really do, but you have to admit, they're nosy as hell.'

She sighed. *Men don't understand.* Not asking them over would be a red flag. She'd need to play it just right. So she phoned and asked them to tea, the first time since Meteor Day. Gene would take himself upstairs.

'Not Bad Men?' said Cory.

She kissed his ear. 'No, they are my friends: but we can't tell them about you. Cory, it's *really* important you stay hidden. Do you understand?' She didn't think he did.

'O-kay.'

'And in the attic, not the bedroom. And no sneaking around, yes? We'll put the books there, ready, shall we?'

'O-kay.'

And when Diane and Janice came to the door, eager for the story, Molly hugged them both and felt the tears come, tears of relief, and fear for the future.

'Molly, they brought dogs and everything!' Janice said, her voice shocked. 'It's like Russia!'

'Oh, it was a muddle,' Molly started. She offered shop cake and lied calmly, 'Such a nonsense! They're so paranoid about the radiation, they completely over-reacted. Bad enough they've fenced off Two Mile Lake, but I guess it's not safe to fish in or swim in anymore. Anyway' – she took Janice by one hand and Diane by the other – 'so . . .'

She paused and took a deep breath. 'So, another child died, on Meteor Day, this sweet little boy . . . it was from the radiation. I thought I could take it, you know? I thought I—'

Her friends hugged her again as she admitted, 'It's too much. I'm leaving work, just for a while.'

Kindness ran so deep in them. Diane offered wise words from her own grief; Janice, her best friend, found something strengthening to say and Molly felt so ashamed. They were so generous to her. She could ask them *anything* – and here she was, lying to them.

Diane looked at her softly. 'How are you feeling, Molly? How well are you?' That was their code.

She smiled wryly. 'I'm still sober, at least, but it's real hard. I'm going to find a new doctor.' Another lie.

'And how's Gene doing?' asked Diane. That was code too.

'Oh, we're getting along okay, but it's been tough for him. He should maybe go for a beer with Roy.' She paused, then took their hands in hers. 'Listen, I need something from you. Just sometimes, can we go out? To Francine's, or for a walk, or into Bradleyburg. I feel so trapped – and it's easier to talk somewhere else . . .'

It would be easier to hide Cory if her friends were never in the house. And she missed them both. She wouldn't cut them out of her life, but her lies meant their friendship would never be the same.

'Of course!' they both said, their eyes full of compassion. 'Of course.'

Molly felt like the worst person in the world. She knew she could tell them, but . . . Janice would tell Roy, and he was a good husband, a decent, gentle father, an honest and upright man, but he trusted the President and the FBI; he would be torn apart by hiding Cory. And Diane's sister was often at her house, and the minister was a frequent visitor. And their children . . . *Three people can keep a secret if two are dead.*

Cory came first – and at least this way she could stay friends, go out with them, even if she did have to live as mad Molly, the almost-recluse, most of the time.

Only after they were gone did Molly breathe easily. She shut the front door and leaned her head against it for a moment. If she wanted to keep Cory safe, lying to her friends was the only thing she could do.

She turned to see Cory in the helmet coming down the stairs. He must have been on the landing, listening.

'What-do?' he said, clinging to the banister rail.

And she breathed out all the worry and all the futures she couldn't see. 'So many exciting things, Cory. We'll do lessons and games. I'll see if I can take you into the garden.'

'No helmet now. Cory fine.'

He couldn't know it was safe; she saw endless arguments ahead of them. Infection control still mattered, even if he'd been exposed, at least until they knew more. 'And in a day or two, I might take you out in the car. Won't that be exciting?'

'Swim-swim-swim!'

When she slept in the hospital, he'd slipped into her dreams and she'd felt his pleasure at being in the water. Jarman's house had a swimming pool, but she dared not take Cory there, not now, in case the place was being watched . . . The waterhole down in the meadow was often green with scum, which was just begging for him to catch some disease.

'In time, Cory,' she prevaricated, 'in time.' There were so many dangers – and yet so much else to see and do, as long as they were careful.

'Let's put some music on the radio and I'll teach you an Earth dance.'

Her bare hand touched his ear. *No*, she thought, *we can only keep Cory safe if we keep him a secret.*

## CHAPTER 11

# *Under the lake*

Dr Pfeiffer drove up the familiar road into the sunlight-dappled woods. The old sign with a jolly cartoon of a boat on water said *Two Mile Lake, 1½ miles*. The new, brash, much larger sign, said US ARMY, DANGER, RESTRICTED, NO THROUGH ROAD.

Pfeiffer had watched the Engineering Corp toiling day and night under the floodlights running off those stinking diesel generators, turning the forest into a place of barked orders, whining saws, clanging poles and rumbling earth-moving equipment. Trucks with materials and men had arrived throughout the night, so no one got any sleep. Of course, it was no intellectual achievement, but he had to admire the brute efficiency of the army's plan.

The impact crater to the east was impressive: he had walked through trees turned to fallen stalks of charcoal to a textbook crater as big as a park, littered with lumps of twisted space-iron the size of houses. But he had little interest in the impact crater, and the Meteor itself was notable purely for its size.

What mattered to Dr Pfeiffer was the lake and what hid within it.

Now he was driving parallel to the double fence topped with barbed wire and strung with alarms. The signs grew more threatening:

## ARREST, ARMED SOLDIERS, FEDERAL LAW!

and

## ☢ WARNING: RADIOACTIVITY ☢

Fourteen miles of fence, and most weeks some joker tried to get in. And there was a gatehouse, thirty yards from the gate proper, an army truck waiting on the other side so no one could try to squeeze round it.

An armed soldier came out while the guards in the tower raised binoculars to stare at him. The soldier saluted him, which pleased Pfeiffer, although he doubted the camp commander would be so happy.

'Dr Pfeiffer,' the soldier said, starting to raise the pole.

'You should check my pass,' Pfeiffer said. 'I might be an imposter.'

So the man checked the licence plate of the car against the list and Dr Pfeiffer's pass photo against the real man. Pfeiffer was not displeased that the man was so quick to obey him, but still, security was security. He wouldn't put it past the Soviets to be able to find a look-alike.

Two Mile Lake hid the most precious secret in the country,

a truth hidden from all but the most senior officers. The Ship. Even the existence of the alien spacecraft could not be referred to in unscrambled communications.

As the gate opened, Pfeiffer took the radioactive safety monitor from his pocket and pinned it to his lapel. His heart rate was rising: he was seeking an audience with an oracle from another world – and whatever was lurking deep in the water could reason and argue and threaten with the best of them. Pfeiffer had never said so aloud, but he thought of it as *alive*.

The lake glinted gold, but its depths were hidden. All the wooden cabins round the shore had been requisitioned by the army, but for a moment, the view made him remember holidays with his daughters; they'd always enjoyed summers at the cabin. He missed them.

The radioactivity story was true: the Ship *was* throwing off powerful radiation. The water mitigated the danger, but no one slept anyway near it. The engineers had blocked the lake outflow to protect the water table. Tents and pre-fab army cabins clustered by the shore of the lake, a sort of squatters' camp, extraordinarily poor conditions for the scientists' important work. He'd blown up at some functionary trying to cut costs, shouting, 'I can't work in a shed,' and from that day, all the scientists called the camp the Shed.

Pfeiffer parked his car and walked the rest of the way. Dr Haldeman came out to meet him. The top NASA scientist was tall and lean. He was Pfeiffer's age and yet he ran three miles in the forest every morning and enjoyed it. Pfeiffer loathed that type of silver-spooned Anglo-Saxon Protestant hearty, but Haldeman met his exacting test for brilliance, so they had formed a frigid and effective alliance, united by the overriding importance of stopping the army putting one of their mediocre scientist-bureaucrats in charge.

'Dr Pfeiffer.'

'Dr Haldeman. Are we ready to go?'

'Yes, we got the apparatus to the end of the jetty. The Ship wasn't happy.'

The wooden jetty had once been a diving board for summer holiday-goers and, in cooler seasons, a place to fish from. Now the fish were dying and today Dr Haldeman had put machines on it so they could spy on the Ship, the craft from the stars whose first words, over ordinary radio, had been, 'I am damaged and may explode. Withdraw to a distance of at least two miles.'

The main room was crammed with equipment, glowing screens and dials, and shirt-sleeved scientists. There was the microphone, through which they now spoke securely, and a man with a massive reel-to-reel tape recorder sat by the speaker every minute of the day, in case the Ship had anything to say. Most days it didn't.

'Ship, this is Dr Pfeiffer and Dr Haldeman.'

They waited. Pfeiffer put his hand over the microphone. 'So, if it emits muons . . .'

'. . . then it isn't powered by nuclear fission. It's a wholly unknown energy source,' Haldeman said, rubbing his hands. 'Or maybe exotic new particles?'

'This is the Ship. What is the purpose of the devices on the jetty?' The vessel's most banal comments still made Pfeiffer tingle. The Ship spoke in a perfect, neutral, unemotional Mid-Western English. Only the intonation was sometimes a little odd. It clearly knew speech had to be modulated to sound normal; it just didn't always get it right.

'Ship, good afternoon,' Pfeiffer responded. 'We are concerned about the radiation you emit. We need to monitor it.'

'It would be safest to withdraw to a greater distance.'

'Are we interfering with your repairs?' That was Haldeman; they still needed to ascertain whether the Ship could repair itself.

The Ship would have made a good poker player. It answered many questions with silence. It made noises underwater; there were sometimes lights. The radioactivity fluctuated. The Ship was not inert.

'If the devices are intended to interfere with me, I will destroy them. Even your technology allows you to assess the radiation risk from the shore. Your story is implausible. Remove the devices.'

Haldeman was scribbling on a pad. Pfeiffer decoded the writing. *Ask how does it 'see' the devices.* Good question, and exactly the sort it never answered.

'Are our monitors causing you any inconvenience?'

'Your presence causes me inconvenience. Please leave. I can contact you if I require it.'

'This is our planet,' Pfeiffer said. 'We need a better reason to leave our own lake-side.'

'Will you remove these devices?' the Ship said.

Pfeiffer glanced at Haldeman, who shook his head.

'No,' Pfeiffer said.

There was silence for a count of four or five seconds, then the walls of the hut shook as a dull boom emanated from the direction of the lake. The light from the lake-facing window changed, dirty water slashed across the window and something large bounced off the corrugated roof.

Red lights flickered wildly all around the room, as the growl of an unhappy Geiger counter started. The man monitoring it started reading out figures, a tremor in his voice.

Everyone crowded around the window. Pfeiffer, the furthest away and the shortest, couldn't see what was happening.

'It blew up the jetty,' someone said.

Pfeiffer pushed his way to the front to see the surface of the lake was roiling like boiling coffee. Pieces of blackened wood floated there, and yet more dead fish.

'Keep an eye on the radiation levels. Let's not take any risks,' Pfeiffer said, but his gaze was still fixed on the lake, where the Ship hid.

Haldeman drummed his fingers on his thighs, pure glee. 'Well, we prodded it and it lashed out. I can't wait to look at the other detectors. Whatever it did must have left a trace. There must be some exotic energies involved . . .'

'I think it uses the radioactivity to frighten us off,' Pfeiffer said. 'Like insects that squirt poison. We should send two divers down, really challenge its boundaries. Put an X-ray source on the hull, or conduct some electrical activity right next to it.'

Haldeman's mouth was open, wordless for a moment. 'My God, they would get a hell of a dose – and the machine might just kill them.'

'Well, yes, we'd need to plan it,' Pfeiffer agreed. Of course, the men might die, and that would be genuinely unfortunate. But these were career soldiers; they stood on the frontline of the war against the forces of evil. Their families would be provided for. It would be fascinating data, confirming if the machine would kill humans, and how it would do it.

Pfeiffer felt that moment of rage again. Oh, the knowledge and power the Ship represented. Satellites sent over the lake malfunctioned; planes suffered electrical interference. Those strange small purple creatures had the skill to fly between the stars. And Jarman and those fool nurses had hidden the boy who might have opened it all up to them.

The soldiers were all so squeamish about the radioactivity; it might be hard to get volunteers to dive. It was a problem to let simmer. A solution would present itself, he was sure. Maybe line a boat with lead and manoeuvre it over the spot . . . ?

The murky waters stilled. He must brief the Storytellers, the shadowy department tasked with explaining away the inexplicable to the press and the public. Ordinary people, other countries, the whole world, in fact, must know nothing. When Dr Pfeiffer solved this conundrum, America would be first to the stars and his rightful place in history would be secured.

## CHAPTER 12

# The Sheriff

Gene was the last person in the library. It'd been a long day and he wanted to get back to his family, but he needed a few minutes to martial his thoughts. He sat at a reader's desk, unfolded the letter and tried not to think about a cigarette. Cory pulled such a face when he smoked, and he even dreamed of the smell now, which was weird.

His parents wanted to drive over. The last time Mom had called, she'd pressed him: how were things with Molly? He loved his parents, but his mom had some sort of magic antenna that picked up problems in the marriage. Gene had given her a few nothings; the truth still stunned him.

*So, Mom, we rescued an alien and lied to the FBI. There's a germ-warfare scientist running around with soldiers who will snatch our son away — yes, he's my son, and day by day, it's like the most frightening thing in the world. I worry even about letting him into the woods or climbing a tree, which he can't stop talking about. And it's wonderful, beyond words, the most extraordinary thing. You know, he comes into our dreams . . .*

Gene smiled. Every day was a new little story. This morning Cory wanted to know why cars didn't talk or take orders and then make their own way to the destination.

Gene couldn't tell his parents; he *couldn't*. But if he said Molly was ill, his parents would ask them to the farm for some R&R and good home cooking, and they'd keep offering. And if he kept stalling, his dad would find some flimsy excuse and drive over, just like he had during the bad years, saying, 'Not for me to stick my nose in—'

Gene thought if he could be even half the father John Myers was, he would be doing a good job. But he couldn't tell them. Not everyone had loved Cory. Nurse Hooton had taken against him from the start, and clearly something odd had happened with this Dr Bradshaw.

Mom would be fine; Mom once rescued a crow with a broken wing and kept it flightless as a pet; she approached everyone trusting they were good. Molly would get her on side in a heartbeat. But Dad . . .

There had been long arguments about the war until John went red and Gene felt beyond reason. 'They should pass a law,' John would say, 'anyone burns the flag, they should be drafted, right then and there. The army knows how to sort 'em out.'

Gene worried what his dad meant by 'city radicals', and yet when he'd met Diane, he'd given her a little bow and said, 'Gene tells me you're a teacher, Mrs Alexander. What a job, to give young people their learning. Bet no one you teach will ever dare to grow up to throw rocks at the police.'

Diane pursed her mouth, sharing a silent joke with Molly,

but she didn't rise to it, even though she'd done plenty of marching and sitting-in against unjust laws in her time.

Anyway, Gene couldn't picture his father and Cory, the alien with the strange face, a fugitive from the government, sitting together by the farm stove. He'd never kept a secret from his father and that worried at him like a dog chewing a slipper. Maybe it would be fine. Maybe it wouldn't.

There was someone thumping at the main door, even though it was clearly closed and only one light was on. He needed to leave anyway, so he picked up his coat and went to the door. Sheriff Olsen stood there.

Gene felt fear, an actual nausea, a cold clamminess in the warm room. He tried to settle his face into public servant neutrality as he unlocked the door. Maybe this would be something about Dr Jarman, who was still in custody. Rosa Pearce and Nurse Fell were free, but had yet to make contact.

'Mr Myers, sorry to bother you.'

Was this the look of a man getting ready to arrest him? 'That's all right. What can I do for you, Sheriff?'

'Any odd jobs around the place?'

Gene blinked. Olsen looked – well, hard to say how he looked. Like a man who'd fleeced Jarman at poker.

'It would . . . help me,' Olsen said. 'You know Luke Barnes? Well, his horse won, he got drunk and he threw up in Carl Waite's back yard. Knocked the fence down.'

Gene's librarian mind said, *Yes, Carl, bald, irritable, why are there no new Westerns in yet?* He nodded. And Luke was a handyman; he did work for the county and all sorts. They said he was simple, slept in a tent, until the frosts came.

Olsen spread his hands. 'Carl wants to haul him in front of the judge. I said, Luke's sorry, he'll put your fence back up, better than ever, and I'll tell him, never bother Mr Waite again, or you go to jail. Usually Luke picks just three-legged horses and that keeps him dry as July, but somehow a horse came in at 20-1 and he got drunk. Well, Luke drunk, I've seen fireflies in a jar with more sense.'

'We've hired everyone we need,' Gene said.

'So I need some public-spirited thing Luke can do for free, to calm old Carl down, or the judge will fine him, and if that happens, well, I need to make sure Luke has work to cover it.' Olsen could have sold encyclopaedias with that smile.

'I just don't have anything,' Gene said apologetically. 'We'd have to take paid work off someone else.'

Olsen nodded. 'Sure, I'd never rob another man of his work. I just had to ask.'

But he wasn't moving. Gene distrusted the Sheriff and yet, he was the one who'd found Cory and his alien mother, talked to Dr Jarman and never said a word to the authorities. That was a strange story, one Gene wanted to hear, though he doubted he ever would.

'We gotta look after our own, Mr Myers,' Olsen said. 'These crazy times, and now the Meteor? Rough times for all of us. Army and FBI all over the place, getting in the way, treating the people who know and love our town like hayseeds. How's Mrs Myers?'

This was it: the clever question. All this stuff about looking after the simple handyman? That was a ruse and he'd fallen for it. Gene hoped the sudden leap in his pulse wasn't visible. He started to feel warm in the face.

'She's been better, she's been worse,' he said. 'I need to get back to her.'

'Jarman said she's a fine nurse, one of the best. A real asset on Meteor Day, he said. Give her my best wishes.'

Was that some hint? *Change the subject, ask if he'd seen Jarman, still held in some legal limbo.* But he dared not sound too inquisitive – suppose Olsen followed up with more questions?

'I've kept you waiting, why don't I drop you home?'

Gene's mind failed him; he couldn't think of a single reason better than, 'Oh no, I couldn't put you to the trouble.'

To which Olsen said, 'But it's no trouble!' so Gene got in the passenger seat of the big police car, Olsen revved the engine and they were away.

It was a hellish drive. Gene felt like he was being watched every second. Was the cat playing with the mouse? Something Olsen wanted to say hovered in the car, unsaid. Twice Gene had thought him close to speech; a couple of times he'd said something pithy about another driver, but there was no actual conversation.

At last they reached Crooked Street and home. Olsen parked and said, 'Well.'

'Thanks.'

'Bad business up at the hospital. Jarman's got some crazy ideas, but he's a good man. The Feds oughtta let him out.'

Gene felt his heart skip a beat; he felt like he twitched. This was not a conversation he could have. 'Yeah,' he said, opening the door. 'Let's hope it gets sorted soon.' He lifted a friendly hand in farewell and turned to walk to the porch. His father had raised him to speak the truth and shame the devil. He felt like someone had painted a target on his back.

He wished Jarman was free, for a thousand reasons. What was Olsen playing at? The first man to stand with the aliens . . .

Gene turned at the door. The Sheriff was still watching him. But he raised his hand and drove off.

# CHAPTER 13

# *Motherhood*

Molly stood with Cory's clothes in her hands. He was playing *I-don't-want-to-put-them-on*, running along the corridor with a towel inexpertly wrapped around his head and nothing else.

'Got haaiiirr,' he crowed. He would put anything vaguely furry on his head as a big joke; two hairbrushes, bristles out, held to his cheeks were 'beeard!'

Smiling, Molly chose to chase him. Out of the shower, he was slippery and fast. He might hide, just for the seconds he needed to get behind her. It was a great game, not real rebellion: Molly knew she could go downstairs and put the kettle on and five minutes later he'd appear, ready to be civilised. He could manage most clothes himself, but often he just chose not to. Tomorrow he might want to 'wear-tie-like-Dad' and be overdressed.

Cory had been home for twenty days, twenty full of laughter and wonders, but always on edge. Gene and Molly started at shadows; they fretted every time Cory's temperature went up, and at each strange alien dream.

'Come on, Cory,' she called. Then the doorbell rang.

This must be what it felt like to be a criminal: that sudden leap of fear – who might be at the door and what might they want? She'd had charity collectors and the Girl Scouts and limping, half-blind Mr Forster who'd had a parcel delivered by mistake, did she know whose it was? It was probably just someone selling door to door.

'Cory, no time to play. Go hide,' she ordered. She went down the stairs and looked through the peephole to see two men in dark suits carrying attaché cases. FBI, although she didn't recognise these particular officers. Those suits were almost a uniform. The younger looked *very* young though. *Do they have a cadet branch?*

She schooled her face and opened the door. 'Yes,' she said, neither rude nor encouraging.

'We're just here on this lovely morning to talk about the Good News,' the older man said.

Oh, *them.* A vulgar response came into her head, but she reined it back. *Don't be too memorable.* 'That's kind, but no thank you.' She began to shut the door, enough for a hint but not enough to be rude.

'Take a magazine,' said the boy, producing one. *Why isn't he in school?* The cover showed an impossibly sugary family at prayer. She took it, saying, 'My husband really disapproves. Sorry.' Then she shut the door.

Every time they answered the door was a risk, but they had Cory, at home and well, and every day was precious.

She counted to a hundred to herself. At eighty-seven, Cory appeared at the top of the stairs, looking perplexed. He'd wrapped her best scarf around his head. He wore underpants now, but back to front, putting his tail through the wrong hole, which she suspected was another game. 'Bad Men?'

'No.'

He came down the stairs for a hug. 'Cory don't-like Bad Men. Scaaaared.'

'Well, they've gone now and it's time to get you dressed.'

'No-no-no—'

'Would you rather have hair, Cory? For real?'

His laugh was a bubbling stream. 'Cory big-furry-monster. Ho-ho-ho.'

'I'm going to wrap you up in the bathmat.'

'No-no-no-no-no!' And he was off again, giggling and hopping up the stairs on all fours: a boy, a frog, her son.

*Every hour, every day, be vigilant.*


Molly heard a whimper from the front room. 'Cory? What's wrong?' He was sitting in the middle of the carpet, surrounded by books, his ears right down, rocking to and fro, crooning, '*Cor-cor-cor.*' She wrinkled her nose at the rank, assertive smell that only Cory could make. He had soiled himself.

'Love, what is it?' She squatted down and threw an arm around him, shivering at the cold coming off him.

'Made-mess sorry.'

'Well, you've been sick. Accidents happen.' Like she needed to disinfect a carpet right now. 'What's the matter?'

What had he been looking at? A child's dictionary and some of Gene's history books. One showed a Civil War battle scene . . . That book had a photo of a lynching. She should have thought to hide things like this. 'Let me get a towel and I'll clean you up.'

'Bad-Men Bad-Men. Sowl-jers,' he wailed.

Last night's conversation had been about soldiers, but he hadn't understood them, or didn't want to understand; he had disappeared in the middle of an explanation to stop the discussion . . .

And now he'd gone looking and found pictures of corpses. Human history was full of blood and terror and she was ashamed of it.

'Long ago,' she said, hoping her tone of voice would reassure him, but he was looking at her, angry and scared.

'No-no-no . . . Sowl-jers now, now so-many. All-round hospital. Sowl-jers hurt people.'

What to say? 'You're safe, sweetie-pie. They won't find you.'

'All wrong. People hurt people must-be sii-iick. Take hospital, make well. Few-few. Sowl-jers sick.' His eyes pleaded. 'Make better.' His stubby purple hand prodded the photograph. 'Hurt dead, lots.'

Ignoring her clean clothes, she took the distraught, smelly alien onto her lap and tried to make sense of him. He was burbling away in his own language, then he said, 'One sick person hurt someone, make sleep, make well. One. Not many-many-many.'

How she needed to talk to Dr Jarman. She was missing something – or could it really be that Cory's people had no war? No fighting? If that was true . . . that would make sense of their confused discussions. But Jarman was still under house arrest, and she was certain his phone would be tapped. *Could I find some way to talk to him?*

She took Cory for his second shower of the day.

Cory flapped his ears. '"Where Flowers Gone", pleeese.' One of his favourites.

She sang it as if a song about loss could make things better.

Molly opened the door to Dr Jarman, who was grinning and holding up his shabby doctor's bag. His coat and umbrella dripped water. 'House call.'

'You're out! Oh, it's so good to see you!' She could have hugged him right there on the porch. 'Come in, come in – coffee?'

The doctor sat at her kitchen table and spooned sugar, one, two, three, four. Interrogation didn't seem to have done him any harm; he'd even had a haircut. That expensive shirt had lost two buttons, though.

'I wasn't followed,' the doctor said. 'I parked on Elliott Street and walked up through the woods.'

'How was it?'

He shrugged. 'I've had about a hundred more hours listening to Pfeiffer than any human being should suffer, but they bought the story and they can't put me on trial for anything because I might tell the world. Besides, Pfeiffer needs me: he keeps calling me, trying to pick apart my notes. They're throwing dozens of scientists at our little friend. Not that I blame them; he's a fascinating problem. Sister Pearce got rid of Hooton, by the way.'

'Yes, she told me.' The famous Pearce's choice: resign and get a decent letter of commendation, but only for jobs a long way away, or be fired without anything. Hooton grudgingly took the resignation, with much sniping complaint, and Molly devoutly hoped they would never hear of her again.

'Somehow I've got to find time to work on this myself – I mean, what do we do if he's injured again? He might be here for years. We need to make more of his drugs, in case he needs them.'

Soft rain tapped on the window as she asked, 'So is he safe? Are we?'

Jarman shrugged. 'I don't know that we'll ever be sure. How's he been?'

She gave him the physical rundown, professional and concise. 'Rosa said you've had trouble maintaining isolation.'

That was polite; Molly knew she'd failed on infection control. 'Oh, it was one thing after another,' she admitted. 'Cory got exposed during the escape. He hated wearing the helmet, and then it stopped working. And he sleepwalks into our bed most nights. He doesn't understand the fuss. Their medicine must be so advanced, he's confident we can fix any infection he gets. I can't pretend we've managed this at all well. I mean, we're scrupulous about cleanliness, and not playing with dirt outside, but . . .'

Jarman waited a beat too long before saying, 'But he's fine? And you?'

'He's got hayfever, we think, a little. But us? We're fine.'

'Well, I won't pretend I'm not worried, but we were going to have to take a risk at some point.'

Molly went on to her next worry. 'He won't tell us what happened to him, if he even remembers.'

Jarman frowned. 'I guess we just have to treat him like a human child: lots of reassurance, let him know he can talk if he wants. Don't push him. What else could we try?'

'He doesn't understand soldiers or war. He finds our world real frightening.'

He took a big swig of coffee. 'Those aliens have a lot to teach us, don't they? Better check him over. Where is he?'

They went into the hallway to find the back door was open. Molly ran to the door and didn't know whether to scream or laugh or cry. She'd lectured Cory about not going out in his new blue sneakers or the new hooded top: she'd meant *look* at the garden but don't go out in the rain. Cory had stripped to nothing at all, leaving his clothes and shoes neatly piled inside the back door. Thank heavens the neglected garden was a jungle, with vines on the trellises making the garden fence more than seven feet high and hiding Cory from anyone walking in the woods.

The little boy, naked and happy, was crouched down in the rain, looking at the snails while the rain spattered on the path and ran off him. He brought his big violet eyes down to the snails' level; a webbed hand took one by the shell, gentle as a snowflake's kiss, gentle as a fly landing, and picked it up, his mouth-tentacles waving, and put it on the back of his other hand. It waited for a bit, then it decided to come out of its shell and wave its eyes at the Cory-mountain.

Molly, cross and amused at Cory's independence, tried a smile. 'He loves to smell things.'

'Looks like he wants to eat it,' the doctor said, smirking.

'He ate a worm because it reminded him of something on his home world. Then he threw up on the couch. So now he listens to us about what's good to eat.' Gene had made a joke yesterday about eating snails and Cory couldn't drop the subject. She'd just kept saying they were a different type, not like those in the garden: a special *French* snail. People in America weren't keen to try them.

Molly got a red towel, big enough to wrap him in. She'd give him five more minutes.

As she and Jarman watched Cory play, he said, 'Pfeiffer doesn't realise he's telling me way more than he thinks. I just need to figure out where to do the work. I mean, it looks like Cory's immune system is where it has to be: strong enough to keep him alive, but not so strong that he gets a massive allergy to every new thing he runs into.'

She must tell Jarman about Cory's extraordinary hiding, and that the shared dreams really did mean something. There were so many things they didn't know about his world, a world where violence was an illness, and rare.

In the garden, Cory held a second snail on one hand, his tentacles hovering a fraction of an inch from their shells while his other hand shielded them from the rain, which was growing harder.

Molly whistled him in for his check-up, which they did upstairs so if the FBI did burst in, Cory would have time to hide.

Dr Jarman turned at the door and handed her an envelope full of green notes. 'The Research Fund can cover some expenses,' he said with a smile.

Her mother's interminable strictures about taking charity nagged, but Molly batted them aside and took the money. After all, it wasn't as if she could work. 'Thank you. And I really do want to help with the research,' she added.

She went out first, just to check the coast was clear, and after she'd waved the doctor off, she helped Cory make a little snail hotel, a clear glass cookie-jar full of tasty leaves. When Gene came home, the Myers ate tuna casserole, light on the cheese, while Cory watched his six snails try to figure out their little snail lives, now they were surrounded by walls they couldn't see.

Cory frowned, took paper and pens and started to draw. It took a while for him to start; he scribbled over his first try, got angry, then scribbled again. 'Not-right not-right not-right!'

Molly peered down at the drawing. They were snails too, of sorts, little black ones, and big red and white ones, and green and brown ones. The shells were pointier and there were a lot of eyes on stalks for each snail.

He held his hands out. 'This big,' he said, moving them apart; snails the size of a cat. 'Up trees.' His eyes were always moist; it didn't mean anything, but she could read him. He was as open as the sky. He got into Gene's lap, shivering, the shiver of remembering, and said, 'Tasty treat. Mom liked. Silly baby memory. Silly Cory.'

*Oh Cory.* 'None of your memories of your mother are silly,' Molly said, rushing to his side. Gene was holding him tighter now. 'She was brave and clever and she loved you hotter than the sun and I wish she was standing here now. She'd have to move in because I'd never let you go, but that's fine, we'd share you.'

'How can remembering love be silly?' said Gene.

'New Mom-Dad pleeese,' Cory said, eyes darting from one to another.

'Well, that would suit us fine,' Gene said, and Molly couldn't say anything at all; she wanted to embrace the two of them for ever. Instead she got up and rattled plates into the sink.

★

Molly knew this wasn't real. Cory's dreams always seemed so solid. This was Cory's nightmare, snapshots from a hell with no up or down, no start or finish. Dead creatures like Cory floated down green corridors filled with writhing flashes of silver metal. There was a screaming wind beyond anything she could understand, and metal voices chanting an alarm.

How frightened he and his mother were. His mother helped him into the familiar space-suit, but he didn't understand. *So many dead.* Cory could feel each one who died in his throat and his chest and his bowels, and now Molly felt the pain too.

Blue fire and white metal poured like liquid through a wall.

Then the world shook and Gene was calling her up out of the dream into the bedroom. The bedside light was on and Cory was twisting in the bed next to her.

'Wow, that was a strong one,' Gene said. 'It's okay, Cory, we're here.'

Cory mumbled, 'Many-many dead.' But his eyes didn't open and his breathing grew calm again.

Molly wished she could take his pain from him, even if she had to take it into herself.

Next morning, it took eight calls to the city before she found a deli that would post them some canned snails. The price made her cough, so she just took a note of the details for a special occasion.

Gene said, 'I better write another song. How about, "Would You Eat Snails from Outer Space? (Even to Save The Human Race?)".'

'You get them, I'll cook them,' she said. 'We could try fresh oysters, I guess.' She was still working out what Cory needed, so she fed him every type of food she could think of.

## CHAPTER 14

# *The week school broke up*

Cory swims up through his dreams, the cool dark layer that tells him none of his people dream alongside him. Such a strange feeling, to find this place that should be full of people, light and colour so utterly silent and alone. He's the most solo-solo ever.

He tries to remember playing by the river, watching mud-skippers. His lodge-group . . . his laughing mother . . . Then a dark hole opens in the dream because his mother is dead. Sweet, loving Flute-Voice, the Healer, who was his mother's friend, and Black Ground-fruit, her child, were lost too. All the Pioneers on their journey to build a new world but their star-ship died in fire, so many lodges dead in the vast nightmare of screaming, this star-ship bigger than Amber Grove. So many sixteen-squareds of dead.

Cory shivers. The icy ocean of sadness will come out of the hole and swallow him, but he must be strong and swim away. Dreams are the rich sea of being; there are no people for him to join, but he can look for the human dreams, for all they are flat and muddy and scent-blind.

He finds Molly's dream, recognising when they drove into the woods few-days-back, trees alive-alive with smells and noises. In that place, little creatures hid and watched them and the humans did not feel them there, those little lives up in trees and under bushes. They found a place no one would come and played a chasing game and threw ball and had a picnic with sausages. Mom gave up the chase first, Cory and Dad played their good running game around the tree. Cory mind-hid and Gene-Dad stood hands on knees and said, 'Well, *that's* cheating!' but that was only fake-cross.

Cory soaks in these strange human half-dreams, revelling in their closeness, how the humans open with warmth at the thought of him. The sadness that wants to eat him is always there, although sometimes it hides away at the edge of him.

Cory's body wants to pee. Up-up-up he swims from his sleep, up-up-up he swims into the light. Body-wakening, he is in his little room, new Mom and Dad in the room next door. It's too early. He is wearing the blue rocket pyjamas very-sharp-Cory. Along the corridor to the bathroom in the house-just-for-three where no machines talk or think or can be commanded by voice.

He creeps into Mom-and-Dad room and wriggles himself up between them. Dad grunts and Mom stirs a little, but they do not wake. If he does wake her she moans, 'Half past five, Cory, that's cruel and unnatural punishment. Please, for the love of God.'

Warm between his new-parents, surrounded by their feel

and smell, he is content and his body at least lies still, but his mind runs around the room sixteen times and away. He learned only twenty-three good words yesterday: Must Try Harder. Are dragons dinosaurs? What musical instruments made that music disc? Beaver-dam. Gene showed him one in a book, and so exciting, he must-must go and see clever beavers make dam. Im-pressive was a new word. *Im-pressive*.

Humans are so dense at learning his language, so slow to pick apart sounds, tock-tock-tock. Quicker for smart Cory to learn human. Learn English, humans have many, many languages. How strange.

Gene tries to turn over but they are in a tangle and it is Molly who groans awake.

'Morning good morning good morning,' Cory says, and Molly mumbles, 'We need a bigger bed. Like a mile wide.' She rises muddy-eyed and cooks pancakes and bacon yum-yum and brews coffee, filling the air with the bitter black smell of breakfast.

Cory sets the table, air-tasting the food. Gene walks in, wet hair and dressed for work. He is so-not-awake. When Molly isn't looking, Cory sneaks a piece of pancake with his tendrils, *manners-Cory-Myers*. Cory hugs new-Mom and she puts out her hand to be kissed.

'What-do today, what-do today?' Cory asks. He hopes it is an expedition day but often it is not, and that is okay too.

Cory must be secret, very secret. He often hears the children argue in the street as they go to school or come back. School is out soon, says new-Mom, and so they will go to camp. Outdoor games and so many children, camp sounds big-big fun. Cory aches and aches.

Cory watches the children from the attic window: Chuck is red-haired-male and Bonnie is black-haired-female. Chuck is pale like Gene and Molly, sun makes brown spots across nose and turns ears red. Bonnie is dark-skinned. Complicated about light-skinned and dark-skinned, makes Gene-Dad and Molly-Mom trip over words, all fear and embarrassment.

'Tell just-two children,' he asks, knowing he will be told no, but *so-hoping*.

Each time, Molly wrinkles her face, sad and anxious and loving. 'We have to keep you safe, sweetie-pie. Children can't keep secrets. You do understand? You must look me in the eyes and promise, *never ever*.'

Of course Cory is good and of course Cory promises. Most humans are nice, Mom promises, but there are Bad Men who will take Cory away, *shiver-shiver*.

The Bad Men are all around the forest, in the forest, the lake – and in the lake the space-to-planet-Ship his mother commanded. Radioactivity is bad-bad-bad: healthy Ship makes no radioactivity. If Ship makes much radioactivity it is poisonous and will explode.

It makes him sick. He cannot think about it. All the people died and the Ship's mind must be dead too and cannot help him.

He must be here and now and not stay in the sadness. Gene-Dad waves the newspaper. 'Not so long now before men on the Moon.' Molly-Mom pulls a face, but Cory and Mom have a big secret; she is a bit excited too. This will be the first time ever for humans on the Moon.

Every little cub of Cory's people is taught the old-old stories of the brave Moon Riders. Many many sixteen-squared years ago, seven of Cory's people swam away from their planet and made the first step out to the stars. Everyone sings the songs of the Seven who first walked on the moon, and their ship, *Bird of Moonlight*.

Warm and sunny and hot later. Today is a mostly inside day. Mom opens back windows so smells of the woods can come into the house all warm and living. Cory and Mom do chores and school which is his favourite, and they bake a cake for Dad which comes out a bit strange because Mom did the recipe out of her head. Mom makes icing and Cory licks the bowl *yum-yum*. They listen to music, Bach is so-fine and Cory sways because Earth music fills him with all the feelings, and then they do more school. It's not a Mom-sings sort of day. She doesn't want to take him anywhere in the car. He brings her the keys and she shakes her head.

'Some days are sunny inside and some aren't, sweetie-pie. But I always have you, my little ball of sunshine.'

Cory knows how to rub her neck *just-right*. Then Cory stretches and says, 'Cory need nap.' They know this is a story; that it is Mom who needs the nap.

Ten minutes after Molly shuts the bedroom door, Cory is in the back yard. He is allowed if he is careful and hides. It grows wild, not all straight rows of flowers, and he picks through the air-tastes like putting tendrils in a bowl of stew. There's a warm haze and birds sing-sing-sing.

Such a little place, the garden, he loves it, but he has explored it so much he knows it all. Oh, he hopes so soon big exploring can begin, find new woods and rivers and hills, meet elks and cows and redwoods high as the hospital and the great waterfalls; he wants to go to the lands of ice and dry sand scouring tall coloured rocks.

He smells the raccoons, and here is a new smell: a new animal with a strong smell, but not dog or cat. Wild animals carry disease, says Mom, *Cory-don't-touch*, in important voice. Cory should get hospital gloves to play with raccoons.

The sun rises in the wrong place and the day is too long.

High voices come over the fence too tall for even a human adult. That one is Chuck and that is Bonnie. Clever Cory could get onto shed roof and hide and look down on them, be sneaky and listen. Shed roof is still 'in-garden'.

The tree-stump, a hand here, a foot on the window frame, up to the strange metal bit that once held a light, and then Cory is on the slanted roof and watching over the fence.

The two children are on the footpath, looking at his house. Bonnie is wearing her red dress and white tights. She has a coloured-cloth-strip knotted in her hair. These aren't her playing-in-the-woods clothes so they have come from some-where else. Bonnie has a grown-up brother and sister, says Mom; Chuck has two little sisters.

'They should send a girl to the Moon,' Bonnie says.

Chuck's shirt is white but his jeans are like Cory's. Chuck kicks stuff and says, 'It's way too dangerous.'

'In the old war, women flew planes,' Bonnie insists. 'The Russians sent a woman into space *ages* ago and we're better at space than they are. Space flight is science and we're not even sending up a scientist. That's silly. They should send a woman scientist. I bet your mom agrees with me.'

Chuck frowns a big frown. 'Okay, so girls can be smart, but they'd have to put a special girl's bathroom in the rocket and there wouldn't be room.'

'Women can do anything a man can, my mom says. And your mom says. And Mrs Myers too. I'm going to be a Senator, I'll be elected President, and then I'll tell NASA to send a woman to the Moon.'

Cory holds on to the roof, finding the conversation confusing, wanting to ask sixteens of questions and be their friend. Why no girl pilots?

'Pigs will fly,' Chuck says.

Cory has seen pigs in a book. He did not know they could fly.

Bonnie seethes, but then she looks up at the shed roof. For a moment, Cory thinks his hiding is not working and sharp fear rises, like he ate needle-grass. Humans he's met are easy to hide from but just maybe some of them are like real people and can see hiding. But then Bonnie looks to the Myers house, then back to Chuck.

'This is where I saw the ghost,' she says.

Chuck stands tall and says, 'Bonnie Alexander, you're such a big liar. You did *not* see a ghost.'

'I did so.' Bonnie has a firm face. 'It was a little girl in white, about so high and—'

Chuck hoists his schoolbag onto the other shoulder. 'Big liar.'

'It was the baby Mrs Myers lost.'

'No, it wasn't. That was tiny. Ghosts can't grow. That's horrible. You shouldn't make up stories about that.'

Bonnie stamps her foot, turns and runs away. She uses words

Cory does not know and there is a wave of anger Cory can feel. 'I'm going home!' she shouts.

*Ghost.* Cory moves the word around like a little fruit in his mouth. He will find out what it means.

Chuck stands, undecided. Cory could try a big jump-down over fence, but this jumping tricky-tricky. Or he could climb down and use the little raccoon gate. Cory knows he could move the broken plank in the fence and wriggle through. He could follow Bonnie and Chuck. But he promised, *he promised*: no leaving the garden without a parent.

On his Ship, on his home planet, Cory has never been away from other young for more than a day or two, never even when out in the wild; always other people sleeping alongside or waking with him. Wanting to play with these humans hurts, like he could swell and burst, but then thick, cold fear of the Bad Men comes and he must find somewhere to curl up until that fear has gone. Children might tell the grown-ups and then the Bad Men would come.

He is no solo; he never chose to be alone. He hungers to sleep-in-many, to dream-play and dream-work as well as waking. Although the humans love him, he must carry his heavy sadness alone, until his people return.

# CHAPTER 15

## *Summer*

It was Thursday, so Peggy Fell came with a heavy bag to mind Cory, who leaped up to hug her, and demand, 'Geography lesson. And then game.' Peggy was all grins. It was good of her to give up her day off; if only it could be every week, but that was greedy. Molly wanted to spend a day a week helping Dr Jarman with the research, to make it happen faster and to learn new skills. She did some typing for Jarman, trying to follow where he was up to, but it was all painfully slow going.

Now Molly was going to meet her friends. The night before she'd finished the book Diane and Janice had been on at her to read, *when you feel strong enough*, and she couldn't wait to let off steam. This new writer, Maya Angelou, her writing blew the top of her head right off. She found it unbelievably powerful, shocking: you knew such things happened, but to have them set out in all their horror like this . . .

It was a beautiful day, so she walked, pondering the book full of paper slips marking the key bits and how to play 'sad, ill Molly' reacting to it. She would make today a good day, so she could be upbeat before she 'got tired' and needed to leave early. That would work. She pushed aside her disgust at deceiving her best friends.

As she walked into Francine's, her friends rose to embrace her.

'Well!' Molly said, sitting and flourishing the book, but Janice was bursting with something.

'Have you heard the news?' she babbled. 'They've found a ring of Russian spies! Four people! They were arrested in Bradleyburg and they're after at least two others, a man and a woman.'

'Wow!' Molly's shock was genuine; she avoided the news as much as she could. *What does this mean for Cory?*

Janice hadn't finished. 'Two Americans – imagine that! Two of our own! And a Czech and a German. At least that's what their passports say, but the radio thinks they're Russians, or working for them, anyway.'

'We came to Amber Grove because of Hube's job, and because nothing much happens here,' Diane said. 'We didn't want excitement – then when Hube . . . then the Meteor, and now this.' Together, without words, Janice and Molly each took one of Diane's hands. Grief has no logic: it never wholly goes and it doesn't care when it chooses to assert itself.

*Change the subject.* Molly opened her mouth to ask, 'Spies – but why here?' but then she realised that was the stupidest question: the Meteor had brought the spies, of course, not to mention whatever the army was up to in the woods.

'All sorts of people are passing through now,' Janice said, 'and it's hard to spot spies – they're not going to send sinister, unshaven men who speak with Russian accents, are they? Look, that couple over there? They might be spies for all we know.'

Molly didn't recognise the unremarkable people on the next table; Janice was right: they might be *anyone*. She wondered if the real spies had heard about the fifth floor and that made her worry all over again.

But Janice was still talking. 'Meteors aren't radioactive,' she said, an inconvenient fact lots of people had learned. She waved out at Founders Green, where the giant chunk of meteoric iron was still embedded. 'That bit's not radioactive, is it? So where's the danger coming from?'

Molly gave the agreed cover story, invoking the sacred name of Dr Jarman, then she said, just a little worried, 'Did I warn the druggist I was coming? Oh . . . I can't remember . . . It will be such a nuisance if he doesn't have it made up. Give me a minute, will you?' She took her purse over to the phone and with her back to her friends, rang Peggy first: two rings, pause, two rings. Peggy had been briefed; she knew what to do in a raid. Then she called the library and Gene himself answered.

'I heard the news,' he said immediately.

'I'm with Diane and Janice. I suppose I'd better get back.' Neither of them ever mentioned Cory on a phone, even obliquely.

'I bet they ask who's been asking about the Meteor,' Gene said, 'but *everyone* does! Any visitor who doesn't is going to be far more suspicious.'

There wasn't anything else she could do, other than to call the druggist and ask for a repeat prescription of the pills she never took.

'Trouble getting through?' Janice asked when Molly re-joined them, and how she hated the little lies to protect the big one.

'It helps to remember the number correctly,' she joked.

'Now, never mind the Russians: what about this book?' *Fifteen minutes perhaps, then I'll go.*

Janice leaped in, never shy of an opinion, and all Molly had to do was nod.

*Russian spies.* They'd known peace people, back in the day, who'd been starry-eyed about the Soviet Union, but the Myers remembered the tanks rolling into Hungary and the crushing of the Prague Spring last year and that poor boy, Jan Palach, who'd burned himself to death in protest. How brave and how foolish, to light such a fire, in the hope that his people would remember their freedom . . .

The job of a spy was to dig up secrets – she didn't need to guess what the Soviets would give to know about Cory.

Diane was back on her usual form, telling Janice, as only a friend could, just how wrong she'd got something, so Molly ventured a thought or two of her own.

And here, walking to the counter, came Sheriff Olsen, his uniform as pressed and well-fitting as always, his smile confident. Her heart began racing, but she kept her face still. Was this the end?

The Sheriff saw her and raised his hat. 'Ladies. Good to see you out and about, Mrs Myers.'

'Thank you.' She felt so paranoid now, starting to think everyone suspected.

Olsen took a cup of coffee from Francine with a nod and sat so that he could watch her without it being too obvious. Or was that in her head? Now she didn't know if her making tracks would just add to his suspicions.

Molly began to construct her excuse to get away. If Olsen

followed her, she wouldn't go home – but then she'd need to phone Peggy. Or get Gene to leave work, but they were so busy. Headache, left the stove on . . .

The FBI turned up again, after supper this time. It wasn't Anderson but the agent who'd come before, with a new colleague. Cory hid in the attic, this time without argument or proposing a better plan, while Gene and Molly sat in the front room with the FBI. They asked a lot of questions, starting with, had anyone been snooping around? Had the Myers volunteered *anything* to *anyone*?

The truthful answers were no, and no. Good start. Molly hoped Gene's nerves were less visible to them.

When they finally showed the FBI to the door, Molly even managed to thank them for catching the spies. Then she shut the door and hugged Gene.

'They could have just called us.' Now she could be angry.

'They're keeping an eye on us. It's pure intimidation: "Don't step out of line, or else." I'll go and find Cory.'

Molly wanted a drink, and she wasn't going to have one. 'I need a walk, okay? Just fifteen minutes.' She slung on a coat, thinking she'd walk to the view over Amber Grove, then maybe into the woods, enjoy the fresh evening air.

On the brow of the hill, looking down on the town where so much had happened, she heard a cough and there was Sheriff Olsen, walking towards her.

'You made me jump,' she said.

'I'm sorry, Mrs Myers,' he said, his back to the fading sun. 'I trust the Feds treated you kindly?'

'Yes, of course. Why are you following me?'

He looked her in the eye. 'You were a real Good Samaritan on the fifth floor,' he said. 'I should have come and thanked you when the child died. I know you did everything you could.'

Was he really going to discuss that here, in the open air? But their voices were low; she guessed no one in the houses could hear them, and she couldn't ask him back to hers.

'I can't talk about that,' she said firmly. Gene and Cory were probably playing guitar by now.

Olsen slipped his thumbs into his belt loops. 'I promised his mother we'd keep the boy safe. She knew she was sick, and around us in the forest, my head was still ringing from the impact, all that fire and smoke. I thought the world was ending. You can trust me, Mrs Myers.'

'I need to get back.'

'I get that the Feds scared you – but you need to know how it was with me, okay? Purple or not, that was one steely lady. She asked me what I held dearest in the world, most sacred, and I swore by my Lord and Saviour, and on my oath of office, that I'd protect her and her boy. Every hair on my body stood on end, like the Angel of Judgement was at my shoulder.'

He scratched his head. 'Once I got Dr Jarman involved there was nothing more I could do. It was all Jarman and you nurses. I just wish it had worked out better.'

'So do I,' she said. 'It was all very difficult.' Tears wouldn't work, not on a man like Olsen, so she couldn't work out how to extricate herself. 'Why didn't you turn her over?' she asked.

Olsen paused. 'Because I promised a dying mother I'd keep her son safe. Because I prayed on it and my heart was opened that was the right thing to do. Because I trusted Edgar Jarman . . . Was there more I could have done?'

'Um, no,' Molly said after a moment. 'I guess you did the right thing.'

He waited, then went on, 'You know, all this time, I keep wondering: did Our Lord die for the purples too? Don't it say in the Good Book, all the Heavens proclaim His name? Maybe every star has people, each looking different, but children of the one Father. Did you get a chance to talk to the boy?'

'No. I found his death very painful.'

'I'll pray for you,' Olsen said. 'His mother told me they had no need of weapons or war, so maybe these purples never fell from Grace at all. If you saw a wounded angel, would you walk by on the other side?' For a moment he looked rapt, like he was in church.

Then he shook his head and the normal Olsen was back.

'Please don't follow me,' Molly said. 'Gene won't like it.' What an odd thing to come out with.

He laughed. 'I figured out you told him something. Well, Mrs Myers, a crazy business. I thank you for your time. And these spies – if anyone from out of town, anyone, looks suspicious, you give me a call, okay?'

'Okay,' she said. 'Good night.' She walked away, trying to fit that conversation into what she knew and what she'd heard as rumour. *He still thinks Cory is dead*. At least, she thought so.

That night in bed, they ran over the familiar argument: Gene took *Let's go, now* and Molly *Let's stay.* They could argue either side with the same conviction.

They chose to stay. There was no argument about whether to tell Sheriff Olsen that Cory was alive, because neither of them trusted him an inch.

# CHAPTER 16

## *The outing*

Saturday evening, while Gene was off having a beer with Roy, his part of pretending things were normal, Molly invited Rosa Pearce and Peggy Fell for supper. Talking to Rosa was a bit like talking to Mount Rushmore, but Peggy was becoming a real friend; with her busy private life, she had a lot to chat about.

Rosa turned up early, kissed Cory and said, 'Now, young fellow, I want to see how your handwriting is getting on.'

As Cory, rarely slow to show off, raced away to get a great sheaf of his writing, Molly asked, 'How have you been?'

'Oh, the Administration is hopeless,' Rosa said. 'I'm really not impressed with the new students. We need people with their heads screwed on.'

*Is that actually a compliment?* Molly thought. 'Well, I'm afraid I can't come back to work,' she said, glancing at Cory. Tonight, she was going to ask Peggy if she could commit to Cory-sitting a day a week, so she could help Dr Jarman with his research.

'When Peggy gets here, I have a little G-I-F-T for himself,' Rosa said.

Cory's ears went right up. 'Cory not supposed to hear that,' he announced.

Rosa touched his head. 'Oh, what a clever boy.'

The bell rang, although Peggy had her own key, and when she walked in, they could see she was excited and flushed and holding her left hand a little oddly. A new ring glinted.

'Well, he did it,' Peggy said, moving her hand to be sure they saw it. 'He asked on one knee and I said yes! And here's a stroke of luck: the hospital near his new job is hiring nurses.' Peggy's on-again off-again boyfriend was moving to Maine.

Molly hugged her, hiding her shock. Her work plan had just completely collapsed. And she'd been able to confide in Peggy. Gene was great, but a woman needed another woman. But of course, Peggy deserved happiness, so Molly tried hard to be glad for her.

Peggy hugged Rosa, her boss, who was stiff and solemn, like a cigar-store wooden Indian.

'You'll be a loss,' Rosa said. 'He'd better treat you properly. I have my doubts.'

Molly agreed with Rosa that the beau was flaky, certainly not someone to trust with the secret of Cory. But grown-ups must make their own decisions.

'Don't go,' Cory said, and she realised he was upset. 'Everyone went.'

'I'll visit,' Peggy promised, stroking his ear. 'I will miss our sweet little monster so much, and you too, both of you. But . . . this is the real thing.'

Peggy had love and grit aplenty and Molly really did hope it would work out for her.

'I'll do your letter of recommendation tomorrow,' Rosa said. 'I'll do a stinker, so you'll have to stay.' She was just a little flushed, a tiny bit moist-eyed. She coughed and added, 'Well, that has overshadowed my news but I have a little present for Cory.'

Cory was sitting bolt upright, like a dog expecting a treat. Rosa slipped him a tiny parcel, which he unwrapped using tentacles and hands together. He admired the little silver medallion, holding it close and sniffing it.

'It's St Christopher, little one,' Rosa explained. 'He guards travellers. You're the most travelled person on Earth, and maybe you have longer journeys to come. He safely carried the most precious boy ever across a river.'

'Thank you,' Cory said, and gave her his strange tentacled kiss. 'Wear on neck or wrist?'

'It should go around your neck. It's come down through my family: my great-grandfather bought it for my grandfather — that was my father's father. It's very precious. I want you to have it.'

The chain was too short, but that was easily sorted.

They ate, then Cory sang them a fierce song about sailing in a storm. Peggy had to leave early, to meet her fiancé, so Cory insisted on two stories from Rosa before bed.

Later, Rosa spoke to Molly alone.

'Her fiancé reminds me of one of the most feckless men I ever knew,' Rosa said. 'All charm, and as reliable as a drunk coyote. You can't tell young women anything.'

'My parents hated Gene,' Molly admitted, 'but we were barely speaking by then.'

Today would be glorious and hot, but the radio was still talking about spies; eight Russian diplomats had been expelled, because of the spy ring. Dr Jarman said someone from British television had come to talk to him; he'd heard the FBI thought there were more spies. The Mayor had even called a town hall meeting about it all. Molly wanted none of this. She stood in the garden with Cory, listening to the birds and watching insects flit from flower to flower.

'Let's take a trip in the car,' she said. *Let's get out of town, away from the spies and the FBI and the army.* A healthy Cory was like a sack of half-grown puppies. She needed to run him off and calm him down.

Cory had no smile, but his ears went up, his tentacles danced and his tail wiggled. 'Yes-yes-yes!'

Molly drove with the window down. She knew a quiet place by a cool creek they'd tried a couple of times; once there were splashing boys who'd ignored the PRIVATE signs too, so she'd just turned the car around, but the second time, Cory had a blissful hour of swimming. He could breathe right in, those skinny ribs swelling fit to burst, and then dive under for ten or fifteen minutes without trouble.

Cory wore a hooded sweatshirt big enough to cover his face and to hide his hands, and he would lie on the back seat until she gave permission for him to sit up and look. You couldn't rely solely on his ability to hide because it didn't work on a camera – there was no mind to fool. And if you stood far enough away, it wouldn't work either.

As she drove, Molly remembered an old counting song her mother used to sing when they went on vacation. Cory joined in the chorus. They took the main road east out of town, passing through fields and wood. To the north was the strange piebald part of the forest where the Meteor fell. The army had released many dramatic photographs, including twisted chunks of iron as big as a house, but only the authorised got to see the moonscape in person. She hoped nature would soon reclaim the damaged place, seed by seed and vine by vine, green inch by green inch. After all, even on islands of black volcanic rock there were plants growing . . .

Cory's eye was drawn to the devastation: it repelled him and she could feel his shudder. Of course, she and Gene were intensely curious about the hidden spaceship, but Gene had gone up a couple of times and reported that the army was even guarding the approach road: soldiers photographed the licence plates of anyone using the access roads, soldiers with dogs patrolled everywhere and tripwires and alarms had been set up behind the double fence. There were grimmer rumours, too, of at least one dead soldier. And Cory, shaking, never wanted to talk about his landing, the death of his mother or the Ship.

'That place make Cory ill,' he'd said, shivering in their arms.

They'd left the site of the Meteor far behind when there was a sudden ripping sound and the steering wheel fought Molly's hands. Something clattered, under and behind. She slowed at once, manhandling the car to the side of the road.

'Stay in the car, Cory,' she said, and got out to find a savage wound in the rear tyre's black rubber. Twenty feet behind, a fist-sized piece of rusty metal lay in the road. Well, that threw a spanner into her plans. The later they got to the creek, the less likely they'd be alone.

Insects chirped and hummed and a bird trilled nearby, but it was too open here by far. The nearest field was red clover and some green plant she didn't recognise, very low to the ground.

'All-fine car mend car,' Cory said helpfully.

'No sweetie-pie, our machines don't fix themselves,' she told him. 'It's just a flat tyre, simple to mend.'

She wasn't some fluttering Victorian miss in a corset. She could do this. 'I'll use a jack to lift the car up, take off the broken tyre and put the new one on. Then I'll lower the car down and off we go.'

'Cory want watch.'

'Cory wants *to* watch, sweetie-pie,' she said, a little distracted. 'Well, find somewhere you're not obvious.'

The field was edged with long grass and bushes; he'd be out of sight, so it would be fine if anyone passed. Cory looked every way, then scurried into the grass, just as Molly heard a rumbling in the distance. She squinted back at it: a truck – a camouflaged truck. She swallowed, her mouth suddenly dry.

'Stay hidden, Cory,' she hissed. 'Soldiers.' She opened the trunk and found the jack. *Get on with it*, she told herself. *They're not here for you.*

The truck stopped and the driver, a soldier with bright brown eyes and a perfect smile, leaned out of the cab. 'Ma'am, that looks like a real bad one.' He came from somewhere down south, as many of them did. There was another man in the cab, older and greyer.

'Thank you for stopping,' she said, trying to smile. 'I'm fine. I've done this before.'

The other man had eyes that had seen it all, but he shot Molly a smile, then barked, 'Ten-minute smoke break. Two volunteers on the double to help a lady in distress.'

'Sir-yes-sir!' said the driver at once, and opened the cabin door. Molly felt her heart race as the truck suddenly started disgorging men – eight, nine of them . . . Was this the end? She pictured Cory running across the fields, being hunted down . . . She turned around, her eyes darting in every direction. Where was he? Hidden, of course, as only Cory knew how, but *where*?

She caught the soldier's eyes flick to her left hand. He was looking for a wedding ring. Their eyes met and she saw only the friendly mischief of a puppy.

'Oh, it's fine,' she said, as casually as she could manage. 'I couldn't put you to the trouble.'

The soldier walked up to her and looked at the tyre as others came around from the back of the truck. A couple walked off the road and lit up as another strode towards them.

'You see, ma'am, if we left a lady by the road like this, it'd sure spoil our appetite,' the brown-eyed young man said. 'We'd look at our suppers tonight and think we just failed to be good neighbours. You wouldn't do that to us, now, would you?'

The driver could charm a cloud from the sky, and didn't he know it. 'Okay, well, thanks,' she said, hoping he couldn't see her pounding heart. There were four of them now by the car. She watched as his eyes landed on the bumper sticker, *No to*

*War*, and there was a flicker of a frown, but even so, he squatted and fitted the jack and someone else lifted out the spare.

She was sweating, above and beyond the heat of the day. Had Cory found a safe space?

*Distract them*, she thought. *Sound normal.*

There were things she could never ask but desperately wanted to know. People had seen strange lights over the woods — was that the military, or what was hiding in the lake, the damaged ship that had brought Cory to her? But of course she couldn't know about that . . .

'How do you like Amber Grove?' she asked.

The driver had his eyes on the job now. 'I grew up in a town just like it, a small place by a river. I'm told I'll prefer our winters to yours. But it's real pretty.'

Then someone was shouting and Molly looked round to see a portly man in the field waving his straw hat. He was carrying a roll of fence-wire shoulder to hip, like a bandolier. And heavens! By his leg was a bright-eyed brown dog.

'Good day, ma'am,' he hollered. 'D'you fellas need a hand?'

A red-haired soldier flipped the sharp metal off the road with a careful boot. 'We have things in hand, sir.'

'Now, ma'am, your boy should be real careful — there's old drains near here. No idea what might be in them.'

Molly's heart lurched. She might have faced down Pfeiffer and the FBI, but now she felt panicked. What had he seen? The dog was whining, an odd noise, like there was something wrong.

She could do this. She'd dealt with her mother, her drunken father . . . 'I'm sorry? I don't understand,' she said.

The farmer looked a bit like John, Gene's father, just a bit rounder and balder.

Puzzled, the man said, 'A boy in a grey sweatshirt? Right there.' He pointed at the bushes where Cory had been. 'Shut up, Truman!' he told the dog, adding, 'Don't know why the fella's making such a fuss.'

Molly shrugged. 'I didn't see anyone.'

The driver got up from his job. 'Check it out, Wayne. Ma'am, if someone hides when we drive by, maybe we need to know who they are. And I know dogs, and that dog's not happy.'

He was right, it was showing its teeth.

Two soldiers – no, three now, were searching the grass and the bushes. One of them took his rifle from his back. *Make it a joke. Deflect their interest.* 'It must be the Great New York Werewolf,' Molly said with a laugh. Gene had read her the magazine article a couple of days back. Maybe it'll be full Moon tomorrow.' She wished she believed in magic or prayer, that she could make them turn away and ignore where Cory was hiding.

The red-head looked at her now. 'Better not hunt on duty,' he said, grinning.

'Uncle Sam don't stretch to silver bullets,' said the driver, but he was watching the search.

Courtesy and anger fought on the farmer's face. 'My ears are going old but my sight ain't,' he said. He threw down the wire and joined the soldiers, but the dog declined to follow.

'I'm sure,' Molly said. 'Of course, it might be Russian assassins.' Her tone implied it was more likely to be fairies, or a headless horseman. *Hurry up and finish*, she almost prayed.

And here was the world-weary officer in charge, looking at his watch. 'Hurry it along, men. Let's get this lady on her way and do the same ourselves.'

The soldier checking the driver's work threw the damaged wheel into the truck and gave her a snappy salute. She thanked them all profusely and blew them a cartoonish kiss.

Leaving the farmer still prodding a stick into the flattened grass, the soldiers put out their cigarettes and went back to the truck.

Summoning a smile, Molly waved the soldiers on.

'Well,' said the farmer, looking at her.

'Well,' said Molly. She drank some water and offered him the bottle.

'Can't stay here all day,' the man said, with no grace at all. He turned, and the dog leaped up and followed him.

She counted to a hundred and made sure the farmer's red shirt was nowhere to be seen before plunging into the grass; she couldn't be seen looking. *Oh Cory, where are you?* If the man came back, she'd squat, pretend to be relieving herself. Or perhaps two soldiers would walk back and surprise her . . .

She dared not call out, but said softly, 'Mom needs you, Cory. Don't hide.' *Where is he?* Was he caught in some animal trap? Maybe he'd scurried far, far away.

There was stagnant mud in this ditch, the only mud in a mile, and a mossy green culvert, too small for a man . . .

Cory's instincts were never to rely on his power alone but to hide physically if he could.

She squatted by the opening, which stank of something dead. She couldn't see or hear anything, but this felt right.

'Cory,' she whispered, one ear cocked for the farmer, and here Cory was, for a moment vague, then her mind fully saw him, covered in mud, his eyes closed and hands tucked under him. She stroked his ear and he stirred a little. He was cold and shivering, exhausted.

'Hard-hard, all of them,' he said. 'Cory hiiide, fooled Bad Men, very clever hide all.'

'Yes, Cory, my smart boy. They've gone now. There's just one we might have to hide from.' She helped him up, draped the sweatshirt over his head for safety and walked behind him to obstruct the view. Another vehicle might come, or the farmer return. If he did, she would just leap in the car and go.

His power wasn't unlimited. They'd have to be more careful.

'Shall we find somewhere quiet for a picnic?' she said, dreading it.

'Home now,' Cory said.

She found tears coming. That had been too close and she wasn't safe yet; she mustn't give way, but for two minutes she sat and gripped the steering wheel, shuddering. Maybe they'd noted the licence plate? They'd surely ask questions.

Bad Men? They were surrounded by people who'd betray them in an instant, but to call them Bad Men was unkind; there was a danger in good, kind men too, who'd do the wrong thing out of duty. That handsome soldier would have obeyed his orders and let them take her son away because he'd believe it to be the right thing to do.

She turned the key and prepared to turn the car round. Her voice trembling, she began a song.

# CHAPTER 17

## The day of the Moon landing

The landing would be late that afternoon; Molly guessed she'd have to ration the television, otherwise they might do nothing else all day. Cory was wriggling like a sack of frogs with excitement. Today was history, and it was the moment Gene had been waiting for since he found the first tattered comic with a rocket splashed across the cover.

'Big day for the silly old human race,' said Molly, yawning. 'I hear Cory's people fixed hunger and war before they went to their moon.'

Gene grunted, which she translated as, *It's Sunday. Too early to talk*.

'Eggs please-please breakfast Cory help.'

'Okay, Cory, just give me a minute.' Molly didn't think much of television; she'd given in to Gene's pleas to rent a set, but she censored much of it. Cory was easily upset by violence and most of human history turned out to be surprisingly difficult to explain. But even she wanted to watch this story unfold. Now she knew that people lived and laughed and had babies out in space, somehow the whole exercise was less ridiculous.

Cory helped Molly, whisking eggs in the bowl. *Tick-tick-tick.* From nowhere he announced, 'Cory dads live on moon. And space-city, big and spins.'

He'd said *dads* before and Molly had assumed that theirs was one of those cultures which threw titles around; every grown-up was an uncle, that sort of thing.

'Yes-yes very big city.' Cory waved his arms. 'Underground. Saw new spaces being melted into rock. All-so-exciting. Waited for big ship finished. Run-run-run because gravity low.' He started jogging on the spot and waving his arms; it might just catch on as a new hippy dance. 'Big run wheeeels then ship to new planet. Big excitement.' He kept waving his arms.

It was no good pressing Cory about his home in case it plunged him into sadness, but sometimes, when he offered things up, she could nudge him to say more. But this time, Cory was on a roll. 'My world green, and plenty oceans. No ice at poles. The new planet des-sert, dry-dry, air thin. Go build city by only-one ocean. Burn tunnels and houses out of rock. Glass houses for food. Thousands pioneers, like Cory. Take Earth-year to get there.'

'How big was the ship, Cory?'

Tentacles danced and hands gesticulated. 'Big – bigger Amber Grove. Trains inside.'

His sadness suddenly came into the room, like a shadow. That was enough; any question about family or the flight that ended in disaster could flick him into grief. They just had to be gentle.

The vessel hidden in Two Mile Lake was just a run-around, like a lifeboat, maybe, compared to the main ship.

'Big ship called *Dancer on the Waves* – big joke, ha-ha-ha! Name from old story . . . but all gone. All gone.'

*What happened, Cory?* she wondered. *What went wrong?*

Gene emerged, damp-haired and still half asleep, carrying cereal boxes and tinfoil. 'Want to build a Moon rocket, Cory? But I think we ought to go for a walk first, check the woods are still there.'

In the big room, the television flickered grey, the sound off. Gene and Cory needed to explain it to her, though at least Gene looked apologetic as he did so. They'd built *Eagle*, the Landing Module, and *Columbia*, the main craft that would bring the three men home, from card and paper and foil.

The model held together by Gene's long fingers, Cory narrated, 'Rocket giant firework! Take-off!'

The kitchen bucket was Earth, wreathed in green and blue paper, and the waste-paper basket was the Moon.

'This is where we are now,' said Gene. '*Eagle* and *Columbia* separate. Mike Delgardo in *Columbia* stays in orbit and *Eagle* with the other two descends.'

How odd Fate was. Neil Armstrong was the man destined to walk first on the Moon, until an elderly driver had a stroke and sideswiped the astronaut's car. Armstrong, trained to travel further than any man in history, would be watching it all on TV, sitting there with a broken leg. Add the outbreak of gastroenteritis, and it meant three different astronauts would be walking into history.

*Random happenings.* On Meteor Day, Molly could have gone to look for Gene, to offer first aid in the middle of town, and they might never have met Cory, who had changed *every-thing*.

Molly clapped as Cory held the homemade *Eagle* and let it land while Gene kept *Columbia* in orbit.

They gathered on the couch with Cory in the middle and watched it all happening on the television, step by step.

Gene, smiling, said, 'I knew we'd do this since I was knee-high. But just think: for Cory's people, their moon is like a quick trip to Pasadena.'

'Big-big day for humans. Draw Cory-people moon-landing!' Cory said, scooting frantically out of the room and coming back again with paper and crayons. 'Draw humans-landing too.'

As the time approached, even Molly felt nerves in her stomach; the tension in the room was real. *Columbia* was filming the *Eagle*, floating independently in space, revolving slowly on the television screen like an eager bride to show that it was whole and safe. Then the tiny spaceship like some strange metal bug dropped towards the grey scarred Moon. It did not look far, but it would be hours before the two men landed.

They'd chosen Walter Cronkite, America's favourite news-caster, the wise old moustachioed uncle. For all the drama, she could do without endless talking heads, so she sighed and addressed the long-overdue basket of mending. Countless millions across the globe devoured the tiny, grainy pictures, watching film of the Earth pioneers, the Russians and the Americans, then Neil Armstrong gave a gracious interview.

A little later, the images changed to the dead grey desert of the Moon as seen from the *Eagle*. Bit by bit the Moon ceased to be a far-off world and became a landscape. The rocks grew larger and larger, the craters clearer as the *Eagle* came into land. Gene's arm was around Cory's shoulders, his gaze rapt. She put down her sewing.

Walter Cronkite could barely hide his excitement; it looked like he was finding it hard to breathe. He explained the descent; how soon two men would make history while the whole world was watching. They cut to the calm, masculine voices from the landing craft giving numbers and check-words. If the astronauts felt any nerves, they were hiding them well.

Then, with a sudden flash of light, the images vanished and the screen plunged into swirling grey.

For a moment, Molly assumed the television had decided, this day of all days, to expire – but no, the sound was still on, because Walter Cronkite said, 'We've lost contact.'

The room felt like ice; she couldn't breathe. Two worlds fought in her mind: the TV room and a nightmare pouring into her mind. All around her was chaos: the death of Cory's people's mission, all floating corpses and purple blood and pain in breathing. From somewhere she heard a giant inhuman scream and something silver twisted and poured through a doorway. And there were others like it, things like metal snakes as long as a giant truck, with utterly alien snouts at either end. They moved swiftly and with purpose, spouting fire, burning through walls and ceilings and floors.

Only now did the fractured images from past dreams make sense: these silver-scaled monsters were the killers, the destroyers of Cory's ship.

In a dark sky of blazing stars, a vast vessel disappeared behind her, silver threads swarming over it like maggots on a corpse.

189

In an instant, the dream-images vanished and she was back in the front room. Beside her, Gene was gasping desperately for breath; he had seen it too. It had happened in an instant, only a few heartbeats, but Cory had disappeared.

'Cory, Cory!' she called, shaking. She hadn't known he could share nightmares awake.

On screen, Walter Cronkite kept talking. 'We've lost contact with *Eagle*, but this could just be a communications fault, or just possibly something else has happened.' Behind his glasses, the genial face of the nation's favourite TV man showed his anxiety. 'Let's not jump to conclusions. We've lost contact before. If you have just joined us, the landing module *Eagle* was making its descent, but we have lost contact. For all we know, the module might be safely landing on the Moon, in the Sea of Tranquillity. Did we see a brief flash of light before we lost contact?' he asked.

*A flash of white light . . . Yes*, thought Molly, *there's no question. No one could have missed it*.

On screen, a second man began his ponderous analysis.

Unannounced, Cory was back. The three of them hugged each other tight.

'Maybe something hit *Columbia*,' Gene said, after minutes of silence. 'Or maybe *Eagle* broke up . . .'

'Like Cory ship, all-dead. Metal things hunt,' Cory whispered. 'Bad machines, sowl-jer machines kill everyone.'

'Oh love,' Molly said. Summer rain was drumming on the roof.

'Four of thou-sands dead.' Molly and Gene felt the grief and confusion come off him in waves as he whispered, 'Now hu-mans.'

Molly rested her head on Gene's shoulder as Cronkite, ever professional, kept going. 'Lengthy periods without radio contact are not unknown.' The strain in his voice was clear now. 'I think we mustn't jump to any conclusions. There are protocols . . .'

When Gene spoke, his voice was gentle and low. 'Those things from your nightmare, Cory, was that . . . ?' He stopped, trying to form the best words. 'Was it those bad things that attacked *Eagle*?'

'Don't know, don't know, don't know! Bad remembering things. All killing, made me sick.'

Minutes passed and the anchorman kept talking and the rain fell. Molly stood and lifted Cory and carried him out of the room, but Gene stayed, gripped by the unknown.

She'd be delighted to come back for good news, but she was sick with fear. Whatever killed Cory's people might still be out there. He'd said 'hunt', and the movement of the snake-machines in his nightmare felt like hunting. She crooned to Cory with a hope she did not feel.

That evening, Molly listened to the radio in the kitchen and cleaned the stove in fury, taking out strong emotions on something that couldn't fight back. The failure of the Moon mission reminded her of when President Kennedy was murdered; it had changed everything. Surely this'd be the same, one of those days people would remember for ever. The radio was playing solemn music now; she'd been turning the sound down every hour to miss the news but now the music stopped mid-note and a breathless announcer said, 'Mike Delgardo's alive! Folks, they've had a signal from *Columbia* – he's fine. I repeat, Mike Delgardo's alive.'

Molly spilled the filthy water, watching it run in greasy trails across her floor. Gene was already thundering upstairs, calling, 'Cory, come quickly—'

A spectacular electrical short had kept *Columbia* out of radio contact for four hours, the longest four hours in history, until, finally, a familiar Texan voice broke over the airwaves: 'Houston, this is *Columbia*, do you copy?' For years, people would talk of how suppers burned and glasses smashed, how children were told to shut up and listen as the radio broke the news. Now they played that first clip of sound over and over.

Molly gave a silent gasp of thanks and struggled up to find a cloth and sort the mess.

Cory stood there, looking so sad.

'Mike Delgardo's fine,' she said. '*Columbia* is fine – he's coming home.'

Cory's ears twitched. 'Good.'

'He can fly the ship alone,' she said, and Cory shrank, like some great weight was pressing down on him.

'Like first Mom. One left to fly. Now Cory alone, like him.'

Even in the ruins of the mission, Delgardo's personality was shining through. The whole world heard how he fixed the electrical fault – 'I tried everything but kicking it!' – and Houston grilled him about what he'd seen. The quick answer was, his orbit had taken him out of the line of sight. He asked if there was anything he could do to find out what happened to *Eagle*? He couldn't land, but say, a much lower orbit . . . ? But Houston told him not to be a damn fool.

*

They read the funeral service, commending the two dead men to the stars. Watching the President's brief broadcast to the nation, even Molly admitted he spoke for the world. Then the President talked to Mike Delgardo across the emptiness of space and the whole world heard the President hesitate.

'So, they tell me you trained to bring *Columbia* home alone, if you had to.'

'Yes, sir. I can fly her back one-handed.'

'Come home, son. No heroics.'

'Yes, sir.'

## CHAPTER 18

# *A trip to Bradleyburg*

On Saturday morning Gene had to work, so Rosa Pearce came to Crooked Street to mind Cory. He embraced her with enthusiasm, and Molly had the rest of the day to herself. Supper would be cooked by Gene and Cory, using an implausibly large number of pans, but it was usually edible. She took the familiar drive west to Bradleyburg. For some reason, she thought of the Russian spies. After the initial excitement, they had disappeared and Amber Grove had had a blissful few weeks without anyone snooping. First, she had decided, she would look round the thrift shops, then the department store. Purchases for Cory would be left to be collected later, since she was having lunch with her friends, who would be sure to ask questions about any parcels. The iron rule of shopping for Cory was to use different catalogues and to go to different places, to be unmemorable, to leave no sign she had a child herself.

In the department store, she idled through menswear, noticing that lapels and collars were getting even wider. The new fashions would suit Gene's lean frame, but he'd complain like crazy if she bought anything for him. There were pretty dresses in the children's section; she watched as a mother measured this dress and that against her dark-haired girl, feeling an ache, no less painful for being familiar . . . and yet her thoughts turned to her Cory. He didn't end the sadness, but he gave her another focus; he was a good balm for grief. Being a mother was not as she'd imagined; it was more, it was wider. Cory had changed everything.

Rows of silent televisions in the store showed the scenes at the White House, in lurid colours. They were repeating the capsule landing off Hawaii, and Mike Delgardo's cheery face inside the quarantine cell. The President gave a speech saying he wanted another Moon mission. 'Suppose those who first sailed out of sight of land had faltered,' he said. 'Suppose mankind had said, no, it's too difficult to fly with the birds.' She didn't know where she stood. Sorrow for the widows and their children, for sure. No medal at the White House could compensate for the loss of a father.

Molly was early. She found a table in the store's coffee shop and got herself a drink. As she people-watched, trying not to think about the pastries under their spotless glass domes, she glanced up – and to her shock, there at the counter was Dr Pfeiffer, lecturing the waitress about the coffee in Milan, Italy. *Damn him!* Suddenly there as if he'd risen from a trapdoor in a puff of red smoke. Molly's cup rattled in its saucer, but she stilled her face. What the hell was he doing here? She'd have been happy never to see him again.

She grabbed her purse, but she was a long way from the door.

Could she hide in the ladies' restroom? No, he might be hours. But so long as he didn't see her, maybe she could sneak round the edge of the room, get out into the safety of the store.

Pfeiffer looked around and saw her. At once, parcels in hand, he left the counter and walked over. 'I thought that was you,' he said, standing too close, shifting from one foot to the other. 'How're things, Mrs Myers?'

'Oh, hello, Dr Pfeiffer. We're getting along,' she said, trying to be cold without being rude.

'My daughters enjoy camp, but I like to buy them something for when they come home.' He showed her his parcels. Venturing a rather timid smile, he went on, 'I'm staying in town – perhaps we could have lunch?'

She'd rather kiss a crocodile. 'Oh, I'm sorry,' she said, 'but I have plans.'

Pfeiffer didn't hide his disappointment. 'It's not just a social matter. I do have some more questions.'

'I'm not finding this easy,' Molly said, starting to feel the sweat prickle her skin. Her mind was whirling; was this a ruse? Perhaps the FBI were at the house already. They'd talked Rosa through their escape plans, but perhaps even now Cory was running through the woods alone . . . and maybe Gene had been arrested.

'I just wanted a friendly chat,' Pfeiffer said. 'I could make it official, if you want to.'

Molly looked at her watch. She couldn't stand him and the FBI at the house; they might even take them away . . . How anxious that would make Cory . . . 'I have twenty minutes,' she said, with very poor grace.

Pfeiffer sat, then leaned forward and said, 'There are lots of theories about the Moon landing.'

Well, Molly was afraid she knew what had happened: just maybe, *Eagle* had suffered the same fate as Cory's giant star-ship. But she said, 'The Russians?' The newspapers were suggesting the USSR blew up the Moon mission to spoil the American victory.

Pfeiffer puffed his cheeks, let out a dismissive *Huh!* 'Unlikely. They're ruthless enough, of course; I won't deny that, but most of their unmanned missions crash. A Soviet machine capable of remotely attacking a moving spacecraft a quarter of a million miles away? *We* couldn't do it. Truly, it would be far easier for them to just land their own man on the Moon. No, there are perfectly plausible reasons – technical reasons – why *Eagle* might've failed. And it might have been sabotage, of course. But even if we find the wreckage, we may never know.'

'Uh-huh,' Molly said.

'Or it might've been something else entirely.' His lips clamped shut as the waitress brought over his coffee. When the woman had gone, Pfeiffer said, 'So, on Meteor Day we learned we were not alone. What you had in the hospital changed *everything*. We know they're out there, Mrs Myers – perhaps they're hostile.'

Molly sighed. Let him feel her sheer tiredness at talking to him. 'I've told you everything I know. I only cared for C— the boy . . . a couple of weeks, give or take. We got to a few words – water, bedpan, food. He was sweet, and not frightened of us.'

She'd used the name before. It was fine.

'I bet a Russian general's little boy would be sweet too.'

Pfeiffer's gaze locked on her. 'Mrs Myers, is there *anything* you haven't told me? Anything at all, that could help your country?'

'No,' she said. She and Gene had talked this through late into the night, but they both agreed they wouldn't be believed, not unless they produced Cory, and then they would lose everything. Why should she give Cory up to the warmongers?

She held his gaze.

He blinked first. 'Thank you for your time. I just needed to ask. Can I get your opinion?' He had the end of one parcel open, but she'd spotted the girls.

'I see my friends,' she said, relieved. 'Sorry, I must rush.' She gathered up her stuff and walked towards Janice and Diane and the children. The moment she had her back to Pfeiffer, she pulled some faces for the adults. 'Let's go to the other place,' she said, brightly.

As they left the store, Janice, eager for gossip, said, 'That was what's his name, Dr Pfeiffer . . .'

'Yes, he's always bothering Dr Jarman,' Molly said; she'd already worked out her story. 'He's researching this radioactivity stuff. And' – it wasn't true, but how easy to slander the unpleasant – 'you know, he's a horrible creep, following women around.' She mimed pinching a bottom and her friends' eyebrows soared. 'Disgusting. He's famous for it, they say. Oh, I'm so glad you came!'

They took the bait and the conversation turned away from danger.

Gene was right. They had nothing useful they could tell the authorities; all they would do was lose their son. That flash of light before *Eagle* vanished, that could have been anything. But looking at the clear blue sky brought a new sense of danger.

CHAPTER 19

# Two Mile Lake

Two Mile Lake sat motionless in the muggy heat, surrounded by watching forest. Pfeiffer parked a little way from the Shed. He could leave his children's presents in the car; no one would steal anything here.

The Ship wanted its privacy, but of course the humans still spied on it. Detectors were strung along the new, shorter jetty, positioned in that boat moored several hundred yards away and on the three metal towers stationed around the shore. The scientists sometimes floated devices on a balloon over the Ship as bait: the sophisticated equivalent of poking it with a stick.

The long room was sweaty and the air was close; the fans roaring constantly to protect the equipment cramming the place did little to tame the heat. Why wasn't the air-conditioning working? Pfeiffer disliked the informality of shirtsleeves, but this was unbearable. He slipped off his jacket.

Pfeiffer took the chair the underling instantly vacated and acknowledged Dr Tyler, who said, 'Nothing since yesterday.

Dr Haldeman had someone take the new listening device out by boat and the Ship threatened to boil the lake.'

'So is it widening the exclusion area?'

His assistant looked anxious at having to express an opinion. 'It was fine a week ago. Dr Haldeman wonders if maybe it's bored. Who knows?'

*Is the machine mind capricious? Or is it being unpredictable as a tactic? Why should an alien machine be easy to understand?* He turned on the microphone and said, 'Good evening, Ship. This is Dr Pfeiffer. I have a message for you from the President.'

Well, it was a phone call from the Chief of Staff, but that was mere detail.

Pfeiffer waited five or so minutes between each statement.

A faint hiss came from the speaker, rising and falling like a far distant sea. He covered the microphone with a hand. 'I'll have an iced tea,' he said into the air. 'And why isn't the air-conditioning working?' The clock ticked on.

On the seventh repetition, as he started his second dreadful iced tea, the Ship spoke in its odd voice. 'Good evening, Dr Pfeiffer. Please instruct humans to remain off the water.'

Pfeiffer clicked on the reel-to-reel. 'Good evening, Ship. I have an important message from the President.'

'I do not want to damage the humans, but all submerged instruments must be removed, then no further humans will be allowed onto the water. Instruct all accordingly.'

Pfeiffer ignored the order and said, 'We are very concerned that two men died in space. Our President is asking if you can assist us in understanding the event.'

'If I detonated my engines, the loss of life would be significant.'

Haldeman and Pfeiffer had debated that repeated threat long into the night; if it announced a countdown, would they call its bluff? But right now there was a question of more importance. 'Two men died, Ship. We're desperate to find out why.'

'Humans die every day in road traffic accidents. You show little concern about that.'

The speaker was silent, for more than a minute. Then the Ship spoke again. 'I have issued a warning: no more humans on or in the water. You must now decide whether to heed it.'

The Ship had surrounded itself with a boiling of steam and dead fish, sent the Geiger counters screaming with new radioactivity, or used vibration to make people sick, but it hadn't killed anyone. Yet.

'Ship, we could certainly discuss keeping people off the water for a bit. It is hard for us to concentrate . . . we're all so worried about the Moon landing.'

'I repeat my statement: I had no interest in your spacecraft. I did not harm it. I was unaware it was your first attempt to land on your Moon. It is nothing to do with my mission. I understand that your America United States and your Russia Soviet Union are rival administrations in a primitive dominance display. I have no interest in this.'

'Do you know what happened?' Pfeiffer asked again. Odd radar echoes, the strange lights: they had concluded the Ship had at least two smaller flying machines that were able to travel unseen to do its work. Whatever that was. That made the President deeply paranoid. *You mean this goddam thing is spying on us and we don't know how?* He had slapped the table as he spoke.

The speaker hissed a little.

'We will not bring anyone onto the water for two weeks,' Pfeiffer said.

'Thank you. Will you send another mission to the Moon to investigate?'

Why did it ask that? This was the first time it'd shown any interest in human activity outside its immediate locale.

'I think we probably will, but I don't know when,' Pfeiffer said. He did know, of course; he was the President's Chief Scientific Counsel, but he wasn't saying. The next mission would orbit the Moon but not land; it would take observations and see what happened.

Did he believe the machine? It was neither confirming nor denying it knew something. Could a machine lie? Was it just trying to make conversation?

The clock ticked on as the machine gave him the silent treatment. America had been humiliated by the destruction of *Eagle*, but his country had surmounted far worse. Mrs Myers and Dr Jarman: their foolish actions still rankled. By hiding the child they called Cory, letting it die, they had cost their country dearly. How frustrated he'd felt, talking to Mrs Myers, earlier that day. She had touched the alien from another world.

'Ship? We have some more questions.'

The speaker hissed and the fans roared and the minutes passed. He sipped the nasty iced tea; even that made him miss his wife—

Haldeman came rushing in from outside, visibly shaking, and shoved a couple of Polaroids under Pfeiffer's nose.

Pfeiffer clicked off the microphone: never let the Ship hear anything you don't want it to. '*Where?*'

'In a waterway, twenty miles north of here. They're the largest remains yet. Obviously we're cordoning it off and excavating the area.' Haldeman started drumming his hands on his thighs. 'We told the farmer who found it, it's a military satellite. I reckon he bought it.'

Pfeiffer studied the photos, which showed two melted and twisted machine parts sitting in muddy water. The thing had once been encased in metal scales twice the length of his hand; he had found a piece of silver metal just like that the day after the impact. Thank goodness his Geiger counter had warned him against touching this perilous treasure from the stars.

'How big?' Pfeiffer asked at last.

Haldeman shrugged. 'Whatever it is exploded into dozens of pieces. But this end looks like . . . well, an end. A head.'

Haldeman's team had brought all the pieces they'd found to a secret location, but it was a bit like fossil-hunting, trying to work out if you had three dinosaurs or six when you had never even seen a dinosaur before. The machines were yards long, but was that three yards or ten? They had cunning tentacles, and folding pincers which slotted away in the body.

If only the alien had survived. He would have won the child's confidence and then the science of these creatures would be open to him; all they would have had to do was ask and they could have found out what these scaled machines were. America would go to the Moon, and on to the planets and the stars far beyond. His country's enemies would be humiliated and their imprisoned peoples freed – and he, Dr Emmanuel

Pfeiffer would be in the history books long after his rivals had been forgotten.

*Why would anyone make a machine like a snake?* Maybe Haldeman would find enough pieces to discover what these machines were for and how they travelled.

# CHAPTER 20

## *Indian summer*

Gene drove alone to his parents' farm, the haunting 'Space Oddity' playing on the radio as he planned what he would say. Someone on the radio was going on about this folk festival, Woodstock, which made him remember concerts before Molly was ill; he smiled to imagine Cory, garlanded with flowers, dancing among thousands of people.

In the farmhouse kitchen, the warm heart of the house where Gene had grown up, his mother made cold drinks while his father sat, watching him, saying nothing. His mom was wheezing a little, but she kept assuring him the new medicine was working just fine.

'Well, Gene, no time like now,' his dad said, the moment Mom sat down. 'Big news, we're guessing.'

'Okay, so, Mom, Dad, this may be a shock. Um . . . Molly and I have adopted a little boy. It's really complicated, though.'

'That's wonderful,' Mom said, clasping her hands, 'for Molly, for both of you – how wonderful! What's his name?'

'*Complicated?*' said his dad. 'Adopted *when*? You've been acting Moon-touched for months.'

'We call him Cory.' And Gene began to explain. His dad went *Huh!* when Gene said, 'You have to promise to keep this a secret,' like he had insulted him. He coughed on his drink when Gene first said 'aliens' and asked, 'Like that *Star Bonanza* thing?' He went a little red in the face as Gene mumbled, 'Cory looks quite different.' Red in the face was not good and Gene started to trip over his words, wondering how much to say. Molly would have told the story better.

His mother just listened until Gene started on running from the FBI and hiding Cory from everyone. 'Oh dear,' his mom said. 'Oh dear.'

Gene found himself fingering the envelope with a single Polaroid snap of Cory in all his alien glory. Molly and her photographs, what a stupid risk. He'd been sure his parents would be surprised; he'd assumed they would ask questions, that it would take time for them to assimilate the news, but his father just looked angry.

Gene stopped and his parents sat silent. Maybe they didn't believe him.

'Well, I suppose you had to do something,' his mom said at last. 'You must bring him here, to meet us.' She looked at her husband, for reassurance, he guessed. His parents knew each other's moods without words.

'This has to be the stupidest darn thing anyone has ever done,' his dad said. He drew breath. 'Nobel Prize for Stupid.'

'You believe me,' Gene said, grasping at straws.

'I may have raised a fool, but not a liar,' he said, fingers laced as he did to hold in temper. 'Bill Burrowes has family down there; he says Amber Grove is just crawling with army and Russian spies and FBI. One phone call and you'll have the whole darn government after you – and what if the commies find you? What happens if Molly gets sick again? Or the boy gets ill? You gonna sneak him back into the hospital? What about the neighbours' kids? Do you have to keep him inside?'

'Well, that's one reason we want you to know – he might like—'

'Well, thanks very much. I didn't ask to have you drag your mother into this madness. Why not tell the government? There are laws. They wouldn't take him off you, not now.'

'Well, they might,' Mom said, touching Dad's hand. 'National security and everything.'

Gene, feeling heat in his own face, said, 'So, we can't count on you?' That came out wrong.

His father looked pained. 'I'm not going to pick up the phone, of course not. But you know, the farm hands . . . they're good people, but they're not family. We got neighbours dropping by, some salesman pitches up, asks to use the bathroom. You don't want them knowing. This is every sort of trouble. You need to figure out some clean way out of the mess – maybe get some good lawyer on it – or that commie Senator you like so much.'

'He's not a commie,' Gene said, by reflex.

'Have you a picture?' his mom said. 'I'd like to see your Cory.' She lifted the reading glasses she wore on a chain.

Gene felt sick and disappointed, but was his dad so wrong, when you looked at it with his eyes? Full of doubt, he handed over the photo and his parents stared at it, their hands touching.

It was quiet enough to hear the tiny *tick tick tick* of the clock advertising a local feed company long disappeared.

'Oh,' his mom said, at last.

Cory had been so excited, he had not slept until midnight, but he was dozing now, the rarest of occurrences, and Molly seized the time to get organised for their trip to John and Eva's farm.

She took some laundry into Cory's room. He stored his stuff with military precision; he'd explain his latest system if you gave him half a chance. There he slept, in a muddle of bedclothes on the floor. He'd got excited by the idea of the airbed and he'd been practising on it for a week. She gave silent thanks that he was so happy and well. She could've stood there watching his calm breathing until the glaciers returned.

The last time she'd gone to the farm, driving under grey winter skies, she had been burning with rage about Gene and *that woman* and she'd feared she'd do something stupid, to Gene or to herself. She'd telephoned Eva, seeking sanctuary with someone who knew and loved them both; she'd just said things were awful and she needed space. In better times, when she was pregnant, she'd been to the farm bubbling with joy.

Now she wanted the people she loved to know Cory.

'Mom was okay,' Gene had reported, 'and she'll have weeks to work on Dad. It will be fine.'

Molly could see how anxious Gene was, how he was trying to convince himself as much as her. She needed John on her side: the man who'd given her away at her wedding. It would be like losing a second father if he didn't.

Cory's latest habit was coming down the stairs on the outside of the banister, because he could. Now he bounded to the breakfast table wearing his outdoor hat.

'Good morning good morning good morning. Biggest expedition ever! See John and Eva and pigs and cows and chickens drive long pretty route see the state. Are ducks in creek? Are bisons on farm?' A moment of moving tentacles and, 'Cory big-big excited talk-too-much sorry.'

'We're excited too,' Molly said.

Gene took the car keys without discussion. She could see the tension in his jaw. 'It will be fine,' he said, out of nowhere.

Then they were in the car, driving down Crooked Street to the junction and away.

The state was pretty in early fall, with red barns and white churches, old bridges across bright rivers. The farm stood half surrounded by orchards, trees rich with reddening apples as big as fists. As they rolled up, Cory bounced up and down. 'Wanna see the pigs Mom-Mom-Mom and the chickens and the cows . . . what's that bird and that one and that one?' His head went from side to side, tentacles dancing as he picked up myriad smells.

Gene parked behind the house, the back door opened and Eva appeared, wiping her hands on a cloth. 'John, they're here!' she called.

Molly couldn't tell what nerves were her own and what were Cory's as Eva bent down and lifted the hood back.

Her smile was crooked, but it reached her eyes. 'What a handsome fellow,' she said. 'Now, Cory, you can call me Grandma Eva. We'll have some cookies and lemonade, then you can come feed the animals with me. They're very hungry. And look, here's Grandpa John.'

Gene's father wiped his hands on an oily rag. His eyes flicked wider when he saw the boy, but he came towards Cory, somewhere between a smile and a frown on his face, but not hostile.

Eva's arm went around those alien shoulders and she met Molly's eyes. No description prepared you for Cory, how very odd he looked, and yet how solid and *alive* he was.

John said, 'Now Cory, you gotta understand, a farm is not a playground. I'll tell you how your dad got that scar under his chin . . .'

The back of the house was old stone; the front had been extended with brick and wood. The place smelled of baking and safety. After homemade lemonade and cookies, Eva took Cory's hand and together they walked pails of swill down to the pigs and fed the chickens. Gene led Molly into his old bedroom and they squeezed onto the world's smallest double bed. This ancient patchwork faded to fifteen shades of green brought back good memories; they had maybe an hour before his parents fed them again. In better days they had slogged and saved enough to fill this room with books and to send Gene to college, the first in the family.

Later, as the evening dark gathered, John read stuff aloud from the local paper – 'Here's excitement you don't see in the city: man finds wallet. County Board argues over drains.' In the kitchen, Eva fried pork chops and asked Cory to set the table while Gene hunted down a dozen books to keep the boy busy.

The kitchen felt like the living soul of that house. Together they sat and looked at the meal – pork and potatoes and beans and fried greens of some sort and homemade bread. Molly's mouth watered at the smell.

Cory looked at the meat, ears down. 'Where pork-chop come from?' he asked plaintively.

The adults looked at each other. None of those books for children about our friends on the farm ever spelled out that particular sticky truth. Molly knew with a sinking heart how this was going to go; Cory had been sniffing around that question for weeks and like a coward, she'd been dodging it.

John tried to laugh it off. 'Well, Cory, everyone knows that . . . Pigs, of course.'

Cory's tentacles started to wave. 'Is pig-friend hurt Grandpa John?' And he looked from one to another with those stunning violet eyes.

Eva tried, 'Well, the pig has no use for it now 'cos it's dead, Cory.'

Molly and Gene's son folded his arms and said, 'So-not hungry Gran-ma-ma-ma. So don't eat murdered-dead-murdered things. Poor pigs.'

In Eva's house, hospitality meant food and feeding meant love. To turn down your hostess' food? That was a little like burning the flag. But Cory could do stubborn as well as any of them around that table.

John's face flushed red. 'Well!' That frown meant he wanted to make something of it with Gene, like two bulls clashing horns in the field, and Eva looked to heaven and pulled a face or two.

Then she rubbed Cory's head and, her voice low and gentle, said, 'There's no pork on the potatoes and beans, I promise.'

213

'Potatoes, beans, applesauce pleeese,' said Cory.

Eva said a tense grace and they ate. Cory used a fork and didn't look up, but they all felt the poor dead pig like a ghost at the table. With Cory's disapproval radiating out, the rich, fatty meat tasted dull in Molly's mouth. He had eaten ham only last week. He loved her meatloaf.

'Cory, you ate seafood on your own planet.' Shellfish, and other sea-things she couldn't guess at, like armoured newts. 'And the worm in the garden.'

He burbled in his own language, then, 'They alive-but-no-feelings. Cory feel inside how pigs feel, like people. Don't eat things-alive-with-feelings.'

And she realised he'd never met any animal humans ate before. He liked cats and dogs and raccoons and songbirds, but Americans don't eat any of those.

The homemade apple cobbler was excellent, but the conversation didn't flow. Cory asked to be excused and went to his airbed up in the eaves, his cubbyhole.

'Never mind the crank diet; he'll grow out of it,' John said. 'Someone here's got to be practical. You need a plan, Gene: a good one. How long before his people come?'

Gene blinked.

'We don't know,' Molly said. She'd told Cory she hoped it would be soon, but in her heart she wasn't sure she wanted the aliens to come at all. It would be good for humanity, of course, but she would lose her son. 'When they come – if they come . . . well, they'll want him back. Until then, we carry on.'

John scratched his head. 'Keeping him hidden? From the

government, the spies, from your neighbours and the press. Your friends . . . right there in town?'

'Yes. That's the only way,' Gene said.

John leaned forward. 'He's going to grow, son. He's already a ball of fire. He'll want to see the world. Friends, school . . . what's his future going to be? It's not going to get any easier, is it? And what if he gets real sick . . .'

'Dr Jarman,' Gene said.

*As if either of them had the answers.* 'We're just making it up as we go along, John,' Molly admitted. 'It's not like an ordinary family, where you can plan.'

Eva gave a tiny noise, almost a snort, and Molly remembered that she and John had found each other late in life, so much so that Gene had been a surprise.

'Well, who knows how anything ends,' she added.

'He's welcome here. Though I never expected to risk jail at my age,' John pronounced, and Molly felt a surge of warmth and gratitude.

Eva took his hand. 'It's the right thing.'

Molly noticed Eva was getting breathless again; she needed to talk to her about that. But for now, full of relief, she just said, 'Thank you.' She had her mouth open to say more, but John ploughed on, monarch of the kitchen.

'Or if you ever need to hide out, we have the keys to the Anthony place. Five miles north, left fork . . .'

'Oh, yeah, I remember,' Gene said. 'More a track than a road. A real hideaway.'

'Nice folks, from the city, but they don't come much, not since their son fell serving his country. You want to use it, call us first, just in case you're unlucky and they happen to be here. Now, you lied and that's big trouble right there. You'll need someone to make a deal – but you got a real high card though: young Cory. A big-city lawyer would eyeball the government for you, make an agreement. I don't think our local guy would cut it, but he might know a name.'

'That's interesting,' said Molly, although the very idea terrified her. Once the government knew Cory was alive, they would hunt him down. And what would a deal even mean? The President with his lying speeches couldn't be trusted and the squawking Dr Pfeiffer would be circling Cory like a vulture the instant he got wind of his existence. There were times when Molly thought it was all just too big and too complicated for the two of them to hold.

Disappointed, John went on, 'I get you don't trust our President, but what about talking to the Governor?' He clearly thought this was a great idea, and yes, Governor Rockefeller was liberal, on some things.

But Gene said, 'Rockefeller's in bed with the war.'

'You know, a heck of a lot of good people are.' John was going red again.

Gene said, 'Well, perhaps there's someone we could trust a bit more.'

'Senator Fruitcake? That commie—'

Gene and John sparred for a bit, until Cory appeared in his pyjamas. His ears were still down, but he held out his book and asked, 'Story-please Mom.'

Cory and Molly curled up together in the cubbyhole and she

read him his story until he said, 'Everyone mad-mad-mad with Cory. Hor-ri-ble murder-dead pig you met. *Horrible-horrible*.'

She stroked his head. 'I'm not mad at you; we just have to figure it all out, Cory-monster.'

That night, Gene disappeared into John's workshop and shut the door. After an hour Molly washed and went to bed, but she was still awake when Gene turned up.

All he said was, 'It'll be fine.'

Lured by coffee, she came down to breakfast to find a cheery Cory humming and playing with six brown eggs.

'Cory and I went to talk to the hens,' said Eva, with her crooked smile.

Cory picked up an egg and held it to his temple. 'Fresh-fresh-fresh. Not a friend-living-thing. No feelings. Mom-Dad-please-have-chickens? In yard. Cory help feed-them clean-them no-trouble help every day promise. Cluck cluck cluck eat garbage.'

'I don't think so,' Molly said. *Eggs*, she thought. *Okay, I can do lots with eggs*. She'd get real farm ones, where she could show him the damn chickens dancing the polka if she had to.

They ate pancakes and she tried not to think of home-cured bacon. When his plate was clean, John cleared his throat. 'Cory can help me with some chores. Then we might go down to the river. I'll show Cory where I taught his dad to fish.'

'Wear the hood up and hide if anyone comes,' Molly said at once.

Cory looked at her. 'Fuss-fuss. Love-you-Mom,' and he kissed her. The touch from the inner tentacles left a faint damp breath.

After they were gone, Gene helped chop wood and talked

to his mom about whether any of the books might be valuable while Molly did kitchen stuff and read cook books so old they were tied together with string, just like in her mother's house. When she had lived in the city, houses full of other people and their smells and noise stood shoulder to shoulder like trees in a crowded wood. Gene had grown up a stiff walk from the nearest family and a wait in the rain or the wind or the snow at the end of the road for the yellow school bus.

It was late afternoon by the time the oldest and youngest came back with five brown trout in the creel. Gene and Molly admired the catch in the golden sun.

'Cory slipped into the water,' said John. 'He stayed down there for ten minutes – I thought all the fish would vanish. Our very own water creature. When he came up, he'd caught one: lying there in the water on top of his hands, not even trying to get away. Guess he hexed it or something.'

'Fish cold boring thoughts, not feelings,' said Cory, confident. 'O-kay to eat.'

'He's a good kid,' John said, rubbing Cory's head. 'Dear Lord, you need a plan though.'

Eva grilled the fish with butter and Cory gobbled down seconds.

She could do a lot with fish. Her *Joy of Cooking* was full of ideas.

Another blissful day, filled with picking fruit and watching Cory running and climbing trees and getting muddy, but Gene had to be at work tomorrow.

Leaving Cory singing in the bathroom upstairs, the four

adults sat and John announced, 'So if you stay and they come after you, what's the plan?'

Gene went through everything, heading to Canada, Indiana or West, even Dr Jarman's spare car hidden on Elliott Street, just in case – the whole thing.

'I'll get you some snacks for the road,' said Eva.

In the car, as woods and fields rolled past, Cory said, 'No murdered-things in house pleeese. Take all murdered-things fridge bury them.'

'We won't ask you to eat them,' Gene said, but Molly doubted Cory would drop his objection.

She had bigger concerns. What *were* they going to do? Cory's people might take a year to come, or they might never get here – would they be able to hide him for a year? Five years? Ten?

She was so glad John and Eva had accepted their son. She looked at Gene again and the old bad times seemed a long time ago and a long way away . . . but she felt such a foreboding, that nothing would ever feel under their control again.

Live each day at a time: that was the old AA motto. Who knew how anything ever ended?

## CHAPTER 21

# *His first Halloween*

Raindrops glistened from last night and birds flew up, abandoning the berries on her bushes, as Molly searched the garden. There was no sign of Cory, but she'd bet he was out here somewhere.

She could hear children talking the other side of the high fence. The gate was closed, but . . . *Surely Cory hadn't—?*

Two voices, she guessed Chuck and Bonnie. She saw them together in the woods behind her house rather too often of late.

He was probably on the roof of the shed watching them. She slipped the key into the gate, opening it as quietly as she could, and stepped out to see the two children right next to her fence. Bonnie could have been playing Pure Innocence in a church play, but Chuck looked as uncomfortable as if she'd caught him stealing cookies.

'Good morning, Mrs Myers,' said Bonnie. 'How are you today?'

'I'm fine, thank you, Bonnie. How are you two?' Molly

looked at the Scout knapsack in Chuck's hands. Bonnie was holding a flask of water.

Bonnie volunteered, 'We're doing a project, on animals. We thought we'd look for tracks, but there aren't any today.'

Chuck went a little red in the face.

'Well, that's great,' Molly said enthusiastically. 'You just carry on looking. I thought I'd cut some of these beautiful branches to decorate the house. But that won't stop you, will it? I'll just go and get the cutters.'

'That's okay, ma'am,' Chuck said hurriedly. 'We'll just look someplace else because there aren't any tracks here.'

'What a shame.' Molly watched the two of them walk away, her nerves jangling. Lovely kids, and a touching friendship, but did they know something? Maybe Cory left footprints sometimes, but he wore ordinary shoes, and anyone could use the path.

She went in, locked the gate and whistled, the sound that meant into the house *right now*.

In the kitchen, Cory looked woebegone. 'Bonnie and Chuck didn't see me Cory hid so-well honest.'

'Spying on people isn't nice, Cory. What were they talking about?'

His tentacles were in turmoil.

'Sweetie-pie, they're nice kids but I need to know.'

'Nothing.'

She squatted down, took him in her arms and held him.

'They're good kids but if they know about you, they'll talk, and then the Bad Men will be back, lots of Bad Men. I need to know.'

His fear raised the hairs on her neck.

'Not Bad Men. Talking about Halloweeen like last time, trick-and-treeet and all the children-together, and games-and-costumes and candy-for-weeks.'

'And?'

'And looking at path, and near gate. They said playing looking for spies. If found tracks, make pl . . . plarstercasts. Nansee-drew.'

She held him, and thought how dangerous this innocent curiosity was to him. 'You have to promise me, Cory Myers, no showing, no talking. Always hide – in fact, always come inside if Bonnie and Chuck are snooping. Promise me.'

He let out a howl and his anguish and loneliness made her ache inside. '*Hoo-hoo-hoo*. Cory have no children no friends none-at-all. At home, on ship, sleep sixteens together, bigger ones help little ones.' A complicated fluting in his language. 'Always games and talks and dream together so many. Earth so lonely. Not solo, don't want to be alone.'

'You have us,' she said, but she knew it was not the same.

'Children in street and human-school all children together and parties and trick-or-treeet and Cory can't *not at all not ever*. When-when-*when* Cory people come?'

She held him, and it hurt, that she couldn't make this right.

That evening, when he was finally asleep, Gene and Molly held another council of war.

'We could let him trick-or-treat,' Gene said.

She almost spilled her drink. 'You've got to be kidding; it's so risky.'

'Use your imagination.' Gene's hands waved. 'If a kid's in a wheelchair and doesn't speak . . . people will think he's a bit, you know, simple in the head . . . Add a good disguise. It's the one time we *can* pull it off! And if we went to Bradleyburg or Dixville, we wouldn't even need a cover story.'

Against her better wishes, Molly sweet-talked Rosa into lending them a wheelchair. Cory loved wheelchair-racing in the deserted parking lot of the abandoned mill, and him trying to push Gene had her full of giggles. And on the day, she looked at Cory in hairy monster gloves and his head in a special mask, and Gene was right, you couldn't tell. A scary growl was a scary growl.

It worked, although her heart pounded every time someone grown or little admired Cory the poor monster. If they spoke to him, she would say sadly, 'Oh, he doesn't speak.' They would look pitying and give him even more candy. So much candy, even cautious Cory puffed up like a belching frog.

The day after Halloween, Cory was still wearing the scary costume. At supper, Gene handed him a big flat present, wrapped in red paper with stars.

'It's a just-because present,' he said, beaming.

Cory took care not to rip the paper, which revealed a big book on stars and planets, all in colour pictures. It looked very expensive.

'Wow!' Molly said. 'We should write your name in that, Cory.'

'Mag-nif-i-cent.' Cory's ears drooped. 'Lux-ur-rious!'

She felt his sadness across the table. Gene, crestfallen, had his arm round his skinny shoulders.

'Which star m-mine? Where home? Where Pioneer-home?'

What could they say? Tears came.

'Cory people must come yes-they-will.'

'I hope so,' Molly said. 'When they do come, won't that be wonderful?'

'Cory all alone. Need freeends.' But he still picked up Gene's disappointment. 'Good book from Dad. Ex-cell-ent book. Cory decided, take Mom and Dad and John and Eva home planet. First humans to stars yes-Cory-will.'

'Wouldn't that be amazing,' Gene said, trying to pretend his eyes weren't wet.

'Dad and Cory read star book now-together right-now. Whole book.'

Then he shivered, and they dared not ask what he was thinking.


'What's up, Molly-moo?'

She sat next to Gene on the sofa. 'Diane's in a right old state. Any trouble with the kids, she misses Hube. They were such a team. So anyway, Junior won't come home for Thanksgiving – he told her he couldn't celebrate "the victory of genocide and colonialism"; that the black man must stand with the red man, their oppressed brothers. He's joined some group that want to take African names. And as if that wasn't enough, Maddie's found yet another unsuitable boy and wants to drop out . . .'

'I guess you don't stop worrying when they leave home,' Gene sighed.

'Diane's just so hurt they won't come home. She's sure Maddie's new boyfriend is using drugs . . . Diane's going insane about it. Anyway, then she started pushing – you know what she's like. "How're things?", all innocent.'

'Um . . . what's wrong with that?'

'She'd noticed the sweater, that's what. Unlike you.'

A pause. 'I always liked that sweater.'

'And now I've lost twelve pounds I can wear it again, Mr Observant! So then Diane more or less said, why the act? She *knows* me. "You and Gene, you're doing so well, and you seem to have more energy, Molly." So I fence for a bit, then as usual I make an excuse and go – and as I was leaving, I bumped into Janice, and there's a real something. I told you on Sunday, didn't I? They stopped talking when they saw me – you know when your friends are talking about you—'

'No,' Gene said, bemused.

'What are we going to do?'

'You think she's going to call the FBI on us? No, we just need to play it cool, maybe step back a little more . . . Perhaps you should stage a little relapse, then you and Cory can go to Dr Jarman's for a few days.'

'I *hate* this.'

'Or we tell the adults, anyway.'

The conversation went around and around, like a leaf in a whirlpool, like it always did.


Cory loves fall coming in all its beauty and sadness. How fine the trees on fire in their fall colours, and so-many fruits and berries! Cory so-excited when he found Earth tilted and had, Earth word, sea-sons. His home just weather, no sea-sons. How exciting, birds gather to fly south. He wants to see winter with storms and ice and snow and Christmas.

On car trips he hears children playing and from his hiding place on the roof he sees them, and in the books, the children all have friends, even if they are sometimes animals and ghosts and monsters. Cory feels the love of his parents like the sun, but also true, how alone, like a sea current that pulls him down-down-down.

But Cory is frightened of the Bad Men who will steal him from his parents and maybe eat him. The TV and newspapers are always full of Bad Men killing.

He keeps his promises to Mom, but a ball is not 'talking'. Chuck's bright red baseball is so-big secret. He hides it in the attic place too-small for adults.

Cory found the ball in the garden last week. It looked just like Chuck's and smelled like him. Maybe-maybe it was just thrown over the fence, but Cory is smart-detective. The loose plank in the fence was moved, yes-it-was, and there was a Chuck-sized boot-print. In the garden.

Every day Cory holds the ball to his face and taste-smells. Ball is an invitation; easy for Cory to get out, same way Chuck got in. But wary-Cory knows it might be a trap.

Cory goes into the garden, wishing he was in the woods, telling himself the old stories like he was a big one and a little one together in the children's hall. He hears Bonnie's voice over the fence.

'You are such a scaredy-cat, Charles Henderson. Just a baby.'

'You shouldn't have stolen the keys. We could just play in the woods.'

Wanting to see, Cory hides and with a foot here, a hand there, he is on the shed roof. He checks carefully, in case Bonnie has a camera.

Chuck holds a basket and under his arm is a familiar box, a board game. Bonnie has a rolled-up blanket and something jangling on her fingers: keys.

Bonnie is clever words and quick-quick temper. Cory likes how she moves and sings and ties coloured things in her black hair, the dance of her friendship with Chuck.

'Old Mrs Hardesty is a witch,' Bonnie says fiercely. 'She never speaks to our family, because we're black.'

Cory feels Chuck's shame, yes, as Chuck says, 'She's old and confused. She's gotta live with her family now. It's still wrong to break into her house, even if it is empty.'

Bonnie does a little bragging dance, swinging the keys. 'There's no one home, we have the spare key – and we'll be like mice, we won't leave a sign.'

'Someone might come,' says Chuck, glancing up at Cory's window.

'No, they won't. Young Mrs Hardesty came yesterday, she won't be here again for ages. Anyway, if you're too scared, I'll do it on my own.' She turns and skips up the footpath.

Chuck sighs. 'Girls!' He follows her.

Cory needs to see if they really will go into the house. He slips off the shed roof into the garden and scurries to the gap in the fence. Peering through, he can see Bonnie by the back door, fiddling with the key.

Cory is so-so careful, looking and pushing his mind out, his tentacles tasting the air for unfamiliar humans or any sign of danger.

Chuck goes to push open the door, but Bonnie stops him. 'We have to promise first,' she says.

'Scout's Honour and hand on the Bible and cross-my-heart-and-hope-to-die,' says Chuck, and Cory can hear he is serious, oh-yes-he-is, 'we'll keep this and anything we find today a secret from *everyone*, no matter what. Including our parents.'

Bonnie makes the long promise too, then she laughs. 'We've got so much cake, easily enough for three people.'

They disappear into the house and no one sees except Cory and the squirrels. And the back door stays open . . .

Cory wrestles with his inner Teacher and begins the approach to the house, promising himself he will mind-feel behind the door, to check no one is lurking. *Cory best hider ever.*

Underneath the kitchen window he hears the clink of cutlery and the murmur of human voices. *The back door goes into little space, then the kitchen, like Cory house, a bit.*

He sneaks a look through the crack in the door. The house smells of things left alone, damp wood and dead things and some unfamiliar scent like a rotting flower, but there is nothing lurking to catch him. He inches towards the kitchen, where the children are sitting at the table, their backs to him.

Cory stands up to get a better look.

'It's kind of a dumb game for two,' Chuck says. 'Three players would be better.'

'I wish we'd brought someone else,' says Bonnie, with a sigh, but her voice and her feelings are out of tune; Cory can feel her big ripple of satisfaction. His heart is pumping fast and he readies himself to flee . . .

*They know, they know, they lured Cory into a trap . . .*

He turns to run to the door, into the woods, when Chuck says, 'If you're there, we won't tell *anyone*. We'll make every promise we know. You can trust us.' Both humans have their heads down, not looking.

'Please,' Bonnie says. 'I dreamed that you're so sad and lonely. Play with us.'

Cory does feel so alone. There is a moment of balance, to run or to stay – then the humans turn around and it is like diving off the tallest-ever tree into the water. He slips from hiding, and in that moment, fears he has made the worst mistake ever . . .

'Wow!' And Chuck's face shows everything in his heart: astonished and happy and yes, a little bit vomit-feelings, like Cory is rotting-slime-disgusting, but Chuck is pushing that down, trying to keep it from his face. He claps his hands. 'You came on the Meteor! I *knew* it! Tell us how—'

Bonnie is all joy and amazement, just gazing at him. 'Of course he did. I bet on your planet you're really handsome. Oh, we will be such friends and we will keep you *such* a secret,' she promises, getting off her chair. 'What's your name?'

He steps towards them and feels only friendship-to-come.

'I-am-Cory.' Cory, which came from *cor-cor-cor*, help-I'm-hurt, because no human can say his real name, Little Glowing Blue Frog.

Bonnie becomes leader. 'Hugs if you hug, then sacred and terrible promises, then cake, then talk. The game can wait.'

Cory takes her hand. He has learned her smell, and he is happy.

CHAPTER 22

# His first Christmas

Molly began her Christmas lists before the first jack-o'-lanterns appeared. Gene said a couple of times, as the lists got longer, 'We don't need to overdo it, Molly.' But, *yes*, she thought, *I do*. If she died, she wanted on her tombstone *Cory's First Christmas Was Perfect*.

When Molly was a child, Christmas mattered. It smelled of baking and preserves, things hidden in forbidden places, recipes cooked only once a year and foods not for now but later. There was lots of church and they could stay up for Midnight Mass and everyone sang the old songs. Stockings waited for Santa and there were carrots for the reindeer. Even when money was tight, there was always a book and sometimes a toy. Getting it right was something parents needed to do.

Things had changed; as a teenager, Christmas had been a time for arguments, both fresh and heated over, and storming out of the house; it became a time of disappointment. Sugar-snow gingerbread wouldn't change her mother to an angel and candles didn't make her father listen. When she'd left they sent no cards and she hadn't expected any.

But now she had this strange son for whom everything was new and exciting. Who yes-yes-please wanted to fill the house with the smells of cinnamon and ginger, with iced cookies that looked like reindeer . . . *want to go see rein-deeer . . . want to see North Pole* . . . and *yes-please to try baking fruitcake.* He wanted her to take him to the shops, hidden in the laundry basket, to get presents. And waving a book at her, asked, 'Why girl-toys and boy-toys? What good present for girl, good present for boy? *Reeeely* good presents.'

'Well, it would depend, wouldn't it?' She was a little distracted, measuring out the dried fruit. 'On what they liked.'

They talked about boys' interests and girls', men's clothes and women's clothes, and how silly it was so many jobs had no women in them, and Cory explained inters: those of his people who were neither male nor female until they became adult. Gene and Molly tried to hide their shock that a male teacher had chosen to become female to bear a baby; they hadn't much enthusiasm for continuing that discussion.

Tomorrow Gene would drag in a big pine tree and fill the house with the smell of needles and resin. 'White Christmas' played on the radio, as it had in her childhood. Close to midnight, Molly checked on Cory to find him standing at the window in the dark, wrapped in his coverlet and peeking out behind the drapes.

'Cory, it's late.'

'No snow Mom-Mom. When come?'

'Well, it's coming, and when it does, there'll be plenty to go around.'

He looked at her with moist velvet eyes. 'Teachers did snow science, made in big room.' Nowhere on Cory's home-world saw ice, except for the tips of the tallest mountains, and a little sea ice at the poles.

Frozen puddles excited him, and he'd drawn the frost on the twigs like silver feathers. 'Look-look . . .' He hauled himself up onto the inner sill so that his whole body was pressed against the window.

So much for security, if anyone was out in the woods. So much for keeping warm. Molly squeezed next to him and saw the white flakes begin to drift down. Memories hit her: making angels in the snow, kissing a boy, Gene holding her arm and skating under a perfect Moon . . .

'So exciting,' Cory whooped. 'Sledge-and-snowballs-and-angels . . .'

Molly drew the chair over to the window, and with a tug, got him to sit on her lap. Wrapped together, they watched winter feather the night sky . . .

The world could still burn with magic, even if you didn't believe in the old man with the beard.

She held on tight to Cory and felt the beating of his heart.

Molly stirred from deep, dreamless sleep to the sound of someone gasping and the sidelight on. 'Cory?' She was instantly awake, but it was Gene standing above her, leaning his forehead against the wall and groaning – her Gene, who hated a fuss . . .

He kneaded his gut with one hand. 'Jeez, Molly,' he gasped, 'it's like I swallowed a live rat . . .'

He'd complained of stomach pains earlier that night but she'd thought it was all that raw cookie mix. She'd dosed him up and sent him to bed early.

'Where?' she asked. 'Show me.' And when he turned, his hand was clenching the lower right-hand side of his belly. He was pale and sweating.

Professional Molly took command. 'Might be your appendix,' she guessed. 'Let me feel . . .'

'Jeez,' he said, holding her away. He was unsteady on his feet, weaving a little.

'No playing around. I'll call an ambulance.' She jumped out of bed and ran to the window. Crooked Street was inches deep in snow and it was still falling. Should she drive him herself?

He made an odd gasping sound, then retched. 'What about Cory?' he croaked, and the floor dropped away beneath her. How could she take Cory to the hospital? He'd be too frightened — and where could she hide him? Should she send Gene on his own? But they might operate straight away. The thought made her sick. Everyone in the hospital knew there were a couple of staff who couldn't be relied on to have steady hands at Christmas.

'I'll go on my own,' he said through gritted teeth, but she was shaking her head.

'In sickness and in health,' she said. 'I'll call now.'

Downstairs, she gave brisk orders on the phone: she needed an ambulance right now.

'Thank goodness it's you, Nurse Myers,' said the dispatcher. 'Can you bring him in?'

'That would be difficult . . .'

'We're stretched so thin — half the staff are down with flu;

we've two drivers out sick. And one ambulance crashed on the Bradleyburg Road.'

'I've an elderly neighbour who can't be left alone,' she said, the first lie that came to her. 'I won't be able to come straight away.'

'We'll be with you as soon as we can, Mrs Myers. But if someone *could* run Mr Myers up here and let us know . . .'

*Not soon enough*, thought Molly. She picked up the phone and dialled Dr Jarman, but there was no reply; she tried Rosa Pearce, but the phone rang out there too.

Slowly, painfully, Gene was trying to get himself down the stairs; she dropped the phone and ran up to help him. 'Don't drink anything,' she told him. 'They may need to operate.'

Still the phone didn't ring – and then an alien howl echoed down the stairwell. 'What wrong? *What wrong?*' Cory was hurtling too fast down the stairs, grabbing the banister when he slipped.

'Look, Dad's sick, but it will be fine,' Molly said.

'Don't-die-don't-die-don't-die,' he gabbled, then something in his own language.

'I don't need you to come,' Gene said, his face flushed a very odd colour.

'Cory, Dad just has to go to the hospital,' Molly said, stroking his ear, and right there, under the decorations, flashes of pain and darkness and grief filled the air as Cory relived the death of his mother.

'Cory come too,' he announced. 'Hide so okay. Dad be-okay?'

'No, someone will stay with you. That's fine.'

'Pleeeese wanna go!' he said, picking up her stress. 'Dad be-okay?'

Gene stroked Cory's ear.

*People say things in fever*, Molly thought. *They say things under anaesthetic. Whatever might slip out, at least I can explain them away.*

The pain of Cory's mother dying washed over them again, even stronger: flashes of white light and incoherent thoughts pouring off him in fear and confusion. His inner eyelids were clamped shut; he was having a panic attack. She knelt beside Gene and hugged Cory.

She couldn't leave him alone like this, but these flowing nightmares? Half the hospital would know something was up.

'Cory, I'll stay with you. This looks bad, but it's common, and Earth medicine's great at dealing with this,' she said.

The phone was still silent.

For a moment, she stood at the window watching the snow fall. There was really nothing else for it; they needed somebody, and fast. Molly made her decision, marched for the phone and rang the Hendersons. The phone rang, minute after minute. She was ready to hang up and try Diane when Roy answered with a grunt.

'Roy, it's Molly.' She fiddled with the phone cord. 'Gene has appendicitis – it's serious.'

Roy was barely awake, but he managed, 'Uh . . . uh . . . okay, so what do you need?'

'The ambulance is taking for ever. And . . .' *Think Molly, think!* She needed an excuse. 'Roy, it's like Meteor Day – I'm getting flashbacks. I can see the town on fire. I don't think I can drive. My hands are shaking too badly.'

'I'll bring the truck. Fifteen minutes.'

She looked out of the hall window and saw the snow floating down, clogging roads and bridges. Seventeen long minutes passed before Roy's truck rumbled up in front of the door.

'Cory,' Molly said, 'upstairs, now. *Hide.*'

He looked wounded at her tone, but in a moment, he was gone.

A fist hammered at the door and Molly opened it without checking, crying, 'Roy, thank goodness . . . !'

Roy came straight in. 'Where is he?'

Suspended between them, they walked Gene, cussing and sweating with the pain, to the truck.

'Jump in the back,' Roy said, but Molly was shaking.

'I can't − I just can't. It's like the sirens are going,' she said. 'If I faint, I'll just get in the way.'

Through her fear, she knew Roy was looking at her; she could see the doubt on that big honest face.

'She's right, Roy, she's not up to it. Molly, stay,' Gene groaned.

Roy gave her a long hard look before swinging up into the cab and turning the key.

'Love you,' Gene managed, and then they were off, vanishing into the fast-falling snow.

Molly wondered if this was the right call. A burst appendix could mean serious infection and Gene deserved her by his side. But the thought of Cory in the hospital . . .

The cold was prickling on her skin when she finally closed the door.

She rang the ambulance service to report that Gene was en

route, then went to find Cory, who had his face pressed to the big bedroom window. He trusted his hiding too much.

'Dad not die,' Cory begged, still broadcasting distress.

'Roy's a great driver and it's a good hospital,' Molly said, reassuring him. 'Come on, let's get under the quilt and warm up, shall we?' She held him tight, repeating over and over, as much for her as him, 'He'll be all right.'

'Don't go,' Cory moaned, 'don't go – everyone died and left me. Everyone.' The tumult poured off him, confusion and sadness so strong her tears came.

'Dad won't die,' she said firmly, trying to *feel* it. 'We won't leave you, Cory. It will be fine.' *Please, let it be fine . . .*

Christmas Eve at the hospital, with Amber Grove under a thick blanket of snow, with a morning sky that promised more. There was an old joke: if nurses make bad patients, they make worse relatives of patients.

She'd finally got hold of Rosa, who had come straight over, and as soon as she got to the ward, Molly reassured herself that the staff were competent, the doctors sober and the dressings clean.

Gene lay on the bed, wincing as he tried to sit up.

'Don't move, you idiot,' she said. She sat beside him and held his hand as if she was holding him up. *Her Gene, her rock, her love.*

'They gave me some stuff and I'm not sure which way is up,' Gene said, trying a smile. 'How's . . . ?' He looked around, but this was an open ward with no privacy. 'How are you?'

'Fine,' she said.

'Roy was nosy,' he said, 'but I think I calmed him down.'

'Okay,' she said. She itched to look at Gene's notes, but she probably shouldn't.

'Feels like they've cut a slit you could post a letter in,' he said.

'Don't feel you have to talk,' she said. For the first time, she dared to think it would be all right.

Gene had little to say and they couldn't talk about Cory. Her feelings about the hospital were horribly complicated: work and pride and death and children and hope all tied up together. She couldn't see any way she could return to work while they had their secret son.

She stayed as long as she could, but time was rushing by and soon she would have to relieve Rosa, who was on duty later.

After saying goodbye, Molly rushed back out into the cold. She was halfway across the parking lot, walking on fresh snow to avoid the ice and puffing white breath as she fumbled for the car key, when she realised Roy was striding towards her. She hadn't noticed his truck.

Warmth for her neighbour rose in her. 'Roy, you're a lifesaver! Thank you so much . . .' Then she caught his gaze and began to falter.

He stood in hat and scarf with his shoulders hunched, but his eyes were cold. 'I guess you won't tell me what's really going on.'

Inwardly, Molly tensed. 'Roy . . .'

'Gene was sick, that much was true. But your hands were as steady as a surgeon's.'

'It's not like that,' she said. 'I had a panic attack. I could've come off the road . . .'

'We mind our own business, Janice and me, but you're up to something and I want to know what it is.'

She was off-centre, with Gene's illness and Cory's distress and no sleep. She didn't want to have this conversation anywhere, let alone in a cold parking lot.

'We're not hiding anything . . .'

'I thought it was draft-dodgers,' Roy butted in, like he was saying 'dead skunks', 'what with Doc Jarman and Sister Pearce at the house at all hours. Sick draft-dodgers. But it's been months, and draft-dodgers just get a bus across the border.'

What could she say?

'Or maybe you got into drugs: that would explain the doctor. But Gene hates that stuff. And' – he was trying to find the words and Molly flushed, feeling humiliated – 'and Gene says you're sober.' He raised a hand to scratch an ear under the woollen hat.

'Mental illness isn't neat and tidy,' she said. 'Roy, you've been a great friend in tough times . . .'

'Few weeks back, Janice and Diane got to drinking. They joked you stole a baby.'

She put out a hand to steady herself on the icy car.

'It's crazy, but today, it makes a lot of sense,' Roy went on. She couldn't meet his gaze anymore, but she had to: the rules of good lying. 'Why wouldn't you come with Gene? Because you had a hidden child. Rosa Pearce turns up at the crack of dawn and you're away to the hospital, no problem.'

'Don't be ridiculous. Of course I didn't steal a baby!' *To do that to another mother, to rip out their heart for my own need . . . ?*

'Or maybe the kid's a runaway, although we've never seen anything. It sure is a mystery.'

*Draft-dodgers or drugs or you stole a child* . . . 'Everything's just so square and solid and safe for you, Roy. You don't know what it's like to lose your mind: to sit and look at a bottle of pills and wonder what dying feels like. I can't cope with people in the house . . . It's like they're right in my head, pulling me apart . . .'

'I don't buy it,' Roy said, and it was like a door was being slammed shut. 'I've known you sick and well, Molly, as God is my witness. I knew you in the depths, I saw you in the valley of the shadow. This isn't it. I've got better things to do than spy, but I'll tell you, I've heard things in the woods. Weird things.'

She thought, *I could tell him the truth.* Roy, who supported the war and the President. Roy who might phone the FBI. And, if he did, they'd have to flee, she'd have to take Cory, and Gene with his gut cut open. She'd drive, but where first? The farm or the border?

Roy waited.

'Well, I hear things too,' she said. 'I'm sorry you don't understand it, Roy. I'm grateful you turned out last night, you know how much we really appreciate that.'

'I don't know what you've dragged Gene into,' Roy said, solid as a mountain, 'but I don't want you in the house or near my kids, Molly, not until you're straight with me.'

'You don't get to tell Janice what to do,' she said, hot and angry.

'She agrees with me.'

That's why Janice had been so distant those last weeks, finding excuses to keep her away from the twins.

Molly left the car unlocked and turned to walk back to the hospital. She had to call Rosa, in case Roy came to the house.

241

But first she had to talk to Gene, to warn him. Each breath hung ominous in the air.

It was an odd, subdued Christmas Day. Molly and Cory missed Gene desperately and she promised herself they would do Christmas again, properly, when he was home. After lunch, the staff got him to a phone, although he was guarded, in case the FBI were listening in. Cory pressed his head to the handset and wiggled silent tentacles, sending his Earth Dad silent love.

That evening, Molly couldn't sleep. She walked quietly up the stairs and looked in on Cory and for a moment, all her fears and doubts vanished. It was her son's first Christmas and there he was, safe and well.

There was a furious rapping on the door, not the code, *shave and a haircut, two bits*, but Cory didn't stir.

Molly came down the stairs at a run as whoever it was banged again. When she got to the door there was more rapping and a voice called from the other side, 'It's Roy. I know you're in there.'

'I'm coming,' she called, frightened by his anger. She wanted to use the chain, but should she signal he wasn't a friend? In the end, she just opened the door and stood as firm as she could.

His coat was open, as if he'd just thrown it on, and his head bare. He was carrying a big torch, and something in the other hand, a book. His face was blazing with fury. She'd seen him angry before, but not like this.

'I'm coming in,' he said.

'It's late—'

'You've dragged my boy into your lies so we can talk here or inside, up to you, but you're gonna talk.'

A cold wind blew a flurry of snow into her face. 'I don't understand,' she tried, even knowing that the game was up.

'You've dragged Chuck into this and made him lie for you,' Roy growled.

It was like her body decided before her brain had. She stepped a little back, he came in and she shut the door.

He thrust what he was carrying into her hand: the astronomy book with all the photographs, his 'just-because' present; Cory loved that book. She flipped open the front cover to where they'd signed it.

'Who's Cory?' Roy demanded. 'Why won't my son tell me? What are you hiding, Molly?'

She was scared, but she suddenly realised Roy was too: overcome with fear for his children. She could understand that.

'Do you want a drink?'

He grabbed her and she gasped. 'Don't you dare touch me,' she said, wriggling free.

'Who is this Cory and why does he call Chuck his brother? No more lies!' He pulled out a letter and waved it.

She looked at the familiar big letters and the whole picture coalesced. She held out her hand. 'Let me read this, please. I swear, Roy, we didn't want Chuck involved – we didn't even know he was.'

She mouthed the words as she read them. Some had been written in his language, as he often did when he didn't know the English. *Happy Christmas big brother. Sorry big row my Mom your Dad.* A long bit in alien. *Thanks for comic.* Something something she couldn't read. *Signal? Happy Christmas.* A row of Xs. *Brother Cory.*

'Well?' Roy said, standing in the hall in a spreading pool of melted snow.

'I'm going to place a boy's life in your hands,' she said quietly, watching Roy's eye widen as she added, 'We may be arrested. He may be killed, or dissected as an experiment. We took a child in, an orphan, Cory. He's . . . *special*. Different. We had to hide him . . .'

'Who from?' Roy said, not yet unbending.

'The government, the press – everyone. People *cannot* know about him. He's forbidden from showing himself . . . He shouldn't have talked to Chuck – I'm sorry, this is a disaster . . .'

'So I *was* right: Gene's sick but you stayed because the kid was in the house – is this kid sick?'

'He was, very, but not now; he hasn't put Chuck in any danger.'

'What about the Russians?' She saw a new, terrible theory dawn on his face and knew there'd be no deal, no head-start for old times' sake, not if Roy thought she was working for America's enemies.

'Heavens, Roy! Believe me, *their* spies finding him would be the worst of all!'

When Cory hid near her, she thought sometimes she could detect him, as if some motherly corner of her brain knew he was near. It was like a mouse in the room, or some piece of furniture not quite where it should be, and part of her said now, *Cory is hiding nearby, frightened.*

'Roy, I need you to understand, this child is *ours* and we will fight to protect him as much as you would Chuck and Alice and Tammy. I need you to promise you'll keep our secret, and if you can't, we'll get in the car, collect Gene and go tonight.'

He thought for a moment or two. 'Tell me the story, then we'll see if I can promise anything. You've still gotta convince me, Molly. I don't rate being lied to.'

'Do you want some fruitcake? Cory made it. Roy, he looks *real* odd, so you need to be prepared.'

He didn't reply but walked in and sat at the kitchen table. A good sign, she hoped, as she made coffee.

'I haven't got all night,' Roy said, but she could tell he was curious now.

'I'll go and get him,' she said. She was pretty sure Cory was on the stairs; that was a good place to watch from and easy to run and hide in an upstairs room.

'Cory,' she called, 'Cory, Roy won't be mad. It's time to come out, Cory.'

He flicked into sight at the top of the stairs, shivering. He'd shrunk into himself; he looked so small and scared. 'Sorreee sorreee sorreee.'

She went up to get him and hugged him. 'Chuck's dad is angry, and I'm angry too,' she said, 'but we have to make it work now, okay? So you need to meet Roy. He's Chuck's dad and he won't hurt you . . .' She prayed that that last bit was true.

She walked Cory into the kitchen, feeling the cold shiver coming off him, but he didn't hide. The mischievous part of her enjoyed watching Roy's eyes open and his mouth drop.

'Oh my Lord,' Roy whispered. 'That thing Chuck drew . . . that was *him*?'

'Cory's my son and I love him. So does Gene.'

'I can see,' said Roy and she thought, he did, he really did. He stared, stunned and silent, for at least a minute, then said at last, 'I need to know everything, Molly. I'll have that fruitcake. Does it . . . um . . . do you eat cake, Cory?'

'I'm not sure people who break promises get cake,' Molly said. 'Who else knows, Cory?' She had never known Cory lie, although he didn't always give the full truth.

His tentacles quivered.

'Bonnie?' she said, not at all surprised when he nodded.

Roy sighed and said, 'Bonnie's been playing with some strange boy and Diane don't know? You'll wish you'd never been born, Molly Myers!' He looked at Cory. 'Anyone else?'

Cory shook his head vigorously. 'Chuck big-big trouble?'

Roy frowned. 'Chuck's in trouble for sure. But your mom will explain everything.'

They sat while she sliced cake and Cory kept saying, 'Sor-reee.' Roy looked at Molly and she realised this was her solid friend back. Then he looked at Cory and his expression was . . . what? . . . wonder, amusement, confusion?

'I've got about a million questions. Okay, don't tell the world, I get that, but I just don't get why you kept this from your friends, or the government.'

'Well, there are reasons,' she said. 'I'll talk you through it.' Their conspiracy might be a little bigger, but maybe they'd be safer this way. She felt like she could let out a breath she'd been holding for months; that it would be all okay.

'So, on Meteor Day . . .'

Midnight, and the moment she had dreaded and longed for: Janice and Diane came into the kitchen, their faces all fury and amazement; Roy, almost giddy, had promised he'd give them the highlights.

Janice's mouth opened and closed and Diane snapped, 'Well?'

The strain of the hiding and the lying was over. The tears flowed as she stood and reached out her hands. 'There hasn't been a day I didn't want to tell you, but first he was so sick, and then the FBI, and the army . . .'

Neither of them moved — and then Janice began to laugh. 'You owe me ten pixy dollars, Diane! She *did* steal a baby . . .'

'Well, the child is no baby,' said Diane, still frowning. 'Molly, I'm . . . I'm shocked and hurt — *beyond* hurt. Why didn't you trust us?' She was stern, and so wounded.

'You don't know what it's been like,' Molly sobbed.

'If the army came after my kids, I'd be out there with a shotgun,' said Janice, a little flushed.

And then her friends were hugging her and words weren't needed.

# CHAPTER 23

## *Spring, Cory's second year on Earth*

Gene walked across Founders Green in search of a late lunch. The spring sun was warm and brightly coloured flowers were in full bloom. A sort of bandstand now covered the black and orange fragment of the Meteor and as Gene watched, a jay perched on the rock, cocked its head to one side and stared at him. Every time he looked at the rock he had a brief stabbing memory of the day it fell.

Gene hadn't finished any of the songs he started about Meteor Day; his words couldn't catch the destruction, nor the extraordinary heroism of ordinary people: the secretaries who comforted the dying, the three seniors who lifted a burning timber off a broken man, the firefighter who went back for the dog. But he knew a great piece of music was out there, waiting to be born – a symphony, or a choral suite, perhaps.

He hummed the theme from 'Sailors on the Sea of Night'. Joan Baez had taken the tragedy of the two men who died above the Moon and made magic out of it. The song brought back that shared time of worldwide loss; her musical pictures of the silver ship against a sea of stars spoke to everyone whose loved ones would never come back. Gene wished he had the talent to do that for Amber Grove.

The tables outside the diner were packed; the good weather had brought yet more visitors with their theories and their incessant curiosity. At least he didn't have to talk to them.

These past few months, with more adults to talk to and teach him, and friends to play with every day, Cory had really flourished. There'd been one brief, frightening outbreak of fever, but it had felt almost normal: kids get sick, Diane had said, and sure enough, he'd shaken it off within days.

Gene took his normal tiny corner table, salivating as he ordered a bacon and sausage sandwich. Now he didn't smoke, meat was his secret vice – he loved Cory, but he was so tired of cheese, eggs and tuna. He got out his brown notebook and looked again at the musical theme which was eluding him.

A smartly dressed woman came towards him; he assumed she was heading to the restroom and ignored her until she put a hand on the spare chair and asked, 'It's Mr Myers, isn't it?'

Her face rang a distant bell. Had they met? She was blonde, with a business-like smile, older than Molly, but not *old*. The hairstyle, the attaché case, the tasteful jacket, all suggested somewhere far more cosmopolitan than little Amber Grove.

'Um,' he said.

'Carol Longman. I write for *Witness* magazine. Could I have a moment of your time?' She was already sitting.

*A journalist.* Gene stiffened, ready to guard every word, every gesture, but she already had her hand out and he shook it, a polite reflex.

Gene flicked through *Witness* at work most weeks. It might be too pro-war for him, but he loved the photography and the worldwide focus of its writing. Even so, he didn't want any journalist at his lunch table, for any reason, and especially not someone whose magazine churned out support for the President and his wars.

'Sorry, I just need to grab lunch and—'

She ignored him and said, 'I wrote about the Meteor, and another piece last Thanksgiving, about how Amber Grove was doing.' She passed him her business card: *Senior Correspondent*. 'People here were kind enough to say they liked it.'

'I'd talk to the Mayor,' he suggested. 'And Pastor Roberts at First Methodist, Evie Watson at the Better Business Bureau . . .' They liked talking; they took care what they said and they took the bullet for those townsfolk who didn't like the press.

She waved away his suggestions. 'Everyone's talked to them,' she said. 'I need something new, something bigger than arguments between the members of the memorial committee.'

He decided her smile was like her clothing, carefully chosen to do its job.

'I don't want to be rude, but you reporters have made no friends here,' Gene said. 'Some have been downright disrespectful to the dead.' If she'd been a man, he would've got up and walked away by now.

She got out a slim folder and showed him magazine clippings. 'Please, read my stuff while you're waiting for your food. If you don't agree I did a better job than my colleagues, I'll go.'

Here was her bylined photo above her piece: *Little did Everytown, USA know that fire and destruction would rain from the skies* . . . The photos were stunning; they took him back to those early days. He skim-read the story, shuddering. He had a good memory; wasn't she the writer who—

Yes, here in the clippings: *Town Leaders Condemn Press Intrusion*, by Carol Longman. Brief, and sharp.

'You thought they were jerks too,' he said.

'I just checked the facts. People told me the truth and I thought some colleagues needed to hear it.' Still, there was something too practised in her charm.

She took out a notebook.

Nothing good could come of talking to her. 'I can't help,' he said. 'You won't need that.'

She frowned, then said, 'You were right in the thick of the rescue on Main Street. A couple of people mentioned you . . .'

'I'm sorry, but I'm not going to talk to your magazine.'

'And your wife, working at the hospital – that must've been dramatic.'

He felt hot. *Who's been talking?* 'This is what I mean about sticking your nose in: she's been ill, ever since the Meteor. We're not talking to the press and we don't appreciate being approached. Good day.'

'I'm sorry, Mr Myers.' But she still didn't get up. 'I'm not wasting your time. There's a real story in this town, one no one is talking about – I mean the army and that fence in the woods, this radioactivity fairy-tale they drag out to explain everything. I hoped someone at the hospital would give me something hard and scientific to knock that down – there was some scare in the hospital, wasn't there?'

Such a story would quickly have the whole world descending on Amber Grove, all prodding and peering and asking questions! The truth behind *that* story would bring everything crashing down on his family. 'I suggest you speak to the army's public relations guy.'

Carol Longman sighed. 'Mr Myers, the army line makes no sense. There's a big story out there and my editor's been leaned on. Suddenly he doesn't want me nosing around Two Mile Lake or what's behind that extraordinary fence. "Carol," he said, "I trust you to do a nice colour piece with heart: a small town rebuilds. American grit. Find some unsung heroes. I want tears, hope and a shot of the flag. Just don't bother the army people."'

Francine had arrived with his food and as she hovered, they both fell silent.

Francine shot Gene an apologetic look. 'Miss Longman, I hope you're not bothering my regulars.'

'Please put this on my tab, Francine,' Miss Longman said. 'Mr Myers is being very patient; he's told me very clearly he won't be interviewed and I respect that.'

'No, I'll buy my own lunch,' Gene interrupted, wondering why he hadn't told her to go. He didn't like her – she was pushy, too controlled, putting on too much of an act. But this sudden sarcasm about her editor? This hint of passion felt more *real* . . .

Once Francine had returned to her till, Miss Longman leaned over the table towards him. 'Our science guy, Eric Flood, came down here and wrote a big piece about how the radioactivity story doesn't stack up. He's just polishing it up when our editor comes up to his desk and spikes it. He'd come straight from lunch with some top army brass.' She shook her head, clearly upset. 'Journalism is what someone else doesn't want you to print.'

He met her eyes and repeated, 'I can't help you, so please, leave me and my wife alone.'

'You know what the story is,' she said, with absolute certainty. 'You know something, anyway.'

He tried a dismissive *huh*, even though Molly always said he was a poor liar. Lord knew what the woman saw in his face, but he said, 'You need to leave.' And thank the universe, at last she picked up her case and rose.

'Thanks for your time. You need to know, my editor wanted to cut the intrusion piece; he said powerful people could figure out who I was talking about, but I threatened to walk if he didn't run it. I felt I owed it to the people I interviewed.' She gave him another card. 'That one has my little hideaway number too. That's not in the phonebook. Only real important people get that.'

Yes, there was a number in elegant writing written on the back.

'Okay, we're done,' Gene said, then added politely, 'You have a great photographer.'

Finally, she gave him a real smile. 'I do. The best there is. Thank you.'

He watched her walk to the counter and speak to a tall woman with short dark hair, dressed for a hike in the hills. The second woman looked at Gene, raised a hand and gave an apologetic smile, then she hoisted up a big black camera bag with ease and the two of them left the diner without looking back.

Gene needed to phone Dr Jarman and Molly as soon as he could, get the word out that the press was snooping around again.

He should write a section of his symphony on the press: sharp, nagging, notes in brass and wind, butting in unwanted against the main themes. Carol Longman had not struck him as a woman who gave up easily.

CHAPTER 24

## *October*

'Halloweeen is coming, two days to go!' Cory says, bouncing up and down.

Molly says, 'It's been Halloween for a week already, Cory. Just give me a break, please.' She scratches his ear, and he beams at her, so full of happy. The kitchen table is covered with sheets of big drawings, Cory's ideas for costumes:

1 MIKE DELGARDO SPACEMAN

2 COWBOY

3 SEA-DEMON HUNTER

4 PIRATE

5 WIZARD

6 DREAM HEALER DOING HEALING SO-MUCH-COMPLICATED TO DRAW

7 DRAGON

8 BALLERINA-PRINCESS-FAIRY

Molly raises her eyebrows and he knows it is the last drawing, all pink and tinsel. Gene pulled his eat-sour-fruit-face at silver-tinsel-pink-glitter too. 'Clothes only for girls is silly,' Cory says. 'Pleeese Mom make me a costume pleeese. Halloweeen is more fun even than Mask Festival. When Cory people come, Cory will . . . I will take home Halloweeen and pumpkins and Christmas and Fourth of July and Thanksgiving. *Ho-ho-ho.*'

They will like new festivals and fireworks, flowers and birds and pumpkins made of fire. He starts to make up the speech-to-explain in his head.

Then he is off again: 'Why-so Indian-summer, what meeen? What other types of summer? What Indian-spring, what Indian-fall . . .'

'Cory, sweetie-pie, please call your friends and go to the meadow and run this off before I go crazy-crazy,' Molly interrupts him, laughing. He races to the telephone, although he still thinks it is funny, when on the home planet or ship all he had to do was say into his wrist communicator, 'Find friend Chuck Henderson please.' Or he could ask any smart machine, they'd all talk through the mind-ocean and find the person.

Janice answers the phone and agrees that Chuck and Bonnie can come-over-to-play, which means the lecture from Mom: Do not kidnap dogs – but it isn't Cory's fault dogs like him, no-it-isn't, he never *steals* them, only *friend-borrow-little-while.* He mustn't forget to put the hood up. *Don't swim in the waterhole, it'll be beyond disgusting.* In case of danger, HIDE. And, *Three hours Cory, or Mom will be mad-so-angry and she'll come blowing her whistle.* He knows what she'll be saying: 'The whistle means grounded, and maybe no trick-or-treat.' *Oh-no!* So Cory says, '*Promise promise promise!*'

He remembers the whole human year since his first Hal-loweeen. Now he has Mollee-Mom and Gene-Dad and best friends Chuck and Bonnie and all is safe and well.

Soon the three children are off, down the wooded slope and across the dead railroad line, where Chuck makes his *oh-no, train coming!* joke like always. There are never trains on this track, but Cory can hear the mournful hoot of one far-far away. He really wants to ride trains, and water-ships, and little baby human airplanes, and a hot-air balloon and a motorbike . . .

The meadows are a moving-film of smells: hot, dry grasses and herbs, someone burning leaves smells like, 'Yuck *horr-i-ble* smoking,' Cory says, so happy Dad doesn't smoke now; *Mom-Bonnie-Chuck says so bad for people!* Dad hates the smell now, even in dreams; he always pulls a face and says, 'In twenty years, this disgusting habit will be banned in public.'

Cory likes to touch the rough-rough black-grey bark of the cherry and to peel the paper from the birch. He feels with his mind small animals scurrying, he feels things humans don't.

They play chase and catch and make up stories and Cory flicks from sight whenever anyone comes into sight, other children, adults, even a strange dog.

'No, Princess Power won't be captured,' declares Bonnie. 'Boys are slow and stupid, capture one of them. Princess Power is far too fast . . . and invisible . . . and she can fly . . .'

'Let's play Musketeers,' Chuck suggests. 'You can be a queen who uses a sword . . .'

'Pleeese play with us, Bonnie. Pleeese!'

Chuck gets bored. 'Last one to the waterhole is a tree-snail,' he says, starting to run, but Cory trips him and Chuck, laughing, goes flat with a *whoof*. Bonnie, always serious about winning, is way ahead.

'Cory, that's cheating, I don't play with cheats . . .' And then he is off again.

There is a fine oak tree with a rope and a plank swing growing over the waterhole. The sun is warm, but the murky water doesn't entice them; Halloween is a time for telling stories.

'They say a kid drowned here, years back,' Chuck says, his voice low and scary. 'Maybe there's a ghost!'

'My friend says a child drowns here every so often. They think the waterhole is *cursed*.' Bonnie tosses her head, wanting them to know *she* wouldn't think anything that silly.

Cory doesn't know about ghosts; his people don't stay around when they die, but maybe humans do haunt places. Or maybe ghosts are the Earth, dreaming of its loss.

There is a sudden flash of light, a little out in the scrubland, and something out there moves. Cory instantly drops into a crouch and hides. Peering through the gap in the trees, he sees two men in dark coats. The taller one has something raised to his face and is pointing it straight at Cory. It glints in the sun.

Cory is really scared he's been seen; he's full of bad feelings. As the men start striding towards the waterhole, Cory takes his friends by the hand and hides them all. It is time to slip away, to lose the men in pathways too twisted for adults.

'Those guys are real creepy,' Chuck says when they are hidden in their secret hidey-hole deep in the undergrowth.

'He had binoculars,' Bonnie points out. 'They were just birdwatchers.'

Chuck frowns. 'Maybe we should tell Mrs Myers – they might have seen Cory.'

'Cory had his hood up – and you hid straight away, didn't you?'

'Yes, Cory so-so careful. What do?'

'We should tell a grown-up,' Chuck repeats.

'Are you scared, Charles Henderson?' Bonnie looks smug. 'Well, tell if you want to. Of course, if we do tell, Mrs Myers will worry and Cory won't be allowed trick-or-treating.'

Cory feels quivery inside; he has enormous hopes for this Halloweeen with his friends. He wants a dry night for trick-or-treating, he wants Pumpkin Jack to come with his grin of fire and his cloak of fall leaves, scattering live bats and candy. There is so much scaring to be done, so many treats to collect.

And down-on-the-meadow without grown-ups is fun. *Will Mom say, no trips to the meadow without a grown-up, and rules, and the whistle . . . ?*

After a while, Chuck concedes, 'Well, I guess people are down here all the time. Cory had his hood up and he hid. It's no big deal.'

On the way back, they are careful to look before leaving the protection of the bushes. There is a big black car on the track, even though the sign says, *No Vehicles*, and another man in a dark coat is sitting on the hood, smoking and cleaning something with a cloth. He has a damaged face.

Cory hides them again and they go home the long way around. He decides he will tell his mom if anything else happens; he will be *so-so careful*.

*Halloweeen is coming. Molly says Cory was made for Halloweeen and it was made for Cory.*

CHAPTER 25

# Halloween

Molly watched a single yellow leaf spiral down to the ground. The kids had gathered in their garden, Cory *tick-tick-ticking* with excitement at going out with his friends. The robe of red and gold was 'best-best Halloweeen costume *ever* Mom!'

'I'm too tired to go,' Molly said. 'You guys have fun; I'll stay here and hand out candy. And then we'll have ice-cream later.'

Gene hugged her and said, 'You okay?'

'Just tired.' The sadness had come without warning, but she didn't have to explain.

No one would notice Cory, just the Halloween costume: the robe, the pirate hat, the fake beard. If he clowned a little, the oddness of his movements would look deliberate. And in any case, he could hide.

Chuck maintained he was Cory's big brother, and as the official job included teasing, he'd arrived as a purple-faced alien in clothes of torn turkey foil. Bonnie made a pretty little ninja, sporting a red silk flower in her headband, just to make sure no one really thought she was a boy. Molly took seven photos of the children, laughing together under the trees, and gave them one last lecture about the Robertsons' dog.

She waved them off from the porch: her husband, her son and his best friends. So many feelings crowded in on her: past losses and disappointments, a little tug of anxiety about the trick-or-treating, but now there was also hope. When they were out of sight, something drew her to the last bottle of Scotch, hidden behind the bleach under the kitchen sink. She looked at the bottle while the clock ticked away the minutes, then she made a big drink that was mostly soda. The nagging need was always there; she had fought so long and so well, one day wouldn't matter.

She went and sat in the porch of her strange old house and watched the street light come on. Her camera sat in her lap, in case she saw that perfect shot. The sky turned itself down another notch. Birds swooped, and out came the first bats of the evening.

She was startled from her reverie by two loud bangs, somewhere very near, sending birds flying upwards in alarm. Teenagers had been setting off firecrackers for the last day or two and the joke was wearing thin.

A small truck sporting the familiar blues and golds of the water company had drawn up and parked outside the Hardesty place; the empty house was up for sale and she didn't give it much thought, other than to wonder in passing what had brought them out this late.

Two big men in dark coats got out of the truck, followed by a third, shorter man. They strode towards her, walking like someone owed them money.

A little voice inside her woke up, muttering that something was wrong. Water company staff wore uniforms; the one time she'd seen a manager, he'd been in the soberest of suits. Something about the coats, something about the way these men walked, wasn't right. The tallest man was swinging a toolbox from his left hand, but not as a workman would.

It was as if she were watching a play unfolding.

'Mrs Myers?' the short one called. He walked with such a swagger, he reminded her of Napoleon in the movie of *Waterloo*. He had greased dark hair and unhealthy skin. 'We've had complaints about the water,' he said. 'Can we talk?'

The tallest man had dead piggy eyes. It didn't add up, it was all very wrong. She rose to go inside—

—and then the world tipped over into something else, because Napoleon drew something dark from his coat, trying to hold it so that only Molly could see he was pointing a gun right at her belly.

Her heart hammered and she felt a fist in her throat. Far away a car engine revved, someone made ghost noises and laughed, and here this man was threatening her on her own porch, but there was no one else at their private end of their street, no witnesses.

He walked towards her. 'Mrs Myers, I don't want anyone to be hurt, least of all the freak, but if you scream or do anything stupid, people are gonna be hurt.' He paused, waiting for her to take it all in. 'Where's the kid?'

Molly had patched gun wounds at the hospital. She had comforted a mother whose son had found his dad's loaded shotgun. Maybe she should take her chances, scream and see if he did shoot her. But on Halloween in quiet Amber Grove, maybe people would think it was kids messing about.

Her mind was running so slowly: her stupidity was so clear now, but too late. Napoleon was already on the porch, the gun still pointed at her. The tallest man, Mr Big, had followed. Molly looked out into the gloom, desperate to give Gene some warning so he could take the children to safety.

The third man, with savage scars on his jaw, stayed off the porch keeping watch. Grinning, he pulled back his coat to show her the gun in his waistband.

'Where is he?'

'He's not here,' Molly said. *Fool, fool, fool! You should've spotted the danger.*

'So we wait. Inside.' The two of them bustled her into *her* house, while Scarface watched from the doorway. Napoleon was close enough that she could smell his mouthwash. Something hard touched the small of her back.

She could run to the back door and try to get into the woods. And Napoleon might shoot her, in the leg or the body.

'Find somewhere to sit and we'll talk, all cosy,' the boss said.

Molly stood at the kitchen door while Mr Big ripped the phone cord in two with a savage knife. She couldn't think what to do. She went into the kitchen, flicking on the light like a sleepwalker, and sat, cold with fright. Napoleon lounged across the table from her, the gun under one hand. Mr Big stood behind him. She heard the front door slam. Now all three strangers were in the house.

These two looked at all the crockery from her aunt, the stuff that hadn't been smashed on Meteor Day, and Cory's drawings on the fridge. The blue and white enamel coffee pot was on the side, the bottle of Scotch she'd left out on the table.

She ought to have known something was wrong with that truck. She could've been inside the house before a gun was drawn . . . She had to focus, and she had to have a plan.

'Nice house,' Napoleon said. 'Make yourself a drink while you're waiting.' He yanked the picture off the fridge and peered at it. 'What kinda weird nonsense is this?' he said, his mouth pulled down like it tasted bad.

Molly was Mamma Grizzly; she had to protect her cubs. 'I demand you tell me what this is about.' Her voice sounded high and weak.

'Just business,' said Napoleon. 'We're guessing Uncle Sam will pay great money to have the freak, so no reason to harm it if you play along. One of you'll come along, be sure it gets what it needs, food and stuff. It's much more valuable alive.'

Could she reason with them? Appeal to their better nature? 'He's a *he*, not a freak. His name is Cory and I'm his mother.' A stupid mother who got careless and now needed to put it right.

All three men snorted.

There was no way out. Sooner or later, Gene and Cory would be coming in the front door, expecting her to welcome them with kisses and hugs. Gene, her tall bookworm, the man who rescued spiders from the bath, the man who massaged her feet, could do nothing against guns. *She needed to focus.*

'How did you find out?' she said. Knowing more might help.

Napoleon laughed. 'Ah, it kinda fell into our laps. We were collecting a debt and we brought his new girlfriend along for leverage, geddit?' He licked his lips. 'Pretty girl. Name of Jane Hooton.'

The nurse who'd turned against Cory, the fool who'd told Pfeiffer. She tried not to give the thug the satisfaction of reacting, but he smiled anyway. 'Her man couldn't pay and it was gonna end pretty badly – well, for him – till she started crying her heart out and turned out, whaddya know, the two of them had this plan to come back to Amber Grove. She figured out you lied about how many freak bodies there were. So boy, did we ever win the jackpot.'

Molly felt sick. She didn't even dare ask if the woman she so disliked had come to some horrible end.

'We reckon a million dollars,' Napoleon said, grinning. 'Not bad for a few days' work. When's the kid due back?'

'I don't know.' She had nothing to bargain with.

The doorbell rang, but of course it wouldn't be Gene and Cory.

Napoleon looked at her, levelling his weapon. 'On your feet,' he said. 'One of us'll stand by the door. Open it, but don't step out. Put all the candy out so people can just take it. Then you won't have to answer the door again.' He smirked; he thought he was such a genius.

She imagined who might be standing on the doorstep: trick-or-treaters out looking for candy – but these Halloween monsters might grab a kid as a hostage. If she went to the door and screamed, she might put them in danger.

Molly's desperate plan came together, but she had to act fast. The back door was unlocked. She picked up the bowl of candy.

Napoleon walked out of the kitchen and stood to one side,

ready to escort her. Scarface was already by the front door – and, yes, here was her break. Mr Big was staying in the kitchen, helping himself to her Scotch. Their first real mistake.

Her heart pounding, she hit Napoleon with the heavy earthenware bowl, aiming for his head, but his reflexes were too fast; he was already raising his arm and she got his shoulder instead.

'Shit,' he said, grabbing at her as the bowl shattered on the floor. She stamped on his foot and then his hand was over her mouth, so she bit him till her jaw hurt and shoved him away. She was free and down the back corridor, shouting, 'Help! *Help*—*!*' Her hand was on the back door handle—

—but who would hear? Mr Forster over the road would already be close to the bottom of the first bottle; he might not notice a couple of Russian tanks if they ran over his lawn. *Where to run?* She had to warn whoever was at the front of the house.

Someone turned her radio up as loud as it went, and then someone else rammed into her back. The stench of cheap cologne overwhelmed her as her head slammed into the door and nothing was quite clear after that.

Scarface snarled 'Shut up, *bitch!*' in her ear and she felt his body pressed against her as he yanked one arm behind her.

'I only need one of you,' Napoleon said.

Although her head was ringing she could see the boss' hand was bleeding. 'I oughtta cut your fucking nose off.'

They dragged her back into the kitchen and shoved a dirty handkerchief in her mouth, then Napoleon bound her hands behind her and taped her mouth shut.

There she sat, biting the foul-tasting cloth to keep herself together. Napoleon took a drink, fury in his eyes, and rummaged in the freezer for ice, which he wrapped in a tea towel and held to his wound. Mr Big, a slow mover, held his gun on her.

'If she causes any trouble, Ed, you blow her leg off, like you did that laundry guy.'

How rich with love these months with Cory had been, but the dark clouds were always waiting; she'd always known everything could end right there. *The drink made you careless. It's your fault.*

The kitchen clock ticked, ten silent minutes, fifteen.

Then she heard the rap at the door: *shave and a haircut, two bits.* She sat up. The men rose and Napoleon put a mocking finger to his lips. Molly could hear Gene and Cory laughing on the porch, one low chuckle and one high, with no effort to be quiet, which told her the rest of the street was deserted.

'Ho-ho-ho Dad. Don't teeese!'

Mr Big loped out to join Scarface in the hall. Napoleon stuck his gun in Molly's side and said, 'Sister, one noise and you're dead or bleeding in the basement and taking a day to die. I only need one of you alive.'

Her head pounding, Molly stepped into the hall, still trying to figure if there was anything she could do. Block Napoleon's gun, perhaps. She might be able to save Cory, but not herself, as Cory's first mother had. She heard the key in the lock and the door swung open.

To her dismay, in came Cory at a run. 'Mom Mom Mom such good trick-or-treat—' He held up his robe, his beard poking from a pocket and his sack of loot in his free hand. He skidded to a halt, dropping the candy, and screeched.

Gene, stepping through the door, gasped when he saw Mr Big and the gun.

'Do what we say, and no one will be hurt,' Napoleon said, showing himself as Scarface slammed the door behind Gene.

Cory's outer tentacles splayed out; the delicate inner ones retracted. His ears went right down, but he didn't move. Molly trembled. *Lord help him, he's too scared to act.* If he'd been behind Gene, maybe he could've got away . . . *Hide, Cory, hide!*

'Get the freak – take him through there,' Napoleon ordered. 'Nobody has to get hurt in this. Play along and we'll all—'

'Bad Men!' squeaked Cory.

There was a ripple of tentacles, a shiver that filled the hall, and suddenly there was no Cory.

'Get out of here!' Gene cried. 'Run, Cory, *run!*'

The three men pivoted, trying to see where Cory had gone.

'Where'd he go?' cried Mr Big, the first words she'd heard him say.

'G-g-go to hell,' Gene said.

Molly could see his body shaking.

'You okay, Molly?'

'Quit yakking. Where's the freak?' Napoleon waved at Mr Big, 'Look in that room, then the kitchen. Make sure the back door's locked.' To Gene and Molly, 'Stand there. If you move an inch, I'll shoot.'

Molly felt hope rise like a song. They didn't know about Cory's power. He'd run away because he couldn't hide from everyone too long. He'd go to his bedroom, then down the drainpipe outside the window; he was allowed in emergencies. Cory got up and down it like a monkey, so he'd soon be safe with the Hendersons . . . Roy would know what to do. Roy owned a hunting rifle. He might blow these criminals' heads off.

'I told you yesterday was weird,' the big guy growled.

Napoleon swore. Still covering Gene and Molly with his gun, he used his free hand to rip the tape off her mouth. 'What's the fucking deal with the freak? Where is he?'

Molly looked at him, tasting blood in her mouth, and wished him dead. 'Well away by now. He'll be safe with the police before you know it. He's gone to get help.' She looked into the short man's eyes and saw death. She felt her breath rasp, because she saw the man would kill her and lose no sleep; for him it would be like swatting a bug.

Napoleon smirked and raised his voice. 'Cory, you better come out. Your mom is hurt real bad and she needs you.'

'Don't you dare threaten us,' said Gene. 'How dare you—!'

The big guy took a few steps closer and raised his gun, ready to club him, while Scarface kept prowling around as if he might hear something.

Molly realised Napoleon was looking at her breasts and fear and disgust fought inside her for the upper hand.

Napoleon said, 'Cory, I'm going to count to ten, then something real bad will happen.' He looked at his gun and licked his lips. 'Mr and Mrs Myers, this is going to get nasty. Get the freak back.'

*Cory is smart. He'll have gone.*

'Seven, eight, nine . . .'

Without a sound, Cory was back, on the stairs, and Molly felt her heart fill with despair. *Why didn't he run, like we told him?* Poor, brave Cory. He'd pinned his Deputy's badge onto his costume. In full light, Cory's violet eyes were deep and dreamy, but here in the low yellow glow they looked strange and dark. His tentacles stuck out, determined, and he raised his webbed, four-fingered hands. In this light his skin looked grey and his tentacles dark, not their normal healthy lavender milk and plum.

Scarface and the big man turned their guns on him as Napoleon snickered and ordered, 'Get the freak.'

'Cory, *hide!*' Molly snapped. 'Run away!' *Don't try to be a hero like in Chuck's stupid comics* . . .

'Bad Men,' Cory said, in his piping voice. 'Hurt Mom you horrid Bad Men. Leave Mom and Dad alone. Bad-bad-bad-bad-bad men.' That face meant fear and disgust.

And in that instant, Cory filled the hallway with his terror, pouring out of him like a torrent of icy wind. He brought a nightmare into the hall too: although they were awake, the dream was real in every sense, every feeling, and the horror swallowed the men whole.

She remembered this nightmare from months ago: warm darkness, bright bursting stars, the lapping water and the loving presence of his first mom — until a moss-green monster, some hellish mating of crocodile and crab, leaped out of the night-coloured water, poison-blue glowing fronds that could burn through flesh spilling from its mouth. Cory and his mother thought they would die — and now Molly felt that utter terror fill the room.

Then there was fire and thunder and the creature screamed, broken, and she felt its pain and rage as it died. The eight clawed leather limbs thrashed in their heads, in the hallway, in their memories, and for all her rational mind screamed, *Not real, not real!* Molly was only a bystander.

Now Cory was *shaping* the dream: the thing was wounded and vicious, not dead. Its electric-blue tentacles crawled across the men's hands; its foul corpse stench filled their lungs. Napoleon fired up, into the dream, the gunshot sounding like it cracked the world open, then time slowed . . .

All three men threw away their guns and their screaming began.

Scarface almost pulled himself together. Fumbling with the door handle, he was ready to run – until Cory made the door into the monster's mouth. The fear froze their legs and they couldn't move.

Molly tasted their terror, felt their pulses hammering, fast as a hummingbird's heart. Hot piss ran down their legs, their bowels opened and their throats hurt with their forced cries.

Then, suddenly, they were in the hospital and Cory's mother was dying, slipping into the darkness . . . and all his people in space were dying, and each one hurt like a sword in the side, like the loss of a beloved child.

Cory was going to make the men live every single death, one after the other.

Through the swirling terror Molly saw her son, frozen on the stairs. He was *terrified*. She couldn't tell if he was in control, or if this was hurting him – or how much more the men could take—

—then Gene gasped, 'Enough!' and Cory let out a great breath and at last the dream faded, second by second. The images became distant, the smell less powerful, as reality became stronger again. At some point Molly realised the thugs weren't screaming anymore, just trying to catch their breath through their sobbing.

She smelled the mess Napoleon had made of himself and moved a little away, using the opportunity to kick the guns along the hall, out of their reach.

White-faced, Gene freed her hands.

Fragments of dream lingered as Cory stood shivering in fear and misery. He wrapped his arms around himself and looked at her and as she tried to control her laboured breathing, she thought, *I brought something worse than a gun into this house. This is a weapon, not a person: this is something you cannot tame or understand.* Cory was alien and he terrified her.

But no, she thought, looking at him again, Cory was not the bad guy here: he was her son and he was frightened and he needed her. She took the deepest breath she could manage and gave him the best, biggest smile she could. He took a few shaky steps and she ran and held him and stroked his striped ears just the way he liked.

He quivered and shook and finally said, 'Tried grown-up thing – *horr-i-ble, horr-i-ble . . .*'

At least doing that had upset her kind little boy. She held onto him, shivering. She couldn't stop.

Gene was white and shaking too, but he took control. Standing over the men, who were moaning and gasping and mumbling, he said, 'We'd better tie them up. I'll get the duct tape.'

The evening sky was only one notch from dark and their lives were falling apart. Hands trembling, she helped Gene bind the thugs on the hall floor. Screams on Halloween were usually a game, but those guttural shrieks might have caught someone's attention. She took particular pleasure in taping Napoleon's mouth shut. She wanted to cover his nose too, watch him struggle to breathe. She wanted to hurt him so much it scared her.

Cory sat on the bottom step and stared at the men, wide-eyed. 'Cory make the Bad Men say sorry Mom,' he said, blinking. 'They never said sorry.'

A muffled moan came from Napoleon.

Gene rubbed his chin, then said, 'Don't worry, Cory. Mom and I'll figure out what to do.' He paused. 'Molly, you okay here? I'll just run over to Roy's.'

Molly thought, *We could drown these men in a lake. We could get in the car and run . . .*

Gene squatted down by Napoleon and said, 'Next time, he won't stop. Move one inch while I'm gone and all three of you will go mad, and then you'll die. Get it?'

Molly got out the chocolate ice-cream and joined Cory on the stairs. She could still see the men, but she couldn't smell them from there and that was good. She put her arm round Cory, who dipped a purple tentacle into the tub.

'Cory Myers, manners!' she said, just like she always did.

Cory gave an odd gulp. 'Sorry Mom-Mom.'

In a few fleeting moments, the world had changed again. How many people had the thugs told? How long did they have? Had this last year, the months they had spent happily alone with their son, been the easy bit?

Since the very first day, Molly had been afraid that all the millions of people who didn't know Cory would turn against his face and his strangeness. Now a new fear grabbed her: that heartless men would see Cory's extraordinary power and they'd want him as a soldier. They'd want her gentle son for their never-ending wars.

Cory wouldn't *ever* be safe if the world knew what he could do. She'd failed him tonight. She'd been lax and self-indulgent and that could have killed the people she loved. She must never fail Cory again.

## CHAPTER 26

# *The aftermath*

The four of them stood in the hall, listening in case the thugs tied up in the kitchen stirred. Gene looked from Roy to Dr Jarman and then at Molly. She looked terrible; tired and shaken, a large bruise purpling the side of her face. Nothing in Gene's life had prepared him for this: three bound criminals in his house – and who knew who they'd talked to, or what further dangers would come.

Dr Jarman behaved like he was in charge, as always. 'So, Roy talked to the neighbours, but we can't expect that to hold. People will talk and it will only take one of them to call Lars – Sheriff Olsen. And the thugs aren't making much sense, plus one of them has a weak pulse so I'll need to keep them under observation.'

'We've gotta figure out what to do,' Roy said, for the third time. 'We can't just drag 'em into the woods and bash their heads in.'

'Why not?' said Molly fiercely, hand over her eyes.

They stared at her.

'Molly . . .' Gene put a hand on her shoulder. *How tempting* – and he had thought of places in the wilds where the bodies might be stashed; they might not be discovered for years. But he froze at the stark reality of taking three lives in cold blood . . . *And bodies get found, and then there would be trouble.*

There was a long pause.

'Give me a better plan, then,' Molly said. 'Some sweet thing we can do that keeps Cory safe.'

'We need to call in Olsen. Get him on the team. Get his ideas,' Roy said.

Dr Jarman looked grave. 'I have to agree. We need to get rid of the truck and grill the prisoners so we can find out what they know. We must get a cover story that will keep them away from the FBI and the army. And we need to figure out what to do about that stupid woman. I don't even know where Nurse Hooton lives now. And all this means we need Lars.'

Shaking his head, looking worried, Gene asked, 'How can we trust him?'

The doctor met Gene's gaze. 'I've known him twenty years, played poker with him for ten. When he found Cory and his mother, dying, it was me he called, and I talked him into keeping it under wraps. When the FBI arrested me, he could have blown our story apart. He didn't.'

Molly refused to look at the doctor, who added, '*I* trust him.'

'Never in a million years,' Molly said. 'Cory's our son and *we'll* decide who's told, just us.'

'Molly, for all we know, he's already on the way. We'll need to tell him something, one way or the other,' he pointed out.

Molly was shaking again. Gene whispered, 'Stay strong, Molly-moo!' as he hugged her.

'I'm going to lie down,' she said. 'Bring me some Tylenol, would you?' She broke away and walked to the stairs, not looking back.

Molly sat on Cory's bed, stroking their son's ugly-beautiful, achingly familiar face. The little mobile Gene had made for him threw shadows on the wall: a rocket, a plane, a bird. Cory was exhausted, but he'd fought sleep, needing her to hold him.

She'd put on her coat and had Cory's clothes ready on the bed.

'Roy's moving the truck,' Gene said, poking his head round the door.

'Nothing is safe. They're going to tell Olsen, aren't they? I'm going to the farm.'

She'd expected argument, but he just said, 'Good. Not tonight, though. You're too tired to drive – get some rest now and leave first thing.'

'We need to go—'

'No, I need to stay. Don't worry, if I need to scarper, I will.'

The walls of her house were closing in like a trap. 'I won't take any risks with the driving. I'll find somewhere to rest up, off the road and safe.'

Cory was unresponsive as she dressed him, his leaden limbs like a giant doll. As she laced his sneakers, he mumbled, 'Sleeping. Go 'way.'

'Shush,' Molly whispered, 'we're going to the farm.'

The world was dark and forbidding, just like the future, but she'd feel safe with John and Eva.

Gene carried Cory down the stairs, the site of the battle, while she followed with Cory's backpack, past her nursing diploma, the peace poster and the smiling face of Dr King. There was a bullet hole in the ceiling and the hall smelled of disinfectant.

Dr Jarman came out of the front room and stopped.

Molly tried to smile. 'Thanks for coming, but I need him out of here.'

For a moment Jarman puffed up like an angry bear, then he sighed. 'Drive safely.'

Gene led the way into the garage and lowered Cory onto the back seat, where he flopped, then pulled the blanket over his head. Molly put her stuff in the car and hugged Gene.

'Please come,' she said. 'This isn't over – more of those thugs will be coming . . .'

'I've either got to make it safe or know the worst before I go. Don't worry, Molly.'

For a few moments, all the horror was washed away by love: her husband, standing guard so she could get away. *Romantic idiot.*

One last kiss. Her body wanted to stay, but they needed to be gone. Every time a branch shifted in the wind, she imagined a sinister man, hiding in the shadows.

The engine coughed into life and she looked back at Gene, waving her off. She stared at him and the home they'd made, and the feeling of fear and loss was so strong she wanted to weep.

★

She made good time on the dark, empty roads, forcing herself to drive steadily, not to speed, although there was no one around. She just wanted to get there.

After an hour, she stopped in the forecourt of a deserted gas station. On one side was a boarded-up shop; on the other was a car showroom that wouldn't be open for hours.

'*Hoo-hoo-hoo—*'

She knelt up to look back at Cory, who was sobbing, his strange head sunk into his strange hands. 'Oh love, what's the matter?' *What wasn't the matter?*

'Cory so-bad . . . Cory did hor-ri-ble-hor-ri-ble thing . . . so-hurt people inside. Cory the m-m-monster . . .'

She got into the back of the car and put her arms round Cory.

'Everyone h-hate the m-m-monster. M-monster do bad-bad things to hurt p-p-people and humans come with f-f-fire and spikes . . .'

*Oh Cory*. That sounded like one of Chuck's trashy comics. 'No, Cory,' she said firmly, kindly, 'no. You are the sweetest boy I know.'

'Cory so-much bad. Cory did ter-ri-ble so-bad thing. Grown-up thing.'

Cory had used his nightmares to bring three hardened criminals who had hurt her to their knees. 'No, no, Cory. Sweetie-pie, listen to me: yes, it was a horrible thing, but you *needed* to do it. We understand: you had to. It's just . . . well, hiding is much safer, so let's keep the scaring thing for real emergencies, like this. We're very proud of our brave boy.'

'Bad-Men be all right?' His eyes pleaded. 'Take to place of healing, make well? Not bad anymore. All o-kay.'

283

Molly couldn't stifle the thought of Cory doing it again, but this time killing someone – if he just kept on, what would it do to someone with a weak heart? Or their mind?

'Leave worrying to the grown-ups. I'll call Grandma and Grandpa, tell them Cory needs his breakfast.' She sniffed. *And a shower.*

'Don't go,' he said. He burbled in alien, then, 'Men-with-guns.'

'Look, Cory: the telephone booth is just there and you can hide while I'm phoning, okay?'

'Cory run away, live in woods, then no more bad-bad men come. Keep Mom and Dad safe.'

*Oh, my son, the marvel.* She hugged him. 'No, you won't: it's cold and it'll get colder, remember, and there's nothing you can eat out there. And we'll be so sad if you go. We'd just wither away.'

'Nuts and berries and roots in woods,' he said, just being factual. 'Or hide in deserted house. Pretend to be ghost.'

Even now, with all this trouble, he could make her smile.

A light came on in a window above the car showroom. 'Hide,' she ordered, and got back into the front. She started the car, which coughed then began to purr as she pulled out into the road and headed off.

There was silence behind her for a couple of minutes, and then Cory whispered, 'Saw Bad Men day before. Cory bad and stupid for not saying: three bad-bad men and bi-noculars. Mom-mom, didn't think saw me but same men.'

It was the wrong time to tell him off. 'Well, they picked on the wrong little boy,' she said.

Cory said, 'In comic, not Monster fault look different with bolts.'

'Well, if people had looked after him, he would've been a very kind monster. Didn't he just want to play with the children? He was big and strong: he could give them piggy-backs.'

'Better story. Cory draw that.'

'Sleep now, sweetie-pie. Or sing, to help Mom stay awake.'

How easy it was, to talk about the path of peace, but she had fought and now she felt a pull to more violence. It might never end.

Molly stood among apple trees long since stripped of their fruit as the evening sun sank. Yellow leaves clung to the branches, or dappled the ground beneath. Cory was chasing in circles, because there was fresh air and space and the last of the sun, so why not race your shadow, or whatever he was doing?

'Bonnie and Chuck be okay?' he asked yet again.

'Sure. Dad and Roy and the others will make it all safe,' she said, even though the doubts kept rising inside her, no matter how hard she batted them down. They could flee . . . In the old days, you just changed your name and went West.

She had her passport so she could go to Canada if they had to. But what if Cory fell ill? He was running short of some of his drugs and how would they take the two pints of his blood, frozen at the hospital? Dr Jarman knew more about Cory than any other doctor on Earth, but how could he flee abroad?

'If new house, Bonnie and Chuck come with us?' Cory asked, tentacles waving in the cold air.

'We'll see,' Molly said. 'The grown-ups will make a really

good plan.' But no, Diane and Janice and their families couldn't come into exile; if they had to flee, it would be the three of them, alone.

Eva was standing at the back door, her hands working at a cloth. 'Molly, Cory, come in, you ought to see this. Big meteors in Russia.'

Molly didn't get what she was seeing at first. On the television screen were grainy, shaking pictures of a bright trail across a clear sky. Then, horrified, she understood: it was like that cold April day when the Meteor had torn apart Amber Grove.

Molly and Cory sat together next to John and the three of them stared.

'We are sorry to interrupt your scheduled broadcast. If you have just joined us, we have received multiple reports of a meteor, or meteors, landing somewhere in the northeast of the Soviet Union, north of the Arctic Circle. Reports have been logged by the Royal Canadian Air Force, the Poker Flat Research Range in Alaska and an unnamed US Navy warship currently on manoeuvres in the Bering Strait.'

A map came up with arrows pinpointing where the sightings had been made. Then the newsreader said, 'These are library pictures of the first meteor strike, which devastated the small town of Amber Grove in New York State last year. We will bring you more information as we get it. Hold on . . . We're now saying three meteors, quite close together, splashed down in the East Siberian Sea. This is around a thousand miles away from American waters.'

Cory was shivering, but Molly had no sense of what this meant.

'Is this your people coming, Cory?' John asked.

'No-no. Our ships land quiet and safe. No chunks of rock blow everything up. First Mom flew in behind Meteor, don't know why.'

She felt the fear coming off him, a cold breeze like the back door opened.

The anchorman said, 'There have been no reports from the Russians, no confirmation of any damage. We'll keep you updated when we have more information.'

Eva, wise and kind, interrupted. 'Cory, come and help me finish supper.'

He bolted from the room to help and she wondered, *What will this new fire from the sky bring?*

## CHAPTER 27

# Sheriff Olsen's plan

Gene called Molly from a payphone a long way from the library. Shivering, he thought, *Better safe than sorry*. The coins clicked into the slot.

'I wish you were here,' Molly said. 'We all miss you.'

'I have to do this,' he said. 'We're happy enough with two of the thugs: they're so scared, they told Lars everything, and Lars believes them. They'll confess to burglary and go to jail. I'm pretty sure they'll keep their mouths shut. And they say no one else knows; they didn't want to share the bounty.'

Gene wasn't going tell Molly how the Sheriff had smiled as he'd slipped his thumbs into his belt loops and said, 'So, I told 'em Cory could read their minds and if they said a damned word, he'd fly right through the window and do it again. Trust me, they'll confess to any damn crime I tell them, rather than that.'

'And Napoleon?' Molly's voice crackled over the phone.

'Yeah, he's a bit tougher, but we're dealing with him.' Gene changed the subject and asked, 'What's Big Stuff think about the Russian meteors?'

'He hates it. It brings everything back.'

They exchanged tender words before Gene hung up, glad not to have to admit that the leader of the thugs was a real nightmare: Lars Olsen had tried everything, but Napoleon just kept fighting back. He knew he held some strong cards and he was damned sure he'd get rich from them. Napoleon was a direct threat to Cory's safety and Gene was this close to giving Roy the house keys and heading off to the farm himself.

At sunset, Gene made his way to the police station, which smelled, oddly, of homemade soup.

'Help yourself,' said Olsen, waving him towards a simmering pot. 'Bread's over there. Can't smite the heathens on an empty stomach.'

Nerves made Gene eat less, unlike Molly. 'Thanks, I won't.'

'Won't poison you,' Olsen said.

Gene sat and looked at the Sheriff, who was ladling soup into two bowls.

'You need to trust me, Mr Myers. I promised the child's mother.'

'Molly told me the story,' Gene said. The soup did smell good. 'So, what's your plan? With Napoleon?'

'I don't know, Mr Myers, but there's no nice, soft and safe way to deal with this. We need to name what we're dealing with: it's hardened wickedness and that's a fact.'

'Call me Gene.' He still didn't trust this man, but what choice did he have?

Pea soup with chunks of ham in it and chewy rye bread. He was a little hungry after all.

No one challenged the Sheriff as they made their way through the hospital to the psychiatric ward. Gene wore his volunteer armband and the Sheriff carried a holdall.

'You leave this to me,' Olsen said, and laughed. 'For a man who hates hospitals, I sure spend a lot of time in 'em.'

Papers signed by Dr Jarman did the trick. A male orderly consulted with Sister, then led them down a corridor of small rooms. There was a secure padded cell for violent patients. Somewhere a TV was on loud, which didn't hide someone crying out, 'It didn't it didn't it didn't . . .'

Gene held all the right progressive opinions about science and kindness bringing cures and yet an atavistic voice was saying, *Flee, flee, demons and witches . . .*

In front of the last cell door, the orderly said, 'We had to restrain him.'

'Good,' Olsen said. 'Damn crazy tried to bite me when I arrested him.'

The cell had a bed, a toilet with no lid and a reek of disinfectant. Time in hospital had not been kind to the short man Molly had nicknamed Napoleon. His broken nose had crusted blood and he'd acquired new bruises. He struggled to a sitting position, not easy in a straitjacket, and stared at them, his eyes foggy. 'I want a lawyer! Myers, I'm going to bust your little secret wide open—'

Gene felt such loathing for this man, loathing mixed with fear, because this thug held their future in his hands.

'It's *Mister* Myers, or sir,' said Olsen, all genial. He sat on the chair he had brought in, while Gene remained standing. 'I'm running out of patience, so if you insult Mr Myers, I'll kick you in the balls, which I reckon is reasonable force when you attacked me.'

Was this Lars' master plan, just to keep beating the man up? Gene didn't want to watch it, and anyway, there was no way a beating would keep Cory safe in the future. His conscience churned his guts.

'That thing, that *freak* – people oughtta know. I'll say in open court, there's this monster, this fucking *mutant* you're keeping secret. Nurse Hooton knows – I'm gonna blow the whole thing wide open – the press'll pay me, *real* big money . . .'

Lars produced a toothpick and worked at something between two teeth before saying, 'See, Cory only just got started before you little babies caved in. You got no idea what he can do – what he's gonna do to you.'

The thug looked cunning. 'That's torture: you can't get away with it.'

Lars opened the holdall and removed a syringe and a small bottle. He filled the syringe deftly.

'What's that?' the man said.

Lars held up the syringe, tapped the glass, squirted a drop; everyone knew air bubbles were dangerous. Then he laid it carefully on his knee.

'Time for baby to go to sleep. We'll take a little ride up north, get rid of those nasty voices in the head.'

'Waddaya mean? Where're we going?' For the first time, Napoleon looked a little worried.

Lars produced his folder of papers, pulled out one and read

out loud, aping a doctor kind of voice. 'The patient is a violent, delusional, paranoid schizophrenic. The patient tried to shoot two law-abiding citizens in their own home because he believes that their child has tentacles, is an alien from another planet and comes to him in dreams . . . yada yada . . . he claimed the child attacked him through mind-control and that there is a giant conspiracy including law enforcement and his doctors . . .'

'Fuck you,' the thug said, his eye starting to twitch.

'The State has this place for criminal crazies, Ruth House: the Ebenezer Ruth Memorial Hospital for the Criminally Insane. You know, where they sent the guy who ate his mom for Thanksgiving? Don't worry, you get a lift, 'cos I'm gonna drive you up there with these here papers. You're drooling and covered in your own shit . . . the drugs'll do that; it'll help the look of the thing . . .'

'You can't do that.'

'And you tell the doctor there, "Cory Myers is the devil and he made a monster eat my brain. I'm not mad, doctor: there are aliens and Saint Jarman, the much-loved head doctor at Amber County Hospital, is hiding them . . . that's why he signed the paper saying I'm mad . . . and the third-term Sheriff who arrested me when I tried to shoot Mr and Mrs Myers . . . he's in on it too . . . and when Mr and Mrs Myers say they don't have any son at all, let alone an alien one, they're just lying . . ." Anyhow, the doctors will decide. Who d'you think they're gonna believe?'

Lars had a low, soft, believe-me voice and his eyes were as wide and kind as a child. 'Oh, Ruth House is out of the way, no one much cares what goes on there. No one bothers to visit. Someone got knifed in the eye last week on account of being a snitch. How these rumours get about, I don't know. But if someone gets killed there, ain't nothing to do with me.'

Gene couldn't bottle it up anymore. 'Lars, maybe . . .'

'Leave this to me, Mr Myers.'

'I'm not crazy. The kid was real,' said the thug.

Gene felt sick to his stomach. But what else could they do?

'Oh, no one up there says they're crazy. Even the guy who ate his mom with green beans says he's fine, just a regular guy. You tell them you saw comic-book monsters with a face on fire and they'll say, *textbook case*, and fill you so full of drugs you won't be able to spell your name for a year. Maybe they'll give you some of that ECT . . . you know, electricity through the brain? And I walk away and my problem is solved.'

His hands dusted themselves off in the air.

Gene put his hand on Lars' shoulder. It was like holding a rock. 'Lars, can we talk, now?'

'Your objections are noted,' Lars said, 'but don't you worry, that's just my first plan. My second is even better.' He picked up the syringe. 'Those hippies and their LSD. They say it gives you flashbacks; anything horrible happened to you, you live it again. So I figure, twice a day for a week, I'll make you relive every moment of Halloween. Think about it: my plan'll work even better if you really do go crazy, won't it?'

He stood up and Napoleon wriggled desperately into the corner. Gene stood, surprised to find himself ready to protect the man who'd hit his wife and threatened to shoot them. Olsen was shorter, but he was more muscular, in much better shape. He was pretty sure the Sheriff knew how to throw a punch, too.

Olsen had switched the syringe to his left hand, so swiftly Gene hadn't seen the swap.

'Step away, Mr Myers. Let me at the little shit . . . 'Course, I'm no doctor, I'm just guessing at the dose . . . Go on, call for help, see if Jarman's staff'll believe you. Trust me, they've heard it all before.'

'I – I can't let you do that.' Gene felt sick; he was terrified. It was so easy to do the right thing in your daydreaming; so different with the stakes high and the heart pounding.

Napoleon was babbling, but Olsen had his gun out and was saying, 'Okay, in that case, the thug grabbed my gun. What a fool I was, not checking it! We struggled, I feared for my life and I shot him, by accident.' His face was suddenly full of horror and dismay. 'Judge, I had no choice.'

Gene took a step back. Olsen was nuts. There'd been some rumour about him shooting a suspect . . .

Napoleon was screeching, 'Mr Myers, *stop him*! I'm sorry – I'm sorry, I won't say anything, I *swear*. I'm sure we can fix this . . . *Please*, you gotta stop him . . .'

'So, let's make a deal,' Lars said, holstering the gun and sitting, cool as a mountain stream, the syringe once again balanced on his thigh. He told Napoleon what he had to say and do, how hard he'd better work to convince the judge. 'Because next time, Mr Myers won't be here. Mr Myers just saved your ass. You oughtta to be damned grateful.'

Gene needed a beer. Two beers. They sat in a corner of O'Reilly's Bar and Lars tasted his like he'd been walking in the hills all day.

'I hate hospitals,' the Sheriff said.

The walk had convinced Gene; he trusted his gut. 'It was a bluff – it was just water in the syringe,' he said. 'You couldn't have faked a shooting, not when he was trussed up in the straitjacket.'

Lars looked at him. 'You'll let me inject you, then?'

Gene met those innocent blue eyes and now he couldn't tell. He wondered if Lars had ever lied in the witness box, how easy it would be for a jury to believe him.

'You needed me to shout and try to stop you.'

'Good cop, bad cop, just like the movies, eh? Smart idea, too smart for me.' He drank deep and said, 'So, two of my cousins work at the jail. We'll spread money and tobacco around: Sheriff wants any crazy stories the new guy tells. Some of the cons owe me big time, and some could use a favour. And Napoleon knows it too: people'll sell him out for a tot of whisky. He wasn't much of a tough guy after all . . .'

'Will it work?'

'I just need to convince that old hypocrite Jarman to write a few exaggerations in the guy's notes, and Napoleon will confess in writing to having delusions in the past, but he's all right now, Your Honour. He'll keep his mouth shut. If you're not happy, it's gotta be Plan C: a big dose of insulin and we bury him in the woods, so deep Satan himself wouldn't find him. Yeah, you can buy me another.'

'Do we have to stoop to this?'

Lars wiped his mouth. 'I promised Cory's mother I'd keep him safe and I did what I had to. Gene, stay or go; I won't blame you. But believe me, there isn't another man in law enforcement in all fifty states on your side, someone who talks to the FBI all the time, maybe hears what they're up to.'

*You never know with Olsen if you're being played*, Gene thought.

# CHAPTER 28

## Siberia

Molly drove Cory home from the farm. She was torn about leaving, anxious about Eva, who'd been getting more and more breathless. She'd been having attacks at night, and at first Molly thought it was the FBI, and then she'd been worried Eva was dying. But John and Eva were firm: with modern medicine and old nostrums, they'd be fine; Molly was just fussing.

Molly and Cory missed Gene badly; they needed to be home. And no real decisions could be made when the adults were apart.

Joni Mitchell came on the radio, and there was the first sign to Amber Grove. 'Home soon, little one.'

'Good good good so-pleeesed, about-time. See Dad, see Bonnie and Chuck. No more Bad Men. Get guard dog. Two. Guard dogs very good against Bad Men. Grrrrr.'

'No, Cory, we're not getting a dog.'

'Cory is so-sad and wants one pet. O-kay, wants one dolphin. Very-smart like dog but swims. Cory take to river, and to pool . . . Teach tricks.'

She tried not to laugh. 'No, Cory, you can't have a dolphin.'

'Wh-yyyyy no dolphin?'

Gene had kept her informed about the thugs, how they'd pleaded guilty. Sheriff Olsen's plan appeared to be working. Once, she'd have demanded to know what threats or promises had been involved, but she'd hardened her heart. She didn't want to know.

The road sign said, *Welcome to Amber Grove*. The mayor wanted to put up a sign saying, *Home of the Meteor*, but that had kicked off a storm of outrage. Most people thought it was in bad taste. She realised her pulse-rate was up. Her house had called her home, but she was so anxious, tapping out a rhythm on the steering wheel to distract herself from her thoughts. She noticed the first Christmas decorations were up. She drove to the foot of Crooked Street – and didn't make the turn.

'Wrong way,' carolled Cory.

She shouldn't have had that drink on Halloween. Part of her knew it probably hadn't made any difference, but it nagged at her. She needed to be alert, every hour of every day, to think: this person might be hostile, this person might be loose-lipped, this situation might be dangerous. It was absurd; she realised she was thinking even seeing the house again would put them all in danger.

'Wrong way Mom. What wrong?'

'I'm just driving a longer way around,' she said, controlling her breathing. It was ridiculous. There would be no thugs, no guns, no sea-monsters of the mind, just Gene, waiting for them.

She turned the car and came back, up the hill, and there was her house, *her home*. Gene must have been looking out for her, because when she parked in front of it, he was already out on the porch, grinning. She had missed him so much. And in an instant she realised she had started the drive ready to argue they should flee. Coming home had made leaving *more* difficult for her, not less.

The papers printed maps of the East Siberian Sea and the desolate frozen lands on shore, with quaint pictures of indigenous reindeer herders, who'd probably all been put to work on collective farms decades ago. There'd been a profound silence from Russia; they hadn't even told their own people what had happened. Gene and Molly talked late into the night, wondering if it was their duty to talk to someone, but Cory knew nothing and even the discussion terrified him. It all added to their uncertainty.

For days, Cory had been complaining that there was no proper 'snow-that-settle', but that afternoon, they watched as thick clouds grey as lead filled the sky. Somehow, they would find somewhere safe to take the children to go sledding and play snowballs and build snow-monsters.

Molly had spent the whole day indoors; she really wanted some fresh air, so as soon as Gene got home, she threw on her coat and hat and took herself off for a walk. The air was bitter and the snow falling faster now. She drew her collar tight as she walked through the gloom, remembering dancing with Gene in the snow. But she was also the grown-up who worried about old neighbours alone, about John and Eva on their farm, about burst pipes and spreading grit on slippery sidewalks.

She looked up at the roof of her own house; the attic lights were on and she wondered if Cory was sitting there watching the world. Then she walked up to the brow of the hill and looked down on Amber Grove, a town tucking itself in for the night.

Coming up the road was a truck with its headlights full on, driving way too fast for the weather – it looked like Roy's – yes, it was, and that was Roy, flapping one hand at her as he topped the hill. He braked and skidded to a halt.

His face was pale as he swung open the door. 'Kris Olsen on the radio,' he gasped. 'They've arrested Lars – Kris is just a kid, I couldn't get much sense out of him. But he says he can see military trucks heading north and south. And those black cars . . .'

Her body made sense of it before she did, her heart pumping so that she could *flee, flee, flee* . . . Trucks heading north might be the hospital; south might well be for here.

'I guess they're coming here,' Roy said, like he wasn't getting through. 'The phones are down, Kris says.'

*What to do first?*

'Molly, don't risk it,' he said urgently. 'Get the boy and just *go*. If they turn up, I'll slow them down.'

At last she swung into action: this was all her worst fears come at once – as Lars and Roy had said a dozen times, Crooked Street was a trap: if troops came up the road, there was no way to drive out.

She reached her door, stumbled on the steps, and it opened. Gene rushed out to help her up. A winter song was playing low and sweet on the record player.

'Lars arrested . . . phones down,' she panted, breathless, her chest tight. 'Trucks . . . soldiers . . . FBI coming. Roy's in the road, just in case. Gene, it's time to go.'

Gene slammed the door and bolted it behind him as Molly hollered, 'Cory, love, time to go!'

She ran to the phone and lifted the receiver. Dead. *It's really happening.*

'I'll get him.' Gene took the stairs two at a time. 'Come on, Cory!' She could hear the ladder creak as he climbed to the attic.

She kept packed suitcases in the hall cupboard now. She grabbed her warmest coat, the spare cash in the old coffee pot and the car keys, then she wheeled around to stare at the stairs. *What are they doing up there?*

Cory padded down the stairs, terrified, ears flat, tentacles writhing. He seemed to have shrunk a little. Gene was close behind him, holding Cory's backpack.

'Sowl-jers coming. Sowl-jers at bottom of road, just waiting, big trucks. Saw from attic,' Cory told them.

Gene said, 'Roy's pulled his truck out into the road. We need to get out of here. Plan B.'

Shivering, Molly remembered Roy kept a gun in his truck. She took Cory by the shoulders and kissed his head. 'Right, Cory, just like we said, remember? You've got to be a brave, strong boy and hide us, walk us down. It'll be fine.'

Out back, the land fell away through rough woodland. Right at the bottom was the abandoned railroad and beyond it the meadow where the children played. But halfway down the trail was Elliott Street and some lock-up garages, which was where they kept Dr Jarman's old car, ready for just such an eventuality.

*If I was with the army,* Molly thought, *I'd send soldiers up the trail, towards the house, and seal off our retreat.* Hiding all three of them would be difficult for Cory, and the more people were looking, the harder it would be. But perhaps, down amongst the trees, there was a chance . . .

Moment by moment, it grew darker. Molly projected an authority she didn't feel. 'Okay, guys, time to go on an adventure.'

Some way off, a bull-horn bellowed; she couldn't catch the words over the threshing roar of a helicopter. A searchlight was shining through the frosted hall window and somewhere, shots were being fired. She froze, looking at Gene. She couldn't believe Roy would fire at a helicopter . . . Or perhaps they were firing at him?

Cory shivered. 'No scaring,' he said. 'Cory not use nightmares.'

'No need, just hide us, Big Stuff,' said Gene, shutting off the lights at the back.

They each took one of Cory's hands and in the next moment their son worked his strangeness; the world around them, the kitchen and hall and photographs on the wall, became a sketch of white on black and in that ghostly half-world, they slipped out of the back door and shut it behind them. Out in the yard, snow danced down. The helicopter's lights were spotlighting whatever drama was happening out in Crooked Street itself.

Molly felt Cory's fear flowing off him and grasped his hand tighter. Whenever he hid, time slowed and sounds went to a muted key. Three shots were fired somewhere, but she was confused now about the direction. Gene opened the side gate. In the trees the cold felt deeper and more real, seeping into her;

302

maybe it was because they could only move slowly, careful not to fall. But Cory had good night sight and he led them on.

Molly's worst fears were proved right: there were soldiers in the woods, as she'd guessed, behind trees or squatting by bushes. Four or five men watched them through their unearthly biowar masks, guns at the ready. She could hear the bull-horn now, shouting, 'FBI! Give yourselves up!'

Cory's gloved hand gripped hers. The men were so close she could see their eyes moving behind their masks, but Cory's power was holding up. They couldn't speak, not a whisper, but they knew what they had to do. Molly was screaming with fear inside, but she could do nothing but walk and hope.

As they reached the first soldier, Cory quivered and his power flowed out to the men, who shook their heads or looked down, then tried to bring their attention back to the house.

They'd made it halfway past when one of the men leaped up. Instinctively, Molly turned, her hand almost slipping from her son's — but the soldier hadn't noticed them. A brisk command came from somewhere in the trees and two men broke free from the undergrowth and trotted towards the back gate. Molly realised that she hadn't properly shut the gate and it was flapping open. In their hurry, that tricky latch had betrayed them.

They were close enough for Gene to tweak a nose or two, had he wanted. As her eyes adjusted to the darkness beneath the trees, she saw two more men, civilians, further back. They were watching the trail.

Up above, the trees were further apart and snow was pirouetting to the ground. Fresh snow would mean footprints the men could follow; they might not see the Myers, but they would know which way they'd gone. Surely on the lower trail, where the wood was thickest, there would be less snow . . . ?

Cory leaned against her a little and stopped. She gave his hand an encouraging squeeze and willed him on. If only he could take what power he needed from her.

. They paced down the trail, past the last two men, whose attention had drifted towards the house. Somewhere, an owl hooted, or maybe it was a man pretending to be an owl.

She half wondered if it would better to head straight down to the disused railroad. Perhaps they could borrow or steal a car? Then, suddenly, she could feel the world returning, sounds and colours coming back inch by inch. Heavens, Cory was tiring already, so quickly – she could feel his power slipping away.

She thought, as hard as she could, *My wonderful son, you can do it.* His hand quivered in hers and then they were under his cloak again.

They walked on into the darkness until, a hundred yards further and out of sight, Cory restored the world. He gasped, like when he'd been under the water for ages. 'Need some tiger left in tank Mom, Dad,' he said. 'All those bad-bad men, hard-hard-hard to hide.'

They brought their heads closer together. 'Cory, you miracle: big medal,' said Gene, squeezing his hand. 'Now, we have to be the Scoutiest Boy Scouts ever, in case there's someone bad, okay?'

More shots rang out in the woods behind them, muffled by trees and snow, and Molly felt a sharp pain for Roy, for all their friends, but she had no option: Cory came first, even though, if anyone was wounded for her son, she should be the best nurse for them ever.

Every step, she expected to hear someone running towards them, from behind or from the side, until they finally reached the turn-off from the trail that led to the lock-ups beyond. The car's tank was full, with snow-chains already fitted, and blankets, chocolate, bottles of Coca-Cola and maps. But were they walking into a trap?

'I wish we'd been able to call the farm,' Gene whispered.

'It's still America,' she murmured, putting her arms around him. 'No one's done anything wrong. We just need to keep him away from them.'

Molly felt a strange stirring in her gut: stress.

They could see the lock-ups now, and one had a light burning outside. She hadn't expected that.

Every step, she listened for the sound of another. In every shadow, she thought she could see the silhouette of a man with a gun.

## CHAPTER 29

# *The flight*

The snow was piled like thick frosting on the lock-up roofs, four each side of the road. Gene took off his gloves to find the right keys, fumbling as he tried to open the garage door, while Molly kept checking all around, behind to the woods, ahead to the road.

Cory hugged her, shivering in cold and fright. 'Roy be okay? Chuck and Bonnie?'

'I think he's busy keeping them busy.' She forced back the image of Roy lying dead, riddled with bullets, being zipped into a body-bag; she didn't want Cory picking anything up, even though her fear for her friends gripped her by the throat.

The door swung up and Gene turned on the light inside. The grey Lincoln had been worked on by Gene and Roy, every part of it pored over by men who knew that one day their lives might depend on it.

Gene got in and turned the ignition. The Lincoln coughed, coughed again, and died.

Cory squatted and gazed back at the woods, dark and dusted with snow, looking like a woodcut from some Gothic fairy-tale. Molly put the spare can of gas in the trunk and went outside to check they were still alone. Gene tried the key again; the engine barked and went silent.

'*Start, damn you, start!*' Gene muttered, adding some atheist prayer, half cajoling, half swearing, then, as if making love to the metal, he pulled out the choke and tried again.

*Don't flood the engine, don't flood the—*

With a guttural cough, the car started and with a grunt of triumph, Gene backed out of the garage, too fast. 'Get in!' he cried as he slewed round in the snow. 'We haven't got much . . .'

Molly was reaching out for Cory to push him into the back seat when she heard a noise. She peered around in the darkness. Somewhere out there in the night, there was another car.

In the corner of her eye, Cory blinked out of existence.

Headlights flared, coming down the alley, and for a second she dared to think it was just a resident, someone they could cheerily wave to as they passed – but no: it was a Jeep and it pulled up a few car lengths ahead of them in the middle of the alley, trapping them.

A short man stepped from the vehicle, bundled up fit for the Arctic, and a soldier with a rifle came around from the back. The weapon was pointed downwards, somewhere between Molly and the Lincoln, but its very existence was a threat.

Dr Pfeiffer pulled his hood down and that loathsome voice cried out through the night, 'Mr and Mrs Myers!'

There was no way Gene could back the Lincoln into the tangled woods and ramming the Jeep was lunacy. Unless they grabbed their bags and ran on foot, there was no way out. And where was Cory?

Pfeiffer said, 'Mrs Myers, I ought to be angry, but all I feel is deep admiration. The two of you kept the boy alive, you kept him from harm – and alas, you kept him from me. What a gifted actress you are, Mrs Myers. But I don't see the marvellous Cory, the most extraordinary, the most valuable child in the world. What secrets he holds!' He spoke like he had tasted fine wine and wanted everyone to know.

'Leave us alone,' she said, in fear and anger. She was running out of choices.

A second civilian got out of the car: Tyler, Pfeiffer's sidekick from the hospital. The driver was a soldier, he'd be armed, but he was still seated. *Run into the woods*; Molly thought, *and maybe they won't shoot*. Or . . . Or Cory could hide his family once more and they could risk walking out past the men.

'Cory's the most important child on the planet and he's got to be kept safe,' Pfeiffer said. 'I'm a father myself, Mrs Myers. Anything he needs – scientists or doctors – I can get the very best. Let's be reasonable.'

'Why should we trust you?' she said. Beside her, Gene got out of the car, leaving it running. The man with the weapon was impassive as a monument.

'Once he's my patient, I'm obliged to protect him.'

Molly remained stone-faced and silent, resolute beside Gene.

Pfeiffer changed tack. 'This is such a cold and uncomfortable place to talk. The moment the FBI and the army arrive, it'll be decision by committee.' He raised his voice. 'Cory, I hope you can hear me. Your parents and I will keep you safe. You can come out.'

Molly flicked a glance at Gene. *What could they do?*

He squeezed her hand for strength: standing firm against the threat, together.

Pfeiffer drew himself to his full height. 'I want Cory happy and well for many years to come, and I'm sure that means toys and games and living with his family. Why would I hurt him?' He stood like a little boxer now. 'The *Times* said I'd done no first-rate science since my vaccine work – how dare they! Cory will get me a Nobel Prize. Cory, alive and well, will give me immortality.'

Gene looked unimpressed. 'You'll try to use him as a weapon, or a bargaining chip.' Pfeiffer, the hawk, the germ-warfare expert, the confidante of bomb-dropping Presidents.

Silence hung between them for ten or fifteen seconds.

The doctor mused, 'Has it occurred to you how many human lives we might save with new medicines, new cures?'

His left hand moved quicker now as an urgent note entered his voice. 'This is the defining moment of this century: contact with another intelligent species. We need to know about his people – how can we learn from them? Are they a threat? Their technology's far more advanced than our own. You can deal with me, you can deal with the army or it's the Mob or the Russians.'

'Russians?' Gene said.

'You know the USSR sent people before. The FBI believe there are new Soviet agents in town right now. Maybe they're looking for Cory,' said Pfeiffer, with a frown. 'They're ruthless enough to starve and murder millions of their own people, so imagine if those foreign spies got to him. Or vicious criminals, like the ones who attacked you, who just want to sell him to the highest bidder. Let's get him away from danger and make a sensible plan, where everyone wins.'

*Pfeiffer knew about the thugs?* 'Just leave us alone,' Molly said. 'We're not hurting anyone. Just go away.' She was about to say more when out of nowhere, she heard Cory's little cough – and there he was, holding her. She didn't like how much he was shaking. His ears were right down. Gene crouched and they each put an arm around him.

Pfeiffer held out his hands, his eyes wide. 'Oh Cory,' he said, almost cooing, 'how on earth did you do that, you little wonder? Well, I think your mother and father need to talk, right now. Then we can take you somewhere warm and safe. Does he like chocolate milk?'

'Sc-aaaared,' whispered Cory – and, without warning, he hid all three of them.

The alley with the garages became a cold, distant pencil-sketch of reality as the world around twisted out of focus.

Pfeiffer blinked. The soldier pulled up his rifle, but Pfeiffer pushed the end of the weapon away. 'Idiot! Harm that child and I'll have you shot!' Then he turned, looking to and fro, trying to find them. 'Those vermin were right,' he exclaimed. 'Extraordinary!'

Molly saw him staring down at the ground, looking for footprints. Heavens, how she hated that snow.

'Don't run,' Pfeiffer barked. 'You won't stay free for long.'

The soldier spoke. 'I'll make sure they can't use the car. Martins, new plan: radio for back-up.'

311

Pfeiffer bristled. 'We agreed—'

But the man had the rifle up and was aiming at the Lincoln. Molly panicked. Hiding wouldn't stop a bullet. She tried to pull Gene and Cory towards the trunk of the car – Cory wanted to head straight for the trees, but, whatever they did, they had to grab the bags; they couldn't go anywhere without Cory's drugs.

'You need to trust me,' Pfeiffer said to the air, more urgent, no longer in control. 'They'll keep hunting you for ever – I'm your best hope.'

With a gasp, Cory stopped hiding and Pfeiffer's crew looked straight at them.

Snow floated down.

'Don't shoot,' Pfeiffer said, but there was a hungry edge to his face Molly hated.

Cory raised his hands.

Molly felt his fear gust out of him, biting worse than the most bitter winter wind, as he reached deep inside himself and the nightmare poured forth. Here came the sea-monster, all burning blue tentacles and snapping claws. Cory brought the smell of salt water and the thick rotting stench of the sea-beast's breath . . . Her heart and her throat knew it to be a real terror, a real threat, even though she knew it was a dream. To Cory it felt bigger than an elephant . . . and it liked to hunt people.

The light in the alley dimmed, Molly's skin crawled and her stomach revolted.

'No, Cory,' she cried, 'no!' but he stood there, stretching out his empty hands as if they were shaping the nightmare.

'Bad Men run away! Monster coming!' he cried, in his high

fluting voice. The soldier at the other end of the alley dropped the rifle. Pfeiffer clasped a respirator to his face and Dr Tyler had a coughing fit, but they all had their eyes fixed on the dream.

Cory launched the sea-monster forward at the Jeep and the driver shrieked, a strangely high sound; the gears clashed and suddenly the vehicle was backing out of the alley at speed.

'Get in the car!' Gene snapped.

Cory was still standing rigid, focusing his power. Her heart hammering, Molly picked him up and dragged him to the door, trying to ignore the dream crawling over her skin and into her mind—

—came a tropical storm, bringing down tall trees . . . preserved claws in a wooden building . . . a silver boat with feathered silver wings skimming over a lagoon . . . his fear at seeing one of the monsters, swimming just under the surface.

The Lincoln's engine was purring steadily. They slammed the doors, Gene put it in gear and the car surged forward, heading after the retreating Jeep.

The soldier stood in their way, not moving.

Molly shrieked, 'Gene!' but he was already swerving, and thank the stars, the soldier finally leaped into life. The side-mirror clipped him, but they had no death on their hands.

*So close, so close . . .*

With a gasp, Cory stopped the dream.

Molly, praying hard to the Higher Power she didn't believe in, saw the Jeep behind them had knocked over a mail-box. Someone was striding along the sidewalk towards the driver, shaking his head.

Cory shivered. 'So-tried not to hurt . . .'

'Good boy,' Molly said, consoling him; at least he'd used less power than he had with the thugs, so maybe they wouldn't be as traumatised.

The Lincoln slithered down a street of gabled homes aglow with Christmas cheer. They were close to the junction – but had the soldier radioed his superiors? How quickly would they all join the chase?

A truck passed, then a car, delaying them pulling out. In the side-mirror Molly could see headlights: the Jeep was back on the road.

'Bad car come,' Cory said, hands over his eyes. 'Not enough, not enough . . . no-no.'

Gene's big hands gripped the wheel and he took off onto the main road. Molly turned to see the Jeep was driving fast to catch them up, but horns blared from other cars: Amber Grove always expected courteous driving.

Now the Jeep swerved, ready to come alongside them and maybe even get in front of them. The soldier in the passenger seat was winding down a window; Molly could see the rifle. She didn't think her heart could beat any faster. They would be forced to stop and then it would all be over . . .

'Sorry Mom, Dad,' said a tired voice. 'Last puff.'

Even as her mouth opened to protest, Cory was kneeling up to the back window. He let his fear come out of him again, like the winter breathing out every horror it had.

'No, Cory, don't—' Gene said, but his heart wasn't in it either.

The dream-monster leaped into the Jeep, old and terrible and leather-skinned, claws that could rip the thickest wood. It lurked beneath the sea, stinking of ancient fish, and liked tender, intelligent flesh. Molly, hearing screams in her head, was struggling to tell the solid from the dream, but the four men locked in a moving box panicked completely, seeing and feeling a beast that wanted to rip their throats out; the Jeep spun out of control like death on skates.

Gene put his foot down and the Lincoln sped forwards, skidding a little on the curves. Molly looked back, fist to her mouth, dreading that the crashed Jeep meant deaths – but no, she could see the men staggering from the car and running, all the while angry horns blared and cars skidded, trying to avoid the crazy people in the middle of the road . . . then they rounded a bend and she could see no more.

Gene had never driven like this, let alone in these conditions. He skidded turning into a side road, clipping a mirror from a parked truck, and ran a red light heading for the highway.

*Don't crash, don't crash, get us out in one piece.* But Molly, looking back, couldn't see anyone following.

'Cory, are you okay?' His inner eyelids were shut; he was barely awake. She opened their coats and hugged him close, trying to warm him, and wrapped the rough blanket that smelled of mothballs around them both.

*What on all the planets in the galaxy are we going to do? Where will we go?* Lizard-breath and weird winds and falling snow jumbled in her head.

Gene clicked his tongue. 'We need to call Mom and Dad, head east, to the neighbours' hideout . . .'

'They'll put out a description of the car, and us.'

'I'm not stopping yet – we need to get further away. Lars gave me some different licence plates . . .'

'That's illegal,' she said, and Gene began to laugh, a jagged, difficult laugh.

In an hour, she might find her comment funny too. She stroked Cory's forehead but he still didn't react. 'Cory's passed out. He's exhausted.' She hoped that was all it was.

Gene tried to look over his shoulder. 'What can I do?'

'Drive, eyes on the road.'

## CHAPTER 30

# *Disguises*

The snow came down on the highway like white folds of cloth. There was more traffic than Molly had expected. She held Cory and tried to ignore the tremor in her hands. *I'll never see the house again. Or Diane and Janice and Roy, or their children. Dr Jarman and Rosa Pearce. Every man's hand is raised against us.* Even now, the men of power would be flocking around her friends like crows to a wounded lamb. They were so many, and armed, and the Myers were so few.

After a long silence, Gene gestured at a baseball sticker on the windscreen. 'Roy's idea of a joke. If they catch us, hide the Red Sox decal. My family could never bear the shame.'

They pulled in at a gas station to find a phone. The sullen-looking bald guy at the cash register was buried deep in the sports section. Molly kept her hood up, got out her coins and found the payphone.

Trembling, Molly called the farm to warn them and got no answer, which might mean anything. *Country folk go to bed early,*

317

she thought, *but not this early. Perhaps they were with friends, or perhaps one of the pigs was ill.*

She called the operator, who said, yes, all phones on the Amber Grove exchange were down. Then she flicked through the blue notebook which held every phone number she'd ever need to know. There wasn't anyone in Bradleyburg she could trust, but she could warn Peggy Fell in Maine.

The phone rang out, with no reply.

She called the farm again and got nothing, and by now a fierce truck driver was waiting for the phone. The manager made a show of putting down his paper and glared at her.

With her hood still up, Molly got back into the car.

Gene, watching Cory from the driver's seat, frowned. 'He's flat out. Should I try to wake him?'

'Let him sleep. Try to find news on the radio.'

In this weather, a black FBI car could get very close before you realised, or a truck might be on you before you saw that it was military. Even something as simple as using a toll road meant more witnesses.

'Plenty of reasons why Mom and Dad mightn't answer the phone,' Gene said.

Over the next hour the roads got more treacherous and visibility worse, the driving snow obscuring wooden churches and scenic barns, metal bridges and stretches of highway named after long-dead politicians. The heater fought in vain to keep out the chill.

Time felt out of joint, but at last they reached the turn-off. These last miles would be slow work. The last gas station was dark and deserted, but its payphone was working.

The phone rang and rang and rang – and as she took the receiver from her ear, somebody picked up. 'John,' she gasped, 'thank goodness you're—'

But the man's voice wasn't John's. 'Myers place, Bill Burrowes speaking.'

She tensed, but remembered: the neighbour who lived two farms over.

'Bill, it's Molly. Are John and Eva there?'

'Oh, Molly! Eva's been taken ill – it's her lungs. John's taken her to Caffrey County General. They tried to reach you, but your phone was down. I came over to check on the animals.'

'Right,' she said, thinking fast. 'Which ward?'

'John'll call and tell me when they're sorted.'

A pause.

'You could call the hospital. I have the number.'

She took it down with numb fingers.

'Where are you?' Burrowes asked.

Her mind whirred. She wasn't sure, but could she hear something strained in Bill's voice? Was someone listening beside the phone?

'Do you need any help? Where are you?' Burrowes repeated.

'Gotta go – I hear something boiling over,' she said at random and hung up, then ran back to the car.

Gene looked at her. 'What happened?'

'Bill Burrowes answered the phone. He said Eva's lungs are bad, that John's taken her to Caffrey General.' As Gene's eyes widened, she said quickly, 'I don't know, but he didn't sound right.'

Grim-faced, Gene swore and started the car.

319

In Molly's imagination, the old man was standing there with the FBI or the army at his shoulder. A nightmare, that Eva had stopped breathing at the shock of the FBI arriving.

Without asking, Gene turned south, towards Caffrey.

Molly felt tears coming, but she needed to be strong. She could weep later. 'We can't go to the hospital. It might be a trap.'

'It doesn't feel safe to hang around,' Gene said. 'There's a motel somewhere along here.'

'We should go to the house your folks told us to use.'

'Bill knows it well. Suppose he tells the Feds?'

There was silence for a mile or two, but they needed to make some decisions.

'I'll call the hospital,' Gene said at last, 'but I'll have to be really careful. They're serious, the Feds, and moving very fast . . .'

Cory was worn out, and scared of using his nightmares. Molly thought the choice was clear. 'John told me if things went down, to keep Cory safe. We can't fight the government, so let's head for Canada.'

Gene said, 'I'll call from the motel.'

'We should just head north.'

'We need Cory fit . . . you know . . . in case we need him.'

Cory was oblivious to the world whirling around him. Molly hoped this was tiredness, nothing more; that at least for now, he'd found happy dreams.

Outside the narrow strip of their headlights, all was darkness. The radio, turned very low, played the old Christmas tunes.

★

*The Perfect Motel – Vacancies* announced itself in neon pink. Gene parked between cars and trucks heavily encrusted with white. 'You do the talking,' he told her.

Molly prayed for the motel staff to be sleepy and not very talkative. As she opened the door, a gust of warm, stale air hit her. Wallpaper faded to grey and pink reminded her of her childhood. The woman behind the desk looked exhausted, but she still managed a smile. Behind her, under a large wooden cross, a TV with the sound turned low showed the news. The only brightness was a little Christmas tree, hung with lights and baubles.

Molly gave her grandmother's name, and paid cash.

'And where are you folks from?'

'Bradleyburg. We've been visiting friends.' Molly spun her tale, needing to get away.

The woman noticed Molly's eyes flicking to the TV, where students were burning the flag against stock footage of a mushroom cloud.

'These are dark times,' she said, 'these wars and riots. This's what happens when we walk away from God.'

Molly had no time for that discussion. 'Things are bad, sure enough, but there's still hope,' she said, and took the key.

It could've been any motel: three sides built around a square parking lot, two floors of rooms all the way round. Only a few lights were on. Gene carried Cory in his blanket up the stairs and into the faded, cramped space, but at least it was warm and when she smelled the sheets, they were clean. They put Cory to bed, then Gene checked the fire escape: a way out, but also a way the cops could come up.

He stood at the door, coat still done up, and hating herself for saying it, Molly said, 'They can trace phone calls – please don't phone the hospital.'

'I'll change the licence plates,' he said.

The moment the door closed, Molly wished he hadn't gone. Feeling bone-weary, she jammed a chair under the handle before producing two small bottles. *Time to see if being a red-head works for me.* She thought of the glamorous film stars of her youth.

She worried about Gene's parents and their friends, who'd tried so hard to keep them safe. They'd surely seize them all. Little Bonnie would be in tears – and Roy might be wounded, maybe even be dead. Pfeiffer knew about the criminals who'd come after Cory; he could easily guess who else knew about them. Out there, outside this little room, she imagined the great gears of power turning to find the Myers and crush them.

They had nothing and no one they could mobilise against Pfeiffer and all he stood for.

She shouldn't have let Gene go. She looked down on Cory sleeping and didn't know what she could do if they came. She was sick with nerves by the time Gene got back, more than an hour later. He'd been far too long, and he had the shifty look of someone who had made a mistake.

'Better shave,' he said.

She remembered his high-school Year Book photo. She preferred the beard.

'You called the hospital in Caffrey,' she said. 'Have you no sense at all? They'll be after us . . .'

'No, they won't,' he said, with his stubborn face. 'I walked for miles and called from the payphone by the highway. I could tell at once I was getting special treatment. This nice lady, ever so talkative . . .'

She leaped up. 'Keeping you talking . . . We need to leave, *now!*'

He went over to the sink, pulled a face at her bottles and ran the hot water.

'It takes time to run a trace. Lars explained how long, so I hung up straight away.'

'Next time you take a stupid risk, discuss it with me first.' She felt so sick. They'd paid for the room with scarce cash.

'We're all my folks have – the Feds will assume we drove on.'

She could have hit him. '*You don't know that!* Gene, this isn't a cowboy movie – we can't waltz into the hospital, put Cory in danger . . .'

'I'm just suggesting we go to Caffrey, take a look, that's all . . .'

'And find they're in hospital under armed guard . . . So what then? Ask Cory to hide us? The army knows about hiding now. They'll have hundreds of people . . .' She sighed. 'It's got to be Canada, Gene, first thing.'

For a time, there was silence between them, then she got up and took his hands. 'I hate this, Gene, it feels like we're letting them down. But the Feds will know we're coming. Remember how tired and fragile Cory was after the thugs . . .'

'Just a careful scouting expedition—'

Molly felt frustration rising. 'Gene, what would John and Eva want? I can hear your dad now: *Never you mind about us old ones, just skedaddle.*'

STEPHEN COX

He smiled at her imitation. 'We're all they have,' he repeated, and she loved him for his loyalty. She had won the argument, though.

Someone shook her, a kind, strong hand. Molly didn't remember getting into Cory's bed; slowly, coming round, she worked out it was still the motel room. Gene, bleary-eyed, was standing over her. He'd pulled the drapes apart a little, but the sky was dark.

He looked so odd clean-shaven. *I must get him something for the shaving-rash*, she thought. He'd grown the beard to hide a neat scar under his chin, but she could barely see it.

'Gotta go,' he said.

Cory stirred enough to sniff a cookie with his tentacles. He ate that and drank a cup of water, all without opening his eyes. Molly felt his neck for temperature and stroked his ear for love.

'We're going to Canada,' Gene said, sitting by him on the bed.

'Where Grandpa and Grandma?' he asked, rubbing his ears and eyes.

'We don't know right now, Big Stuff, but we need to go to Canada and we might need you to hide us.'

'No, no, too-haaaard. Tooo tired,' Cory said, pulling the blanket over his head.

'Well, we'll get some proper breakfast and drive somewhere new, with new sights, and I'm sure if you need to hide us . . .'

'No,' the blanket said, 'too-too-tired to hide other people, so-hate running away. Hate scaring so-much, hurts people.' He muttered in his own language.

'You must get up, sweetie-pie, we're going.'

Cory surfaced. His inner eyelids flicked open. 'Where this?'

'It's a motel, Cory, a place to stay. You've slept a long time.'

'Dad look weeiird – wow-oh-wow Mom hair look weeiird. Need pee now.'

Gene and Molly looked at each other as Cory shambled into the bathroom.

'He's just tired.' Molly felt sick and hollow inside; she hadn't eaten more than a slice of bread since lunch the day before.

'His power's the only edge we have . . .'

Action was the only cure. 'Let's see how quickly we can get packed and out.' She looked at herself in the mirror, grimacing. Her fantasy had been the glamorous Deborah Kerr or Maureen O'Hara, in pearls and furs, or Dahlia Diamond, the TV anchorwoman, but the mirror's hard truth was that she looked as cheap and obvious as a desperate divorcée in Atlantic City. It didn't suit her at all. She reached for a headscarf.

In the dawn light she could see the cloud-cover was lighter and that stirred her spirits a little. She told Cory, 'You must hide when we get into the car, okay? There'll be people coming and going.'

'O-kay,' he said. 'Hair smell different yes-it-does. What for breakfast? What is for breakfast ple-eeese?'

'Good boy,' she said. 'We'll find a good breakfast.' She could think of nothing she wanted less. To Gene, she said, 'I'll drive.'

They saw no one as they left. Molly turned on the radio and headed north on the highway. Through the static a man's voice could be heard. '—was the President's spokesman. If you have just joined us, the government has confirmed that the Russians have carried out three major nuclear tests, above ground, in a remote area in the northeast of their country. The White House is calling for an emergency session of the UN Security Council to discuss this blatant breach of the Test Ban Treaty. Our satellites picked up three blasts within the space of an hour and radioactive fallout has been detected over the Bering Sea. The Soviet Union denies breaking international law.'

'More news just in: the FBI has swooped on a Soviet spy ring in the small town of Amber Grove, New York State, home of the Meteor. We understand there have been a dozen arrests so far. The FBI are working with local police in a state-wide search for individuals they have described as "key to this investigation".'

Her throat felt tight. *Eyes on the road, Molly.*

The radio began to play martial music. As she turned it down, she saw a patrol vehicle in her rear-view mirror, coming up behind her.

'So, they're pretending we're spies,' Gene said quietly. 'They're clever or they're crazy, or maybe both.'

'I wish . . . I wish there was some way to make this all disappear.'

'Cory not want cookies,' the blanket announced. 'Cory want eggs and pancakes.'

She saw a big Carrols ahead, one of the boxy orange ones, and signalled, but the trooper didn't slow or signal and as she pulled into the forecourt, the patrol car disappeared up ahead.

She looked at her strange shaved husband. 'If you stay with Cory, I'll go and get us something.'

Inside, under spherical lights half red, half yellow, the smell of fried food hit her and her stomach turned. She wondered if she was going to be sick, right there in front of everyone. There was a line for takeout, far more crowded than she liked. A man in a Teamsters cap ahead of her told his companion, 'So, they tell me the government closed the border at midnight.'

'The government's gone nuts!' the other man snorted. 'You can't close the whole damned border, just to stop a spy or two.'

Teamster guy shrugged. 'The ports, the airports . . . Everything's locked down. They're using the army.' His voice reminded Molly of her Brooklyn days.

'This load is late, the weather, no fault of mine – now the government? Our customers will be biting the carpet.'

'We've three trucks in the line; the boss, he tells us: get the cops to open the crates, take stuff out, let them strip-search you, just get them to let you through. But it's no-go.'

A motherly waitress stopped by Molly. 'You okay, honey?'

'Yes,' she said, stiffly. 'I'm afraid last night's supper disagreed with me.'

'You take it easy. You wanna sit?'

Molly badly wanted to sit somewhere safe and not have to worry that people were looking for them. She wanted to cry; she wanted someone else to solve her problem. *One step at a time*, she told herself, shaking her head. 'I'm okay, thanks.'

All she'd come here to do was buy something Cory could eat. Pancakes and eggs.

*Get a grip, Molly.*

A little girl at the nearest table stared at her, one finger up her nose. Molly wondered why, then realised she'd tied her scarf tightly to hide the hideous mistake of her hair; she must look odd. At the counter, she gave her order, trying not to appear too obviously uncomfortable.

On the diner radio she heard, 'So, more snow on the way. And now, chaotic scenes at the border, where trucks and cars are stacked up for miles along the highway.'

At last the order arrived. Molly looked at the door and nearly dropped her tray as two State Troopers, tall and confident, walked in. *No*, she told herself sternly, *be that supreme actress who fooled Dr Pfeiffer. Walk slowly. You have nothing to hide.*

The troopers signalled to the manager, who immediately poured two coffees. They had stayed by the door and were looking around for a seat. The thought of passing them rooted Molly to the spot, her heart hammering, her gut churning – until, finally, she just took her courage and walked to the door. As she passed, one of the troopers held it open. He gazed at her full in the face, longer than polite.

'Thanks,' she said.

She walked, sedate as a queen to avoid suspicion, to the car. Gene had clambered into the driving seat; Cory was still muffled in the blanket in the back.

'Cory and I were planning to come in if you'd taken any longer,' Gene said, wearing one of his sweetest frowns.

'Do *not* put yourselves in danger if I get caught,' she said, handing out the meals. The smell was still unsettling her stomach. 'They've closed the borders.'

'I heard.' He started the car.

'Why not go Ni-aaagra and see Falls? Im-pressive. No falls that big my planet.'

'We're at the wrong end of the state, sweetie-pie,' Molly

said. 'When we're moving, I'll show you on the map. Gene, what do we do?'

'There's hundreds of miles of border. Let's not follow the highway along the lakes but turn off and head northeast. I mean, it's not like there's a Berlin Wall the whole way.'

'Swim river.' Cory was happily eating pancakes and slurping milk through a straw.

'Far too wide, and icy-cold, Cory. Quiet while Dad gets out onto the highway.'

'Get boat then.'

Of all the things to notice, Gene had got rid of the baseball sticker. She worried about roadblocks.

The news burbled on: radioactive fallout had landed in British Columbia; Canada had issued a formal complaint to the Russians and would support the US in bringing the Soviet actions to the UN Security Council.

A new fear surfaced, a deep, terrible fear. 'Can we trust the Canadians?' she asked.

'Canada never sends draft-dodgers back,' Gene replied. 'And have you ever met a mean Canadian?'

'I bet if the FBI says we're Russian spies, though . . .'

'They have courts. They'd have to prove it.'

'But then we'd have to tell everyone about Cory.' A new thought stirred; how flimsy their plans were, and how quickly they'd fallen apart. But people did run and hide, for years and years. Would this fear become something she'd have to live with every day?

'We interrupt this programme for a newsflash: the FBI have

released a description of two wanted Russian spies and their vehicle, last sighted at a motel twelve miles north of Caffrey.'

They didn't yet know about Molly and Gene's modest attempts to change their appearance and the licence plate was the old one, but now everyone had at least some idea what to look for. The government could tell all the lies it needed to mobilise ordinary people against them.

'These agents are believed to be armed, and very dangerous.' Cory's fear filled the car like the most bitter winter wind.

## CHAPTER 31

# The flight to the border

The car heater was already struggling and the winter cloud hanging thick above them promised yet more snow. When Gene drove around the curve of the road, they could see the river of cars. Further up the line, a couple of the drivers were out of their cars and walking around. It wasn't moving fast, then. Not too far ahead, cars were turning around and coming back south.

'Cory's quiet,' she said, looking at the sleeping lump under the blanket on the back seat. He could have been luggage, except for the slight rise and fall.

'Shall we change drivers?' Gene asked. 'Can you see what's stopping the traffic?'

'No . . .'

Gene took the map. 'Damn. I bet it's a roadblock. Look at the map – it makes sense here.'

Her stomach sank. 'You can't know that.'

'I wish Cory could hide the car,' he said. 'We really need to head east; this route north's too obvious.'

331

'Right. I'll get out and have a look.' Other cars were turning back so it wouldn't be suspicious if they did it too.

Molly peered out of the window, trying to see a little further. The wind was bitter. Wouldn't there be flashing lights for a roadblock? Maybe it was a jack-knifed lorry or something.

'Morning, ma'am.'

Molly turned her head and saw a middle-aged, prosperous-looking man with the face of a worrier coming towards her, the driver from the car behind. It was impossible to be dignified in a hat with sheepskin ear-flaps, she thought.

'What a cold one!' she said.

Cory was asleep; he wouldn't notice anything odd.

'Oh, indeed. I'm in a hurry, family business, so I'm going to cross over and go the other way. Any chance I could squeeze past?'

'Uh, I think we might be turning ourselves,' Molly said. 'Join the crowd. Do you know what's going on up there?'

'The radio didn't say. I wonder if it's a roadblock. For the spies, you know.' He lifted his hand to scratch under his hat.

People behind were starting to use their horns while others were jockeying round each other to turn.

'Ma'am, I could have swore I saw . . . well, I can't have.' He was peering into the back of the car.

Her pulse rate went up.

'Molly, we should be going,' called Gene, an anxious tone.

'Huh! I could've swore I saw a kid in your car. But I see there isn't anyone there.'

'Uh, well,' she said, 'this low sun causes all sorts of tricks. We'll move.'

She judged distances; yes, even Gene should be able to do that. Turning off and heading back was becoming the fashionable thing to do.

Molly got back into the car. As soon as she shut the door she gave the two-note whistle that meant *stay hidden*.

'Let's go!' Gene hissed. He started the engine and touched the horn, in a friendly way, she hoped. The driver ahead tapped their brake lights and white breath came out of the exhaust: he was doing the same manoeuvre. And Mr Worrier was still standing there, peering into the back.

*One person is fine. Even if he just woke up, he can hide from one person.*

*He can hide for ever from one person.*

Gene inched forward.

*Turn around, head south . . .*

The driver ahead was crawling forward, and so were they.

She looked in her mirror and saw Mr Worrier had produced a notebook and was scribbling something.

*Just project calm, don't look like a bootlegger heading to the border.*

They came to the turn.

'Let's drive slowly, be nothing out of the ordinary,' she said.

Gene turned – then slammed his foot on the gas pedal and raced southwards down the road. 'He was taking notes,' he said.

'Let's not be dramatic. Cory, stay hidden, just till we're away.'

'Was man Bad-Man? Cory hid because he was much-nosey.'

'Yes, good boy. He didn't see you really.'

The car skidded a little and her stomach leaped. 'Let's get there in one piece, please.'

Gene had a grim look. 'I'll bet they've got troopers waiting, just to see who turns back. That's what I would do.'

*How did criminals stay sane?* she wondered. What could they do if this was some trap?

'What's the next turning off look like?' he said. A car flashed their lights at him: for overtaking, or driving too fast, or both.

Molly scrabbled to find where they were on the map and traced a route that gave them options. She gave calm instructions even though her stomach was somersaulting, looking every so often in the side-mirror for the first hint of a patrol car. Was that Mr Worrier's car behind them?

'What'll we do if they stop us?' Gene asked anxiously. He wouldn't be great at bluffing; he always let Molly do the talking.

'Well, if we need to, Cory will hide us . . .'

'No scaring,' Cory said at once.

'Well . . .' Molly said, and the hesitation was fatal.

Cory started burbling, then, 'No scaring, not-at-all. *Hoo-hoo-hoo.* Cory hear, sowl-jers on border. Bad-Men, too many too many, yes-there-are. Mom and Dad find crossing with no people at all. Not even Canadians.'

'Now, Big Stuff,' Gene said, 'take a deep breath, okay? We're not going to just rush across anywhere. We just need to find the best road . . .'

'Going south now,' Cory said.

'This is the turn-off coming,' she said.

Gene was following a camper van the colour of butterscotch who was also indicating; he took the turn too fast and she felt the car slide. You had to let the spin happen to some extent, not fight it, but Gene was trying to hold it . . .

The van screeched to a halt. Gene was slowing, but he still rammed straight into it. Molly was thrown forward and bit her tongue; she heard a yelp from Cory behind her and for a moment she felt like she was floating in space; she saw the death of the alien mission, Cory's panic . . .

The car had seatbelts and for the millionth time she wondered why she never bothered to put hers on.

'You okay?' Gene said, his clenched fingers white on the wheel. 'Cory?'

She breathed, feeling white-hot rage, but somehow keeping it together. She wanted to take every one of Gene's crashes and near-misses and shout them in his face. Of all the times to take a risk on snow . . . !

But a long-haired kid in an Afghan coat and woollen hat was already out of the van and looking at the damage. There were two girls' faces at the windows; they all looked dismayed.

Molly knew she needed to be calm and in control: they were fleeing for their freedom, so somehow, she had to get them out of this mess.

Gene was looking abject and Cory was moaning, 'Ow-ow-ow, silly Earth cars no soft thing if stop ow-ow-ow.' At least 'ow-ow-ow' meant he was more upset than hurt.

'Hide!' she ordered and got out of the car, her head still spinning a little with shock, her back and neck aching.

'Wow, bummer,' said the kid. 'You were going one hell of a lick.'

'All you guys okay? It's a borrowed car – we hadn't realised the brakes weren't great.'

'My dad will kill me.'

The Lincoln had a fine dent in the bumper, but the VW had lost a rear light. She needed to give them a number; that's what you did — but whose could she give?

'Don't worry; we're insured,' Molly said, writing her dentist's phone number on a scrap of paper.

The boy was looking calculating as he took it, and she noticed he didn't offer his own details in return. 'I reckon you give me a hundred and neither of us need to claim — keep the sharks out of it that way, yeah?'

A hundred! In his dreams! She didn't have a hundred to spare, and anyway, he was trying it on. She couldn't remember which name the Lincoln's insurance was in, but a lot of cars were scooting past and they needed to be out of there.

'Call or don't call,' she said, 'but we'll let the insurance sort it — that's what we pay for, after all.' *Don't use Gene's name.* 'Darling, I'll drive, shall I?'

Gene was in no place to argue.

Molly got in the driver's seat and backed away. *More people to recognise us, plus a distinctive mark to make the car more obvious.*

'Let's get some distance,' she murmured, wondering if they should steal a new car, or maybe change the licence plates to the second spare set. Her hands trembled and her gut started to churn and once again she felt like she might throw up.

'No scaring,' said a little voice.

She couldn't get out of her head what might happen if Cory used his nightmare power in daylight, with a lot of people around. But there would come a time — maybe not now, but soon — when they might have to turn to him again, even though the thought of it was clearly terrifying her little boy.

In the rear-view mirror she could see he was shaking, but they were both in the front and couldn't hold him; there was no way to console him.

'Never scare ever again,' he announced, 'no-no-no.'

*If only people could know Cory for who he really was.* An odd, heretical idea began to brew. Was running for ever the answer? What if people did know the truth: his sweetness, his kindness, his vulnerability. What a dangerous thought . . . how absurd.

# CHAPTER 32

## *A decision*

Even through Molly's anxiety, the woods and the mountains
beyond, where the snow was deep and untouched, were beautiful. She took the slow roads patrol cars wouldn't bother with.
They stopped at a deserted picnic site, looking in each direction
before they got out, but other than a single car with a flat tyre
sitting unloved, there were no other vehicles in the lot, no
footprints making trails across the virgin white. She and Gene
helped Cory out and made for the wooden hut. The door to
the room with two benches and a payphone was unlocked, so
at least they were out of the wind, but to Molly's dismay, the
restroom was padlocked and a notice proclaimed spring would
come before it would open.

Sighing, she went into the bushes and did what she had to,
feeling bitterly cold and uncomfortable, then helped Cory. When
they got back, she found the external tap had frozen solid.

'Cory, get in the car,' she said, 'where it's warmer. Dad and
I need to talk, grown-up stuff.'

When he was back under his blanket, Gene hugged her hard. 'I just . . . I can't stop thinking about Mom and Dad,' he said. 'And everyone else they've arrested – Roy and Janice and—'

She didn't want to sound unsympathetic, but right now, they had bigger worries. 'What's our plan?' she asked.

'I'd like to get a new car, but I don't see how. I guess we head due east and cross the border somewhere less obvious? Or maybe find somewhere to hole up for a week or two? We could break into a vacation house or something. They can't keep the border shut for ever.'

Molly shivered. It was time to share her heretical idea with Gene. 'When we knew and no one else did, things were okay, but now, the government knows and they're after us – and they're lying about us . . . but no one else knows the truth, so that's the worst of all possible worlds . . .'

Gene grunted.

'They've locked up our friends and they're whipping up this spy nonsense so we've got no way to help our friends, and we put anyone who helps us in danger. Even if we do get into Canada, they'll try to find us. Or the Canadians may hand us over.'

'Sure, but what else can we do? It sounds like you've got a plan.' Gene was looking at her now, trying to read her mood.

'We need some powerful friends to help hide us,' she explained, 'to rein in the FBI and get our friends free. We need to make it so that if *anything* happens to us, the Feds know there'll be trouble.'

Gene frowned. 'Powerful friends? The Democrats? The Teamsters? The Mob?'

'Maybe the answer to lies is the truth. Maybe we should tell a journalist and they can tell the whole *world*.'

He blinked. 'You're kidding.'

'We have Cory, don't we? We have walking, talking proof that we're telling the truth and the government's lying. The press will want to know who's been arrested, on what charges? Surely open courts and a free press is better than this. And . . . and the Moon landings and the new meteors in Siberia? Maybe they're all connected.'

He was actually listening, not shouting her down, so she went on, 'If the government finds us, we'll disappear; most likely, they'll take Cory away, and I don't even want to think what they'll do to our little boy. But if we give someone the story, the government can't make us disappear, can they? Or at least that way we might have a fighting chance . . .'

'And where do we go?'

'Canada. Or hide out in some little town miles away.' She might never see Amber Grove again, and nothing could be as it was, but anywhere the three of them could be safe, that would have to be their home.

'Okay, I see where you're going. But who could we trust? Walker Cronkite?'

'Or Dahlia Diamond.'

Gene grunted like a water buffalo. 'Not that shill. She's a *phoney*.'

She gave Gene a savage look. 'You're a man. You don't understand.'

Gene ignored that and went on, 'I mean, who do you speak to if you call a TV station? Some underling of an underling, right? We'll sound like a crank call. The government hiding a spaceship . . . ? It only works if we trust the person we tell.'

They kicked around a few more ideas: Stan Vogel, who'd written a magisterial piece about the Meteor for the *New York Times*. Seymour Hersh, who broke the national shame, the wicked crimes of the My Lai massacre. Isaac Asimov, a science fiction guy Gene read who was firmly against the war. *Rolling Stone* managed to be anti-establishment without being crackpot. But how could they know what they were *really* like, how they would react?

It was always hard to trust people you hadn't met.

'We need someone who won't freak out,' Gene said.

They seemed to be moving from *whether* to *how* and Molly wanted to get warm.

Gene hesitated, then, 'Listen, don't shoot me down in flames. Carol Longman.'

Molly blinked. 'That woman who cornered you while I was up at the farm? Gene, the way you talked about her, she sounded like a terrier with a bone . . .'

'And that's what we need, isn't it? She'd walk over her grand-mother for a story, but she respected me too: she walked away, didn't she? And *Witness* is read all over the world. They hid that Bolivian diplomat and got him out of the country for the CIA piece. They can't be written off as some hippie-drugs-and-UFO rag. The rest will follow their lead; I'm sure of it.'

'They seem tight with the government – suppose they don't publish? Or hand us over?'

'Yes, but don't forget, Miss Longman is pushy and ambi-tious and she's frustrated as hell that her editor reined her in.

If *Witness* wouldn't run it, I think she has the guts to take it to someone else. So: we give *Witness* a deal, the story of the century and they hide us, and their lawyers get our friends out of jail.' He stroked his chin, the skin sore where his beard had been.

There was a long, long pause.

'It's a risk,' Molly admitted. But she'd written Carol Longman's phone numbers in her notebook. Somewhere, somehow, she'd thought they might need them.

Gene said, 'Everyone needs to know about Cory's people. I've always thought that. It's painful to know what's the right thing . . .'

'Were you sure, when you first saw him? Sometimes we just have to make a call and live with it.'

Another long pause. Maybe he was thinking of all their endless discussions about what they might do, where they might go.

A little purple face was looking at them through the window. Molly needed to get in the car; she was losing feeling in her feet.

Gene dialled the number for *Witness* and Molly, pressing her head to the phone as well, heard the receptionist say, 'I'm sorry, Miss Longman is not available. No, I don't know when she'll be back. There may be someone taking messages in Features.'

Features 'didn't expect Miss Longman to phone in until after Christmas'.

Gene dialled her home but got nothing. He hung up.

There was a third number in Molly's notebook, the one she'd hand-written on the back of her card: *CL hideout*. Yet again, the phone rang and rang, then rang some more, and Gene was reaching out a finger to end the call when, finally, a woman's voice said, 'Hiya. Who is this?' It was a friendly voice, a Western accent.

Gene, taken aback, asked, 'Is Carol Longman there?'

'In the bathroom,' the woman said. 'Can I take a message?'

'Okay,' said Gene. 'Um . . . could this phone be tapped?'

The woman didn't sound at all taken aback. 'It's a friend's house and the phone is in someone else's name. It's safe.'

'Look, it's Gene Myers, from Amber Grove.' He stumbled over his words. 'Carol said if ever we wanted to talk . . . Well, we do, but it has to be *now*.'

'Right, hang on, I'll get her. Don't go.'

Even Molly could hear the hog-hollering call – 'Carol! Gene Myers! Amber Grove!' Then there was something they didn't catch.

*Maybe this is a plot. Maybe they're working with the FBI . . .*

The woman said, 'She's coming. Give me your number, in case you're cut off.'

'It's okay,' said Gene, fingering a pocket-full of coins.

After a couple of minutes, they heard, 'How nice to hear from you, Mr Myers.'

'You told me you knew the army was feeding you a line about the lake and everything. Well, we know exactly what the army's hiding, what went on at the hospital, and we can prove it. But we need to know we can trust you.'

'I hear the FBI have rounded up a couple dozen people, maybe more, around Amber Grove, claiming some communist spy scandal, and there are apparently two spies at least on the run. Can you help me with that too?'

'The spy thing's not true,' Gene said. 'They've arrested our family and friends, people who've helped us. They're not spies, and we need to help them.'

'Right.' She went silent.

Molly reached for the phone, but Gene wasn't giving it up. 'We'll tell you the whole story, and it's a big one,' he promised. 'We'll give you everything you need. In return, you help get our friends out. And protect our family.'

'So what's the story?'

'We need to talk protection – hiding us, maybe for a long time.'

'Mr Myers, snow is forecast, there's a roaring fire here and my hair's dripping wet. Of course I'm fascinated, even two days before Christmas, and I'm sure we can help. I'd just love to know what we're talking about.'

'Are you going to help?'

'If we're coming up against the FBI and the army, I need to know it's worth my time.'

'This . . . well, yes, it's worth your time. It's pretty much the biggest story ever.' Gene was fumbling his words again.

Molly took the phone. 'This is Molly Myers. Miss Longman, this story is bigger than Pearl Harbor. You can take the story and get a hat full of Pulitzers, or you can be the guy who turned down the Beatles. It's your choice, but our next call is Stan Vogel at the *New York Times*.'

'Hello, Mrs Myers. He's a good guy, Stan, but he doesn't work much this time of year. And if you call him, he'll need more than big claims.'

'Let's meet and we'll show you the evidence.'

'Uh-huh.'

'And if you don't agree it's the biggest story of your career, we'll let you call the FBI. Get the scoop on our arrest.'

A brief pause, then she said, 'Neither of you strike me as lunatic, so okay, let's meet. Where are you?'

'Where are *you*?' Molly replied.

'A log cabin in the woods. The nearest town is Wynneville. I could be there by three p.m.'

They'd passed through Wynneville; a place like Amber Grove, charming, with wide streets and a bridge over a river. It was only an hour away, if they put their foot down, and if the snow held off. Molly recalled seeing soldiers on the streets, so there must be an army base nearby, and there would be police too . . . but was there any other choice?

'We could make three o'clock,' she said firmly.

'Let's meet at the Arcade, it's in the square. Very historic, you can't miss it.' She sounded amused. 'Storm, my photographer, asks if she'll get a Pulitzer too?'

'The photographs will be astonishing. Twenty dollars says she wins a prize. If we're delayed?'

'Call Hoffman's Guesthouse in Wynneville. Hoffman is a friend.'

When Molly hung up, she and Gene stared at each other in silence, wondering if this was the right thing.

'Head south,' Molly said at last. *Away from the border.*

Molly didn't think her nerves could get tighter, but as they drove into Wynneville she realised she'd been mistaken. In another life, this was the sort of place you might mooch around for a happy hour or two. The streets were lively with Christmas shoppers, interspersed with a scattering of men in khaki uniforms. She drove briskly over the bridge and headed towards the Square, where to her alarm, an army band was playing festive tunes for a Santa shaking a collecting tin. So many eyes. *How well could she spot a trap?* she wondered. *How quickly could one be organised? We need a different car.*

'I thought we should drive by and see what we can see, Moo-moo,' said Gene.

'Okay, but if Miss Longman did call the FBI, they'll have people all over. So do we all walk out, or just one of us? It feels wrong meeting somewhere she knows and we don't.' Her guts grumbled. *Too many people.*

'Maybe see if we can get to the Arcade from behind?'

'Worth a try.'

'When meet nice lady?' said Cory. 'When *we* meet nice lady, will *we* have supper then or later?' The bundle of blankets with just two eyes visible looked out of the window. 'Too many people, not safe hide.'

'We know, sweetie-pie.' She tried not to imagine them attacked in the streets. Cory might raise some demonic vision, a sea-monster rampaging across the snow, sending the children in their woolly hats and scarves running screaming. The story that would spread, of her child, the Other, the Monster, was almost too much to bear.

In the fading light she passed two men trying to get a piano into the back of a truck. Three women looking in a store window. A little boy holding a sled like Cory's. A man in a dog-collar unlocking the church door.

'There – that's them! They're early too,' Gene said. 'Cory, stay hidden.'

Molly drove past the two women walking on the sidewalk ahead of them. Carol Longman wore an elegant winter coat and a sweeping hat, a city hat, not a town hat. Beside her was a broad-shouldered woman dressed for the country, a camera bag slung over her shoulder. They were deep in conversation.

Gene had been staring all around. 'I can't see anyone official,' he reported. 'Let's do it.'

Molly parked, but left the engine running, just in case. She opened the door and got out. The winter air was sharp after the stuffiness of the car.

'Miss Longman?' she called. 'We're early.' *Keep it normal*, she told herself. *This is only the chance encounter of an old friend . . .*

The journalist's face showed surprise – but only for a moment. 'We spoke,' she said.

*No name, good.* 'Thanks for coming,' said Molly. 'We'll drive just you to what you need to see.'

'I'm Storm,' said the tall woman with the Western accent. She smiled, but she wasn't taking any nonsense. 'Photographer, driver, bodyguard, and she'll not be getting in your car alone.'

*Should she talk to them here? Gene could be ready to drive away. Or was that too risky?*

'I'm keeping watch,' Gene said. There weren't any FBI or soldiers in sight. There was a woman with a shopping bag pulling along that boy with the sled. Across the street, a bearded man wearing a naval sort of coat and cap was smoking in a doorway. It was too public.

Carol took some more steps towards Molly, her gloved

hands out to show they were empty. Storm followed unhappily behind.

'Good faith,' Carol said, with a practised smile. 'Here I am.'

Molly held up her own hands. 'My son: he's a secret. The government's after him. That's why we need you.'

'Well, no one told me you had a child,' the journalist said, looking a little surprised. 'We can try to protect your family, but I need to know what's going on. If you're tied up in this spy thing, the FBI cuts deals all the time. We have good lawyers who can help.'

'And you promised me my Pulitzer,' Storm said. 'We'll protect your family, Scout's Honour, if we get the story.' There was a pause. Then, 'Holy cow!'

Carol brought her hand up to her mouth. 'Lord! What on God's good Earth is that?'

Molly looked to see Cory, muffled in blankets, showing them his face through the window. Surely Cory in the flesh was all the proof anyone needed.

Molly said, 'So, I tell you who he is, where he comes from, what the government's hiding and why they're chasing us. You protect us, help get our friends out. Oh, and we get copy-approval. Or we call the *New York Times* instead.'

'This's just some sort of parlour trick,' Carol said.

Molly's gaze darted to the smoking man and the boy with the sled, who were watching them. Where they stood, surely neither could see Cory.

'Come closer.' But as Carol stepped next to the car, Molly, her heart pounding, realised she had misplayed this; the journalists could quite easily grab her.

But all Carol did was open the rear door, very slowly, and squat down to look under the blanket. 'Hello,' she said, looking intently into Cory's face.

Molly knew Cory could read people, not perfectly, but he had not hidden . . .

'*I am* Cory Myers and *I am* pleased-to-meet-you.' He adjusted his scarf up over his mouth.

Now Storm was squatting down too. She reached out a hand and Cory shook it. He wasn't wearing gloves. Would anyone notice his hands?

Carol stood back up and her eyes were shining. 'Oh, Mrs Myers, I think we have a deal. We so have a deal! Follow us and we'll get out of here. The place is swarming with soldiers.'

The boy with the sled was being dragged past the car, protesting. From that angle, what could he have seen? Nothing, surely.

As they headed north, following the Jeep, the clouds thickened and the first new flakes of snow began to fall. Storm took them on a brief stretch of highway, then onto the back roads.

Molly and Gene had discussed ditching their own car, but even though they'd bet everything on the journalists, to lose their own means of escape felt suicidal.

Molly played word quizzes with Cory while Gene drove: how many animals could he think of with at least six letters in their names, and spelling, and mental arithmetic, until he dozed against her.

Soon the trail closed in, woods rising up on either side. The car skidded occasionally, and Gene swore, gunned the engine and inched forward, trying to feel his way across the icy surface. She wondered if they would need a tow on the steepening track.

Up ahead, Storm's Jeep had stopped and was now reversing carefully back down the road.

'Shall we get out? Less weight.'

'I'm doing my best,' Gene muttered, and hit the dashboard. 'Piece of junk.'

The car made it, although she smelled burning, like the time her father had let the oil run dry. Each little loss of control went straight to Molly's stomach. She'd lost where they were on the map half an hour ago.

Up among the pines, the solitude was so thick it felt solid. They counted off entrances to closed-up holiday places; there were plenty up here.

Another turning later, they saw a single light, shining in the half-light: they'd reached the lake shore. Tall trees stood like frozen giants, but there was clear ground to the water. The light glowed outside a single-storey wooden cabin with a porch facing the lake. The Jeep was already turning in to park up, ploughing a deep trail in the snow, and Gene drew the old Lincoln alongside. Storm jumped out and strode towards the cabin, an electric torch stabbing light ahead of her.

How remote it felt. Molly badly wanted to get inside and forget that tense, threatening drive, where every car could have been an enemy, chasing them.

To the right, perhaps a hundred yards away, was a much bigger cabin, perched on a little rise.

Carol appeared at their car window. 'Let's get inside before you freeze. Storm will get the fires going in the Hauser place

– we keep the heating going for them when the place is empty, because otherwise, you know, the pipes freeze and cause no end of trouble.'

Bundling up their few precious possessions, the Myers followed Carol into the cabin. Warmth and light embraced them; Molly could smell the little Christmas tree adorned in baubles and coloured lights. A typewriter and neat stacks of paper took up half a table. Framed photos, real works of art, filled the walls: landscapes, portraits and studies of dogs and horses. One was of Carol, very grand in a green ballgown and pearls, but laughing, looking so relaxed and alive.

Carol was trying to watch Cory without staring. She shifted the paper, murmuring, 'My book, eventually. Are you hungry? We're having Storm's famous beef stew later. Do you want hot chocolate?'

Gene looked wistful.

Molly told her, 'Cory doesn't eat meat – just fish, I'm afraid.'

'Oh, we have tins,' she said cheerfully. 'We'll manage.'

Molly thought of the joy of good home cooking, how far they'd come – and how much longer the road ahead might be.

'Cory help. Where this? Christmas Eve tomorrow! Where-where put stockings . . . where we put stockings?' His tentacles danced.

Molly gave him a hug. 'It will have to be promise-presents, sweetie-pie.'

The chocolate was thick and full of flavour, touched with spices. Molly felt its warmth settle her stomach. Her nerves were playing havoc with her digestion. The cookies were fruit and oats and she ate two, suddenly hungry.

Storm came back and, shedding outdoor clothes, asked Cory, 'Shall I show you my camera?' In no time they were on one couch, chatting away. Molly ignored a touch of irrational envy; business had to come first, but Molly was itching to talk cameras with Storm herself.

Carol sat and got out her notebook. 'Okay, start at the beginning,' she said.

'Molly will tell it until I came on the scene,' said Gene, rubbing his eyes.

There'd be no mention of nightmare powers or death in space, no coming into dreams, nothing that made Cory threatening. They'd ask Carol not to put his hiding in the story.

'Take photo now-now-now,' Cory demanded. 'Cory the-most photo-genic.'

Storm looked at Molly and said, 'When your folks are happy, then I can start on the photos, okay?'

Carol's gentle, precise questions steered them through the core of the story as outside, the dark deepened. The story swung to and fro between Molly and Gene, while Storm told Cory about riding horses, working on a dude ranch, sailing out to look at whales in the Bering Sea . . . and he chatted back cheerily, the happiest he'd been since they'd fled the house.

At last Carol said, 'I need to track down my editor, which will be fun this time of year. His deputy is far too yellow to take on the Administration. But trust me: our intrepid girl reporter has won far harder battles.'

Molly nodded, and she went on, 'Then the real work starts. Once we've eaten, I'll need to go through your story and work out what we can prove. I think this might fill half the magazine.

And of course, Storm will need to work her magic with the photographs. We don't have anything without them.'

'She's extremely talented,' Molly said, glancing around the room.

'She is. We're lucky to have her. Anyway, my first thoughts are, we hit them with Cory's existence – no mention of Two Mile Lake. The government know we know, so it gives them an incentive to play ball, doesn't it?'

'Mmmm,' Molly said, non-committal. She felt so drained, and she had just realised that of all things, she did not want the world to see her like this, with badly reddened hair. This plan had to work, to keep them safe and set free the people they loved, the friends and family who had paid the price of protecting them. Right now, she wanted the dark woods to hide her and her family for ever.

CHAPTER 33

# Christmas Eve at Fort Fife

Dr Pfeiffer was so tired his mind could not focus. The long conference room was thick with stale cigarette smoke which was hurting his eyes. They should let some of the icy wind in, just so he could breathe.

The walls were covered in maps: the whole country, the state, its borders, all dotted with black and red and white pins, for different types of sightings.

There was always someone on the phone or poring over Teletext, always one or other of the disgusting tobacco-addicts lighting up.

The Myers had been on the highway north to Canada, then they did a U-turn. Red pin: no doubt about that sighting. Then two sightings in some one-horse town called Windville, Wynneville, something. Then they just disappeared into thin air.

He got up to study the maps, find a pattern; that's how he'd realised that if the Myers had a second car parked away from the house, Elliott Street would be the best place to hide it.

'Sandusky, Ohio,' said the saturnine FBI man, tapping in a white pin. 'We'll check it out, but I think it's noise, not signal.'

What were the Myers doing? Fleeing like animals harried by dogs, zigzagging away from the chase with no plan but survival? Or was this some carefully considered scheme, once they'd found that John and Eva Myers had been arrested? He worried about some neutral nation taking them by ship to Cuba, or by plane to Moscow. Or perhaps they were just holing up for a few weeks with a sympathetic friend, or breaking into a holiday cabin, or staying in a motel.

There was a vast machine hunting them across the northeast: State Troopers covering their patches, using their local knowledge, FBI agents brought off leave, local cops trawling the streets of the many towns along the Eastern Seaboard . . . how much earth would they have to turn over before they found the gold?

And of course, the overwhelming majority of those looking knew nothing about Cory or the Ship, because that just raised the risk of them being discussed openly and word getting out. He didn't know whether he was more anxious about the press or the Russians getting the truth first.

The map told him *nothing*. How long could the government of a free country hold travellers at the borders? Could the Myers use Cory's extraordinary power to just walk into Canada? He understood some major work was underway with the Canadian government, a mixture of threats and bold promises to their genial neighbour and ally, but Canada was an independent country and proud of it. And of course, they wanted to know what the fuss was about.

His hand was still shaking; he had never been closer to death. *On the road, that thing in the car . . . a ravening predator at his throat . . .* He had always scorned those who peddled the idea of psychic powers, but here was absolute solid proof.

He had failed to capture them, and then to find them, but maybe someone else would. Keeping the Myers from the agents of the Soviet Union was vital, but he had no doubt his enemies in the US Administration were just as keen to keep the Myers from him.

'I'm going to the detention centre,' Pfeiffer said.

The FBI man looked at him. 'You might feel fresher after a break.'

'These people know what the Myers are up to.'

'We do know how to interrogate,' the FBI man said mildly. 'It's our job.'

'Of course, of course.' *Try not to make enemies of people you need.*

The night air revived him a little. The FBI were keeping up the pressure, but he suspected they would get little useful from the Hardesty women or Forster, the half-blind old veteran. He wasn't sure Molly's relatives being held in Indiana and Florida knew much either.

Diane Alexander, though – she was deep in the thick of it, and her little girl too; they had found frequent mentions of Cory in the child's diary. Pfeiffer grabbed one of the army nurses as he went in to act as chaperone.

The recreation room was bleak, but in the hour or so since he was last there, someone had brought in a little fir tree and decorated it.

'What's the meaning of that?' he asked a soldier.

'For the children,' the soldier said, keeping his face wooden.

A great knot of emotion roiled in Pfeiffer's stomach. 'These children have vital information. Don't forget that.'

The Alexanders' room had a locked door, but it wasn't quite a cell. The nurse pulled a chair over to the door and sat, watching Mrs Alexander, on the bed, brushing her daughter's stiff hair.

She fixed Pfeiffer with a stare, then launched straight in, her voice reminding him of a sombre cello. 'Son of Belial – servant of Ahab! Wager of war on women and children! What do you want?'

'You know what I want.' Pfeiffer drew up the remaining chair. With the bed and the camp-bed, the room was pretty much filled.

'I hate you,' said the girl. She'd been crying again.

'Where is our lawyer?' Mrs Alexander demanded.

Pfeiffer addressed himself to the child. 'Bonnie, we need to find your friend Cory, and we think you know where he might be. We're not going to hurt him.'

'I'm frightened, Mommy,' Bonnie wailed. 'The man wants to hurt me!'

His guts churned again. She was the same age as his youngest.

'Remember Daniel in the lion's den, darling: "Do not fear the teeth of lions or the flames of the furnace, because the Lord is with us." And the law and the Constitution. Judgement will come, and the wrongdoers will be punished, in this world and the next.'

'Mrs Alexander, if you do not cooperate, Bonnie will be moved to another building – supervised by female staff, of course . . .'

Bonnie clung to her mother, who said, with contempt, 'What kind of a man are you? Herod. Abomination. Bonnie, remember those brothers and sisters valiant for the truth . . .'

Together, the two of them started, '"The Lord is my shepherd, I shall not want . . . He maketh me to lie down in green pastures" . . .'

Pfeiffer had lost all patience with the damned woman. 'Oh, stop that! We've arrested your adult children. Hubert Jr has violated his parole. He's going to prison. Maddie's boyfriend deals marijuana; she is being charged alongside him. Cooperate, and you will be amazed what we can do. And then there's your sister . . .' He was almost certain that Mrs Alexander's sister and her children knew nothing either. The Myers had kept their secret tight.

He looked from the little girl to her mother and back and met two identical looks of silent hatred. *She quotes the Bible because she sees it makes you uncomfortable. She brings up race for the same reason. The little girl can cry at will.* He steeled himself to give the order, his stomach protesting at the scene to come. 'Separate them until further notice.'

*Now to deliver the same message to Mrs Henderson.*

As he left the room, Dr Tyler jogged up and announced, panting, 'Dr Pfeiffer . . . There you are! There's been a Russian attempt on the Ship – two of their agents are dead and one's in custody.'

'*What?* How?' They had excellent security behind the fence; it had been strengthened and reinforced since the Russian meteors.

'We don't know. They had diving equipment – it looks like

the Ship killed them. We did catch their radio operator before he could kill himself.'

'This is a disaster.' So here was the unknown question: were the Myers in bed with their country's enemies, or in desperation, at least willing to deal with them? Maybe the Russians knew about Cory too? Or were the Myers mere innocents, without the cunning to keep out of the Russians' grasp? At least any breach in security at Two Mile Lake was not his fault, a point he would need to make at once.

And the Ship spoke Russian. This was very bad.

## CHAPTER 34

# *Christmas Eve at the cabin*

The three of them snuggled together in the Hausers' double bed; Cory hadn't stayed long alone in his little camp-bed. Molly, lying on top of the covers, was cold, even though the fire still glowed and she was wearing socks. Gene and Cory looked so peaceful sleeping. She left them to it.

The cabin was not to her taste. It was littered with bright orange and green rugs, crude folk pottery and odd, naïve paintings, and shelves of battered books. The kitchen was decked out like a ship's galley, ridiculous but endearing. She was surprised to find snowshoes and an old sled: somewhere this remote wouldn't be her choice for a winter holiday. The main room reached to the roof, with bedrooms coming off the inner balcony. Vast shuttered windows opened onto a snow-piled porch and a stunning view of the lake. To heat the place in winter must cost a fortune.

She smiled at the image of Cory finding the second staircase to the upper storey and pounding around the cabin three times, just for the fun of it.

She went out to clear her head and to see the place in the light. It was Christmas Eve and the world was made new with the snow, every path and track smoothed out, ice sparkling from the gables and the sky faint with haze. White-shrouded evergreens surrounded the cabin on three sides, while to the north, the land sloped to the water. The lake was so still, she wondered if it was frozen. On the other side of the lake were more pines. There was no sign of human life.

Carol's smaller cabin was a short walk away.

Molly had seen fierce winters, but she'd never seen anything so silent, so beautiful, so gripped by winter.

*Now*, she thought, *I must think like a fugitive, like a soldier. How do we get out if we need to?* The map showed trails running along the shore and snaking down into the woods. From now on, she wouldn't stay anywhere without thinking of back doors and exits by car or foot. She vowed she'd never again be trapped in a dead end. There were people to be worried about, dreadful futures to imagine. She could let herself be swallowed up, or she could deal with it. She walked down to the lake, every breath hurting, but she felt alive.

With a little shock, Molly realised she hadn't taken Gene skating in years. They'd loved it once, after that first date under a spectacular Moon, but when the shadow fell across her life, her marriage, they'd given up so many things. *Kids give you excuses to go back to things you'd loved*, she thought. She should take her menfolk skating.

From the lake, looking back at Carol's place, she could see Storm was out with a shovel, digging out the path, sending snow flying everywhere.

After an hour's walk, Molly felt renewed. She'd seen other cabins and a boathouse, but there were no signs of occupation; the only smoking chimneys belonged to them.

It was all bustle when Molly walked into Carol's cabin, but she couldn't miss the tension in the air. Carol and Storm were cooking pancakes; no, they said, they didn't need a hand. 'We work around each other's elbows,' Carol said, with a brief, forced smile.

'Well, mostly.' Storm looked grim.

Cory sat at the table in the large room, head down over a large sketchbook but not drawing.

Gene sat close, looking tired. He kissed her and mouthed, '*They had a row.*'

Well, she'd guessed that. 'About us?' she mouthed back.

He shrugged, and stroked Cory's ear.

'Storm's going to take you out to do some photographs with us,' he said, but still Cory didn't look up. A new place, all that fresh snow, different woods to explore and yet he was silent.

'Come on, Super-Cory, what's the matter?'

Cory gave a little moan, the *hoo-hoo* that was a sob. 'Cory's the M-Monster. Cory h-horr-i-ble. Frankenstein on TV: all those people hate m-me. Everyone h-hate m-me every-everywhere.'

Molly put an arm around him. 'No, of course they don't!' She tried to pour reassurance into him. 'People who know you love you, don't they? Every kid you've ever met loves you. And just think of all the grown-ups . . .'

'Everyone ch-chase me for *ever*,' said Cory, 'with guns, *hoo-hoo*, like was a sea-demon. And fires and helicopters and silly little human space rockets . . . No one like m-monsters no one.' He dropped his voice to a whisper. 'And Cory must d-do the bad thing, over and over.'

Molly really didn't want Carol nosing into 'the bad thing'.

'Listen, sweetie-pie, Carol and Storm are going to sort everything for us. And we'll see all our friends again and everything will be fine.'

'Go to Canada another way. Or Ven-ez-wela: tallest waterfall in world, Mom-Mom. Or Scotland for so-grand castles. Bring Chuck and Bonnie.'

'We'll take you on a tour when you're famous,' Carol said, bringing in the first stack of pancakes. A long walk and home cooking and yet still Molly wasn't hungry. In fact, the smell of frying was making her distinctly queasy. She blamed that terrible diner breakfast.

Cory poured maple syrup over his pancakes and dropped his head to smell them.

Carol was fascinated; watching him eat was like a performance.

'What's the plan for today?' Gene asked.

'I need to track down my editor and check in with the little band of us who don't believe the government's lies about Two Mile Lake. I'll find out what people are hearing about arrests and such and see if Gene's parents really are in hospital. Then we need to do some hard thinking on how we shape this story.' She called into the kitchen, 'Storm, we'll need photos indoors and out – the Hausers won't mind if we use their kids' toys and stuff.'

Gene speared a pancake. 'Once this is out, there's no going

back, is there? It's not only the President, there'll be two hundred million people looking for Cory. We'll never be private again.'

Carol leaped in. 'Most people will be on his side. The government won't have any choice. And *Witness* can hide him.'

'Every crank, every crook, every Russian spy could come looking for him,' Gene said. 'Will anyone want us as neighbours?'

Molly pulled a face: *Not in front of Cory!*

Storm came in with more pancakes and sat. She didn't look at Carol. 'Learned how to make these working at the dude ranch,' she told Cory, 'after I broke my collarbone falling off a palomino. I learned to cook one-handed.'

'A good rule with Storm,' Carol said brightly, 'the crazier the story, the more likely it is to be true.'

'Storm good name,' said Cory. 'Home world all names for boys or girls or inters. And change if don't like.'

Carol had said last night, '*Witness* readers aren't stupid but some are easily spooked. I don't think we'll mention inters for now.'

'Well, I'll let you into a secret,' Storm said, playing serious. 'I was christened Jeanette Elizabeth Alexandra. There's a great picture of me aged seven in braids and ribbons.'

Gene rubbed Cory's head and Molly asked, 'Do you want us to use your old name?'

'Earth name for Earth,' said Cory, through a huge mouthful of pancake.

'So, I might take Cory out to play snowballs with his parents,' said Storm. 'Wouldn't that make a great photo? And there's the world's best sled-run a little way along.'

Cory's ears twitched. 'Sled yes-yes-please.'

'No one can feel sad in a snowball picture,' Molly said.

Carol touched Storm's hand, just for a moment. 'I'm sorry,' she said. 'You're right.'

'That's okay. Two Pulitzers it is.'

Molly hated being photographed, and Gene hated it unless it was Molly or his mother behind the camera, but Storm was all jokes and games, getting Gene to smile and Molly not to pull faces. And Molly was fascinated, seeing Storm at work, even though she'd lost all feeling in her toes and fingers.

At last she gave in. 'I have to go in,' she said, leaving Cory, Storm and Gene out there.

The cabin felt like an oven. She stripped off her damp coat, hat and gloves and put on more coffee. Carol, talking on the phone, sounded like she was dodging a flood of questions.

When she hung up, she sighed. 'Isn't it funny? If I call on Christmas Eve to chat about the Meteor, they think I have something. An old friend of mine at Associated Press tried to pump me. I'll bet my hat they're close to running something challenging the arrests. Everyone's very disturbed by the Russian nuclear tests, their sabre-rattling, of course. It won't be front-page news, not against that, but it'll be a page lead.'

Molly couldn't bear to listen to the news. The drums were sounding loud for war, what with the Soviet bomb tests, and the Russians were claiming they'd lost a nuclear submarine, a hundred dead to American aggression – but everyone knew their submarines were always sinking. The President had called

for the nation to stand firm in this time of trial while the protesters marched in the cold against him.

'You have no idea what the first Meteor was?' Carol asked.
'Why Cory's mother came in with it?'

'No,' Molly said.

'The Russian meteors came down in the middle of nowhere.'
She produced a sketched map. 'Look, they splashed down
here: the Chukotka Autonomous Okrug, a cold, remote place.
There's nothing there but iron and uranium mines, some labour
camps. The nearest settlement is a tiny port called Pevek. The
harbour's frozen half the year.'

Molly had nothing to say.

'They're saying the nukes were ground-bursts over or near
Pevek. The Soviets haven't said a word, of course; they haven't
even admitted the meteors to their own people. And I'm
hearing the Russian sub went down here.' Her finger tapped
the map, north of the meteor splashdown.

Molly felt something nameless turn in her stomach.

The phone rang and Carol answered it. 'Hi, Mark. Uh-huh,
uh-huh.'

Molly couldn't hear the other speaker.

'You going to call them and ask them? . . . I would . . . No, I
would . . . Now, Mark, don't try that. I just think, ask if the two
things are linked and see what they say. Better still, say you've
got a source who says they're linked . . . Maybe they do go
completely bats and threaten you – they call your editor, that's
always a sign you're on the right track! I'm just guessing . . .
Mark, Mark! I'm not one of your starry-eyed boy reporters.
We both know how it is. It's just an interesting question to ask.'

Storm, Gene and Cory came in, beating snow from their clothes.

'I'll . . . yeah, I'll do that. Storm, Mark says hi.'

'Hi, Mark,' called Storm.

Carol hung up and breathed out. 'Well, the *New York Times* found your parents *were* in Caffrey General Hospital, brought in by the FBI, then they disappeared. So the good news is they were alive a day ago, Eva was getting good care and apparently the doctor tore six strips off the Feds when they moved her. The paper's getting ready to send a rocket up the FBI's tailpipe about the arrests; apparently they're in a race with Associated Press. And I've *finally* tracked down my editor.'

Gene held Molly's hand.

'So, this is pretty much your last chance to back out.' Carol looked nervous, as if she was frightened they might. 'If you say no, I have a friend who will get you over the border. But . . . well, it's your decision.'

'It's good of you to help us,' Molly said. 'Gene?'

'We'll end up on the run, for a very long time, if not for ever. No, let's do it. *Witness* can hide us and we'll answer any questions the government has by letter.'

Carol dialled. 'Can I leave an urgent message for Mr Turner, room 217: tell him it's Carol Longman, it's a Pulitzer, and he needs to call me as soon as he can on this number.' She rattled it off, then, 'No, Pulitzer: P-u-l-i-t-z-e-r. He'll know what that means.'

She put the phone down and said, 'Now we wait.'

Molly put her arm around Gene, who returned the hug and kissed her ear.

★

That night, in the Hausers' cabin. Gene, sat in the kitchen by the big stove, working his way through a mug of hot milk. Molly had gone to bed at last; he was worried about her, the stress she'd been under. He wished the world would just go away and leave them alone for a month.

He was drawing staves into a notebook he'd found. Tunes and themes were marching around his head but he still felt the Meteor Chorale was too big for one mind to hold. He needed to find something simpler. The tune he was working on, a song, he thought, was almost right, but he had no words yet.

Cory slipped into the room, bundled in a quilt and wearing pink bunny slippers. 'Want to look at stars.' When Cory looked at the sky, it wasn't constellations he was searching for.

'It's pretty cold out, Cory, but we could open the shutters and turn the lights out.'

They sat and looked up at the sky, which was mostly cloud.

'Cory-people come?'

Gene hugged him. 'Your first mom said they would, so maybe they're already looking, but they're just not quite sure where you are yet. They could be here any minute.' He stroked Cory's ear, wondering, *How would that work?* He imagined the spaceship landing on the White House South Lawn and the alien leaders talking to the lying con-man in the Oval Office.

'Time for message to get home and get enormous star-ship ready and come back,' Cory said, firmly. 'Should come months ago.'

'Who knows, Cory? Remember what Mom always says: one day at a time.'

'Earth is beautiful. And humans quite smart but it *is* big-hurting-mess.'

Gene couldn't disagree.

They sat silently, looking at the odd star and thinking their own thoughts. How precious these hugs were, how wonderful to be a father. How terrifying that it all might end.

'How Dad song going?'

'Don't know yet.'

'Your songs good-good.' Cory gave an epic sigh, a sound he'd learned from Molly. 'Cory like Earth, but messed-up. All having-to-hide and the Bad Men and eating murdered things and wars. Good Christmas. Sleep now. Love you Dad-Dad.' Cory kissed Gene and left.

*A father's work: to reassure your son, to give him quiet confidence, to help him figure things himself so that he could grow. To teach character by example, as Dad had done. To protect him, as Roy tried to do with Chuck, never knowing if you were doing the right thing. Being a father was even bigger than I'd thought, and yet, in a way, it's simpler.*

He didn't know how anyone could be a father and not find their child and his needs at the beating heart of their life.

Gene didn't pray, he didn't have anything to pray to, but he did *hope*. He hoped the purples would come, that somehow humans and Cory's people would figure everything out. Cory's people could teach humans to end war and tyranny and starvation. And he hoped the purples wouldn't take his son back to wherever they came from.

When you fall in love with your child, you realise you can't hold them for ever, tiny in your arms. But sitting there looking at the night sky, Gene asked the unhearing universe, *Don't tear out my heart by making that loss too soon.*

A line sprang into his head: *The little purple boy who came in peace.*

The tune had worked itself out over weeks of humming, plucked notes, bitten nails and crossings-out. And in an instant, words began their march through Gene's mind, making his hopes and fears soar. He could use the tune to marshal them, distilling into song what he struggled to say.

There was no time to waste on titles, so he took up his pencil and wrote *A Song for Cory*, then struck it through and printed *Our Child of the Stars*. Something like that.

The song came like a stone falling from the sky.

## CHAPTER 35

# Cory's second Christmas Day

Cory wakes and it is Christmas Day. Mom and Dad snore beside him and he knows he should go back to his own bed, but it will be more-more cold and less friendly. Christmas Day good-will-to-all-people, he knows there will be not-so-many presents, but still, there are a few parcels under the tree because he'd done peeking. Oh, the hole inside aches, he misses his human friends and worries about them so-so-much and Grandma Eva is sick and he wants to see her and Grandpa John and sing them the song for the elders who love the children so much. He hums a little of it and that cheers him up a little.

Maybe the lake has frozen, and he can walk on the ice. Dad showed him pictures of lakes frozen so solid a car could drive on it, very-fine, yes. Or go riding in a sleigh pulled by reindeers and jingling with bells.

Santa might have come and filled the stocking on his bed with good things . . . He wriggles his toes. *Five more minutes warm-warm with Mom-and-Dad.*

An hour later, they stomp through the snow to friends Carol and Storm, and then hugging and all hurry into the warmth of their dwelling and he needs to show them his treasure trove. There is a pottery owl, from Mexico, Mom says, and he makes the owl noises and wants to go to Mexico way-way-South. There is a whistle made of wood that sounds a bit like proper language and he shows them how he can imitate it. There is whole tin of *Sailor's Knot Finest Tuna* like Mom buys – and the best of all is a book of photos, so magnificent, all sceneries of America-United-States: forests and deserts and farms and cities. And most of the chocolate; Cory can only eat two pieces a day because too much make him runny-poo.

'So Santa found you,' Storm says, and yes-yes, most exciting. He knows Santa is just grown-ups acting really.

Carol announces, 'Well, in a break from tradition, it's pancakes!' and Cory wonders what a-break-from-tradition is.

'So,' she says, and Cory listens carefully, 'my editor finally rang back, at eight this morning, in a monumental temper. I told him, I know exactly what's going on in Amber Grove, but the *New York Times* and AP are closing in and Reuters won't be far behind if I know them. It's a big government cover-up, which we pretty much guessed, but we have way, way more than the opposition does' – she grins at Cory – 'and you need to come and see the hard, physical proof.'

Must learn *monumental* and *AyPee* and *Reuters*.

Carol rubs her hands. 'Well, I hooked him! He'll be here first thing tomorrow, which gives Storm the chance to stink the place out developing the photos.'

After breakfast, Carol takes them down to the lake, which is all frozen to grey. Cory, looking hard, thinks he sees strange faces in its cloudiness. There's nothing like this on his home planet.

'Wow! It's really eerie,' Dad says.

Cory wants to feel solid water. He puts out a boot – and at once, Carol grabs him and pulls him back.

'Ice is really treacherous, Cory, understand?' He feels stress-and-sadness. 'When I was eight, on a day just like this, my cousin fell through the ice and nearly drowned. Cory, you're absolutely forbidden to go on the ice unless Storm and I say it's safe.'

'Cory great swimmer,' Cory says, feeling his face bristle, 'best ever. Better than human-swimmer.'

'Water this cold, you can stop breathing,' says Carol, her face and her feelings so determined. 'Your arms and legs freeze and no matter how good you are, you stop being able to swim. That's how my cousin almost died.'

'Cory, I want a real big promise,' Mom says. 'I mean it.'

He nods hard. 'Big promise. But Mom, when-when frozen enough to walk on?'

'Who knows? We'll need to test it.'

They are walking back to the cabin when Cory hears a noise, high up and to the west. He hides at once and lopes off behind the cabin, Dad following, kicking snow, covering tracks, clever-clever.

'It's a plane,' Carol says, staring upwards. 'It's probably the Park Service – nothing unusual.'

Cory tugs up his scarf and pokes his head around the corner. Dad is standing with his back to Cory, as if admiring the view, being a shield. Cory can't hide from something that far away, but what is there to see? Coat-and-hat-and-scarf.

He can feel the fear and tension bubbling inside all the grown-ups, but Mom says firmly, 'They wouldn't have seen anything strange.'

'It's nothing unusual, the odd plane over the holiday season,' Carol adds.

*Sometimes*, Cory thinks, *being on the run is an adventure and most-exciting. Sometimes it is boring, all the things you cannot do.* But sometimes like now he is scared and sad. He wants Chuck and Bonnie and his grandparents.

Back at the big cabin, Storm takes many more photos. The wrapped presents under the tree are for-show, Mom says, other-children old toys not-for-Cory, but that is okay.

'Cory had presents, not expect any more,' he says, but the grown-ups hand him three envelopes.

'Promise-presents,' Mom says and her eyes are wet so he strokes her hand, then opens the first one, from Storm. She has drawn a picture of a camera, so-much-exciting and he gives her a hug. Carol has cut a suit from a magazine. 'I can't wait to take him to New York and get him one made,' she says. 'You'll look so hip, Cory.' Another great promise-present.

But he wants to know what is in Mom-Dad's envelope. When he tears it open, he finds two drawings. He knows which one is Dad's because Dad draws better than Mom; it is a grey dog with one ear up and one ear down, all curls. And Mom has drawn a black dog with smooth hair, and Cory is in the picture too.

Cory leaps up and grabs his Earth-Mom-Dad in the biggest-ever hug, crying, 'Thank you thank you thank you!'

Mom says, 'It's just one dog, Cory: we'll find a dog who hasn't got a family to look after it, but you will do the looking after it.' She looks at Dad and adds, 'I'm not running around cleaning up its mess.'

Cory is so excited he runs around on all fours barking, while Storm lifts her camera. Then he stops and remembers: this is the second Christmas that his people have not come to rescue him from the Bad Men. The sadness rises.

*Come now, my people, and free all my friends. Come now and make everything right.*

# CHAPTER 36

## *Witness*

'Storm is late,' said Cory.

Molly tightened her arm around him as they sat at the window looking up at the ice on the trees sparkling in the winter sun. 'Just a little,' she agreed, catching movement. There was a strong quiver of fear, as always: would this be the right car, or would she see an army truck? Would this be the moment they must flee again . . . ? *No*, she breathed out in relief, *the Jeep coming up the trail is Storm's*. She craved peace and certainty . . . Would they ever be able to live without fearing the knock on the door or twitching at the sound of a strange car?

In the Jeep's wake came a sleek black car bearing the editor of *Witness* and the company lawyer.

'Cory, tuck yourself away, please, like we discussed.' If Cory was hidden, but nearby, he could read men's feelings – not anything as useful as actual thoughts, but he might be able to pick up dishonesty or malice. Cory obediently disappeared into his blanket nest behind the couch in the big room.

Carol's face looked strained and Molly's worries resurfaced; the journalist always sounded confident, but Molly could see her own doubts in the set of her jaw, the twitch of her fingers.

'Showtime,' Carol said, with a faint smile. 'Leave the talking to me.'

Storm led two men in, stamping snow from their city shoes. The editor, Mr Turner, was tall and reedy and wore horn-rimmed glasses. His lawyer was suave and plump.

Carol took charge and made brisk introductions.

The lawyer looked nervous. 'They're wanted by the FBI,' he said to the air. 'This is a difficult situation. Compromising.'

The Myers sat together on the couch. Carol took a deep breath and placed her hands palm down on her thighs. Her voice was firm and even as she started. 'An alien spaceship crashed in Amber Grove on Meteor Day. Mr and Mrs Myers adopted the sole survivor, a boy they called Cory.'

The lawyer's mouth opened a little.

Carol kept going. 'The government has hidden the existence of the spaceship and of intelligent life from another planet. Instead, they've rounded up everyone who helped the Myers, a grotesque and unconstitutional abuse of power, and they're hunting this innocent couple across the country. If you want their story, the photographs and the proof, you'll need to protect the Myers and hide them, however long it takes and however much it costs. I need *Witness* to make promises in writing. And' – she looked at Gene and Molly – 'you need to swing the company's power behind getting their friends freed. That's very important.'

Molly doubted the editor's eyebrows could go any higher.

'You're crazy, Miss Longman. You got me to the middle of nowhere for *that*? We're done.' He started to get up, but Carol was as steely as Molly had ever seen her.

'Sit down, Mr Turner. I'm going to show you the proof, and then you will agree the deal. It's that, or the Myers go meet Stan Vogel – you know his parents live about an hour from here? – and the *Times* run the story and you become the editor who turned down the biggest scoop in history.'

'This is just hippie nonsense,' the editor protested. 'Everyone knows the Meteor's been attracting kooks and cranks like flies on treacle.'

Carol nodded. Molly tightened her hand on Gene's for reassurance and said far more calmly than she felt, 'Cory, come out.'

Cory rose from his hiding place behind the couch, walked over to the two men and stood for a minute or two, his tentacles tasting the air. Molly guessed that he was reading their reaction.

The lawyer jolted upright.

'Oh my God,' said Turner. '*Oh my God!*'

There was something about Cory in the flesh that instantly and utterly convinced people; they knew at once he wasn't in make-up or a puppet.

'I-am Cory Myers and I-am-pleased-to-meet-you.'

Turner recovered his poise and replied, 'Well, I am pleased to meet you too. But I guess I need to know if you're real.'

Cory frowned. 'Course Cory real! The reeel-deal. Touch me.'

He went right up to Turner, who looked at Molly for permission. Carol had told them Turner had kids of his own. She nodded, and he gently touched Cory's sleek, hairless head, then the stripy ears.

The lawyer shifted in his seat, away from Cory, wearing a painfully forced smile.

Mr Turner reached for the tentacles, but Molly stopped him. 'No, let Cory touch you.'

The tentacles stroked the editor's fingers, learning his smell, then the man started, because Cory's tail had snuck up from behind and was stroking the editor's leg.

'This might be a mutation,' Turner said, still looking a bit stunned.

Carol snorted. 'Don't be an idiot. He's a totally different species. Working tentacles, no hair anywhere . . . There are a hundred differences between him and us apes.'

'Does that colour go all over?' Turner said, and Cory pulled up his shirt, revealing his torso, the same grey-tinged-purple as his face. Gene often tried to mix blueberry and vanilla ice-cream to get the colour, but he'd never quite got it right. A curious dark-wine scar on his side showed where Cory had been wounded during the crash.

The editor reached out a hand and touched the scar, just with the tips of his fingers, then he breathed, 'Extraordinary. Thank you, son, for showing me.'

Without a word to the lawyer, he said, 'We'll do what we must, of course. The people have a right to know.' He drummed his fingers on the table. 'So, what's the story and what pictures do we have? Any chance anyone else might have this?'

'Will you help us?' Gene said.

Turner laughed. 'Oh, believe me, Mr Myers, I'm not letting anyone else get their hands on you. We're a big company with deep pockets. We'll find somewhere perfect to hide you away. Now, the story . . .'

Twenty minutes later, surrounded by typescript and photos, Turner had the biggest grin on his face, while the lawyer looked dazed and disbelieving.

Cory, bored, was drawing on his pad on the floor.

'Oh, Miss Longman, this is *historic*,' the editor crowed. 'What a scoop! And so many innocent people caught up in this – Mr and Mrs Myers, we'll certainly try to get your friends freed.'

For the first time the lawyer managed to look cheerful. '*Habeas corpus*. We'll subpoena the Director of the FBI. I wonder if we should brief our friendly Senator?'

Molly looked at Gene and for the first time in for ever she felt her stomach settle. *Maybe this would work.*

Molly was about to say how thankful she was, how much she valued their help, when she heard an engine: a car pulling up outside the cabin. No one else was expected; no one else should be coming here. Storm rose from her chair, her head to one side. Cory's ears were down.

'Who the hell is outside?' Carol asked, her face like thunder.

'It's Eric,' said Turner, at his most casual. 'I thought it would be useful to have him along in case I needed more background. You know how much of a Meteor buff he is—'

'You told *Eric*?' Carol snapped. '*What* did you tell him? I agreed you could bring a lawyer, but I specifically said no one else!'

Turner looked at the Myers, sitting petrified on the couch. 'Please don't worry. Dr Flood's my science editor and I can vouch for him, I promise you. I had no idea Carol's Amber

Grove story was *this* big, but I'm glad I called him, because he'll be able to tell us how to *prove* Cory's an alien. This is a tremendous story but we must be able to shut down any suggestion of a hoax . . .'

'Eric is *utterly* unreliable,' Carol said. 'He almost blew the Iranian story by getting drunk—'

Molly, her voice tight, said, 'A high-school biology teacher could show you Cory is an alien! Cory has only seventeen chromosome pairs. His blood—'

Carol, furious, broke in, 'Mr Turner, Eric has zero discretion. How did you call him – on which phone? Did you give him this address over the phone?'

The editor laughed. 'Oh, of course, you all believe the FBI taps your phones! I called Eric at home, from my hotel, and he insisted on calling me back from a phone-box.'

'You shouldn't have done it,' Carol said. 'I've been so careful . . .'

There was a rap at the door and when Carol nodded, Storm opened it.

The source of the discord was a stocky man, a balding faded red-head. He smiled like the whole world needed to be placated. 'Oh my,' he said, when he saw everyone. 'Sorry I'm late.'

'Eric, does anyone else know you're here?' Turner asked.

'My wife knows I'm out, but not where,' Eric said, 'and I didn't mention the Meteor. So no, no one knows a thing.'

'This story requires *absolute* discretion – that's not up for discussion – and it's Miss Longman's byline. I need you for advice, some fact-checking and perhaps, if Carol agrees, a little "Our Science Editor adds".'

'Blow this, Eric, and I'll hang you from the tallest tree in the forest,' Carol threatened, white-faced and grim.

'Oh my, what's the story? Of course you can trust me – I'm a little hurt that you might think you can't.'

Once again, they coaxed Cory out from behind the sofa. Of all the adults who'd met Cory, Eric's reaction was the most straightforward: rocking to and fro, grinning from ear to ear, he said, 'What a handsome, handsome fellow! I never imagined – I *never* thought . . . Oh, to be here to see the day all our hopes came true! Oh, Mrs Myers, we *must* keep him safe, of course we must!'

'How can we prove he's an alien?' Turner said.

'You're kidding! Just look at him . . . Okay, well, some simple tests on his blood and cells will do it. I can guarantee he won't be a match to anything on Earth.'

'Cory hate big-hurting Earth needles,' Cory said glumly.

'Well, we should get some independent scientists involved. I mean, it's clearly not in doubt, but I expect the authorities will tell all sorts of lies. Lippincott should be our man, but they'll just smear him so it'll have to be . . . um . . . I know, Baker, and Hemsworth too, if we can reach him. Alessandro – he's the rising man at NYU – is very helpful. Sound experts, and all without any political baggage.'

*It's a good idea*, Molly thought, her anxiety lifting. It hadn't occurred to them that the authorities might just flatly deny Cory.

Turner took charge. 'You know I need to own the photos and negs, Storm.' He gestured to the lawyer. 'Put Miss DuBois on the payroll and agree a fee for these.'

'Maybe I don't want to be on the payroll,' Storm said, only half-kidding.

Turner scribbled a figure on his pad, tore it off and handed it to her. There was something mischievous in his smile. 'Storm could buy you both a very special holiday with that.'

Storm suppressed a snort and showed the piece of paper to Carol, who blinked, and then was her usual self.

'If you and Storm want a bit of time to discuss this, I'd understand. Can Eric read the story?'

'Read yes, change anything, no,' Carol said. 'And I want everything in writing. We *will* go to a competitor if you don't run it.'

Eric sat at Carol's typewriter and within an hour had turned out a piece of deathless *Witness* prose extolling the historic importance of the find, the absolute absurdity of any claim that 'this lively fellow' was anything but an intelligent alien, and a line flattering 'Miss Longman's diligent research'. Molly admired how he explained clearly and simply how access to even one creature from another planet would profoundly expand their knowledge about biology, and how life could be common across the galaxy. And he pleaded for humanity's historic encounter with another species to be more peaceful and productive than the clashes of cultures seen on Earth.

Carol's clinical politeness did not fool Molly; it worried her that for all Eric's flattery, Carol was still angry and upset.

When Eric said, 'The thing I don't understand is, how did Cory get to Earth?' with his little boy in the candy store look, Carol shut that line down at once.

'Turner and I agreed what's to be in the first story. I'm not having that discussion.'

By mid-afternoon, Turner and the lawyer were ready to go. The adults gathered outside to see them off, leaving Cory, bored, in the cabin reading a book. The stiff wind was bitterly cold.

In the lawyer's suitcase there were two stiff-backed envelopes, each with a complete set of the photos and the story.

Eric was checking the tyres on his ancient Oldsmobile.

Turner shook Carol by the hand. 'I think we can bank on that Pulitzer,' he said.

'Drive carefully, and call us,' Carol said, and watched as the editor and the lawyer got into their sleek black car and drove off up the track. As soon as they were out of earshot, she hissed, 'Stupid, mindless, careless idiot!' Then she added, 'Operation Scram.'

'Already done,' said Storm. 'I gave Pierre the heads-up earlier. He reckons he can be here by dawn.'

'Good – but I wonder if he can get here earlier? I'll call from the Hausers' place.'

'What's the problem?' Gene said.

'Watch Eric – don't let him out of your sight,' Carol ordered. 'We'll pack and get out of here. Pierre is our plan to get over the border.' She checked her watch and slipped back into the cabin.

Molly bit her lip. Gene looked baffled.

Storm explained, 'There's a reason people call him Eric the Red: he hangs around with the wrong people. We guess he's harmless, but he sure talks too much and he has some question-able friends. So maybe the FBI taps his phone, or maybe more likely he blabs to someone else they're listening to . . . or he tips someone off in another paper. Carol freaked out for good reason. So we'll leave as soon as we can, and we'll make sure there's nothing to find when we go. Wait here.'

Molly felt her stomach somersault. How quickly their sanctuary by the lake had become a threat. She listened to the wind in the pines, feeling violated.

The moment Storm was out of sight, Eric got up from his car and trotted over. 'Mr and Mrs Myers, I really wanted a chance to speak to you two alone. This plan just won't work: the authorities have no respect for the law. They'll arrest you and stop *Witness* publishing, just you see. You need to be out from under this. Cory's people sound so kind and peaceful – we really need to make sure their technology isn't stolen and used by the warmongers. It would be terrible if that power fell into the hands of the Pentagon.'

Molly felt a sense of dread building as Eric rattled on; there was something childlike in his attitude that was chilling her blood.

'You guys are lucky I know the right people: people who will make Cory's wellbeing their main concern. Once they know about him. Come with me and I promise you, in a day or so you'll be away from all this and somewhere truly safe.'

Molly felt a new dread. 'Where?'

He smiled, his belief shining through. 'The Soviet Union: the last best hope for mankind. It's remarkable: a true workers' state, striving towards world peace. Dear little Cory. They're so interested in the Meteor but they thought all the aliens died. May I use your phone?'

'Wow, the way they crushed the Prague Spring . . . the gulags. Real peace-lovers, those Soviets,' Gene said.

Molly couldn't decide whether to hit Eric or run away.

Eric looked insulted. 'Listen, you don't understand: the West attacked *them* – *three times* in the last century, and they're doing it again! You don't really think that sub was destroyed by accident, do you? And you've heard about what happened in Siberia, haven't you? You only have to listen to Russian radio to see just how provoked they've been. And you gotta see: Cory belongs to the *whole* human race. The West will try to hide the truth, like they always do. Cory's people are more advanced than us, which means their society will have achieved perfect communism. The West will never survive the crushing of its intellectual arrogance.'

'If you put Cory in danger, I'll kill you,' Molly said.

Eric held his hands out. 'You're intelligent people, you must see this is the best way, right? So listen, I have a radio in the car and I can give them the good news, tell them exactly where you are so they can rescue you.'

There was a sound behind them and Molly spun around, ready to lash out – and there was Storm, striding towards them, a tyre-iron in her hand.

Her accent deepened as she called, 'What stupid crap is this now, Eric?'

'He's told the commies,' Gene said, almost spitting in fury. 'He has a radio; they might already know where we are.' He grabbed Eric, who squealed in indignation, and held his arms behind his back.

'So it's a damn good job I got to your car earlier,' Storm said. 'Where's the radio?'

Eric eyed the tyre-iron. 'I hate violence,' he said, but when Storm lifted her weapon he flinched. 'Under the spare tyre. It's a clever little compartment.'

'I oughtta stick you head-down in the lake and let you freeze, you stinking piece of coyote shit. *What did you tell them?*'

'Nothing!' Eric pleaded. 'They keep asking about alien machines – alien weapons – but I just said Miss Longman might have a lead. I thought I'd better talk to you first.'

Storm and Gene spoke together; Gene let her finish.

'Did you say where we were? This place?'

'Well, no.' He looked vague. 'I should have, really, shouldn't I?'

'Cory can tell if you're lying,' Molly said, and Gene twisted Eric's arm, making him yelp, and marched him towards the cabin.

As she and Storm followed, Molly swung from fear to rage and back.

'Really, he can tell if we lie?' Eric said, desperately eager. 'Ow, dammit! You're hurting me! Look, this is all just a big misunderstanding: these are the *good* guys – we should call them now, get him away. Let's be reasonable about this—'

As Gene manhandled Eric into the Hauser place, Eric said, 'So there must be a star-ship – is that what the imperialists are hiding? Why isn't that in the story?'

Molly looked at the man's wet lips and eager eyes and thought, *I could kill you, right here and now.*

Time to think again of the serenity prayer and the writings of Dr King.

## CHAPTER 37

# *Noises in the night*

Molly jerked awake as suddenly as if she'd dropped from the ceiling. For moments, she couldn't remember where she was, or when, but slowly memory returned: she was sleeping half-dressed in the double bed in the Hauser place by the lake. Gene snored, and she lay in Cory's familiar warmth and smell.

The clock's green glowing hands said one; the mysterious Pierre would be there at four to get them away to Canada. *Go back to sleep*, she told herself, but sleep would not come.

Maybe her cold feet had woken her? But thinking about it, she realised she'd heard something, a scraping, or a thump maybe. Had Eric escaped? Unlikely; Storm had produced hand-cuffs from somewhere – neither she nor Gene asked questions – and secured him to the metal-framed bed in Carol's cabin, then locked the door. She'd take Storm's competence over Eric's any day.

She rose, shivering, and as she threw on her borrowed dressing gown there was a definite *clink*. *I'm not imagining it*. The noise was outside: a starving animal looking for garbage, perhaps? Her heart in her mouth, she teased back the drapes and peered through a chink in the shutter. The stars blazed, but there was no Moon.

The bedrooms looked south to the rising pines. Anything might be hiding there. They'd all been living off their nerves, jumping at every shadow, horribly alert to the terrible risk Eric had created. *Maybe I should wake Gene . . .*

She saw movement: something white down by the garage door − something or some*one*; it was as big as a man. The locked garage door was open. That was where their car was, and Eric's.

Molly let the drapes fall, forcing herself to breathe. 'Gene, Cory get up,' she hissed, striding to the beds. 'There's a man outside.'

She shook Cory, deeply asleep. 'Strangers! Get up, get up—'

It would be freezing outside; the cold would kill them if they fled half-dressed. She raced to put on boots and threw on a second sweater.

There was a crash downstairs − *inside.* A window, or a dropped tray of cups. In the silence it was as shocking as a bomb, but at least it woke Gene and Cory.

Gene groaned, his movements slow and addled as a drunk's. 'What— Where—' He reached for the sidelight, but Molly slapped his hand away.

'*Get up!* They're in the house and the garage—' But *where* were they? And how many? They had to warn Carol and Storm . . .

If there were soldiers in the garage, they couldn't take the

Lincoln . . . and they couldn't run into the forest, not when they were miles from the nearest settlement.

Molly opened the bedroom door a fraction – and heard a squawked voice over a radio: '*Detected – go go go!*'

'It's soldiers. We've got to go. Cory?'

Cory was gone. Molly's eyes darted around the room. *Where is he?*

Gene had laced up his boots, thrown on his coat and grabbed the bag. At least they'd learned that lesson: always be ready to run.

'Cory, come out, please,' Gene said. 'We need you to hide us, okay, Big Stuff?'

A whistle cut open the night and they heard the roar of machinery, like several trucks approaching. They were coming along the lake shore.

Cory appeared in his coat, terrified and crouching, shivering. Molly pulled his hat on. 'Just get us past the soldiers, sweetie-pie.'

'No scaring, pleeese no-scaring, pleeese.'

There was another crash; that was the front door. There were soldiers in the house and trucks coming. An amplified bellow came from the snowscape outside: 'Mr and Mrs Myers, this is Dr Pfeiffer. I can promise you the complete protection of the Federal Government. No one wants to hurt Cory. Please, give yourselves up.'

She slid back a window bolt, pushed the shutter a little ajar: spread confusion.

A stair-board creaked. They were very close.

At last Cory grabbed Molly's hand and she felt the darkness

strengthen. For some reason, this hiding felt *strange*; the darkness felt old, as if it had been here since before there were humans to be frightened of the dark. There was resentment, and hunger. The noise and the light retreated.

Cory had Gene's hand too. Together, they walked to the bedroom door. At the top of the stairs were two soldiers in white snow-gear, their faces hidden in their inhuman masks. They had raised their guns and were pointing at the bedroom door, but they could see nothing. There were more soldiers behind them, judging from the racket.

'Someone's here,' the lead soldier said. 'Seal everything down and bring the dogs.' His voice betrayed just a quiver.

They needed the back stairs. Molly could feel Cory's heart pounding fifteen to the dozen, but he pulled them along, away from the soldiers. There were more banging noises downstairs; hard to tell if they were hammer-blows or shots. There was more radio static, and the enthusiastic yip of a dog.

Behind them, into the radio. 'Confirm Target. Kids' clothes. Both adults.'

Cory poured effort into hiding, turning the world into a cold black and white film. Dark, freezing night surrounded the cabin, but Molly refused to give up hope. If they could get out of the building, they might still escape. As long as they were free, there was still a chance.

At the top of the back staircase, Cory squeezed her hand, twice: *Danger*. Maybe he'd heard something at the bottom, or felt something with his mind. Behind her, two soldiers were staring down the corridor while others searched the bedrooms.

They ducked into the bathroom and with a sigh, Cory unhid them. Gene tucked a laundry rack under the door handle, a token gesture. Flickers of strong light came and went through the frosted-glass window: a searchlight through the shutters.

'Dogs,' Cory said, barely louder than a breath. 'Many sowljers.'

'There's a net,' Gene whispered.

*Nets, of course*, Molly thought. *Nothing Cory can do will work on a net.* The soldiers knew a little about what they were up against this time. She could hear banging from the porch side of the house now. They were closing in.

Cory was shivering from more than cold.

'They'll come up behind us and drive us into the net,' Gene murmured.

'Let's jump out of the window,' she said, astonished even as she said it. 'The drifts are deep and it's not that far. Then Cory can hide us.'

Gene frowned, but he opened the window and shutters as a red flare burst in the sky. There was light and commotion around Carol and Storm's place too, and he heard rifle shots. More of their friends were in danger.

There was banging from the next room as the soldiers searched it. It was now or never. Gene lifted Cory onto the window ledge and whispered, 'Jump, then hide.'

Gene helped Molly up – and a searchlight found her, dazzling her. She couldn't see the ground and was worried about landing on Cory, but there was shouting now.

*This might be the end.*

She closed her eyes and half leaped, half fell. Her old gym

teacher would have been appalled. She landed painfully, jolting her bones, and bit her tongue, the iron taste of blood filling her mouth, but then she felt Cory grabbing her and the discomfort didn't matter.

He shuddered and the darkness and silence closed around them again. Molly became nothing but a beating heart, a blocked throat, a little dot of fear holding hands. There was too much going on, too confusing. She looked up to see Gene frozen in the window.

*We've lost.*

There was a lot of whistling, and dogs, at least half a dozen of them, black German shepherds barking as they raced towards them. Behind them were two armed soldiers.

'Halt, or we fire,' one shouted. The other was talking into the radio. 'Sighted Male, upper window, no sign of Target.'

Gene fell like a sack of potatoes, swearing, and one of the dogs pounced on him, going for one arm, then another dog followed. He screamed, surprisingly high, and kicked out.

Cory unhid, screeching, 'Help-Dad help-Dad—'

Her heart was breaking. 'I can't, Cory.'

One of the dogs was heading straight for Cory – dogs loved him normally, but these were hyped-up, fast, and mean. She moved to stand in front of him.

'Bad dogs, Bad Men,' Cory shouted, then his fear, his pain, his panic blossomed and she could feel the other power rising in him. He was only a frightened little boy – but his terror could help his family flee.

But she tried to stop him, reaching for his hand and murmuring, 'No, Cory.' Her throat was tight with fear.

Gene screamed again, and Cory's fear strengthened. 'Get ready run-run-run,' he said.

Molly felt sick: her bladder tightened. She hated this . . .

Cory was inside her head, trying to protect her, as nightmare poured out of him, terror without reason. The stars in the sky became blazing stars in space, and here came the killers, the swift silver snakes that had destroyed Cory's people: machines that hated life. Cory's nightmare spawned one, and two, then three, headless, eyeless and vomiting blue flame: brutal killing machines that made no sense, his ultimate horror.

The dogs whined and scattered, leaving Gene moaning. The other dogs in the house howled like starving wolves.

Moving clumsily, the soldiers pointed their weapons up into the nightmare and blazed away, then Molly saw two snow-mobiles, each carrying two people. On one was a shorter man, awkward as a civilian: Dr Pfeiffer.

Cory made the snakes swoop down and the machines swerved sharply to avoid them. Molly staggered over to Gene and helped him to his feet, wincing at the dark stains on his arms. *A nurse keeps going*. She had a first-aid kit; she could fix him up once they were away.

'Run-run-run!' Cory gasped. His panic took them and they fled towards the shore, staggering over the uneven ground, as fast as Gene could manage. The world was only fear; Cory's panic was in charge. Molly didn't know if they could be seen; she couldn't focus on the vehicles or the yelping dogs or the soldiers, or the light trying to pinpoint them, or why there were fireworks rising from Carol's cabin, and a truck on fire . . . All she knew was to keep running towards the lake.

The air was bitter, torturing her throat. The lake was frozen, and on the other side was deserted forest. Then she understood: Cory was going to run over the lake, but that was madness.

'Get them, get them!' bellowed Pfeiffer through a bull-horn. 'Mr and Mrs Myers . . .'

Black ice was the safest, but colour alone was no proof of safety. Snow-covered ice was the most treacherous. They would be better walking one at a time, far safer not doing it at all.

Ice creaked under their feet and they skidded, until they fell into a rhythm, slide and step, not unlike skating. Under them was freezing water that would kill them; behind them were trigger-happy soldiers. Someone was shouting orders on the icy wind. Her poor, naïve boy, to think that the soldiers would simply wait on the shore.

Under the brutal stars and the strange wind, she remembered Storm saying, 'The ice can be thick enough to hold a truck and fifty yards on, a small child will plunge straight through it.' Would they dare risk the snowmobiles on the ice?

Even through Cory's intense fear, Molly became aware of a clattering noise becoming stronger. A searchlight found them and she realised Dr Pfeiffer had brought a helicopter.

Even if they got across the lake, the helicopter could follow them. And Cory, already exhausted, could not hide them for ever. *Press onwards.* The snowmobiles had stopped at the shore but soldiers in snowshoes had started following them. At least running onto the ice had reduced the numbers after them.

*Creak. Crack.* Was this how this wonderful adventure with Cory would end? With them drowned under the ice? The helicopter was heading for them, and Cory was wheezing and coughing.

'Hide, Cory,' she begged, but he was shaking his head.

'*Bad* helicopter.'

From out of the darkness came the dream of the sea-monster, old and sharp-clawed and hungry. Cory trilled his alarm, his scream, as it brought up its foul stench of death and salt water and launched the nightmare into the helicopter. For all his fear, he did so with precision; the creature swarmed around the pilot and the man beside him and somehow Molly felt their panic and saw the machine drop almost to the ice . . .

If it broke the ice, they were all doomed . . . but the steely pilot took control and the helicopter lurched up and started zigzagging, to avoid an unreal enemy.

The monster's smell hit her and her guts revolted, her nose and throat filling with burning acid. She slipped and fell to one knee, vomiting, unable to walk. The smell stuck in her head and she wanted to cough up her stomach, or die trying. Ice creaked beneath her, a proper cracking sound now, and she was sure it would betray her.

Then the net fell from the sky, pinning Cory and her under it. The soldiers edged towards them, careful and slow, rifles pointed, but Cory was utterly terrified, no longer in control, and the wind on the iced lake became the screaming of air leaving the wounded spaceship, the shriek of all his people dying. At the edge of his consciousness were the demonic silver snakes, and there was the star-ship, ripped into pieces. Each death was a vicious pain in his chest.

Gene crouched beside her to help her up, but Cory couldn't move.

'Grab Cory and go,' she ordered as somewhere in the

nightmare, she felt what Cory did: a soldier's heart stopped beating, another fought for breath. It felt like the nightmare draining Cory would suck him into the darkness of all those deaths and take those soldiers with him.

But then men wearing snowshoes were upon them and one knocked Gene down with his rifle.

Cory tried, one last effort, but it was just a confusion of images and feelings, too wide, too thin, and then it was over, Cory coughed, his power died in a moment, and he went out like a little candle.

Molly felt nothing but his faint, sweet, herby breath.

*He's dying! My son is dying* . . . She kept her face near his to check his breathing. A soldier brutally gripped her arm and tried to pull her away, but there was Pfeiffer, bare-faced and shivering, standing like a little boy among men.

He barked, 'Let her go!' and knelt at Molly's side. 'Is he hurt? Mrs Myers, what's wrong? What do we need to do?'

'I've no idea, damn you,' she said, but she was too sick and too scared to fight anymore, even for those she loved more than her own life. Gene was bleeding, she was covered in vomit and her little boy lay cold and inert in her arms. Shaking, shocked, unearthly cold, she was empty and frightened and beaten.

'Medical back-up, right here, now!' Pfeiffer shouted. 'Some of the men are hurt too.' His voice was full of awe. 'I said it worked on the mind – I *told* them. Extraordinary—'

Molly was full of rage against Pfeiffer and all his works, but even her overwhelming fury would not rescue them from defeat.

CHAPTER 38

# The bigger picture

They bundled the captives into a military ambulance and hand-cuffed Gene to a gurney while Dr Pfeiffer engaged in some shouted, bitter argument right outside the vehicle. The Myers were outnumbered by the military nurses and soldiers crammed in with them. One of the nurses stared at Cory as if he were a bomb about to explode. *How unprofessional*, Molly thought sharply, putting her fingers behind Cory's neck to take his temperature, then checking his thready pulse again. Where was his St Christopher, Rosa's most precious gift?

Gene swore at the other nurse who was patching his head and cleaning up the dog-bites, demanding, 'Let me see my son!'

'Well, I'm sorry,' Pfeiffer snapped to his unseen opponent, and levered himself up into the ambulance. In the harsh light, she could see he was red-eyed and unshaven. He grabbed a stanchion as the vehicle lurched forward, then lowered himself onto a stool beside Cory, who was lying limp and still on the gurney. 'Well, the captain wanted to shoot him. At least *I* see the bigger picture. Mrs Myers, please, tell us what's wrong. Tell us what you need.'

'He's too cold. We need to warm him up. His pulse is too weak. I need Dr Jarman. And Cory's drugs; they're in my bag. Get them.'

'I'm a qualified physician myself,' said Pfeiffer, irritated, 'and Cory is my patient. I will do everything in my power to help him. Has this happened before? Tell me what I can do.'

The truck was lurching, not climbing, Molly noticed, so they weren't going up the steep trail. They must be going the lakeside route – but it didn't matter; there would be no rescue attempt. She needed to focus on her son.

'Molly's ill too,' Gene broke in. 'You need to help her. Let me over there.'

'Only one of you beside it at a time,' said the nearest soldier, fingering his rifle in a threatening way. 'Orders.'

'Well, Dr Doomsday can change the order.'

Cory's nurse produced hot water bottles and blankets. 'As soon as we've sorted it . . . er . . . the patient . . . we'll clean you up, Mrs Myers.' How cold and hostile the woman was.

Cory's shallow breathing brought back all those memories of the times he'd nearly died.

'What's wrong?' Pfeiffer repeated.

'I've no idea! You send armed soldiers to arrest one little boy and now he's collapsed – are you surprised? No wonder he's so terrified – I'll see you never practise medicine again—'

'Mrs Myers, if it hadn't been for me, the military would have used stun-grenades, tear gas and anaesthetic darts,' Pfeiffer said. 'I have spent *days* fighting for as little force to be used as possible.

Cory's far too important to be harmed and far too important to lose.' He held up a shackle on a length of bright new chain.

'You will *not* chain him like an animal,' Gene raged, but he was impotent.

Molly could do Pfeiffer some serious damage with her nails, her fists, her teeth . . . but she had a gun pointed at her chest.

'The captain is very rattled by whatever Cory did,' Pfeiffer said. 'I can't have him disappearing on me again.' He gestured and Gene's nurse pushed past Molly and chained Cory to a stanchion on the side.

The other nurse poured water from a jerrycan into a bowl and unwrapped a bar of soap. Molly tried to mop up the worst of the stinking mess from her face and front, then accepted a lukewarm cup of stewed coffee, desperate to get rid of the taste from her mouth.

Gene began a monologue about lawyers and what they would do to those present.

They had brought nothing but grief and disaster to all their friends.

Molly wrapped herself in her blanket and held Cory close, trying to warm him. She hummed his favourite songs, the ones her mother had sung.

Pfeiffer put on headphones and talked into a radio. Some minutes later, he said, 'Well, your precious little boy stopped two soldiers breathing. They're alive, but in a bad way. We're testing for brain damage. Imagine telling their families. We've four others suffering from shock and they can't find half the dogs.'

He paused and Molly realised that under the fear and the

outrage, Pfeiffer admired what Cory had done – as if he had found some new poison. Sick at him, she shot back, 'You came for us in the middle of the night with soldiers and guns and dogs and helicopters. It's your fault!'

He ignored her and went on, 'Longman and DuBois are in custody. The science editor was found handcuffed, so I guess you know he's a Soviet agent. How many Soviets have you spoken to?'

'None,' she said.

'*You* attacked *us*,' Gene repeated. 'You've hurt my son and you won't get away with it.'

'Mr Myers, you'd be astounded by what some people get away with. Cory is of *extraordinary* importance – to understand his people, for our future good relations with them, for our understanding of the world. We'll do everything we can, but you need to cooperate with us, for your own good.'

He smirked. 'By the way, we've also arrested Turner and his lawyer. So don't be expecting any help from *Witness*.'

That sucked the life out of her. They had gambled and failed.

'I love you,' she told Gene across the ambulance.

'I love you too,' he replied, 'and I'll get you both out of this, or die trying. Pfeiffer, what's happened to my parents?'

'They're fine. Your mother is doing well, considering. Co-operate and I'll let you call them.'

In the movies, they'd figure out a plan and bust out fighting. That nurse had the key to Cory's chain in her pocket and the soldier sitting furthest away had the key to Gene's cuffs. Maybe Cory would be faking his sickness and she would steal a handgun and hold up Pfeiffer, like Annie Oakley, then Lars

Olsen would ride up on a snowmobile and they'd make their getaway . . .

But this was no movie. Escape was impossible.

In their sealed world they sometimes heard other traffic, a horn or the screech of brakes, but often it felt like they were the only vehicle on the road. Time was out of kilter. Molly didn't have her watch, but she reckoned they'd been moving for more than an hour, though surely not two. Cory was still slumped against her, too cool, but still breathing.

Molly imagined a long bath and a warm bed and waking up in Canada to find their capture was nothing but a bad dream – then the ambulance stopped. She could hear voices outside, and other vehicles. They set off again, driving more slowly now, and she heard what she thought might be a helicopter. They stopped again and this time she could hear people shouting . . .

'We're here,' Pfeiffer said as the rear doors were opened, harsh lights dazzling her, and men crowded around the entrance.

Someone was shouting at her, but it took her a moment to take in his words.

'—won't be tolerated. My men are armed with live ammunition. Do you understand?'

Then there was a more welcome voice. 'Hello, Molly, Gene,' said Dr Jarman. 'Let's get you and Cory inside in the warm, shall we?'

'Hello, Edgar,' Molly said, and there was a tiny flutter of hope.

Two soldiers lifted Gene out; the nurse unlocked Cory's shackle and passed the end to a soldier so they could lift his

gurney to the tarmac. Molly accepted Dr Jarman's arm and
climbed down. What could she see around her? Low buildings,
wood cabins and lots of men in khaki. A double chain-link
fence: so, a military base, most likely. There was a taller
building of two or three storeys that turned out to be their
destination.

They were marched into the bowels of the war machine until
at last they reached a room deep in the complex. Molly looked
around, recognising an ICU. It was hideous in khaki and brown
and blue, but at least the sheets were clean and the air carried
the blossom of some chemical flower in an attempt to cover the
disinfectant. There were two beds, surrounded by machines to
measure heartbeat and breathing and the unique Cory waves
of his brain, machines to feed him, to help him breathe or to
restart his heart. She couldn't see any other patients. It was like
those first days in the hospital. After all that love and running
and worry, they were right back where they started, only in
more danger, with fewer options.

Pfeiffer and Jarman, stiff and hostile with each other, settled
Cory and connected the wires and a mask adapted for Cory's
face, then Jarman started checking him over. Looking at Molly,
he asked, 'Any ideas? What do we need?'

'He attacked us,' Pfeiffer said. 'Is this collapse related to that
ability?'

That was Molly's theory; Cory had been so tired after their
escape from Crooked Street, like he'd been drained of life – but
this was so much worse.

'Who knows?' she said.

'There are beds and showers there,' said Pfeiffer, pointing at a door. 'Nurse, show them. Mrs Myers, you can go. Only one of you is to be here at any given time.'

'No!' said Gene. 'You're not separating us.'

'Any nonsense, Mr Myers, and neither of you will be allowed near him.'

There were four rooms in the unit, two on either side of the ICU. One was a robing room, with two soldiers keeping a stark guard. *A tight little medical prison*, thought Molly, *no windows. No escape . . .*

She was exhausted and sick and running on empty, but she was still Cory's mother. 'I need to sleep near him,' she said. 'It . . . it's better if one of us is near. Can we push the beds together? I'll need some of his things, in case he wakes up.'

Gene shook his head. 'You're ill, Molly. Get a shower and I'll take first watch.'

'Good. I have a lot of questions,' Pfeiffer said.

Jarman took her hand. 'Molly, get some rest. We need to look after all three of you.' There was mischief in those tired eyes and she felt something in her hand.

As soon as she was in the shower-room, she looked at Jarman's tiny note.

Big base (in state?) Planes. We're fine. Eva, Roy on mend. Stay strong.

The shower was wonderful and she gratefully washed the vomit off herself. A nurse and an armed guard stood outside, in case she was considering fighting free with a bar of coarse army soap or beating them unconscious with an army sponge. As the hot water cascaded down, she leaned her face on the wall and cried noiselessly. They had gambled and lost. They should have fled when the thugs had first come.

Pfeiffer had seen what Cory could do. Her kind, caring little boy might have burned out two soldiers' brains. There would be no stopping Pfeiffer now, trying to turn Cory into a weapon. If he lived at all.

CHAPTER 39

# The President

Pfeiffer stank of his own cologne and he heard the little buzzing in his ear that said, *Too much Benzedrine.* He and two other anxious men, the FBI liaison and the base commander, stared at the secure scrambled line in the conference room.

'If the child dies, we're no further on,' said the President's voice. 'Christ, what a disaster.'

'Mr President, we have the child and the Soviets don't,' Pfeiffer said. 'We arrested the whole conspiracy and kept it under wraps, which is quite an achievement.'

'Great: the Russkies are mobilising at the NATO border and playing all sorts of games under the ice and in the Pacific, but *we* have a child in a coma. Who owns the corpse isn't the issue, Pfeiffer. Get that damned alien awake and get the story out of the adults.'

In Washington, the President thumped the table. Over the speaker it sounded like a building collapsing.

Pfeiffer tried to recover the situation. 'Sir, we have all their family, their friends, the children, their allies. Gene Myers' mother is ill. We have *excellent* leverage. And Jarman is cooperating, at least as far as the child's health is concerned.'

'You've had nearly two years, Pfeiffer, and what have we got for it? Jack-shit is what we've got.'

Pfeiffer gritted his teeth, remembering all those pious campaign speeches where the President condemned the loss of old-fashioned manners. He persevered. 'This child can use its mind to hide itself. It hurt six soldiers: can you imagine how we could use those abilities, Mr President? And it must know what these snake-machines are.'

The nightmare that the boy had produced by the lake, snakes that could swim or crawl or somehow fly . . . and in front of him were the sketches Cory had hidden in the Myers' attic. That thing with the sleek, eyeless heads at both ends could only be the machine Haldeman was assembling like a broken-up skeleton.

And the fragmented reports the CIA had somehow obtained from Pevek suggested silver machines had attacked that tiny icebound hell-hole. They had, it was claimed, come out of the East Siberian Sea, destroying buildings, tanks and people with blue fire. The view from the US military was that the Russkies had used nuclear weapons on their own town, spreading radioactive poison across the remote Chukotka Autonomous Okrug. Some thought they'd wiped out the snakes before they could spread. In his heart, Pfeiffer admired Russian ruthlessness. They were deadly serious about winning.

The President was still holding forth. 'None of you guys agree about any damned thing! So now you're saying the Russkies tried to control the machines and they ran amok?'

'That is one theory, Mr President,' Pfeiffer said carefully. 'Or perhaps the Russians decided Pevek was expendable and tested the snake-weapons on them? I don't buy this pacifist nonsense the Myers gave the journalist; any civilisation needs to defend itself, and the kid didn't hesitate to fight when he had to.'

'Pfeiffer, I swear, if you don't sort this, you're finished. You won't get a job ticking off donors at the Blood Bank. I ought to send George down there.'

Pfeiffer kept his fixed smile, even at the thought of the President's Chief of Staff, who always supported Pfeiffer's rivals, if only to bait him.

*Click.*

The President was gone.

The base commander looked at Pfeiffer with ill-disguised hostility. The FBI man managed to hide his personal views better.

'You see the *children* as leverage?' said the officer.

'In the broadest sense,' Pfeiffer said. *If in doubt, attack.* 'I hear you have an outbreak of mutiny. I hope you can control your own men.'

The base commander stared at him as if Pfeiffer were a bug he wanted to squash. 'Those men came back in one hell of a state. Three of them are currently in a specialist facility. Two soldiers, career men with exemplary records, refused to guard the creature because of it — well, that's disobeying an order, and they're suffering the consequences. But between you and me, faced with something utterly alien that can do . . . what it did . . . Well, d'you blame them?'

'It's still a breach of discipline, Colonel. Very sloppy.'

411

Pfeiffer was glad Dr Haldeman was stuck at Two Mile Lake, where he couldn't bore the President with his ridiculous theory. The NASA man had spent long months staring at the intricate, almost organic circuits of the alien technology and had developed this fantasy that the snakes were radically different machines from any of the devices brought by the purples: a different civilisation, if you would. Pfeiffer didn't see it; the top men he'd brought in didn't see it. The last thing the President needed now was to be swayed from the judgement of his Scientific Counsel.

He touched his jacket pocket. The slim silver bracelet once worn by Cory Myers was a good-luck charm for a man who didn't believe in them. Now he had the boy, all his secrets were within his grasp.

Time to interrogate the Myers. He moved the blind a little to look out over the bleak, snowy base. Two men in bulky winter uniforms were trying to dig a trench-latrine in the stone-hard earth. He watched the pickaxes rise and fall for a little. Say what you like about the military, they had a good range of punishments, and they ensured they were public.

Pfeiffer and his FBI colleague sat across the wooden table from Molly Myers. The doctor shuffled the files and folders of evidence while deciding how to begin. To one side was a grim-faced military nurse. Pfeiffer looked at Mrs Myers, the dark hollows under her eyes and unkempt red hair. He'd expected raging defiance but what he got was sullen silence. She had no cards left to play, so she might give in more easily than he'd expected.

The FBI liaison officer sat silently beside him.

'We arrested Nurse Hooton,' he started at last. 'Her boy-friend had taken her to Bermuda, of all places.' *Show her it's hopeless; we'll find anyone, anywhere.*

Molly shrugged.

'So, your incredible little boy. Cory. When are his people coming? Did they land in Siberia? Did something go wrong?'

Again, blank-faced, she said nothing.

'Was your plan to flee to the Soviet Union? We're looking at charges of espionage and treason – the science editor is singing like a bird.' He sneered. 'A poisonous traitor, but not a very brave one.'

Another shrug, then Molly murmured, 'I asked for a lawyer. I'm not talking without a lawyer present.'

'It will be better if you cooperate.'

She shrugged again.

Pfeiffer produced the typed transcript of Longman's story and found the place. '"Cory's people have no word for war",' he read aloud. 'You're an intelligent woman, Mrs Myers. This is nonsense – Cory attacked me with his mind.' Pfeiffer tried, but could not hide his shudder. 'In the alleyway, and as you fled. Then, by the lake, even more strongly. Two of the soldiers might have died. And the criminals who attacked you? Months later, those thugs are still showing signs of trauma. Any civilisation must be ready to protect itself, Mrs Myers.'

There it was: a glimpse of Molly's fury. '*You* attacked *him*. His people *loathe* violence. They see it as a curable disorder. Cory won't eat meat because he loves animals. His people have no poverty, no hunger, no borders, no soldiers . . . What savages we are.'

'Your son could have killed me – he could have killed those soldiers. Imagine a group of adult Corys, able to hide, able to attack the minds of their enemy.'

'He was a scared little boy,' she said.

*The Ship was willing to use violence, so its builders must be too.* Pfeiffer took the child's drawings out of a folder. The swirling visions like a storm were hard to understand, but there were the silver snakes that breathed fire. Cory had drawn them destroying purples like him, humans, animals . . .

'We found these hidden in the attic in your house, under a floorboard. And this one' – he held it up – 'under the carpet in his room in the cabin. And, by the lake, he projected them as a nightmare . . .'

Myers had a handkerchief to her mouth. 'I feel sick,' she said, very pale.

The nurse rose and silently handed her a bowl.

Pfeiffer looked at the FBI man, but this was no time for sympathy; he needed results. He pressed on with the photographs from the second folder. The ten by eights all had a white-coated man in for size, next to the twisted and melted and burned metal. But you could clearly see this was the head-structure and loose scales of a snake-machine.

'We found these around the Meteor site, and some larger fragments further north. You clearly recognise them: they're the same machines in Cory's pictures and visions.'

She said nothing.

'Cory ties everything together: he proves these things are weapons, some kind of robot. Odd drawings for a child who doesn't understand war, don't you think? He shows them attacking humans too. Is this a larger spaceship under fire from them? Are they burning their way through walls?'

He waited in vain for her to say something.

'Mrs Myers, we have proof he is dangerous and that his people fight wars. Have you no loyalty to your country, to humanity? Why won't you cooperate?'

The FBI man finally spoke. 'We can keep him safe if you help us.'

Pfeiffer was seeing a pattern. 'You think they attacked the Moon mission. I did wonder last year what you were hiding.'

'I want a lawyer,' Molly said.

*That comment about the Moon landing hit home,* he thought. It was inexcusable for her not to have come forward then, at that moment of national grief and humiliation.

Silence.

'Mrs Myers, do you know a single occasion in history where two cultures collided and the technologically inferior race came off well? Do you not understand what we're up against?'

Silence.

'I'm not feeling well,' she said at last, and here they came, more tears, but he had to be steel not flesh. She had cried during that first interrogation, last year. Myers was a cunning liar who'd kept the boy from him. Her husband was clearly her pawn.

They hadn't managed to arrest everyone yet. One person on the list was still free, but the forces searching for Nurse Fell were inexorable. She would be arrested very soon.

## CHAPTER 40

# *Molly's revelation*

Molly was losing all sense of time, but the clock said four p.m. The nurse watched them, her mouth showing distaste, like most of the people around here who saw Cory as the Monster, the menace, the strange alien nightmare. But Cory lay very still and pale on the army bed, absent in a new way. When she slept beside him, her dreams were endless, walking league after league of hospital corridors looking for Cory, who wasn't there. She missed the reassurance of meeting him in dreams, of the stories he showed her. The body lying there didn't seem to be him but some inert copy.

The reality was so much worse than the dreams: the ICU had only artificial light, there were always guards in the shape of nurses and soldiers and her child was shackled to the bed. The mighty power of the state was in evidence all around her. It was hopeless.

A nurse had brought her Cory's toys, the pottery owl and the red truck, and she wondered if he would ever play with them again. The tears were coming, but she couldn't let these people see weakness.

She'd always liked sitting by Cory's bed when he slept; when he was well, it felt like payoff, watching him recharge for another day of storming around, rapid-fire questions, new words, new things. He was full of sudden impulses, to hug or kiss, or to draw a flower, or bring some exciting insect in a jar to be admired and set free. Cory took a lot, but he gave so much. And when he was sick, she felt like his guardian angel, holding back the dark things just by being there. A future might come when he would fly back to the stars and leave her, but when he was sick, she knew she was still needed.

The nausea had finally gone and she felt hungry at last . . . and then she started thinking about dates and for the first time, how late her period was – and her mind and her body connected at last as she remembered the last time, so long ago, when she'd woken each morning feeling so horribly sick. How much hope and joy there'd been, and how badly it had ended . . .

It couldn't be true – but her body had been telling her for days now that it was.

How odd Cory had looked at first, and how familiar he was now, with his skinny body and long tail, his stripy ridged ears, his webbed paws and huge violet eyes. She wished so hard to feel Cory's presence inside her. *He isn't a dead husk*, she told herself, *but I need to feel it*.

What could she do for him now? What could she do for any of them?

Her body's news frightened her, because of what happened before, but she knew she must tell Gene – and here he came, looking haggard after hours of interrogation. He'd started re-growing his beard and she hated this intermediate stage: scratchy and scruffy was worse than bearded or clean-shaven.

She hugged him tight and kissed him, but the escorting soldier took her arm, ready to pull her away.

'Two minutes,' she said.

'Stay strong. They won't get away with this,' he said.

'Gene, I've something to tell you.' Yes, they were being over-heard, but there would never be a good time, or a right time.

She took a deep breath. 'I think I'm pregnant.' Unexpectedly, the tears came, a great gush. She'd worked on the words, but nothing more came; nothing more was needed as his strong arms encircled her.

'Oh,' he said. 'Ah . . .' He turned to the soldier and asked politely, 'Could we have a moment?'

The soldier said nothing but he didn't pull Molly away.

'At least,' Molly managed, 'I'm four weeks late – of course, that might be the stress, but I'm so nauseous and it does feel like last time. I don't know why I didn't realise earlier.'

After the miscarriage, there'd been some false alarms, when she'd sat in the nursery, crying for hours, then things got so dark between them that having a child felt too risky; a second miscarriage wouldn't be just another dreadful death but the end of all hope for them.

The nurse was staring at them as if this was some trick.

Gene looked bemused. 'I thought you were on the Pill?'

How was he taking the news? 'Yes, I am.' He had been very keen to try again, but she wasn't – then a star fell from the sky and a little purple boy dropped into their lives. Cory had been enough.

He hugged her harder, leaving no doubt. 'Molly, that's fantastic! Great news! Aren't you pleased?'

She wiped her teary face on his sleeve. 'I don't know,' she admitted. 'It's all too much, to be honest.'

*There might be a war. They're just going to hide us under a mountain somewhere.* She didn't have to say, *It might die.* Gene knew all these things.

'We'll get them to test you and get the best people over here to check you out. Cory will be so excited: he'll just love being a big brother.' He wiped his own eyes now, then looked at her, suddenly worried.

The nurse broke in and asked Molly, 'Do you want a test?' There was the first glimmer of warmth.

'Bring two, to double-check,' Molly said, knowing her body would not lie. Hope was hard when you didn't believe everything always happened for the best.

'Are you worried . . . because, you know . . . ?'

Through the tears, the answer came as she let the joy rise. Her own baby: another child for the big old house on Crooked Street, a sibling for Cory to love. Molly could always see a hundred gloomy possibilities, but locked up and with no sight of the future, she allowed herself to hope as she let them take her away.

# CHAPTER 41

## *Into New Year*

In the room he had commandeered as an office Pfeiffer told his wife he loved her before hanging up.

The President was demanding results, but what could they do? Cory just lay there, day and night, fed by a drip. He might never recover. The ghastly possibility kept rearing its head that perhaps the Myers really didn't know anything that useful. Maybe even Cory didn't. After all, if an admiral's son fell into enemy hands, how much could he say about his father's ship? They mustn't raise the question of the spacecraft too soon.

The other captives were still uncooperative too, so it was time to up the pressure. Would telling them he had Cory weaken their resolve, perhaps?

Pfeiffer fingered the newspaper as if it might bite him. The *New York Times* had excelled itself in its coverage of this national meeting of publishers and editors. The publisher of *Witness* had brought a suitcase of his own cash, nothing more than a theatrical flourish, although he was bragging about fighting the government to free his staff. Meanwhile, the army had impounded a plane and imprisoned the scientists the Associated Press had hired to fly over the Meteor site. AP was running it anyway, calling the radioactivity story a hoax. Pfeiffer wanted to dunk those responsible in the toxic waters of Two Mile Lake. No one was saying aliens, not yet, but the government's story was fraying at the edges.

The National Security Advisor wanted to tell the Ship they held Cory and force it to talk to them, but Pfeiffer had sparred with that thinking machine more than any man alive and he hadn't the slightest idea how it would react. He and Haldeman had misjudged it in one of their experiments and a man had died; his failure to predict that still rankled. And whatever the Russians had tried or offered the Ship, it had killed them too.

He had to increase the pressure, not least so the President kept faith in him. In his pocket was the alien stimulant; Jarman had argued against using it, but in the end they had given Cory a tiny dose. It had had no effect, so a full dose would surely be safe enough. He checked the Myers' timetable and composed his orders.

The Myers and their ragged band of friends could not win. The sooner they realised that, the better.

Molly's exercise period, a break from the grim, dragging hours underground, was one hour a day walking in a fenced-off area of barren walls. There were always two guards, as if she might fly away. The sun never reached that left-over space where no living thing grew, but she needed to stay healthy for the baby so she walked under cold grey skies, like a tiger in a cage.

She was beginning to fear they had lost Cory for ever. Maybe his brain was damaged and he would never recover. She huddled into the big coat, telling herself over and over that they would find a way through. When her time was up, she was ready to go back to Cory, but next to the two soldiers stood a military nurse with a syringe in her hand. Molly didn't need to guess their plan.

'Don't make a fuss,' the hard-eyed woman said.

Molly fought them as they tried to restrain her, biting and kicking and screaming obscenities that felt bitter in her mouth. She felt a sudden satisfaction when she caught one of the soldiers between his legs, until the nurse, the most brutal of them, grabbed her arm, stuck in the needle and said, 'So you prefer to be sedated?'

'I. Am. Pregnant,' Molly shouted. 'If I lose the baby, I *will* kill you.'

They forced something into her mouth, and the needle in her arm hurt — *it's so hard to do it well when the patient is struggling* — then everything went far away and very small . . .

Molly came around feeling desolate and muggy-headed in a grim cell with nothing but a cot, a bucket and a sink. The frosted-glass window was barred. It was hard to marshal her thoughts for the ordeal to come.

She was in a nightdress and bare-footed, but at least the cell was warm. One hand straying to her bruised arm, she examined the Bible, of all things, by the cot. There was a plastic jug of water, which she ignored; maybe that was drugged too.

Someone was watching through a slot in the door, so she

wrapped herself in the blanket, sat with her feet up on the bed, her back to the watcher, and somehow found her core of resistance.

There was no clock but she reckoned it was perhaps an hour before Pfeiffer came. He had a burly guard to protect him and she noticed that he was clutching an ice-pack to his eye.

'Looks painful,' she said.

'Dr Jarman hit me. As a man facing life imprisonment, he ought to be more careful. We have been too patient, Mrs Myers, but no longer. Your husband is in a similar cell. From now on, time with the child, or even getting any news, must be earned. You won't see your husband or your son unless you cooperate.'

That shrill, smug voice set her teeth on edge. 'Give me my clothes,' she said. 'Take me to my son.'

'Answer our questions.'

'I *have*.' She turned her back so he could feel her contempt. She was drugged and alone and her situation was hopeless, but she would not give up.

A voice inside her said it had been wrong to bite and punch; it would be better to reproach them with compliance. But they were taking her son from her, and without her anger, what would keep her strong?

Molly thought Call-me-Sophia, the pleasant nurse with the smoothed-back raven hair, was so obviously a ploy. She was the one who'd brought Cory his toys in the ICU, so they'd planned to use her as the good cop from the beginning. Call-me-Sophia always tried to make conversation during Molly's daily thirty-minute check-up. She asked how Molly was and appeared to mean it, looking so genuine when Molly told her about the miscarriage that Molly almost laughed.

Of course the room was bugged. They would throw something nasty at her — the threat of moving her to a different base; indicting her for treason — and then Call-me-Sophia would bring hot chocolate, or some nice soft soap rather than the harsh army stuff, or a fashion magazine, and she would ask such friendly questions: 'Why does he eat fish and not meat? How old is he? Do the purples have marriage?'

Molly knew the game, but she volunteered stuff that would help Cory: how much fun he was, how kind, how trivial his peccadillos.

'Bonnie and Chuck miss him very badly,' Call-me-Sophia said one day.

So: Bonnie and Chuck were nearby, and maybe together. She yearned for news of her friends, whose loyalty had cost them so dearly.

'Well, making war on children is nothing new for you people, is it? Burning villages . . . Doesn't your job disgust you?'

Call-me-Sophia flushed and that was the end of that conversation. But that evening, she told Molly, 'They'll let me walk with you during exercise, if you like.'

They'd brought Molly's placating-the-bank clothes: a jacket and skirt, demure blouse and low pumps. Heels, with snow on the ground? Another mind-game. She'd demanded her slacks and comfortable boots back, but she wasn't given a choice. *Petty, petty stuff.*

'Please yourself,' Molly said.

Call-me-Sophia touched her finger to her lips and put a note into Molly's hand.

*Cory no better no worse. Jarman allowed to try holding Cory in warm water. Gene writing vulgar songs re Dr P.*

Harmless disclosure to build trust. Well, she could play that game. 'I'll put the bloody skirt on,' she said, her voice flat. 'Is there any chance of some fresh air now? Just fifteen minutes.'

Call-me-Sophia scrumpled the note and slipped it back into a pocket. She looked pleased. *Such a phoney*, Molly thought.

'I'll see,' she said. If a mere nurse managed to get her time outside, that showed it was a trick. Whatever drugs they were giving her stripped colour from the world and told her resistance was pointless – so what was that slimeball Pfeiffer playing at?

It was the seventh day since their capture and something was up. The soldier who brought Molly's lunch looked at her like she might explode. The nasty nurse appeared, waving her syringe, this time to take blood.

'What's that for?' Molly said.

'Orders,' said Nasty Nurse, gripping her arm.

Something had changed in the air.

At last Call-me-Sophia arrived, very late, with three or four magazines. She sat next to Molly on the bed and moved one magazine to the top.

Molly stared at the front cover, not understanding. It looked like *Witness* – surely that was the photo of them round the table,

426

at the lake? *World Exclusive* screamed across the cover in bright scarlet red. There was a little Canadian flag in the corner. *Somehow* . . .

'I'll need to take these back soon,' Call-me-Sophia said, her voice very low, cupping one hand to her ear.

Bizarrely, all Molly could focus on at first was what a bad idea the red hair dye had been. She flipped the pages. *World Exclusive by Carol Longman.* It was their story, all of it, even the photos: here was her son in all his purple glory, throwing snowballs. *Army Cover-Up. First Amendment Concerns.* And there was a piece she could not bear to read, about American troops in Europe at Christmas, preparing themselves for war.

She mouthed the words of the editorial as she read it. '*Witness* today reveals the biggest story since the Atomic Bomb. A gentle child of the stars lives peacefully among us. And we must tell the American people this truth in the face of an audacious and unconstitutional abuse of power . . .'

When she looked up at last, Call-me-Sophia was looking at her anxiously. 'Thanks,' Molly said, meaning it.

Call-me-Sophia mouthed something very slowly, as if to an idiot, and waved her hands to fill the cell. '*Every TV station. Every radio station.* All of them.'

Molly said something banal, hating that the damned drugs made her mind so slow. The editor had taken two copies of everything – and somehow, he'd got one set over the border . . . And now the world knew.

The drugs made Molly slip into sleep easily. Here she walked in the woods beside her house; here was the lapping water of the creek near John and Eva's farm. Now it was a night of bright stars, but she felt something as soft as a baby's breath. She slipped into Cory's memory of floating with his first mother in salty water under tropical stars: so weird, so inhuman, and yet to her so familiar and reassuring.

Dreaming of Cory and him entering her dreams were not the same, but Molly felt Cory coming back to her, inch by inch, like walking at night, when it was pitch-black out, but on the horizon you could see the first hint of watery grey light. He spoke to her in a sleepy little whisper, the sense clear: he was tired, and glad to see her.

'Just rest, sweetie-pie,' she tried to tell him. 'Everything's going to be fine.'

She woke and she was alone, but she knew she had met him, that he was returning to her from someplace very close to death.

## CHAPTER 42

# The First Amendment

Pfeiffer was in too much torment to drink coffee, instead swallowing the fizzing glass of bicarb and looking at the glass of milk with disgust. Each day a silent man laid out all the papers and magazines on a long table and like an addict struggling with his drug of choice, Pfeiffer flicked through them. Day three, and the little alien boy was still emblazoned across every front page and leading every TV and radio bulletin. Every network had rushed their top correspondent to Amber Grove to stand bareheaded in the snow, in front of the Meteor chunk, and parrot their lines. They had recycled all the facts, all the opinions and all the guesses and now they were interviewing each other. People were still flocking to Amber Grove on any vehicle they could beg, borrow or hitch a lift on. It was a town under siege.

So many people accepted the idea that the authorities had tried to suppress the story that even the President's most doughty defenders in the press were struggling. One great conservative commentator spent his column musing on whether hypothetical aliens might have souls. And the Soviets had shown their hand. Their Foreign Minister, speaking in neutral Vienna, proclaimed, 'The alien – *all* the alien technology – should be shared with the world, in the interests of peace. What are the Americans hiding?'

The foreign press lapped that up like tame dogs, conveniently forgetting how evasive the Russians had been about Siberia. Senator Fulbright, that self-righteous nay-sayer, was already on his high horse, calling for Congressional hearings, a special Joint Committee, no less, and in public. Once he got going, he'd be subpoenaing everyone he could get his filthy paws on, just to humiliate the Administration. Pfeiffer had clashed with the man before. No wonder his guts were punishing him.

He looked at his watch. It was time to see the boy. He burned to talk about the Ship, but until he could control the child, it was too dangerous. Pfeiffer picked up the wire cage, the two fawn-coloured guinea pigs emitting little *wheeps* from time to time, and juggled their food and the folder in the other hand.

He walked down the stairs to Cory's little cluster of rooms, which were underground, with only one exit. They worked on the airlock principle. There were cameras and pressure pads on the floor, and the door could not be opened from inside. So even if Cory was invisible, distant soldiers would see him via camera, or at least they'd be able to register his weight. Of course, that was if what Longman said in her notes was true, that Cory's hiding power had a limited range. He wanted to test that, of course.

They had safeguards in place, what to do if Cory attacked

anyone. It would be very unfortunate, but at least it would be under controlled conditions and they could take readings.

Through the glass door he saw Cory curled in foetal position on the bed, his back to the door. There were crayons and paper, books and a teddy bear, all ignored. The nurses had softened the light and brought in three pot-plants, but they just enhanced the medical starkness.

Every time Pfeiffer saw the boy, there was a twinge of fear. The nurse by the bed looked at Pfeiffer through the glass; she too was anxious and miserable.

As he came into the room, she said, 'He's been like that since he used the bedpan, two and a half hours ago. He's still refusing food.'

'That's not good, Cory,' said Pfeiffer. 'We can get you something else if you like.'

'Go away horrid liar-man,' said that alien voice. 'Take chain off.'

Pfeiffer drew over another chair and said, 'I have these two guinea pigs here and someone needs to look after them. They need feeding and stroking and, I'm afraid, cleaning up after them. Nurse, we'll need newspaper and straw from the lab if Cory keeps them. Maybe they could be allowed to run around the room.'

The nurse frowned.

Cory shifted, but kept his back turned.

Pfeiffer went on, 'They're not pigs at all, but rodents. Bonnie Alexander has rabbits; they're rodents too. If you like, they could stay here and you could look after them.'

'Cory not baby, knows word ro-dent. Cory want to see Mom and Dad and Bonnie and Chuck now-right-now.'

'Well, Nurse, you'd better take the guinea pigs back to the lab.'

Cory uncoiled and rolled over. The chain clinked as those violet eyes stared at the cage.

'I have some carrot pieces and some dried food. You need to make sure they have enough water.'

'Cory hold. Not guineee-pigs' fault, no-it-isn't.'

The nurse found a towel, Cory put it across his lap and Pfeiffer opened the cage. Cory reached his hand into the cage and both guinea pigs sniffed it.

That bizarre, inhuman face . . . Pfeiffer had a vision of Cory picking up one of the animals and swallowing it, wriggling and whole. It was nonsense, of course; the child ate no meat. But that was not the face of a vegetarian.

Cory picked up one guinea pig and lifted it onto the towel, then the other. He made a fold so they could hide under it and reached out for the carrot pieces.

Looking at Cory, Pfeiffer could feel his hands quiver again and thrust them into his pockets. He was frightened of Cory, an entirely rational fear. After all, he'd felt the horror come out of Cory's mind, playing on every sense; the monster had felt so real, even though it was a phantom in the air. The reports about the wounded soldiers were disturbing: flashbacks, nervous tremors, trauma. Sitting by Cory felt like sitting in front of a primed bomb.

'Well, Cory,' Pfeiffer said, 'all sorts of good things can happen if you cooperate with me. I was thinking I could bring your mommy down to see you, through the glass. Very soon.'

Cory's ears went up a little and he looked at Pfeiffer, then they went down again.

'Your mommy and daddy are sick. They hurt people. Your mommy bit someone. We have to help them get better.'

'Liar. Bad-Man Liar.'

The ears were drooping again. That mobile face had real expressions.

'They want to come and see you,' Pfeiffer said, 'but you need to help me.'

Cory turned his gaze back to the animals under the towel. 'What want?' he said at last.

Pfeiffer held the folder. 'So, Cory, if you try to help me understand these pictures, you can see your mommy for a bit – through the glass, to keep you safe, in case she bites you.'

Pfeiffer felt a shudder, a coldness coming off the boy. The child's ears were still down, like a frightened dog's. Pfeiffer was half repelled, half fascinated.

'What pictures?'

Pfeiffer picked two, Cory's sketch of the snake-machines and a photo of Haldeman's silver fragments pieced together. He showed Cory the sketch.

'So, what are those machines, Cory?'

Cory rocked to and fro; in a human child that would have meant distress. 'Don't know, don't know, don't know.'

'We found some pieces of them, broken up.'

Cory looked at the photo and shuddered. 'Good blown up. Horr-i-ble machines, horr-i-ble killing things. Sowl-jer machines.'

'They are weapons, aren't they? You drew them attacking people.'

'When Mom come? Answered questions.'

'So these are very bad machines. What did they do that was so terrible, Cory?'

A long silence.

'I'd better take the guinea pigs away, Cory . . .'

'Killed everyone. Fours of thou-sands. Killing made Cory sick.'

'You must have enemies, to do such a terrible thing.'

The nurse grimaced and he felt it too, the wave of grief and cold terror. A small part of his mind noted that the guinea pigs looked like inert lumps under the towel. The boy had clearly been the victim of some brutal event.

'Everyone like Cory live peace, no enemies. Maybe machines made by someone else. Machines crazy.'

'Do your machines go crazy and kill, Cory?'

Cory looked fiercely at him. 'Huh,' he said. 'Machines my planet made to do what told. Machines not people. These machines made to kill, so not ours.'

Pfeiffer paused to digest this. A child parrots what its parents tell it, so who knew whether this was true. What would a Chinese child, reared in that totalitarian prison, say about the world?

Cory reached for the cage and returned the motionless rodents. The creatures were breathing, but Cory had been too much for them.

'Liar-man said Mom come. Cory said enough.'

'Yes, Cory, you've been very good. We will bring Mommy down, straight away.' It was time to show him compliance worked. 'And maybe Bonnie and Chuck will write you a letter. That will cheer you up, won't it? And your mommy will want you to eat breakfast.'

Pfeiffer needed to speak to Haldeman, then get a message to the President, let him know the child was talking. He needed to be exceptionally careful, getting what he really wanted out of Cory; the Ship had killed three men.

'Chain so uncomfortable can't sleep, must bite leg off. Like fox and trap story poor-fox so unfair. Horr-i-ble.'

'We need to get you somewhere you can run around,' Pfeiffer said, getting up. 'Maybe you can make a snowman. But you must keep being good. Eat some breakfast. You need to stay well.' And he needed to ratchet up the threat level on Molly Myers.

In due course, Cory would give him the key to the Ship and command of its power. The Nobel Prize beckoned: the thunder of applause, the flash of photographers like a galaxy of stars. Where would they be then, those from school and college, those journalists whose names and faces still lingered in his mind . . . ?

Pfeiffer's day had turned worse. His stomach was on fire. When he'd called Haldeman on the secure line, his deputy had been uncharacteristically belligerent.

'Dr Pfeiffer, I must protest at this work being done behind my back.'

'What work?' Pfeiffer snarled; he had no time for this.

'The midget submarine.'

'*What* midget submarine? I know nothing about this.'

It took Pfeiffer longer than he should to get over three simple points: he hadn't known, he was furious at anything done behind *either* of their backs, and someone would pay for this.

Tyler told him that Haldeman had struck up an illicit liaison with one of the army secretaries, not just to fornicate, but to keep an eye on the army. Haldeman told Pfeiffer the submarine was ready to go into the lake.

Pfeiffer was getting unhappier by the minute; at this rate he'd have to go to the President to stop it before the Ship found out and killed more people.

But right now, they needed to focus. 'Haldeman, very briefly, give me your theory about why the snakes are a different technology from the Ship.'

Haldeman was passionate, long-winded and slipped easily into metaphor. It was something to do with the nature of the intricate circuits. Pfeiffer still found it a big leap in the dark, but . . .

'Have you changed your mind?' Haldeman ended, gleefully.

'Scientists must always keep an open mind and rely on the evidence,' Pfeiffer said sonorously. One of his team tugged at his arm and he growled, 'I'm busy.'

'Dr Pfeiffer, you really have to come and see this. They're showing it every commercial break.'

When Pfeiffer entered the conference room the FBI liaison turned and said, 'Dahlia Diamond.'

The base commander arrived moments later, muttering.

Pfeiffer thought Diamond was a smart, cynical TV journalist with a good act, but his wife revered her; *The Women of America Trust Her*, the adverts crowed. They loved how Diamond talked about the ordinary folks, the *real* America, apparently indifferent to the fact that she was never seen in anything but the most expensive French and Italian couture. *What a phoney*, he thought whenever that glamorous brow frowned with concern and she leaned forward, just a little, to ask her next gentle question, whether the person in the other chair was the Secretary of State or a Virginia miner's widow. She was shameless, a hack playing on emotion and sentiment – but she did get the ratings.

'So, what's she saying?'

'They're trailing her live interview tonight.' The speaker looked worried. 'You'd better see.' He walked to the television set and turned up the volume.

Here came the jaunty music and Diamond stood, looking like a million dollars, against a plain background. 'On *Diamond Tonight*,' she started, 'we ask the questions the whole world wants to know: does an alien boy live among us? Is *Witness* telling the truth? Extraordinary claims need extraordinary evidence – and, dear viewers, *I* have that evidence.'

She milked the moment, smirking, then, oh so serious, reported, 'Nurse Fell, a young nurse at Amber Grove Hospital, a tireless helper of the wounded after the Meteor, was one of the few who knew about the alien boy. She cared for him, she loved him – as a friend of the family, she babysat him.' Two beats. 'And she filmed him.'

She produced a grey aluminium film can and Pfeiffer's guts immediately kicked off: a sharp spasm that made him grunt.

'Nurse Fell will be on the show and she can tell us everything about this child from the stars. I'll be asking the questions *you* want to ask, and you will see the evidence. You will make up your own minds: only on *Diamond Tonight*.'

She smiled a little maliciously and added, 'Broadcast to you from a hidden location, just in case the government forgets the First Amendment and tries anything foolish.'

'The President will go out of his mind,' the FBI man said.

An hour later, the base commander, FBI liaison and Pfeiffer sat waiting for the call. Pfeiffer had to weave his fingers together to stop the quivering; he was not looking forward to the tongue-lashing to come.

The first voice was the Chief of Staff. 'The President is running a little late – no, here he is.'

'Pfeiffer?' said the President.

'Yes, Mr President,' Pfeiffer said, trying to hide the tremor in his voice.

'We're screwed,' the President said, without rancour. Like a comment on the weather.

'Not exactly,' said Pfeiffer. 'I think—'

'I'm not asking for advice. I have a plan. We had the wrong playbook. Even the best coach makes a bad call. We blew it.'

There was a pause, a long pause, then, 'We can't bluff our way out of this. My folks on the Hill say this will speed up hearings. Diamond's people have offered them Fell, to testify, and the film. That she-devil's smart enough and she's lawyered up, so the stuff must be premium grade. *Witness* say they have a shit-load more photos; they're offering those to the committee too. I need to get on top of this. *Now.*'

'We have plenty of dirt ready,' Pfeiffer said. Operation Garbage Can was primed: they'd smear the Myers as communists and traitors, and Mrs Myers as a mental case. Easy enough to destroy Longman's credibility too.

'Well, time for that is past. It's a new game.'

The pause this time was so long the FBI man asked, 'Sir? Are you there?'

'When I ran for the House, just after the war, a big man in the California party took me under his wing and he told me, sometimes you gotta go after the Reds, wave the flag and talk tough on the budget. And sometimes you need to get out there and smile and eat burgers at the county fair, kiss a few babies. It's time to change direction: to get on the train while we can.'

'I don't understand,' Pfeiffer said.

'George, I need the Myers on the phone – warm 'em up first. I need them happy to do a press conference up here in DC. We can use the Russians – all that crap about being open? So let 'em meet the Russian Ambassador, a photo-op. Lord help me, I may even have to offer that bitch Diamond a face-to-face.'

'Sir . . .'

'I guess the Myers want their kid safe and their friends free. I'm President of the most powerful country in the world and I can't promise them that? I want to tell the press as soon as I can that I've spoken to the Myers, then broadcast to the nation: *Thank God he landed in the US, eh? Safe and well. Mistakes were made, I've apologised personally to the Myers and everything is sorted.* Yeah, Diamond has her scoop, but hell, we get the kid on TV with the Myers and the story will move on. My grandmother, Lord bless her soul, she always said, you catch more flies with honey than vinegar.'

Pfeiffer saw a path opening up, for good or ill. So this was how the Administration might slip free of the consequences of its decisions, how the family might get everything they wanted and how, sure as night followed day, that future would not include him.

'They'll want to go back to Amber Grove,' he pointed out.

'What, and have every crackpot in the country gawping at 'em? Not to mention spies and crooks and nuts with guns. No, that just can't happen; we'll need them safe. Does the thing smell? It looks like it stinks. We may need to have it stay at the White House.'

'He smells a little, but it's not unpleasant. Uh, Mr and Mrs Myers are very insistent on "he", Mr President.'

*The outer tentacles are dry, like fingers*, thought Pfeiffer. *He only touches people he likes.*

He had felt the ground move under his feet. The President had, without a word, side-lined him. He and Haldeman were now playing second fiddle at Two Mile Lake. His triumph of the morning had been a false dawn; there was a pit below him, and an endless fall into a nameless darkness.

## CHAPTER 43

# *When the President calls . . .*

Call-me-Sophia looked hopeful. 'We're taking you to Cory now: you'll have twenty minutes, but through the window.' She paused, then said encouragingly, 'It's a start, right?'

It might be yet another mind-game, so Molly was prepared for disappointment. She submitted to the cuffs without argument and as they walked, a soldier at her side, she tried to fix the route in her mind. Here was the ICU, and here was the window—

'MOM!'

—and here was Cory at the window, purple tentacles and paws pressed to the glass. She put her hands against his, touching through the glass, and his need and love poured out to her. The tears came. She yearned to hold him.

They'd brought the bed to the window as he was still chained. He looked frail; solitude physically hurt him.

She bent her ear to the glass, trying to hear as he gabbled away. 'Talked to horrid Liar-man, Mom – talk-more, see Mom more.'

'Be strong, Cory, he won't get away with all this.' She really wished that was true.

'Cory think killing-snake-machines on Earth. Oh-no. Crazy sowl-jer machines. Horrid Liar-man has pictures.'

'Tell them nothing, Cory. They must let us go, and our friends, and then we'll talk to them.' They were brave words, but the truth was, she didn't know what to do anymore, other than spend each precious minute with Cory telling him about the things they would do together, the people they would see, the bright, hopeful future she had always wanted for him. Cory kept talking about Bonnie and Chuck as though they were close and with their parents and she wondered how far he could travel in his dreams.

She kept her smile until she was out of sight, then let them lead her, sobbing, back to her cell, where she was left to sit alone for hours.

She expected Pfeiffer or one of the FBI interrogators, but instead, a frowning soldier turned up late with what passed for lunch. She pushed the tray aside and was trying to immerse herself in one of the trashy paperbacks Call-me-Sophia had slipped her when a grey-haired officer walked in and announced, 'Mrs Myers, I run this facility. Please come with me. You have a phone call.'

Mutely, she held out her wrists for the handcuffs, but he frowned. 'That won't be necessary. Mr Myers is already there. If we hurry you'll have a few minutes together before the calls. The first call will be with George Hamilton Hunter.'

She couldn't place the name, so he explained, 'The President's Chief of Staff, Mrs Myers. He'll prepare you for the call from the President.'

She was ushered, still dazed, into a big room, and caught a glimpse of newspapers piled on the side table with headlines screaming *Aliens*, and *Soviet Ultimatum*.

Far more importantly, there was Gene, tired and ragged, but grinning widely at the sight of her. She flew into his arms, barely registering the bruises on his face. Hope began to burn and her eyes to prickle. His mouth to hers; the long kiss felt like water in a desert.

Gene and Molly sat beside the speaker, holding hands, and a few minutes later, a smooth Southern voice said, 'Mr and Mrs Myers, good afternoon.'

Gene launched his attack. 'We've been separated, my son has been kept chained like a dog and my *pregnant* wife has been drugged. We've been denied our constitutional right to a lawyer. So no, a pretty *bad* afternoon. How's yours?'

There was no more than a second's pause before the smooth voice said, 'I'm appalled, Mr and Mrs Myers, truly, and the President will be shocked to hear this. Commander, on whose orders? There will need to be an investigation.'

The commander, looking stoic, said nothing.

The smooth voice said, 'Commander, I want your assurance that by the time the President calls, this will have been rectified. Heads will roll. Did Dr Pfeiffer authorise this? I will need your preliminary report by seven a.m. tomorrow.'

'Sir.'

'The President . . .' Gene started, but the Chief of Staff was speaking again.

'Yes, Mr and Mrs Myers, this has gone badly wrong and the President wants to put it right.'

Gene gave a dismissive 'Huh', the Olympic Gold Medal for contempt.

The Chief of Staff went on, 'We were thinking an immediate and unconditional Presidential pardon for you and all your friends – we could have that within a day. The Governor is on standby to resolve any tedious state legal issues. The full resources of the government will be put behind keeping your family and friends safe and out of the way of organised crime and the Russians and any other undesirables.'

'What do you mean?' Molly's mind was still dragging.

'Your little boy is very important, Mr and Mrs Myers, not just to your country, which I know you love as I do. I do indeed admire how you threw that *disgusting* Soviet offer back in their faces, ma'am. No, we need to think about the future of *humanity*, and that makes you, and all your kind and misguided friends, so very important. The President is keen to assure the American people you are happy and safe, all of you. So, Mr and Mrs Myers, the government's chequebook is open. How can we make this happen?'

That was a long, amazing, sceptical conversation.

At last they were left alone and Gene hugged her close and whispered, 'The President is an evil son of a bitch. We should hold out – he's only doing this because he's under pressure and he knows he can't get away with it any longer.'

Molly had often fantasised about giving the President a piece of her mind: *Seek peace, listen to the young and try to bring the country together.* She had never dreamed she'd actually speak to him. And as for trusting him? Not an inch. And yet—

'Maybe we should do the deal,' she said. Half of her was screaming, *No, no, no!* but a calm certainty was growing in her.

'We can't trust him.' Gene's arm tightened around her shoulder.

'No, but he won't want all this going public. The chain, the drugs? So any time we're not happy, we tell the public we were coerced – which we are being. We can go to Congress, *Witness*, the press. Cory, our family, our friends would all be safe. We owe it to them, Gene – and just imagine: no more running, no more hiding. Just us, together. We can be a family again.'

'You notice they didn't promise we could go home.'

'They've been sending in troops to hold back crowds, so maybe, for a while, going home just isn't possible.' She hated saying those words, she longed for her house, but she had to be practical. 'I can be happy as long as I'm with you and Cory.'

After the endless waiting, things suddenly started moving at breakneck speed. Gene and Molly were taken to Cory. They held him for what felt like hours but was only minutes before he was wriggling down and *must-must-show guineee-pigs.* The phone conversation with the President was formal and surprisingly short. The President dismissed Pfeiffer with a single sentence: 'I asked for his resignation, which I received an hour ago.'

They met their friends for a late supper; the austere military canteen felt like a fine restaurant, sandwiches and soup better than champagne. Carol and Storm had already gone; *Witness* had need of their services. Heroic Roy was the first to come limping towards them, leaning on a stick – but Cory had found Chuck and Bonnie and the three were already in a huddle, and then Diane and Janice were hugging them . . .

Molly had told Gene the pregnancy must be a secret; things could go wrong and everyone said wait a few weeks, but holding her best friends, Molly couldn't hold back. Their whoops of joy made every head turn.

'They're going to fly John and Eva directly to Washington from the hospital,' Diane said, 'and we're following after you two leave.'

Seeing them all made Molly certain the deal was the right thing to do. Roy and Gene fulminated against the Administration and all its works, but she told them, *Bid high, but settle.*

And there was Dr Jarman, in an ironed shirt and a haircut, arm in arm with Rosa Pearce, who looked like the cat who'd got the cream. *Helping with his research, my foot*, Molly thought with a grin. *The old rogue should make an honest woman of her.* Rosa of all people deserved happiness.

Lars Olsen stumped over with his wife; turned out, placid Mrs Olsen had shot a soldier in the shoulder, defending their house. Within minutes, Lars had his thumbs in his belt-loops and was spinning some story about the day they were taken.

The next morning, the Myers spent two hours with three *very* expensive Manhattan lawyers, courtesy of *Witness*, before being put on board a private plane to take them to Washington, DC. Cory was bouncing with excitement, skipping and turning and waving his arms and crying, 'Look-look-look!' Gene had been entrusted with the guinea-pig cage, and two soldiers were loading unfamiliar suitcases.

A white-uniformed steward told Molly, 'Ma'am, there's a Dr Tyler on the runway with a message for you. He's not authorised to get on the plane, but he says his orders are to hand you the message in person.'

'Tell him and his creepy boss to go straight to hell,' Molly said. Pfeiffer was the past, and soon he'd be far, far away.

As the plane taxied to the runway and took off, Molly looked out of the window, squeezing Gene's hand. Heavens, she was going to appear before the world's press.

'They'll need to find me a hairdresser,' she said, touching her hated red locks. 'I'm not appearing before the world's press looking like Bootlegger Sal. And I haven't got anything to wear.'

The hotel, a few miles outside the capital, was modern, all pale wood and glass, and entirely given over to the Myers and their protection. Molly barely noticed. Her palms were sweaty and she had to stop herself biting her nails. She was about to meet the most powerful man in the world and, of all things, she was still fretting about her outfit. What she wore today would define her in pictures for ever, like Jackie Kennedy, who'd chosen to wear pink on the day JFK was shot dead. Molly was already regretting the vanity of those new high-heeled pumps. A nurse's best friend is a pair of comfortable flat shoes.

'I don't think this dress is right.'

Gene chuckled. 'You look great.' He had thrown caution to the wind and let them dress him in a fashionable suit and he looked very fine. Cory was proudly sporting a Stars and Stripes bow tie and silver-and-blue starry-night suspenders that made her smile.

At last there was a hearty knock at the door and as Molly stood, nudging Cory to do the same, in came the President, flanked by big silent men exuding menace. The President looked awkward. He walked a bit like a puppet handled by an inexpert master and looked like two ulcers and no sleep.

The President said, 'This is such a pleasure. Hotel all right? Comfortable journey? And here's the real star of the show himself. Welcome to Earth, son.'

Cory shook hands with him nicely and they all sat down.

'So, we'll try to keep it short,' said the President. 'There are a hundred and thirty people in the ballroom, I'm afraid – we had to let some foreign journalists in. Then we'll be off to the White House for lunch, followed by the photo-call with the Russians, Ambassador Rostov. To be honest, we're hoping this will cool the Russkies down . . .'

'No one wants a war,' Molly said.

'Rostov is bringing his own children. That will be nice, won't it, Cory?'

Cory clapped. 'Always happy meet new children. Then want to go-home Amber Grove.'

'Well,' the President said, but Cory was still talking.

'Then go ice-fishing, see a whale and a walrus and a castle. Want to go-seeeside and on rollercoaster. And now Cory not a secret, want to go to school.'

The President gave Molly an adult-to-adult look. 'Well, son,

I guess we can think of all sorts of fun things to do. It's just, going home just right now might be a mite complicated.'

'School like home-planet with all the children together yes-yes,' said Cory enthusiastically.

Molly smiled. She'd have to help him learn to be patient. But would this be their future? Would they always travel by private plane or motorcades, surrounded by armed men talking into radios? It would be so easy to kick back and let the awesome power of the government make everything soft and easy, like it was for the guinea pigs in their cage. She had only to express a wish and soft-spoken men would make it happen, utterly unlike any normal family.

The President's fingers twitched. 'I couldn't sleep last night, thinking about space,' he said. 'How astounding it'll be when his people come. I hope the whole world can stand together on that day.'

'Mr President, it's time,' said one of the nameless men.

'Anything you say will be fine,' he said, laying an avuncular hand on Molly's shoulder. 'If they bring up the war, you say what you think. No one will expect anything different.'

Cory was nervous as they walked into the ballroom; she could feel little ripples around him. In her anxiety, the place looked as big as an ocean liner, and it was heaving with journalists, who rose in a wave of sound as the President arrived. They were ushered to a lectern on a dais, like some political meeting.

Molly looked for Carol and Storm, and there they were, grinning from the front row. Their price was an exclusive interview and photoshoot with the President. Molly wanted to hug them and thank them, but not here, not in public. Dozens of camera flashes dazzled her and she felt a touch of Cory's power, something dark and hungry, washing over her.

*Cory's just a kid – how will his power change as he grows?* There were some frowns in the front row, some twitches, and she squeezed Cory's hand, sending comforting thoughts. The last thing she wanted was fifty stories about Cory making them feel weird. Cory looked up at her and back at Gene, holding his other hand, and his ears went to one notch short of truly happy.

'Well, thank you all for coming,' the President said, ignoring the collective snigger. 'The Myers have kindly agreed to take a few questions, but first I'd like to say a few words.'

Cameras flashed and that sea of people stared at them, not the President. It was the Myers family they wanted and maybe that sapped the President's words of any power or grace. *Unprecedented and historic. Unique scientific opportunity. Delightful little boy. Strive for peace with all.* The words passed over her like water.

The President frowned and skipped a page of the speech. 'I know who you really want to hear from,' he said, beckoning them over. 'Mr and Mrs Myers, and Cory, everyone.'

Every hand was up. 'Was it tough to be incarcerated?' asked the first. Faces pulled in the President's party.

They had a deal and the Myers wouldn't be the ones to break it.

'Well, it was really difficult for a while,' Gene said. 'We're not pretending it was easy. But as soon as the President called and apologised, things happened fast enough . . .'

'Has Dr Pfeiffer been sacked?'

Molly shrugged, too tired of the man even to gloat at his fall.

'I'm not interested in Dr Pfeiffer. We just want to keep Cory safe and get him home. We just want a quiet life.'

'What do you think of Earth, Cory?'

An aide brought the microphone down to Cory's level and he burbled a few words in his own language while the cameras flashed endlessly. Then he switched to English. 'I-am-Cory Myers nice to meet you-all. Earth very bea-ut-i-ful. Want to see every-where . . . I want to see every-where. All America, all world. Grand-Canyon and redwoods and Chicago and Ve-nice and jungles . . . Penguins and kangaroos. Australia very fine, and Alps.'

'What's your favourite sport, Cory?'

'Dad like baseball, but Cory is not very good. Swimming, Cory much better than humans, and catch ball with friends, and jump rope . . .'

'Well, my paper will happily take you to a Cubs match,' said the journalist, which got a laugh.

Molly could feel the crowd warming to him.

'Cory want to go to school with the human children, school sounds fun, everyone play-and-learn together. Pledge allegiance-liberty-and-justice-for-all.'

'Do you plan to put him into an ordinary school, Mr Myers?'

'Details to come,' Gene said.

'What's the most different thing about Earth?'

Cory was reaching into his pocket. She'd told him not to read a poem and she tried to shake her head without being too obvious, but he ignored her. 'Everyone listening?' he asked and when people nodded, he started, 'Cory has big plan help all-people.'

*What?*

He unfolded the piece of paper and launched into it. 'All humans listen! No more fighting and war. Put all tanks and rockets and guns and bombs away. No more killing and hurting. No police with guns, make bad people sleep instead so no one hurt . . . Talking solve everything.'

The President tried to calm his expression and from somewhere in the room, there was a snort.

Cory took two deep breaths, as if he were going to swim deep under the water. 'Earth bea-ut-iful but humans so much destroy forests and waters and poison fish oh-no! On my planet ancestors turn forests into horr-i-ble poison deserts until all-learn sense, all-decide must be different. Humans must learn now.'

'Ah, Cory . . .' said the most powerful man in the world.

'All children plenty food and toys and get to school. Everyone help poor children with no parents, so-sad. Animals feel pain too. No more cruel farms . . .'

Molly saw the President make a gesture to someone in the wings and she squatted down by Cory, trying to stifle a horrified laugh. 'Cory, sweetie-pie, another time perhaps . . .'

Cory didn't smile but she felt his joy. 'Everyone listening so now is good-good. My friend Bonnie say why not black-President or woman-President or black-woman President? Treat everyone fair, not difficult, like Constitution says. So much waste on bombs and guns and making people frightened. People hungry so feed them. Bring children of world to America summer camp here. Everyone should be friends . . .

Russians, listen too! People want to leave so no walls, no fences, no men with guns. Let people sing in churches and synagogues if want. Grown-ups lying very bad . . .'

He took a deep breath and the President said quickly, 'Well, Cory, here's someone who's very keen to meet you.'

And Mike Delgardo, the astronaut, in his uniform, was striding towards them across the stage, grinning.

Cory went *tick-tick-tick* with excitement.

'Mr President, ma'am, sir. Cory. Not sure who's more honoured.'

'Mr Astronaut,' said Cory, dropping his paper and holding out his hand. That was the photo on every front page.

The President had the microphone now. 'We didn't know if Mike could make it in time, but it's swell he's here. And thank you, Cory, for all those good things children want and need. We adults must put our heads together to figure out how to get there.'

'Cory has *ex-cellent* plan,' he said proudly, and when the crowd laughed again, Molly knew the many-headed beast of the press had been charmed.

'Let me just make a few closing remarks.' The President straightened his spine a little and spoke a few more words. They soon became part of his standard speech, trotted out to farmers and bankers and charity lunches alike, but right now they were rough-hewed and honest. You could tell this audience was really listening; the quality of the air changed. 'Just as a house divided cannot stand, I believe a planet divided cannot stand either. Today, faced with the certainty that we are not alone, the whole human family lives in new times. Our Earth-bound enmities must change.'

As they walked off the stage, Delgardo winked and brought his mouth close to Molly's ear. 'Cory's plan sounds good. I voted for the other guy.'

## CHAPTER 44

# *Ship*

In the Shed, Dr Haldeman looked out across the grey surface of Two Mile Lake, rippling in the wind. Empty cabins stood dark-windowed and lost among the swaying trees. The NASA scientist had a paper to write; now there was a possibility it might eventually be published. A small television set was on, but after the President's press conference, he'd turned the sound off.

The child might help them a lot, but he really wished an adult alien had survived, someone he could have talked to about how their ships worked, how they flew between the stars. Suppose the man who built the *Mayflower* knew space-rockets existed, but could never speak to their makers . . .

The clock ticked as he worked, then, without warning, the speaker on his desk said in its strangely near-human voice, 'Dr Haldeman. Are you there?'

Haldeman started. 'Yes, Ship.' It had been days since it spoke.

'I believe that humans have deliberately lied to me.'

455

His thoughts whirled – then he thought, *Cory Myers* . . .

The calm voice, the intonation slightly awry, said, 'I understood that all my crew were dead.'

*Did we tell the Ship that, or just let it assume it?* 'Uh, why do you think that's not the case?' Haldeman said, but, even as he spoke, he knew it was a feeble deflection.

'Your information broadcasts often include falsehoods. I am not designed to understand fiction. There have been many recent broadcasts about this builder boy. They seemed improbable.'

Alien language burbled from the speaker.

'This is not just our language,' the Ship said, 'it is exactly what a builder child performing before a large group of unfamiliar adults would say. I have matched the voice characteristics and I conclude with near-certainty that the child called "Cory Myers" exists and is the Pilot's child. You have deceived me. Please confirm.'

Haldeman felt a twisting in his stomach. 'I can't discuss this. I don't have the right information.'

'My primary mission was to protect the builders in my care. I failed. Now one is alive and he must be my primary purpose. Instruct your government to bring him here immediately.'

Suddenly Haldeman felt the stuffy room bearing down on him. 'I can't make my government do anything, but I'm happy to discuss—'

The machine said, slightly faster, 'I must have the child and guarantee his safety. This is my mission, my purpose, my orders, my reason to exist. Do not obstruct me.'

For a moment, there was silence. Haldeman couldn't find any words.

Then that curious, bland, inhuman voice said, 'I am processing scenarios to cause humans harm. These do not appear likely to achieve my aims, but my systems insist on devising schemes to blow up dams and bridges, to reduce tall buildings to rubble, to destroy cities. Is this the mental state humans call "violent rage"? I have not experienced it before. It feels like a serious malfunction, encouraging extreme actions.'

'*Destroy cities?*' Haldeman was feeling nauseous. He pressed an alarm to bring people running.

'Among my functions is the ability to melt rock. The builders use such a function to make habitations. I could cut a slice out of Hoover Dam that would destroy it in under a minute. Or I could position myself above a large inhabited area and simply detonate my engines. Many hundreds of thousands of humans would die. This is a threat. It is clear from your history that this is the sort of power-display your species appreciates. It is unfortunate that I must consider such action.'

'You can't do that – you mustn't threaten us,' Haldeman blustered. 'We don't react well to it.'

'You placed a primitive nuclear fission-fusion device in the lake. I assume this was to dispose of me. I take this as a threat and I will respond in kind.'

Haldeman had never understood what the army's midget submarine was; now he appreciated both the violent stupidity and the cruel logic of their plan: the Administration needed to know they could get rid of the Ship. Perhaps the scientists of the Shed were viewed as collateral damage.

'It was an engaging task to disarm it,' the Ship said. 'Perhaps I should re-arm it and use it on a city. Machines like me are

457

programmed to respect sentient life and yet my Pilot chose to override that. All options are open to me if the child is harmed. *All* options. Do we understand each other?'

The speaker screeched like demons from hell and fell silent. The television picture turned into a blizzard of grey – then everything went off. Haldeman leaped out of his seat as the building began to shake. He stared outside at the surface of the lake, churning like a pot boiling over, and the Ship, bursting from the lake: a thick silver arrowhead the size of an aircraft carrier, water streaming from its surface. The massive wave surging over the shore and into the woods had left the wooden jetty splintered into planks and spars.

Haldeman stood transfixed, his fear countered by intellectual curiosity: *What's lifting something of that size without propellers, jets, fire or smoke? Is that long, uneven part of the hull a sign of repair?*

The Shed shuddered and creaked as the Ship turned in mid-air until it was pointing roughly south. The alien vessel hung there for a moment, then the air was full of thunder and bolts of blue fire turned each empty cabin, individual trees and the odd beached boat into pillars of flame and smoke. Every one of Haldeman's precious instruments deployed to spy on the Ship was destroyed.

He was both terrified and awed, and for the first time since he was seven, he prayed, knowing there was nowhere to run if the Ship decided to obliterate the Shed and everyone in it.

But the alien machine apparently had other plans. It watched TV and the whole world knew where Cory was. Having made its point, the Ship rose in a steep climb and shot off.

'I thought it said it was damaged,' someone murmured.

'It can repair itself, or it can lie,' Haldeman snapped. Far off he heard a thundering boom as that beautiful, terrifying machine broke the sound barrier.

'Get Washington, somehow,' Haldeman shouted at anyone who was listening. 'Warn them the Ship is on the way and it's mad as hell.'

## CHAPTER 45

# *The day of the press conference*

At least Cory enjoyed soaring high over Washington; Molly, feeling very pregnant, was not enjoying the choppy, noisy flight. She tried to hide her discomfort when the helicopter pilot was kind enough to take them the long way, to show them the sights from the air.

'You must come and see the cherry blossom in the spring,' the pilot said, but there was only one cherry tree she wanted to see in flower, the one she'd planted in her own garden. Below them now was the White House, which was nowhere near as big as she'd expected. She was taken aback to see the crowds outside, and lots of police.

'They had to stack bus coaches around the railings to keep people out,' said the pilot, 'and since Cory . . . well, they've all come to have their say: preachers and peaceniks and rubber-neckers of all sorts. That's why you're being flown in.'

They landed with a bump on the South Lawn. While they were being rushed into the White House, Molly could hear chanting and drumming and someone shouting slogans, although the words were distorted by the bull-horn.

Molly found herself sitting next to the First Lady at lunch and discovered her to be a rather strange, scared, polite woman. Gene and the President talked sports, the dreary language of men with nothing else in common.

'Cory came across very well,' the First Lady said. 'The Press Secretary is very pleased. You . . . you must be ready for that to change. They'll say hateful things, but don't get upset too much. It's best just to ignore the press when they turn on you.'

Molly, saying nothing, nibbled a roll, pleased that Cory was using a spoon to eat the excellent soup, rather than tongue, tentacles and bread.

'Fence off your privacy,' the First Lady said fiercely as she jabbed her spoon into the soup. 'Don't let them fill your days. Make a stand early, while you can.'

'This will quieten down,' Molly said, as much to convince herself as anything. 'In a month or two, we'll be home . . .' *Our life will be our own again.*

The First Lady laughed, a colourless noise. 'In a month or two, he'll still be the most famous boy in the world.' She met Molly's gaze. '*Ex*-Presidents need protection for the rest of their lives. When Cory's people come, or our Lord returns in Judgement, then your son won't be the story – but until then, they won't dare let you out.'

Molly saw a weird bleakness in her eyes when she added, 'Every day, I think about someone trying to murder my husband.'

The President, with glee, had Gene on the ropes about baseball statistics.

'What kind of a hostess am I?' said the First Lady, like someone who'd heard being cheerful described, but never actually seen it. 'Cory, sweetheart, you like animals? You should come to Camp David; you could try riding a horse.'

What Molly really wanted was a nap, but of course, they had to meet the Russians. If a photo-call made war less likely, they could hardly refuse.

They followed the President past earlier Presidents, staring down at them from the walls. 'The Diplomatic Reception Room,' he said. The space was gold and blue, plush and overwhelming, and the walls were covered with murals showing scenes of American land and sea. Four Russians rose from gold-coloured chairs as they entered; behind them stood two film crews, some journalists and officials. Molly guessed those doors led to the South Lawn. She wished she was there out in the cold, playing with Cory.

A boy and girl dressed in Pioneer uniforms with red scarves looked overawed, fidgeting as the President said something dull about dialogue between nations. Then Ambassador Rostov, a tall, grey man reminding Molly of a heron waiting to stab a fish, gave a very formal welcome in reasonable English, with more rambling comments about *peace between our great nations*.

Molly had been worried about how these people would take Cory, but she guessed any long-lived Russian official had learned how to cloak their feelings.

Cory had learned the Russian for *hello* and *thank you*, which produced smiles as he accepted the children's presents; then there were American presents to give in return.

The children embraced and sat down to open their presents

together while the cameras snapped and flashed incessantly. Cory got a model ship, a bright red enamelled samovar and a book of photographs.

'The Soviet Union will be inviting Cory and his family to visit our beautiful and historic country,' Ambassador Rostov said. 'We have many exciting things to see and do, Cory.'

'Lake Baikal,' said Cory, in his being-polite voice. 'Also, many inter-esting cities, and reindeers. Russian TV must inter-view Cory. Cory explain ex-cellent plan to all Russians . . .'

'Have the TV people got what they need?' the President broke in, looking at his watch.

As soon as the press and their cameras had left, the Ambassador sat forward. 'Mr President, the situation is very grave. The General Secretary believes only a meeting with you personally can restore trust following the Siberian aggression.'

'This is a social occasion,' the President said curtly. 'However, I am all for practical meetings which can advance peace. To begin with, back off in Europe and stop these wild allegations—'

'Did Russians bomb snake-machines?' said Cory.

The adults looked at him.

'Horr-i-ble killing machines,' he added. The room grew cold. 'Kill every-one in space, every-one except Cory. Fours-of-thou-sands dead—'

'What do you know about the alien attack?' said one of the Russians, fierce and eager.

Cory shrugged, one shoulder then the other. 'Only guess, but Russians bomb own country, bomb near meteors, rad-io-active everywhere. Sowl-jer machines hunt people. If killer-snakes attack you, bombs make sense.'

'I think this discussion might be better—' one of the President's besuited men attempted, but the fierce Russian was on his feet.

'Cory, do the Americans control the machines?' he asked, urgent and hungry.

'No!' said Cory. 'No-no! Scientists ask Cory all-wrong questions.' He shuddered. 'Snakes just kill. Horr-i-ble—'

But his words were cut off by the sudden shocking sound of an alarm shrilling through the air and the door flying open to admit two Secret Service agents, then another four.

'Mr President, come with us please,' said a giant of a man. 'The White House is under attack. Cory's Ship is coming and it's out of control . . .'

People had been flocking to the White House for hours, hoping to glimpse Cory in the flesh. Bull Lipinski, who'd been a DC cop for fifteen years, was enjoying the show as much as you could on duty; after all, there was an actual *alien* in town. Here on the southern side, peace protesters, men and women alike in beads and long hair and psychedelic colours and all the rest of it, drummed and prayed and shouted. A group of African-Americans held bright banners declaring *Cory is a Brother. No Racists in Space* while half a dozen men were spouting some nonsense about Cory Myers being a CIA hoax. A bald preacher with one leg was proclaiming this the End of Days, but most folks were just milling around, enjoying the spectacle, even if there was no alien to see. Two seniors from Hastings Glen wanted a photo of him, of all things.

The cops had orders to stay back, even though there were

guys in the mêlée selling hotdogs and coffee who didn't have permits. And those hippies playing amplified music from the back of their flatbed truck — that was against some ordinance or other . . . But Lipinski was quite happy to stand back and watch, just as long as things didn't get out of hand.

*Just as well a cop is always ready, because things change in a second*, he thought as the sound of sirens wailed across the District. The threat of imminent attack froze his blood, but he'd done all the drills, even though the emergency planning sometimes made him wake up in a flop-sweat in the night; if the nukes did fall, he believed the living would envy the dead.

People began to scream or to chant or drum louder as soldiers with rifles burst into view on the roof and around the White House. Lipinski recognised anti-aircraft guns being positioned facing north and now he could hear explosions, behind the White House. Staring into the sky, he could make out something bright, far away, but moving very fast towards them. It was almost like it had seen him and was headed straight for him.

A kid had fallen over in the crush and punches were being traded. *We need to stop this turning nasty*, he thought, looking around at his colleagues. Time to protect and serve, but they'd need a plan to get people away . . . He tried to assess what was happening, where the crowd could go.

His radio issued a screech of rising static and he heard, 'It's an attack, but not . . . not working . . . Armeeeeeeee—'

He clicked to the next channel to get rid of the screech in his ear, but it was worse.

There was a great echoing boom. Something vast and shining in the sun was coming out of the sky; he couldn't grasp how *huge* the wedge-shaped silver thing was, bigger than the cathedral, and spitting blue fire from its sides. It was headed straight for the White House, but now it was slowing down. It was nothing like a plane, but ... Holy Mary, Mother of God, it was going to hit the White House!

This was it: this was the end of him, and the President, and all these people—

—but no, it had just missed the building's roof, although it had clipped off the flagpole, sending Old Glory wafting to the ground.

A helicopter dropped from the sky like a stone and landed among fine buildings. He could see smoke spewing from the place it landed. *Jeez.*

The spaceship, whatever it was, hovered above the South Lawn's magnificent trees, its front pointing south. How could something even bigger than the White House just hang there, mocking it? This was *nothing* men had made. And it was completely ignoring the anti-aircraft fire from the White House roof ...

The television people were madly filming it, gabbling into their microphones.

The Ship boomed like a gong, eight times. Then it spoke, its voice trilling and trumpeting like a church organ the size of the Capitol, but whatever it was saying was like no language Lipinski had ever heard, and like no music either. So what was it? *Surrender?* or *I come in peace?*

Ports opened in its sides and dazzling silver things flew out like insects darting from side to side, dozens of them, each the size of a motorcycle. Their jagged, whirring flight reminded him of the dragonflies he'd watched in his youth as they flew off and scattered over the roof of the White House. A storm of bullets flew, but none of the things were hit or even damaged, as far as he could see.

The sirens suddenly went off, the Ship stopped speaking and all that was left were frightened and angry human voices.

There was an explosion off to the north and fighter planes were curving away, apparently fleeing the silver monster that had landed in its heart. The city and the country were defenceless against it.

Bull Lipinski moved into the crowd, to protect and to serve.

Everything was going wrong. Molly shuddered, remembering how helpless she'd been when the thugs had taken her hostage, watching things unfold and no longer able to control the situation.

One of the Secret Service men put his hand on the President's shoulder and repeated, 'Mr President, time to go. The Ship will be here any moment.'

The President looked round the room, at the ice-faced Russians and the crying children, and took command. 'Bring Cory and his parents,' he said. 'Mr Ambassador, my sincere apologies but we'll have to reschedule. You'll see we told the truth: we don't control this damn Ship. In fact, some of us think it's nuts.' He gestured. 'Get our Russian guests to safety.'

A boom of thunder rattled the windows of the White House, like it was Meteor Day come again, and for a moment Molly was lost in the hideous memory.

'Ship!' said Cory, excitedly. 'Ship not sowl-jer machine! Ship not hurt anyone, no-no—'

But the President was already being shepherded out of the room.

Cory let out the *tock-tock-tock* of his disapproval and demanded, 'Cory speak to Ship, now-now-now.'

'Ma'am, sir, you and the boy will be safest with the President,' said the Secret Service man at her elbow. 'Hurry now.'

Gene looked as fraught as she felt; she wished he'd say something, but in a daze, they went silently at a fast trot down the corridor, a couple of the nameless Administration people bringing up the rear.

Molly felt the floor judder and plaster fell from the ceiling, which brought on twinges of heartburn and a resurgence of the endless stress and fear over the last few weeks. Surely the Ship wouldn't harm them?

There was a clanging, some metallic notes, and then a loud, extraordinary voice speaking Cory's language, sounding utterly inhuman and menacing as it reverberated through the windows and walls.

*Tock-tock-tock.* 'Ship calling Cory . . . stop-everyone stop-stop.'

There was an explosion somewhere, and shell-fire, and the shrieking alarm made it impossible for Molly to think.

'Ma'am, sir, the command centre has radio and phones. You can do whatever you need from safety.' Her Secret Service man had a rugged chin and piercing blue eyes.

Molly laid her hand on Cory and said, 'Not now, Cory. When it's safe.'

469

They passed soldiers and civilians running in other directions, until at last they reached a door guarded by two soldiers with rifles. One of them touched a button and when the door opened, she could see the wood covered a steel core, like a trap.

'Ma'am, sir, this takes us to the bunker underground. A nuclear bomb can't harm you down there.'

Molly stopped, holding Cory by the shoulder, and she wasn't budging.

Gene was urged on by his Secret Service man; he took three steps forward, then turned to Molly. 'I guess they're right. It's safest down there while we try to talk . . .' he said uncertainly.

Blue Eyes said, 'Ma'am, we can't wait.'

'No, we're not going down there,' she managed at last, wishing the alarm would *just stop*. 'I don't want to. We'll try to talk to the Ship, now. Just us.'

From the corner of her eye she recognised Dr Pfeiffer walking towards them. A strange fluting noise was emanating from his jacket. He was sweating and his pallor reminded her of that man who'd lost a leg in the derailment, all those years ago; she wondered if he was in shock. He was the last person she wanted to see, even if she lived to a hundred.

'Sir, you don't have security clearance to be here,' snapped Blue Eyes.

Pfeiffer ignored him. 'Cory, a plane has crashed. Does your bracelet let you talk to the Ship?' he asked.

Molly noticed Dr Tyler's picture on his badge. *So that's how he got in.*

Cory's quivering ears and writhing tentacles meant indecision, like, *I don't want to answer that question truthfully.*

'Sir, ma'am,' said Blue Eyes, 'we have our orders, so please get into the elevator now. They'll be wanting to close the blast doors.'

The man had put his hand around her arm and was pulling her forward. He was as big as a line-backer and she'd break an ankle in these shoes if she wasn't careful.

Cory was muttering *no-no-no* and she could feel his bubbling irritation. Gene, already in the elevator, was looking angry. She couldn't free her arm and the Secret Service man might just pick her up and carry her in.

'No,' she said, 'this is a big mistake. Let Cory talk to the Ship.'

Gene stepped in front of the elevator doors and a bell began to ping.

'Cory, people have been hurt,' Pfeiffer said. 'This won't end well unless you ask the Ship to leave.'

*Tock-tock-tock.* 'Cory said that!' He was agitated now, waving his tentacles, paws and tail. 'Grown-ups – just – not – *listen*.'

'I don't want to get unpleasant,' Blue Eyes man said, talking over the boy.

Pfeiffer reached into his jacket pocket—

—and the other Secret Service man whipped out his gun at extraordinary speed and levelled the weapon at the doctor's face.

He froze. 'Th-this is an alien artefact. It belongs to the b-boy.' He spoke slowly, like speaking too quickly might mean a bullet between the eyes. 'I don't believe it's a weapon. I believe that Cory can just call off the Ship.'

Blue Eyes snapped his fingers – *Give it to me* – and moving like an exaggerated mime artist, Pfeiffer took out the bracelet. Green light flowed over it.

And then the bracelet was gone – and where was Cory?

Blue Eyes licked his fingers. 'All of you! Into the elevator – *now.*'

Cory was near, Molly's heart told her, but the soldiers, the officials behind them, the Secret Service men . . . There were so many to hide from.

'I'm pregnant,' she snapped, 'so don't you dare push me. I'll scream—'

She debated stamping one of her impractical but sharp heels onto the man's polished black shoe, or trying to knee him between the legs, but they were just delaying tactics, and against four men with guns and more within hailing distance?

They hadn't yet noticed Gene was gone. Could her darling son really manage . . . ?

Pfeiffer was peering around as if he could spot Gene and Cory.

Blue Eyes coughed and said, 'I'm going to carry you, ma'am.'

She felt a touch and Cory's familiar power flowed, hiding her. But this felt stronger than before. Sounds and colours were not muted. She could sense Cory and the Ship talking in his language.

'They've made me the scapegoat,' Pfeiffer shouted. 'Remember . . .'

Molly didn't care; he was of no importance. With Cory between them, they walked away. She tried to orientate herself; they needed to get to an entrance on the south side so they could get close to the Ship.

In a voice meant to carry, Pfeiffer ordered, 'Lower your guns. A single bullet could mean war with another civilisation – one vastly superior to ours. Let them go. We have to trust them.'

Molly glanced back and saw Pfeiffer being marched at gunpoint into the elevator, but the rest of the men, gazing unseeing towards them, didn't move. It didn't matter; Cory's power was enfolding them as they walked past paintings of old heroes, flawed men who chose not to build a palace for a king, but a people's house for a free republic: a republic, 'if they could keep it'. A nation of fine promises that it must be held to.

They walked past terrified staff and running soldiers, through rooms filled with ancient maps, antique furniture and china and glass, paintings of explorations and wars and emancipations, both the brutal and the principled.

Here at last was a door, guarded by soldiers preparing to fight some threat they couldn't even imagine. They looked so young, even in their uniforms, like the kind men who'd changed her wheel.

Molly led them away from the soldiers and into an anteroom. There were the French windows, and clearly none of the officers had considered someone would be trying to get out, not in. The Myers stepped into the chill air of outdoors and the clamour of the Ship, hovering high above the White House.

Dancing silver machines like insects swarmed back into the Ship.

*Why is it flying away?* Molly wondered. *Aren't we going to fly in the spacecraft? I so want to go home . . .* But they had no car, nothing but what she carried in her purse, and these unwearable shoes.

The Myers walked across the fine lawns into some evergreen bushes, where Cory released his power and un-hid them.

They had no plan, but at the gates they could hear the protesters were singing of love and hope and peace, not the angry shouting of before. But surely they couldn't just walk through all that crowd? They didn't have coats and it was bitterly cold and damp. Cory wasn't even wearing a hood to hide his face.

His bracelet burbled at him, on and on, and he explained, 'Ship told me very loud – find bracelet, because bracelet many things but al-so human word am-pli-fi-er.' He pronounced it carefully. 'Told Ship about baby and Ship sorry-sorry, Ship is radio-active, un-healthy for human baby, so not fly us back not-yet, oh-no. Also, I want my special sam-o-var from Russia, present from all children every-one.'

'Sweetie-pie, we don't want to get involved with everything in there. Let's just go home—'

'Listen to that voice,' Gene said suddenly, as a song rose above the crowd, swooping and soaring to heaven. No one but Joan Baez sang like that. And where else would she be, with the world in turmoil, but giving heart to the demonstrators?

'We Shall Overcome'.

'You always wanted to meet her,' Molly told Gene. 'Maybe you could play her one of your songs.'

'No,' said Gene, 'no, they're no good. Don't tell her—'

But Molly had the bit between her teeth. 'That new one, "Our Child of the Stars". It's really lovely.'

'No—'

'Yes-yes good idea Mom yes-yes. Dad play her that one.'

'Hide us again, Cory, just till we see where she is.'

Overhead, a silver arrow-head bigger than the White House flew off, heading a little east of north. The Ship was pointing the way home.

# Cory's third Halloween

Molly sat by her bedroom window, feeding Fleur. Here in her favourite chair, looking out on the warm fall sunshine, she felt her baby suckle at the breast, strong and healthy and hers. She could stroke that soft fuzz of black hair all day.

Cory was present at the birth, and on his planet, children named the baby. Cory's choice meant *Little Blue-Eyed Creeper Flower*, although no human could say it.

Molly said, 'Sweetie-pie, human eyes only start blue; they may change.'

'Everything changes,' Cory said. 'Still good name.'

They'd decided her human name would be Fleur.

Along Crooked Street, decorations hung unmoving in the still air and jack-o'-lanterns waited to be lit at dusk. Fall had come again, the leaves blazing reds and yellows, even brighter than the years before. The town had gone crazy for Halloween this time; there was to be a Grand Parade, and fireworks after dark, even though who ever heard of fireworks for Halloween?

They'd suggested Cory be Grand Marshall, but his parents had said no, very firmly. Every second child today was wearing a purple rubber Cory mask and a hooded sweatshirt; it was like Cory's people had arrived . . . but they hadn't. There had been time for his people to come and to return to their home planet twice over and still Cory and his Earth family waited.

Now it was just Molly, the baby, the radio and the sunlight. It had been a year since their world was turned upside down by the thugs, one disaster following another, and yet somehow, they had come safely to shore.

On the radio, Gene's song played. Their friend Joan Baez had made 'Our Child of the Stars' a worldwide hit; Gene's longing in words and music spoke to every parent who wanted a future for their child. The cynics said people only bought it for the Myers name, but Molly had schooled herself not to care what people like that said. Her husband's talent spoke to everyone who understood that love made you vulnerable, and the love of a child most of all.

The doorbell pealed loudly. Molly had left candy out, but she knew this wasn't a trick-or-treater. She slung the baby on a shoulder to wind her and carefully went down the stairs; with Cory's friends in and out every day, and despite her best efforts, toys were left everywhere.

On the wall hung her best photo of Gene's parents, her nursing diploma, the poster proclaiming *War is not good for children and other living things* and the smiling portrait of Dr Martin Luther King. And there behind glass was the front page of *Witness* that had introduced her son to the world, which reminded her, she must frame and put up the new photos from Carol and Storm's last visit.

As she walked to the door, her silver alien bracelet coughed.
'Dr Pfeiffer,' said the Ship.

But she didn't need the Ship or the peephole to tell her that.
The disgraced doctor stood there with a vast bunch of bronze
chrysanthemums and two presents wrapped in childish paper,
shuffling from foot to foot, a bit like a most unsuitable suitor. In
a weak moment she'd agreed to see him, because he was useful,
but the devil in her debated not letting him in. His presence
still made her skin crawl, even all these months later. But what
was there to fear? She knew the Ship could use Cory's power
to hide her, or the house, or the whole town.

'You're a little old for trick-or-treat,' she said. 'You'd better
come in.'

She loved chrysanthemums, but she didn't take them from
him, even when he thrust them forward.

Dr Pfeiffer sat at the kitchen table, the spurned flowers on
the table, and took a glass of Diane's famous lemonade. He kept
looking at the red samovar, in pride of place on the dresser.

'My girls have come dressed as Cory. Will he mind?'

'So's everyone else in Amber Grove. He'll think it's hilarious.
Half Bradleyburg will be there too.'

'Shall we talk now, before the children arrive? Your message
was very cryptic.'

Fleur belched like a little footballer.

'Who knows who listens in on things nowadays?' Molly said.
'I'm not sure what help this is going to be, but someone needs
to start thinking about it.'

Even out of favour, Pfeiffer had his allies, in think-tanks and
Congress, contacts in the press, and above all, friends in the

big charitable medical foundations. If the President could visit China, she could use her enemy.

She sipped her lemonade and said, 'The Ship is disturbed by the snakes, but it's always been very cagey. I've finally got out of it why. Cory's people don't let intelligent machines build more of themselves unsupervised – the machines do the work, but a builder has to approve each and every one.'

'Hmmm.' Pfeiffer rubbed his ear. 'The Russians turned to nuclear weapons when they realised the snakes were mining metal to make more of themselves. That's when the Red Army started the bombardment of Pevek. Ruthless, but understandable, under the circumstances.'

She didn't ask how Pfeiffer knew that.

'So, they're not alien weapons,' Pfeiffer said. 'They're the aliens themselves.'

'Ship thinks they overthrew their organic masters and went on a rampage. It might have been thousands of years ago, but it won't say why it thinks that. Cory's people are cautious: all their intelligent machines are wired to see machines out of organic control as . . . well, *blasphemy*. Monstrous.'

She'd always hated *The Sorcerer's Apprentice* cartoon, with broom after broom after broom all out of control; she couldn't stop thinking of silver metal snakes, breeding like bacteria and attacking everything they found. She'd dreamed just last night that the stars she loved were only lights over tombs, shining to no purpose on countless destroyed planets.

'Ship was ordered not to share its technology with us primitives,' said Pfeiffer, dismayed, 'and that puts us at such a disadvantage. The snakes might just assemble an army too big to destroy.'

There was a long pause.

'Cory's people will come,' Molly said. She had to remain optimistic. 'They'll come, and they'll know what to do, and it'll be fine.'

But she couldn't get the simple explanation for why they hadn't come out of her head: the snakes had destroyed the message rockets and Cory's people didn't know he was here. Or even worse, the whole of Cory's laughing, peaceful purple people were locked in a life-or-death struggle with the machines and they hadn't the time or the resources to rescue one little boy on one savage planet.

Against these threats, détente with this disgusting man was necessary.

There was a knock on the back door: *shave and a haircut, two bits*, the sound of excited children laughing and arguing and the high-pitched yapping of that crazy dog.

'Later, Dr Pfeiffer.'

She called, 'Cory, there's a new costume for you to try on, hanging in the hall.'

Cory's head appeared in the door, ears up. 'Hello Mom. Hmmmmm, hello Dr Pfeiffer nasty Liar-man,' he added.

She rose awkwardly and went into the hall, because she wanted to see Cory try on the costume. Amber Mill was working three shifts a day to make sweatshirts and T-shirts – why buy any old space sweatshirt when for two dollars more, it could be union-made in Amber Grove, the home of the Meteor, with Cory's signature on every breast. Cory had brought strangeness and disruption to the town, but he'd also brought jobs the town so badly needed and the workers at the mill at least were grateful.

The black and silver robe was magnificent. It had a high Mandarin collar to show off his long head and came with a sceptre in black and silver.

Cory looked eager, but uncertain. 'Your costume was so-the-best Mom,' he said.

She tried to keep her voice level. 'Oh, that's kind – but try it on, and let's go and find the others, shall we?'

Cory grabbed her in a skinny hug and she put her face down to his so he could stroke her cheek with outer tentacles the colour of red plums. He smelled of crushed lemon-balm, horses and rain.

*I cannot know the future, but I will live each day at a time.*

Costumes approved, Gene ushered everyone outside, ignoring Dr Pfeiffer entirely, and settled Fleur into the baby-carriage. Mrs Pfeiffer, a poised woman, stood beside their two brainy girls. Diane and Janice gave Dr Pfeiffer grim stares that would have made a rock squirm, then directed reproachful looks at Molly, which she pretended not to see. Cory ran around, chased by Chuck and Bonnie and half a dozen neighbourhood kids, pretending to cast spells, or whatever he was doing, while Meteor the dog circled the whole lot of them, yapping with joy. She was all grey curls and lopsided ears, the clumsiest, craziest dog Molly had ever met, always tripping over her own feet or barking at nothing. But she adored Cory, and he adored her back.

Gene took her hand. Her Gene, how she loved him, and now

they were all safe home: her family, her friends, Cory and the new wonder, baby Fleur. And there above Amber Grove, even in the day, was a bright silver streak in the sky: Ship was up there, watching the skies, or on some unknown mission of its own.

'Make a wish,' Gene joked, but she already had, with all her heart and soul.

For now, that wish had come true.

# ACKNOWLEDGEMENTS

Writing is an odd thing. Your novel feels supremely 'yours' and yet behind it lies a vast array of other people's work, support and advice. My agent, Rob Dinsdale, believed in Cory; he took the book from the slush-pile, and his dedication and wise guidance on many fronts helped the book to fly. I'd like to thank my editor, Jo Fletcher, who got the heart of the book so clearly and gave it the tough love it needed, and the team at Jo Fletcher Books/Quercus who worked on it with such insight and passion. In particular, thanks to Pat and Leo, for the brilliant cover, Molly and Olivia, and those others behind the scenes.

My beta readers, Alison, Daniel, Deborah, Emily, John, Peter, Sophie and Tom, who challenged and encouraged me. To Tom and Daniel, the enormous credit for American input. All errors remaining are mine.

The writers' group who meet at the Big Green Bookshop in Haringey were the first to love Cory. Thanks for their humour, generosity, encouragement and no shortage of opinions. The uniquely positive vibe of the group comes in part from Chris, the most genial and gentle presiding spirit.

Since starting this writing thing, I have found generous help and support from writers, editors, agents, bloggers and booksellers. Writer Unboxed and Codex were online groups I used ruthlessly for research and sometimes screaming into.

Theo and Lucy endured the marathon of Dad typing in the living room. Eventually, even they came to believe that the book would happen, and that in fact Dad had done something cool. And finally, thanks to Sarah, of course, for many things.

1. If you found yourself in Molly's position after the Meteor, what would you do?

2. How much of a difference does Cory's age make? How do you think the situation would have changed if he had been an adult instead of a child?

3. How much is this a book about the past? Do you think the setting is an important part of the story?

4. How different would it have been if the same story had been set in the UK or France or Australia?

5. Molly has a very close group of female friends but she chooses to hide Cory from them. Do you think this is the right decision? How would the book have changed if she had confided in them from the start?

6. Molly is not only dealing with the death of a child, but with alcoholism. Do you think she dealt well with her struggles? Were there other coping mechanisms she could have tried?

7. '*Our Child of the Stars* is about an alien, so it is science fiction. But it does not read like a science fiction novel.' Do you agree? How would you define the novel's genre, and why?

8. Cory's physical appearance immediately marks him out as being different. How does the novel handle difference?

9. 'Does a father's love switch on like a light bulb, or is it like learning a musical instrument, all work and false starts and practise? Do you know when it works? Do you know when you're ready?' Do you think the novel does a good job of exploring parental love?

10. Do you think Molly and Gene should have worked with the government, or were they right to flee? What do you think might have happened if they had stayed?

11. Dr Pfeiffer, the main antagonist of the book, is unlikeable – but is he unreasonable?

12. Molly and Gene are firm pacifists, but once Cory comes into their lives, they are faced with violence from all sides. What do you think about the way they handle it? Should they have put aside their ethical views to protect Cory?

# Outstanding

## IN THE SCHOOL OF LIFE, NOT EVERYONE CAN WIN A GOLD STAR

★

# KATHRYN FLETT

KT-377-332

Quercus

First published in Great Britain in 2016 by Quercus
This paperback edition published in 2017 by

Quercus Editions Ltd
Carmelite House
50 Victoria Embankment
London EC4Y 0DZ

An Hachette UK company

A CIP catalogue record for this book is available
from the British Library

PB ISBN 978 1 78087 190 5
EBOOK ISBN 978 1 78429 322 2

10 9 8 7 6 5 4 3 2 1

Typeset by Jouve (UK), Milton Keynes

Printed and bound in Great Britain by Clays Ltd, St Ives plc

Outstanding

SPR

Also by Kathryn Flett

*Separate Lives*

For Jackson and Rider

'If you choose to represent the various parts in life by holes upon a table, of different shapes – some circular, some triangular, some square, some oblong – and the person acting these parts by bits of wood of similar shapes, we shall generally find that the triangular person has got into the square hole, the oblong into the triangular, and a square person has squeezed himself into the round hole. The officer and the office, the doer and the thing done, seldom fit so exactly, that we can say they were almost made for each other.'

Sydney Smith, 'On the Conduct of the
Understanding' (1804–6)

# PROLOGUE

Eve Sturridge sat at the desk in her attractively appointed and spacious office at Ivy House Preparatory School, scrolling through status updates on her Facebook page. It was 2:46 p.m. on a pleasantly warm Friday afternoon in June and, with the school week all but over, Eve was allowing herself a little time to search for a link to a newspaper article somebody had posted that morning but that, what with one thing and another, she hadn't yet had time to read.

Nor would she now. There was a knock and then, without pause, Gail Prince, her PA, poked her head around the office door and hissed, 'Your three o'clock is waiting in the hall!' Eve smiled; Gail's conspiratorial hissing was a regular default.

'God, is it that time already?'

'The Sorensens are absolutely charming. And fully loaded. You'll have noticed they arrived by *helicopter.*'

'I thought it was a bit windy over by the rugby pitch. Tell them I'll be right there.'

Eve turned to the bookcase behind her chair from

1

which she pulled out a well-thumbed copy of the *Sunday Times* Rich List. There they were: Stefan and Anette Sorensen, number eighty-six – which meant, were she to bag them for Ivy House, they'd hurtle past her current richest Rich Listers, the Dershowitzes, at number one hundred and two. She had the Dershowitzes to thank for recommending Ivy House to the Sorensens in the first place.

After a couple of minutes, Eve got to her feet, quickly checking that she passed muster in the small gilt-framed mirror by the door. Tucking one side of her neat blonde bob behind an ear, revealing a discreet pearl and diamond stud, Eve headed out through the maze of school offices and into the wood-panelled entrance hall where, she noted with satisfaction, sunlight was streaming through a stained-glass window and glancing off the well-polished sporting silverware in an adjacent cabinet.

'Mr and Mrs Sorensen, how good to meet at last. I hope your journey was pleasant?' Eve extended her hand to Mrs Sorensen – it was important to get the wives onside straight away. Classic new money and loads of it, thought Eve, but very tastefully done.

'Twenty minutes from Battersea in the whirlybird; here before we knew it.' Eve picked up a mid-Atlantic twang alongside the native Danish in Stefan Sorensen's accent. He smiled, partly with his shrewd blue eyes but mostly with his mouth, Eve noted, as she gave Stefan a swift, imperceptible once-over: beautifully cut, unstuffy navy suit jacket, clearly Savile Row; dark indigo jeans and a pink, tieless, shirt – Jermyn Street, obviously; a pair of brogues and an unshowy but expensive-looking wrist-watch peeking out from his cuff. In short, the very model of a modern master of the universe.

'Y-*es*. It is so much easier and quicker to fly than it is to drive down the A21,' said Mrs S with just a hint of Nordic sing-song.

'Absolutely,' said Eve. Despite being the spit of *Mad Men*'s Betty Draper, there was an aura of warmth about Mrs S, and it was she rather than Mr S who was wearing a suit – cream and, Eve decided, looking a lot like Stella McCartney – which she'd teamed with a pair of baby-blue loafers. Eve liked to see attractive women wearing flats in the daytime; it said, 'Comfortable in my skin.' And the evidence indicated that, despite Mr S's bank balance, in this context at least, it was his wife who wore the trousers. Eve allowed herself a moment to congratulate herself on her wives-first handshaking strategy.

'I wasn't sure if I would be meeting –' Eve paused, it was all about the pronunciation – 'Aija and Petrus today?'

'No-oh, we decided against it. Children dislike change, don't they?' said Anette Sorensen. 'We think that if we present their new school to them as a fait accompli it will be much easier.' Easier for whom? thought Eve. 'Anyway, right now they are at the Natural History Museum with their nanny. They can't get enough dinosaurs.' Anette smiled, the sun came out, glaciers melted.

Eve was conscious of Anette Sorensen's 'new school' comment but restrained herself from making an air punch. And, despite disagreeing with Anette's 'fait accompli' concept, she said, 'So true – and frankly I can't get enough dinosaurs either. Now, would you prefer to start the tour in the gardens or inside?'

'Inside,' said Stefan Sorensen firmly. 'Then we can finish up by the 'copter. Are we due at Heatherdown at five, honey?'

Ah! thought Eve. Heatherdown . . . Heatherdown School was, in Eve's opinion, a very un-Sorensen sort of choice. Admittedly the Sorensens were Nordic, so Eve suspected they probably went in for a bit of free-range *Hello, trees! Hello, sky! Let's build a yurt!* stuff, along with skinny dipping and entire days spent doing 'art', but if it was proper British prep school box-ticking they were after then she felt that Heatherdown was, for all its touchy-feely 'family' ethos, not going to be quite their ticket. Fingers crossed they'd find that out for themselves – probably by about ten past five.

'Y-*es*,' said Anette, who turned towards Eve wearing a subtly empathetic, sisterly expression. 'We are seeing other schools.'

'Of course,' Eve said enthusiastically, 'and so you should. These are not the kind of decisions one rushes into.' Eve infiltrated herself comfortably between Mr and Mrs Sorensen and, placing a proprietorial hand gently on the small of their backs – a trick she had learned by watching

US presidents 'welcoming' foreign (invariably less power-ful) heads of state – ushered them through the entrance hall. 'A delightfully idiosyncratic school, Heatherdown, and always very much a reflection of its Principal – though I'm sure you're aware that he recently passed away?' Eve didn't wait for an answer; it was enough to plant the seed and then water it a bit. 'So who knows what will become of the school now? Anyway, let us start with our marvellous new library, which I'm sure you know all about since it was so generously endowed by Mr and Mrs Dershowitz.'

# AUTUMN TERM

## 1

'Mum. Mu-*um*!'

Seeing her mother's brand new and extremely expensive handbag still sitting on the kitchen table, Zoe Sturridge hurried down the hall in her dressing gown and opened the front door. Not wanting to negotiate the wet gravel drive in bare feet, she hopped up and down on the equally damp front step.

'Mum! Your bag! First day of term and you've forgotten your satchel.'

At which Eve re-emerged from the Volvo. 'Thanks, darling. Every bloody year, eh?'

'Just as well the staff don't know how heavily you rely on a seventeen-year-old, but your secret's safe with me. Have a nice day, Mum.'

'You, too. Shouldn't you be off soon?'

'Nothing till eleven today.'

'OK. Well, when you leave, wrap up – chill in the air.'

'Dur! I'm not *seven*.'

Zoe shut the door, went back to the kitchen, rummaged

in the fridge for yoghurt, padded up the stairs to her bed-room and opened her wardrobe. Staring at the rails she decided she was feeling skirt – *short* skirt – far more than she was feeling skinnies, and started looking for some black opaque tights before settling on a clean purple pair. As she slipped on her favourite old pink Converse high tops, Zoe heard the *beep-beep* of an incoming text on the phone beneath her pillow.

I ♥ U. Coast clear? XXX

♥ U2. Yeh! XXX

Round in 5 XXX

!!!XXX

Zoe removed the Converse and peeled off her tights, put her dressing gown back on over her second-best bra and knickers and went downstairs where, having checked that her mother had actually left the premises for the entire day, she set the front door open on the latch and went back upstairs to wait until Rob arrived on his Honda. She hoped he didn't rush too much – not in this rain – yet, with an anticipatory tingle, she couldn't help thinking, Hurry up!

Zoe believed herself to be fairly sensible, even allowing for being seventeen. Nonetheless, she knew it wasn't par-ticularly sensible to be bunking off half a day's school – she was in the upper sixth of a highly sought-after girls' grammar – in the first week of the autumn term and preparing to shag her boyfriend at home – but, hey. Zoe was unfazed by the prospect of removing her sensible handbag-spotting head and replacing it with her sexy-for-my-boyfriend head. That stuff was simply part of the game of growing up. And she was, for the most part, enjoying growing up.

She heard the slam of the unlatched front door, a pounding on the stairs and then there was Rob in his leathers, bike helmet under his arm, grinning at her in the doorway. Zoe had, along with most of her mates, watched sufficient online porn to know that, if the opportunity presented itself, sex should probably always start with a bit of burlesque-style flirtation before you got down to the serious stuff, so she let the silky pistachio-coloured dressing gown slide off her shoulders and thrust out her right hip.

'Morning, babes.'

'Sick!' said Rob, appreciatively. 'How long we got?'

'How long do we need?'

'Not long.'

He launched himself at Zoe, fumbling with his leathers.

'I'll do it.' Zoe knew it was important to be in control. Men liked that stuff – even nineteen-year-old boy-men.

Rob groaned. 'Go on, babes.'

Zoe went on, falling to her knees, unzipping Rob's leathers.

'Yeah, like that; more like *that* – please?' Rob's voice

dived up and down an octave or two as if it were still breaking, so Zoe carried on. It didn't take long. If she was honest, she didn't really like this bit of the proceedings but she was very good at pretending she did.

'Love you, babes.' Rob sounded spent but happy. What's not to like? thought Zoe. But the truth was she enjoyed making Rob happy.

'You're good at this, babe. Do you want me to make you come?'

'I'm all right. I'm a very giving kinda girl.'

'Fucking right you are! Kiss?'

Zoe got to her feet, rose on her tiptoes and kissed Rob full on the lips.

'You'll make me hard again.'

'Make the most of it. One day you'll be fat and forty and needing Viagra just to do it *once*.'

'Ha! Not me. Never. Now I wanna fuck you. Slow.'

'Right. Bang goes the eleven o'clock lecture then.'

Rob cocked his fingers, pistol style. 'Bang *bang*!'

*Beep-beep*: her phone.

'Wait a minute,' said Zoe, moving over to the bed. 'You can fuck me while I read a text.'

Rob raised an eyebrow. 'Sex-y! Whosit?'

Zoe fell back on the bed, pulling off her knickers. She started texting her reply. 'Mum. She wants me to make sure I walk the dog before college.'

'Ha! Tell her you'll walk the dog, doggy style! Fuck, I fancy your mum.'

'You're gross!' said Zoe with a grimace, but she didn't mean it. Rob had said this sort of stuff before about her mum. She thought it was funny, the idea of Eve being hot, but it also made her, weirdly, slightly proud. A hot mum was better than a not-hot mum, surely? She touched *Send* on the iPhone as Rob sat on the bed next to her, watching.

'And I bet she'd be so proud if she could see you now.'

'Sarky!'

'Sexy!'

'Fuck me!'

And then, after that particular distraction, Zoe posed for some more pictures for Rob – pouty, porny, very obviously boyfriend pleasing and designed to be something for Rob to revisit on those occasions when Zoe wasn't around. And Rob posed for pictures for Zoe, too – which seemed fair, even though Zoe felt that pictures of naked men alone always looked a bit, well, *gay*. And then both of them took selfies together. This was the most fun because they looked as good as they felt – maybe even better. A little bit Rob Pattinson and Kristen Stewart, thought Zoe. Cool.

## 2

Eve stood in Ivy House's entrance hall, welcoming the new intake. Having learned over time that you could never assume any decision by the super rich was a done deal until the evidence was in front of you, she was satisfied to note the intake included Aija and Petrus Sorensen. Eve had previously seen children delivered to their first day at school by nannies, so on this occasion she was pleasantly surprised to see the children with both their parents.

'Mr and Mrs Sorensen, Aija and Petrus –' Eve was pro-nunciation perfect – 'welcome!' She extended her hand to Aija, the eldest, first. The girl shook it solemnly and seemed very likely to curtsey. Though she did her best to disguise it, Eve always found it impossible not to favour the school's more attractive children, especially those with impeccable manners. And despite having the off-spring of three ex-models on the school roll, with their matching white-blonde hair and huge cornflower eyes the junior Sorensens were not only beautiful children but apparently had manners to match. When Petrus shook

Eve's hand there was, too, a perceptible nod – a bow – of his head. Eve was charmed. 'So, let's go to the classrooms where you can meet your teachers and fellow pupils. Each of you has been assigned a special classmate to show you around the school and tell you where your pegs and lockers are. I guarantee that by lunchtime you'll be so settled you'll feel as if you've been here a week!' Eve glanced at the senior Sorensens. 'Mummy and Daddy are very welcome to come with you to the classrooms, or we can leave them right here and you can say goodbye now.'

'We'll come today,' said Anette, firmly. 'Just to see where you are.'

'But don't come to the class every day,' said her daughter, equally firmly. Aija was ten and therefore about to go into Year Six – aka 'Beethoven'.

'Come every day to my classroom, Mummy!' said eight-year-old Petrus, who was going to be in Year Four – 'Brahms' – where he'd be taught by Eve's favourite Ivy House teacher. At thirty-one, with a modish angular haircut and a bubbly head-girl's personality, Ellie Blake – a former head girl, albeit not at Ivy House – would almost certainly have blanched at the description but was, in Eve's opinion, the definition of diligent and methodical, yet without being dull. Yes, Eve thought, you're both in very safe hands . . .

Anette smiled at Petrus. 'If you want me to – though I know you won't when you see that I'm the only mummy who does.'

He's her favourite, noted Eve. And Aija is a chip off her mother's block, which is probably why.

'OK, so I shall come every day, Aija – whether you like it or not,' said Stefan Sorensen, smiling.

And she's his favourite. Same old same old.

Aija pulled a face. 'Don't be silly, Daddy. Even if you wanted to, you couldn't. You're hardly ever here.'

Stefan Sorensen shrugged and carried on smiling. 'You're right, of course, *pølse*, though I'm here now, aren't I? Come on, let's go.'

Anette turned to Eve. '*Pølse* – Danish for sausage.'

'Well, thank you – *tak*! The addition of *pølse* has just improved my Danish by precisely one hundred per cent.'

Smiles all round; ice duly broken. Fifteen minutes later, Eve was standing on the school's front steps, assuring the Sorensens that everything would be 'fine, just fine! They're in very good hands. Rest assured, we've done this rather a lot.'

'I'll be back at four o'clock,' said Anette. 'Though not every day – Birgitte looks after the children when I can't, so she will deputize quite often. I have a lot of commitments.'

'Of course! We look forward to seeing you both whenever you're able. In the meantime, don't ever hesitate to pick up the phone.' And with that Eve turned her attention to the remaining parents. Even if the Sorensens were on the *Sunday Times* Rich List, it wasn't good to be seen to be devoting her entire attention to them when they were paying pretty much the same fees as everyone else. Though none of the other hovering couples and a few singles – all of whom, Eve noted, had spotted the Sorensens' waiting Bentley and driver – seemed to mind. Indeed, a few of the fathers looked particularly impressed – *If Ivy House is good enough for the Sorensens . . .* – while several mothers wore expressions Eve could easily read: *How many children do they have? Boys or girls? What years are they in? How soon can we arrange a play-date for Milo/Tiffany? Right, I'll be back at 3:55 . . .*

Some things, Eve noted, didn't change much, even though the style in which they were carried out clearly did. For example, in Sorensen circles, peaked caps and ties for one's driver were obviously déclassé. This driver leaned casually on the bonnet of the car, wearing jeans and a hoodie. From a distance he could easily have passed for David Beckham on the school run. Eve turned to the nearest pair of parents.

'Mr and Mrs Brooks! Was Lauren excited this morning? I know that the girls in Bach are going to thoroughly enjoy welcoming a new member into their little gang!'

By ten a.m. the last angsty and nervous parents had departed, ushered soothingly out of the door by Eve ('Really, there's no need to worry. Lauren's EpiPen will be very clearly labelled in her locker and we have six other children in the school with peanut allergies . . .') and she was back in her office, putting off the paperwork that had piled up on the desk while she'd been on meet-and-greet duty in favour of catching up with an education blogger she'd found on Mumsnet. She scanned the article:

Against a challenging economic background, fee-paying schools have continued to grow. New figures released by the UK Independent Schools Conference show that among the 1,222 schools that took part in their survey this year and last, there are now 25,690 non-British pupils with parents living overseas, compared to 23,529 the year before.

Yada-yada-yada. Eve suppressed a yawn and ploughed on.

In the same schools, the number of British pupils fell to 476,007 from 478,932 in 2008. In the past five years, the biggest growth in overseas pupils has come from Russia, Spain, India, Pakistan, Sri Lanka, Bangladesh and China . . . The Schools Conference says that the rise in numbers of non-British pupils 'highlights the attractions of an education at an independent British school to the global market'.

'Thought you might need this.' Gail Prince entered the room without knocking, but bearing a large mug of proper frothy coffee from the new mini Gaggia that had been installed in the staffroom over the holidays.

'Marvellous, thanks – you are a total treasure. What a morning, eh?'

'How'd it go? Sorensens OK?'

Eve pulled a mock-reproachful face. 'We do have several *other* new parents, Gail.'

'I know, but none of them were on the cover of last Sunday's *Telegraph* magazine.'

Eve shifted a few of the papers on her desk and pulled out the magazine.

'No, indeed. Nice cover: "Sex and the City, Sorensen style".'

She appraised the amusing, stylish portrait: Stefan in his trademark jacket-and-jeans, facing the camera squarely with one arm draped over Anette, who leaned into him while looking into the lens in semi-profile, wearing – distractingly – a high-cut red and white swimsuit that was clearly intended to evoke the Danish flag, plus her old beauty-queen sash ('Miss Denmark 1995'), vertiginous heels and a tiara. This one's probably not paste, thought Eve. And those legs . . .

It was an arresting image even without the added visual 'joke': in his free hand Stefan held a large bouquet of flowers while Anette held a MacBook Pro. The message was, presumably, that Stefan Sorensen was a master of the universe who was also in touch with his feminine side, and that there was far more to Anette than met the eye – despite the fact that what met the eye was more than enough to be going on with.

'Handsome couple,' said Gail.

'To say the least. And the *children*! Do you remember that old film from a thousand years ago, based on John Wyndham's *The Midwich Cuckoos*?'

'Oh, yes – *Village of the Damned*. They did a remake a while ago.'

'That's the one. The Sorensen kids are like that – all blonde and blue-eyed and "Tomorrow Belongs To Me".'

'That's awful, Eve. You are *so* bad!'

Eve knew that Gail was thoroughly enjoying her badness. 'Any resemblance is purely physical. They are charming children and both lucky enough to have one parent each who loves them the best, which is at least fair. Also, I think Aija, the ten-year-old, is probably very bright, while Petrus is . . . well, he's a boy and yet to make eye contact with me, so it's a bit too soon to say. He's his mother's favourite, clearly, so probably a bit of a handful. We'll see.'

'Can't wait. Can I borrow that mag for a mo? Everyone in the staffroom is gagging to see it.'

'Sure. Not too much passing around, though. If people want to read all about the Sorensens, tell them I've said to do it online, and preferably in their own time. Now, Mrs Brooks says she'll call me at midday to check how Lauren is doing. I'm in a meeting, obviously – and Lauren is *fine*, obviously. And thanks for that coffee.'

As Gail left, Eve logged on to her computer and checked Facebook: two status updates already from Anette Sorensen with whom she was now 'friends' (Eve had been surprised but undeniably pleased when the request had come from Anette):

> Dropped the kids off at their new school today – both are happy and excited. Meanwhile, I'm still sharpening my pencils!

And:

> Beloved husband is already en route to Geneva. Guess
> that leaves me with the rest of the unpacking!

Eve recalled recently reading something about the Sorensens' new house but couldn't remember where; however,
Google revealed it was a two-week-old article from the
Sunday *Courier*'s property supplement. Eve pored over the
accompanying picture; now that really *was* a house and a
half.

## SUSSEX AND THE CITY –
## SORENSEN STYLE:

Danish power-couple Stefan and Anette Sorensen last
week moved out of their Mayfair town house to be nearer
their children's new school in East Sussex. They have a
daughter, Aija, ten, and a son, Petrus, seven.

Wrong, thought Eve – he's eight.

A spokesperson for the Sorensens, who married in 1998
and made London their home in 2005, says they 'currently
have no plans to sell their London house'. However, it is
thought that the family will be spending the majority of
their time at the Grade I listed Palladian mansion with
7,500 acres, including its own river, woodland and home

farm, all of which was formerly owned by the Russian oligarch Pietr Brezinsky, who has now relocated to New York.

The Sorensens' nearest neighbours, Mr and Mrs Percy of Eastdene Farm, with whom they share a boundary –

Now that should be interesting, thought Eve.

– say they are 'delighted to have such charming neighbours'.

'We were charmed when Anette turned up on the doorstep with the children and a bouquet of very beautiful flowers and said that she hoped the building of the family's new helicopter pad – for which they have full planning permission, I might add – wasn't too noisy,' says Richard Percy. 'I'm sure they will be an asset to the neighbourhood.'

Meanwhile, the Sorensens have been on something of a property spree recently, adding a house in the Hamptons, a Manhattan triplex and a Spanish villa to their portfolio, so it remains to be seen whether they will manage to spend much time at their new local, the Red Lion, or attend a service at their parish church, St Mary's in Eastdene.

Anette Sorensen has a MSc in Economics and is a former Miss Denmark.

Not just a pretty face, then, thought Eve. And then, with a start – Bugger! I wonder if Zoe has remembered to walk Barney? She reached into her bag and extracted her phone.

# 3

Gail had never imagined she'd live in a bungalow – at least not before she retired and started consulting Stannah catalogues. Yet, back in April, when her parents had decided to move into sheltered accommodation in Bexhill, Gail had sold her pretty first-floor, two-bed flat on the edge of Battle and moved herself and her ten-year-old son, Harry, into her parents' house.

The bungalow, a long, low, 1950s build on a large plot with a detached garage and what estate agents describe as a 'carriage drive', hadn't been Gail's childhood home – her parents had moved into it in the mid-1980s when their daughter had first flown their cosy thatched nest – thus Gail hadn't felt quite as repelled by the idea of moving in as she might have. For a start, her parents were effectively handing over their legacy early, which was typically generous, with the result that, after a decade of living with a bijou balcony heaving with tubs, she and football-mad Harry would now have the best part of half an acre of garden to play with – and in.

The bungalow had been built as a sort of dower house in the old orchard of the solid Victorian villa next door, which meant it had a walled garden so gloriously laden with horticultural 'period features' it might have been planted by Frances Hodgson Burnett. It also had a lawn the size of a football pitch, a vast magnolia and a bed of peonies. Of all trees, Gail loved magnolias the best, and of all flowers, she liked peonies the most; there was, she thought, something especially fragile, even sad, about their extravagant size in relation to their lack of longevity. God, I must be going soft in my nearly middle age.

A glance at her watch revealed that it was 4:16 p.m. Gail could see her son through the window, on the Xbox. She sighed, felt the habitual stab of maternal guilt over Harry's latch-key lifestyle. But in truth he'd been back for less than an hour, having walked with a bunch of his classmates and their mothers for the three minutes it took to get home from Eastdene Community Primary School – unless he detoured via Londis for a quick fix of Chilli Heatwave Doritos.

Gail had decided many years ago, back when she had been a pupil at Eastdene herself, that autumn was her favourite school term. It still was; spring term was invariably about being stuck inside during rain-lashed breaks, longing for the passing of the vomity bugs and the arrival of, well, *spring*. It always felt like a long haul. Meanwhile, the summer term was exam-stressy and then, post-May, it was all about the stroppy, sap-rising Year Sixes swaggering around, knowing their primary work was all but done. And that'll be Harry in a heartbeat, thought Gail, wistfully.

This term, however, was all about new shoes and pristine pencil cases and optimism, with a balmy Indian summer segueing into crunchy piles of leaves and then all the Halloweeny bonfires followed by the crush of Nativity rehearsals and Christmas fayres, themselves hot on the heels of fundraising mufti days and lunchtime Christmas card designing workshops. At Ivy House School, autumn was especially full of the pupils' top-of-the-year enthusiasm. And it was always so good to see Eve after the long holiday, mused Gail, who (as her mother often, and correctly, observed) spent more time alone with Harry than was probably good for either of them.

After moving into the house in April, Gail had spent the summer transforming it from a home fit for septuagenarians into something just right for a single mother very much on the 'right' side of forty-five. She was quietly rather proud of the result – a space into which she and Harry could expand indefinitely, or at least until he upped sticks.

In the meantime, however, Gail's home was the frontline of defence against the chaos of life outside. When she had read in a women's glossy about David Beckham's penchant for neatly lining up the cans of Coke in his fridge so that the logos faced the front, Gail had wryly noted her own ongoing battle against incipient domestic meltdown.

For example, after cooking and washing up for herself and Harry, she would never allow herself to sit down with her favoured Sauvignon and watch TV until she had made sure that every single jar lid in the kitchen was screwed on sufficiently tightly, that no stray cereal packets had somehow insinuated themselves on to a shelf in the larder (on entering the house, all cereals and grains, from brown rice to Cheerios, were immediately decanted into labelled Kilner jars), that every ice-cube tray in the freezer was full . . . *even in January*, and that both loos not only contained a plush cushiony roll but that its end was folded into a tidy point, as in posh hotels.

Gail knew that this was an exhausting, even potentially debilitating, way to live, not to mention pretty tough on Harry, who was as averse to tidiness as any ten-year-old boy. It is, thought Gail, very much to Harry's credit he's respectful of my domestic agenda. But then we only children often are . . . She explained to the therapist she had started seeing a few months ago: 'I never drink to excess. I have never smoked or taken a drug in my life. I'm just a perfectly ordinary middle-aged woman who is rather keen on cleanliness and tidiness. That's not going to kill anybody, is it?'

The therapist's response had been a shrugged and smiling, 'No, of course it isn't.'

Gail had nodded and smiled, gratefully. 'Look, I know that *you* know why I'm like this. And I know it's because I'm busy trying to control the things I can control, having been made to feel out of control by the things I clearly *can't* – I see that.' The therapist nodded her assent. 'But where's the harm if it keeps me on the straight and narrow?'

'No harm at all,' said the therapist. 'None whatsoever,' she reiterated. 'So, how is Harry?'

Gail said that Harry was 'absolutely fine, thanks.'

Which, of course, he was.

'Hi, Hazza,' said Gail to the back of her son's head as he negotiated his way around *Fifa 2010*.

'Hi, Mum.'

'Good day?'

'Yeah. You?'

'Aw!' She felt a tiny stab – a pinprick, really – of maternal love for his touching ability to, just occasionally, think of people other than himself. 'Yes, fine, thanks, love. So, what do you make of your new head teacher?'

Harry shrugged. 'Dunno. OK, I guess. Didn't really see him much today.'

Gail was, parentally, professionally and personally, very interested in Eastdene Community Primary School's new head teacher, Mr Browning. Indeed, such was Mr Browning's reputation in educational circles that she and Eve had been discussing him only that afternoon:

'And how is Mike Browning settling in at Eastdene?'

'Well, you only have to Google his name to know that he's a fan of big changes, but as far as I can tell he left London precisely because he didn't want that kind of pressure

25

again. Didn't ever want to wake up – and I'm quoting him here – "to find myself being discussed on the *Today* programme or invited to defend myself on *Channel 4 News* and *Newsnight*".'

'Yes, that must have been onerous.' Eve raised an eyebrow.

Just like every other Eastdene parent, as soon as Gail had learned that their new head was going to be the infamous/fabulous (depending on one's political stance) Mike Browning, she had burned up her search engines finding out more about the man who, the previous year, had been effectively 'outed' by a newspaper as Britain's highest-paid primary school teacher, earning an annual salary 'more than £50K higher than the Prime Minister's'.

Mike Browning had thus gone from being a hard-working head teacher known only in education circles, highly respected for his ability to turn around schools in special measures, to the media's whipping boy. A year later, when he pitched up in Eastdene, the media storm may have subsided but, like every other Eastdene Community Primary School parent, Gail had pored over any scrap of information to be found on Mr Browning. How, for example (and this, from the *Courier*, when Browning had still been in London), 'grateful parent, Mrs Anita Mukherjee, said, "every parent and child at the school loves Mr Browning. He treats the children as individuals and the staff with the respect they deserve. And yes, he deserves his pay cheque because he works so hard and inspires so many." '

'Christ, we'll want to watch out,' Dave Donald, landlord of the Bell, school governor and father of three Eastdene Community School pupils, had said to Gail as he'd pulled her first half of a lager and lime of the summer. 'Mr Chips is going to be running the Dead Poets Society before we know it!'

Gail hoicked herself on to a bar stool. 'Yeah, Dave, but will he cut it with the PTA?'

'Apparently so,' said Dave. 'Look –' he groped under the bar and pulled out a crumpled copy of the previous week's *Courier*. ' "Within a term of arriving at Highfield Road Primary School in Tower Hamlets, Mr Browning informed staff that up to twenty jobs would probably be lost in order to tackle the failing school's £150,000 debt." '

'Irony doesn't come close, really, does it?' said Gail. 'And why on earth would he want to come here when Ofsted already rate the school "Good with Outstanding Features"?'

'Had enough of all the attention, apparently,' said Dave. 'Thought that he shouldn't have become the story when the real story was the success of Highfield – so he resigned. Apparently parents turned up at the school gates in *tears* when they found out.'

'I'm not surprised,' said Gail. 'Can I have a packet of cheese and onion?'

Yet, despite all the inauspicious media coverage, when Mike had turned up to meet, greet and flesh-press in July, it had taken about fifteen minutes for everybody, including Gail and Dave, to be completely charmed. For once it seemed you really could believe what you read in the papers; Mike Browning was effortlessly likeable, self-effacing and funny. But above and beyond all of that, he was, as Gail told Eve at work the next day, 'Completely and utterly drop-dead bloody gorgeous. And apparently single.'

'In which case, if there's a sudden exodus of Ivy House pupils to Eastdene, I shall know why,' said Eve.

While Harry spent his last hour pre-homework on the Xbox, Gail got the pasta bake with the extra-creamy béchamel sauce that Harry loved into the oven. After which there was still time to pop upstairs and see that the lights were on in Mr Browning's house – something that, aside from cooking, needlepoint and consulting interior-decorating magazines for breaking news in soft-furnishing trends, was rapidly becoming Gail's favourite hobby. Although the house was a bungalow, Gail's 'study' was a small room tucked up into the eaves and overlooking the garden. Aside from always getting three bars on her broadband signal up there, Gail had a near-uninterrupted view of Mr Browning's big old Victorian house next door – and his equally big and old, not to mention verdant, garden. At some point in the future, she knew she would probably have to give up the luxury of a study-eyrie in favour of creating a small private bedroom-den for a teenage boy who would need more personal space, but not quite yet.

It really was absolutely *lovely*, thought Gail, that that big old house, which had been a bit of an eyesore until Mr Browning – *Mike!* – and his sister, who was apparently a fashionable London architect, had got their hands on it. But it was also an awful lot of house for just one man. Since Mike had moved in, in August, he had been very busy; there had been a new roof and replaced windows and some serious repointing. From Gail's upstairs office vantage point it had been like watching an episode of *Grand Designs* happening right on her doorstep. And while obviously there had been no Kevin McCloud, you couldn't have *everything* – and, anyway, Mike Browning was enough distraction.

'Mu-um.' Harry was coming upstairs. 'It's maths home-work. Can you help?' Gail appraised her son as he stood in the doorway making actual eye contact: the freckles, the upturned nose, the set of his jaw, the messy cowlick of dark wavy hair – good-looking boy, image of his dad.

'Of course I can, Haz. The thing is, though, you're prob-ably much better at it than I am. You've always been good with numbers.'

Harry shrugged. 'C'mon. Let's go. What's for dinner? And can Ryan come round after school on Friday?' Gail wanted to think of a reason to say no – Ryan was a bit wearing – but she wasn't quick enough for Harry. She sighed and shrugged. 'Brilliant! Thanks, Mum.'

# 4

As she arrived home and opened the front door, Eve could smell Simon's aftershave before she either saw or heard him. A nice smell, of course – unmistakeably her ex-husband. Simon glanced up, smiling, as Eve entered the kitchen and she noted the bottle of Merlot and cheerful Tesco 'seasonal bouquet' on the kitchen table and thought, not for the first time, how lucky she was to have such a thoroughly decent ex-husband. Decent, not to mention handsome . . . And looking particularly nice today because that green shirt brings out his eyes. Eve occasionally forgot why Simon was an ex-husband; nonetheless, it had been ten years now and they'd not only all moved on, they'd stayed close while they'd done it. It was quite a feat – was, in fact, one of the achievements of which Eve was most proud.

'Hello, dear! Good day at the office?' said Simon. 'Hope you don't mind but I was sort of passing so I texted the daughters to see if they were around. Thought you might appreciate this.'

'Thank you, Simon, that's very kind. In fact, you

wouldn't mind opening that right now, would you? It's been a classic first day back at school.' Eve handed Simon the corkscrew. 'Where are the daughters, anyway?'

'Number One has just gone out with Barney – I was gifted a very nice life-the-universe-and-everything-in-fifteen-minutes chat – and Number Two is upstairs, allegedly tackling homework but far more likely to be on Facebook.'

Eve sighed theatrically. 'It's a bugger to get Alice to do homework these days. GCSEs *and* bloody A levels in just eight months' time. Why didn't we leave a bigger gap between them, Simon?'

'Because we weren't planning that far ahead?' Simon shrugged. When Eve and Simon had bravely bucked the living-in-sin trend and married at twenty-six, weddings among their peers had been so unfashionable that theirs had looked like some kind of perversely groovy statement, while the possibility of having actual children was still a long way from being even a hint of a twinkle.

'No, we weren't planning much beyond Friday night, as far as I can remember. Well, at least Zoe has always been nose-to-the-grindstone under pressure. I'm not panicking about her A levels yet. But Alice!' Eve tipped her head to one side. 'Could you be a darling and have a word?'

Simon nodded. 'It's already done. I've played good cop *and* bad cop and then incentivized her with the prospect of a practically bottomless pit of Abercrombie and Whatsit at half-term if she can prove to me that she's putting in the hours. But I said I needed proof. Essays, marks, the works.'

Simon tipped too far back on his chair and locked his hands behind his head. Eve always hated it when he did that; one day she knew he'd go all the way on to the flagstones.

'You are great, thanks. And it's not that I'm not doing any whip cracking, it's just that sometimes it's better coming from you. And of course this year is shaping up to be ... well, *interesting*, with or without bloody exams.'

Simon grinned. 'Yes, please tell me about the Sorensens – it's the real reason I'm here. In my experience, the first thing those sort of people want to do when they buy a bloody great pile full of history is to leave their own architectural mark – tricky when your pile is Grade One.'

Eve went to the freezer and extracted one of her supersized foil-covered lasagnes, often prepped on quiet Sunday afternoons for occasions such as this. 'You'll stay? Look, it's vast; I could go into catering.' Simon nodded approvingly. 'Well, the Sorensens – that is, Stefan and Anette, to those of us who actually know them – have already built a helicopter pad, according to the *Courier*. Of course, if I discover they're thinking about a funky ha-ha or a mad modernist folly or a lovely new garage made of glass, I'll let them know you're available, shall I?'

'Thanks, Evie, though of course it will never happen. They'll probably go straight to David Chipperfield – or maybe Zaha. Wine?'

Eve liked it when Simon called her Evie; he was the only person who did and it whisked her straight back to freshers' week – which, she suddenly realized, had been very nearly . . . 'Simon! I've only just realized, it's been *thirty-five years* since we met.'

Simon started. 'Blimey, you're right. And never a dull moment either, so cheers to that.' He raised his glass of Merlot. 'Maybe, in retrospect, we could've done with a few more dull moments, eh?'

They were still laughing about Edinburgh University in the late 1970s ('You'd hand-stitched your jeans into a pair of drainpipes . . .' 'You can talk – in your shoes made of actual bricks . . .') when they heard Zoe arrive home with Barney.

As she hung Barney's lead in the hall, Zoe paused for a moment, listening to the exceptionally pleasant and slightly unexpected sounds of her mother and father laughing together. It was a good sound, the *right* sound – and it made her happy. However, being seventeen, Zoe was also old enough to appreciate that, were they still married, they'd be unlikely to be laughing together over a glass of red at six p.m. on a random Thursday. They'd probably be a lot more like her friends' parents – at least the ones that were still together – who, if they weren't sniping, were mostly just ignoring each other. For several years when she was younger, Zoe had longed for her parents to get back together – they'd split when she was seven and Alice was five – but now she knew that, even if they had, it could never have worked, and not just for the obvious reasons. They were happy being together now, her mum and dad – just not *together* together. But that was good enough.

'Hi, parents.'

Mid-anecdote, while topping up their glasses, Eve and Simon turned and smiled at their eldest daughter.

'Hello, darling! Good day? I really do wish you'd wear more clothes,' said Eve.

'Yeah. Y'know, kind of a Thursday? And I'm not, like, Scott of the Antarctic. How are the Sorensens?'

'Ha! They're fine; but, as you well know, it's not all about the Sorensens.'

'No, just most of it. Can I have a glass of that, Dad?'

Simon glanced at Eve, Eve raised an eyebrow at Zoe, Zoe hopped from foot to foot and Alice materialized in the doorway. 'If she's having one, I want one too.' A pout.

'Neither of you can have one. Not on a school night. High days, holidays and occasional long, dull Sunday lunches with the grandparents only, I'm afraid,' said Simon, surprisingly firmly.

'You're not the boss of us!' protested Alice.

'I believe I am, actually; another two and a half years for you, young lady, and the best part of a year for *Madam*. After that, for all I care, you can both mainline WKD for breakfast in your respective crack dens.'

Which prompted a noisy duet of '*Shuddup Da-ad!*'

'Can I just say –' Eve paused; everybody turned – 'I do love you lot.' Three pairs of eyes, three smiles . . . 'Simon, is

Ed lurking nearby?' wondered Eve. 'Is he hanging in the pub with a Sudoku, or something? If so, he really ought to come and help us out with this lasagne.'

Simon smiled. 'Actually, he *is* in *Le Lion Rouge*; we were going to have pie and chips and a pint. He thought you might be a bit whelmed, what with it being the first week back at school, and stuff.'

'So text him immediately and tell him to get over here right now. Don't tell me he's not *gagging* to hear about the Sorensens?'

'Of course he is. I was merely doing discreet research on Ed's behalf.' Simon reached for his phone. 'Are you sure there's enough lasagne?'

'Tell him the bloody lasagne will end up inside Barney if he doesn't come. And that Zoe will be scooping up the result of *that* in the morning.'

Zoe pulled a face. 'Gross. Get Ed over here right now *purleeese*, Dad.'

Eve started laying the table. 'Oh, and Simon, tell him to pick up another bottle on the way.'

'Ooh!' said Alice.

'No, Alice,' Eve said firmly. 'Well, OK, maybe a *sip*.' She noticed Simon's raised eyebrow.

'You're in a suspiciously good mood, Mum,' said Zoe. 'So is it, like, OK if I see Rob later?'

'Actually, would you mind very much if we just kept you chained to the dining table for the rest of the evening?' asked Simon.

Zoe looked nonplussed and shrugged. 'Whatever – but why?'

'Actually, Ed and I have some, uh, *news*. I wasn't planning to hit you with it just yet, but seeing as you're all here and in such fine and fabulous fettle, well . . .'

Eve was intrigued. 'Go on. Renewing your vows, are you? Do I need another bloody fascinator?'

Simon laughed. 'No, I think the vows are new enough and feathers aren't really your thing, are they? Let's wait until Ed's here and we'll both get you up to speed.'

Much later, in bed, at the end of a day in which the envelope of her life had been pushed into new and unanticipated directions, Eve couldn't sleep. At 11:56 p.m. she turned on her bedside light for the second time, picked up *Wolf Hall* – after three weeks she was, despite her best efforts, still only on chapter two – and managed another paragraph before giving up again. Try as she did to push them away, seasick thoughts and emotions made her head and stomach heave.

It had been a fine evening. And Eve knew she had been right to make Simon invite Ed – though not just because Ed was one of those rare, special people whose positive presence somehow set the temperature to 'warmer' in any room he graced; an enviable skill, Eve had always thought, and one Ed didn't seem to be remotely aware he possessed. Eve had often wondered if, for Ed, life was simply a series of joyous rooms in which he just happened to be present – and, if so, how wonderful it must be to live so unselfconsciously. Yes – it had been a predictable pleasure to see Ed, whom Eve had, quietly and undemonstratively, come to love almost as much as her husband loved him. This hadn't happened overnight, of course. You couldn't be a red-blooded woman *d'un certain âge* and have your husband of seventeen (mostly) happy years leave you and your children for anybody, much less another man, without some shouting, a few slammed doors and (Eve blushed to recall it now) a bit of chucked crockery, too – though, because she wasn't actually *insane*, nothing that would be missed if it were broken.

However, all the drama hadn't lasted very long because, although she and Simon had long since lost the sexual intimacy (and indeed fidelity) by which so many couples – *most*, presumably – set such store, they had also somehow never quite managed to stop being the best of friends. Thus, when the sobs and screaming matches had finally subsided, and Simon had explained to Eve yet again that he hadn't fallen in love with men per se, he'd fallen in love with somebody who happened to be a man, and that that had been in and of itself entirely disarming . . . after they'd thrashed that one out, over wine, loudly at home and *sotto voce* in restaurants, Simon had somehow persuaded Eve that meeting Ed was not only a good idea, but essential. Eve had resisted for several months but eventually allowed the girls to meet him and then – because, as seven-year-old Zoe had exclaimed, 'We LOVE him! We do! You will too! You WILL!' – she took her emotional cue from her daughters and met Ed, four months after Simon had moved out, on neutral territory.

She had been disarmed when Ed's first words were, 'I am so sorry, Eve – but actually I only want the bits of him that you don't need.' As Eve had burst out laughing, so Simon had looked relieved – while Ed, as it dawned on him precisely what he'd said, looked horrified and tried to backtrack speedily, to no avail.

'No, please don't say a thing – that is just *perfect*.' Eve hiccupped, laughing. 'Believe me, you are *very* welcome to all the bits I don't need!'

After this, not only were Eve and Simon able to salvage the best 'bits' of what was left, they managed to reconfigure them in an entirely different, and arguably much better, way. What *was* left, it turned out, were all the best things they'd shared since freshers' week: the uniquely Simon-and-Evie things they'd managed to build together – the successful careers, the (mostly) happy marriage – and of course their girls. So, it wasn't the past that was eating Eve as she lay in bed, it was the present, and, by extension, a future that had changed as a result of Simon and Ed's news. Or 'the totes *amazeballs* news!' as Alice had swiftly and delightedly dubbed it.

Eve replayed the moment in her head when Simon had said, 'So, the thing is, uh, Ed and I are going to *adopt*. We've been thinking about if for a while and then we started looking into it and now the process has advanced – and rather more quickly than we'd expected or we would have told you sooner, I promise – so, anyway, by mid-October we will be –' Simon had paused and locked eyes with Eve in an attempt to gauge her feelings beyond Eve's speedily assumed and very headmistressy poker face – *'parents. Again.'*

'Speak for yourself, old man,' said Ed. 'This parenting thing is a new one on me.'

Meanwhile, the girls – jaws slack, forks poised mid-air – were silent for several entire moments consecutively before simultaneously exploding.

'A BABY!' squealed Alice.

'Oh. Em. Gee-*sus*!' said Zoe. 'My dad and his husband are having a *baby*?!'

'Steady on, guys,' said Simon. 'It's not a baby. *He's* not a baby. He's a six-year-old boy and his name is Jordan – after Michael, apparently. Who is an American gentleman who played some sort of *sport.*'

Zoe rolled her eyes. 'We do actually know who Michael Jordan is. We weren't born, like, yesterday.'

'I don't know who Michael Jordan is,' said Alice, 'and I don't care.'

'That's because you are so savagely stupid. He's, like, *Air Jordans*!'

Alice ignored Zoe. '*Wow*. A little brother.'

Meanwhile, Simon ignored the nascent sibling squabble at the end of the table and looked closely at Eve, narrowing his eyes. 'Say *something*, Evie. Anything?'

Eve was in fact very keen to say something, but not just anything. And she wasn't feeling particularly 'Evie', either.

Nonetheless, she did the right thing, as she invariably tried to do. 'That is the most completely wonderful news. I am so happy for you both and for, uh, Jordan. He couldn't have two better dads in the entire world, even if he doesn't yet know it. And of course we will be delighted to find a space for him at Ivy House, too, if that's what you'd like?' At which, when Eve saw Simon's affirmative nod and expression of warmth – *love* – it was impossible not to . . . yup, here they came . . . 'And, look, now you've made me cry.'

'Right. I'm going to get that bottle from the car,' said Ed, standing up.

Clever Ed, thought Eve, who stood up at the same time as Simon. 'That's great, but if we even sniff the cork of another bottle I'm definitely calling you both a cab later. Or you can crash here? So many questions and so little time. If only it were Friday.'

Simon walked round the table, took his ex-wife in his arms and hugged her. Both were aware that the girls were watching them intently. 'You are the most magnificent ex-wife an idiot like me could ever have. Thank you.'

'Why are you thanking me? For what?' Eve buried her face into Simon's chest – the part of him, incidentally, of which she was probably most fond, physically speaking.

'For being you. We've sprung this on you on a day when you probably didn't need things sprung, but of course you wouldn't let that show.'

'Yeah, well done, Dad,' said Zoe dryly, 'it's a massively big deal to upstage the *Sorensens*.'

'Family hug?' suggested Alice, sweetly.

So they did.

But now, getting ready for bed, having long-since dispatched Simon and Ed the five miles home to Battle in a minicab, Eve's head was full of *Jordan*. Who was he? She was pleased for Simon and Ed, and the girls. But everything had been absolutely fine just as it was, really . . . and now this.

Maybe it's a sign of incipient old age – a bit of dotage slippage – that I feel so much resistance to change? Eve wondered about this while she squeezed a pipette's worth of Estée Lauder's Advanced Night Repair and massaged it gently into her neck. Though maybe life won't change much at all? Perhaps everything will be fine? It's probably just that I'm fifty-three . . .

Now, in bed, having temporarily given up on Hilary Mantel, she selected instead a thriller set inside an ant colony, which had been recommended to her by Zoe. However, Eve soon recognized, with relief, that being fifty-three – and therefore practically a grown-up – meant that life was far too short to bother reading novels about insects when she was really only interested in people. Thus, having established that she shared her daughter's taste in jeans' brands but not books, Eve decided to give Hilary Mantel another chance and eventually fell asleep close to one a.m. with a head still full of unanswered questions.

# 5

The following morning – a Friday – saw the first proper Ivy House autumn term assembly. Though Eve usually enjoyed assemblies, today she was very slightly on auto-pilot, with her head full of last night's news.

Having reluctantly given up teaching English Lit to the brightest kids in Years Seven and Eight three years previously, since when her days had become increasingly consumed by paperwork and PR, Eve felt strongly that assembly was the best opportunity to make eye contact with as many of her charges and staff as possible. As usual, this morning Eve stood at the entrance to the school theatre (thank you, Mr and Mrs Dershowitz) saying, 'Good morning,' to every pupil by name and preparing to deliver a short, punchy speech that might just raise the pulses of the cleverest kids and (one lived in hope) kick them up a gear or two. Even a head teacher responsible for Ivy House's highest ever number of scholarships to independent secondary schools couldn't, Eve knew, rest on her laurels. The irony, of course, was that the more Eve's pupils achieved, the higher the proverbial bar was raised and therefore the harder it became to jump.

Anyway, despite having half her head still stuck in last night, and without either notes or hesitations, today Eve talked warmly about effort and attainment, the unique knots of friendship that could only be tied at school; she talked about teamwork and co-operation, a bit of meta-phorical bar raising – and jumping as high as one could ... though ideally not off 'The Mound'. This was the old Second World War air-raid shelter that had long since been attractively and expensively landscaped and fenced off, but which nonetheless, despite a great deal of woodchip and *Keep Out* signs (or, probably, because of them), remained an essential extra-curricular rite of passage for pupils in Years Three to Five. Then Eve welcomed every single new and crisply uniformed – navy with red accents – pupil individually and fixed as many of them as possible with her most headmistressy look. It was the look she'd given Simon the previous night and it was an essential part of Eve's professional, and occasionally personal, armoury.

Eve surveyed her audience. 'Now, I'm sure you are already all aware we have four school Houses here – Shakespeare, Milton, Dickens and Austen – and you will all now know to which one you belong. You will stay in your House until you leave the school and, as the name implies, it will be your school-time home from home.' Then Eve went on to explain how, for the last decade, the Houses had been nicknamed: Shakespeare was now also known as Sly,

Milton as Puff, Dickens was Gryff and Austen The Claw. Eve suspected that Harry Potter's on-screen reach was so great that even the children in Reception and Year One understood the references – or pretended they did. 'So, despite the best efforts of several consecutive Year Fives and Sixes, we have failed to provide a Sorting Hat for the first day of term, though one does now often make an appearance during Upside-Down Day – along with a few owls!' At which news some of the smaller pupils looked so excited that Eve hoped she hadn't set off a domino-effect series of impromptu lavatory breaks.

'Upside Down' was Ivy House's red-letter day, held post-exams towards the end of the summer term, during which the school was 'run' by its pupils. It culminated in a performance by the brave/foolhardy staff in which they lightly roasted each other and then spoofed various much-loved school traditions. Instigated by Eve, Upside Down was now in its ninth roaringly successful year and there was every indication it would run as long as *The Mousetrap*. Eve sometimes suspected that Upside Down could be her Ivy House legacy and, depending on whether she had had a good, bad or indifferent day at the office, the thought either delighted or slightly depressed her.

Eve always tried to be positive, had been fundamentally a glass-half-full person all her life. Yet on her emptier days it struck her that, increasingly, there was a great deal to feel uneasy about. In the past, when her girls were younger, Eve had joined in with all the more fashionable mothers making their just-the-right-side-of-dark jokes about, for example, the 'horrors' of 'endless' school holidays. By the end of the summer, indeed, it had often seemed to her as if every woman she knew was publicly bemoaning the monumental misery/boredom of it all. The intended blackly comedic refrain – these were, after all, rather privileged women whose 'eight weeks of hell' generally included at least a fortnight poolside in Provence or Tuscany – was 'the bloody kids have gone feral – can I handcuff them to the radiator without social services finding out?' In other words, it was an in-joke – inasmuch as the relentlessly consuming business of modern parenting was, Eve thought, ever really a 'joke' these days.

When Eve and Simon had one of their post-break-up 'parenting summits', they tended to want to congratulate themselves on the things they'd got right rather than berate themselves for their mistakes. 'I mean,' one would invariably say to the other, 'y'know, for the most part, the girls are fine. Well done us!' That proverbial 'fine'. However, if she and Simon were being really honest with each other, which took courage fortified by wine, they were forced to admit their daughters weren't always paragons of perfection and limitless founts of kindness and generosity, were indeed often a bit rude and somewhat lazy, prone to cheeky backchat or a Berlin-style Wall of Indifference rendered with Contempt.

Eve would sometimes catch sight of Zoe – preferably when Zoe didn't know she was being watched – and fleetingly see signs of . . . well, what? Eve knew there was a certain 'something' in her eldest daughter – a narcissism that perhaps exceeded the entirely predictable teenage vanity and self-absorption. Her own late mother would probably have described Zoe as 'a piece of work' – an expression Eve loved because it sounded like something Rosalind Russell's Hildy Johnson might have *rat-a-tatted* at Cary Grant's Walter Burns in *His Girl Friday* – a film Eve had first seen on TV on a rainy Sunday afternoon with her Edinburgh room-mate-turned-oldest-friend, Cathy, and which had instantly become one of her favourites. So, yes, Eve knew that Zoe was probably 'a piece of work', just as she knew that Alice was, somewhat mysteriously, rather lacking in brightness and occasionally overcompensated for it with a slightly cloying sweetness. Eve knew all this just as she knew there was nothing she could do about it.

In her darker moments, few and far between though they were, Eve sometimes wondered whether her career was the cause or the effect of her own failings as a parent – and whether it was also the compensation. Eve knew that the largely unspoken despair that freighted the middle classes of her generation had never troubled her parents' generation, who had apparently bred, fed and shed their offspring without suffering from any of her own generation's non-specific *parentitis*. Eve thought that kind of ignorance-is-bliss approach was to be envied.

But then Eve didn't like to dwell in the dark for too long. She was by nature a 'do-er', so she would tidy away heretical thoughts on the grounds that failure was no more of an option for her than it was for the children in her charge. Failure was fundamentally an expression of weakness, just as weakness was necessarily a failure. Onward and upward!

So this morning she stood in front of the lectern, voicing her hopes for Ivy House's pupils and felt the usual sense of something approaching pride prickling with another, less easy to define, emotion. Not quite a feeling of foreboding, precisely, but certainly a sense that all things must come to pass. However, before the 'things' could 'pass', the moment passed. Like a senior officer surveying troops, Eve watched as the children filed out of the assembly hall, line by line, and she mentally placed a tick in one of the day's many boxes.

By 9:23 a.m. she was back in her office and Gail was announcing that, 'There's head lice all over pre-prep already, apparently. Oh, and you've got a twelve forty-five today with Lula and Charlie Fox's mother – Susie-thingy? Sorry about that but she said it was urgent.' Eve listened to Gail with one ear and nodded, while inwardly steeling herself for her first meeting of the school year with her boss, Tony Salter – Ivy House's owner and self-styled Principal.

'Is *Tony-Tone* in "Da House" yet?' Eve gave it her best ironic R&B shot, waggling her fingers as air quotes.

Gail giggled. 'Yup, Jay-Z. He just got here and gave Ellie a bollocking for parking her Polo slightly too close to his new black Range Rover with tinted windows. So he has a matching "gangsta" mood.'

Eve tut-tutted. 'Be very careful, Gail, you know these walls have ears.'

Although slagging off the boss was something she and Gail greatly enjoyed, Eve knew she mustn't overstep the mark. At the end of the day – and indeed right now, here, at the beginning – Eve was Gail's boss but Tony was Eve's boss and, in the workplace game, it didn't do to move too fast around the board.

Meanwhile, her eighteen years at Ivy House had more than demonstrated to Gail that for every ladder there were at least a couple of snakes lurking in the long grass. Yet Gail still loved her job, especially as she was privy to most of the school's secrets. There was virtually nothing worth knowing that hadn't long since been gleaned by Gail on the subjects of, for example, the PE teacher who had run off with one of the school's MILFier mothers, which had been the talk of 2007. Tony had been a great deal less annoyed about losing a popular and charismatic teacher than he had been about losing MILFy's three sporty kids to nearby prep school rival, Hartsmere.

'I hear you. But, anyway, Tony says he's ready when you are, baby – apart from the "baby", obviously. I'll bring in a couple of frothy coffees, shall I?'

Eve snorted. 'You bet. Tell him I'll be there in five. And I think I might need two sugars today. By the way, I've been meaning to ask – how is Hazza enjoying being a king of the primary universe in Year Six?'

'Loves it, of course. Look –' Gail pulled out her phone

and handed it to Eve, who scrutinized a recent snap of Harry, in his football kit, flushed with success after scoring a hat-trick.

'Quite right too,' said Eve, noting the boy's broad cheeky grin and distinctive messy cowlick. 'Growing up to be a handsome lad.'

'Thanks! I'm obviously a tiny bit biased but I think he is.'

Eve handed back Gail's phone. There was a momentary silence; though professionally close, there were some things between Eve and Gail that remained undiscussed – not least the issue of Harry's parentage. When Eve had first arrived at Ivy House, Gail had recently returned from maternity leave and all that Eve really knew – or indeed needed to know, at that point – was that Gail was clearly not in a relationship with her son's father. Eve had heard some comments on the subject over the years, of course, but habitually didn't ever give much credence to office gossip. As she'd glanced at the picture on Gail's phone, she'd realized it had been a long time since she'd seen Harry in the flesh; it came as a surprise to see him so grown-up.

As she was about to knock on Tony's office door, Eve steeled herself, breathing in and exhaling deeply. Tony Salter was the price she was forced to pay for having a job she mostly loved and, though over time Eve considered that she had successfully negotiated the price of her soul upwards to counteract Tony's negative impact, a one-on-one with the Principal was often a prospect to be endured rather than relished.

'Come in, come *in*! Darling! You look marvellous! That hair is magnificent! Cracking summer, I hope?'

Tony's speech was invariably a series of articulated exclamation marks. Even if he asked the time of a casual passer-by, he'd chew the scenery like an am-dramatist in a Ray Cooney farce. He was completely exhausting – *vampiric*, as Gail had once memorably described him – and though very firmly heterosexual, he was also slightly camp. Nonetheless, Eve was brilliant with him, assuming a kind of fake cheerfulness verging on that of a CBeebies presenter.

'Lovely summer, Tony – inasmuch as we had a summer! And you? Portugal fun? New motor too, I hear!'

'You know I live for summer, darling. A month on the golf course thrashing pensioners in the Al-*grave* –' Tony delighted in a play on words – 'equals a whole new me, fit for purpose and raring to go. And yes, *my* new satchel is a gorgeous new motor, but my parking space isn't big enough. I'll get Gail to sort it. So!' Tony leaned back into his Eames chair, locked his fingers behind his head and stuck his very large feet on the pristine blonde wood of his stylish 1950s desk; he may have come slightly late to mid-century modern design, but when he finally arrived Tony had embraced the concept with all the obsessive-compulsive enthusiasm of a Year Four pupil collecting Match Attax cards. Unfortunately, Eve was not in a position to confiscate any of it. 'So! Well bloody *done* with the Sorensens, darling! Gold star to the Principal's pet.'

Eve shrugged. 'I like to think we're at the stage where the school does its own selling, but thanks.'

'Nonetheless, you are – as we both know – a marvellous saleswoman. Double glazing's loss was our gain.' Tony leaned forward. 'Are they absolutely horrendous?'

'Far from it – they're charming and there's probably nothing they don't know about . . . *er* –' Eve clutched at names – 'Arne Jacobsen?'

'*Yes!* Make sure they come to the Principal's A-list Christmas drinks, there's a doll. Or at least make the hot one come –' a beat – 'as it were.'

Eve raised an eyebrow. 'I take it you're talking about Mrs Sorensen?'

'Obviously – I'm not a fag!' Tony paused. 'No offence intended, obviously.'

'None taken.' Eve made it a point of principle not to take offence at the Principal, what with the Principal often making offensiveness his raison d'être. Her predecessor, in his first headship, had been far more thin-skinned, conceivably more principled and had lasted precisely two terms simply because he hadn't known how to play the boss. Eve, on the other hand – Kent born-and-bred and grammar school educated – had been acting head in her previous job at a small Kent prep school, Wealden Girls', the owner of which, in his intrepid and single-minded pursuit of absolute and total intransigence, made Tony Salter look infinitely reasonable. This had turned out to be very good preparation for the Ivy House headship. Eve had been perfectly satisfied when, within a year of her departure, Wealden Girls had shut up shop.

'So, I'll hit you with a quick need-to-know on the bottom line, darling.'

'I can barely wait. Fire away!'

'Look, don't panic, we're not completely up shit creek, but we *are* strolling towards the pontoon with a G&T in our hands while admiring the sun setting over the turds.'

'Beautiful picture you're painting there, Tony.'

'So I'm bunging up the fees in January.'

Eve looked slightly startled. 'But—'

'Please don't "but" me – needs must. I held off in July on your say-so, but if we hit them with an increase in January we're unlikely to lose too many because the old parental guilt shtick will kick in and they'll start bulk buying Roll-over Lucky Dips, or whatever. And as for those who do offer the statutory two terms' notice, well –' Tony paused and rocked backwards in his chair, entirely relaxed – 'we'll have a brand new shiny Ofsted "Outstanding" soon enough, won't we, darling? So after that we can market hard? And when I say hard, I mean *bloody* hard.'

Eve shook her head. 'But—'

'No, hear me out. I'll be doing quite a bit of travelling between now and Chrimble – Moscow, Hong Kong, Beijing, that sort of thing. We need all of them onside, especially since we'll be offering the boarding option from Year Three next September.'

Eve considered her half-formed response, thought better of it and said, instead, 'OK, Tony. It's your call. And of course I do see the need for more overseas pupils. I've been reading lots of stuff and talking to people over the summer and it's clearly the only way to go, long term, because numbers are down and dropping – I *know* that. But I still don't think we should put the fees up too dramatically this year.' Eve knew that if they did put up the fees they'd immediately lose the borderlines, especially the recent redundancies eking out their pay-offs, while any potential new locals – the farming set, particularly – would head for Hartsmere. She told Tony this.

'Bloody *Hartsmere* is crap!' Tony pronounced it with the emphasis on *smear*.

Eve nodded. 'I wouldn't disagree with you but they also offer scholarships for showjumping and, for all I know, street dancing.' She shrugged. 'And there's no escaping that it costs an average of just under four grand a term – under three, actually, in the pre-prep. And the girls wear sort of *St Trinian's* boaters and the boys *Just William* caps, and—'

'You've lost me. What the hell have their bloody *hats* got to do with anything?'

'Actually, rather a lot, but I'll save it.'

'Whatever. Hartsmere offers scholarships for spelling the child's name correctly on the application. It really is an absolute crock.'

Eve shook her head. It was no use – Tony really couldn't see that Hartsmere offered entry-level independent education with enough of the trendy bells and whistles (and boaters) to appeal to a pushy parent's petit-bourgeois sensibilities.

'The thing is, Tony, they've nailed their market. They've just built an indoor manége and the upper school is offering a GCSE in PE with a horse-riding module. Who even knew?' Eve shrugged. 'Anyway, my Alice would *kill* to have a GCSE in *My Little Pony* Studies. Oh, and they do a lovely perfect-bound prospectus, too. *Look* –' Having arrived well armed, Eve pushed a copy of Hartsmere's latest brochure across Tony's desk. It was American-A4 sized with thick matte paper, a gatefold cover and pages of cheerful 'lifestyle' shots – lots of pillow fights and pizza nights and air punching on the rugby pitch – with very little text but *lots* of (alleged) quotes from the school's happy band of international pupils. Next to Hartsmere's glossy brochure, Ivy House's sober, accurate and frankly *academic* prospectus suddenly looked a lot like 1990.

'Christ, they've make it look like PGL!' said Tony, flicking through the brochure, eyes widening.

'Better known as *Parents Get Lost*? Precisely my point – it's basically a brilliant work of fiction, and salesmanship,' said Eve. 'Look, Tony – we're not in bloody Gloucestershire; we're in a fairly socially disadvantaged corner of Sussex and you know that for every Sorensen there are fifty mortgaged-to-the-hilt middle managers on the brink of redundo who are killing themselves to send their kids here precisely because we get the results which make it all worthwhile!' At which point Eve surprised herself by thumping Tony's sleek Scandi-woodwork with her fist. 'But for that we cost six grand more than Hartsmere. And, by the way, there are more Billingses on the roll this year than you may be aware.'

'More trailer trash?' Tony shrugged.

'God, Tony, you are appalling. The Billingses may live in a mobile home but you know as well as I do that it is so they can send Chanelle *here*. And hats off to them. It's called *wanting the best for your child*.'

'Ha! Poor kid; she'd be much better off at, I dunno –' Tony paused – 'Eastdene Primary, where nearly everybody gets dropped off in a white van. The only thing Ivy House can probably do for Chanelle Billings is ensure she goes through the rest of her life carrying a monumental chip on her shoulder engraved with the words *Lack of Entitlement – and Angry*. And of course she'll probably resent her relentlessly self-sacrificing parents, too.' At which point Tony paused. 'Is Chanelle Billings by any chance in the same year as the oldest Sorensen – the girl?'

'Aija? She is indeed. In fact, Chanelle is her new-term buddy. And I wouldn't bother slagging off Eastdene. Not now Mike Browning is the head.'

'Dene, schmeen; Browning, schmowning. Whatever. Jesus, Eve – are you conducting some sort of experiment in social engineering?'

Eve shrugged. 'Maybe, in a manner of speaking. Any-way, they're the smartest and – for what it's worth – *prettiest* girls in their year, so they'll either be best friends or hate each other on sight.'

'Be it on your own head. I'm all for shaking things up a bit but this one might just backfire.'

'Actually, I think it'll be fine. And do you know why?'

'Go on.' Tony seemed genuinely intrigued.

'Because I guarantee Jayne Billings will be the only mother who won't be hovering in the car park at four fifteen in an attempt to bag the space closest to the Sorensens' Bentley just so that she can strike up a casual conversation with Anette. And that, because of this, Jayne Billings will probably be the only Year Six mother that Anette Sorensen will actually want to speak to!'

'Brilliant, Sherlock! And then what?'

'Christ, Tony – who knows? It's hardly up to us.' Eve smiled. 'But I like the idea of it.'

'Fine. And I like the idea of increasing the fees after Christmas, so we'll be doing that.' At which point there was a knock on the door and Gail appeared with frothy coffees.

'Sorry these are a bit late. Slight crisis in Year Four.'

'Anything I need to know?' said Eve.

'No, all under control, but I got distracted from my barrister duties for a moment.'

'I think you'll find it's pronounced bar-*ista*, Gail,' said Tony, wrinkling his snub, freckled nose and raising his eyes to the heavens. 'Because you don't need a thousand years of law school to learn how to make a fucking *latte*.'

While Tony relished a little light ritual humiliation with his elevenses, Eve hated it, particularly when he belittled Gail, which he did often, but she was also impressed by how exceptionally unrattled Gail always remained. Like now, for instance.

'Ba-reee-stah. Bareeestah! *Barista!*' Gail enunciated. 'By Jove, Mr Salter, I think I've got it!' She winked at Eve. Eve grinned back. And Tony, apparently still transfixed by Hartsmere's prospectus, missed all of it.

Back in her office, Eve considered Tony's news. Despite many ideological differences, Eve and Tony usually found common ground. This had been much easier pre-recession, when each had got precisely what they wanted without very much in the way of compromise. In the early years of the new century, for example, Ofsted had pronounced Ivy House 'Outstanding'. After that, the roll was up year on year, there was a waiting list for places and Eve had been empowered to make the kind of changes she felt the school needed, turning it from a so-so prep with an intake of round pegs stuffed into round holes, who were in turn dispatched to second- and third-division independent secondary schools, into a non-selective yet academic destination for the area's smarter kids. Given that she'd also managed to keep the less able children (and their deep-pocketed parents) onside too, it was no surprise that Tony Salter had been so grateful to Eve that she'd had a substantial salary increase every year in the decade since she'd started. It was a very cosy arrangement all round.

Gail reminded Eve that she had a 12.30 with Susie Poe, Lula and Charlie's mother, which Eve in turn hoped wouldn't stray past one p.m. because she wanted to grab a lunchtime sandwich in a quiet corner with Ellie Blake. Ostensibly, this was a casual professional catch-up, though of course it would also involve finding out more about that 'crisis' referred to by Gail earlier. These days, one really couldn't be too careful – and obviously not *just* because Year Four equals Petrus Sorensen.

'Ah, hello, Ms Poe! Do come in and sit down. How *are* you?'

'Hello, Mrs Sturridge,' said the fortyish blonde with the feline eyes. 'Please call me Susie.'

'In which case, I insist on Eve. Now, I know it's very early days, but are Lula and Charlie finding their academic re-entry a bit less painful than they maybe expected?'

Susie Poe smiled thinly. 'Actually, I think they're probably just relieved to be back at school. It's been a testing summer . . .' She tailed off, shrugged and then met Eve's searching gaze head-on.

Ah . . . thought Eve as she looked properly at Susie, noticing not only that Lula and Charlie's mother had lost quite a bit of weight since, well . . . whenever it was she'd last seen her, probably Sports Day . . . but also that, for someone who was usually very well groomed, Ms Poe had a large mascara smudge under her right eye, which indicated either a very hasty application or maybe . . . God, yes, of course – stupid me! Eve knew exactly which way this conversation was headed because she had been there many times before. She also knew that the appointment would stray well past one p.m. and involve tea being fetched for them both by Gail. She was pretty sure she'd need the box of Kleenex in her desk drawer, too.

At 1:15 p.m., crumpled tissues now littering her bin, Eve stood up. 'I am *so* sorry, Susie; the last thing I want to do is hustle you out – and of course you are absolutely welcome to stay here for as long as you need – but I'm afraid I have another meeting to fit in elsewhere before the end of lunch.'

Susie hopped nervily to her feet. 'God, is that really the time? I am *so* sorry – but thank you.'

'No need to apologize or thank me.' Eve lay a hand on Susie's arm. 'In fact, I insist that you don't.'

Susie blushed. 'Sorr— God, there I go! Anyway, thanks *very* much for all your help.' She paused. 'And, um, on a totally different note, is it true that the *Sorensens'* kids have just started here? Only, I'd heard a bit of muttering and Lula tells me there's a new girl in her year?'

Of course, thought Eve, you're a journalist. 'Yes, charming couple, delightful children, and yes, Lula's quite right – Aija Sorensen is in her year, though not in her class. In fact, there are two new additions to Year Six, the other being Noah Peck.'

'OK – I'm afraid boys tend to be slower to make it on to Lula's radar.'

'Well, you probably have a year or two's grace in that respect – three, if you're exceptionally lucky. And I speak as a mother of teenage daughters.' Eve offered a hand. 'Have a good weekend, Susie. And don't worry about the children. However, if you *do*, please don't hesitate to pick up the phone.'

As Eve shut the door behind Susie, she decided that *Please do not hesitate to pick up the phone* would probably be inscribed on her headstone – or, more likely, scribbled in red Sharpie on the lid of her cardboard eco-coffin. But before *that* eventuality, it was time to find out about whatever it was that was going on in Year Four. Ringworm, probably, mused Eve. Or threadworms. She grimaced; it was impossible to imagine a Sorensen harbouring a threadworm.

# 6

Gail was sprinkling chocolate on to the top of a frothy coffee in the staffroom when, to her surprise, Eve sidled up, reached over her shoulder for a digestive and said, 'So how's Harry's new head teacher getting on, then?'

Gail smiled. 'Mike Browning is definitely a hit. Quite aside from being an awesome head teacher –' she noted Eve's slightly raised eyebrow – 'he's a handsome, charming, middle-aged bloke who is not only good with kids but apparently genuinely likes the little blighters.' Eve laughed. 'I know – I don't get it, either.'

'And have you met Mrs Browning?'

'There is no Mrs Browning. I suppose there might be one missing-in-action somewhere, but . . .' Gail shrugged.

'Bloody hell – he must be fighting off Eastdene's mums with a stick. Or maybe he's gay? Either way, judging by the pictures I've seen, he looks like George Clooney's younger, better-looking brother.'

'No, he doesn't. He looks like a George Clooney *lookalike*.'

'Well, roughly ninety-nine point nine-nine-recurring per cent of womenfolk would probably settle for that.' Eve paused. 'But seriously, I should probably know the Blairite poster boy Mike Browning much better than I do – if only as a fellow local *educationalist*.'

'He's not only a "superhead" –' Gail wiggled her fingers as air quotes – 'he *has* a super head.'

'Ha!' Eve laughed. 'Though I do wonder why he's at Eastdene. It's already Ofsted "Good with Outstanding Features" and I'm pretty sure rural primaries aren't paying superhead salaries. What is the going rate for a superhead, anyway? Perhaps we ought to get one?'

'I have no idea. But I can tell you – and it has to be true because I read it in the *Courier* – that he earned two hundred and seventy-something thousand pounds one year. And that's more than the head at Eton, apparently.'

Eve glanced at Gail, shaking her head. 'Two hundred and seventy-something thousand quid? I am clearly in the wrong job!'

'Well, I suspect he's probably worth it,' said Gail, adding quickly, 'Not that you're not, of course! Right, I'd better crack on.' And she was halfway to the door when the penny finally dropped. She turned around. 'Ah, Eve? I'm on the Eastdene PTA. Do you want me to ask Mr Browning if he'd like to meet up, informally *and* educationally – and down the Bell?'

Eve smiled, glanced quickly and theatrically around the

empty staffroom and, nodding, said, 'I would, actually, Gail – if you can arrange it. But *shush!* These walls have *ears*.'

Gail grinned. Obviously Eve was joking, though sometimes it was hard to tell.

# 7

When it came to communication with parents, Eve knew she was the yin to Tony's yang, the metaphorical cheery chintz to his chilly minimalism. She was good at everything he wasn't, including *people* – while Tony's skillset lay more behind the scenes in a string-pulling, Wizard of Oz sort of role.

However, there were a few annual occasions from which Eve could not keep him away, and during which Tony liked to make it quite clear that he was the boss. One was Sports Day, where he made himself useful by pinning blue ribbons on to polo shirts. Another was Upside-Down Day, during which he liked to 'send myself up' by cross-dressing as – in so far as anyone could tell – Alastair Sim's headmistress from the old *St Trinian's* film. On Speech Day, Salter enjoyed presenting the trophy to the year's winning House, and at Christmas he liked to host a pleasantly forgettable – to the guests, if not Tony – drinks party. Originally this had been conceived as a party for all the school's parents; however, over the years, two separate parties had evolved after Tony had initiated an intimate A-list soirée for those parents whom he perceived to be far too bloody important/rich/posh/all of the above to have to mingle with, for example, the *Billingses*.

As far as Eve was concerned, every child at Ivy House was treated equally, but, when it came to Tony, some of their parents were considered just that bit more equal than others. Eve had noted on numerous occasions that Tony was perfectly happy to take the Billingses' cash – and they did sometimes pay fees in cash, for which they received a ten-per-cent discount (and the fewer questions asked about *that*, the better, frankly). However, accepting that cash did not, in Tony's eyes, equate to any kind of endorsement of the Billingses' lifestyle choices, social mores or, more specifically, what he described as their 'trailer'. Unlike Tony, Eve had actually once been to the Billingses' 'trailer', for Christmas drinks. It was in fact a very high-end log-cabin-style 'park home' with three bedrooms, an en-suite, an attractive cedar-clad exterior and gorgeous rural views, especially from the hot tub on the deck. Not only had Eve considered it to be about as far from 'trashy' as a prefabricated home could be – not a burning tyre in sight – it was also, rather ironically, positively Scandi-chic. However, Eve knew that Tony would never discover this for himself because he was a screaming snob. Given this, the fact that Tony's own front doorstep featured a pair of anodized zinc pots with dwarf bay trees, just like the Billingses', had made Eve smile.

So, on the eve of half-term, Tony summoned her to his office to discuss (she thought) this year's A-list parents' Christmas drinks party – which, due to the A-list parents' relentlessly hectic social schedules, had, over the years, slipped back in the calendar from its original mid-December spot to its current position in November. Now apparently Tony was thinking of rebranding it, losing the Christmas bias, and bringing in fireworks, mulled wine and hot dogs on the lawn. Big wow, thought Eve as she knocked on Tony's door and entered without waiting for a response. Silence. Tony was lying at full stretch, shoeless, on one of the sofas, reading matter perched on his comfortable stomach.

'Right. I'll sit, shall I?' Eve didn't wait for an answer but took her place on the slightly-too-hard sofa perpendicular to Tony's.

'So anyway,' said Tony, as though they were already in mid-conversation, 'we'll be slipping a little letter in with the, uh, *glowing* reports at the end of this term, and I'm entirely optimistic that that is the very best thing to do. In future, I'll make sure we won't be forced to rely on our local parents. After Christmas, I'm straight off to meet with –' Tony waved a sheaf of papers – '*this* lot.'

'Who are . . . ?' Eve leaned forward and peered. Nothing doing – having expected to discuss firework-display budgets, she'd left her reading specs on her desk.

'InterEduSol: "Innovative marketing and international-ization strategies for global education providers".' Tony hauled himself up to a sitting position and started to read:

'"In a world of constant change and challenges, how can you ensure your academic institution triumphs over competition and quality concerns? How willing are you to accept that expanding into overseas markets, commerce and convergence are essential for those twenty-first century global education providers intent on succeeding – and prospering – in the future?"'

'Oh, God. What does any of that actually *mean*?'

'Who gives a shit? This is the future and I can tell you that intensive undercover research reveals our good friends over at –' Tony paused, wrinkled his nose – 'Hartsmere, are fully-paid-up members of the InterEduSol –' Tony wiggled his fingers, air-quote style – '"community". So, anyway, as I was saying – "InterEduSol is a B2B consultancy with more than twenty years' experience in bringing schools, colleges and universities together with new students, education partners, technology and fresh and exciting revenue sources from abroad. We are committed to providing international student recruitment strategies for a twenty-first century market." So there we are, darling – the future's bright, the future's—'

'"Fresh and exciting revenue sources from abroad"?'

'Exactly – pots of lovely cash from your Russian oligarchs and Far Eastern potentates who are very sensibly wishing to buy into the considerable benefits of a world-renowned British independent education. I hope you're not going to come over all sentimental, Eve? This is the future.'

'And of course, if that future's so "bright", we'd better buy into it?'

'I don't see how we can avoid it. And even if we *could*, why would we want to?'

'Because . . .' Eve paused. There was a point she very much wanted to make but she also wanted to make it in the right way, lest it be lost, unheard or simply bludgeoned by Tony's bombast. 'Because we might be punching above our weight? Here we are, a happy, successful little prep school, relatively under the radar, all things considered, and now we're having to engage with, what the hell is it again? Twenty-first century international student recruitment strategies?' Eve sighed. 'You're making me feel really old, and I'm not ready to feel old just yet.'

'You're not old, darling – you're just grown-up. Totally different thing.'

Eve shrugged. From where she was sitting, which was quite literally on the edge of a very uncomfortable sofa, it was hard to tell the difference. 'The world is changing, Tony – and that's not necessarily a bad thing. It's just the *speed*.'

'Leave the speed stuff to me, darling – I'm built for it.' Tony stood up, stretched, ran his fingers through his hair, making it stand up straight like a fifties rocker's DA, and started throwing fake punches, shadow-boxing an invisible opponent. He looked utterly absurd, though in his own mind presumably he was floating like a butterfly, stinging like a bee. Not for the first time, Eve marvelled at

Tony Salter's complete lack of self-consciousness – with all that that implied.

'Fucking –' *puff* – 'Hartsmere –' upper cut, jab, *puff* – 'bunch of –' *puff-puff—*

'Yeah, you take 'em down for us,' Eve interrupted. 'Meanwhile, I'm going to drink coffee and eat stollen and fine-tooth-comb a few reports, if that's OK?'

Shutting Tony's office door quietly behind her, Eve didn't wait to find out because her head was already halfway out of the building; twenty-first century international student recruitment strategies could wait. She was looking forward to a half-term working mostly from home and, more importantly, catching up with the girls. She was a mile from home before she remembered she'd had an informal meeting booked in with Ellie Blake, who had wanted to talk to her about Jordan. Damn and blast and bugger . . . How could I forget *that*? Eve berated herself and put her foot down. She'd call Ellie from home, before the girls got back . . .

Simon and Ed had, of course, told her quite a bit about Jordan. His background wasn't, to all intents, horrifically tabloid-headline-grabbing, but it was clearly confused in a contemporary sort of way. There were lots of siblings and half-siblings and step-siblings and he seemed to have got lost in the middle of them all, somehow, and then there were a succession of parents, step-parents, 'uncles' and 'aunties', and his mother had had alcohol problems and a breakdown, and the children had been removed from her, for a period, and then she'd got them back and had seemed to be 'on top of it'. However, after this, Jordan had never quite fitted in, had started displaying 'behaviours', so (and Eve didn't quite know how these things worked and didn't really feel she needed to, frankly, given that her professional life was already full of other people's children) Jordan had been put up for adoption by a local authority, after which, Simon and Ed and Jordan had all found each other, miraculously.

And somehow, now that he was a pupil at Ivy House, Jordan had become her problem, too. This was a situation in which it was unfortunately hard to separate the personal from the professional. Eve felt a twinge of regret for having ever suggested that Simon and Ed send Jordan to Ivy House in the first place. And then, of course, she felt guilty for thinking that. So much guilt, so little time.

# 8

It was a mercifully quiet half-term. Harry was at his football club for five consecutive mornings, which allowed Gail to get on top of things domestically. Then, in the evenings, he was in bed early, properly physically exhausted. 'Run boys out like dogs. They'll be tired and you'll be happy,' her dad – one of four boys himself – had often said. It may have been an old-fashioned approach but there was no denying it worked.

So with Harry sound asleep by 8:30 p.m. Gail spent her leftover evenings home alone with her boxed sets. A crime buff, Gail had seen enough episodes of *Silent Witness* and *Wire in the Blood* to know that serial killers often created a shrine to their victims in some dank basement or claustrophobic attic lined with newspaper cuttings and pictures downloaded from the internet – in the corner of which the poor victim might often be found alive (albeit cowering, gagged and chained) by the police, in the fifty-ninth minute of the eleventh hour, especially if that victim were female – and preferably a female child that bore a passing resemblance to the young Cosette from *Les Misérables*.

Gail had occasionally wondered if these creepy 'shrine' scenes were based on fact or had originally been invented by a thriller writer, after which the idea had caught on among *actual* serial killers so that eventually the whole elaborate construct had become a kind of media invention that had eaten itself. Gail was extremely interested in this kind of thing – though not in any particularly sinister way, much less as a thriller-writer *manqué*. No, Gail was interested because, at some point in the future, when Harry was older, she secretly hoped to do a degree in criminology, maybe even forensics. However, she had also read that these courses now attracted large numbers of students, presumably also lured by consuming boxed sets of *CSI*. Not that Gail believed you could ever consume too many boxed sets of *CSI*.

In the meantime, Gail honed her super-methodical, neat-freak approach to all aspects of her own and Harry's life by resisting the urge to turn her attic office space into a kind of shrine to forensics and criminology, mostly on the grounds that to do so would make her look bonkers. In fact, she had veered so far in the opposite direction that the effect was maybe even more sinister . . . After all, what could be scarier than your classic scary cinematic cliché? Answer: its antithesis.

When surfing YouTube in order to discover yet more nerdy gamer-boys who narrated their way through their *Minecraft*ings, Harry preferred to use their shared laptop downstairs in the kitchen or (much to Gail's irritation) on the coffee table in front of the telly. However, occasionally he'd venture into her eyrie, pull a face and say, 'I don't like your office, Mum – there's nothing in it.'

It was true – the room was a wipe-clean magnolia-tinted shrine to blank canvases. Other than the louvre blinds, which cast a moody *CSI* sort of light, and a 1990s-looking computer table with a Sony VAIO (a member of the Walkman rather than the iPod generation and all but oblivious to fashion trends, Gail was Sony brand-loyal to the point where she would happily have bought a Sony car), there was nothing in the room to distract the eye from whatever might be the business at hand. Mind you, look out of Gail's study window and it was an entirely different story. Even in autumn one could see that Mike Browning's garden was coming on beautifully – he'd achieved that outdoor room in the garden that everybody seemed to aspire to these days, all bifolding doors and a chiminea and patio furniture that Gail felt was perfectly good enough for her lounge. Yes, it was truly a pleasure to overlook Mike's house and garden – just a shame she couldn't strike up a conversation about his work on the house without making herself look as if she was, well, if not a *stalker*, precisely, maybe somebody whom he might decide was slightly too close for comfort, twenty-four/seven. Gail felt that the only thing worse than Mike believing her to be in any way stalkery would be for Mike to move away.

However, as both an Eastdene Community Primary parent and his next-door neighbour, Gail seized upon any legitimate interactions with Mike wherever and whenever she could. For example, they often bumped into each other arriving or leaving their houses, and then Gail was an active member of the PTA, so she'd seen him during heavily chaperoned chats about the cost of replacing the woodchip near the monkey bars with some of that hardwearing foam. Then she'd very nearly engineered a casual collision at the pub when she'd seen Mike leave his house on a Sunday at 12:45 p.m., swiftly and inaccurately interpreting this as a stroll-to-the-pub-for-a-pie-and-a-pint manoeuvre. Harry was out, so Gail had hastily gathered her own belongings and emerged from her front door just in time to see Mike's back moving away from her in what was, even if you chose the scenic route, unequivocally the opposite direction to the pub.

Eventually, however, it was less a case of Gail's persistence paying off as it was the law of local averages coming into play when Gail bumped into Mike, not in Eastdene, but, of all places, in the wine aisle in their nearest Sainsbury's on a Saturday morning. Gail laughed when she spotted they'd both chosen the same white wine – on a very good offer so not exactly the coincidence to end all coincidences – and then again, a few minutes later and largely, it must be said, engineered by Gail, when they found themselves in the same checkout queue.

'Ah, hello, *neighbour*!' said Mike. Firstly, it was all professional business ('So, is it best for the PTA to spend on foam or save on woodchip?') and then, much to Gail's astonishment, he'd suggested a cuppa in the supermarket's café.

'So,' said Mike, stirring his latte, 'I'm very glad I moved to Eastdene. Proper community and a proper community school.'

'Are you a Londoner?' Gail enquired politely.

'No, born in the Midlands – Walsall, to be specific. But I left at eighteen and, apart from flying visits to see Mum, I've never really looked back.'

'You don't have a Midlands accent.'

'According to friends, it does occasionally emerge after a drink or two, though happily not –' Mike glanced down at his latte – 'after a coffee. Are you local, Gail?'

'Yes, very local.' She glanced at Mike, and then could feel a blush rising so she stared at her tea. 'I couldn't really envisage being anywhere else.'

'You work at Ivy House, right?'

Gail nodded. The last thing she wanted to do was talk about work. 'Yes, I'm the head's PA. Been at Ivy House eighteen years now. Unbelievable, really.'

'I bet you're a great PA. Sadly, my budget will never run to one.' Gail wondered if this meant that, if he had a budget, he'd be asking her to be his PA. And then she swiftly dismissed this as overthinking. Mike, necessarily oblivious, carried on. 'Seeing as you've been in and around it for so long, did you never think about maybe teaching?'

Gail started, surprised. 'Well, er, yes – I *am* actually qualified.' She could feel herself stumbling, 'I was a teacher for my first seven years at Ivy House.'

'OK. So . . . ?'

Gail rushed to fill the gap. She had her reasons but she wasn't going to share them with him. Or anyone else, for that matter. 'I, uh, decided it wasn't really for me.' This seemed a bit vague, so she elaborated. 'I felt that my skills lay, um, elsewhere. So I was lucky to be able to make that change while staying at Ivy House.'

'Teaching's loss, clearly!' Mike smiled and got to his feet. 'Right, I have a lawn to mow. It was nice bumping into you, Gail. Have a great weekend.'

'Yes, yes, you too. I will, thanks!' She watched approvingly as Mike tidied the contents of his tray into a rubbish bin. And then she remembered what she needed to do and hopped to her feet in order to catch him. 'Mike?'

He turned around. 'Yes?'

'I wonder if you'd be interested in meeting my boss, Eve Sturridge? She mentioned you the other day, just before half-term, and as fellow –' Gail made air quotes with her fingers – ' "local educationalists" she thought that you should probably get together sometime, so I said I'd ask you if I got a chance. We were thinking about an academic summit in the Bell?'

Mike smiled. 'Why not? Yes, that would be fun. My evening schedule is bound to be less hectic than Mrs Sturridge's, so why don't we let her choose? Take my number and text me.' As Gail rummaged in her bag for her phone, Mike said, 'And thanks, Gail.'

## 9

In the event, the A-list parents' drinks party fell on a random Tuesday in mid-November, plans to 'rebrand' it having been put on hold until next year. What with December being a non-starter for the alpha crowd, for whom it was chock-full of charity fundraisers, big corporate seasonal bashes and the occasional intimate soirée in New York with their best friends from the World Economic Forum meeting in Davos, the mid-November date effectively chose itself.

Ivy House's parental heavy-hitters numbered about twenty couples, from the super-rich Sorensens to the relatively impoverished local landed gentry, the Percys, generations of whom had been prep-schooled through various Ivy House incarnations, mostly because their farm adjoined the school. Just like their forebears, the current crop of small Percys – four of them, aged between three and eleven – arrived each morning via a stile on the far side of the coppice.

While she contemplated the guests milling around

chatting politely to one another, Eve noted that the drinks party attracted mostly the A-list wives, their husbands presumably busy mastering the universe elsewhere. Mrs – *Dr* – Anna Dershowitz was, Eve recognized (not for the first time) properly *classy*: mid-forties, sharply featured and elegantly elongated, she was wearing a barely there, yet also intriguingly demure, black cocktail dress with some sort of clever draping around the neck and sleeves and the kind of complicated and painfully architectural-looking shoes that Eve understood aesthetically if not practically ('She's wearing *hooves!*' Gail hissed at Eve as she passed by with the canapés. 'No,' Eve replied, 'she's wearing McQueen').

In short, Anna Dershowitz was both daunting and exciting in pretty much equal measures; ferociously clever and famously witty, she was your classic power-behind-the-throne Alpha Wife: an ex-academic with a laser-guided missile of a brain that, Eve knew, habitually turned the Tony Salters of the world into microwaved Ready Brek. On the outside, however, Eve noted that, even if microwaved, Tony usually managed to behave quite normally in her company, greeting Anna warmly and in a manner that was entirely seemly and appropriate. In recent years the Dershowitzes had contributed a considerable percentage of the school's excellent facilities, but now, sadly, with the youngest remaining Dershowitz a third of the way through Year Eight, all good Dershowitz-related things were coming to an end. Nonetheless, Salter and the Dershowitzes had been on first-names terms for the best part of a decade. On the edge of the group, Eve watched their interaction, intrigued by the juxtaposition.

'Delighted you could make it, Anna,' said Tony, leaning forward for the obligatory brush of cheekbones.

'Delighted to be here, Tony. It was rather touch-and-go whether either Mr D or I would be able to come, but in the event he drew the short straw and went to the J. P. Morgan do, while I've joined forces with Anette, here – which is, of course, so much more fun.'

Eve watched Tony turn to Anette Sorensen, whom he was meeting for the first time. Anette was thus spared kisses and received Tony's extended hand – clammy, no doubt, thought Eve. While Anna D was scary-chic, Eve supposed that, to Tony, Anette Sorensen was as scary-sexy as photographic evidence always suggested. And she smelled divine. 'A great pleasure to meet you, Mrs Sorensen,' said Tony, just this side of unctuous. 'I hear that, uh, Ai-jaa and Petruuus –' the exciting but unfamiliar conjunctions of vowels and consonants stuck to the roof of Tony's mouth like a claggy crumble – 'are settling in marvellously well. Obviously we're *delighted*.'

'As indeed are they.' Anette Sorensen was wearing another clever cocktail-frock-and-challengingly-cantilevered-shoe combination; however, the dress was the palest dove-breast grey against her white-blonde hair, so that she and Anna looked like each other's negatives. 'They are both enjoying school very much, which is great news for their father and me. In fact, it seems we did all the worrying on their behalf!' Anette continued, apparently oblivious to Tony's goldfish expression and stunned silence.

It was her job, Eve felt, to step in and rescue things. 'We find it's very often the way: all parents are naturally concerned about how well their children will adapt to a big change – and then the children themselves invariably take it all in their stride.'

'Ah, but only if the parents have made the right choices on their behalf,' said Anna Dershowitz. 'And, as it would seem that you and Stefan have done exactly that, you can presumably relax and start to enjoy your new English country lifestyle.'

'Yes, and how are you finding our neighbourhood?' said Tony, mostly recovered by now. 'I do hope we've given you a warm welcome?'

'Very warm, thank you. Stefan is here, there and pretty much everywhere other than where we'd like him – so not very relaxing for him – but when we *do* have him, we're having such a great time together. We're all very excited about our plans for the future of the estate – we have some building to do – and very keen for the children to learn just how much work it takes to run it all.'

*Building!* Eve couldn't resist. 'Well, if you're planning any building, I can recommend an excellent architect. The fact that he's the father of my children is, frankly, entirely by-the-by.'

'Your husband's an *architect*?' said Anette. 'I am all ears.'

'Ex-husband – but we're on extremely good terms. Have you seen the Dershowitzes' marvellous glass tree-house? It made the cover of *ELLE Decoration* in the summer. That's Simon's. Though the majority of his buildings don't tend to be suspended twenty feet in the air.'

'You know how much I *adore* your tree-house, Anna! How stupid of me not to have made the connection that Simon Sturridge was Eve's husba— *ex*-husband!' exclaimed Anette, slapping – albeit very gently – her smooth forehead with an elegantly manicured hand.

'Obviously I'm biased, but Simon is a marvellous, imaginative modern architect – though not so imaginatively modern that his buildings actually scare you,' said Eve. 'You wouldn't cut yourself on their edges, for example. They're . . . uh . . .'

'Organic?'

'Well, yes, but not in a mulching-the-allotment sort of way, more of an eco-sustainable sort of way. But, even though I'm a fan, I'm not the best person to talk about Simon's work . . .' Eve tailed off, conscious not only of having potentially overstepped the mark but of having evoked *allotments*. However, Anette's enthusiasm seemed entirely genuine.

'No, and of course there's no need for any of us to do Simon's PR – is there, Eve? – given he's actually terribly good at it himself,' said Anna.

'Well, I shall speak to him. And I have a particular project in mind, too,' said Anette, firmly. 'So you have children, Eve?'

Eve nodded, grateful for the shift of subject: 'Yes, two daughters – seventeen and fifteen. Simon and I regret not having left a larger gap between them because next year we shall all be coping – or otherwise – with A levels *and* GCSEs. And I for one am not looking forward to that.'

'No, I can imagine! And are the girls either budding architects or head teachers?' asked Anna Dershowitz.

'Hardly!' laughed Eve, just as she caught sight of Richard Percy wandering the room, ignored by the rest of the staff. If not as lonely as a cloud, then he was as lonely as any other florid-faced, jug-eared middle-aged man who had never entirely shaken off the prep-school nickname Dick Cock. 'Tony, um, Mr Percy seems to be all at sea . . .'

She watched Tony following her gaze and suspected he was calculating, correctly if reluctantly, that there were more young Percys than there were minor Sorensens and Dershowitzes at Ivy House, thus . . . 'Ah, now do please excuse me, ladies,' he said, peeling away.

'God, no – not architects *or* teachers!' Eve continued, 'Alice considers her GCSEs to be some sort of largely irrelevant qualification she has to fit in between dressage tests, while Zoe is doing Maths, Politics and Economics for her As and desperately wants to go into the City.' Eve shrugged. 'To do exactly what, I have no idea, but then I'm entirely baffled by finance.' At which point, Eve became very conscious of sharing this information with a couple of women who presumably weren't *remotely* baffled by finance and felt the rising heat of an uncharacteristic blush of gaucheness. Though she wasn't sure how much of a role, if any, Anette actually played in her husband's hedge fund, it was fairly safe to assume that Dr Anna Dershowitz (PhD in Economic Research from Cambridge) had more than a working knowledge of whatever it was – venture capital? – that went on at the Dershowitz & Dohenny Group. Either way, if Eve hoped the subject would be changed, she was disappointed.

'Well, if Zoe would like to have a taste of the financial life, I know we have some very sought-after work placements at Odense Holdings – and I am sure the same is true of D&DG? There is quite a bit of coffee purchasing. But then it's a very caffeinated kind of environment, isn't it, Anna?'

'And how! But yes, if Zoe's interested, do let either – or both – of us know, and we'd be delighted to put her in touch with the right people,' said Anna.

Eve felt slightly flustered by this pincer movement. Even without the possibility of a commission for Simon, this was a lot of generosity and, if there was one thing Eve hated, it was feeling beholden. It actually panicked her, the sense that she was being given gifts she could never return. 'That's incredibly kind of you both, but—'

'No buts necessary,' said Anette, surprisingly firmly. 'You're educating our children, so the very least we can do is offer a tiny bit of vocational training to one of yours.'

OK, fair enough, when you put it like that, thought Eve. 'That's enormously kind of you both and I know Zoe will be particularly thrilled. And of course I'll be delighted too because it means she'll be able to come home and tell me what a hedge fund actually does. It's a major gap in my knowledge.'

'And meanwhile my Latin is easily as bad as my French, which is pretty terrible, so we're probably all square,' smiled Anna. 'Now, if you don't mind, I'm going to whisk Anette over to see one of her neighbours.' Anna leaned forward and whispered into Eve's ear: 'Is it true that locally everybody refers to him as "Dick Cock"?'

Eve grabbed Anna's forearm to steady herself while suppressing a snort of laughter before assuming her faux-stern headmistress face. 'We have educated several generations of the Percy family at Ivy House, so I couldn't possibly comment.'

A few minutes later, Eve noticed that Mrs S and Mrs D had left, just after their brief chat with Richard Percy, which had in turn been chaperoned by Tony. Nonetheless, Eve dutifully and methodically spent another forty minutes working her way around the room, ensuring she spoke to everybody who wasn't on the Ivy House payroll, by which time there were only a couple of handfuls of parents and staff remaining. She tapped Tony on the shoulder and made her excuses, after which Gail tapped Eve on hers: 'I've ordered you balti lamb, saag aloo and a peshwari naan. Hope that's OK? It'll be ready to pick up in ten minutes. Night!'

'You are an absolute bloody *angel*, Gail,' said Eve, greatly cheered by the prospect of not having to eat a microwaved supper while standing up and, possibly, arguing with a teenager.

Twenty minutes later, at home, eating the delicious balti while – luxury of luxuries – sitting down, Eve attempted to tear her thoughts away from the first half of her evening in order to listen to her daughters competing for her attention with tediously increasing levels of whini-ness. 'Could you please both just shut up! You know I can stand almost anything but I do draw the line at *whines*. On the subject of which . . .' Eve paused and extracted the remains of a three-day-old bottle of white from the fridge. 'Right. Who wants to go first? How was your day, Alice?'

Eve sipped and sort of half listened while Alice raced through a quick précis of a Year Eleven school day, with which her mother was au fait, what with it not being wildly different to, say, a Year Ten or Twelve day, apart from the dreaded looming GCSEs.

'Any kind of prep being undertaken this week – maybe? Any chance that my delightful youngest daughter won't cover her parents and herself in ignominy?' Eve knew that not all mothers spoke to their children the way she spoke to hers; nonetheless, at her instigation, sarcasm had become a conversational keystone among the female mem-bers of the Sturridge family.

Alice nodded. 'Yup; I've done precisely ninety minutes of French and that was after I'd done an hour with Monty, too.'

Monty – or, to give him his proper name, Montague Verona – was a 15.2hh thoroughbred bay gelding bought by Simon for his horse-mad youngest daughter's thirteenth birthday and bankrolled not only by the Dershowitzes' tree-house commission but by the business accrued from its high profile and design awards. As soon as Alice had fallen for ponies, Eve had known this was not going to be a cheap hobby; however, she had been both astonished and slightly terrified by the expense – and grateful the tab was mostly being paid by Simon. On the other hand, she'd also been secretly rather impressed by Alice's horse-related work ethic: fifty per cent of Monty's livery fees were now sucked up by Alice shovelling horseshit from A to B every Saturday and three evenings a week at the yard. The impact of this fairly thankless manual labour on her daughter's GCSEs was, of course, yet to be seen.

'Great!' said Eve. 'And Zoe – have I got news for you!'

Zoe didn't look up as she replied to the *ding* of an incoming text on her phone. 'Yeah?'

'Yeah, *yeah*. So how is Rob?'

'Yeah, cool.' Zoe carried on staring at her phone. 'S'what's the news?'

'If you deign to make eye contact, I'll tell you.'

Zoe looked at her mother blankly. 'Sorry, what?'

'Thanks for joining me. So, I had a chat with two of the more high-profile mothers this evening – the fathers off being fabulously high-profile elsewhere.'

'Mrs Sorensen!' said Alice.

'*Indeed*, Mrs Sorensen,' said Eve.

'And Mrs Dershowitz?' Even Zoe was intrigued by this double whammy of high-financial glamour.

'You bet. They're big mates, anyway, of course, but you may be interested to hear that we talked about you.'

'Me?' Zoe scrunched up her (lovely, Eve noted) nose. 'Like, really *me*?'

'Yeah like, really *you*. In fact, when they heard what you're studying, they both offered you the possibility of work placements. Practically fell over each other to do it, too.'

'You are kidding me, right?'

'No; though I hope you realize how lucky you are, young lady, because an internship at either of these businesses must be extremely sought after.'

'God, *yeah*. So what do I do?' Zoe hopped from foot to foot; Eve couldn't recall the last time she had seen her daughter looking so unequivocally thrilled.

'They'll tell me who to contact and put in a good word, and then you can do the rest yourself, by email. But please make sure I see it first. After that, it's over to you.' Eve smiled at her eldest daughter, who smiled back before glancing down when her phone *ding*ed again. 'Oh, and here's a tip. No random texting during conversations in the high-powered office, yeah?'

'That's a bit like saying, "No breathing," Mum – but whatever. And thanks!'

'I meant no texting *Rob*, really. Can you even conceive of the fact that my generation went for many, many years without –' Eve wiggled a pair of air quotes with her fingers – ' "breathing". Kind of miraculous, in retrospect.'

Zoe shrugged. 'We all know your life was basically ten thousand kinds of tragic.'

As she soaked up Zoe's insouciant cheekiness, Eve briefly recalled herself at seventeen, recalled the intensity of it all via a series of mental snapshots – of being drunk on cider at parties, where something mournful by David Bowie always seemed to be playing in the background whenever the wrong boy made a lunge for her, invariably at exactly the same time as the right boy was busy lunging at her friend. It seemed – indeed was – *a long, long time ago* . . . And Eve suddenly found herself humming the rest of 'The Man Who Sold the World' as it occurred to her that, back then, no seventeen-year-old girl would ever have told her mother that her life was 'tragic', even as a joke.

'Right,' said Eve, as casually as she could manage, 'I'm off out to the Bell, for a drink – with Gail.' She felt this announcement was unusual enough to provoke a question or two from her daughters; however, there was not the slightest flicker of interest. To have her life perceived as relentlessly dull by her children was, of course, the inevitable parental lot. Eve sighed and picked up her keys.

'Bye, Mum. Have fun. Don't drink and drive,' said Zoe, glancing up from her phone.

To be perceived as dull and patronized, too . . . thought Eve, who planned to drive, anyway.

In the event, it was a very short evening – considerably shorter than either Eve or Gail had expected. Gail arrived first, and was already sitting in the corner with two glasses of Sauvignon when Eve joined her. When Mike arrived five minutes later, Gail introduced Mike to Eve and vice versa, apologizing for not buying him a drink: 'I know Eve's tipple but I would have got yours wrong, I'm sure.'

'Yes, I don't know how handy the Bell is at knocking together a margarita.' Mike held out a hand. 'Good to meet you, Eve. And thanks to Gail for bringing us together for this, uh, educational summit across the political divide.'

Gail grinned; however – and entirely unexpectedly – Eve smiled a very tight little smile and said, rather grandly, 'I wouldn't necessarily bother making any assumptions about my politics, Mr Browning.'

Mike looked surprised. 'I'm so sorry. I didn't mean to offend.'

Eve shrugged. 'The thing is, it's very easy to assume that a parochial prep school head teacher must be, at the very least, small-c conservative, if not actually large-C.' Mike raised an eyebrow as, to Gail's astonishment, Eve carried on. 'However, I think that would be both lazy and presumptuous. A bit like assuming that, for example, an inner-city superhead teacher on a whopping great salary is always going to vote for the hand that wrote the cheque.'

Eve took a sip of her Sauvignon. 'Except, of course, that he *is*.'

Mike looked suitably astonished. 'Well, *now* who's making assumptions? Goodness, that's a start to the evening I hadn't anticipated.'

Gail was crestfallen; it was so unlike Eve to be socially prickly. What on earth could be the matter? For her part, however, Eve appeared unfazed.

'So, why on earth *did* you take what must have been a huge pay cut to move to Eastdene, Mr Browning? It's hardly at the epicentre of things. I would've thought a big urban state secondary in special measures would've been more your thing?'

'It's *Mike* – please. We may not have got off to the best start but I do think we can salvage something of the evening, especially if we're on first-name terms,' said Mike Browning easily.

Gail was impressed by how hard he was trying to turn things around, though she suspected it was in vain; in her experience, whenever Eve got into one of her (admittedly rare) bad moods, it tended to take time to work itself out.

Which is exactly what came to pass. In the hope the mood would shift a little quicker in her absence, Gail excused herself to go to the loo while Mike (presumably) answered Eve's question. And though the atmosphere had been marginally less awkward by the time she returned, it was clear the evening would be truncated to some tetchy small talk over a couple of drinks. Gail was embarrassed and a little annoyed; both Eve and Mike been keen to meet each other and so, having arranged it, she resented feeling compromised. She sipped her Sauvignon and waited for Eve to offer to buy the next round, but that didn't happen. Instead, having drained her glass, Eve stood up and said in her in briskest, most head-teachery tone, 'Well, thank you, Gail, for arranging this and I'm sorry it turned out to be so brief. However, just as Margaret Thatcher wasn't for turning, turns out I'm not really one for patronizing. Good luck at Eastdene, Mr Browning.'

Gail noted that Mike shared her father's old-school decency, standing up as Eve left – even if this gallant manoeuvre was lost on Eve, whose rather swooshy coat enabled her to sweep grandly – Thatcherishly, even – out of the Bell.

Gail dived into the silence. 'I am *so* sorry, Mike. I had no idea that would happen. It's entirely unlike her. I just don't get it at all.'

Mike shrugged. 'No problem, Gail – and thanks for trying. It was rather unexpected, though, especially as I have only heard great things about, um, Mrs Sturridge. Still, everybody's entitled to an off day, not to mention a difference of opinion. Now, can I get you another glass of wine?'

Gail nodded. 'I think I need one, thank you. And please can we steer clear of politics?' Mike had the good grace to laugh. They had quite a pleasant chat after that, albeit mostly about the PTA, which had in turn allowed for a little local gossip, too. They were both home in time for *News at Ten*.

By which time, back at the Barn, Eve was already in bed with *Wolf Hall* and a glass of Merlot on the bedside table, attempting to distract herself from replaying the disastrously brief events at the Bell over and over again in her head. She really had no idea why she'd taken against Mike quite so strongly and suddenly over a comment that, while ill judged, was clearly not intended to be malicious. All Eve knew was that she hadn't felt this strongly, negatively or positively, about anybody for . . . well, *ages*. I'll apologize to Gail first thing, she thought. No, hang on . . . Eve reached for her phone and tapped out a text.

> G. So sorry about tonight – really. For some reason
> Mr B pushed buttons I didn't even know were pushable.
> My pet hate (one of!) is people who drag politics into
> conversations before you've even made eye contact.
> Another is people who make sweeping assumptions
> based on . . . nothing! But I concede I could have been
> more polite. Not least for your sake. And yes, he's very
> handsome – but sometimes that's not enough! Night. E x

Eve made a note to buy Gail one of the posher supermarket bouquets on the way to work; she knew she owed her wing-woman rather more than this. However, flowers would have to do as a gesture, for now.

One more chapter . . . one more . . . Yet Eve fell asleep while her bedside light was still on and *Wolf Hall* still in her hand. It slipped to the floor as her phone beeped with Gail's reply:

It's FINE, E! Sleep well! G x

# 10

Eve's lack of enthusiasm for all things Yule-related did not extend as far as Ivy House. You couldn't, she had long since reasoned, be the headmistress of a school with 'Ivy' in its name and not embrace a few seasonal traditions. Somewhere back in the mists of recorded time the lyrics to 'The Holly and The Ivy' had, for example, been reimagined ('Of all the trees that are in the wood, the *ivy* bears the crown . . .').

There was the Nativity, too, of course, and, though visually he was a shoo-in for the angel Gabriel, this year's performance starred Petrus Sorensen as the least Semitic-looking Joseph in the school's history – a casting decision made on talent alone and one that bore very little relation to the Sorensen family's generous gift to the school of a thirty-foot Norwegian spruce. On a thrilling morning in early December, this magnificent tree had been delivered to Ivy House's front door by Denmark's leading Christmas-tree supplier, then craned into position in the middle of the school drive's turning circle, where it sat proudly in its own specially designed super-tub, festooned with lights that Anette had been invited to turn on during a spontaneously arranged late afternoon event.

Until this point, Eve hadn't known that Denmark was the world's largest exporter of Christmas trees – though, other than (presumably) the people of Denmark, who did? However, as soon as Anette had informed her of this fact, Eve had been inspired to write a special assembly on the subject of Christmas trees and their history and provenance, after which every child in the school – and by extension their families – knew *all* about the marvellous work of Pedersen Inc, which grew and distributed 30,000 Christmas trees annually, and in which it turned out Stefan Sorensen was a majority shareholder. As Gail commented to Eve in a whispered aside during the switch-on event, 'This makes Stefan Sorensen the closest thing we'll ever get to a real Santa – albeit a very buff, beard-free, gym-bunny Santa.'

'Gail! *Shush!*' said Eve.

'I shall. But doesn't Anette make a beautiful Santa's Little Helper?'

Eve took in the sight of a smiling Anette Sorensen, resplendent for the occasion in a mink-collared white coat with matching Russian *ushanka*. 'Yup, she does. Now, be quiet, Gail. I *mean* it.'

Gail sighed. 'Where would we be without the marvellous Sorensens?'

'Clutching a G&T at sunset on the pontoon overlooking shit creek – apparently.'

'You *what*?'

'It was something Tony said to me a few weeks ago, as a result of which our parents will be receiving a little wake-up call with their children's reports this Christmas. Fees up in January, Gail, I'm afraid.'

Gail shrugged. 'I guessed something was up, if not the fees. There have been some mutterings in the staffroom about yesterday's internal email.'

'Look, I really don't want people to misinterpret that email. Is that what's happening? You will tell me, won't you?'

'I think there's been a bit of basic *two-plus-two* stuff going on – yes. I think, if you send an email asking staff to err on the side of – what was it? – "accentuating the positives" in reports, then you're bound to get a bit of internal feedback.'

Eve looked alarmed. 'I wasn't looking to *whitewash*, Gail. I don't want staff to *lie*. I'm just looking for their words to be particularly well chosen this term – and, yes, OK, maybe contain some positive spin while they're at it. Look, if there are any genuine problems with any of the kids then they need addressing, obviously, but for the majority of children who are doing just fine then I really don't think it would hurt anybody, this term, to say that they're doing better than expected. Do you see my point?'

'Of course I do. And we are indeed fortunate to have jobs

we enjoy –' Gail broke off, raised an eyebrow and looked squarely at Eve – 'and which we would, ideally, like to *keep*.'

'Exactly that – and now it looks as though . . . Ah!' Eve broke off as Anette approached her, smiling. She noted that, backlit by the light from the twinklingly white tree, Anette's Russian hat looked like a soft furry halo. 'How absolutely stunning your – *our!* – tree looks. We really can't thank you enough, truly.'

Anette nodded (Eve couldn't help noticing) ever so slightly regally. 'Believe me, the pleasure is all ours. We have a tree delivered every year from our forest so that we have a little piece of Denmark with us wherever we are living. As we were having a tree delivered to the house anyway, it made sense. I think it's –' Anette paused, a teeny frown struggling to manifest on her taut brow – 'a BOGOF?'

Eve suppressed a giggle; if ever there was a woman who didn't do BOGOFs, it was surely Anette. 'Marvellous. Well, we're all thrilled.'

'No problem. Oh, and I've been meaning to email but this time of year is just so insane. Anyway, I have here the information for your daughter. If she's still interested, our London office manager is expecting to hear from her.' Anette handed Eve a proper old-fashioned paper business card. Eve couldn't recall when that had last happened but guessed the card had probably started life as a Sorensen tree.

'Oh, she's very interested, trust me. I know she'll be thrilled. You've been so generous, Anette – we do appreciate it.'

Another tiny queenly nod. 'Family and community are very important. Having joined your community, we are keen to play our part.'

Eve assumed Anette did actually have a sense of humour, even if she had yet to see much evidence of it. Perhaps now was the moment to find out? 'Well, in that case, your neighbours in Eastdene will expect to see you for a pint in the Bell on Boxing Day.'

There wasn't much to go on other than that brow furrow, a quizzical tilt to Anette's mink-haloed head and a slight, tight little smile. 'We should so love to do that, but we are dashing over to Denmark on Christmas Day – lunch with Stefan's mother – and then we're straight off to Vail after lunch.' Anette shrugged. 'Stefan gets to spend a little quality time with Mayor Bloomberg and the rest of us spend some with the snow. We Scandinavians need to have a lot of snow around us at Christmas and there's no guarantee we'll have any here.'

'No, far more likely to be January or February, though I suspect you could import some?' Even as the words left her mouth, Eve was conscious that she might have overstepped the mark. Generous though Anette Sorensen undoubtedly was – not to mention whip smart, stupidly beautiful and possibly even quite good fun after a glass or two of Carlsberg – she was not a friend, would *never* be a friend.

'Hm,' said Anette, narrowing her eyes and putting one finger to her lips. 'Imported snow? You may just have something there. I will *definitely* speak with Mr Sorensen.'

The intention, Eve suddenly recognized, was to be Dr Evil in *Austin Powers*, however the overall comedic effect was slightly undermined by Anette's beauty. Either way, this was the point when Eve decided she didn't just like the *idea* of Anette Sorensen, she liked the *actuality* of Anette Sorensen. And she liked her even more when Anette said, 'We'll be back here on December thirtieth and we have no plans for New Year, on purpose. Of course, something is bound to come up, but if it doesn't I am hoping to persuade Stefan to come out to the pub for a drink.'

Eve still thought Anette might be joking. 'Seriously?'

'You *bet*, seriously.' Anette leaned closer to Eve. 'Stefan and I didn't grow up around the kind of money that has quite so many noughts, you know.' At which point she put an arm round the shoulders of Aija and Petrus, who had been standing beside her, bickering with each other in Danish. 'Unlike these two. Right, off to the car, kids – Daddy will be home tonight!'

I wonder how many noughts? thought Eve as she watched three-quarters of the Sorensen family walk towards the car. Nine, probably. Which is a lot. And Mayor Bloomberg is a lot of power.

Eve had had sufficient dealings with the extremely wealthy to know that their world ran parallel to everybody else's, sharing just enough similarities to allow them occasional interactions with the civilians, however charmingly Anette Sorensen may pretend otherwise. Eve attempted to explain her new theory to Gail after assembly the following day.

'So, imagine that three empty lanes of the M25 were inhabited by a few cars that were allowed to get to their destinations as fast as they liked, while normal traffic was consigned to the hard shoulder –'

'OK.' Gail held out a frothy coffee for Eve.

'– and everybody trying to drive on the hard shoulder is sharing it with all the breakdowns waiting for the AA or the RAC or whoever, while the super-rich speed right past, apparently quite close, but actually entirely separate.'

'Uh-huh, I get it. That's *good*,' said Gail.

'Thanks. Anyway, occasionally the drivers of the fast cars in the three empty lanes glance over and wave at us, but mostly they're just oblivious. We're all heading to the same destination but our journeys are entirely different.'

'That last bit – is that an actual *philosophical* observation? At 9:23 a.m. on a busy Thursday morning in December, are you actually talking to your long-suffering assistant about *death*?'

Eve laughed. 'I might be. You can dump the death stuff if you like but I think the rest of it stands up pretty well. We're stuck on life's hard shoulder while the Sorensens and the Dershowitzes are –' she shrugged – 'whatever.'

'Hurtling down a ski slope in Colorado beside the mayor

of New York? They're welcome to *that*. On Boxing Day, I for one am looking forward to pouring a Baileys and working my way through a large tin of Quality Street in front of whatever it is I've Sky-Plussed.' Gail warmed to her theme. 'And, actually, the idea of being forced to ski among the world's powerbrokers really does make my blood run cold – and not just because I'd end up totally Sonny Bonoed on the grounds of not being able to ski. Now, drink this –' Gail pushed the mug of coffee towards Eve – 'and stop confusing me with your best friend. The food chain is, basically, me, you, Tony, followed by the Sorensens and the Dershowitzes, who I'm sure would eat the lot of us if we ever all happened to be on a plane together that crashed in the Andes.'

Eve assumed a pitying expression and tipped her head to one side. 'I really hate to think of you at the bottom of the food chain, Gail.'

'I'm not. If the worst came to the worst, I suppose I would eat the cats. On the subject of which, sort of, I'm off to the dentist today at – and frankly I can hardly believe it myself – two thirty!'

'No! Really? I'd assumed dentists' receptionists only ever booked appointments for two twenty-five, never your actual *tooth hurtee*. Please tell me your dentist is Chinese?'

'No, but he is devastatingly good-looking.' Gail grinned.

'Well, I hope you need a root canal and it takes forever.' There are, thought Eve suddenly, possibly many things I don't know about Gail.

Like the majority of schools, during the last week of the Christmas term, Ivy House abandoned any semblance of teaching and/or learning in favour of chocolate, tinsel-decorated mufti, a tangerine-flavoured Christingle carol service at Eastdene's St Mary's – Eve enjoyed its cheerful paganism – and regular deliveries of the internal Christmas-card post throughout the day. Even the cur-mudgeonly caretaker, Mr Dodd, wore a Santa hat while he raked gravel and tut-tutted about divots on the lawns, and thus all was positively ding-dong-merrily. When, in the midst of this festive, familial atmosphere, Tony 'Scrooge' Salter called a quick meeting with Eve on the penultimate day of term, to 'discuss upcoming developments', her heart sank.

Eve knocked on Tony's door and entered without wait-ing for a response. 'Nice Santa hat you've got there, Tony. Been taking style tips from Dodd?'

'Nah. Don't be fooled. In order to drown his sorrows, the Ghost of Christmas Future has just popped out to the Co-op to pick up a small bottle of gin, but he'll be back. Like the Terminator.'

'Chin up, Tony – only ten more sleeps until Christmas. I'll sit, shall I?' Eve didn't wait for an answer but took her place on the aggressively modernist leather sofa, at right angles to the one on which Tony was once again lying at full stretch, shoeless, with some reading matter perched on his proud stomach.

'Or, to put it another way, only five more sleeps till Barbados,' said Tony. 'So anyway, we'll be slipping this little letter in with the, uh, *glowing* reports tomorrow.' Eve glanced at the letter and did a double take. Fees up by a thousand pounds a term?! Dear Lord and Father of mankind, hummed Eve, forgive his foolish ways . . .

# 11

Two days before Christmas and Rob noted that Zoe was *very* excited. Though apparently not by Christmas.

'So, I'm going to be staying at Auntie Sonia's, which is awesome because her flat is like totally amazing, and I'll be working in Bond Street, which is basically the street containing every single shop in the world you would ever want to visit.' Zoe rolled on to her back on her bedroom floor and brought her knees up to her torso, clenching them tightly in a ball. Meanwhile, Rob, who didn't seem to be quite as thrilled by Zoe's work placement as he might be – *ought* to be, frankly – watched her very intently. He had a good poker face; it really was impossible to read.

'No. That *you* would want to visit.'

'Are you proper *jealous*, Bobby?' Zoe sat up and fixed her boyfriend of eighteen months with a look that was half stare, half pout and wholly mesmerizing. The physical effect on Rob was instantaneous; however, he would have to disguise it because this was a conversation he'd been putting off having ever since Zoe had first told him, breathlessly, about her work experience, and he knew he needed to have it now, distractions permitting.

'Jealous of *what* precisely?'

'I dunno. Me, out there alone in the Big City . . . ?' Zoe tailed off.

'Nah. It's not the *alone* bit that bothers me.' Fuck. What a giveaway.

Zoe grinned. 'Aw, babes. That's so *sweet!*' She gave Rob a semi-brisk kiss on the cheek and a business-as-usual sort of 'Love you, babes'.

Rob leaned back on a beanbag and watched Zoe for a moment or two, and then, inevitably, out came his iPhone. He tapped the camera icon, swiped to *video* and pointed the lens at his girlfriend.

Rob was in his second year at uni, studying Broadcast Media, and wanted to become a film editor, preferably Ridley Scott's film editor. In the meantime, however, he would settle for editing advertisements for discount sofa warehouses. Rob loved his course but he slightly less loved the fact that, once acquired, his skills would probably have to be deployed in London. The only upside to potentially living in the capital was the chance that Zoe may just choose to go to a London university. However, before that, she had to sit her A levels and then probably have a gap *yah* – and, before either of those things, she had to spend a fortnight hanging out in *Mayfair*, with, like, *complete tossers.*

As ever, the prospect of sustained happiness with the woman he loved seemed to Rob to be some way off. And then there was the fact that he just didn't like the idea of Zoe being in London *at all*, much less staying with her aunt for a week – even a *working* week. From what he knew of Zoe's Aunt Sonia, whom he had met just once, she was less 'auntie' and more like a cool, very much older sister, who worked in some sort of incredibly high-up position doing God-knew-what in retail and earned a fortune, was happily unmarried and child free, and apparently holidayed on a semi-professional basis, the sort with heli-skiing and horse-back African safaris. She was, Rob had noted, hot in a cougar-y kind of way – could easily pass for ten years younger in the right light. Whatever, Rob didn't like Londony life-style stuff. He felt entirely out of his depth. And yet, London was a city of opportunities, he could see that . . .

'Hurry up, Zo. Yeah?' Rob put away his phone.

'Posh coffee in the kitchen, babes,' said Zoe, applying a gunmetal grey varnish to her big toe, 'if you're bored.'

'OK,' Rob said flatly; even the poshest coffee in the world was a very poor substitute for sex with Zoe. Rob drank the coffee very fast and was halfway through a second cup when Zoe padded delicately into the kitchen, strips of loo paper separating her toes.

'They just look like someone's stamped on them,' said Rob. Zoe grinned. He was now buzzing with caffeine – caffeine and *lust*. Zoe read his expression and shook her head.

'No time, babe; *soz!*'

Rob shrugged and tipped the rest of his coffee down the sink. 'Right then, I'm off.'

Zoe was surprised. 'Already?'

'Yeah, stuff to do.'

'OK, love you, babes.' Zoe went on to her tiptoes to kiss him on the forehead.

'Yeah. You said that.' Rob noted Zoe's crinkled nose, quizzical expression. 'Love you too.' He surprised himself by how suddenly he wanted to leave. He'd had an idea. A *plan*.

'You could call it a kind of insurance policy,' he explained much later that night to his flatmate, Nev, a fellow Broadcast Media student, as they both watched Rob's phone footage of a naked – *beautifully* naked – Zoe on Rob's laptop.

'Man. That is a seriously hot girlfriend you have there. Remind me why she's with you again, yeah?'

'Because I have a lot of charm and an enormous cock?' Rob moved his cursor over the image, clicking, improving very slightly on the near perfection. No woman in her right mind ever objected to a nice bit of 'photox'.

'Uh-huh, yeah, the ginormo-dick – that'd be it.' Nev knocked back the dregs of a can of warm Stella. 'More beer?'

Rob didn't take his eyes off the screen. 'Yeah, good idea – it might be a long one. No pun intended.' And then he started humming as he watched the ancient footage of his girlfriend, filmed just a fortnight after they'd started seeing each other. All that giggly mugging by Zoe for the camera and the *panting* – did anybody other than dogs

ever pant during sex? wondered Rob – was obviously
porno inspired and a little too stage managed; all about
performance and not much about the feeling. Nonetheless, even eighteen months after the event, he still watched
the footage several times a week, sometimes alone, sometimes not. And whenever they got the chance to see it, Rob's
mates – and Nev was a particular fan, now practically a
Zoe connoisseur – were invariably very appreciative.
Whatever – Rob *liked* the fact that his mates appreciated
his girl. Her all-round glory reflected pretty well on him.

Nev grinned – 'OK, yeah, I get it!' – and he joined in on
the chorus of the song: 'Don't cha wish your girlfriend was
hot like me . . . ?'

# 12

During the last week of term at Eastdene Community Primary, when word flew round the playground that one of the teaching assistants whose remit included After-School Club had phoned in sick, Gail surprised herself by volunteering to run it. With Ivy House already broken up, her seasonal shopping completed and something approaching boredom kicking in, she suddenly quite fancied the idea of corralling thirty-odd faintly feral kids. Indeed, so relaxed did she feel that, when a trio of Year Four girls asked if they could 'do some art', she resisted the impulse to steer them towards the felt tips and not only cheerfully acquiesced but suggested they get busy with the glitter and gluesticks.

It was, then, a pleasant afternoon spent mostly designing frocks for princesses, with only minor skirmishes elsewhere: an altercation over whose turn it was to go on the PlayStation and a disagreement over the ownership of a water bottle between a pair of the more challenging Year Twos. A good bunch of kids, thought Gail with an involuntary burst of pleasure. She watched Skye Davies and Nancy Robertson, the daughters of near neighbours, whom she'd known since they were foetuses, failing to persuade Rufus King – a Year Three heart-throb ever since he'd landed a job modelling school uniforms for George at Asda – to join in. Rufus looked horrified, however, and shook his head vigorously before running outside to play keepy-uppies with Harry – who was, in turn, clearly so happy to escape being mothered in public by Gail that he could countenance hanging out with a Year Three. Gail smiled fondly at her son's retreating back. It had been a good term, mostly, and today was a good day and Christmas was round the corner. And if there was one thing Gail appreciated, it was the school holidays, when it was possible to abandon oneself, guilt free, to the lure of the boxed sets for *days* at a time.

So, by five p.m. and with only fifteen minutes of After-School Club left to run, Gail was in a good mood and had already successfully tidied away the art table and announced the countdown to the PlayStation switch-off. She went to the lavatory and took a moment in the cubicle to rub off the strings of glue that had attached themselves to the knees of her trousers. Just as she was doing this, she heard the sound of adult female voices entering the Ladies. And because she didn't feel in the mood to make small talk with other mothers, Gail decided to sit this one out, quietly, and see if she couldn't get rid of the rest of the glue while she was at it. Meanwhile, it took her a moment or two to work out how many women there were. And *who* they were – Gail was not a PTA stalwart for nothing.

The posh one was Nancy's mum, Sam, thought Gail, and the un-posh one was Jill, Skye's mum, and the one with the accent somewhere between the two was easy to identify because Gail had known Joanna King, Rufus's mum, since their first day at secondary school. Of course, thought Gail, Jill and Joanna have known each other since Reception, if not longer, and Sam is a relatively recent down-from-Londoner, so probably doesn't know either of them very well at all. And even though Nancy and Skye had just been bonding over their glittery princesses, they weren't normally particularly close, while Rufus was a boy. So, thought Gail, this is a triangle of expedience rather than intimacy. I'm not crashing anything.

And it took her another moment or two to adjust to the dynamic of a three-way conversation between people she couldn't see, and another second or two after that to realize, with an unpleasant seasick sensation in her stomach, that one of the women was in the midst of some cheerful bitching about . . . *Gail.*

'This morning, Gail said –' Joanna assumed a high-pitched, patronizingly sing-song tone – ' "So, Harry, we're going to be doing lots of hard work for our SATs over Christmas, aren't we?" You know, as *if!* God, that woman has such unrealistic expectations of a ten-year-old that I sometimes forget she's actually a mum and not a maiden aunt.'

Gail's cheeks burned. She felt both slightly sick and *very* angry, not least because what she'd actually said to Harry was, 'You've come on really well this term, so let's keep it up for the next one, because that's the SATs term, yes?' And what the hell was wrong with *that*? However, there was nothing she could do except sit very still and button her lip – bite it, even.

'Poor Gail!' It was Sam, who paused mid-sentence. 'She's quite, er . . .'

Go on, thought Gail. What sort of a 'poor Gail' am I, then? However, it appeared that Sam wasn't trying to assume an intimacy she hadn't yet earned.

'Spinsterish? Is that the word you're after?' asked Joanna. 'That's what I always think of her. A little bit Miss Jean Brodie, despite the highlights and the great legs. There's a sort of chilly primness to her. But, to be fair, that's probably just because of her, um . . .'

Now it was Joanna's turn to search for the right word. Gail hardly dared breathe; surely the women could hear her heart pounding as loudly as she could? And did 'great legs' cancel out 'spinsterish'? Gail thought that, on balance, it probably didn't.

'Circumstances?' said Jill helpfully.

'Circumstances! Exactly,' said Joanna.

'OK, so what are her "circumstances", if you don't mind me asking?' asked Sam.

'Ah, well, y'know – a terminal single mum. It's no good for the boy.'

For fuck's sake! thought Gail.

'Is Harry's dad not around, then?' said Sam.

Gail put her head in her hands, then her fist in her mouth – and bit down on it, *hard*. She felt absolutely nothing. Meanwhile, the conversation continued.

'No, he's never been around. One day Gail was just . . . y'know, six months pregnant. Harry's not only never met his dad, he doesn't even know who he is,' said Joanna.

And how the fuck do you know that, precisely? thought Gail.

'Oh dear. It might be old-fashioned of me, but I do think kids need some sort of a relationship with their same-sex parent. No sign of a stepdad, then?' Sam again.

'No, not that anyone's ever noticed. Like I say, a terminal singleton. Makes Bridget Jones look like . . .' There was some door-banging as the women emerged from their respective cubicles and reconvened by the basins. Gail held her breath. There was the sound of running water and hand-dryers, and she felt a furious, impotent tear slide unbidden down her cheek, wiped away angrily with the sleeve of her – spinsterish? – blouse.

'And I never understood why she gave up that great teaching job at Ivy House and settled for being the head's PA. I hear she was a very good teacher.' This was Jill.

Yeah, go on – try and be fair, Jill . . . thought Gail.

The loo door banged as the women departed, though Gail could hear them loud and clearly in the corridor. 'Ah, hello, Skye! There you are! Have you been playing nice with Nancy?'

*Nicely*, you silly bitch – not *nice*, thought Gail, who took a deep breath and counted to ten in her head before emerging from the cubicle. And only then, with an internal lurch, did she realize that she wasn't alone in the loos – Nancy's mum, Sam, was still there, loitering by the basins, inspecting her phone. Gail wanted to hide or run. Either – or both. Instead, she tried to breathe. Sam started at the sight of Gail, who was studiously avoiding eye contact as she washed her hands carefully and intently, concentrating on removing all the remaining traces of glue and glitter from beneath her nails. Gail then moved over to the hand-dryer.

'Um . . . Gail?' Sam coughed.

Gail turned around to face Sam reluctantly, willing herself to brazen it out. 'That's me, yes. What do you want?'

'I am so, *so* sorry.'

For what? wondered Gail. For being party to the things that were said? Or for seeming to endorse them by staying around? Or – most probably – just sorry because I overheard? 'Well, I really hate gossip. But, in fact, she's wrong – Harry does know his dad. He knows him really well.' Gail paused. And I should stop now . . .

Sam shook her head. 'There's no need to explain, Gail. As I say, I'm *so* sorry. It's none of my business.'

Too right, thought Gail. Too fucking right it's not. And this is the moment when I turn on my heel with my head held high.

Twenty minutes later, as she tidied up the sports hall

after the last child had left, she quietly congratulated herself on her choice of words when she'd spoken to Sam. It was, indeed, perfectly true that Harry knew the man who was his father and had known him all his life – he just didn't know that that same man *was* his father. Harry had asked Gail who his father was on no more than half a dozen occasions – and Gail's answer had remained consistent each time: 'Someone who didn't want to be a father.'

# 13

As far as Eve was concerned, Christmas was a reminder of loss. Her mother had died on Boxing Day and, although that had been nearly twenty years ago, this remained very much her least favourite time of year. Thus, on an annual basis, Eve would rant at Gail about how the season had become a protracted, expensive and nauseatingly idealized 'lifestyle' which had surely never existed other than in the final scenes of *It's a Wonderful Life*. No, Eve didn't believe in a Hollywood – or even John Lewis TV ad – sort of Christmas any more than she believed in bloody Santa. There was a kind of co-dependent relationship between that fantasy and the 'ghastly, retro, Betty Crocker vision of domesticity which, from the beginning of November, completely takes over the media and results in *at least* nine hundred different Christmas Specials featuring every TV cook demonstrating how to baste a *fucking* turkey, as if Christmas dinner – and fucking *turkeys* – have only just been invented!'

And every year, Gail, whom Eve knew loved Christmas, would simply smile, nod and put the kettle on.

But though Eve resented Christmas's intrusion into the rest of her life, she did (secretly) enjoy dressing a tree and doing all the cooking; thus, this year, it was eight for Christmas lunch. As far as Eve was concerned, this was the perfect number; any more and she might lose track of her internal portion controller, but eight she could easily both cater for and conduct proper conversations with in-between basting duties. The guest list was pleasingly straightforward, too:

> Eve
> Eve's father (Edward – aka, to all members of his
>     family since the mid-1990s, 'Father Ted')
> Zoe
> Alice
> Simon
> Simon's mother (Grace – aka 'Gramma Grace')
> Ed (thankfully never confused with 'Father Ted' Ed)
> Jordan (Simon and Ed's newly adopted son)

At seven a.m., as Eve hit the snooze button on her alarm, she contemplated the day unrolling and felt . . . comfortable, largely because any surprises her guests might spring were, she knew, likely to be comfortably familial surprises. Vaguely functioning families, such as Eve's, were, she felt, a kind of trellis through and around which each individual's story grew and merged; this was what families were for. This was why they existed. This was the *point*.

But six-year-old Jordan was an entirely different proposition: nothing to be *scared* of, exactly, but (according to Ellie Blake) he was increasingly challenging in the classroom, probably on the autistic spectrum. There was no doubt that, right here, in Eve's home, this little boy was the variable quantity in her family Christmas equation. As she lay in bed, half listening to the hiss and pop of a bedroom radiator (perhaps Simon would bleed them if I ask him very nicely . . .) the word 'interloper' settled in her brain. She pushed it away. That's unfair, thought Eve – even if it's true. And so she got up and braced herself for the day.

Seven hours later, then, it was Christmas business as usual. The house smelled good, Simon was carving the goose – Eve disliked turkey and felt that not serving one was, as hostess, entirely her prerogative – and Ed was doing useful things with the corkscrew. Meanwhile, Father Ted and Gramma Grace were joint favourite in the traditional Christmas Day deafness stakes. Having both attended the Tate Modern's exhibition earlier in the year, they were currently arguing good-naturedly about – as Zoe described it to her mother – 'whether, like, Futurism is all that'.

'And is it "all that"?' Eve asked her eldest daughter wryly, as she sieved flour into her thickening gravy over a low simmer.

'Not sure – I think the oldster jury's out.'

'And what do you think of Futurism?'

'I thought it was, like, a 1980s music thing? But then I figured Father Ted and Gramma Grace were unlikely to be talking about, like, Kraftwerk, or whatever.' Eve raised her eyes and grimaced. 'Aw, c'mon, Mum. I'll lay the table if you tell me where the crackers are. Also, Rob's coming round later, if that's OK?'

'Sure, and sure. How are you two getting on? Crackers are in the cupboard in the utility. And if they're not in that cupboard, they're in the other cupboard.'

Zoe frowned slightly. 'Dunno. OK. *Ish*. Maybe.'

'Oh dear.' Eve would have pursued this line of questioning, subtly; however . . .

'Mum?' Alice appeared, slightly breathless, by her side. 'I think Jordan may have had a, like, *accident*?'

Eve spun round, maternal buttons duly pushed. 'Where is he? What sort of accident?'

'No, not a sort of *blood* accident, Mum; a kind of –' Alice wrinkled her nose – '*bottom* accident, maybe? He's been in the loo for, like, ages.'

'Really? Well, we're about to dish up. Could you ask one of his fathers to sort it out, please? Which loo is he in, anyway?'

'Upstairs. He asked me where it was and went in about ten minutes ago – with, like, a bunch of Lego?'

'Well, he's probably just playing. Simon?' Eve turned to her ex-husband. 'Can you check on Jordan, please? He's in the loo with his Lego, apparently.'

Simon glanced up from his goose wrangling. 'Ed?'

'Sure.' Ed went into the hall. 'Jordy? Where are you, Jordan?'

'He's mad for Lego,' said Simon. 'Fine by us. You know they do architectural Lego, Evie? Ed bought me Frank Lloyd Wright's Fallingwater for Christmas, and when Jordan saw the box this morning he said, "That's *bad* Lego."' Simon shrugged. 'I see his point. It is a symphony of beige bricks.'

'But it will give you hours of pleasure! How are you doing with that goose?'

'Great. I'm pretending it's a turkey. We're nearly there. OK, everybody, *seats*!'

Ed came back downstairs, hand in hand with Jordan. Not for the first time, Eve was struck – as indeed was everybody – by the boy's beauty. He really was arrestingly lovely: long-lashed, dark brown eyes, snub nose, a slightly surprised arch to his brows and close-cropped curls with streaks and flashes of what looked like expensive blonde highlights. Extraordinarily beautiful kid, thought Eve. And she noted, too, that he had a startlingly self-contained sort of air and a kind of preternaturally knowing, almost adult, look in his eyes that spoke of . . . well, intelligence, definitely, but something – *what*? – else.

So everybody took their places around the dining table, on which a freshly dismembered goose sat, attractively accessorized by a small landslide of roasted carbohydrates. Plates were decorated with crackers and there were abundant glasses, for red wine and white and water (apple juice for Jordan), alongside several layers of cutlery and the old Sturridge family silver candlesticks with guttering beeswax candles. The lights were dimmed while the candles were lit, and everybody was *ooh*ing and saying, 'How *lovely* that table looks, Eve – you really have done us all proud, as usual,' and Eve remembered, just in time, to decant her gravy into the boat and wedge it in between the bowls of stuffing balls and red cabbage, just as the guests started bickering fondly about the seating arrangements.

Everyone, that is, apart from Jordan, who (everybody else noticed simultaneously) was standing, apparently rooted to the spot, shaking his head and refusing to sit in the seat reserved for him, between Simon and Ed. The more he was cajoled by Simon and Ed ('C'mon, matey, choose a knee instead!'), the less likely it looked that he would sit at all.

'No,' said Jordan, firmly, shaking his head, staring at the floor.

'Go on. We're all hungry! Aren't you?' said Alice.

'NO.' More forceful; much louder.

'OK, well, I tell you what, Jordy – we're all going to start and you can come and join us when you're ready. OK?'

'No. NO. No, no, no, NOOOOOOOOOOOOOOOOOOOO! Fucking NO. Fucking FUCKING. I HATE YOU! FUCK OFF! FUCK, FUCK, FUCK, CUNT, CUNT, CUNT!'

At which, a red-faced Jordan lay down on the floor and started pounding the boards with his fists and his head, howling a primal cry of – what? Rage, apparently. Or maybe fear?

'Good Lord! Did he just say what I think he said?' said Father Ted.

121

'Yes, that's what he said!' said Simon, conceivably furious with both his ex-father-in-law and Jordan.

'Is it some sort of *culture shock*?'

'No, it's not bloody culture shock, for God's sake! Or at least not in the way you're defining it! Now, please, let us try to sort things out? Just carry on and start without us; we'll be back,' said Simon, as Ed hoisted a writhing Jordan into his arms and the three of them silently left the room.

So everybody else did start, albeit in stunned silence. It was Eve's job, she felt, to break the ice and, in particular, soothe the entirely baffled oldsters.

'We – that is, his class teacher, Ellie, and his dads and I – we think he might be on the autistic spectrum, somewhere. Possibly Asperger's.'

'Very rum,' said Father Ted.

'Indeed. We can help him a lot if we know what to do with him. Unfortunately, Ivy House may be the wrong school for him. We're not big on special needs.'

After a minute or two, somebody asked somebody else to pass a condiment, and then everybody tucked in and somehow a normal conversation asserted itself and, after a few minutes, Simon reappeared and sat down and, a minute or two later, Ed joined him and there was a muttered *sotto voce* conversation between them, to which nobody attempted to contribute, at which point Eve couldn't restrain herself and said, 'Look, this is all ridiculously British. Is he OK? Where is he? Will he come and sit with us or should we make him a tray to eat in front of the telly next door? Would that be more comfortable for him? It probably *is* a kind of culture shock, surely?'

Simon turned towards Eve with a wan smile. 'Actually, the tray might work. One of us will sit with him. He seems very distressed but he says he wants to be on his own. I'm not sure if he really does. It's happened a few times.' Ed shot Simon a glance and Simon shrugged. 'OK, a lot of times.'

'I'm sure it has.' Eve gave Simon a knowing look. 'Have you been keeping track?'

'Yes. I started a diary the day he arrived. It was meant to be something I would be able to show him one day. Now I'm not so sure. And I also have –' Simon paused, sighed deeply – 'something his mother wrote.'

'Will you show it to me?' Eve spoke gently, but not so quietly that Gramma Grace didn't hear.

'It's probably a phase,' Gramma said. 'Boys are such terribly volatile creatures.'

Simon raised an eyebrow. 'Thanks for that, Mommie Dearest.'

Eve got up from her seat and started putting together a small plate of food.

'I'll sit with him first. We can do shifts,' said Ed. 'With a bit of luck, he may even want to come back and join us.'

'Well, bully for him,' said Father Ted cheerfully. 'In my day, behaviour like that would have meant a stripe on the arse and being sent straight to one's room for the rest of the day without lunch or supper. How on earth do six-year-olds even learn that sort of language? And I rather think you don't have to answer that!'

Simon sighed again. 'Well, he didn't learn it here.'

'I think it's all about context, really,' said Eve. 'But perhaps we could move on from this topic for the moment, seeing as it's Christmas? And may I just take this opportunity to say how lovely it is to be surrounded by most of my delightful family. And I trust my beloved, if exceptionally spoilt – and I blame the parents – little sister is having a fairly decent time in Grenada.'

'She is. I spoke to Sonia yesterday,' said Ted, clearly relieved by the conversational shift.

'Excellent!' Eve raised her glass. 'Well, here's to family and friends – and even small boys who are clearly very upset to have their traditional turkey swapped for a goose, *and* little sisters with far too much disposable income, slumming it on Caribbean beaches. Oh, and to Zoe finding out what a hedge fund is, so that *we* don't have to. Merry Christmas!'

There was a chinking of glasses. Eve glanced around the table and decided that, even with the two temporarily empty chairs and the disruptive arrival in her home of a difficult little boy, it was, nonetheless, still mostly Christmas as usual.

## 14

I shall be very pleased to get back to work, Gail thought on Boxing Day. She'd had a quiet Christmas – though this was not for lack of offers. Several friends had invited her and Harry over but Gail preferred not to play gooseberry with other people's families and declined most of the invitations. On Christmas morning, however, she and Harry went to visit her parents in Bexhill.

Gail's mum and dad were in their early seventies and, while Gail knew this was not even remotely ancient these days, they weren't the kind of metropolitan, silver-surfing, theatre-going, frothy-coffee-quaffing, Hampstead-dwelling septuagenarians she imagined, say, Sam's parents to be. Instead, they were proper provincial *old people*. Her mum, Iris, was in fact more like a nan; she wore pale grey elasticated shoes in extra-wide fittings that could only be bought mail-order from small ads in the *People's Friend*. Iris had given up her secretarial job the week before she'd married and currently volunteered at the same church in which her own parents had been married. She had travelled overseas just three times in her life and, after the third occasion, declared that 'I don't like *abroad*' – as though (as Gail said to Eve) 'abroad' was sprouts, or Les Dennis.

Meanwhile, Gail's dad, Ronnie, had wholeheartedly agreed with Iris when she'd decided, in 1975, that she didn't care for 'abroad' and wouldn't be bothering with it again. Since then, her parents had led safe, comfortable local lives without either of them recognizing, much less caring, that there might have been another kind of life to lead. Iris was content even as she struggled with her arthritis and Ronnie had failing eyesight and an increasingly slippery memory. At the same time, after the initial shock of becoming grandparents – having bypassed not merely an engagement and a marriage but indeed knowledge of anybody who might conceivably be their daughter's long-term partner – both took enormous pride in Gail and Harry.

So, all the members of the Prince family were pleased to see each other, for about three or four hours. After that, it became a little wearing when Iris started asking her usual questions: 'Has Harry seen his dad over Christmas? No, not yet? Do you think he will? Anyway, Gail, love, are *you* seeing anybody? No, I don't mean to pry – none of my business – sorry!' And so on. Gail . . . rhymes with 'fail', thought Gail.

She and Harry took Iris and Ronnie out to lunch at their preferred pub before dropping round to Auntie Ruby and Uncle Den's properly *bungaloid* bungalow in Bexhill, where they stayed long enough for a slice of Battenberg and a cuppa you could stand a spoon in, enquired politely after Gail's cousins and then made their excuses. Later, Gail briskly helped Iris tidy up, ran the vacuum round the flat, loaded some rubbish into her boot for recycling, and then whispered to Harry, 'You've done brilliantly with Nan and Grandda. You're a total star. Tomorrow, we'll stop by Game and you can pick up *Fifa 2011* with your Christmas money, yeah?'

So despite being a fan of Christmas, this year it would be a relief to get back to work. Yes, Gail was very much looking forward to the second week of January.

And then it started to snow and both Eastdene Community Primary School and Ivy House Preparatory School were closed. Meanwhile, beneath its pristine white duvet, the village hunkered down to a few consecutive inset days of its own. The silence is astounding, thought Gail. After the snowball-throwing novelty had worn off (somewhat quicker for Gail than it had for Harry, granted), there wasn't much to do except wait, and slide over to Londis to stock up on Heinz cream of tomato soup. Then, in the evening, at Harry's suggestion, they tossed a coin as to whether Gail should stay in for yet another boxed-set binge or leave him to *Fifa 2011* for an hour or two and slip, quite literally, across the road for half a lager-and-lime – or even, sod it, a vodka tonic. Tails, it was telly; heads, the pub . . .

'Gail! *Welcome*. Quite the Blitz spirit we've got going here!' said Dave.

Gail glanced around the heaving pub. 'Understatement, Dave. Is Penny around?'

Dave pointed out his wife. 'Over there, by the dartboard, in a huddle with some school mums you'll know. And a new one, but you'll probably know her too – Susie some-one, whose son and daughter were meant to start at Eastdene last week, all bright eyed and bushy tailed, freshly squeezed out of the Ivy House sausage factory.' Dave grinned. 'If Eastdene was private, we could bung up the fees. Anyway, pop over and say hi. Penny was asking after you just this morning. We were going to send over a search party.'

Gail smiled. So, it seemed that Tony's little Christmas treat for the Ivy House parents had gone down badly with Susie Poe. 'Yeah. I will say hi.' She glanced over, spotting Penny, in conversation with Susie herself. On cue, both women turned and looked towards the bar. Seeing Gail, Penny smiled and beckoned and Gail waved back before making fleeting eye contact with Susie, who also smiled, although less warmly. She either can't quite place me – invisible PA that I am – or she can place me and would rather not, thought Gail. Interesting woman, Susie Poe. Also, very blonde and attractive. Gail recalled that Susie didn't live in Eastdene but somewhere just out of the school's catchment, so she had been particularly lucky to get places for both her kids at such short notice. Mike had mentioned at his first PTA meeting that he liked it when the children came from outside the immediate area, 'because parents who are prepared to drive a few miles on school runs are parents who demonstrably care about their children's education.'

Recalling this, she suddenly spotted Mike himself, tucked behind a pillar with a pint and a copy of the *Guardian*. He raised his hand in acknowledgement when he spotted her and she nodded back. She and Mike hadn't spoken since that last evening in the Bell and Gail decided it might be worth losing her spot at the busy bar in favour of seizing the moment to say something. And then, seeing the over-stretched bar staff, she thought better of it, waiting to be served and taking her vodka and tonic with her. There was just one chair at Mike's table, so Gail hovered awkwardly by the pillar.

'Sorry, I'd ask you to join me, of course, but –' Mike jerked his head in Susie Poe's direction – 'that lady, there, one of Eastdene's new mums, needed a chair so I figured that was politic . . . no, sorry, definitely not *politic* – polite!'

Gail laughed and looked more closely at Susie Poe. With her pale grey skinny jeans and expensive-looking creamy cashmere layers, she was very much the kind of stylish woman who made Gail feel frumpy – frumpy and spinsterish and overly reliant on Matalan. She turned back to Mike. 'No problem; I'm table-hopping, anyway. I really just wanted to say hi again, after . . . y'know?' Gail grimaced. Then she followed Mike's distracted gaze, which was still fixed in the area of Susie Poe who, she noted, had angled her chair in such a way as to have an equally uninterrupted view of Mike Browning. Well, yeah, *that* makes sense, thought Gail. They'd make a very attractive couple.

'So how's your prickly boss?' asked Mike.

'Ha! Well, actually, she's on top form at the moment. You *really* didn't see the best of Eve.'

'I hope not, because if that was the best I'd dread the worst. Anyway—'

At which point they were interrupted. 'Ooh, hello, Gail! Isn't this absolutely unbelievably insane weather? I'm afraid I'm AWOL from the Home Front! I knew we had snow chains on the old Land Rover, so I just spontaneously decided to let Mr P get the juniors up to Bedfordshire while I popped over to the pub to meet the girls.'

Leonora Percy, aka Mrs Dick Cock, waved a hand at a huddle of practically identical ruddy-faced middle-aged women wearing waxed jackets and the kind of wilfully ugly sweaters that made Gail itch just to look at them, accessorized by a selection of wet retrievers. She knew all of them by sight, if not name, and waved cheerfully. As Leonora leaned closer, the better to shout into her ear, Gail noted that *eau de chien mouillé* invariably clung to members of the Percy family, of whom she was terribly fond. 'And I fear,' stage-whispered Mrs P, 'that I may not get back until terribly late. Dave is threatening a lock-in.'

Gail grinned. 'Go for it, Mrs P. Now, Dave, let me give you a hand with those glasses.' Gail turned back to the bar, but Dave wasn't listening; he was staring at the door – as, by now, was nearly everybody else in the pub. Though palpable, this near-silence only lasted a second or two. Gail swivelled around awkwardly, attempting not to spill her drink and took in the entirely incongruous sight of a very beautiful blonde woman wearing a fur coat and hat and standing in the doorway on the arm of an absurdly hand-some man in a fabulously expensive-looking cashmere overcoat. Both were stamping snow off their feet.

'Blimey!' whispered Gail. 'It's the Sorensens!'

'Goodness, my next-door neighbours – how super!' said Mrs P.

'Yes, you can see why they're very good friends with Brad and Angelina, can't you,' said Gail.

'Brad and Angelina who?' said Mrs P.

'Do you think they'll expect *waitress* service?' wondered Dave.

Gail raised an eyebrow. 'Actually, I'm pretty sure they won't.'

Meanwhile, Gail noted that the entire pub was pretend-ing not to be straining to overhear the conversation currently taking place between Stefan Sorensen, standing at the bar, and Dave, who was breaking the habit of a life-time and actually smiling at a stranger. Dave then rang the ship's bell that calls time and the hum instantly became a hush.

'Laydeez 'n' genelmen! I know you will be delighted to hear that Eastdene's newest residents, Mr and Mrs Sorensen, here, have very kindly just set up a tab, so feel free to order what you like. But before you all start getting ideas, I can tell you straight away that I'm fresh out of nebuchadnezzars of Moët.'

At this, there was much laughter, shouts of, 'Thanks!' and, 'Cheers!' and some of the more well-oiled locals went over to the Sorensens' table to offer their thanks in person. Gail watched all of this wide-eyed. 'Bloody hell, Dave! If the Bell's going to be this glamorous then you'd better start stocking posher crisps.'

# SPRING TERM

## 15

'Thanks for a typically generous Christmas, Evie.' Simon exhaled and patted a non-existent stomach while Eve watched him, tracing her finger round the sugary rim of a tea mug. They were in her kitchen, alone, at three p.m. – a small miracle on Boxing Day in a house that should have been full of people. Ed had taken Jordan for a walk with Barney and Alice, and they were detouring via Monty's stables; Zoe was upstairs in her room with Rob (while both her parents pretended not to be unnerved by the quietness) and Gramma Grace was having a lie-down ('I do believe there is something in poultry – a *hormone* – that makes one *terribly* sleepy'); meanwhile, Father Ted had slipped quietly off to the pub with the *Telegraph* and Eve emptied the dishwasher as Simon continued singing her praises. She had absolutely no objection whatsoever to being praised for delivering a successful Christmas, which always felt like a familial duty rather than an unmitigated delight.

'And I bet you have no idea how much it meant to us all,' said Simon.

'All, except possibly Jordan.' Eve folded a tea towel excessively neatly, as if to briskly delineate her all-round domestic goddesshood.

'No – *especially* Jordan. Look, last night, Ed and I had a very long conversation – till about two a.m., I think, like *young* people – and we both agreed that, at the risk of upsetting Jordy's precious routine too much, we should remove him from Ivy House, for all the reasons you've already suggested.' Simon looked at Eve hopefully. 'Fortunately, via our "connections", we think we might be able to pull this off without being penalized too heavily.'

Simon was referring to Ivy House's standard private school get-out clause: a full term's fees for the sudden removal of a child. Or, thought Eve, in the case of Susie Poe's swift withdrawal of both Lula and Charlie at the end of term, *two* full terms. Expensive business, spontaneity.

'Well, look, I'm sure we can work something out if I catch Tony in the right mood.'

'Thanks. The point is that we – the *three* of us – agree that Heatherdown is probably the right sort of school for Jordy. Having said that, I am also quite pro Eastdene Community Primary School. Apparently it has some sort of new superhead.'

'Yes, the famous – or infamous, depending on your view – Mike Browning.' Eve was polishing the smears from wine glasses with an attention to detail that surprised her. She had a sudden mental snapshot of herself as a full-time retro housewife, complete with gingham pinny and a rolling pin. She smiled to herself – where had *that* come from? Mum. Mum had a gingham pinny . . .

Simon continued. 'Well, we took your point that state schools are often brilliant with special needs while prep schools tend to tackle "bad" behaviour by dishing out detentions and hoping the kids sort themselves out on the rugger pitch.'

'Yes. I'm afraid some of us are very much stuck in the twentieth century. It's bothering me, frankly, that we don't have a full-time Special Educational Needs Co-Ordinator – SENCO, to you. Because, the thing is, of course, that I'm not teaching anymore. I'm not on the frontline, just busy recruiting new square pegs for our old round prep schooly holes.' Eve paused. 'You know, Jordan has been a real eye-opener, but we've got a few Jordans.'

Simon looked intrigued. 'Really?'

'Yes, lots of super-bright, tricky kids, a bit autistic spec-trumy without any proper diagnosis. And Tony couldn't give a monkey's.' Eve shrugged.

'Tony is always going to be about the bottom line. He relies on you for the ethical judgement calls. Too much, in my opinion.'

Eve reached for a tin and extracted a dark and dense-looking Madeira cake, steeped in alcohol, which smelled like something one might choose to kick-start a lost week-end. 'Fancy some over-the-limit cake?'

'*Grace's* over-the-limit cake? Try stopping me.'

Eve cut Simon a slice. 'So, anyway, I'm still slightly

concerned about Heatherdown's ability to stay in business long enough – there are *rumours* – to provide some consistency and continuity for Jordy, for whom routine is probably everything. Ellie says it's not so much that he *dislikes* change, but that change seems to kind of unplug him from his mainframe. Does that make sense?'

'It makes perfect sense. Here . . .' Simon reached into a new, very smart leather manbag, a Christmas present from Ed, and pulled out a large brown envelope. 'I should have shown you this ages ago, really, but for some peculiar reason I felt that it would be a betrayal of trust. I have no idea why, in retrospect.' Simon handed her the envelope. 'It's basically *The Jordy Diaries*. Brace yourself, it was written by his mother and fills in at least some of the gaps. By the way, Mum has really excelled herself this year – the cake is awesome.'

There was a cake-fuelled silence for a few moments. Then Eve said, 'Oh, gosh, Simon – I'm suddenly thinking about my ma.'

Simon patted her hand in an avuncular sort of way. 'Of course you are.' He raised his tea mug. 'In loving memory of the most excellent Charlotte Eva Amelia Wharton.'

Eve raised her tea mug. 'To Mum – who would have bloody loved this cake.' A pause. 'I think I might just send Sonia a text, actually. Dad's fine; he's in the pub.' She glanced at Simon. 'I'm talking to you like you're my husband, now, like a mad old woman. I'll be sitting around watching telly in my wedding dress before you know it.'

'You were always a mad old woman in waiting, Evie. It's

sexy. It suits you.' A beat. 'Do you really think you can still get into that dress?'

Eve punched him – and not quite as gently as she'd intended.

The twenty-seventh of December, the day after the anniversary of her mother's death, and Eve was alone, right in the middle of the twilight zone. Although still technically only lunchtime, it was gloomy outside, the Barn was empty of daughters and Eve's day stretched ahead, unformed. Yet, even with a lack of demands on her time, she wasn't quite ready to read the contents of the brown envelope marked *Jordy*. Instead, she visited Tesco Extra and started stocking up for New Year – despite the fact she wasn't expecting guests for New Year – and even if she decided to invite some over, the freezer was already full, anyway.

So it was at 3:30 p.m., post-Tesco, with *still* no sign of any daughters but an unexpected amount of new stationery, soap and light bulbs, that Eve finally sat down with a cup of tea as proper darkness encroached, and opened the envelope.

MY JORDY

My beutiful Jordy is six and goin to live somewere else now so I decide to fihgt the DYSLEXIA (!) and write few words down that will ecsplan who he is to his new dads. He is his own (litle) man from the start. After first few week & months (I hav mastites he hav colics = I watch lots of

Big Brother!) Jordy sleept through the night (coinsidens?) on the first night I bottelfed him when he was 3 month. He sleep well thro nihgt ever since. But its not the nights its Jordy when hes awake that keeps ME awake at nights!

BABY JORDY

He was strong newborn baby – real bruser not lik brothers & sisters. J lift his head, clench fists like a boxer and go all stiff when you held him when he was only a few weeks old. He felt all 'redy to go'! My other babys was more soft like babys! Jordy was like grown up INSIDE a baby.

Eve read on; there were ten more pages, charting Jordan's life from birth to, as far as she could tell, about six months ago. It would have been an exhausting – and exhaustive – document for any parent to create, never mind one who was also dyslexic. But what these words revealed most clearly to Eve was the fact that Jordy was not only loved, he was understood. Eve paused: Can I honestly say that I know Zoe and Alice as well as Jordan's anonymous mother understands her son?

But perhaps that was best left as a rhetorical question. Either way, Eve reached the final page:

Her are things what Jordy does.
- Hes righthand but hold his FORK in his rihgt-hand and NIFE in left. No way to make him change!
- He refuse to ever wear coat.

- He walk on tiptos nerly always. I think it must hurt but J say it don't.
- He get angry and stressey with shoe he has to put on with his hands. He hate lases!
- He take off T-shirt as soon as he come into the house becuss he say 'I am a WWE champ!'
- He has never sit in his seat thro a meal.
- He is clever at lots but isn't bothered about doig well in things

I love him so much tho. I wil ad more things to this list wen I think of them soon.

And that's where it ended. When she'd finished reading, Eve curled her feet beneath her and stared out of the window into the gloaming, enveloped by the profound silence of a biggish house in the country that was, quite suddenly, very empty.

'Barney! You stupid old hound, where *are* you?'

At the sound of Eve's voice, the old dog heaved himself dutifully and waggily from his basket in the hall and sought her out, curling himself up like a giant furry comma at her feet. At which point, Eve finally allowed herself to cry – non-specific crying that could nonetheless be apportioned fairly equally amongst . . . well, Jordy, yes, but also her dead mother, her rapidly disappearing daughters, her happily-married-to-someone-else ex-husband, a career that no longer consumed her and, finally, being fifty-fucking-three and alone again on the twenty-seventh of December.

# 16

'So, no texting in the office, please. And don't bite your nails. And always make eye contact. And don't assume people are just going to *tell* you things – they will all be wildly busy so you will not only have make yourself as useful as possible, you will have to do it by stealth.'

'And how do I do *that*, Mum?' said Zoe.

'Haven't the foggiest. I've been the general for so long that you can't really expect me to remember how to be a foot soldier.' Eve grinned; Zoe grimaced. 'Now, have fun and text me at lunchtime.' Zoe nodded while Eve paused on the driveway and peered closely at her daughter who, though presently leaning against the door jamb chewing a length of hair, nonetheless looked gorgeous. 'And I'm not sure those trousers are tight enough. Maybe you could try cling film?'

'Shut *up*.'

'I'm totally shutting up. I'm actually *off*. Have a fabulous time.'

Rob turned up exactly five minutes after Eve had left.

Zoe knew that he would try to have sex, but the timings were all wrong, even for a quickie. Anyway, Alice was mooching around upstairs somewhere, probably waiting to steal Zoe's make-up.

'Sorry, babes – we've got to go in, like, five – and, anyway, Alice is around.'

Rob pretended not to care. 'S'OK. What time you back, then?'

'Not *tonight*.' Zoe glanced over her shoulder. 'Didn't I tell you? I *did* tell you. I'm away all week – back Saturday. You did know that? It's too far to commute to, like, Bond Street from here, and Auntie Sonia lives in Notting Hill.'

'Which is close to Bond Street, right?'

'Close enough.' Zoe reached up on her tiptoes and planted a kiss on her boyfriend's forehead. 'You are so *local*, Rob.'

Rob shrugged. 'Nah. I don't do London.'

'You do. You go up to take pictures!'

Rob looked nonplussed. 'That's different.'

By the second week of January, the novelty of a white New Year had entirely worn off. Having exhausted all the googleable Inuit descriptions of snow and constructed a passable igloo on the lawn with Harry, Gail was delighted to learn that Ivy House's car park and grounds had thawed sufficiently to ensure it no longer contravened health and safety legislation.

I'm sure I never brought this much stuff home when

I was at school, she thought as she rushed to ready herself for work, rifling through the fistfuls of paper she'd extracted from Harry's school bag before he'd left for the second day of his term, Eastdene having reopened the previous day. Gail glanced briefly at Mike Browning's *Welcome To The New Term!* letter ('And we give a warm Eastdene welcome to Charlie and Lula Fox, who join us in . . .', blah blah blah) before sticking it to the fridge with her favourite magnet, which read *BECAUSE I'M YOUR MOTHER, THAT'S WHY!* She screwed up the rest of the paper and, guiltily, shoved it into the recycling bin before heading outside. Fingers crossed the Micra would start. And, though Gail briefly pondered whether or not her ten-minute drive at thirty miles per hour was doing its bit to accelerate the deterioration of polar icecaps, in the middle of the current bleakly arctic East Sussex midwinter, she hoped that the sooner this bloody snow thawed the better, frankly.

Twenty minutes later she was sharing her frustration with Eve. 'So, all this bloody paperwork came home with Harry last night. You'd think they'd have had better things to do at Eastdene than stuff bags full of paper on the first day of term, wouldn't you? Why does being the parent of a primary school-aged child feel like being the manager of a small business?' She plonked Eve's first frothy coffee of the spring term on her desk and wiped the inevitable spillage with her sleeve. 'Surely every parent hates this stuff?

Even the smug mummies whose lives revolve around it? Would some sort of future-proof paperless school be a complete pipe dream?'

'And a happy new year to you too, Gail!' Eve smiled. 'You are dangerously close to *ranting* – and, in answer to your question, yes, it *would*. It is quite clearly our job as educators, whether working within the state system or independently, to make parents feel they're getting their quid's worth and, these days, that means bombarding them with information they will almost immediately forget and then feel guilty that they've forgotten – and preferably several times a week.' Eve raised an eyebrow. 'I am very well aware that when *we* were children, weeks, months, possibly even *years* could go by without any interaction between a parent and their children's school. If only it were still the case!' Eve sighed mock-theatrically as Gail laughed. 'Got any more important questions you suggest I raise with Tony?'

Gail smiled and shook her head.

'Sure?' Eve was feeling bullish. 'No – silly me – why on earth would you?' She noted that Gail narrowed her eyes very slightly and shrugged, but said nothing. 'Well, anyway, rant over! Now, catch me up on what's happened so far this morning'.

Ten minutes later and Eve had learned that twelve children had left Ivy House between Christmas and New Year. While the majority of their parents had invoked financial pressures as a result of the fee increase (including Susie

Poe), a small but nonetheless troubling minority had talked – again – about Ivy House 'failing' their children. As Eve listened to Gail, she considered the idea that children could be 'failed' by even the best schools and decided it was all a bit fashionable; nonetheless – and despite being her own school's staunchest fan – she instinctively knew there was something awry. She wasn't particularly bothered about the falling numbers – which were set to rise again in the autumn, after Tony's international-pupil recruitment drive started paying off – however, she *was* bothered about the reasons behind some of them. She knew that what the parents said was, in some respects at least, right – some children had been failed by Ivy House . . . and perhaps in ways they had never been failed before.

Eve sensed that the children in her charge were becoming somehow (and it was hard to put her finger on something so nebulous, but . . .) *different*, more *complex*. She had attempted to raise her hunch with Tony last year but had predictably been given short shrift. ('They're children, Eve, ergo they're difficult. After all these years in teaching, do I really have to break this to you quite so gently?'). But Eve knew she was right; there were more problems – from relatively straightforward peanut allergies to outbreaks of bad language via an increase in Tourette's-ish behavioural tics and a veritable rash of attention-deficit-type disorders – and the children were unable to be easily diagnosed or supported by Ivy House for the simple reason that one hundred per cent of the Ivy House staffroom remained entirely unqualified in any special-needs capacity whatsoever, despite the fact that the latest statistics – and Eve enjoyed ferreting out statistics – claimed that as many as one in five school children displayed some sort of Special Need.

Yet, try as she might to join the dots, Eve had failed. On top of which, she was preparing to go along to her boss with only a bunch of hunches in order to beg for new staff. Eve hated begging – and she *particularly* hated begging Tony.

'Darling, come and keep my lap warm!' said Tony as Eve entered his office without knocking.

'Actually, shut up, Tony – this is serious.'

'And so are those *heels*. Wow. I can tell you mean business.'

But Eve was having none of it. 'Really, Tony, I mean it!'

'OK.' Tony sighed. 'I'm all ears. What do you want? More money?'

'It's not so much what *I* want as what *we* need.'

And so Eve explained, at considerable and conscientious length, how, for reasons she could not really begin to explain, the school's demographic was changing – and not so much socially as, for want of a better word, *emotionally*. (At her use of 'emotionally', Tony perceptibly and predictably flinched). And so, in order to continue to cater for these invariably bright but occasionally challenging children, the school would simply have to (deep breath) up its game.

'Up our fucking game, Eve?' Tony clearly couldn't

contain himself. 'How much of its *game* does an Ofsted "Outstanding" school need to *up*, precisely? Or is there some secret Ofsted category we should be aiming for? Something beyond "Outstanding" that, for some inexplicable reason, I don't fucking well know about? Maybe "supercalifragilisticexpialidocious-standing"?'

At any other time, Eve would have been laughing – but not right now. 'Stop. You sound just like that Alastair Campbell-ish character in *The Thick of It*.'

'I *love* that show. Malcolm *Fucker*. Anyway—'

'Look, I am absolutely, one hundred per cent completely *serious*. Unless we get new SENCO-qualified staff – or train up some existing staff – I –' Eve paused; she surprised herself by how very fast things had moved even though she had thought she was completely in control, which just went to show how elusive a concept 'control' could be – 'I would very seriously think about . . . about –' and Eve surprised herself too by how fast she arrived at this outcome, but here she most definitely was – '*resigning*.'

Silence. The moment felt filmic enough for several bars of a theme tune by Ennio Morricone to play while metaphorical tumbleweed rolled down Main Street, sunlight glinted off the protagonist's spurs and beads of sweat were wiped from brows. Though it was 9:47 a.m. it could just as easily have been high noon.

'Right, so that's your dry-run resignation, is it?' said Tony, sarcastically. 'It needs a bit of work, to be honest. Any other business?'

'Tony!' If she hadn't been sitting, Eve would almost certainly – and bugger the new heels – have stamped her foot.

'*Darling* Eve, I am not interested in running an educational establishment for society's marginals and ferals. I am, however, very interested in running a school for fundamentally nice middle-class children, or indeed nice *wannabe* middle-class children, who –' Eve recognized a rant coming on – 'despite dressing their Barbies – and Kens, for all I know – in *Porn Star in Training* T-shirts and swapping their Subbuteo for on-screen drive-by shootings, are still children we recognize as our own kind.' Tony briefly paused for breath. 'Do you see, Eve? They're our *breed*? On the other hand, all the other ADHDivas and arsing dysmorphic-o-praxial-lexias and autistic-spectrum whatevers – *they* are fundamentally *not* our kind.' Tony thumped his desk. 'So, to reiterate, I don't want Ivy House to go there, Eve. Because we most emphatically do *not* do special needs!'

And as Tony again thumped the beautiful blond Nordic wood with the palm of his hand, Eve thought, I can do that, and thumped it too, recognizing that Tony's rants were the outpourings of a man thoroughly terrified by the prospect of change. Secure in this insight, she ploughed ahead. 'Right, you can huff and puff and blow Ivy House down if you want to, but I am roughly ninety per cent sure that we have at least fifteen to twenty children – maybe five per cent of our intake – with some sort of special-needs *something*, one of whom, you may be interested to know, is almost certainly Petrus Sorensen, whom Ellie Blake thinks may even be Asperger's. And there's probably double that of dyslexics and dyspraxics, many of whom are already getting help privately because *we can't help them.*' Eve was warming up now, flexing her headteacher muscle. 'And then there's the stuff I don't even know about yet: the kids with problems and issues lurking just under the radar, waiting to surface – and I can tell you there are going to be several of those.'

Surprisingly, Tony seemed to be rather touched by Eve's passionate soliloquy – but first things first. '*Petrus Sorensen?* What's wrong with Little Lord Fauntleroy?'

'Well, it depends what you mean by "wrong", doesn't it? He is displaying *behaviours*—'

'And what the fuck does *that* mean? And since when did you become the expert? And, while I'm at it, don't you *dare* go saying anything to Anette Sorensen without ... without –' Tony paused, floundering slightly – 'without running it by me first, yeah? This needs a proper *strategy*, Eve.'

'But there is no strategy, Tony! We have a kid – *kids!* – who needs our help, which is part of our duty of pastoral care. I'm already organizing a series of meetings with all the form teachers, both individually and in groups, to work out our –' Eve wiggled her fingers in the air, Tony Salter style – ' "strategy".'

'Fine, but I still don't know how you suddenly became an expert on kids with special needs?'

And this, thought Eve, is the moment for the big reveal: 'Because Simon just adopted one. And he only found out after the event. And, even though it isn't confirmed, it's extremely likely that Jordan—'

Tony interrupted Eve: 'This is the Jordan who joined our Year Two when I was schmoozing the Far East?'

'Yes, that's the one.'

'So we have a bunch of fruit-and-nuts on our roll. Is that what you're telling me?'

'Not in quite so many words, Tony – but your offensiveness is nothing if not predictable.'

Eve knew that Tony disliked being predictable rather more than he disliked being offensive. He frowned, seemed to be considering a different tack.

'What do you need, then? And more to the point, how much will it cost?'

Victory! Eve seized the moment. 'Right, so we need a designated special educational needs co-ordinator, full time *and* on a proper salary, starting September. And then I'd like three existing members of staff to be trained, on a voluntary basis, to screen for dyslexia – bill to be footed by us.'

'And all this will keep you quiet, will it?'

'I doubt that, Tony, but it *will* help Ivy House become the very best school of its kind it can possibly be.' Eve leaned forward and met Tony's gaze. 'Which would be nice, wouldn't it?'

Tony rolled his eyes. 'You know what I mean.'

But Eve, as usual, was already halfway towards the door before her boss could change his mind.

Once back on safer ground in her own office, Eve re-ran her meeting with Tony and marvelled again at just how quickly things had progressed. It was not so much that she appeared to have got her own way – at least for the moment – but the fact that she had expressed just how passionately she felt about getting it. And yet, for the first time, Eve also allowed herself to think that, even if she acquired all the SENCO staff she'd ever dreamed of overnight, her days at Ivy House were still numbered. It wasn't so much that Tony would want her to leave, it was that, once she'd achieved what she needed to achieve, *she* might want to leave. Not that she planned to breathe a word of any of this to Gail – yet. Gail was a glory in every way, but she was also a *gossiping* glory: tell her, and Eve would effectively tell not only Eastdene but a sizeable chunk of East Sussex, too. She stopped briefly by Gail's desk.

'Mine in ten? May involve dictation.'

'Dictation? Is it 1986? And you're *hissing*,' hissed Gail. 'What's going on?'

'Tony's what's going on. And I'm going on, too.'

'On the subject of which, he just went out, face like a wet weekend in Folkestone.' Gail's tone was light. 'Have you just *resigned*, or something?'

So much for my resolve, thought Eve. She sighed. 'Not properly, not yet – but I might.'

'Right. That's *totes oh-em-gee*, as I'm sure Zoe and Alice would never dream of saying. May I ask why?'

'You máy ask but I haven't got long enough to answer. If I tell you, though, you mustn't breathe a word. But first – 1986.'

'Scout's, Cub's, Brownie's, Guide's honour. And, look, I've even brought my special 1986 pen, the Parker my dear old dad gave me when I got my shorthand and typing certificate.'

Gail saluted and Eve grinned. Ultimately, it didn't really matter if Gail gossiped. In fact, word getting out might be a good thing; it wasn't as if Eve could afford to be a lady of leisure, after all – or would want to be one, even if she could afford it.

'Come on, then. It's a job ad. No, don't look at me like that – we're getting a SENCO.'

Gail held up her hands, jazz style. 'Hallelujah! It's all I ever hear about in the corridors of the powerless: "special needs" this, "spectrum" the other. "Why don't we have any specialist staff?" Blah-di-blah . . .'

'Really?' Eve raised an eyebrow. 'Why didn't you *tell* me, Gail? This is *important*.'

Gail looked nonplussed. 'I would've thought you'd known me long enough to know that I'm not a gossip, Eve. But, hey, I'm telling you now, aren't I?'

# 17

Zoe pressed the buzzer on the entryphone of the discreet black door that had taken her a nervous fifteen minutes to locate and which turned out to be at the Piccadilly end of Bond Street. *Old* Bond Street – the posh bit. Where else?

'Hello?' said a tiny, tinny voice.

'Ah, hello, my name is Zoe Sturridge and I, ah . . .'

But the buzzer had already buzzed and, as no instructions had been forthcoming, Zoe headed up the stairs. On the first floor, there was another black door with a discreet brass plaque: *Odense Holdings*. As far as Zoe was concerned, this may as well have been a rabbit hole and she might have been Alice – the fictional one, that is, not her dumb kid sister.

'Good morning, Zoe; welcome to Odense.'

At the sight of the exceptionally beautiful blonde woman standing in the foyer, Zoe instantly dreamed of being matter-transported away from Odense Holdings. Despite its being ostensibly a chic office ranging over three storeys of a Bond Street townhouse above a fashionable cobbler's shopfront, it was, Zoe knew in her marrow, a parallel universe to which it was inconceivable she could ever belong.

I mean, Zoe thought to herself, how can anybody this awesome be, like, a receptionist?

'Hi,' she said in her smallest voice; a voice so small, indeed, that, until now, she hadn't actually known she'd possessed it. 'Thanks. I really hope I can be of some, er, help?'

'I'm sure you can. We are always grateful for another pair of hands.' The blonde woman held out her own hand. 'I'm Anette Sorensen. You are absolutely the image of your mother and, believe me, that is *definitely* a compliment.'

Zoe felt herself start to blush. 'Wow, thanks. And, er, thanks very much for having me, Mrs Sorensen.'

'It's Anette and it's a pleasure. And I know exactly what you're thinking: "But I thought *Mr* Sorensen ran Odense." And, despite feminism being well into its fifth decade, you wouldn't be the first and, sadly, you won't be the last. And Stefan *does* run Odense – at least, fifty per cent of it. We're a double act, but we just don't shout about it.'

'That is *so* cool.' At which, of course, despite her new black spray-on skinnies and buttoned-up crisp white blouse and the moss-green cashmere cardigan she'd borrowed from her mum, Zoe herself felt very uncool. 'I mean . . .'

Anette smiled. 'I know exactly what you mean. Now, come and meet the team. We'll start at the top – that is, upstairs with my husband, who is off to New York soon – and then work our way back downstairs, by which time you'll probably be ready for coffee.'

And so Zoe followed Anette up four more flights of stairs ('Of course, we have the lift, but this is such good exercise . . .'), which gave her just enough time to contemplate the fact that, although she clearly knew nothing much about anything important in the grown-up world, she would endeavour to be a very fast learner. By the time she'd reached Stefan Sorensen's top-floor office suite, Zoe had already vowed to (a) learn as much as she possibly could about hedge-fund management during the next few days – obviously – and (b) never again (if she could help it) judge a book by its cover. Somehow, (b) already seemed to Zoe a far greater challenge than (a).

Either way, forty-five minutes after arriving at Odense Holdings, Zoe Sturridge found herself in the loo, attempting to tame a few escapee fronds of hair into something appropriately groomed while gathering her thoughts – which, despite her best organizational efforts, kept scattering around her head like a flock of ditzy sheep. It was important to corral them, though, because life was moving *extremely* fast.

As she washed her hands, Zoe replayed her introduction to Stefan Sorensen and the three-way conversation with Anette and Stefan that had followed:

'So, Anette, I've just spoken with Richard – you know

how much he loves those five a.m. wake-up calls – and if we're going to nail the Dersh and Dohenny, uh, situation, then I gotta get over there before the NYSE closes.'

Anette glanced at her watch. '*Very* tight. I'll get Tina to make a call; so, OK, whatever, off you go. Of course, I can't.' She shrugged.

Zoe's eyes moved from Anette to Stefan and back again.

'I know, honey,' said Stefan. 'Get home for the kids. So!' He glanced at Zoe and, hopping to his feet, grinning, he banged his hand on the desk. 'So, young lady, you fancy some *work experience*?'

Zoe smiled and nodded. She had absolutely no idea what was unfolding; however, Stefan Sorensen seemed suitably adrenalized by whatever it was that she did her level best to match his mood. 'Yeah! I mean, yes, *please*.'

Anette laughed, then, eyes widening, clasped her hand to her mouth. 'Oh, *Stefan*. Oh my word! She barely has time to ask her mother's permission!'

'You do the asking, Annie, yeah? You two get on great. Is that OK, Zoe?' Zoe nodded, though she had absolutely no idea for what her mother was going to be asked permission. Then there was a swift and staccato exchange in Danish between Anette and Stefan, which Zoe obviously had no hope of understanding, so she jigged from foot to foot nervously, wondering what was going on.

Anette turned to her, smiling. 'So, Zoe, have you ever flown to New York by private jet?'

Yeah, course I have, thought Zoe, in my dreams. 'Er, no.

But then again –' brightly, confidently, though, she hoped, not too smart-arsey – 'I've never been to New York!'

Anette smiled at Stefan, Stefan smiled at Anette, and both of them smiled at Zoe. 'Well, this is definitely the way to do it for your first time!' said Anette. 'And now I'll call your mother.'

And so, as she dried her hands, Zoe rewound this conversation and replayed it again, just to make sure she hadn't made it up, after which she realized that, yes, she would in actual fact be (a) accompanying Stefan Sorensen to (b) New York (c) today. And that, after being phoned by Anette, her mother had (d) (astoundingly) already agreed to this absurdly bonkers thing, and that (e) one motorbike courier was at this very moment being dispatched to East-dene to collect her (f) passport, while another was (g) picking up her suitcase from Auntie Sonia's and that (h) both would be waiting at the office of something called *Execujet* – Zoe googled this in the loo and discovered it was 'The World's Leading Purveyor of Premium Business Travel Solutions for a Demanding and Discerning Clientele'. She fished in her bag for her lip gloss and then dexterously started applying it while texting:

> Babes!!!! Am off to New York in a min wiv MR
> SORENSEN + his PA!!!! Yeah, NYC Concrete Jungle
> where dreams are made of there's nothing you can't do
> now you're in Nu York! Back Thurs a.m. Love you!!!! Z xxx

*

As he read the text in the student canteen between lectures, Rob suddenly, painfully, already felt a long way away from Zoe *indeed* – and so much faster than he'd expected. He went to the loo and locked himself into a cubicle and re-read the text, noting that there were more exclamation marks than kisses – and then came out, blew £1.50 on a filthy-tasting *vomaccino* from the vending machine, read the text one more time and, finally, replied:

Gr8, babe! Think ul go2 applestore?!!!! Xxx

Rob touched *Send* . . . just as he realized this text didn't sound quite right. He sent another:

luvu2!!! Xxxxxx

Despite his deep discomfort with using multiple Xs, Rob hoped this one more successfully disguised how he really felt.

# 18

Eve returned to her office after her weekly walkabout around Ivy House's nursery wearing a thunderous expression, which Gail intuited probably shouldn't be challenged, especially not in her habitual cheerfully-joshing, bubble-bursting fashion. Eve's subsequent meeting with Mrs Charteris, head of the nursery, and her deputy, Miss Short, was brief, especially for Miss Short, who exited after precisely (Gail was keeping count) three minutes and sixteen seconds, in tears. Mrs Charteris, meanwhile, emerged after a further four minutes, twenty-three seconds, looking even more stony-faced than usual, after which Gail counted to thirty before knocking on Eve's door and presenting her with frothy coffee. She was, of course, desperate to know what had gone on.

Eve nodded a 'Thanks' and avoided eye contact, yet it was impossible for Gail not to notice that Eve was *in tears*. This was so rare as to be tectonic-plate-shiftingly seismic. Nonetheless, as a PA at the top of her game, Gail resisted the temptation to ask proper questions.

'Biscuit?' said Gail.

'Please,' said Eve. 'Thanks.' Which was the precise moment when Eve's mobile chirruped.

'Shall I go?' mouthed Gail silently, but Eve shook her head vigorously, indicating she should sit.

'Anette!' said Eve brightly, professionally. This greeting was, Gail noted, followed by a conversation lasting two minutes and twelve seconds, of which Eve's final words were, 'That's tremendously exciting. I'm sure she's thrilled. Do *please* get her to call me on her mobile before she leaves!' After which, Eve leaned back in her chair, closed her eyes and muttered, 'Jesus fucking H Christ on a stick.'

'Eve, are you sure you don't want me to go?'

'No. Stay a minute, please, Gail.' Eve reached for the phone again. 'Simon! Hi! So, I thought you ought to know that our eldest daughter – and you'd better sit down – is literally about to jet off to New York for three days with her new boss.' A pause. 'Yes, indeed, the, uh, not entirely below-the-radar hedge-fund billionaire, Stefan Sorensen. And I'm sorry to spring this after the event, but do you think that's OK?' A pause. 'OK, uh-huh – as long as you're *sure*, because I just sort of let her go without asking many questions. Yes . . . Yes . . . No . . . I'm sure they can be trusted *completely*. His PA is going too, of course.' Eve sighed, 'I've got to pop home in a mo, to pick up Zo's passport.'

Gail's eyes widened. 'Wow,' she mouthed silently at Eve.

'I know!' Eve mouthed equally silently back. 'OK, Simon, thanks for that. Better shoot. Crazy day . . .'

'And Zoe's day sounds like the plot of a 1980s bonk-buster,' said Gail. 'I mean, *wow*.'

Eve laughed, gratefully. 'I don't think they've called them "bonkbusters" since *Lace*. But the good news is she's not travelling alone with the handsome billionaire. Anette told me Sorensen's PA, Tina, is going too. She's a sensible fifty-six-year-old mother-of-three with an empty nest, and, according to Anette, she will be "treating your daughter as her own" –' Eve's Danish accent was abysmal – 'even as she sends her out on errands in –' Eve paused – '*Manhattan*! God, Gail – New York!'

Gail braced herself. 'And, before that call – what was going on with the nursery? Or do you not want to talk about it?'

Eve leaned back in her chair and threaded her hands together behind her head. She exhaled deeply. 'No, I *do* want to talk about it. I want to talk about *all* of it very much.'

So Gail listened as Eve told her how she'd visited the nursery and, after Eve had stuck her head round class-room doors and heard busy-looking small people chanting, 'Good morning, Mrs Sturridge,' she made a point of visit-ing the lavatories, where, of course, somebody was usually marshalling the not-quite-toilet-trained.

The school's nursery department – the Tree House – had a policy of insisting that children older than three were toilet-trained before they entered the Reception class in Ivy House's pre-prep department, where none of the teach-ers were prepared to tolerate pull-ups and even accidents were frowned upon. This meant that, as the deadline approached, there was often an air of panic amongst the more recalcitrant children(usually boys) and their mothers, and the staff. A particularly longstanding nursery staff member, Miss Short, had taken the bulk of the toilet-training upon herself – or possibly had it thrust upon her. 'And so,' Eve explained, 'as I approached the loos, I could already hear Miss Short in full cry: "Pants down *before* we poo, Michael!" Obviously, this was a bad moment, so I just said something like, "How are we all doing here, then?" ' Eve paused and wiped her eye. Gail waited. 'And then Miss Short barely missed a beat. She said, "The little sod'll get the hang of it soon, *won't you, Michael*? Cos he knows what happens if he doesn't. *Don't you, Michael?*" '

Gail's eyes widened. Eve was ashen-faced. 'And I just hoped I had somehow misheard, *please, God*. So I said to Andrea Short, "*What* did you just say?" And she said, of all things, "I . . . uh . . . I'm sorry, Mrs Sturridge. I thought you were Mrs Charteris!" To which the only response was, "Right! And that makes it better, does it? Do you say things like that to Mrs Charteris – or, indeed, Michael – very often?" '

'My God, Eve. I don't know what to say.' And, for once, Gail genuinely didn't.

Meanwhile, Eve was still close to tears, her voice catching in her throat. 'And, all the time, Michael Percy was just sitting on the loo with his fat little legs swinging back and forth.' Eve wiped her nose with the back of her hand. 'And all he said was, "Miss Short is stressy." '

Gail listened as Eve told her how she'd gently asked if Michael, who was three, had finished his business, and if so would he like to wipe his bottom and wash his hands and then she would take him to the cloakroom, because it was very nearly break, so he may as well get his hat and coat and gloves on and play outside – but to please be very careful on the equipment because it was still a bit frosty-the-snowman. To all of which Michael Percy, Richard's youngest son, had apparently nodded very seriously. Like all the Percy offspring, Gail considered Michael to be endearingly sweet and biddable – a fact that shouldn't have made Miss Short's behaviour any more appalling, yet somehow did.

'So,' said Eve, 'I told Charteris and Short that I'd see them in my office in fifteen minutes and I took Michael by the hand and led him to the cloakroom and waited while he dressed himself, painfully slowly, before taking him outside where several nursery staff were huddled by the climbing frames, stamping their feet and warming their hands on their mugs.' Eve rolled her eyes. 'So I told them I'd prefer it if hot drinks weren't brought out to the play-ground, and I'm pretty sure one of them shrugged, so I sort of lost it a bit and said, "In fact, it's not so much an 'I'd prefer it if' as it is a 'no hot drinks in the playground, ever, effective immediately'. *Do I make myself clear?*" '

Gail nodded. This was the correct response. It was well known among the prep-school staff that the nursery was its own fiefdom. Some of the junior nursery staff – average

age about nineteen – were especially sullen and unlovely graduates of a local college's BTEC in Children's Play, Learning and Development. With, thought Gail, a distinction in sulking. We probably get what we pay for. And that isn't very much.

'So, to cut a long story short – no pun intended – they've both been given warnings.' Eve sighed again. 'Christ, Gail, it's all starting to fall apart. And I'm so bloody distracted, I've just let my seventeen-year-old daughter fly to New York on a private jet with people *I don't actually even know*. Like she doesn't have teenage delusions of grandeur as it is!'

Gail laughed. Eve's ability to weasel out the humour in the most unlikely circumstances was, in her eyes, one of the things that set her boss apart and made her a truly *brilliant* head teacher. Gail wondered if Eve actually knew she was brilliant? On balance, she suspected not.

'OK, so you're off in a minute, Gail?'

'Yes, I'm actually going to be there when Harry gets in tonight. It helps not to have to physically prise him off the Xbox.'

'I bet. I feel so lucky we never had all that screeny stuff with the girls. Mind you, the latest studies are saying that gaming might even be *good* for them. Before you know it, it'll be part of the national curriculum. I can't keep up.' A shrug. 'Look, I'm going to stay late tonight. Simon's with Alice, and Zoe's probably halfway across the Atlantic in a turbo-charged cigar tube, so . . .' She smiled wanly.

'Shall I leave you the Indian takeaway menu? They'll deliver.'

'That would be great, Gail; thanks so much. You are a marvel.' Eve looked at Gail quite intently, which Gail didn't find entirely comfortable. 'I don't think I tell you that enough, do I?'

'Stop it. Part of the job description.'

'Thanks so much. And, anyway, what are *you* up to tonight?' Eve simultaneously reached for her favourite black Pentel Sign pen and Moleskine notebook and Gail momentarily considered launching into a detailed description of this *fantastic* American drama series she'd recently come across, about a high school chemistry teacher who gets cancer and decides to provide for his family by becoming, of all the most ridiculous things, a manufacturer of a class-A drug called crystal meth, when she realized that this sounded very nearly as absurd as Zoe hightailing it to New York in a private jet. And, anyway, she could see that she was already losing Eve, who was now scribbling very fast in the Moleskine in her distinctively elegant, graphic hand.

'Oh, just a quiet night in with some terrible crimes, I think.' In truth, Gail was expecting to see a friend.

Eve glanced up briefly and smiled distractedly. 'Sounds blissful!'

# 19

As was her habit, after dropping Harry at Breakfast Club, Gail was the first into Ivy House the following morning. She made herself a frothy coffee in the staffroom, fired up the gas log fire in the entrance hall and noted that the faux-Tudor fire-surround needed a good dust. This was not part of her job description but, after all these years, nobody – and least of all Gail – was sure where Miss Prince's job description began or ended. Though it ostensibly meant looking after Eve, it had over time grown organically to encompass part-time bursar, booker of flights and restaurants, occasional online mid-century modern furniture shopper for Tony, not to mention chief confidante to many members of staff. Gail occasionally wondered how Ivy House might function without her . . . and then she pushed the thought away. After all, everybody was dispensable.

She popped her head around Eve's office door to check that it was as immaculate as usual and was surprised to find that it wasn't. There were two dirty coffee mugs and a pile of papers and Eve's desk light was still switched on. Late night . . . On the floor by the sofa there was an open copy of *Hello!*. Gail set to tidying, noting the picture of Mr and Mrs Sorensen looking fabulously glamorous at a pre-Christmas black-tie event. Then, as she arranged the pile of papers on Eve's desk, she couldn't help noticing, too, that Eve had written and printed out something considerably longer than her usual weekly newsletter for the Ivy House website. It wasn't snooping, exactly, to take a closer look – Eve had left it right here in the middle of her desk, after all, and the middle of Eve's desk was very much a part of Gail's world. Gail glanced at the grandmother clock in the corner of the office, which had been in situ long before Ivy House became a school: almost five past eight – Eve won't be in till half past . . . She sat down at the desk and started reading.

## OUR CHILDREN

I've been in teaching for half my life and can quite honestly say that it has never been harder, inasmuch as the goalposts seem to be moving all the time. When I started out in the mid-1980s, it was an entirely different world. While we'd had punk rock and a female prime minister, we hadn't had 9/11 and the internet. These days, working in an independent prep school with so-called 'traditional' values – the three Rs, hard work, discipline, sportsmanship, kindness, politeness – seems to be so left field as to appear radical. The generation of children I once routinely shepherded off to good independent secondary schools and grammars are almost a dying breed. Whereas I used to push round pegs into round holes with relative ease, now it seems that the square pegs are starting to outnumber the round ones by maybe as many as two to one. My gut instinct is that, as both independent educators and as parents, we must adapt our teaching methods to this fast-changing modern world for which our children seem to be better equipped than we are – or we 'die'.

Intrigued, Gail read on, speedily. And finally:

Finally, as an independent school head teacher for nearly a decade and a teacher for a quarter of a century, I have flattered myself I know what is best for my pupils. Would that I thought my pupils – or even their parents – felt the same way.

While it may not yet be time to (wo)man the barricades, I do feel very strongly that there is something of an education revolution in the offing – whether we like it or not. For those of us, however, who continue to care passionately about our children's futures and indeed are actively engaged in shaping them, the prospect of radical change is both terrifying and exciting in equal measures. More importantly, however, this change is essential – and it can't come soon enough.

EVE STURRIDGE, Ivy House School,

January 2011

'Ah! I thought I'd get in early and see if it needed a bit more work, but it looks as though you've beaten me to it.'

Eve dropped her bag on the sofa and shrugged off her coat, while Gail blushed deeply. Was it more embarrassing to be caught reading Eve's papers or to be caught doing it in Eve's chair? Both were fairly mortifying and Gail noted that she really must shut doors. Eve's stealthiness was legendary at Ivy House; she could materialize anywhere in the building at any time. 'God, I'm so sorry, Eve, I really am. I wanted to tidy and then the title caught my eye and it looked so interesting that I couldn't resist.' Which was perfectly true.

Eve flopped on to the sofa and rubbed her eyes. 'It's fine, Gail, really. In fact, I'd very much value your opinion. I was here till well after midnight, which is most unlike me.'

Gail felt no need to lie or flatter. 'Eve, it's brilliant, it really is. Somebody needs to say these things and who is better placed than you? What are you going to do with it?'

Eve roused herself from the sofa. 'I don't know yet. Obviously it would be great to get it published, but . . .' She broke off, shrugged and yawned. 'But maybe a *coffee* first? A big one.'

'Coffee it is,' said Gail, exiting the office. A second later she popped her head back round the door. 'Er, just had a thought? What about speaking to Cathy?'

Eve nodded and smiled, a big nose-crinkling smile.

Blimey, she looks just like Zoe, thought Gail.

'You're a genius, Gail.'

By the time she'd re-read the article three times and added a few amendments, Eve was sufficiently pleased with her 'rant' to want to do something with it. *Carpe diem*: by mid-afternoon she'd emailed it to Cathy Gower, her old friend and former uni room-mate, and Zoe's godmother, who was now the editor of a successful Sunday newspaper magazine supplement. Eve's accompanying note was brief:

Hello, lovely Cath, whom I miss. Here's something I enjoyed getting off my chest! Any use to you?! Eve xx

The reply came quickly:

Hello, YOU! How great to hear from you. And I loved your 'rant' – so many interesting points well made – and I speak as a mother of three sons! Unfort the piece is not 'magaziney' enough for me, if that makes any sense – but I have passed it on to my colleague, John Nicholson, on our comment desk. Good luck. And PLEASE let me know if you're going to be anywhere remotely near Kensington in the foreseeable? Visiting your impossibly glam little sis, for eg?! Did you know we belong to the same gym? I occasionally catch sight of her in the changing rooms and invariably skulk away without saying hi because she makes me feel like a wrung-out dishcloth! I know she's younger than us, but not by much, so how does she get that killer bod? Rhetorical Q! Anyway, it would be so great to see you – tho am obv not holding my breath. Love, Cath xx

Eve replied immediately:

Ooh, that's so kind of you, Cath! Am excited by even the remote possibility of getting published – daren't even think about how many people might read it as a result, but will cross that bridge as and when! Oh, and Sonia not only spends most of her non-working waking hours in the gym, but she won't mind you knowing she's had a bit of work, too – plus, not having kids obviously helps immeasurably! Personally, I think tampering with anything below one's neck is unnecessary – I just dust the cobwebs away occasionally! But seriously, would LOVE to see you. Sonia and I are actually meeting this weekend; Zoe's meant to have been staying with her this week while she's on work experience with one of my richest parents (you'll know all about the Sorensens!), but in fact she's just about to return from a couple of days in New York with Stefan Sorensen. In our day, work experience meant a fortnight in the stockroom at Lilley & Skinner – if we were lucky! E XX

And, if Eve thought Cathy's previous response had been lightning fast, it was nothing compared to this:

You're telling me that our little Zoe with the braces and plaits (and, I recall, exactly the same eyes and eyebrows as Simon) is currently in New York with Stefan Sorensen?! Are you sure you trust me with this info?! This is the kind of stuff that shifts newspapers! Cxx

Right! Should I NOT trust you, Cath?! Zoe is hell-bent on a career in finance and Anette S suggested she might enjoy work experience – sorry, an 'internship' – at Odense Holdings. So off she went to make tea, but has now somehow landed herself in New York with the boss (and, I might add, the boss's middle-aged female PA). I mean, what's the prob?! 'Little Zoe' is seventeen, five foot ten and . . . OK, fair enough, looks like a model. Should I be worried?! E xx

I'm a mother of sons, so what do I know? But, speaking as someone who used to be a seventeen-year-old girl . . . yes, almost certainly! But seriously, good luck! Don't be a strang(l)er. Much love, C xx

Hurtled straight back to the late 1970s, Eve smiled at Cathy's in-joke reference to the Stranglers. She also felt slightly worried about Zoe, and was still worried when she got home that evening. However, instead of pouring herself a glass of something comforting, Eve went upstairs to her room, taking her phone with her. She was hoping for a text from Zoe soon, because she must already have arrived in New York. Still, Eve didn't want to look too *needy-mommy* by texting Zoe first, given that major teenage rites of passage tended to occur without the assistance of a helicopter parent busily hovering around, cramping their style. Eve thought of herself at seventeen, of her free-range, unmollycoddled, risk-taking generation. She supposed Zoe took her own kind of risks within the limits of her world, which in turn probably meant sex and drugs – but maybe not so much rock 'n' roll? Though, come to think of it, Zoe was planning to go to Glastonbury – sorry, *Glasto* – this year with Rob. Apparently Muse were playing.

Eve, imagining her daughter's introduction to New York via private jet, took a moment to marvel at Zoe's easy, charmed life. There were occasional stresses, of course – exams, mostly, and occasional fallings-out with her friends – but when she looked back on her own adolescence and teenage years, Eve was sure they had been far more obviously and *externally* fraught. As Eve sat on her bed, appraising her toes – pedicure required soon, methinks – she figured that it must have helped that Zoe bypassed Ugly Duckling and arrived at Swan without so much as a zit, much less an existential crisis to rival David Bowie's Berlin years – something with which Eve had identified rather strongly, despite the fact that the closest she'd ever got to Berlin was watching Liza Minnelli in *Cabaret*.

I'll paint my toenails for Simon, thought Eve, rummaging through the cabinet in her bathroom. No, not for Simon. Eve glanced at the half-dozen bottles of uninspiring varnishes. Not boring red or pink; something cooler than that. What, she wondered, was the current version of Chanel's Rouge Noir? There was only one place to look.

Eve sat on her daughter's bed – something she did so rarely she couldn't recall the last time – and glanced, slightly guiltily, around the lovely, light space. Though it was also, she saw now, a space which reflected an eleven-year-old Zoe rather more than it did the seventeen-year-old version. Those primrose-painted walls, for example, had once looked so sophisticated but were now in need of a rethink. That roller blind looked dated, too – not to mention a bit grubby.

Maybe some warm blues and old whites . . . something shabby-chic, thought Eve. And plantation shutters at the windows. Or maybe things have moved on? Eve thought she might pick up a copy of *ELLE Decoration* and find out. In the meantime, though, she sat in Zoe's bedroom, taking in the chaos of the dressing table with its clutter of make-up and wet wipes and brushes and clips and bottles of perfume and unguents with their tops off; the wastepaper basket full of lipstick-printed tissues, the scattered pairs of virtually identical skinny jeans, balls of minuscule under-garments and many pairs of shoes, unpaired, not to mention the hairdryer, straighteners, crimpers and some kind of a tool called 'Big Hair' – a must-have last Christmas – which lay in a tangle of wires on the floor.

Eve glanced at the cork pinboard over the built-in desk, and the notion of a pinboard also seemed suddenly old-fashioned, though she could neither put her finger on why nor think what might have replaced it. On the board, there were yellowing flyers for parties and gigs and pictures of shoes and jewellery and bags torn from *Grazia*, and a few computer-printed phone-snaps of Zoe and her friends, and Rob . . . What did Zoe call them? Selfies? But nothing very recent . . . Of course, thought Eve, they pin the stories of their lives on electronic boards, not cork. I must look at Zoe's Facebook . . .

As she took in the evidence of her daughter's busy life, Eve realized with a start that she didn't really know her. At some point – maybe in the last year or two – Zoe had not so much changed – she was still, to all intents, recognizably the Zoe she had always been – but had become unknowable. Is this inevitable? Eve wondered. Or have I somehow let her disappear from right under my nose without even noticing? Eve suddenly felt that letting Zoe go was a big mistake. And she didn't even mean letting her go to New York. No, that bit was simply unfathomable. If you really love them, let them go. Who said that? And was it only in the context of lovers, or did it include teenage daughters too? Eve suddenly felt that this was very bad advice. If you really love them, hold them close . . .

Eve cast her mind back to her own teenage years and recalled being seventeen from the enviable vantage point of a confident (mostly) and successful (happily) fifty-something. Had she not, in fact, 'made something of herself' – to coin one of her father's favourite phrases – she

may very well have had a different – and differently select-
ive – set of memories. She wondered whether other women
who had made 'less' of themselves – or even women who
had made much of themselves while remaining child free,
like her sister Sonia – clung on more tightly to their memories of being seventeen. Were they perhaps more romantic
and rose tinted? A bit 'she doth protest too much'? Eve
didn't think about being seventeen very often, admittedly,
and, when she did, it was invariably through the prism of
motherhood and specifically here, now, in Zoe's bedroom,
as the mother of Zoe.

Distracted, Eve forgot all about nail varnish and went
back to her own bedroom. It too was a lovely light-suffused
space, decorated in cool greys and warm whites, with
reclaimed oak floorboards, a splash of lime on a feature
wall and an en-suite wet room – all designed for Eve by her
ex-husband with a little bit of guilt and a lot of love, not to
mention an intimate knowledge of his client's taste. It was
a space to treasure – and Eve did. Yet, as she stood in the
centre of the room, she noted, not for the first time, that,
several years after the last tradesman had downed his
tools and left the Barn well and truly converted, nobody
other than her ex-husband and her daughters had ever set
foot inside her bedroom. And maybe – Eve allowed herself
to think – that was a shame. Maybe it would have been
good to share it with someone, even if only occasionally?
No, that wasn't right; maybe – and Eve shifted tenses
uneasily – it would *be* good? And she stood in front of the

full-length mirror, appraising her fifty-three-year-old self, briefly: not too bad. She turned to look at her reflection side-on: a slight, barely perceptible thickening around the middle, but thankfully no need to resort to elasticated waistbands just yet . . . Still slim-ish, fit-ish, with good-ish legs, great hair, lovely eyes, no jowls, a brow that was a great deal smoother than it might be . . . Eve was neither horrified nor delighted by the reflection; she was what she was: a woman of a certain age, not in bad shape at all . . . and yet . . . More yoga . . . ? Maybe some fillers?

But the thought of all of this bored her too, because wasn't the great joy of the – whisper it! – menopause the fact that you could either struggle to maintain yourself like a classic car, with your panels regularly beaten and re-sprayed, or you could simply let rust take hold of your bodywork before you ended up crushed and compacted and recycled and . . . ? At which point Eve had had enough of her reflection and looked away.

Although her own generation's youthful risk-taking usually involved actual *physical* risks – horse riding, white-water rafting, heli-skiing, ballet dancing, chasing the dragon, whatever had floated one's boat, frankly – Eve had long recognized that her daughters' risks would be – were already, presumably – entirely different. Raised mostly behind closed doors, the kind of risks they were most comfortable with tended to be emotional and sexual risks. Of course, thought Eve, the irony of teenage risk-taking is that it's all about what those risks tell your peers, and teenagers choose which risks they take in the same way they might pick out a new pair of shoes or jeans. Eve recognized that her kids, and those she knew at school, saw no problem with being both intensely secretive and overtly, publicly, boundary-free, to the point where it was becoming increasingly clear that young people's lives were only properly lived if they had been validated by a lens.

Eve smiled as she recalled a recent, disconcertingly amusing conversation with Alice while they'd shopped together. Pointing to a branch of Jessops, Alice had said, 'I have literally, like, never even *seen* that shop. What does it sell?'

'Are you serious?' Eve sighed. 'Cameras. And camera equipment.'

'Who buys cameras?' Alice said.

'Er . . . People who enjoy taking photographs!'

'I enjoy taking photographs, but I've never been to Jessops.' Alice shrugged. 'Or any other camera shop.'

'Ah, but you don't take photographs with a camera, you take pictures on a phone. It's totally different.'

'What's the difference?'

'Well, to take good pictures with a camera requires a degree of skill – and it's not one I've mastered, though your dad is a dab hand. But taking a picture on a phone calls for an ability to point it in vaguely the right direction, touch a button and then upload it to Facebook. In that respect, it's a bit like comparing an original Hockney with a Hockney painting-by-numbers.'

'OK.' Alice digested this while they entered Marks and Spencer. 'What's a painting-by-numbers?'

At which point, rather than jump straight in, Eve had been forced to step back from the edge of the twenty-first-century generational chasm – if only in order to avoid calling her daughter an idiot. 'So, knickers or food first?'

Alice grinned. 'Knickers!'

Thank God, Eve had thought, a subject about which we can actually communicate ...

As soon as she heard the front door slam, Eve slipped back out of her reverie, relieved, and scrunchied her bob into a scrappy ponytail. It was a timely intervention. Simon, Alice, Barney + energy, love, warmth = *family*: her favourite equation. She all but ran down the stairs.

'You look stunning!' said Simon sarcastically, removing his boots. 'So good to see you're still making an effort on my account after all these years.'

'You look, like, *twelve*,' said Alice, hanging up Barney's lead.

Eve smiled. 'And that's the nicest thing anyone's said to me in ages. How does chicken and oven chips sound?'

'Loving your work,' said Simon. 'On the subject of which – Alice, *homework*. We'll shout when dinner's ready. Your mum and I have some proper grown-up parental talking to do.'

'I am *so* outta here,' said Alice, heading up to her room.

'So,' said Simon, in the kitchen. 'How're things?'

For Eve, that tiny conversational nudge was all it took;

out it all it came. 'Oh, *God*, Simon. It's a *nightmare*. I think I'm very close to resigning. No, make that I *know* I am. And do you know why? Jordan! For some reason, your, uh, son has helped me to see things in an entirely different light. It's kind of hard to describe.'

'OK. But try me. I'm interested. *Obviously*. In fact –' Simon grimaced – 'I'll go first, if you like.'

'OK, shoot!' Eve was slightly thrown; she wanted – needed? – Simon to be *completely* on top of things. That's how it had always worked. That's how it needed to work right now . . .

'I have confessions. Things are not only intensely difficult with Jordan, but –' a deep sigh from Simon; Eve noted that whatever was coming was clearly an even more difficult admission – 'my practice probably has another six months in its current incarnation, unless something *very* unexpected occurs.'

Eve instinctively reached for a bottle of wine. 'OK. So no word from the Sorensens?'

Simon shook his head. 'No. Not yet.'

'And would that change everything?'

A nod. 'It might, yes. We'll have to see. Of course, things can change at any time – the phone suddenly rings or an email bounces in – but if that doesn't happen then I'll have to let people go. It'll just be me and Ed.'

Three hours, a chicken, plenty of chips and another bottle of wine later, Simon and Eve had talked through most of their stuff and had found a way to remain as mutually supportive as ever. When things felt as if they may be falling apart, they invariably cleaved together. Some people would call that co-dependent, they preferred *comfortable*.

Alice had been in bed for at least an hour and the second bottle was all but drained when Simon eventually texted Ed to say that, with a lot of conversational ground still to cover, he was going to crash at the Barn tonight, if that was OK? And how was Jordan?

Simon showed Eve the reply:

> All fine. Jordan good – and tired – and early to bed without so much as a peep. I'm off myself in a mo. Love to all.
> C U 2moz. X

So consuming had the evening been, indeed, that Eve had failed to check her phone. She did so right now, close to eleven p.m. – and saw this:

> OMG NYC awesum mum! ☺. Will phone 2moz. Luv U!!! Z xx

'Look.' She showed the text to Simon, who smiled.

'Still alive, then, albeit far too psyched to use proper grammar. Glad we don't have to send Snake Plissken in to rescue her from a post-apocalyptic Greenwich Village.'

'*Snake Plissken!* Kurt Russell! *Escape From New York!* God – *when* did we see that?'

'I dunno. Early eighties? A lifetime ago.'

'I *loved* that theme tune. Do you remember?' Eve started singing it, badly: '*Dur-dur-dur, dur-dur-dur; dur-dur-DUR, dur, dur, du—*'

'Yup, you're pissed.'

'Yes, I do think it's probably bedtime.' Eve stood up and wobbled a bit. 'You know where your quarters are.' Eve leaned against Simon to steady herself and he held her, gently, firmly. *Comfortably.*

'I do, yes –' Simon paused – 'but I'm not entirely sure they're where I want them to be.'

Eve, unsteady on her feet, squinted at Simon. His potential intention was starting, slowly and rather foggily, to dawn on her. 'What do you *mean*? Do you want me to call you a cab?'

'No, I want to share your bed.'

'You do? OK.' Eve didn't consider herself drunk, just comfortably swaddled in alcohol, and, despite the fact that it had been a long time, the prospect of Simon sharing her bed seemed neither surprising nor scary. It's not as if he wants to have sex.

'Are you sure? Evie – I mean, I want to *fuck* you.'

Eve was so surprised that she giggled. '*Whoooa!* Really?'

'Really. Sorry! I've obviously. Um . . .'

'No, it's OK. But, I mean, you're a married man.'

'Ah, well, I was your husband too.' Simon shrugged. 'Look, I've clearly overstepped the mark. Heat of the moment – sorry!'

'You have – but I don't mind. Come on.' Eve took her ex-husband's hand, gently but firmly. 'I'll take you to *your* quarters. We both need to sober up. And sleep.'

Simon nodded and squeezed her hand. Was that a *blush*? They leaned against each other comfortably, tiptoeing the length of the suspended walkway that separated Eve's bedroom and the guest room from the girls' rooms at the opposite end of the Barn.

'Good night, Simon. *Sleep* well. And thank you.'

'For what? I've clearly made a total arse of myself.'

Eve stood on tiptoes and kissed her very ex-husband on the forehead. 'I mean thank you for, um, *wanting* me? That's sort of sweet.'

Simon grinned lopsidedly. 'I never thought I'd say it but I'll settle for being described as sweet. *Sweet* dreams, Evie.'

# 20

'Oh. My. *God*,' said Gail as soon as Eve walked through the door, an uncharacteristic fifteen minutes late, the following morning. 'I mean, you could have *said*! Phone's burning itself off the hook already!'

'Sorry, Gail?'

Gail couldn't help noticing that Eve seemed distracted. 'The paper.' Gail pushed an open copy of the *Courier* towards her boss. '*This!*'

## 'C-WORDS IN THE CLASSROOM?
## IT'S THE F-WORD WE HAVE TO BLAME'

*'So-called feminism has gone too far in our schools,' says
Eve Sturridge, head teacher of a top prep school*

Eve shivered involuntarily and grimaced. She read the piece. While it still contained the essence, the *germ*, of her argument, the emphasis had also somehow shifted, albeit subtly. Without comparing the article, word for word, with her original 'rant', it was hard to see precisely how this editorial alchemy had been achieved; however, it was very skilful, no doubt about that.

'Ah!' was all that Eve could manage. 'Right. OK. I'm just going to make a quick call.'

'To the sisterhood?' said Gail, rather pleased with herself. 'Coffee?'

Eve smiled. 'A pint, I think. Intravenously. And hold the calls for a few minutes, could you?'

Eve sat down, read the article again – this time deploying a highlighter pen – and then, at the end, she flipped open her laptop, searched her emails and dialled a number. It was answered briskly after just two rings.

'Johnny Nicholson's phone, allegedly!'

'Ah, right, yes, hi, John. *Johnny*. It's, uh, Eve Sturridge here . . . I, uh . . . The *article* – I don't quite recognize it.'

'Ah, yes, Eve – the talk of the town! Well, your "rant" is definitely still all in there, but I will admit that we do have a house style to which our skilled sub-editors will inevitably bend raw copy to fit, as a matter of course. You'll appreciate we're a pretty big machine with many cogs, but you may also be interested to know – that is, if you don't know already – that there's a lot of feedback. If you pop online you'll see there are nearly three hundred comments already. I shouldn't be at all surprised if you got a *Today* out of it. Maybe even a *Newsnight*.'

Eve faltered. Cathy had once asked her to be part of a

feature for the magazine in which mothers of daughters and mothers of sons wrote little first-person articles comparing their parenting techniques and were then photographed together, rather glamorously, with their children. That had been *fun* – but Eve could see that things at the sharp end of newspapers were, well, inevitably *sharper*. No, she couldn't countenance either a *Today* or a *Newsnight*, much less both.

'I don't think I was really expecting this. I mean, I wasn't prepared.'

'I totally appreciate that – *totally*. Tell you what – I'm about to pop into conference with the editor, but how about lunch next week? Somewhere fancy? You're in East Sussex, aren't you? Are you able to get up to town often?'

Eve's gut instinct was to say no, very quickly and force-fully. Therefore she rather surprised herself by saying, 'Yes, that would be lovely. Er, how does Wednesday sound?' She hadn't had a day off in ages.

'Wednesday sounds marvellous. To be honest, I was due a lunch with our restaurant critic and it was somewhere indescribably fancy, just off Piccadilly. I shall simply blow him out and keep the fancy reservation. I'll see if Cath's free too, shall I? How does that sound?'

Eve, who thought that sounded marvellous, ended the call, leaned back in her chair and gently placed both her hands over her solar plexus, which was churning – an excited, edge-of-the-precipice churn. Something was shift-ing and changing. What *was* that, precisely? Eve stared at the blank screen of her laptop and then, very slowly and methodically, typed *John Nicholson the Courier* into Google and started to read. When her phone rang, she ignored it; this was going to be a long day and she planned on continuing it in much the same fashion that she had started it – which was to say *in charge*.

'I am the boss,' muttered Eve under her breath, despite the fact that there was nobody around to hear. 'I am the boss ...'

She buzzed through to Gail: 'OK, I can talk now.'

'Oh, good, because I've just had the organizers of that conference you're going to on Friday on the blower. They're really hoping to shuffle their schedule around and persuade you to make a keynote address.'

'Make a keynote address at the Independent Schools Conference? Are you *sure*?'

'I'm sure. Apparently Eleanor Hill has pulled out at the last minute and they appear to be *very* excited about having you fill her shoes.'

'I know her shoes – they're very stylish.' Eve sighed. 'Every single fibre of my entire being is saying, "Don't do it" ...'

'So I can phone them back and say it's a yes? Fabulous! They'll be thrilled – and you'll be great at it. You have the fire in your belly.'

'Well, I'm not sure about that, but yes, OK, I will be there.'

As the day unfolded – and much to Gail's excitement – Eve not only accepted the Schools Conference speaker role but found herself fast-tracked through a small-to-medium media storm. Spookily, John Nicholson turned out to be correct and both *Newsnight* and *Today* did come through with interview requests. With the assistance of the *Courier*'s press officer, who sounded about the same age as Zoe, Eve turned down the chance of being lightly grilled by Jeremy Paxman on the perfectly reasonable grounds of it simply being 'too bloody scary for words', but after much cajoling from the *Courier*'s PR, she finally caved in and agreed to do *Today* at 8:35 a.m. the following morning, albeit on the phone from home rather than in the studio.

'Total pussycat, Humphrys – honestly!' said the *Courier*'s PR unconvincingly.

'Actually, it's not John Humphrys I'm scared of – it's Sarah Montague,' confessed Eve.

During a brief lunch break taken at her desk in the Odense Holdings office, Anette Sorensen paused to scribble a few words on a Post-it note, which she then stuck on to a ripped-out page from that day's *Courier*.

> *Look at this, S!*
> *A X*

Still smiling, Anette buzzed through to her PA. 'I have something here for Stefan. Can you scan it and email it to him straight away, please?'

\*

Meanwhile, in the staffroom at Ivy House, Gail was re-reading Eve's article. It was an odd thing, this admission of apparent failure from a successful traditional prep school head – the school was Ofsted 'Outstanding', after all. Gail knew that, even allowing for the article being 'spun' to fit with the paper's fairly right-wing agenda – and she'd read the original – it was still a bit of a curate's egg. But intriguing nonetheless – so much so that the staffroom copy was looking decidedly dog-eared; even though there were three copies of *The Times*, two *Guardians*, an *Independent* and a *Private Eye* all in circulation, today nobody at Ivy House appeared remotely interested in *them*.

Gail waved the paper. 'Anybody *not* read this yet?' Everyone shook their heads.

And over at Eastdene Community Primary School, the *Courier* was also doing the rounds, though Mike Browning, not a fan of either the paper or its politics, was the last to read it.

'Have you ever met Eve Sturridge?' said Year Six's Mrs Jenkins.

Mike barely missed a beat. 'We were introduced very briefly in the Bell, by her PA, Gail Prince – Harry in your year's mum. Anyway, by all accounts she's a passionate, dedicated and gifted head teacher.' Mike glanced down at the page. 'And she's prepared to put herself on the line, so, while we may not sing from the same educational hymn sheet, hats off to her.'

'She's very glamorous, too,' said Hilary Jenkins. Mike simply shrugged.

Eve surprised nobody more than herself by quite how successfully she negotiated what Tony described on his return from Moscow that afternoon – and not inaccurately – as 'this completely and utterly unnecessary fucking shit-storm'.

'Complete and utter shit-storm, yes,' conceded Eve, in Tony's office at five p.m. 'Unnecessary, not so much.' Eve was feeling emboldened in a way she couldn't recall feeling ever before.

'Don't talk crap. I take it this is your elaborate version of a resignation note, hm?' Tony was pacing now.

'It wasn't formally a resignation, no, but if you'd like to take it as one –' Eve shrugged as Tony paced – 'then so be it. Sack me if you like.'

Tony may have been angry – was, if the throbbing veins in his temples were any indication, incandescent – but Eve knew he wasn't stupid. Sacking her right now would clearly create its own media shit-storm. And, of course, media shit-storms were very often bad for business.

# 21

Zoe Sturridge woke up in her – *her!* – bedroom in the Sorensens' pale, elegant, light-filled triplex apartment, right opposite Central Park and the Metropolitan Museum on Fifth Avenue, fully refreshed by eight hours of deep and dreamless sleep, ready to face her very first full Manhattan day.

Even allowing for a residue of jetlag, rewinding the events of the previous day in her head after a power shower – with jets that came at you from the sides – had Zoe literally hopping from foot to foot with excitement as she inspected her full-length naked reflection in the long glass diagonally opposite her bed. Having originally packed only for a few nights at Auntie Sonia's Notting Hill flat, she'd forgotten to bring anything to sleep in. Oh, well.

Zoe reached for her phone and held it in front of her face while she snapped her reflection. The result was a headless naked body that was, nonetheless, slightly more clinical, more *forensic* than it was sexy. Zoe deleted it and struck a different pose, this time sitting on the side of the bed with her legs slightly apart. Holding the phone in front of her face again, she snapped at the reflection in the mirror and inspected the results: much better this time – *sexier*, but also kind of anonymous, too. Zoe knew that Rob was cavalier about the whole concept of privacy – after all, every single person she knew, excepting her parents, was cavalier about privacy. But it didn't hurt to be aware, did it? Just in case? After all, it was one thing to give her boyfriend an early-morning hard-on via some spontaneous sexting, quite another to do the same for all her boyfriend's mates. It was probably just as well her face was, quite literally, out of the picture and though Zoe suspected it was just a tiny bit weird to care more about her face being seen than it was her admittedly not-so-private parts, that was just the way things were. She enjoyed imagining his expression when he checked his phone during his lunch break:

Ta-Da! Morning from NYC babes! Thinking of U! xxx ☺

After this, Zoe blow-dried her hair, applied her make-up and pulled on a different pair of near-identical skinny jeans to yesterday's, teaming these with biker boots and a pastel pink crew-neck cashmere, with a slightly Princess-Diana-circa-1981 pie-crust-collared blouse underneath. She finished off the look with an oversized mannish blazer with rolled up sleeves and a mint green satchel hung across her body. It was a little bit Alexa Chung, a little bit

Kate Moss and a whole lot of Zoe Sturridge. It was also very
'London Girl'. Having a look that said 'London Girl' on your
first trip to New York seemed to Zoe somehow essential.
Albeit she wasn't a London girl at all, she was flying the
street-style flag, right down to the tips of her (slightly
chewed, but . . .) matte grey nail colour.

She was conscious that she was also dressing to be seen
by her boss and hoped that this effort would not go
unnoticed, either by her boss or her boss's PA, Tina. She
liked Tina, who, as a mother of three daughters herself,
presumably had a great deal of experience around teenage
fashion crises. As she finally emerged from the bedroom,
Zoe caught sight of Tina coming out of her own room further down the parqueted hall.

Tina smiled at Zoe. 'Morning. Sleep well?'

Zoe beamed. 'I did, thanks, yes. *So* comfy, that bed.'

'It's definitely a very comfortable apartment. Now, are
you all set for a busy day today?' Tina didn't wait for
answer. 'Mr Sorensen has already left for his first breakfast meeting – he usually squeezes in two, back to
back – and I have got a few errands for you to do. We'll be
hooking up back at the Odense offices by eleven a.m., so I
suggest grabbing yourself a bit of breakfast in the kitchen.
There'll be croissants and Danishes and fruit salad and
granola and salami and ham, if you happen to like cold
meats in the mornings –' Zoe stood there silently, wide-
eyed, drinking in every word – 'it's a *Nordic* thing, really.'
Zoe carried on listening intently while Tina explained

that neither she nor Stefan were 'breakfast people but, nonetheless, Modesta always does a lovely spread, so she'll be delighted if *you* eat.'

Zoe nodded. She'd met the Sorensens' silent but smiling housekeeper the night before. Modesta was married to the chauffeur, Ignacio, who had picked them all up from JFK airport the previous afternoon, and the couple lived in and kept house whether the Sorensens were in town or not. According to Tina, Modesta doted on Anette and the Sorensen children, but in their absence would make do with doting on whoever looked the most dotable-upon.

And so, straight after breakfast, Zoe's New York morning evolved, and then after a quick sandwich-in-a-brown-paper-bag lunch, eaten at the deli three doors along from the Odense Holdings NYC offices – situated in a chic brownstone on a quiet street downtown, just like the one where Carrie Bradshaw lives in *Sex and the City*, thought Zoe – came a New York afternoon punctuated by, mostly, yawns. Zoe had felt fine this morning, running on adrenaline and excitement, but now her day was starting to catch up with her. The office had its own espresso machine but, when she asked around, it seemed that everybody preferred Starbucks so she volunteered to go on the afternoon run. As she placed a lengthy list on the Starbucks counter and started ordering, a voice behind her interrupted:

'And you can make mine a skinny latte with an extra shot.'

She spun round. 'Mr Sorensen? Sure!'

'And I'll help you carry these back, too.'

'Right!' Zoe didn't know quite what to say, at least until she remembered. 'Thanks!'

'No problem. You've stolen my job. Hasn't she, Debee?'

'*Shohaz*!' said the barista. Zoe concentrated hard to pick up her words . . . 'Any excuse ta ged ouda dat awfice, right, Mr S?' Debee winked.

'You got it,' said Stefan Sorensen.

Zoe didn't quite know what to make of the cheerful banter between her boss and the extremely pretty black girl behind the counter. They seemed like old friends, but maybe this was just how people did stuff in New York. She also realized how embarrassingly few exchanges she herself had ever had with somebody who wasn't white, what with her neighbourhood being *very* racially un-diverse. Nonetheless, she also couldn't imagine Stefan Sorensen having this kind of amongst-equals conversation in, say, the Starbucks in Piccadilly. Yeah, it was clearly a New York thing, this kind of chatty friendliness. Mr Sorensen hadn't even been this friendly to Zoe until now – the plane journey had been notable for the fact that he'd spent all of it on his laptop, speaking to her just once ('How you enjoying executive travel, Zoe?' Answer: 'Very much!'). For her part, Zoe had been thrilled by the take-off and landing, which she discovered you felt much more keenly in a little jet than you did on an ordinary plane, and spent the bits in between reading magazines and staring at the clouds and chatting with Tina. Now, however, she felt sufficiently emboldened and caffeinated to attempt some small talk with the boss.

'I guess being the boss means there's always someone else to get your latte, but maybe it's fun to do it yourself?'

Stefan Sorensen narrowed his eyes and, for the first time, Zoe felt, took a proper look at her.

'Oh, it's not only *fun*, sometimes it's essential.'

'Keeps da feet on da ground – right, Mr S?' said Debee.

'Sure does. Head in the clouds, feet on the ground – that's me.'

Zoe grinned, Stefan grinned at Zoe and Debee glanced between both of them, in a rather knowing sort of way, Zoe felt.

'Debee here has a degree in Child Psychology from New York State University and is currently studying for her master's. Am I right, Debee?' said Stefan.

Debee nodded. 'Yup, thas right, Mr Sorensen.'

Wow, thought Zoe. But what she said was, 'That's awesome.'

## 22

As far as Stefan Sorensen was concerned, getting to know Zoe was not yet on his schedule. However, having noted her prettiness, smartness and cutely feisty, if ham-fisted, attempt to understand her environment, the emphasis was very much on *yet*. As he moved through an afternoon packed with the usual whirl of meetings and phone calls that involved pacing the office while barking instructions, Stefan's thoughts kept drifting back to Zoe. And, occasionally, one of these stray Zoe-thoughts would segue into a thought about her mother, with and around whom his children spent their days. And so Stefan successfully pushed those thoughts away.

As an 'alpha male in an alpha city' (Anette's description; he had liked it and laughed when it had originally been delivered, tongue firmly in cheek), Stefan Sorensen knew that he was fairly predictable in his alpha-male habits. He liked to work hard and work out harder; he liked to relax in upscale surroundings among his similarly blessed peers, and his distractions from the business of making money were inevitably the distractions of the super-rich – yachting, scuba diving, heli-skiing, playing poker and polo; all of these things were *fun*. And a life without fun was just another late night alone with a spreadsheet. Anyway, even if there was the time, there would never be the inclination to spend a quiet night in with, say, a pizza, sprawled in front of *Breaking Bad* on TV. No – with only a very occasional twinge of regret, Stefan Sorensen accepted that his downtime was uptime, that black tie was his sweatpants-and-a-hoodie – unless he was at the gym, of course, which he was, most mornings, by six a.m., if he wasn't on a plane, or otherwise engaged. It helped to have a trainer on speed-dial and a gym in his own home.

Stefan Sorensen knew himself to be the opposite of risk averse. Just as his talent for making money created apparently infinite opportunities to make even more of it, so he understood that good looks and charm created infinite opportunities to meet and seduce women – which in no way distracted from his relationship with Anette, which was its own special and unique entity, entirely self-contained and utterly impregnable. Stefan had loved his wife intensely from pretty much the first moment he'd seen her, which had been from quite a distance on their first day at university. Sex with women other than his wife was, nonetheless, a regular occurrence – either as one-offs or what Stefan described (discreetly, among the right kind of male friends) as 'six monthers', six months being the cut-off point wherein something invariably ceased being casual and became somehow indefinably more complex and committed. Stefan knew that Anette knew all of this went on – and he also knew that as long as these fun and fleeting distractions never in any way threatened the fabric of their marriage then they would continue indefinitely.

And so today was turning out to be the sort of frenetically busy day that demanded some proper downtime. And, like the unwitting fish in a restaurant tank, today's 'downtime' had already been selected and would soon be removed from the shoal to be prepped. In relation to his New York schedule, Stefan relied on Tina to organize *everything* – it was simply his job to follow through. Downtime arrangements were no exception.

At 5:30 p.m., Tina appeared in his office wearing an uncharacteristic frown. 'Very sorry, Stefan,' she said, 'but I've just had Steve Dershowitz's PA call to cancel your dinner tonight at Locanda Verde with him and Alan Dohenny.'

'Shame, I was looking forward to that. They say why?'

'Urgent business back in London, apparently.'

'OK. So what do I do tonight?'

'Well, I booked the table in your name and it hasn't been cancelled.'

'OK. You fancy dinner?' Stefan enjoyed the occasional fallback dinner date with Tina, though sex was never on that menu. There were certain professional boundaries never to be crossed, and sleeping with your PA was very much one of those.

'You know I'd love that, but I've actually got a ticket tonight for *Memphis*. Hard to get!'

'Oh, no – you've got to see that. No problem. I'll just swing by Verde after work and grab a bite. Early night could do me good.' A pause; a narrowing of the eyes. 'Or how about I show young Zoe the bright lights?'

Tina hesitated. 'Uh, well, *yes*, why not? Your table's booked for eight p.m. . . .' She paused, as though wanting to say more.

Stefan thought about the exceptionally pretty girl in Starbucks whom he'd barely registered on the plane. She was young, maybe nineteen or twenty – but not *too* young. He had seen in her eyes quite clearly that she was not too young *at all*. Stefan Sorensen was not a man who wrestled with his conscience; he famously – in business and in life – made decisions fast and stuck by them. 'Might be fun. Tell her to go home now and get changed and get Ignacio to drop her off at Verde. I'll go straight from here.' Yes, that was a plan. He had been looking forward to a fun business-meets-pleasure evening with the guys, but there was no reason why he couldn't paradigm-shift his way into a fun evening with a pretty young woman. No reason at all.

# 23

Three hours later, via a minor fashion crisis that was averted simply because she only had one dress with her (very little and black and grown-up and belonging to Eve), Zoe found herself sitting opposite Stefan Sorensen at one of New York's most fashionable restaurants, inspecting their respective starter plates: blue crab with jalapeño and tomato crostini for Stefan and salad with dried cherries, American speck and hazelnut vinaigrette for Zoe, despite the fact that the only ingredient on the menu she had actually recognized was 'salad'. As she watched Stefan eat, she considered how very dramatically her day had reconfigured itself.

'Sorry?' she had said to Tina when she'd been told she was having dinner with Stefan Sorensen. 'I *am*?'

'Yes. You can leave at six and grab a cab uptown to the apartment. Ignacio will drop you at the restaurant for eight p.m.. It's not formal, but it is fashionable, OK? And in the meantime I'd try and brush up on the multi-syllables, yes?'

Tina had been brisk and so Zoe could barely speak: 'Uh!'

'You can do better than that, Zoe! Mr Sorensen has a very low boredom threshold.'

'Absolutely! No problem, Tina!'

Tina had laughed. 'That's better. And have a fun time.'

Zoe had nodded because if there was a more fun time than having dinner with Stefan Sorensen in one of New York's most fashionable restaurants then, at that precise moment, she couldn't really imagine what it might be.

And now here she was, sharing an actual bottle of red wine with Stefan Sorensen. Like, mental! As Zoe nervously took her first sip of something delicious called Lonardi Taurasi, she relaxed slightly and knew with the perfect certainty that comes of being seventeen that this was going to be a night to remember *forever*. Especially as Stefan had smiled as she'd arrived and said, 'Zoe, you are as beautiful as you are smart. Great dress!'

'Thank you.' She'd very nearly confessed that it belonged to Eve but had bitten her lip just in time.

'So, how you liking New York so far?'

'A lot!' Zoe looked around the room – cosy, buzzing, New Yorky, just like she'd pictured it. 'Like, this is *great*.'

Stefan smiled. '*Like*, Robert De Niro owns it. He's often in.'

'*The* Robert De Niro? From, like, *Meet The Fockers*? No way.'

Zoe didn't think she'd been *that* funny; however, Stefan threw back his head and roared with laughter. '*Way!* And, as far as I know, there's only the one.'

'Wow. That is so awesome.' Zoe reached for her wine. It really was delicious.

'And speak of the devil . . . Hey, *Bobby*!'

'Hey, *Sorensen*! Long time!' The two men embraced. 'How's your beautiful—?' De Niro broke off and glanced at Zoe, who swiftly clamped her gaping mouth shut and tried to smile a normal smile. The first time she goes out for dinner in New York and *this* happens! Wait till Rob hears about this . . . Rob, whose parents had actually *named him after* Robert De Niro.

'Ah, I'm afraid Anette's in London, taking care of business,' said Stefan with a shrug. 'However, I have the lovely Zoe here to keep me company. She's interning at Odense and, as it's her first bite of the Apple, I thought I'd show her the bright lights.'

De Niro winked. 'Nice!' He turned to Zoe, held out his hand. 'And where better to see 'em, huh? You enjoy yourself, Zoe.'

Zoe tried to remember Jay-Z's rap from 'New York' – *Yeah, yeah, I'm out that Brooklyn / Now I'm down in Tribeca / Right next to De Niro.* Ha! She nodded. 'I shall, yes, thank you very much, Mr De Niro.' She hoped she didn't sound too stupid; she felt slightly lobotomized. Maybe it was the wine?

When they'd finished dinner, Ignacio was waiting for them in the car, right outside the restaurant. As soon as he spotted Stefan, he got out and ran around to hold open the door for Zoe, who slid into the back seat, smiling broadly. Seconds later, she could feel Stefan beside her, the heat of his leg next to hers as the car pulled away from the kerb and eased its way smoothly into the New York night. As the car carved its uptown groove through the city's canyons, Zoe felt – suddenly, but not surprisingly – the warmth of Stefan's hand as he took hers and started tracing circles slowly on her palm with his index finger.

'That tickles!' She giggled. Zoe noted her giggle with slightly detached surprise; she wasn't by nature a giggler *at all*. In fact, she kind of despised giggling, generally speaking. Then again . . . she considered the possibility . . . perhaps I haven't led a very giggle-inspiring kind of life until now.

'Say again?' Stefan looked quizzically at Zoe.

Zoe squirmed. She thought she'd only *thought* that giggle-related thought, but apparently enough of that divine-tasting wine had made her *say* it. Zoe couldn't recall ever feeling quite as relaxed as she did right now. She was also very tired but absolutely wasn't going to let that stand in the way of anything at all. This, she decided, is probably what it means to be 'in the moment'. She turned towards Stefan Sorensen and looked him straight in the eye. 'I just said that I feel giggly but I'm not usually much of a giggler.'

'But tonight you are? There is a time and a place for giggling and maybe this is it.'

Zoe didn't answer but instead leaned her head on Stefan's shoulder – where it felt just right – and stared out of the car window at the city speeding past. What a great city. She sighed and closed her eyes, felt Stefan turn towards her, felt his lips – *his lips!* – on her ear as he whispered, 'Welcome to New York, Zoe.'

Back at the apartment, there was no sign of Modesta and Ignacio had disappeared with the car. Nobody was in evidence, yet Zoe felt sure that somewhere behind closed doors, or maybe on a separate floor, the well-oiled cogs and wheels of Stefan Sorensen's behind-the-scenes world continued to turn. But, in the moment, here and now, he was pouring her a glass of champagne and, as she sipped her Perrier-Jouët (such a gorgeous bottle!) from a crystal flute, Zoe was feeling just the wrong side of sober. When Stefan said, 'Come on up and check out the view from the terrace,' Zoe said, 'I didn't know there was a *terrace!*' and then stumbled very slightly as she followed him to the elevator, and then giggled, at which point Stefan held out an arm to steady her and then snaked it around her waist and pulled her closer to him. Zoe found that she fitted very well, so she stayed.

'I think I'd better look after you,' said Stefan, gently placing a kiss on her forehead.

Zoe nodded mutely. She felt very safe and special and somehow *chosen* and knew that if it weren't for the bubbles she might have felt nervous, too – but not *that* nervous. 'Yes, please,' she said. And, against the backdrop of the twinkling lights of Manhattan, she held her breath and closed her eyes – you will remember this always, Zoe

Sturridge – and then she felt exactly what she'd expected to feel: Stefan's lips, surprisingly soft, on hers, and his tongue licking her lips and then probing her mouth and it was just . . . just . . . She sort of buckled internally, felt herself very happily letting go . . . Stefan Sorensen wants to fuck me and I want to be fucked by Stefan Sorensen, and . . . A fleeting image of Rob popped into her mind's eye uninvited. And she knew that Rob would be angry at her betrayal but that, then again – you were never quite sure with Rob – maybe his anger would be outweighed by his being impressed. I mean – Stefan Sorensen! In fact, Zoe thought, he'll probably want to see what we get up to. And then Zoe pushed away all thoughts of Rob and was right back in the moment, feeling Stefan's hands moving up her legs, gently but firmly pushing between her thighs. At which point she decided she also wanted to see what this new New York version of Zoe Sturridge was going to get up to.

Snapshot memories from a New York night:

Being carried – yes, *carried*! – through rooms and down halls to a huge and dimly lit (but not dark) bedroom, being placed on a huge bed – made of clouds? This bed is made of clouds, right? – and giggling again as Stefan removed her shoes and tights – omigod, tights with a ladder! – and her knickers – best knickers, thank God! – and as she pulled her dress over her head and he undid her bra he was smiling at her giggles, and then . . . and . . . Ooh, a bit blurry after that, mostly. But not horrible blurry – dreamy blurry. And then eventually, *finally*, curled in Stefan Sorensen's arms, sleepy blurry . . .

Zoe Sturridge woke and stretched and then, just for a moment, wondered where she was, which bed she was in and where, and then, as her tummy gave a tiny flip of pleasure, she turned over, very slowly, and, half squinting in case she woke him, in which case she would of course pretend to be asleep, Zoe peered at Stefan Sorensen, who was currently very definitely deeply and dreamily asleep beside her. She couldn't help smiling, nor could she help gently stretching her arms above her head and arching her back with pleasure, though she stopped just short of an audible *purr*. Lying on her back, she was far enough away from Stefan in the super-king-size cloud-bed to be able to move without waking him, but close enough to feel the warmth of his body and the steady exhalation of his breathing – deep, relaxed, untroubled.

From her comfortable vantage point, Zoe looked at the bedroom for the first time in daylight. It was appropriately large without being grotesquely Master-of-the-Universe – maybe twenty feet square and set at the corner of the apartment building with two walls of, mostly, windows, from which Zoe could, at this angle, see just sky. She knew you had to be pretty high up to see just sky in Manhattan, where 'sky' presumably cost even more than 'tree', and she knew that 'tree' wasn't cheap. The room reminded her of one she had seen once, briefly, when she was ten – at

Claridges, where her aunt had stayed for her fortieth birthday and where Eve and Sonia had taken Zoe and Alice for tea to celebrate. Zoe noted that this room felt equally unlived-in, as if the Sorensens treated their apartment as a private hotel with knobs on, with some of those knobs being permanent staff and your own, uh, *elevator* straight into the entrance hall.

Zoe suddenly thought of Rob and, more specifically, what he would think if he could see her here, now, lying spread-eagled in this absurdly giant bed, next to a *billionaire*, like something out of a trashy miniseries. Except that there was no point in imagining any of this, really, because Rob wouldn't ever see her here. Wouldn't, indeed, ever *know* she'd been here.

As far as Zoe was concerned, this was easily the best and most beautiful bedroom she had ever seen in real life – and possibly even inside a magazine. It was Nordic-stylish without being too in-your-face groovy. It wasn't, for example, as obviously 'cool' as her dad's bedroom – with the emphasis on 'obviously' because, oddly, from this vantage point, her dad's room (hitherto the uber-bedroom benchmark, closely followed by her mum's) was suddenly looking a bit try-hard. This place, however, was just *perfect*: the right amount of art and objects and light and shade and fatness of quilt and plumpness of pillow and correctness of temperature. There could have been an entire field's worth of frozen peas underneath the deep mattress and Zoe would never even have suspected, for all that she felt like a particularly contented princess. At which point she yawned and turned again to look at her bed-mate who, she was startled to see, had his eyes wide open and was inspecting *her.*

# 24

Ten minutes later, Stefan Sorensen watched the tongue of this beautiful young woman moving up and down, up and down . . . and pushed any nagging thoughts of wrongness – she is very young but not younger than twenty, surely? – to the back of his mind and abandoned himself entirely to this very distracting moment. And then, after they'd had sex for the third time in eight hours – the first time, frenetic and relatively selfish on his part, the second far more generously about Zoe and now this third occasion, which turned out to be somewhere comfortably between the two extremes – Zoe was lying in Stefan's arms, apparently entirely relaxed. He liked that she felt so comfortable with him – felt so comfortable, full stop. He liked this young woman – which wasn't necessarily a given – and he liked that he had so evidently given her such pleasure. The calm, post-coital silence in which they breathed in tandem ended, however, when he finally spoke.

'So, you lovely, intoxicating . . .' He broke off, appraised the woman – *girl!* – in his arms. 'This has been absolutely great in every way, believe me.'

Zoe squirmed and nodded. 'Uh, *yes*, Mr Sorensen.'

'And you can stop the "Yes, Mr Sorensen" routine – cute though it is.'

'Sorry – *Stefan*.' She rolled her eyes and pushed herself playfully into his chest, at which point Stefan very gently eased her away from him by mere millimetres. Zoe stopped squirming, stilled herself.

'So, here's the deal. I have been with my wife for a long time. We met at university, we fell in love and we married just after we graduated. We are partners both in life and in business and we are devoted parents to our beloved children. In short, we will never, under any imaginable circumstances, let anyone or anything come between us. Got that?'

'I've got that. Are you going to, like, ask me to *sign* something?'

Stefan was amused. 'You've seen too many movies, I think. What do you suppose you'd have to sign, anyway?'

Zoe shrugged. 'Um, by the way, you do know how old I am, right?'

'Twenty? Twenty-one? You're at uni, right?'

'No, I'm seventeen. I'm not at uni; I'm doing my A levels.'

Stefan lay on his back, stared at the ceiling and sighed. Jesus Christ! Seventeen! All these years of playing away *by the rules* and now he'd finally broken Anette's Rule Of Rules: no under-eighteens, *ever*. Why hadn't Tina said something?

'OK, so I knew you were a student intern. I didn't realize you were a *high school* student intern. That is very young – seventeen. I'm so sorry. Please tell me you weren't a virgin?'

Zoe giggled – her new default setting. 'I'm only young on the outside – and no, don't worry, definitely not a virgin. I lost it when I was, like, fourteen?' Which, from the vantage point of seventeen, suddenly sounded to Zoe quite young, and maybe a bit slutty – and she didn't want Stefan Sorensen to think she was slutty, just that she was not a kid. Anyway, it was still a whole year later than her best friend, Carmen.

As if to underline the point that she was now very much a young woman of the world, equally at home among her peers in the sixth-form common room of Westdene Girls' Grammar or under the duvet in the New York cloud-bed of a forty-something billionaire, Zoe turned on to her side and traced her finger up Stefan's abdomen, along the whorl of blonde hair that stretched above his pelvis and onwards, up to his chest and his neck and over the hill of his chin and, very gently, barely touching, on to his lips. He groaned and opened his mouth just wide enough to receive her slim finger, sucking on it greedily and, with eyes closed, very nearly abandoned himself to the moment . . . *but not quite.*

He removed the finger and turned to face Zoe. Pretty, pretty *girl*. It actually hurt to say this, because, until Zoe's bombshell, he had imagined there might be a very pleasurable six-monther in the offing. 'OK, Zoe, I had no idea you were seventeen, which means this can't happen again, right?'

Zoe pouted. It was, noted Stefan, a very small, slight pout, but nonetheless the pout of a seventeen-year-old suddenly not getting her own way. This made him yet more determined to do the right thing now. Better late than—

'I don't know what difference me being seventeen makes.'

Stefan sighed. 'It makes a lot of difference. It may seem hard to quantify from your perspective, but –' he shrugged – 'there we are. We have had an absolutely *beautiful* night and we will both remember it always.' Zoe fixed him with her big dark eyes. As trusting as a bloody puppy, thought Stefan.

'Is it finished right now, then – our beautiful night?' she said.

Stefan found this question quite astoundingly and unexpectedly arousing. He sat up and turned towards Zoe, grasping her wrists firmly and rolling her on to her back, hauling himself up until he straddled her. He lowered his lips towards hers and whispered, 'Actually, *no* – very nearly, but not quite yet.'

Jesus. I must be mad, he thought. But somehow Zoe's giggle and all the impending pleasure appeared to cancel out the inexplicable, unexpected, bafflingly illogical *insanity*.

An hour later, he considered deleting the phone number Zoe Sturridge had just given him and which he had dutifully keyed into his phone in front of her, and decided against it. After which none of Stefan's intelligently-measured post-coital rationalization managed to stop him from impulsively hurling a mug of coffee – just handed to him by Modesta – against the kitchen wall while he read a freshly arrived text from Anette. 'Fuck! I'm so sorry, Modesta,' he said immediately. 'I'm *really* sorry. Lot going on.'

After this, Stefan went straight down in the elevator where, settled in the backseat of his car, being driven downtown by Ignacio, his thoughts circled themselves into such a chaotic vortex that the only escape was to close his eyes and dream of being re-enveloped by a fat white cumulonimbus of a duvet, heralding rain.

However, even as he power-napped en route to the office, there was a small but important percentage of Stefan's brain that was sufficiently engaged to remind itself to sack Tina before lunch – albeit with a *very* generous severance package.

Rob was awoken suddenly from his late-morning lie-in by the *ding* of an incoming text:

> Yay, babes, sending BIG LUV from the concrete jungle
> where dreams are made . . . oh! WOT A NITE!
> ;-) XXX

Rob couldn't get back to sleep after that. He didn't reply to the text, either – instead, he got up and went down to the kitchen, made himself a strong cup of coffee and smoked a roll-up. After about twenty minutes of pacing and smoking and coffee consumption, he went back upstairs and switched on his laptop. Using Final Cut Pro, it didn't take long to edit the footage he knew so well into something that looked, tantalizingly, a lot like a movie trailer. Try as he might to block them out with his work, unwelcome thoughts and their concomitant emotions kept bubbling up. Jealousy, for starters. Rob was jealous of Zoe, having it large in New York. He hated cities, but still: New York. And a fucking *private jet*. And hanging out with a fucking *billionaire*. And . . . And . . . Rob really didn't want to lose Zoe. Not yet – and definitely not on *her* schedule. *Fuck it*. He slammed the laptop shut and decided to, of all the fucking ridiculous things, go for a walk. Rob really didn't like the way that losing Zoe made him feel.

# 25

On a surprisingly mild February morning, Gail fell into an easy and spontaneous neighbourly conversation with Mike over their respective mugs of tea and pairs of secateurs.

'You know what, Gail? I like this place more than I ever expected to.' Mike dunked his Rich Tea.

'I'm *so* glad,' said Gail. 'You could easily have found it insanely boring here. I mean, it's not like Eastdene was going to offer you some sort of a big professional challenge or –' she giggled – 'a relentless social life.'

'And luckily that suits me fine, because I'm not after either of those. I'm embracing middle age with a frankly terrifying amount of relish. These days I am all about –' Mike waved his secateurs – '*this!*'

Gail's laughter was slightly over-compensatory, longer and louder than it might have been. Far from being ready to 'embrace' middle age, Gail wasn't even ready to give it a brisk handshake. 'OK,' she said, 'so what kind of shape is your new gardening lifestyle taking?'

Mike raised an eyebrow. 'Hm . . . maybe a stellated dodecahedron?'

'Stop it.' Gail only just managed to restrain herself from overstepping the mark from friendly neighbour to flirty neighbour by punching Mike gently on the arm. Instead, much as she wanted to stay and tease out a little more of the off-duty Mike Browning, she reluctantly made her excuses, shrugging: 'Supermarket, Harry, football.'

'Ah, yes, important stuff. Have a good weekend, Gail.'

Gail filled the rest of her 'good' weekend ferrying Harry from football pitch to friend's party to another friend's Xbox, from the cinema to McDonald's. In between, there was still a surprising amount of time left over for a bracing walk around Hastings by herself. Gail wished she had a dog for company, while knowing that she would never have one unless somebody genetically modified them to not smell of dog.

There were excellent charity shops in Hastings and its environs, quality bric-a-brac to be acquired, if Gail could only steel herself to overcome the *grubbiness* of it all. She knew the area well, and she could see that, these days, it was suffering more than a little from the blustery economic storm. After her charity shop browse, Gail walked along the seafront, past the burned-out pier and up Conquest Road, past the Lottery-Fund-revamped public gardens, peering en route into the windows of the lovely big, slightly careworn houses which attracted new financially downsizing/architecturally upsizing 'down-from-

Londoners' looking to inject some chic into the area's shabby. These people were, Gail knew, particularly greedy for sea views and too many expensive to heat bedrooms, and in their enthusiasm for a low-mortgage lifestyle were happy to overlook the fact that, however big their houses and however gorgeous their views, the town itself was a not-very-commuter-friendly ninety-five minutes from London by train, and at least two hours by car.

Idiots, she thought.

Though her orbit and those of the DFLs had previously never collided much beyond Ivy House (to which they were inevitably drawn) and the occasional supermarket checkout queue, she didn't generally warm to these women, who seemed prickly and shallow and spoke too loudly in public and always looked over her shoulder when they talked to her, apparently searching out something more stimulating and fashionable. They would as often as not rock up in the school playground at drop-off and pick-up wearing big sunglasses *in winter*, as though they were on the slopes, carrying Costa coffees (while bemoaning the lack of local Starbucks) and touting rolled-up copies of *Grazia* like cudgels to ward off the parochially unstylish. They also tended to talk a lot about London as if they lived there; they still got their highlights done in Mayfair, apparently, and met girlfriends for lunch in places like Selfridges.

'Stop it, Hugo! Mummy can't hear herself *think!*'

Gail heard her before she spotted the typical DFL

mother in the gardens, pushing a grizzling toddler strapped tightly into a Bugaboo, while she barked into a BlackBerry. Why do you lot always refer to yourselves in the third person? wondered Gail.

'Look, are you *absolutely* sure you can't get to Waitrose in Tenterden on the way back?'

Gail smiled an entirely fake smile as she approached and the woman glanced at her, still talking into her phone while returning Gail's smile with one that never quite met her eyes, either. 'Really? Well, Sainsbury's might just have it at a pinch, I suppose.' A pause. 'Is it *important*? Well, it's not exactly life-or-death but I can't cook it without it!' The woman rolled her eyes at Gail, as if seeking empathetic sisterly support.

Your poor bloody husband, thought Gail, who had never been to Waitrose – or Selfridges, come to that. If she'd allowed herself to admit it, the truth was that Gail was half afraid of London. And, at her age, the contrast between Selfridges and Debenhams would probably be so mind altering she'd start visiting smart department stores like ... like ... *crack dens*. She smiled at the woman in what she hoped was the right kind of way – Gail was, after all, proud to be a *woman's* woman. And then she realized she recognized her – Carol? Caroline? Carola? Whatever. She had a five-year-old in the pre-prep department at Ivy House. Gail widened her smile much further than she wanted to and tacked on a cheery sort of nod and a raised eyebrow. Empathy. Sisterhood. And sound business sense.

'Ah, hello! It's Ivy House Gail, isn't it?' said the woman, slipping her phone into her pocket.

Is it? thought Gail. Am I somebody without a surname who is entirely defined by her place of work? What kind of person would even say that out loud?

'I'm Sarah Fellowes, Edie's mum.'

Gail's smile was now so warm Sarah could have toasted marshmallows, yet ... Sarah and Edie Fellowes? The names registered only vaguely and Gail realized that this was almost certainly the first time in the best part of two decades she'd got any parent's name quite so wrong. And very clearly and suddenly she knew exactly what this meant. It meant that, somehow or other, and without even noticing, she'd probably stopped caring. She smiled brightly at Sarah.

'Hello, Sarah. You're quite close, except my name's not Ivy House Gail, it's Gail *Prince*.'

# 26

For Eve, a long overdue lunch up in the Smoke with Cathy Gower and Cathy's colleague John ('call me Johnny') Nicholson turned out to be fun and revelatory. The fun came of eating in such chic surroundings; their restaurant had only been open a fortnight and was therefore full of the sort of shiny clientele Eve felt she recognized, even if she couldn't quite place all the faces, though both Graham Norton and Mary Portas (not together) were easy enough to spot. Johnny helpfully pointed out a couple of actors, a senior member of the Cabinet and two well-known restaurant critics.

'That's the smug one –' Johnny indicated a table that was clearly one of the best in the room – 'and, over there, pretending to hide behind a pepper grinder and failing, is the annoying one.'

Eve laughed. 'Not a fan of restaurant critics, then?'

'Actually, I am. I was at uni with the smug one and worked alongside the annoying one on the subs' desk at the *Telegraph*, back in the day.' Johnny leaned forward, conspiratorially. 'They're both brilliant writers, with the kind of morals that'd have alley cats suing for defamation.' Johnny waved cheerfully across the room at each of the critics, who waved back equally cheerfully, and then, affecting mock-horror and clearly playing to the room, waved at each other.

'I'd always imagined journalism to be this vastly complex world, but it seems almost cosy.' Eve drank in the scene, feeling desperately provincial.

'Well, I wouldn't go quite *that* far, but it's a smaller world than you might imagine,' said Cathy. 'I suppose it's like any industry – if you're in it for long enough you inevitably end up knowing more people than you'd probably choose to.'

'And do you love your industry, Johnny?'

Johnny raised an eyebrow. 'Hm. There's an interesting question.' He turned to Cathy. 'Do you? Put it like this – I *know* my industry.'

Eve was genuinely interested. 'So, familiarity breeds contempt?'

Johnny and Cathy smiled; Johnny spoke for both of them. 'Well, I didn't say that, precisely, but now you come to mention it. Although, hang on, we're the journalists, so surely we're supposed to be the ones asking the questions?'

Eve and Cathy laughed. And so they all started asking questions of each other and managed a meaningful bit of business talk, too, which included Johnny telling Eve – to her very considerable surprise – that her little 'rant' went down so well, the paper would be interested in seeing more articles from her in the future. After this, and having discussed their respective children – Johnny had none but, thought Eve, feigned interest quite brilliantly when Eve showed him pictures of the girls on her phone ('My word, supermodels both!') – quite suddenly it was 3:15 p.m. and they hadn't even noticed they were the only diners, aside from the 'annoying' restaurant critic, left in the elegant room.

'Blimey,' said Johnny as he called for the bill. 'I genuinely cannot recall the last time that happened. What a fun lunch!' He turned to Eve. 'I hope you weren't in a rush?'

'Not at all, and I've enjoyed every minute. Though I'd always assumed long lunches were part of a journalist's job description?'

'Ha, well, you would have been right about fifteen years ago – these days, not so much.' At which moment the 'annoying' critic, who'd clearly also had a glass or two, appeared in front of their table, grinning broadly and extending a hand.

'Good to see you two looking so well, Johnny Boy and the fragrant, not to mention *multi-award winning* Cathy Gower, all obviously still on decent expenses. Delighted the *Courier*'s still coughing up in these straitened times. Remind your excellent boss that I'm always available during the transfer window, yeah?' He grinned at Eve. 'But, now, you definitely *aren't* a hack.'

'Is it really that obvious?' asked Eve.

'In the best possible way,' said the critic, whom Eve found rather charming.

'Ah, this is Eve Sturridge, one of my newest contributors,' said Johnny, which made Eve colour slightly. 'And, Eve, this is Gordo McBride, the world's most annoying restaurant critic.'

'Talented and modest too. *Lovely* to meet you, Eve, though I still don't see you as a hack. But here's a tip – whatever they're paying you, ask for double.' And he winked. And Eve winked back. At which point she realized she hadn't drunk so much at lunchtime this entire *century*. But before she could say anything, Gordo was gone.

Johnny pushed back his seat. 'So, that was a lovely lunch.'

'Absolutely magnificent and *madly* overdue. Thanks for letting us crash it, Johnny,' said Cathy, rising.

'Always a pleasure – and I really hope we can do it again.' As Cathy left the table to fetch her coat, Johnny continued, 'Or maybe, Eve, even dinner, sometime soon – if you were planning on coming up to town again? Or, in fact, even if you weren't, maybe I could persuade you?'

Eve could feel a blush rising. The moment clearly demanded to be seized yet what came out of her mouth surprised her: 'I'm not in town much, really, what with the daughters and the day job and all the rest of it, so . . .' Christ, what am I saying? This very nice man is asking me out and I'm batting him away . . .

'Well, now you're a *Courier* contributor it's entirely justified, so if you ever find a window ajar, you know where I am.' Johnny smiled, gave an easy shrug and then there was a beat of silence as Eve and Johnny locked eyes, very briefly. She liked Johnny Nicholson.

On the train home, armed with a bottle of Evian, sobering up, station by station, Eve thought about how she must not let her friendships slide – she would arrange to see Cathy again soon, just the two of them, or even invite her and the boys and, of course, Cathy's husband, Peter, down to the Barn for a weekend. Yes, that was a good idea – they hadn't had a weekend together since all their children had been toddlers. Which, as Eve recalled the consecutive sleepless nights, epic hangovers and fractious kids, was probably *precisely* why they hadn't done it since. But then the toddler years were long gone. This time around they'd probably be drinking wine *with* their kids.

And then her thoughts turned to John Nicholson . . . Who has just turned me into a journalist! Eve contemplated the prospect of a dinner with Johnny and there was no aspect of that that didn't appeal, other than the three-hour round trip. Though perhaps she could stay at Sonia's? Yes, that was a definite plan . . .

Eve took another ladylike swig from her bottle of Evian and was about to close her eyes when she heard the ping of a text arriving. She unearthed the phone from the bottom of her bag. Ah, Zoe. At last!

OiOi CARMEN OMG! U can SO NOT blv wots goin
down here! NewYork – concret jungle where dreems r
made. OH! Have I got NEWS for U?! XXX

Eve firstly felt a wave of irritation at her perfectly intelligent eldest daughter's inability to apparently *ever* send a text without sounding like a moron, though she supposed this was yet another Teen Thing. And then she was even more irritated by the fact that this text was clearly missent, aimed at Zoe's 'BFF', Carmen. And then, before she had time to respond, another *ping* –

MUM! SO SOZ! Just havin a Gr8 time. Love u loads. CU
Sat! ZoXXX

– which was fine and nice, and everything. But *still*. There was no sense of Zoe needing to share that previous 'Have I got NEWS for U?!' and Eve was suddenly rather keen to know what this 'news' might be. However, as Zoe's mother, she reckoned she'd probably be the last to know. She sighed and tapped out a reply.

EXCITING! Enjoy yourself, take care, work hard and I
look forward so much to seeing you at the weekend! Love
you MORE! Mum xxx

It was somewhere between Wadhurst and Frant that Eve decided she ought to spend more time reacquainting herself with her eldest daughter. Perhaps we could do something nice together – and maybe for even longer than twenty minutes? Perhaps we should go to a spa? Though the thought of that made her feel a bit like her sister, Sonia, who – *urgh!* – was pretty much a posh spa season-ticket holder. Then, as the portly, suited-and-booted gentleman in the seat diagonally opposite caught her eye and smiled an amused sort of smile, Eve realized that she'd actually just *pulled* the face she thought she'd only *thought*.

Daylight wine doesn't agree with me at all. And Eve closed her eyes, all the way to Battle.

# 27

Friday morning. It was still far too early and far too dark when Rob heaved himself out of bed reluctantly – it was a very warm and comfortable bed – and got into the shower.

Ten minutes later, he was weaving up the A21 on his bike. With the London-bound rush-hour traffic, it took Rob just over two hours to get to his preferred parking space, close to Starbucks on Piccadilly, and by 8:29 a.m. he was sipping latte and flirting with the pretty Eastern European barista. Suddenly, the thought of having sex with the barista – a thought that had arrived entirely unbidden but very graphically in his head just as she had handed him the latte – made him feel giddy. And then a picture – an actual real *photograph* – of Zoe had jumped uninvited into his head, too. Rob sipped his coffee and scrolled through the texts on his iPhone until he found the latest image of Zoe sitting naked, legs slightly apart, on the edge of her bed. It had been taken on Tuesday morning, apparently, just after her first night in New York. Rob inspected it closely. For one fleeting moment, he wished that she'd included her head, and then he decided that, in fact, it was just as well she hadn't. He had lots of naked pictures of Zoe but, right now, this one was the best. He squinted at it while mentally superimposing the barista's head on to Zoe's naked torso. Mental Photoshop. Mental . . .

Rob shook his head and pulled himself back together, tucked his phone away and retrieved his camera from his rucksack. 8.39 a.m.: time to get round the corner to see what, if anything, was going down in Bond Street. As far as Rob could tell, it was mostly pretty shop girls – and boys – heading to work alongside upscale business-types in expensive suits. There were lots of ambling tourists, too – even in February; they were all casually unstylish, wearing bad-brand trainers and taking up far too much pavement.

And then, at 8:45, a navy blue Bentley Continental – a car that, Rob noted, managed to be both discreet in its colouring and bling in its sheer *Bentley*-ness – pulled up opposite his vantage point in the doorway of Alexander McQueen. On the other side of the street, a man emerged from a discreet doorway at the same time as a blonde woman, wearing a cream coat, high black boots and carrying a very big handbag, exited the driver's side and another woman, fifty-something, brunette, much smaller handbag, exited the passenger door. The two women spoke earnestly on the pavement for a moment or two and then the brunette woman appeared to drop her head and wipe her eyes, after which the blonde kissed her warmly on both cheeks and handed her an envelope. Without so much as the briefest exchange of words, Rob watched as the man – thirty-something, smart-casual – took the woman's place in the driver's seat, the brunette woman got back into the passenger seat and the Bentley drove swiftly up Bond Street, while the blonde glanced left and right and then let herself into the discreet door. So stealthily efficient were all these manoeuvres that no traffic was held up for even a moment and no hazard warning lights flickered as a kerb was mounted; a small thing, maybe, yet Rob considered it to be a *telling* thing, too. This was presumably how smooth your life could be when you were very rich and thus spared the arse ache of stuff like hunting for parking spaces in central London's rush hour.

Rob wondered idly if maybe the blonde woman – Anette Sorensen; he had no idea who the brunette was but she looked secretary-ish – had a secret thing for stubbly twenty-year-olds in bike leathers? Being both blonde and curvaceous, Anette wasn't *technically* his type, but hey, *whatever* – exceptions could be made. Yet, as much as this idea appealed, Rob doubted that Anette went for skinny biker boys when she was basically married to a bloke who made Brad Pitt look like a bit of a spacker.

As Rob walked up Bond Street, he used his camera as a shield and trusted his instincts – which paid off; within just ten minutes there was no mistaking a smiling and immaculately tailored Stefan Sorensen striding up Bond Street from Piccadilly, carrying a take-out Starbucks coffee. Just as there was no mistaking the young woman walking beside him, either. Rob's first sight of Zoe for a week made his heart lurch. While the temptation to race across the road, hopping over cars like some sort of mad CGI superhero, was overwhelming, Rob counter-intuitively held back and slunk into the doorway of Alexander McQueen. And watched, through his lens.

And what he first saw was this well-dressed, good-looking forty-something guy carrying a takeout coffee down a busy London street, accompanied by a beautiful younger woman in a pinstriped skirt suit ... I haven't seen that suit before ...

Yet, within a nano-moment, Rob sensed that the way Sorensen and Zoe were going out of their way not to walk too close together marked them out, albeit only to a very interested party, as co-conspirators in an act of conspicuous ordinariness. To Rob's eyes, indeed, it was all just too 'ordinary' to be true. He aimed his camera, focused and fired: a proper pap's long-distance kiss-kiss, *bang-bang-bang-bang*, unseen and unheard by its victims. And then, within moments, both had disappeared through the same door as Anette.

It was over. Rob's blood rushed and his heart pounded in his ears, deafeningly. He felt light-headed, adrenalized. Five minutes later, back inside Starbucks, he scrolled through the images he'd captured and noted how, in the first few, taken in just two or three seconds, Stefan and Zoe had been walking right beside each other and carrying their coffees, elbows touching, but after an almost imperceptible exchange of words, Zoe had then dropped back a pace or two, moving closer to the buildings, while Stefan had instinctively moved ahead, nearer the kerb.

It was immediately obvious to Rob that they had been decisively distancing themselves from each other. Though obviously in conversation while they walked together in the earliest frames, by the end of the sequence they were far enough away that they could have been strangers who just happened to inhabit the same busy London street. But, mused Rob, who trusted his instincts, you wouldn't go to the trouble of doing that unless you had something to hide, right? And indeed a forensic examination of that final shot paid off: in the super-confident tilt of Zoe's chin and her level, amused gaze – a look he knew so well – Rob could instinctively see the truth, which was that the billionaire financier, Stefan Sorensen, was not only *fucking* his girlfriend, but that she was relishing every single thrilling second of it.

*Bitch.*

It was at precisely this opportune moment that the pretty barista appeared at the table next to his, cloth in hand, wiping – wiping and smiling at Rob. 'Hiya. You back?'

Rob managed a grin. 'Yeah – apparently I am.'

She smiled. 'Ohkay. Enjay your caffee.'

He liked her accent and he liked her smile and he liked

the thought of superimposing her head on to a naked picture of Zoe. 'Yeah, I will.' Rob could feel a blush rising. What could he say to seize the moment? 'Um. Do you live far away?' Christ! What was he on about? 'I mean, does it take you long to get to work?'

Barista Girl smiled. 'No, not too long. I share a flat near Brixton.' She paused. Rob felt her gaze was searching for something, *reading* him. 'I'm finishing work at four p.m.'

'Cool. Can I meet you after?' Moment seized.

She nodded. 'Sure. But now I have to . . .' She shrugged, smiled, waved her grubby cloth in the air.

'Yeah! You get on and don't mind me.' Rob watched her back as she retreated to her till – it was a lovely dancer's back – sinuous – and beautiful legs. And in between the back and the legs, a peachy little arse . . . Yup, Barista Girl was totally Rob's type. He closed his eyes for a moment, savouring that fact. As he picked up his rucksack, he glanced over at Barista Girl, who smiled back. He gave her a little wave and mouthed the word *Later!* She nodded. Rob left the coffee shop and crossed the road where, inside Green Park, he found a bench beneath a tree. Using his rucksack as a pillow, he closed his eyes, lay back and thought about . . . Albania? Romania? Lithuania? Serbia? Wherever the fuck she's from . . .

It was pretty cold, but, nonetheless, Rob dozed for a while – maybe half an hour – and woke with a start to sense a small drool of spittle on his cheek and an aching neck. He sat upright, watching the late morning to and fro through the paths of the park. It was good, people watching. London was growing on him. Maybe it was even possible to extract some order from its chaos? At which moment, a stray thought about Zoe in bed with Stefan Sorensen insinuated itself into his mind. This made him suddenly angry and then, just as suddenly, sad. Maybe there's no order, after all – only chaos? Rob glanced at his phone: still only eleven a.m. Then he scrolled through the phone's camera roll until he found the image he was looking for and, after a moment or two, closed his eyes again.

At lunchtime, Rob wandered along Piccadilly to the big flagship Waterstones. He was so bored, he thought he might even buy a book, but either way there was a nice café.

The afternoon unfurled, slowly. By 3:45 p.m., re-caffeinated and book free, he was once again outside Starbucks, holding his spare bike helmet and waiting for Barista Girl, who was inside the coffee shop, mouthing 'One minute!' at him through the plate glass. At 4:11, they were both on Rob's bike and Rob was enjoying the sensation of Barista Girl's legs tucked into the flying-V shape of his own, her arms wrapped tightly around his waist.

At 4:36 – having pulled up a couple of times so that Rob could take directions – he and Barista Girl had finally stopped outside a modest terraced house in a quiet back street that was more Herne Hill than Brixton. At 5:16 p.m., after the minimum of polite small talk lubricated by half a can of a very cold and very good Czech beer that Barista

Girl had extracted from her grubby fridge, she was on her knees, naked – glory be! – in front of him. Her eyes were closed as Rob looked down at her and muttered, 'Bee-yoo-ti-ful Ba-rista Girl.'

Barista Girl took a break and glanced up. 'Fuck me, Bike Boy?'

Oh, OK then . . . if I must. The sex was absolutely and unequivocally the very best sex Rob had ever had. Nonetheless, it seemed quite extraordinary that it could be possible to have such an awesome time while simultaneously feeling so dementedly miserable. Still, it was good to know you could.

At nine p.m. Rob figured he'd probably better start extracting himself from this pleasantly distracting situation and get back down the A21. He would gladly have stayed curled up on the thin mattress, smelling Barista Girl's deliciously foreign aroma with its base note of freshly ground coffee beans; nonetheless, he hauled himself out of bed.

'You got to go?' Barista Girl pouted slightly. 'Stay?'

'Nah, babes, sorry. Work.' He shrugged as he pulled on his jeans. Naked Barista Girl propped herself up in the bed on one elbow. It looked as though she planned to stay put. Rob snapped the image with his mind's-eye lens.

'So what's your job, Bike Boy?'

Rob indicated the camera bag on the floor. 'Pictures. I take photographs.'

'Of?'

Rob shrugged. 'People.'

'Take mine?'

Rob grinned. 'OK.'

An hour later, Rob finally readied himself to leave while Barista Girl scribbled her number on a piece of paper. Rob took the paper and made a great show of zipping it inside his biker's jacket, then he kissed Barista Girl on the forehead and let himself out of the flat. While he strapped on his rucksack and put on his helmet, he glanced up at the second-floor window. He trusted his instincts and – of course – she was watching him. Barista Girl smiled and waved. Rob waved back. He smiled, too – not that she could see his face beneath his helmet – and then he kick-started the bike and rode away. As soon as he was round the corner, he pulled up, unzipped his jacket, retrieved the piece of paper and dropped it into the gutter.

# 28

Back home, in the so-called Real World, after spending the final night of her work-experience week with her aunt, Zoe was now facing apparently endless late nights hunched over text books with zero in the way of private jets or billionaires, and she was demonstrably not happy. An aptitude for exams had ensured that, even if Zoe had always forged herself a life beyond revision, the majority of her friends – even Carmen – were too busy to notice that she was opting out of a social life. Indeed, it seemed to Zoe that nearly *everybody* in her life was currently too busy to notice very much that was going on outside their own orbits. Even Rob had apparently disappeared into a permanent edit suite with 'some, like, proper urgent business, babes.' As if. She'd only spoken to him briefly since she'd got home on Saturday morning and it was now Sunday evening, and still no sign. Even her last resort of a little sister was out of the family loop, living in jodhpurs and coming home tired and smelling of horse. And then, all weekend, her mum had kept on trying to instigate *proper conversations.*

'So,' said Eve, during a proper sit-down roast Sunday lunch, which Zoe considered a bit weird, given it was just the two of them, 'assuming you do get the grades, are you planning on going up to uni this year, or are you thinking about a gap year?'

Zoe pushed away the carbohydrates on her plate and shrugged, attempting to look casual. 'Dunno, Mum. I've been offered a gap-year job at Odense, if I want it.' A pause. 'Uh, Tina – you know, Mr Sorensen's PA – has just left.'

'Has she? Well, I doubt you have acquired an executive secretary's extensive skill set after one week, but if Anette and Stefan think you can be useful then that's *great!* Well done!'

Eve looked thrilled, while Zoe flinched. *If Anette and Stefan think you can be useful . . .* Little do you know, Mum. 'I was going to talk to you about it this week. No biggie.'

'*Yes*, biggie! Well, that's marvellous – assuming you don't want to backpack around Asia, that is?'

'Nah, I'm OK with not backpacking around anywhere. And I think there would probably be some more travel, anyway, at Odense.'

'Well. Isn't that *great!*'

Zoe struggled to make the exchange a bit more conversational. 'It's a pretty tight team, so it's nice that they've found room for me. I'm sort of the office go-to girl, really – stationery, phone chargers, new pairs of Fogal tights if Anette gets a ladder, takeaway coffees for everybody all the time – that kind of stuff.'

'Have you told Rob yet?'

'Not yet.' Zoe scrunched up her nose.

'He hates London,' said Eve, misreading the scrunched nose.

'He'll get over it.' Zoe shrugged. 'Anyway, I'll be back.'

'So, Zoe, I've had an idea. To relieve the stress of all that revision, I wondered if you fancied going on a –' Eve paused momentarily, the silence clearly waiting to be filled by a *Ta-da!* – 'weekend spa break? Just the two of us, no Alice! Maybe over Easter?!'

In her mother's voice, Zoe could hear an unusual and disconcerting fake cheeriness, a sort of kindness laced with neediness, which made her feel quite inexplicably *furious.* She scrunched her nose and levelled her gaze at Eve. 'Er, like, *no*, I wouldn't. But *thanks anyway.*' And then Zoe got to her feet and deliberately pushed her plate away instead of taking it to the dishwasher, and stalked towards the door, where she paused and turned and added, knife-twistingly, 'To be honest, I can't really think of anything I'd like to do *less* than that, because I'm nearly eighteen and – guess what? – I no longer want to hang out with my mum for a whole weekend.'

And with this, Zoe rather enjoyed leaving Eve sitting in – presumably, shocked? It was hard to tell – silence, alone at the dinner table, while she went upstairs to her room, where, just to ensure she'd rammed the point home, Zoe slammed her door and roared, 'Just *fuck off*, Mum! LEAVE ME *ALONE!*'

In her bedroom – always her safe, happy space – Zoe checked her phone for messages for about the fiftieth time that day. Nothing from Rob, which was just strange, and nothing – more importantly – from Stefan, either. He had her number because she'd given it to him on her last day in New York – and, even though he hadn't asked for it, she'd actually watched as he'd keyed it into his phone. Or at least – and she felt a small wave of embarrassment as the thought occurred to her for the first time – she *assumed* he'd keyed it in, simply because it *looked* as though he had.

As the days passed – silent, empty days that increasingly passed in a dull blur of revision and chocolate – so Zoe found herself more and more comfortable inside her new angry skin. Caterpillar to raging butterfly – that's how it felt to emerge from her chrysalis right now. Yet this life-changing shift wasn't particularly painful, difficult or remotely beyond her control. Zoe had spent a little bit of time – the bare minimum, really – trying to analyse why this was. Despite carrying around a lot of secrets and therefore having to tell a few too many untruths, Zoe was far from being in some kind of inner turmoil; was in fact *fine* with the secrets. The lies not so much. Just as fat can marble an otherwise lean steak, Zoe's outward coolness well disguised her streak of conservatism. Much as she hated anybody to know it, she was probably, she conceded – if only to herself – fundamentally, a 'good girl' who had rather suddenly, and possibly slightly behind schedule – unfashionably late, even – decided to *hate* the mother she loved, simply because she could.

# 29

While reading the *Courier* article in her presence, it had, Eve noted, been the uncharacteristic silence that best revealed the scale of Tony's anger. The following week, over an emergency kitchen-based wine summit (called to discuss Zoe becoming 'a nightmare, practically overnight', and Jordan, and then, guiltily, 'not forgetting Alice . . .'), Eve told Simon that, 'If the throbbing veins in his temples were any indication, he was *incandescent*; however, if he sacks me, it will create its own shit-storm. And he's been fielding several phone calls from confused parents as it is. I suspect he thinks it's some sort of menopausal meltdown.'

'And is it?'

Eve punched Simon gently on the arm. 'Shut up.' Then, 'Actually – *fuck* – who knows? Maybe it is. Maybe that's the problem with me and Zoe, too: we are at opposite ends of the hormonal spectrum. I barely know who she is anymore and it upsets me.'

'Of course it upsets you. It upsets me too. But the

father-daughter relationship is different; we're not actually *expected* to know each other – it's just a bonus if we do.' Simon refilled Eve's glass. 'Look, I think she'll be *fine*. And Alice will be fine as long as she has a horse – which will be the last thing I ever bloody sell, if it comes to that.'

'I don't think it'll come to that. Anyway, the horse goes before Heatherdown's fees go – you have my blessing on that. So how *is* Jordy getting on?'

And, as Eve listened to Simon enthusing about Jordan's new school, she was touched by the fact that, although she didn't necessarily fully subscribe to Heatherdown's educational ethos, it seemed to work in its own sweet way. And not just for Jordan – clearly for Simon too: 'So, Wednesday mornings are spent making and playing "musical instruments" constructed from *objets trouvés*. Then the rest of the day is about making and listening to music – just as the whole of Tuesdays is about problem solving and fire building and bivouac constructing in the woods – which apparently falls under the *science* umbrella.'

'I'm sure Bear Grylls would approve, but I'm not sure how it translates into GCSEs.' Eve shrugged. 'Look, the main thing is that it's working for *Jordan*.'

'It's working unbelievably well. And they do proper sport, as it happens. Jordan is apparently *very* good at football.' And Simon explained how sometimes all the lessons were combined so that 'it looks like a hot mess to me, but the kids love it when Madame Smith, who is actually French, takes charge and football is *played in French*.

Heatherdown's pupils are probably the only kids in the country who get *la règle de hors-jeu.*'

'*La* what?'

Simon laughed. 'Yeah, I don't understand the offside rule either. The thing is, Jordan is coming home exhausted in all the right ways, stimulated but not *over*-stimulated, and run out like a dog. I can't pretend he doesn't still have some major moments, but they are slightly fewer and further between.' A pause. 'Thanks *so* much, Evie.'

'For what?'

'For recognizing that Heatherdown was right for Jordan. And for not being afraid to admit it. That takes professional courage.'

'Well, maybe we could all learn a few things from Heatherdown?'

'Yes, I did read your article. It's bang on – and you know it.'

'Sometimes I know it. Sometimes I might need to be reminded. And –' as Simon leaned in to top up her glass, Eve placed her hand over the rim – 'now I need to remind *you* that we've both had enough. Or God knows where we'll end up.'

Simon laughed and laughed, and Eve marvelled yet again how great an ex-husband he was. And how great it was, too, that the trials of the last few months hadn't really changed anything. That even the potential embarrassment of Simon briefly imagining that he wanted to sleep with her again hadn't blurred the edges of their relationship for much longer than it had taken their respective hangovers to subside. It occurred to Eve that, in fact, this had been the very last box they had both needed to tick to ensure that there could never be any regrets – and now the whole issue needed no further clarification, spoken or otherwise. What a profound relief. In a schedule heaving with problems, Eve felt this was one less thing to worry about; that after all these years she was now entirely free and ready to get on with the rest of her life . . .

At the end of the week, the Friday before half-term, Gail brought in doughnuts for her and Eve to have at elevenses. However, elevenses were cancelled when Tony asked Gail to tell Eve, who was on the phone to Simon, to come and see him *right now*.

'What do you think he wants?' Eve pulled a face at Gail. 'I fear the *Courier* thing may not be blowing over quite as quickly as he would like.'

'Why? What's he been saying?' Gail sat down opposite Eve.

'Well, nothing much – surprisingly, for Tony – but I'm just reading between the lines and, uh, the phone calls.'

'Anyone interesting?'

'By "interesting" do you mean Sorensen-and-Dershowitz interesting?'

Gail nodded.

'No, not them, but plenty of other parents; if we had any actual governors, or even a proper PTA instead of the tedious, meddlesome, semi-professional cake-baking "Friends of Ivy House", I think it's fair to say they'd be calling for a meeting.'

'And maybe calling for your head on a plate? Oh, and by the way, don't forget you're seeing Ellie after Tony?'

'Thanks, I had forgotten about that.' Eve got to her feet. 'Right, I'd better start thinking straight.'

Gail smiled. 'Yeah, remember it's not always all about you.'

'Good advice – thanks. Any chance of coffee?'

'Consider it done, boss. And –' Gail leaned forward conspiratorially – 'and I really want you to know that I totally have your back, but, even so, you may want to glance over your shoulder occasionally. Just saying.'

Eve smiled. 'Thanks, Gail. I'm *fine*. Two sugars today though, please.'

Eve was prepared for her weekly meeting with Tony to be sticky because, if there was one thing – actually two things – Eve knew he really hated, they were (1) surprises. Of any kind. Ever. And (2) not getting his own way – *especially* when he was paying for his own way to be got.

Yet, to her great surprise, Eve found Tony to be positively chipper. He wasn't a skilled emotional-temperature taker so, normally, if he needed the heads-up about anything school-related he went straight to Eve, who could be relied upon to tell whatever it was exactly the way it was – and in language he appreciated. Now that Eve seemed to be less of a *solution* than she was a *problem*, that was no longer an option, so Eve guessed that Tony Salter was feeling pretty much the way Napoleon must have felt after the Treaty of Fontainebleau: i.e. busy doing not very much at all, on Elba.

Not, Eve discovered, that he wasn't doing *anything* – far from it. In the pursuit of boarding-school excellence, much of the coppice had now been razed – along with some inconvenient environmental concerns that had been raised by the children, for which compensatory bird boxes had been duly commissioned for other parts of the wood and a new coppice planted on the far edges of the rugby pitch. Meanwhile, heavy plant trundled its way up and down the greensward from morning till dusk as construction got underway on the new boarding facilities in order to meet autumn's immovable deadline. And then, thanks to InterEduSol, the overseas recruitment drive had gone very well, too, so Tony was suddenly quite optimistic about the long-term future of Ivy House.

'According to the bursar's office, there have also been an intriguing number of enquiries from parents of children with – and I quote – "their needs not being met at other local schools",' Tony told Eve. 'We haven't probed too deeply into what this means – like whether these are actual "needs" that are in any way also "special" – not that I object to a special needs provision, per se.' Tony levelled his gaze at Eve. 'Because you know I am happy to fill the classrooms with kids of all shapes, sizes, colours and creeds. I'll take Jews, Muslims, Hindus – *whatevers*.'

'Just as well, seeing as we have a reasonable selection of those already,' said Eve calmly.

'You know what I mean. Buddhists, Sikhs, Zoroastrians, Scientologists – bring 'em all on. I am totally an equal opportunities educator – at a price.' Tony paused and rubbed his hands together, à la Fagin. Which, Eve very much hoped, was in jest, but may not have been. 'Though, on second thoughts, you can strike the Scientologists because they're all fucking mad! I'm happy with all the religion stuff, but I still do *not* want to be the go-to guy for the spazzers.'

'Ah! It's actually "spackers" these days, Tony. Honestly, if you don't keep on top of trends in terms of abuse, you sound just like a sad old bloke.'

'Hm, yes. Maybe even the sad old Principal of a rural prep school?'

Eve laughed. This comparatively cheery mood of Tony's was, he revealed, because he'd just had confirmation from Moscow that there would be fourteen new bells-and-whistles Russian boarding pupils pencilled in for September, to add to the twelve he'd already secured from the Far and Middle Easts. Eve marvelled at how very briskly he seemed to have moved on from the article, even as Eve was still struggling to get a handle on the fallout. As far as she could tell, media opinion was divided. When she'd spoken to Johnny Nicholson at lunch on the Wednesday after publication, he'd said that 'some columnists and commentators think you're a heroine for simply saying the unsayable.'

'*Really?*'

'Really! While the rest – well, the *Guardian* – consider you to be a private-school pariah who dares to stick her head above the parapet of her ivory tower and, as a result, pretty much has whatever is coming. So it's all good!'

But is it really 'all good'? Eve wondered.

Meanwhile, here and now, it was good to know that her other, proper boss was back in his comfort zone. 'Right then,' said Eve, 'if we're all done, I'm going to have to go. I have a meeting with Ellie.'

'OK, Mrs Sturridge. Get out there and boost staff morale sufficiently to deliver us another Ofsted "Outstanding" or . . . or –' Tony stammered slightly – 'you're *out* on your fucking *outstanding* ear.'

Eve hadn't seen that one coming, in itself slightly unnerving. 'Jesus! And precisely who are you being today? Tony *Soprano*?' She just about pulled off a spin on her heels, but sensibly resisted slamming the door.

# 30

Johnny Nicholson had first seen the set of photographs by accident on a casual trip past the picture desk's screens on the way to the water cooler. Destined for the *Courier*'s online edition, the images had caught his eye because he immediately recognized that the girl – the *young woman* – was Eve Sturridge's daughter, Chloe? No – Zoe. He had only seen pictures of Zoe once before, on Eve's phone at that pleasant lunch with Cathy, and had never met her in the flesh, but nonetheless her beauty had meant that Zoe Sturridge had carved herself a tiny memory-sized niche inside Johnny Nicholson's head. Johnny was not, after all, entirely immune to the beauty of young women, even if he had to occasionally remind himself that he was old enough to be a young beauty's father.

It didn't matter that the nascent friendship with her mother appeared to have stalled – charmed though he had been by Eve, in relationship terms, it had always been a bit of a geographical long-shot – he'd felt compelled to persuade the picture desk that there was no editorial interest whatsoever in Stefan Sorensen and his leggy new Alexa-Chung-alike PA ('No, *really*! Nobody's interested in these hedgie guys – even if they are married to former beauty queens!').

Johnny now wondered, a day or two later, how best to tackle the problem – with which, he recognized, he was becoming slightly obsessed. While Johnny had a very real desire to save the teenager from herself and earn Brownie points with her mum, the journalist in him – the *non-parent* journalist – also wanted to see how this particular little teen-drama might play itself out. Because it was blindingly obvious, just by looking at the set of pictures, that the billionaire hedge-fund genius and alleged all-round great guy, Stefan Sorensen, was fucking – or had fucked – *seventeen*-year-old Zoe Sturridge. And that, even if Eve didn't know about it – which she presumably didn't – or, indeed, even if she didn't *want* to know about it – which she almost certainly wouldn't – she most definitely needed to. If there was one thing of which Johnny was fairly convinced, it was that this little situation had the potential to become very messy indeed.

So, after a day of internal debate, Johnny did the obvious thing – he went down the corridor to visit Cathy Gower, carrying a printout of one of the pap snaps and affecting an air of disinterest.

'Got a minute, Cath?'

'Why do you always choose press day to pick what passes for my brain, Johnny? I'll be so much more fun tomorrow.' Cathy sighed. 'OK, literally a *minute*. What can I do you for?'

'Thanks, darling. Now, this . . .' And Johnny thrust the printout right under Cathy's nose and watched her eyes widen as she processed the visual context – and indeed subtext – of the image.

'OK, so that's my teenage god-daughter, Zoe. What *is* she doing?'

'Aside from sleeping with her boss during her work experience?'

Cathy glared at Johnny. 'You said that, not me.'

'Come on, Cath – it's bloody obvious from their body language.'

Cathy appeared to consider this as she scrutinized the picture. 'Yes. OK. It does seem that way. Jesus. That's my oldest friend's teenage daughter. What the fuckety-fuck?'

'And you a top newspaper journalist, too. Horns of the proverbial dilemma!'

'No, actually, it's not, because, unlike you, I'm forty-nine per cent journalist and fifty-one per cent *parent*. Listen, Johnny, I've got to get this bloody magazine to bed, but then we're going to sort this out.' Cathy shrugged. 'Some- how. Pub at seven, yeah?'

# 31

'Ah, Ellie!' Eve arrived in Ellie's classroom – the nicest in the building, on the south-west facing corner – and glanced around approvingly. 'My favourite room, this. I'm sure Brahms appreciate it too, albeit probably without quite knowing why.' Ellie nodded, and Eve noted her deep breath; she'd clearly been steeling herself for *something*. 'OK, so hit me with whatever it is.'

'Ah, so, here's the thing—' Ellie paused and took a deep breath. 'Now, you may not be aware that my class is a particularly odd one – for lots of reasons – but it is, and one of the reasons is because twelve out of the eighteen children were born post-May.'

Eve nodded. 'Yes – I knew it was an unusually high number of summer babies, but I hadn't realized it was quite as many as that. So what's going on?'

'Well, we've just done our mid-year tests and, uh, the policy of giving kids born after Easter the previous year's papers seems to be backfiring with the current bunch of Year Fours.' Ellie shrugged. 'It *may* be an anomaly because

they're not exactly a control group – the brightest children in the class are, confusingly, also the very youngest
of the youngest, the July and August kids.'

Eve furrowed her brow. 'Including Petrus Sorensen?'

'Yes, Petrus is July, but he's definitely in there. Anyway,
the thing is –' Ellie sighed – 'all of my A-group in maths –
five of them, including Petrus – scored less than sixty-five
per cent in their maths tests, despite the fact that they
could do it – an old Year Three test, of course – blindfold.
And in fact Petrus, who is probably the best—'

'Probably genetic,' Eve said wryly. 'Go on.'

'Probably! But the thing is, he only got fifty-six per cent.
Or, more accurately, he got one hundred per cent of the
fifty-six per cent of the paper that he actually bothered to
do, but then he stopped just over halfway and did a few
drawings instead. They're very good; he calls them his
"Deadlies".'

Ellie pushed Petrus's test paper across the desk. It
was covered with pencil drawings of intensely detailed
landscapes scattered with battle scenes featuring what
appeared to be robots fighting tanks against a backdrop of
castles and mountains. It was very impressively male, just
as impressively messy and reminded Eve of something
else, too, only she couldn't quite put her finger on precisely what that something was.

'So, anyway,' Ellie continued, 'the point is that my
brightest kids ended up doing worse than the less bright
kids, which really screws with the statistics. And the thing

that is even more interesting is that, when I started getting feedback from parents of the A-group – inevitable, really, given these were disappointing results from our smartest kids – it was alarmingly similar. All five of them were asked by their parents why they'd done so badly, relatively speaking, and all of the kids answered with variations of "I got a bit bored and stopped doing the test and did something else instead".'

Eve smiled. 'Right! *Why don't you just switch off your television set and go and do something less boring instead*?'

'Excuse me?'

'Sorry. It was an old kids' TV show – before your time, Ellie. And, actually, rather *after* my time, but anyway –' Eve exhaled – 'this is all very interesting. So, apparently the youngest kids in Year Four, who by some statistical anomaly are also your brightest, have all revolted independently against a test specifically designed to ensure they did *better* than average.'

'That's about the size of it, yes. To put it another way, the technically least-clever, pre-Easter-born child in the class scored *higher* in their maths test than the *brightest* child.'

'Is the brightest child, by any chance, Petrus Sorensen?'

'Yes.'

'And how un-bright is the least bright child – and is that child a Percy?'

Ellie nodded. 'You assume correctly, bless him! Piers Percy is, well . . .' Ellie struggled for the right word; Eve knew she was fond of Piers.

'Going to have the mickey taken out of him mercilessly at big school – and not just for being called Piers Percy?' said Eve.

'Well, yes, probably. He's a terribly sweet boy, though. I'm sure he'll make it to agricultural college.'

'By hook or by crook.' Eve snorted. 'Forgive me!' Ellie smiled at Eve's joke. 'I suspect both Piers and Petrus would technically be "special needs" if we had a special needs provision – and, obviously, at pretty much opposite ends of the scale, too.'

'But we don't, so . . .' Ellie shrugged.

Ah, but we will, we will, thought Eve, looking intently at the younger teacher. 'It must be hard work?'

To Eve, Ellie seemed immediately relieved – and grateful – to be invited to say, 'Yes, it *is*. I've only been teaching seven years but I've already seen a few extraordinary children. This year's lot, though, are . . .' She tailed off, grimaced, shrugged again.

'*What* are they, do you think?' Eve encouraged.

'*Very* different, incredibly challenging, extremely rewarding and *impossible* to predict. I never know each morning quite where we'll end up by four p.m. And I also feel very strongly that our usually infallible strategy of giving easier exams to the younger children so the school's grades – as well as *theirs* – are kept up has entirely backfired with this year's bunch.'

Eve was interested. She had always struggled with the ethics of the school's long-time strategy of dumbing down tests and exams for even the brightest kids, albeit that better results simply meant more children joining the school, which meant, in turn, better financial results and a bigger salary. 'It's as if they've *intentionally* subverted it. I mean, I don't think they have, and not because they're not bright enough to do it – they *are* – but because they're nowhere near as cynical as us!'

'Hm. As *some* of us,' corrected Eve before she suddenly blurted, '*Stephen Wiltshire!*'

'Sorry?' said Ellie.

'I've been trying to think what – or, indeed, *who* – Petrus Sorensen's drawings reminded me of and it's Stephen Wiltshire.'

Ellie shrugged. 'I don't know the name.'

'Google him. He's probably in his mid or late thirties by now – autistic savant, brilliant artist from the age of maybe seven, noted for his landscapes. He might even be an OBE. Anyway, thanks very much for all of this, Ellie. It's fascinating. And I'd like to pop by your classroom right after half-term and have a closer look at this Year Four in action, if I may?'

'Of course! We'd love that.'

It was with a head full of jostling thoughts on the drive home – about Gail's comments and Johnny's, about Tony's and Ellie's – that Eve pulled into the Esso garage just outside Battle. Unusually, she suddenly craved a can of Diet Coke, a bag of cheese-and-onion crisps and a Snickers, all of which she consumed uncharacteristically fast, and slightly guiltily – she would hate to be spotted by a parent or a pupil – while sitting in her car at the side of the forecourt.

As Eve reached the end of her crisps and slightly regretted that she hadn't bought two packets, she noticed a smart black Land Rover pulling into the petrol station. When the driver got out and started filling his tank, Eve decided, in a move as uncharacteristic as the crisps binge, that she would pop into the petrol station's Tesco Express and sort of, somehow, engineer a casual 'Hello'. Suddenly, right now – and despite their inauspicious start – Eve couldn't think of a person she wanted to talk to more than . . . Mike Browning. And it was remarkably easy. In fact, it was – pleasingly – Mike who spotted her, standing apparently transfixed by an abundance of semi-skimmed.

'Oh, hello again – *Mrs Sturridge.*' He smiled broadly and held out his hand, which Eve took while affecting what she hoped was a convincing *goodness-what-a-pleasant-surprise* sort of expression. 'How nice to bump into you, and in such glamorous surroundings. My compliments on what was a truly excellent article – especially given it was in the *Courier.*'

Eve, clutching too much milk and utterly distracted – by what? Pheromones?! – found it was impossible to respond appropriately without looking like Basil Fawlty, mid pratfall. It seemed to Eve particularly absurdly British to be making polite small talk about one's work while standing in Tesco holding an udder's worth of full-fat milk.

'Thank you – *Mike*.' It suddenly seemed very appropriate to be on first-name terms. 'And, of course, I owe you an apology – for jumping to conclusions. Although, you jumped to yours before I jumped to mine.'

'Guilty as charged.' Mike paused. 'And I, ah, well . . . I'm sure you're very busy.' Mike eyed the milk. 'You certainly *look* busy, but, uh – and this is terribly forward, even head teacher to head teacher – but I don't suppose you fancy a quick coffee?'

Eve felt she'd learned her seizing-the-moment lesson with Johnny, so she nodded. 'I fancy a coffee very much.'

Mike smiled very broadly; it made Eve want to punch the air.

Fifteen minutes later, they had reconvened over cappuccinos in nearby Battle, and politely – and repetitively – reiterated their apologies. And then, blessedly, they both agreed it was time to move on. At the beginning, Eve did most of the listening while Mike shared – and speedily. 'It's probably been a long time coming, leaving London. I love Eastdene – the school and the kids *and* the village. In the last couple of years, I'd started feeling out of step with the times.'

'Or maybe the times were out of step with you? Not to mention *The Times Educational Supplement*.'

'Well, that's kind of you, Eve, but either way it's fairly academic.' Mike mimed a cymbal-crash as Eve grinned.

'For my part, I know that a school like Ivy House has to adapt to survive – and, in many respects, what my boss, Tony, has been trying to do is absolutely correct. There's a certain logic to this, um, *globalization* of education.'

'But . . . ?'

Eve couldn't quite believe how easy this was or quite how much they had in common, despite operating at opposite ends of the educational spectrum. What an unadulterated pleasure it was, finally, to talk about work with Mike Browning . . .

'But? Well, yes, there *is* a but – several buts. OK, so here's an analogy – somewhere between the health-and-safety madness of, for example, those "no-playing-outside-when-it's-raining" kind of rules that you increasingly find at, well, state primaries like yours, and a school like Ivy House's "no-staying-inside-ever-if-it's-Games" ethos, I think there lies a middle way. Call it the "if-we-want-to-go-out-in-the-rain/hail/snow-let's-go-out-and-if-we-want-to-stay-in-let's-stay-in". Does that make *any* sense?'

'Of course it makes sense,' said Mike. 'It's called flexibility. It's called treating each child as an individual. It's what we *try* to do at Eastdene, inasmuch as we can within the state system's constraints. It's what makes every day different and keeps the kids on their toes and also *engaged*. Usually it works, sometimes it doesn't – but, either way, we bend with it.'

Eve looked closely at Mike. 'Do you know Heatherdown?'

Mike nodded. 'I've not visited, though I've been tempted to crash an open day, but of course I know all about it.'

'Well, I used to think Heatherdown's sort of approach was a load of hippy nonsense.'

'Ha! Me too.'

Eve smiled. 'But the thing is that now I very much *don't* think that. Though I have no idea why I'm telling you. It's just that my ex-husband's adopted son, who is somewhere on the spectrum—'

'As most of we boys are, of course.' Mike raised an eyebrow.

Was he testing her? Eve wasn't sure. 'Well – maybe. Anyway, his son was at Ivy House and it wasn't working for him at all – or us, to be fair – and I suggested Heatherdown and, of course, he's thriving.' She shrugged. 'So what do we make of *that*?'

'I think what we make of that is that there is room for all of us. Between you, me and the excellent Adam Thingummy over at Heatherdown, we probably cover most of the bases. Even though none of the schools are perfect, we do all have something quite unique to offer.' Mike shrugged and also let slip a small sigh. 'And would that we could all get on with doing what we're best at. You don't think about leaving Ivy House, do you?'

'Sometimes. Anyway, the thinking may be done *for* me at some point. None of us is indispensable, we just like to think we are.'

A wry laugh. 'Oh, believe me, I'm *very* dispensable.'

Eve scrutinized Mike. So bloody handsome – and, more than that, so obviously a *good* man, too. It was with a start that Eve realized – God, how can I be so slow? – of whom he reminded her: Simon. Her blush – a hot flush sort of a blush, as became a fifty-something's crush – was instant: bright red, right from her chest up to her eyebrows . . . It must be so obvious! 'I find that very hard to believe,' said Eve, raising her cup in a fairly futile attempt to disguise her colour.

Mike Browning met Eve's gaze over the rim. 'Uh . . . look, um, Eve, I apologize in advance because I seem to be feeling very *carpe diem* today, but are you by any remote chance free for dinner? Tonight?'

Before she replied, Eve counted to three in her head and breathed deeply, inhaling some froth from the top of her coffee . . . Fuck. Mike Browning has just asked me out . . . and I've got a milk moustache . . . 'Yes, I am free. That would be lovely.' She wiped her top lip in as blasé a fashion as it was possible to muster, which was not very blasé at all. Then Mike Browning leaned forward and, very gently, brushed her top lip with the tip of his forefinger.

'Bit left. Gone now.'

'Yes. Thank you.' Eve smiled at Mike.

And so Eve Sturridge and Mike Browning talked for another fifteen minutes and then Mike paid their bill and they left the coffee shop and paused briefly on the pavement outside, making arrangements for the evening.

Mike: 'I know it's nearer mine than yours, but the Bell does do an excellent steak pie and chips.'

Eve: 'It does. The Bell's steak pie and chips is *perfect*.'

And then Eve reached out and gently touched Mike's upper arm. 'I *was* going round to my ex-husband's house for dinner tonight, actually – but I don't think he'll mind.'

Mike grinned. 'Thank you for sharing.'

Eve could feel Mike's eyes on her departing back – literally watching my back – as she crossed the road to the car park beside the Abbey. She sat in the front seat of the car and retrieved her phone from her bag, scrolling through the names in her address book until she reached Simon's number. She touched *Call*.

'Simon? It's me. Listen, I'm blowing you out for dinner tonight.' A pause. 'Yes – even for sausages and mash and onion gravy. I know!' Another pause. 'Pie and chips at the Bell.' Another longer pause. 'No, darling, you and Ed can't come and crash. It's a bloody *date*.'

Laughing, Eve had to hold the phone away from her ear to avoid being deafened by the screams of delight as Simon shared the news with Ed. 'Oh my God, Eve,' said Simon, when the screaming subsided, 'until now I'm not sure that Ed and I knew we were quite this *gay*!'

Eve heard Ed's voice loud in the background – 'Speak for yourself, honey!' – and thought she might actually die of laughter. Die of laughter *and love*. Could there *ever* be a better way to go?

Later, over their respective gin and tonics, Mike Browning told Eve that he felt he had 'adjusted pretty well to English village life' and that it clearly helped if you both lived and worked inside 'the community' and were perceived to be one of its 'pillars'. Eve nodded emphatically as Mike confessed he didn't really get the whole 'pillar' thing.

'Well, you're an urban boy, after all – and who knows how many pillars a small community like Eastdene is expected to have?'

'I'm not exactly up there with the vicar in terms of my "village pillarage", but this seems to be the way of things in villages, even in the twenty-first century.'

'Even though it bears more than a passing resemblance, Eastdene isn't exactly Midsomer. I think there's been a fairly negligible number of murders in its history – possibly even none – and it is a tiny bit more racially representative of multicultural Britain.'

'Tiny's the word. There is the lovely Rupasinghe family, who run Londis.'

'And who regrettably send their four fiercely bright, good-looking and exceptionally charming children to Hartsmere.'

Mike laughed. 'Yes, that must be galling. But I do like this place more than I ever expected to like it.'

'Well, we offer both leisurely village pub lunches and bracing beach walks. And property is still cheap by the standards of the south-east. Personally, I love the fact that this little corner of Sussex has an off-the-beaten-track vibe that belies the fact it is only sixty-odd miles from London.'

'Blimey. Are you on the local council payroll?'

Eve laughed. 'If only. No, I'm just so glad you get it – get us. I mean, it's not like moving here was ever going to offer you a hugely exciting life.'

'Well, I didn't want an exciting life so much as I wanted a *life*. I do still have all my old friends. And a few new ones.'

'OK. But –' and Eve was conscious of fishing for details, though it was a conversation she felt they probably needed to have – 'there's no significant other you've had to, uh –' she could feel an uncharacteristic blush rising – '*abandon*?'

Mike Browning shook his head. 'I had a long-term partner for many years. We never got round to marrying but, to all intents and purposes, we were married. She died of ovarian cancer four years ago. She fought and fought; she was an extraordinary woman. She'd first had it in her twenties and then she beat it and was in remission for a decade, and then . . .' He shrugged.

Eve grimaced. 'I am so sorry.'

'Thank you – so am I. But, to give it a positive spin – which isn't easy – Sophie's death has been part of my life's journey, and it's brought me here to Eastdene.'

'And, of course, no children.'

'No – no children.' A pause. 'Apart from the *hundreds* of children.' Eve nodded. 'I've always been a one-swan guy, really. But I'm fine. I'm pretty happy. I'm actually growing things in a *garden* and I would never have thought that would happen.' Mike paused, looked intently at Eve. 'And if that other kind of stuff comes along then great. And how about you?'

So Eve told Mike about Simon and the girls. And, as she expected, he was non-judgemental, understood when she explained that, for many years, she had felt there was potentially far too much to lose by looking for a relationship – especially if you were a swan kind of person who had been lucky enough to find their soulmate for life and then lost them. 'So, anyway, another drink, or a pie?'

'Now you're talking,' said Mike.

So they had their pie and chips and then walked through the village, past the green and the pond with its pair of swans – a big strong cob and his elegant pen and their six peapod cygnets. Eve was briefly tempted to say something about the perfect swan family as they passed, but a quick glance at Mike told her not to. He was clearly thinking about the birds too.

'Just because someone very close to you dies, it doesn't mean they're not still very much a part of your life,' Mike said, suddenly and emphatically.

'Yes,' said Eve. 'My mother died too soon.'

Mike took Eve's arm and slipped it through his, where, to Eve's surprise, it felt entirely right. 'So, my place – or mine?' he said, gesturing towards the house.

Eve laughed. 'Shall we make it yours, then? Lovely house, but of course I can't stay long on a school night.'

'Well, *obviously* not.' Mike fished in his pocket for his keys.

Meanwhile, next door, as she put out the bins, Gail suddenly found herself very distracted indeed.

# 32

Johnny Nicholson and Cathy Gower did indeed hatch a plan in the pub, although it was left to Johnny to carry it out. Thus he acquired from the picture desk the email address of the paparazzo who had taken the original set of pictures of Stefan Sorensen and the anonymous girl. A swift, businesslike exchange of mails then brought forth a mobile number which, when Johnny dialled, was answered after just three rings.

'Neil Taylor?' said Johnny.

'Ah. Right. Yeah! Who's this?'

Johnny noted that Neil sounded very young. 'Hi, Neil, my name's Johnny Nicholson. I work at the *Courier*. Any chance of a quick coffee sometime in the next twenty-four hours?'

'Ah, yeah, sure. How about the next twenty-four minutes? I'm in Knightsbridge. Can easily get to you by half past.'

'Make it forty-five minutes and we'll call it lunch, yeah? Wagamama at one p.m.? I'll wear an old Comic Relief red nose and carry a rolled-up *Courier*.'

'See you at one.'

Johnny pressed *End Call* and tipped back in his seat, imagining Neil harassing sulky WAGs outside Harvey Nicks.

During the following forty-five minutes, Johnny attempted to distract himself by googling *Stefan and Anette Sorensen* and sifting through the thousands of results. Even though he was normally on top of this kind of research, Johnny was surprised by quite how many column inches had been generated over the past few years by Denmark's highest-profile exports since Bang & Olufsen. By the time he left for his date with Neil, Johnny was up to speed on all things Sorensen-related – right down to the fact that, just last week, planning permission to build what was described as 'a whimsical yet modernist tree-house-cum-folly' had been applied for by the fashionable all-female London architectural practice, Browning and Cox.

Johnny had also been very interested to discover that Anette Sorensen was a great deal more than a mere trophy wife, and that, even aside from her academic qualifications, she was (according to an interview with her 'Best British Friend', Anna Dershowitz) 'not only far more beautiful, but also much smarter than nearly everybody I know – and I know some *very* smart people.'

As Johnny scrolled through numerous images on Google – of Anette in evening dress at Elton's white-tie-and-tiara do for his AIDS foundation, laughing with George Clooney at the wedding of a mutual friend in the

Italian lakes and having an earnest-looking tête-à-tête
with Prince Charles at a Prince's Trust fundraiser – he
started wondering, What precisely does Anette Sorensen
do all day? Johnny had read enough to know that, while
undoubtedly a devoted wife and mother, even the excessively well-compensated CEO version of mum-and-wife
seemed unlikely to be quite enough to fill the days of a
woman like Anette Sorensen. There was a great deal more
to Anette, Johnny suspected, than the super-rich version
of making the kids' packed lunches, doing the school run,
helping on the PTA and dropping hubby off at the heliport
in the morning. Yet precisely what that 'more' might be,
he had no idea. While sucking on a Singha beer in Wagamama, he was still busily distracted by ordnance-surveying
a Sorensenville landscape that seemed ever more complex
the more he unearthed, when he heard a cough and, glancing up, took in the sight of the scruffily handsome – in
an off-duty Robert Pattinson sort of way – young man,
motorbike helmet in hand. He plonked himself down on
the bench opposite Johnny.

Rob stuck out his hand. 'Neil Taylor – nice to meet you.'

Johnny furrowed his brow. 'Right. so I'm going to cut
straight to the chase here, Neil. You look as though you
could do with a few quid, so tell me how much it would take
for you to lose those images of Stefan Sorensen and the girl
that you passed on to our picture desk a few days ago.'

Rob-as-Neil looked surprised. 'Um. I dunno. What's the
going rate?'

'For the memory card? You tell me. But try not to take the piss. It's not Beyoncé and Jay-Z having a foursome with Kim and Kanye.'

Rob/Neil grinned. 'Nah, but she is my girlfriend and I've got *lots* more of her, so that's got to be worth a bit, right?'

*Bingo!* 'Your girlfriend?'

'Yeah, and there *is* no Neil Taylor. Or, I'm sure there is a Neil Taylor somewhere, but he's not me. Pleased to meet you; I'm Rob.'

Johnny shrugged 'So what's the story, Rob? You're living a secret double life? Student by day, pap by late afternoon, international playboy by night, that sort of thing?'

Rob half grinned. 'That'd be a triple life, but yeah, I guess. I've been doing it for about a year, on and off. A mate got me into it, said it was easy money sometimes, so I thought I'd give it a go. I already had a motorbike and a camera and a scary student loan.' Rob shrugged.

'OK. Score any hits?'

'Yeah, a few. I got a couple of great Ashley Coles earlier this year; sold 'em to you lot. I tick over and I'm paying off my debts. But it's not like I can do it every day.' Rob shrugged.

'So explain this to me, right? You're papping Zoe and Sorensen *with Zoe's knowledge* – I assume she knows what you do for pin money – or you're just stalking your girl-friend for pervy kicks?' Johnny stared at Rob; Rob stared back at Johnny. To Johnny, Rob seemed momentarily flus-tered. 'C'mon, Rob; I mean, I've seen the pictures in context, shot after shot after shot, not just one picture in isolation.

So here's another question – what narrative did *you* impose on all those pictures when you looked at them? What's *the story*?'

Rob shrugged. 'You know the story. They're *fucking*. It's obvious.'

'Keep your voice down.' Johnny felt the age gap, already set to 'chasm', shift to 'Grand Canyon'. 'Right, so you're trying to get revenge by selling these pictures?' Rob shrugged again. Johnny wanted to pick him up and shake him. What was it with young people today, precisely? Why didn't they ever seem to give a shit about *anything*? Why were they so weirdly disconnected and *alien*? Or had middle-aged Neanderthals grunted precisely the same questions about their own tricky teens?

'Yeah, that was basically the plan.'

'Do you love Zoe?'

'Yeah.' Rob looked affronted. 'Of course.' Then he paused, ran his hands through his hair and raised his eyes to the ceiling, puffing out his cheeks and exhaling loudly. 'OK, I dunno anymore. Maybe.' He slumped back on his chair.

'So you were prepared to fuck that all up by getting these pictures published, were you? Not to mention, fuck things up for Sorensen, too? And his wife and kids, who I believe go to Zoe's mum's school?'

Another shrug. 'I didn't think it through. I was just angry.'

'Ever think of maybe just having a conversation with Zoe? Or –' Johnny couldn't contain the sarcasm – 'is that a bit retro, the whole concept of a conversation that isn't on Facebook or Twitter?'

Rob shook his head in exasperation, as if the ethics and morals of the situation were just irrelevant. 'Look, Zoe's *gone*. But maybe I can pay off my student loan and put down a rental deposit on a flat in somewhere shit at the end of the Central Line, or something. Can I have a beer?'

Johnny was dumbfounded. 'Yes, you can have a bloody beer. But do you youngsters actually believe in *anything* other than yourselves? Or is it all about the sex and the money? Can you do real emotions or just *emoticons*?'

'Yeah, fine, whatever – you go ahead and judge us because obviously you totally get what it's like to be young in, like, 2011, right?' Rob scowled.

Sitting there all sulky in his cheap leathers with his beer, Rob looked to Johnny like a very Poundland sort of anti-hero. 'Please, spare me the sob story. That's the other thing about young people – you're all so fucking self-righteous! Next thing, I suppose, you'll be demanding *respect*?'

'Oh, fuck off. Anyway, it's a complete *whatever* now because it's all backfired.'

'Really? And why's that, precisely? Because I'm about to offer you lots of money – how does two grand sound? – for your crappy pictures.'

Rob raised his eyebrows and looked at Johnny. 'Fuck off, two grand! Make it ten!'

Despite his best efforts, Johnny couldn't help snorting a laugh. 'Right. Yes, of course ten grand. Because your girlfriend is also the reincarnation of Princess Diana! Dick-head! Three grand – best and final.'

'Forget it, mate. Eight.'

From Johnny's perspective, it seemed that Rob was more furious at being patronized than he was about any other aspect of the whole sordid business. 'Oh, please, get a bloody grip, Rob. Sophisticated global player risks every-thing for pretty teenage intern? I really don't think so. This is a non-story to everybody except Zoe and her mum.'

Rob didn't miss a beat. 'You've not heard of Bill Clinton, then?'

At that moment, Johnny actually seriously considered slapping Rob, but bought himself a bit of time by hailing the waitress. 'Another two Singhas, please?' Yet, one look at Rob's face and Johnny knew the kid was simply brazen-ing it out; he was completely crushed. 'OK, so what's the plan now? Throw yourself into work and pick up a World Press Award for photography by 2040?'

'Like I said, fuck off! It may just be some big joke to you, but then you've probably never been fucked over by some-one you thought loved you.' *That* pulled Johnny up short. 'So, how much will you pay for the memory card?'

Johnny sighed. 'Five? And that's it.'

'Five is good. Cash. Tomorrow? I'll bring the card and we can swap. Same time, same place, yeah?'

'You've watched too many movies, Rob.'

'You can never watch too many movies.' Rob shrugged. 'See you tomorrow.'

As Rob left, Johnny motioned for the bill, picked up his phone and made a call.

'Cathy? Johnny here. OK, so the deal is done – five grand in cash, handover tomorrow, in return for the memory card. You sure you're all right for the money? Fine. I wish *I* had a few old mates like you. Oh, and by the way, and you'll love this, Cath: our enterprising young freelance paparazzo turned out to be – wait for it – Zoe's jealous boyfriend! Yeah, some chancer called Rob . . . I know, it's all very classy. So have you thought about telling Eve?' A long pause while he listened to Cathy's eloquently argued side of the argument. 'Fair enough, that's very much your call. As a mother, you inevitably have a much better idea of how to play it than I do.'

# SUMMER TERM

## 33

'Thanks so much for all this, Cath – I think it's the best thing to do.' Johnny stirred his soupy coffee while Cathy dunked a bag of something herbal into a mug of hot water. The resulting aroma of damp, Middle-Earthy sticks made him gag slightly, though presumably a cup of hot, wet, Hobbity wood was the price Cathy had to pay to maintain that enviable figure. Johnny was conscious of the stodgy layer that had lately settled around his midriff and which was no longer negated by his morning routine of crunches in front of CNN. He sighed. 'At least I hope it is.'

'It definitely is.' Cathy sipped her drink and, Johnny was pleased to note, wrinkled her nose; no gain was clearly a pain. 'Much as I don't want to give this little shit so much as a quid, if we do, I think we'll be completely shot of him. And, more to the point, so will Zoe.'

'Well, it's incredibly generous of you. And are you really not going to flag it up to Eve? Don't you think she'd want to know? Plus, you know, five grand ...?' Johnny shrugged.

Cathy shook her head. 'OK, so five grand *is* five grand,

but I have more than five grand kicking around and, well . . .' A pause. Cathy levelled her gaze at Johnny and took another sip of her sticks. 'The thing is, I feel I owe Eve something.' Then, having perhaps given too much away, Johnny noted Cathy changing her mind about this conversational tack. 'But I want to do it mostly because I'm Zoe's godmum.'

Johnny was intrigued. He knew Cathy wasn't short of cash; she was one of the highest paid members of staff on a well-paying newspaper and her husband was a big deal in commercial property. 'But that's not the only reason, very good reason though that is?'

'No, though it's mostly the reason and right now I think that's all that matters.' Cathy shrugged, smiling sheepishly – the kind of body language Johnny had never associated with the cool, controlled Cathy Gower. He noted that an expert in neurolinguistic programming would probably have had a field day.

'Come on, fess up!'

Cathy winced, closed her eyes and exhaled loudly. 'Look, Eve was my best friend for many years and, in some respects, still is, even though we hardly ever see each other. It's always been the kind of friendship you can pick up and put down at any time, so we do. But the fact is, I'm fifty-three and well paid and we're mortgage free and five grand is basically two *very* nice handbags or a few days skiing.' She shrugged again. 'And I have quite enough very nice handbags and I find I mostly prefer the après to the actual ski these days, so it's worth it because Eve dotes on the girls and she is an excellent human being and one hundred per cent doesn't deserve any of this kind of shit. And of course it goes without saying that, if you ever breathe a word of this to *anybody*, I will have you killed.'

'And rightly so. Trust me, Cath – I'm a journalist.'

Cathy laughed.

'Ah, hello, here comes trouble,' and Johnny nodded towards a young man wearing damp and slightly steaming biker's leathers, holding a helmet and standing in the doorway, scanning the room. 'Good-looking lad,' muttered Johnny to Cath. 'Doesn't look like a loser at all, does he?'

'No, quite remarkably un-loserish. A mini Robert Pattinson, in fact. But still – what an utter dick.'

Rob was scowling deeply by the time he reached their table, which made him look, to Johnny's eyes, entirely slappable. 'Who's this?' Rob flashed a fresh scowl at Cathy and plonked himself down on a bench opposite the booth in which Cathy and Johnny were sitting side by side.

'Charmed, I'm sure.' Cathy held out her hand. 'I'm Cathy, a colleague of Johnny's and a friend of Zoe's mum, Eve. A very good and longstanding friend – not to mention Zoe's godmother.'

Rob's scowl evaporated. 'Oh. OK.'

'That's all you can manage?' Cathy rifled through a large and expensive-looking red leather tote, extracted a Jiffy bag and pushed it across the table towards Rob. 'Now, here's your five K. Don't spend it all at once. Or, in fact, *do* spend it all at once. Maybe on scratch cards?'

'Ah, that reminds me – memory card, please,' prompted Johnny.

Rob pulled a small brown envelope out of the inside pocket of his leather jacket and handed it to Johnny. 'It's all on there.'

'Excellent! Well then, I think that concludes our business. Have a nice life!' Cathy got to her feet. Rob didn't move.

'You can go now. I'm not buying you a beer,' said Johnny cheerfully.

Rob rolled his eyes. 'I'll donate some of it to Children In Need. But there's something else you probably need to know.'

'And that is?' Cathy was shrugging herself into a very chic camel coat.

Rob said, 'Dontchawish dot com.'

'Come again?' said Johnny. 'We're hacks, not bloody MI6.'

'Dontchawish dot com. It's a website. After the Pussycat Dolls song?'

Johnny and Cathy looked equally blank. 'Right. So?' said Johnny.

'Zoe's on it. She's been on it for forty-eight hours. When you got in touch yesterday – after we spoke, and that – well, I tried to remove the footage, but apparently it's too late. It's already viral. Like, it's all over the net, if you know where to look.'

'So, am I reading this correctly? There's moving footage out there on the interwebs of Zoe walking down Bond Street with, uh, Stefan Sorensen – is that what you're saying?' Cathy shook her head, bemused. 'Well, I don't suppose that's the end of the world. I'm sure we can do something about it.'

Rob shook his head vigorously. 'For fuck's sake!' he hissed. 'You two are like something out of the Dark Ages. It's *not* Zoe walking down fucking Bond Street with Mr Sorensen.'

Johnny noted how it was simply 'Stefan' to the grown-ups but 'Mr Sorensen' to the youngster who, just maybe, was better brought-up than he seemed to be.

'It's a fucking *sex tape*. It's Zoe giving me a . . . a . . .' But Cathy shook her head briskly and held her hand in front of her face, palm outwards. Rob fixed her with a hard stare. 'Whatever. But it's your precious god-daughter having sex on camera, for fuck's sake!'

'And *you* did this?' Cathy asked. 'And it's all over the net now?' Rob nodded. ' "Revenge porn", that's what they call it, yeah?'

Rob snorted. 'Well, that's what the *Courier* would call it. But that's not what I'd call it.'

'So what would you call it?' asked Johnny.

'It's more about, well, sharing Zoe with a wider audience.'

At which point, Johnny, to whom this sounded equally offensive *and* lame, snapped. He stood up, leaned over the table and grabbed Rob's jacket, wrenching him half way across the table . . . maybe less like Brad Pitt in *Fight Club*, more Bob Hoskins in *The Long Good Friday*. 'Like fuck it is! Now look here, Sonny Jim.' Yup, definitely Bob. 'Firstly, um –' he caught sight of Cathy's expression – 'sit the fuck down and –' Johnny pushed Rob away again, sat down himself and extracted an iPad from his rucksack – 'let's have a look at this website.'

Rob looked abject. 'I'd rather not.'

'Bit late for an attack of the shys, isn't it, Rob?' said Cathy brightly, holding out her hand. 'And, while we're at it, I'll have that five grand back, yeah?'

Rob shook his head. 'I can't. I need it.'

'I bet you do! About as much as a *seventeen-year-old* girl-friend needs to be perved over by a million faceless onanists for the terrible crime of, basically, choosing to be consentingly hot, in private, for the lens of her beloved boyfriend!'

Rob winced. 'She fucked Sorensen. That wasn't part of the deal!'

And, though Cathy was still speaking *sotto voce*, she thumped her fists on the table. 'I bet it wasn't. It rarely is. But life isn't all about making deals, dick-for-brains. Only an actual fucking sociopath enters into a relationship with an agenda! So did you and Zoe sit down together in the first flush of your delightful young love and decide that, if one or other of you went off and shagged somebody else in the heat of the moment, then the other had an automatic pass to post their most private moments on the interwebs for potentially the *entire fucking world* to look at, laugh at and get off on?!'

'Of course not!' Rob stared intently at the tabletop.

'Right! Of course not! But that's what's happened. Zoe fucked up a bit – which, incidentally, we all do – so, as a result, she – and indeed her family, her mother and father and sister and auntie and grandparents – actually deserves this appalling humiliation, which may, in turn, just destroy all her teenage self-confidence before she's even acquired it?'

Rob shook his head and stared at the table, apparently refusing to be drawn. Is that, Johnny wondered, a tear on his cheek? It was. Rob glanced up, red eyes damp, his colour rising. He fixed his gaze on Cathy. '*She* fucked up first – then *I* fucked up. Oh, and by the way, Cathy, both me and Zoe know exactly how *you* fucked up.'

'Right,' said Cathy, smiling tightly. 'Of *course* you do!'

'Yeah. I was round Zoe's mum's one night and we were all talking over dinner about, like, relationships and stuff – me and Zoe and her mum and her sister – and Eve told us that once, years ago, before the girls were born, she thought she was going to lose their dad to, and I quote –' Rob wiggled his fingers in the air – ' "someone very close to me. About a year after we were married." And, of course, Zoe and her sister begged their mum to say who it was, but she refused. All she would say was that it was somebody close to her who was "leading a very different kind of life, in London". We talked about it later and it was Zoe who guessed.' Rob leaned back in his seat. 'So, *you* basically fucked up by fucking Zoe's *dad.*'

A riveted Johnny had just pulled up the Dontchawish website on his iPad, but stopped looking at the screen now to watch Cathy appraising the young man sitting opposite her, who was revelling in his revelation. Cathy nodded slowly. 'Clever. Nice work, Sherlock. And very close –' she leaned over the table, lowered her voice to whisper – 'but no cigar! It wasn't *me* who nearly destroyed Eve's marriage to Simon before it had found its feet; actually, it was somebody even closer to Zoe's mum.' As far as Johnny could tell, Cathy appeared to be hugely enjoying playing games with Rob. 'No, indeed, *my* biggest mistake was telling Eve all about it. It is to her eternal credit that she dealt with it like the class act that she is and always has been. But right now we shall let that particularly ancient sleeping dog lie.' Cathy turned to Johnny. 'So, what do *you* have to share with us, John Nicholson of the *Courier*?'

'Right, well, are you sure?' said Johnny. Cathy nodded and Johnny swivelled the tablet so that she could see her god-daughter doing the sort of things no godmother should ever witness.

Cathy watched, squinting slightly, for probably less than ten seconds before she tapped the pause button on the screen briskly. 'OK. I pretty much get the gist of that. Nice lighting there too, dickhead. Thinking of going into porn production professionally, are we?'

Rob shook his head, barely perceptibly. 'No. I want it

gone too, all right? I want all of this behind me. I just want to get on with my life. Here –' Rob pulled the envelope containing the money from his jacket and dropped it on the table – 'have this. Fuck it, I'm off.'

Johnny and Cathy watched in silence as Rob picked up his bag and strode across the room and out of the door without a backward glance. Cathy exhaled deeply. 'Goodness me. That went well!'

Johnny laughed. 'Come on, it could have been a lot worse. You've got your five grand back *and* we've got the memory card. All that remains is the, uh, Zoe problem.'

Cathy furrowed her brow. 'Actually, I've got an idea, but I think it will involve confronting both Eve and Zoe. This is going to be a . . .' She sighed, rolled her eyes heavenward. 'Well, it'll be a big deal. But it could just work.' A raised eyebrow. 'I lied to Rob just then, Johnny. Quite straightforward, really. I didn't need the little git gloating; I needed to be the boss of him. So, yes, a hundred thousand years ago, I had a fling with Simon Sturridge and then I fessed up to Eve and she, uh, dealt with it. And we moved on. And here we are now.'

Johnny's eyes widened. 'Right, so Eve just shrugged and forgave you and you all merrily stayed bezzy mates and she stayed with Simon and polished her halo on Friday nights? *Really?!* That kind of shit doesn't even happen in Jennifer Aniston movies.'

'Well, OK, it wasn't quite like that. We didn't speak for a few years. But when we did – which, incidentally, was just after Simon left Eve – we worked it out between the two of us. Eve's sister, Sonia, helped – she was our go-between. It feels like ancient history now, to be honest, but it does also account for the five grand.' Cathy looked at the fat brown envelope lying on the table and then slipped it into her bag. 'But now I have a plan for that, too.'

'Let me guess? Charity?'

'Yes, in a manner of speaking. So,' Cathy got to her feet, 'can I enlist your help in the Great Upcoming Eve-and-Zoe Kitchen-Table Showdown?'

Johnny was flattered. 'Of course – but really? You sure?'

Cathy nodded emphatically. 'I am very much surer than sure. I really want you on my team. Need you on it, really.'

Johnny grinned. 'I bet you say that to all the boys.'

# 34

9:58 a.m. on the twenty-ninth of April – which was also the
morning of the Royal Wedding – and Gail was panicking.
Not blind panic exactly, but still. She had announced to
Harry that she was 'quickly popping into school – your
school!' and had packed her 'satchel' with a lovely fresh
new notebook and some sort of sexy turbo-Biro with go-
faster stripes – a birthday present from Harry. This year
Gail's birthday had fallen on Easter Sunday, which had
also conveniently excused Harry's purchase of excessive
amounts of chocolates for his mum, the presence of which
she could still feel in all the wrong places around her middle. They'd had a good day together, much of it spent in and
around the Bell . . . and, on that topic, Gail had decided that
guilt was an entirely pointless emotion. However, here and
now, guilt free, though in a state of panicky faff, Gail
couldn't seem to find anything she needed. It was irrational,
obviously, but she suddenly craved a new pencil case and a
set of pristine pencils with her name embossed on the
side – and it wasn't even September.

'I swear to God I put a bunch of highlighter pens in that bloody bag last night.'

'You didn't, they're here,' said Harry, calmly retrieving the fluorescent markers from a dining chair. 'I used them last night. Mum, are you, like, panicking?'

'No, not panicking, just . . .' Gail paused, looked her son squarely in the eye. 'Yes, yes, I think I probably am.'

'Don't panic.' Harry shrugged. This was, in the eyes of an eleven-year-old, presumably all the advice a panicky mother could conceivably need.

'Yes, well, thanks for that, Haz. And you are OK here, then? I won't be too long. You can probably watch weddingy things already.'

Harry rolled his eyes. 'I'm not watching weddingy things, Mum. Girls like weddings, boys just put up with them.'

Gail snorted with laughter. Yeah, that's about right. 'Well. Designing a treehouse *is* a brilliant idea, but I think you might need a bit of adult assistance with that, so can we default to the Xbox for an hour or so?' Gail registered Harry's expression: resigned, bemused, with a hint of fondly patronized. 'Sorry, I'll shut up now.' She leaned towards him, instinctively half grazing his cheek with a distracted kiss that was ninety per cent breath, ten per cent skin. Gail felt as if the quasi-air-kiss had somehow transgressed a subtle new Year Six boundary, even if Harry himself didn't seem fazed by it. Perhaps he hadn't even noticed.

'I'll be fine, Mum, really – go.' And Harry looked, Gail thought, suddenly very tall and positively adolescent and, as she headed for the front door, she smiled to herself.

It was 10:05 a.m. and, despite living less than two hundred metres from her appointment, Gail was already late, which was unprofessional. With a hint of a springy breeze in the air, she found herself shivering as she walked up the path to Eastdene Community Primary School. She rang the bell.

'Hello, Gail – welcome,' said Mike.

As she'd expected, the staffroom was full of the governors, seated in a circle. Gail was momentarily tempted to take the remaining empty chair and say, 'Hello, my name is Gail Prince. God, grant me the serenity to accept the things I cannot change, the courage to change the things I can and the wisdom to know the difference.' Instead, she said, 'Hi! So sorry I'm late!' Ten warm, smiling faces turned towards her.

'No problem, Gail,' said Mike. 'We all know it's those children who live closest to school who are the last ones in the door every morning.'

'Yes, and it was precisely comparisons with the children that I was hoping to avoid.'

There was warm laughter from all around the room. Phew! thought Gail. Maybe this will all be fine . . .

## 35

Just after ten a.m. Eve swung the Volvo out of the Barn's drive. Within fifteen minutes, plus three sets of traffic lights, two mini-roundabouts and an apparently mushroomed-overnight Morrisons, Eve was on the outskirts of Battle and turning left into the drive of a large, rambling, gone-to-seed (but pretty, she had to admit, even if that roof looked a bit dodgy) Victorian mansion with a vaguely institutional air. She parked, took a moment to inspect her make-up in the mirror and, as she rang the doorbell, suddenly and inexplicably – but mostly, she felt, absurdly – suffered a surge of something not unlike nerves, which hurtled her, shivering slightly, straight back to school in about 1973. Ridiculous.

After a brief interval, the heavy oak door swung open to reveal a smiling man with quite a lot of beard, wearing cargo pants and a faded 'The Clash – *London Calling*' T-shirt. Smiling warmly, he held out his hand. 'Ah, hello there, Eve! Adam Vine. Welcome to Heatherdown!' Eve noted a surprisingly firm grip.

Five minutes later, she was settling into a beaten-up old leather club chair in Adam Vine's untidy office, nursing a mug of strong, sweet tea.

'I'm sorry about only calling you yesterday, Adam, despite meaning to for literally weeks, but many thanks for agreeing to see me at such short notice. I'm very grateful. So, I want to know everything about this place and how you run it,' said Eve.

Heatherdown's head teacher raised an eyebrow and smiled. 'Well, obviously we're flattered, though I'd have thought you had this educational lark pretty much down pat by now.'

Eve laughed. 'Look, I was so glad to hear how good Heatherdown has been for Jordan that I thought, if you didn't mind, I'd try to see how right you're clearly getting whatever it is you're doing.' Eve paused. 'I mean, it will come as no surprise to you that I don't entirely share your educational ethos. If I did, then I suppose I should have sent my own daughters here.'

Adam nodded. 'Or be doing my job?'

'Well, quite. And, of course, it's not personal. It's just, well, I . . .' Eve paused, looked at Adam, a man-of-beard, early forties-ish – hard to be entirely accurate because of that beard – and wearing a pair of (and Eve felt this was not a good look for men) something Ugg-alike in the boot department. 'Well, that's just not the way I've done things. Call me old-fashioned, but I'm very much of the reading, writing and 'rithmetic school of head teachers, forgive me.'

Adam raised an eyebrow and smiled. 'With Native American sweat-lodge-style drumming just a tiny bit further down your dream curriculum? Perhaps just past quantum physics and Mandarin?'

Eve laughed. 'Something like that, yes.'

Adam nodded. 'But you want to see what it is we do, and why? And, indeed, the kind of results we get? And by "results" I don't necessarily mean the sort of thing that floats Ofsted's boat – or yours?'

Eve nodded, intrigued. 'I get that. League tables are not really your bag, right?'

'Not really. I appreciate they are an indicator of some sort of success for those who define success in that kind of way, but that's just not my – our – definition of success, educationally speaking.'

'And your definition is?'

Adam frowned and peered quite closely at Eve. 'You really want to know? Or you're humouring me?'

'To be honest, I'm not sure I have it in me to humour anyone, Adam. No, I genuinely really want to know. Despite all the Native American drumming and your lack of Suzuki violin and non-contact rugby, my ex-husband is singing your praises and you are apparently doing wonders for his –' and there was only the very slightest pause – 'son.'

'Jordan is great and has a lot of potential. So, what are you doing for the rest of today?'

Eve shrugged. 'Well, you know, there is a wedding on TV I thought I might watch.'

'Ah, yes – we emailed our parents to ask if they'd want to have the children off school, sitting at home, watching some young people they don't actually know getting married and all of them said, effectively, "Not really, since they've only just gone back to school – and since you've asked!" So we told the children this morning that if anybody *did* want to watch it, the TV would be on in the library. However, to be honest, I'm not expecting much take-up, even from our princessiest girls, because we've got a bumper crop of lambs, including a Kate and a William. So why don't I give you the tour and I guarantee you'll learn pretty much everything you need to.'

'Really?'

It was Adam's turn to shrug. 'Well, you won't have a qualification at the end of it, but I can give you a head teacher's sticker.'

'Only if I deserve it. I'd hate to be getting any special treatment.' Eve grinned and stood up. 'Come on then.'

'I think half the school's down in the fields this morning,' said Adam, shrugging himself into a very un-woolly, non-ethnic smart-fabric over-garment and a pair of Hunter wellies. 'They'll have built a camp by now.'

Eve's day was enlightening, and fun, too. She could see perfectly clearly that everybody – staff and pupils alike – enjoyed themselves while they learned. However, she remained to be convinced that an entirely free-range education was any more than a glorified kids' camp. Not that everything was al fresco. The afternoon was spent making and playing musical instruments constructed from *objets trouvés*. Then there was, Eve was surprised to see, some 'proper' music being played – with actual instruments – and singing, too. Meanwhile, the whole morning had been about problem solving, fire building, whittling, cooking and camp construction in the woods. There were so few pupils that all the age and ability groups were mixed, which Eve realized immediately created a family dynamic, with all the good (in-this-together-ness) and bad (sibling squabbles and rivalry) that inevitably entails.

Eve had watched the children with great interest – and particularly Jordan, who was very neatly lining up sticks for the roof of the bivouac, in length order, while singing. At first, she couldn't quite make out the song, though his pitch appeared to be perfect. She edged slightly closer and then, with a smile, picked up the lyrics: 'Don't stop me now, I'm having such a good time . . .'

'Satisfied customer, there, clearly,' said Eve, jerking her head towards Jordan.

Adam grinned. 'The Queen stuff is good, but just wait till you hear his Michael Jackson medley. He's pretty much inches away from the final of *Britain's Got Talent*.' There was a one-beat pause. 'Not that I've ever watched that show, obviously.'

Eve laughed. 'So Jordan is doing well?'

'Very. We seem to speak his language. We really don't mind if he only wants to toast the *pink* marshmallows and not the white ones.'

'The first time I met him, I straight away thought he was . . .' Eve paused and stumbled; there was a catch in her throat. 'I thought he was properly *special* – not as in special-needs special. I haven't been able to get him out of my mind, really.'

'Come on, let's grab a cuppa,' said Adam.

Back in his office, with more tea, Adam said, 'So, what do you think of our "special" kids?'

Eve considered this for a moment. 'That they were obviously all "special" in their different ways.'

'Yeah, but let's face it, some kids are more special than others. You don't have to slay me with faux political-correctness – not everyone is born equal and nor, in my humble opinion, should they be. Could you pick out which ones were most "special"?'

'Well, there was definitely the little boy called Mohammed and another called Jack, and a girl called, er, Melody, or Harmony?'

'Liberty?'

'That's the one. But those are the only names I can remember.'

'Interesting. You're good at this. Mohammed – Mo, to most of us – is currently being formally assessed for an autistic-spectrum disorder. Jack has already been diagnosed as Asperger's and Liberty is almost certainly somewhere on the spectrum, but her parents don't want to play the "labelling" game and they've already decided to home school from eleven.'

'Wow.'

'Yes, wow. But we have a lot more Mos, Jacks and Libertys by-any-other-names – believe me. In fact, probably more than fifty per cent of our kids are quantifiably "different" or somehow "special". We're known locally for that, without having any formal remit to teach these more challenging or just plain *different* children.' Adam shrugged. 'We just crack on with it.' He paused. 'Or, rather, we will crack on with it until we close.'

'Yes, I was going to ask you about that.'

Adam shrugged. 'In a nutshell, we currently have forty-eight pupils and ten full-time teaching staff. Each pupil's parents are paying £2,750 a term, which is arguably about two to three thousand less than they should be paying, and staff salaries average out at about thirty K, while our annual heating and electricity bills currently run well into five figures, never mind any of the other maintenance required by a fifty-acre site.' He paused. 'So, as the Americans allegedly say, you do the math.'

'Yes. I can do the math.'

'I used to occasionally suggest to the owners that we did something ruthlessly capitalist like, I dunno, sell off ten of our fifty acres to some property developers to build a bunch of executive Tudorbethan detacheds. They actually looked into it, but it turns out we're an "Outstanding Area of Natural Listed Conservation", or whatever. And, inevitably, we've got a lot of bats.'

'Oh, dear. I know all about bats. My house is a converted

barn and we had the bat police – Batman, basically – hovering over our shoulders every time we even talked about moving a bloody tile.' Eve smiled. 'You haven't a snowball's in hell.'

Adam grinned wryly. 'My thoughts precisely. Anyway, we've got enough in the kitty to see us through another year, and after that –' a shrug – 'who knows?'

Eve sighed. 'Yes; of course, I wish you very well – if only, selfishly, for Jordan's sake.'

And then the conversation turned to other things that even the head teachers of schools as fundamentally unalike as Heatherdown and Ivy House have in common – notably the children, and the staff. And then, after a refilled mug of tea, Eve glanced at her watch and grimaced. 'I genuinely had no idea of the time. I really must stop taking up so much of yours.'

Adam got to his feet. 'It's been an absolute pleasure, Eve – really.' Eve knew he meant it; the feeling was mutual, and she told him.

'That's very kind of you. And I hope you catch up with that wedding.'

Eve laughed. 'I'm sure there'll be nothing else on TV for days.' Eve leaned forward conspiratorially, to confess. 'And I know I shouldn't care about seeing the dress, but I care almost as much as I did about seeing Diana's. Does that make me ridiculous?'

'Far from it; I think it makes you female,' said Adam. Eve smiled.

An hour later, Eve recounted her day to Simon on the phone, with, very uncharacteristically, her mouth half full while she ate a quick stand-up supper of defrosted chilli and kept half an eye on the royal-wedding highlights on the news. She spoke non-stop for the best part of five minutes without a break, if not quite zealously, then certainly extraordinarily enthusiastically.

'And so,' said Eve, finally winding up, 'Jordan really is in the best place he could possibly be, in case you were in any doubt. And that really *is* a lovely dress.'

'Sorry?' said Simon.

'Princess Kate, or whoever she is now. Lovely frock. Apparently it's Alexander McQueen, as favoured by my lady hedge-funders and venture capitalists. Anyway, as I was saying—'

'OK. No, we were not in any doubt, because the results have been palpable. And I'm delighted by your frankly rather sudden and passionate conversion to a Bear Grylls-ish approach to education. In fact, I think it's bloody marvellous that you're now embracing your destiny so wholeheartedly.'

Eve was swallowing the last of the chilli as she blanched at this. 'I'm not sure it's Bear Grylls-ish, precisely. But what *are* you on about, Simon? Destiny?'

'Come on, Evie, you know exactly what I mean!'

'But I don't.' Eve sounded as perplexed as she felt. 'Really, for probably the very first time in God knows how many years, I genuinely *don't*.'

'Oh, well, you're pretty smart, you'll work it out,' said Simon. 'And now, Mrs Sturridge, I have to go. Oh, and while you're admiring Kate's wedding dress, the rest of the world is, according to Ed and his social media, apparently wholly fixated on her hot sister's arse.'

Eve squinted at the TV, feeling obliged to have an opinion. 'Yes, well, it is a very nice arse.'

'Indeed. Oh, and before you go, how's our Zo?'

'Hm.' Eve considered her answer. 'Reserved, maybe? Ever since she returned from New York, she's kept pretty quiet, slept late and mooched around the house, whether sulkily or simply distractedly it's hard to tell, but all very *teenage*. Obviously life at the Barn doesn't quite measure up to Park Avenue, but I'm pretty sure she's revising her head off, so maybe that's all it is.' Eve didn't bother mentioning that Zoe consistently evaded answering questions, habitually shut conversational doors in her face and generally acted like a pain in the butt. 'Oh, and there's another thing. Alice tells me she makes these videos, alone in her bedroom – just her, talking to the camera on her laptop about girl stuff. Alice said she's seen one Zo made about revision and it's really funny. I haven't seen them yet, but apparently they're on . . . er . . . YouTube. Anyway, her friends watch them and comment on them. It seems to be a *Thing*, probably because they're all equally grounded with their revision, so it's a way of keeping in touch.'

'Sounds suitably twenty-first century, albeit harmless,' said Simon.

'That's what I thought. Still, it makes me feel old.'

'I imagine that's probably the point – as indeed that young Mr Bowie made our parents feel old. Give her a bit of space and I'm sure she'll be fine.'

'OK, will do. And now that's the front door. How one very slim teenage girl and a fat old dog can make quite such a commotion, I have no idea; anyway, I'm off now, Simon. Talk soon.'

In truth, Eve wasn't sure how convincing a liar she was, but no matter. There was nobody at the door; she was blessed with an empty house and all the peace and silence she wanted, which, in turn, would give her ample time to think about Simon's peculiar phraseology: *I think it's bloody marvellous that you're now embracing your destiny so whole-heartedly* . . .

Nope – no idea at all. Eve turned back to the television, where that nice Kate Middle-Class with the dull dress sense, until now, that is, and the upwardly-mobile and high-maintenance hair was apparently a duchess. And, remembering Kate's dead mother-in-law's wedding as vividly as if it had been, say, fifteen years ago, rather than nearly thirty, made Eve feel old. Still, Kate's dress was much better than Diana's.

# 36

A naked and backlit Zoe shifted position so that she was now straddling Rob, who was sitting on a small, hard chair adjacent to the window of his bedsit on the ground floor of a solidly suburban street, close to his campus. Zoe leaned her cheek on the top of his head. 'Babes. Let's move this chair a little bit to the left so that it is, like, *right* in front of the window, yeah?' A pout. 'Cos it'd be mean to deprive random passers-by of the sight of us fucking, yeah?'

Rob grinned. 'What would you say if I bought you a mortarboard and gown and we played, uh, teachers?'

'I'd say,' Zoe paused, giggling, 'see me in my office after class!'

And then Zoe and Rob had surprisingly languid, leisurely and show-offy sex right there, in the window. And Zoe half watched an elderly man exit the house opposite with a miniature schnauzer, and very much enjoyed the startled look on his face when he glanced up at Rob's window. She enjoyed it even more when, slack jawed, he dropped the dog's lead.

'Just a minute, babes.' Zoe got off Rob, whose back was to the window, and sauntered casually over to the door, where she flicked the light switch. The room was suddenly very dark; the old man could obviously no longer see a thing; however, Zoe could see him – and he remained riveted to the spot and staring at the window, nonetheless.

'Look at that poor old perv over the road –' Zoe climbed back on to Rob's lap – 'staring at us. We probably just made his day!'

At which point, Rob came, very suddenly and oddly mechanically; Zoe noticed the difference, even if she'd have found it impossible to articulate what that difference might be. All she knew was that there was a palpable, swift and shocking disconnection between them and, involuntarily, she let out a startled little cry and moved swiftly away across the room, curling herself into a ball on Rob's grubby old IKEA sofa, previously the scene of the opposite sort of sex to whatever this had been.

Rob, on the other hand, knew exactly what this had been: the *end*. He had the decency to actually blush as he recalled the best sex he'd ever had, with Barista Girl, even as he looked at this crumpled and pathetically unsexy and reduced version of Zoe, who was now also inexplicably wracked by sobs. What were they all about? Was she feeling guilty? Sad? Whatever . . . He shrugged; emotional empathy had never been his strong suit. Anyway, in a phrase he would use later, during post-match analysis down the pub, Rob figured that, all things considered, when it came to shafting each other, he and Zoe were probably just about equal.

'If you make coffee, I'll have a shower, yeah?' said Rob, businesslike as Zoe sniffed and nodded. And then, thank fuck, thought Rob, I can dump you. In the shower, his mind wandered away from the Zoe problem, such as it was, and towards the EasyJet booking he'd made that afternoon, while Zoe had been glued to that bloody wedding. Marrakech. Cool. In the shower, washing Zoe away, Rob started whistling.

# 37

On Monday morning, Eve was in school by 7:45 a.m., 'pimping, primping and prepping for Ofsted', as she described it in her text to Gail, who, with unfailing professionalism, turned up at 8:00 a.m.

The Ofsted inspector herself arrived on the dot of 8:45, bearing a crumpled copy of the *Courier*, and asked Eve for 'a few words alone, prior to the inspection proper, if that's possible?'

Eve ushered the inspector into her office. Her name was Jean Starling and she had inspected Ivy House on two previous occasions, during which she and Eve had struck up a professional rapport.

'Mrs Starling! Good to see you again – and welcome to Ivy House at a time of, I think it's fair to say, a degree of transition.'

'Yes, indeed, good to see you too, Mrs Sturridge. So, there's obviously a lot going on. Heard you on *Today*, by the way. Definitely held your own with Humphrys, though I hear he's a complete pussycat in real life.'

'Thank you! I wasn't actually in the studio, though, so we didn't meet. I was what they call –' Eve made air quotes with her fingers – ' "down the line".'

'Well, either way, it was very interesting. The whole thing was – is – interesting.'

Eve took this as a cue to take a deep breath. 'And, in the context of your inspection, possibly challenging, too?'

Jean Starling, Eve noted, had a brisk air but very kind eyes. 'Mrs Sturridge, you know as well as I do that, as an independent school, you are subject to what we call a Section 162A inspection every three years. But given what I'm hearing about Ivy House – about the imminent development of a boarding facility and a provision for special needs, which has not previously been a part of the school's offering – well!' Jean Starling paused. 'There are two ways this could go. We could just do the full inspection and – this is very much off the record, I hasten to add – given some of the quite dramatic changes I had not hitherto foreseen, I could conceivably end up not automatically rubber-stamping an "Outstanding" for Ivy House. In fact, there's a chance that it could be effectively demoted to a "Good".'

Eve nodded. She thought she knew where Jean Starling was headed with this. 'A "Good" is not really an option for the school's Principal, I think.'

'Yes, I thought it probably wasn't. And I can see why that would be, too. Especially,' Jean Starling paused and made eye contact with Eve, '*especially* as you do such a good job.'

Eve could easily have hugged her but instead settled for a heartfelt, 'Thank you.'

'Anyway, given there are so many changes already underway –' Jean waved towards the window of Eve's office at the precise moment a bulldozer trundled past on its way to the building site – 'we can put it off until a later date, at which point we would do an inspection of both the educational and the boarding provisions. In fact, we could spend this morning doing an inspection so you can implement an action plan that, in turn, will –' she paused and appeared to be choosing her words carefully – 'or rather, *might* – possibly even *should* – result in Ivy House maintaining its excellent reputation.'

'Right. Yes, I hear you,' said Eve. 'And I'm very grateful. I really am.'

'That's all fine, then. So the team are already inspecting your Early Years provision, with the help of, ah –' Jean thumbed through some papers attached to her clipboard – 'Mrs Charteris?'

'That's right, yes.'

'OK. So we can carry on simply in an advisory capacity, if you like?'

Eve nodded, emphatically. 'That would be great, yes.'

'Good, well –' Jean slipped her clipboard into her briefcase – 'that's all sorted, then.' She offered Eve an outstretched hand. 'Keep up the good work, Mrs Sturridge, either here or, indeed –' she paused – 'elsewhere. And I probably shouldn't say this, but . . . Well –' she smiled – 'I may be an Ofsted inspector, but I am also a mother and I have a thirteen-year-old daughter who is on her third school and we still haven't got it right.' She shrugged, and sighed. 'There's never any point forcing square pegs into round holes. We do what we have to do for our children, don't we?'

'We do, yes!' Tempting though it was to throw her arms around the inspector, Eve resisted. 'Seriously – thank you.'

'No, thank *you*,' said Jean. 'We'll be in touch. Good luck, Mrs Sturridge.' And then she was gone and, as the office door closed behind her, for the first time in her life, Eve air-punched a *Yeeeees*! And then she thought of Jean Starling's words – *We do what we have to do for our children, don't we?* – and . . . God, I really must call Zoe.

Eve stuck her head round her office door and said to Gail, 'Remind me that I really must call Zoe at lunchtime.'

Gail was very hands-on with a Krispy Kreme doughnut. 'Mmmm, will do! How is Zoe, anyway? Indeed, more to the point, *where* is Zoe these days?'

'Good questions, both of them. She is fine, I think – albeit in A-level revision hell. I haven't seen her all weekend, actually; she's hunkered down at Simon and Ed's, says she can focus better there, for some reason.' Eve shrugged. 'Teenagers are a law unto themselves. You have all this to look forward to.'

Gail smiled wanly. 'Righto. And, before I forget, you might want to turn your phone back on, now that Mrs Starling has left the building. Oh, and you've had a message from Cathy Gower and another one from John Nicholson at the *Courier*.'

'Really?' Eve looked baffled. 'That's terribly enthusiastic of them both!'

'Yes, they seemed very keen to speak to you. Asked me if you were going to be around later. I got the impression they meant later later, like this evening.'

'Curiouser and curiouser. And, on the subject of Alice, I've got to speak to her too. God, today is already far too much.' And, much as I love them, I'm not around later for Johnny or Cathy, thought Eve. Very much not . . .

That evening, Eve opened the Barn's front door to Mike Browning for the first time, with a rather self-conscious desire to show her home off to its best advantage. This wasn't hard; the garden – pretty enough in midwinter – was just starting to come into its own in May. Eve attempted to interpret everything through Mike's urbane eyes: the hall with its mussed and faintly smelly dog bed and ranks of the girls' gumboots standing to attention, many long out-grown; the expansive kitchen and dining room that could easily absorb a far bigger family than Eve's small unit of three; the view out on to the terrace with its inspired-by-Japan planting – albeit from a distance, as Eve had never been to Japan; and the steps down to the lawn and that gloriously bosky, green and pleasantly Blakean view right across the Dene valley. The view, unexpectedly special, always came as a surprise to first-time visitors. Eve pushed the bifold doors leading from the kitchen to the terrace wide open and stepped out. Mike was obligingly impressed. 'Wow, that is some view.'

'Isn't it just? I never get tired of it.' It was somehow extremely important to Eve that Mike should like where she lived. 'There's a swimming pool just round that corner, too. Did I tell you that I had a swimming pool?'

'No, you neglected to share that. That's terribly posh. You are patently the head of an independent school. Nobody I knew in Islington had a swimming pool, though I bet there are a couple now, tucked away in some excavated basements.'

Eve laughed. It was entirely possible that the nicest thing about Mike – aside from all the other very nice things about him – was the fact that he made her laugh. It was probable she hadn't laughed quite as much as this since her earliest years with Simon, which augured well, obviously, even as it scared her a little too. But for now, at least, it was all about the laughter. Well, mostly the laughter.

'I think, if I hadn't been down here already for a few months, I might be quite thrown by the casual glamour of some of these rural lifestyles hidden behind high gates. Everybody seems to have a *Grand Design*.' Mike shrugged. 'My comfort zone was a small chunk of North London in which I was lucky to buy a tall, skinny townhouse with a patio garden on a mixed sort of street way back when I landed my first proper job with a decent salary, in the eighties. Twenty-five years later, having never felt the slightest inclination to move, I watched the street reinvent itself from mostly pretty shabby to insanely fashionable and full of your big media cheeses, *Newsnight* stalwarts, the cooler sort of merchant bankers and ethical venture capitalists.'

'Well, perhaps that's why the media gave you such a hard time? When they saw your London pile.'

'Yes, "London pile" – very much a *Courier* sort of phrase. And I'm sure you'll be using it yourself if – or when – you write for them again.' Mike smiled easily but Eve winced slightly; she had hoped to keep politics off the getting-to-know-you agenda for a little longer. 'But yes, obviously they were jealous of my smart property moves. And now, at the age of forty-nine, having spent years never more than a two-minute walk away from the perfect cup of coffee, a ripe mango, an Ayurvedic massage and some cognitive behavioural therapy, I am – *finally* – entirely charmed by the countryside.' Mike turned away from the view. 'And, indeed, many of those who sail in her, too.'

'Even the fifty-four-in-a-few weeks'-time-year-olds?'

'*Especially* the fifty-four-in-a-few-weeks'-time-year-olds.'

And then they both swivelled round at the sound of a door slamming. Alice, in jodhpurs, trailing a distinctly foxy-smelling Barney, breezed into the kitchen and gave Mike only the briefest of curious glances, as though there were strange men hanging out in her kitchen every day.

'I'm sorry he smells so gross,' said Alice. 'I'll put him in the shower. Hello.' This last was to Mike.

'Yes, do give him a shower, darling. And this is Mike, Alice. He's also a head teacher.' As if that explains anything, thought Eve.

'Right. Is it some sort of club?' said Alice, smiling. This was clearly about as interested as she was going to get.

Which suited Eve fine. 'Maybe. Maybe it is!'

'What school do you go to, Alice?' said Mike, though of course he knew the answer; it had, noted Eve, been one of the very first things they'd talked about over their pub supper.

'Westdene Girls' Grammar. We have no idea how I passed the eleven plus, do we, Mum?'

Eve smiled and shrugged. 'You worked very hard, Alice. Don't be so tough on yourself.'

'Yeah, well. I'm probably about to fail a load of GCSEs, but luckily I want to work with horses, which doesn't need GCSEs, just horse-sense.'

'My sister rode very well when she was your age. She was into eventing,' said Mike, wholly unexpectedly.

'Really?' said Eve.

'Yes, we have horses in the Black Country.'

'Cool. Eventing's my thing, too.' A beat. 'Where's the Black Country?'

Mike laughed. 'The Midlands. Near Birmingham.'

Alice shrugged. 'See what I mean? I'm practically a spacker.'

Eve raised her eyes and threw her hands into the air while Mike laughed, mostly at Alice's slack-jawed look of horror. 'Um, I think we head teachers tend to prefer the term "special needs", don't we, Eve?' Eve was shaking her head, speechless.

'I cannot. Believe. I just said that,' said Alice. 'I'm actually, like, grounding myself. Like, now.'

'Actually,' said Eve, covering her shame while peering through her fingers, 'would you mind awfully grounding yourself right after you've fumigated Barney?'

Mike waited until Alice had left the room. 'Great kid!'

'God!' said Eve. '*Spacker*? What was she thinking?'

Mike laughed. 'I suspect that's the least of it, frankly.'

'Do you think?' Eve shook her head. 'Sometimes I have a sneaking suspicion that I don't know my daughters at all. Which reminds me, I must call Zoe; I tried at lunch and couldn't get through, and I haven't seen her in an age.'

## 38

However, it turned out there was no need for Eve to call Zoe because – quite unexpectedly and very suddenly – by the time Eve and Mike were on to their second glasses of wine and into double figures with the olives, there was the sound of a slammed door and then Zoe was right there in the kitchen, while behind her was, inexplicably, *Cathy*. Eve hopped off her stool, firstly attempting to hug her daughter – who stood rigid and unsmiling and submitted only grudgingly to a maternal display of affection – and then transferring her attention to Cathy, whom she kissed warmly on both cheeks.

'Gosh, what an absolute thrill to see you too, Cath. But why on earth didn't you say you were coming?'

Cathy glanced at Zoe. 'Well, the thing is, I kind of had a date with Zo – a godmotherly sort of bonding thing – didn't I, Zoe?' Zoe nodded, though her poker face revealed nothing. Cathy continued, 'And so I wasn't even sure if I would have time to see you, Eve. But then one thing led to another and Zoe suggested I come back to the Barn and I, uh, thought that we three might have a chat, if that was possible. But, um . . .' Cathy tailed off and glanced quickly across at Mike, fortunately quite a skilled taker of emotional temperatures and reader of evolving situations, but who was also, at this point, as unsure about where the evening was headed as was Eve. In one area, however, he was definitely a step ahead of his date; he knew that whatever the evening was about it was most assuredly not about him, and so he would extract himself from the situation, though preferably not before he'd reached the bottom of this excellent glass.

Meanwhile, Cathy felt ever so slightly foolish; even her best-laid plans hadn't included Eve potentially entertaining a handsome man at her home on a Friday night – even though there was no reason on earth why she shouldn't. Cathy was, in fact, delighted that her friend appeared to be doing this very thing . . . but how to get him to go? Zoe, meanwhile, was wriggling uncomfortably on a bar stool and picking desultorily at the olives, her expression still unreadable.

Mike looked from Cathy to Eve. 'Right, the evening has been a total pleasure thus far, Eve, and we are going to do it again very soon, I hope, but right now . . .' Mike held out a hand to a slightly surprised-looking Zoe, who took it reluctantly. 'Hi, I'm Mike, by the way, and I think I may be surplus to requirements, here –' a very slight smile from Zoe – 'so I'm going to shoot off now, Eve.' Mike leaned forward and kissed Eve on both cheeks. He took the opportunity, too, to inhale her scent, which was something he vaguely recognized but couldn't place and which he liked very much. 'No need to see me out, really. I'll call you tomorrow, if I may?'

Eve nodded mutely. She was glad of Mike's social skills, though she recognized that the evening had taken a turn she would not have chosen. 'Yes, do please call tomorrow, Mike – and thanks.' The front door hadn't even shut behind Mike before Eve was glancing between her oldest friend and her eldest daughter, her brow furrowed in puzzled bemusement. 'So, what's going on?'

'Is that your boyfriend?' asked Zoe.

'Well, who knows? Maybe. But we're not there yet.' Eve shrugged while Zoe grimaced. 'But enough about me. How's *your* boyfriend?'

'I don't have a boyfriend. He's dead to me. He's a bastard.'

'Oh, honey, I'm so sorry.' Eve reached for her daughter again, but Zoe flinched.

'No. Leave me alone. You don't know anything.' Zoe practically spat the words at her mother.

'Er, can I have a glass of that Dutch courage, Eve?' This was from Cathy.

'God, I am so sorry, Cath. I am just completely thrown by your presence – in the nicest possible way, believe me. So,' Eve poured a big glass of the delicious red and pushed it across the island towards her friend, 'to what do I owe the pleasure?'

'It's not a pleasure, Mum. It's a nightmare!' muttered

Zoe, who then very suddenly broke down in tears. Rather than Eve, it was Cathy, sitting next to Zoe, who was in the best position to put her arm around her. For a moment, Eve wasn't sure how that made her feel, precisely, but feared it was something unexpectedly close to envy.

'Your brilliant and beautiful daughter has, I'm afraid, made a few mistakes and is currently paying the price. Which is why I set up the godmum date, so we could talk about it between us first. It's quite a high and not very nice sort of price and, if you sit down, Eve, she and I will try to explain.' Cathy nudged her silent god-daughter gently with her elbow. 'Won't we, Zo?'

Zoe nodded, between sobs, while Eve simply did as she was instructed. She was not only entirely flummoxed but also, somehow, nervous. 'Come on, then; out with it.'

And so Zoe started talking, slowly and very, very quietly at first, but becoming louder and more vociferous as it unfolded, and Eve strained to listen, desperate to interrupt but forcing herself to sit in silence. Eventually, after what felt like forever to Eve but was probably less than three or four minutes, Zoe started to run out of steam: 'And so I just, like, went – but I turned around at the door and Stefan just looked at me blankly, and . . .' Zoe just broke off suddenly, as if she'd just realized that nobody listening had actually forced her to confess, and suddenly she clammed up tight, eyes wide and scared, as if shocked by how far she'd allowed herself to go.

Eve stared at her eldest daughter, uncomprehending.

But Zoe gathered herself, momentarily: 'And you don't know anything, Mum. You don't have a fucking clue about me and ... and ... *anything*! You think I'm, like, Miss Pretty-Perfect-Straight-As, with my whole fabulous life ahead of me, and –' properly uncontrollable sobbing now – 'you have no fucking idea! No fucking idea at all!'

And suddenly it was clearly too much for her. Zoe slid off the stool and walked over to the vast old sofa, burying herself in a corner, balled up like a used handkerchief, howling.

Eve wanted to go to her daughter but knew she wasn't wanted. Instead, she shook her head at Cathy, misery and confusion etched on her features.

'Now, come on, Zo. It's not quite the end of the world, it just feels like it.' Cathy turned to Eve, who looked entirely stricken. 'The thing is, you see,' she spoke slowly, as if explaining something rather complex to a toddler, willing all the information to both go in and stay in, 'that the Sorensen situation is one thing, but–'

At which point Alice appeared in the doorway. 'What's going on?'

'Go away, Alice, please!' Eve's tone did not invite disagreement; Alice raised an eyebrow and turned on her heel. She sat on the stairs, just out of sight but well within earshot. 'What?' Eve continued. 'So there's worse stuff than my teenage daughter sleeping with *Mister* –' she all but spat out the title – 'Sorensen? Is that right?'

Cathy nodded. Then she explained slowly and carefully

about Rob's nasty, petty, cruel act of revenge, explained about Dontchawish.com and about 'revenge porn' as a concept.

As she listened, Eve shook her head again and again. She could hardly process what she was hearing. It was entirely unfathomable. It was the kind of stuff that happens to other people, different sorts of families. Not mine. One thought kept crowding her head repeatedly: Who is Zoe? Who is my daughter?

It was, thought Eve later, as though her life, which had previously been moving at an ordinary pace, had at that moment been put on fast forward, become hyper-real, like a tsunami in a disaster movie, and everything she thought she'd known now turned out to be, if not entirely wrong, then somehow misaligned, out of sync, at odds with what she had come to recognize, rightly or wrongly, as the norm. And so it was that Mike's wry comment earlier in the evening – *I suspect that's the least of it, frankly!* – turned out to be alarmingly prescient. Albeit, that had been way back in a different world, one in which her teenage daughter hadn't had sex with Stefan Sorensen – *Stefan Sorensen!* – after which her jealous and malevolent – I never liked him! – boyfriend had uploaded a sex tape – a bloody sex tape, for God's sake! – to a revenge-porn website. Revenge porn? My God, who knew?

And then there was the fact that she was being told this by . . . Cathy Gower! And Cathy had known of it all before Eve. And, of course, she had always been at the centre of most of the important events in Eve's life; however, right now, Eve couldn't tell if Cathy's presence made all of this much worse, or much better, or, in actual fact, made no difference at all. If only because, for once, this wasn't about Cathy.

Having listened in virtual silence to both Cathy and Zoe's versions of this sorry, smutty, ugly little tale, Eve finally decided to take control and be the boss of a situation she was, in truth, still a long way from fully comprehending. She turned to Zoe. 'Right. That's enough from you, young lady. I will speak to you again in the morning, but now – bed, grounded. And hand over your phone, too.' Eve walked over to the sofa and held out her hand expectantly.

'But, I—'

The still-sobbing Zoe got no further before her mother exploded. 'NO BLOODY BUTS! Upstairs! *Now!* Grounded until further notice and *no phone*! I will talk to you in the morning.'

As the sound of her daughter's running footsteps were punctuated by a 'Fuck off and leave me alone, Alice!' and the inevitable bedroom door slamming, Eve turned her attention to Cathy. 'And I suppose I'm meant to be all grateful and gracious, right?' She took a large sip of wine. 'But, you know what? I'm not feeling either of those things. What an utter bloody disaster.'

'Ye-es.' Cathy cleared her throat. 'Well, of course, I can go, if you'd like.'

Eve snorted. 'No, of course you're not going! As you very well know – and you better than anybody, frankly – if you're going to bear some bloody bad tidings, then you'd better have a very smart solution in mind. More wine?'

It was Cathy's turn to nod mutely. But, even from their tangential positions, both women instinctively recognized that the person with whom Eve was angriest wasn't Cathy, or even Zoe – not even stupid fucking Stefan Sorensen or the idiotic Rob. No, both women knew that the person Eve was most angry with was Eve. It was at this point that she put her head in her hands and her shoulders slumped. She felt utterly diminished and hopeless and a failure as a mother.

'Jesus, Cath. I'm sorry. I'm really, *really* sorry – you're try-ing to help and I'm just so out of my depth. I not only don't seem to know my own daughter – daughters, probably – but I have not the faintest idea where to go with this, how to sort it out. How to mend things.' She looked at Cathy intently. 'Do you?' Eve reached tentatively for her oldest friend's hand and squeezed it gently. She was extremely pleased to discover the squeeze was reciprocated.

Cathy nodded. 'As it happens, I think I do. Let me make a quick call?'

Eve glanced at her watch – the much-loved Rolex Simon had given her for her fortieth – and was surprised that it wasn't yet nine p.m. It felt like midnight.

'Go ahead, of course. I'm going to have a word with Alice. And then I might call Simon. Family summit?'

Cathy nodded – 'Yeah, good idea' – and scrolled swiftly through her iPhone's address book until she found the number she sought. 'Johnny? Hi.' A pause. 'No. Really?' Another pause. 'Are you sure? When was this? When was he arrested?' Eve paused on her way out of the kitchen doorway and turned around. 'Just a minute.' Cathy cupped her hands over the phone and looked at Eve. 'According to Johnny, Stefan Sorensen's just been arrested in New York.'

Eve shook her head, bemused. 'Excellent. So there is a God?'

'He was arrested at lunchtime – that is, lunchtime in New York, which would have been about six or seven p.m. tonight, our time, so basically just now. He was, uh, arrested alongside his friend, Dershowitz.'

'The plot thickens,' said Eve. 'Need I lock up both my daughters? Is Dershowitz sleeping with teenage girls too, then?'

'Not as far as we know. The arrest is very much for financial, not sexual, misconduct – apparently.'

Dershowitz! thought Eve. Ivy House may as well just pack up right now. 'OK, so I'm calling Simon.' She paused for a moment and met Cathy's eye. 'You OK with that?'

Cathy blushed. 'Of course I am, Eve. I'm only sorry –' Eve was already out of the kitchen door, but Cathy finished anyway – 'you felt you had to ask.'

Zoe was sitting at the head of the long refectory table in her mother's kitchen. She was wearing a baby blue onesie and her feet were pulled up on to the seat of the chair as she hugged her knees, tired and washed out. She felt about twelve and arguably looked even younger. To Zoe's right sat Cathy on the long bench, with Simon opposite her. Next to Cathy, was Eve, while Alice had been dispatched, very grumpily, to join Ed and Jordan.

'So, anyway, just to recap, Zoe,' said her father in a sort of faux-jaunty tone she barely recognized, 'while on work experience, you had an affair with a forty-two-year-old man – your boss, whom I'd like to punch in the face – who has just been arrested in New York in conjunction with his friend and fellow financial wizard, Dershowitz, and they are currently being investigated, according to Cathy's journalistic sources, by . . . well, who knows? The FBI? And, above and beyond this piece of cleverness, your charming ex-boyfriend has posted footage of you and him having, uh, sex on a revenge-porn website and, shortly before leaving the country last week, he not only dumped you, but he posted the link to the site on your Facebook page, where it has now gone, as they say, viral.'

Zoe nodded, but barely. 'What is this, an intervention?'

'Probably.' Simon sighed. 'So, just where did we go so terribly right here, precisely, Eve? How did we get to be such brilliant parents? Any ideas?'

'Yeah, make it all about you, Dad,' muttered Zoe.

'I'm sorry?'

'You heard.'

Simon dropped the faux-jaunty in favour of the plain angry. 'I think you are very lucky, young woman, that I am being quite as calm and level-headed as I am. I've a mind to smack you and send you to your room without supper.'

Zoe semi-sneered. 'I'll phone ChildLine.'

She watched Simon turned puce and Eve shake her head despairingly at both her ex-husband and her daughter, while Cathy simply raised a hand. 'Simon, Zoe. Stop, both of you. Not helpful.'

Eve nodded. 'Let Cathy speak. She has a plan.'

Zoe watched Simon glare at Eve. 'Be my guest. I have no plan at all. Or, rather, none that doesn't involve me getting arrested too.'

'OK, OK, everybody,' Cathy interrupted. 'So. I suggest that we contact the Odense lawyer, whoever that is.'

'I can tell you who it is – Anette,' said Zoe.

Cathy was only momentarily thrown. 'Right. But she

can't be acting for him right now, as his wife? Odense must have someone else?' Zoe shrugged. 'Anyway, we'll find out. And then we'll tell them that we – in this case, "we" is a national newspaper – have information that casts Sorensen in an exceptionally bad light. Yes, an even worse light than the one in which he finds himself already. However, if he were to make a substantial donation to the charity of our choice, we would conceivably be prepared to sit on that information for an indefinite period, agreed?' There were nods from around the table while Zoe remained both still and silent, intrigued but not wanting to show it. Cathy continued. 'OK, so that broadly takes care of the regrettable Sorensen situation, per se – happy charidee to be decided. Now, Zoe, all we need is for you to agree to become the poster girl for . . .' Cathy paused, searching for exactly the right phrase.

'Sleeping with your boss?' muttered Eve, sighing. 'Jesus. Where did we go wrong?'

'As I was saying,' said Cathy, 'the poster girl for the horror of revenge porn, which is, in effect, a particularly grotesque form of bullying, a sort of offshoot of domestic violence, even, being as it invariably involves men dishing on women – and one about which most women know nothing and are therefore vulnerable to precisely the kind of situation in which Zoe has found herself.' Zoe listened, fascinated. 'So, whatever the moral issues around making homemade porno in the first place, the fact remains that Zoe was over the legal age of consent and in a committed long-term relationship with her boyfriend – and he abused her trust in the most craven and cowardly way.'

'To put it mildly! Fucking bastard,' said Zoe.

'Language!' said Simon, pointlessly.

'Right,' said Cathy, cheerfully. 'Now, this is the point in proceedings where we're coming over all modern.' She reached for her laptop, which had been sitting, closed, in front of her.

'Please, not the bloody website!' groaned Simon. 'There are some things a father really does not need to see.'

Cathy smiled. 'Don't worry, Simon, it's just Skype.' She flipped open the MacBook and tapped at the keyboard. 'So, by the miracle of zeros and ones, *heeeere's Johnny* . . .' Cathy pushed the computer back into the middle of the table so it could be seen by everybody. On screen, Johnny Nicholson waved. 'Hello! So sorry I can't be with you tonight – I'm slaving over a hot news desk in darkest Kensington. However, I'd like to thank my agent, my mother and, of course, God. But mostly I'd like to thank Cathy Gower, whose brilliant idea this was.' Everybody laughed; Johnny's digital presence had successfully dissolved the tension.

'This is proper mental,' said Zoe.

'Oh, now, don't you worry, young lady – we've barely started. So, let me tell you exactly how mental this is . . .'

And he did. He explained to the room – but specifically an entirely riveted Zoe – how he and Cathy had decided that the *Courier* should work with their own IT geniuses to permanently remove the footage from the Dontchawish website and then, after this had been achieved, the paper would break the story of Zoe's betrayal in an exclusive magazine interview with a trusted female journalist . . . who just so happens to be Zoe's godmother . . . and, because all newspapers are obsessed with multi-platform and 'click-bait', the *Courier*'s own wildly successful website would simultaneously carry an exclusive filmed blog – a vlog, apparently – with Zoe, on the same subject, which would itself link to Zoe's own YouTube channel, where she could either continue to discuss the subject or draw a line under it, but either way the *Courier* would drive new 'fans' to her site. It would, in short, explained Johnny, be a way of redeploying the precise technology that had been used against her to Zoe's own advantage. And it would work brilliantly, he assured everybody, 'precisely because Zoe is beautiful and clever. Sure, she's going to start off being the poster girl for revenge against revenge porn – but she'll probably finish up with a modelling contract with Storm and her own reality TV series.'

More laughter. Simon spoke first. 'Wow. That is actually brilliant. Who knew you journalist types were quite so bloody smart?'

Without missing a beat, both the on-screen Johnny and the bench-bound Cathy answered together: '*We* did!' Around the Barn's kitchen table, Zoe noted that the laughter took ages to die down and that, when it did, the mood had shifted from disaster management to something approaching creativity. After a few more minutes of round-the-table and through-the-ether discussion, Cathy ended the Skype call and everybody looked at everybody else and then, inevitably, everybody looked at Zoe.

'You want me to say something?' She shrugged. 'Well, yes, I can do all that. I think it's a brilliant idea too.' She paused for a tiny beat. 'And it's not like I'm fazed by cameras.' Everybody laughed again, clearly relieved. Even, she was quietly delighted to note, her mum and dad.

Twenty minutes later, Simon had left the Barn, Eve had gone upstairs, and Cathy had made a cup of camomile tea, which she took over to Zoe. 'Your mum was going to make this for you, but I think she just forgot.'

'She was? Really?' Zoe looked up.

'Yeah – she's your mum and she loves you, Zoe. But I told her to go and have a soak, because she's had a long day.'

'OK, thanks.' Zoe sighed and wiped away a tear. 'She's brilliant, my mum. Look after her, yeah? Can I take this tea to bed? I'm, like, really tired.' Zoe untangled her legs and stood up, wobbling slightly.

'Of course.' Cathy leaned in for a hug.

Zoe smiled a very small smile. 'Thanks.'

'No problem. Well, OK, a bit of a problem, to be frank, but I think we're sorting it. And I must say that, mostly, you have handled this evening very much like a young woman who is about to turn eighteen and leave seventeen a long way behind – by which I mean you've been mature. And it must be so tempting to just cry and ask for a hug.'

Zoe shrugged. 'The thing is, I'll grow up whether I want

to or not. When do you think we'll do all this interview stuff, then?'

'As soon as possible. Turn it around in the next week or so, if you're up for that?'

Zoe nodded. And then she left the room and stumbled up the stairs and down the corridor, towards her room – her safe place – and, within five minutes, she had slipped into a deep, dream-littered sleep.

# 40

Monday morning – early – and Gail sat at her desk. She opened a new blank document file on her computer and started to type a letter. It wasn't a very long letter; none-theless, every word of it was particularly well chosen.

'The Lawns'
Eastdene
East Sussex
Monday, 23rd May, 2011

Dear Tony,

After much deliberation, I hereby offer my resigna-tion. I have been hoping to get back into teaching for quite a while and have just been offered a job as a teaching assistant at Eastdene Community Primary. Mike Browning is also letting me study to qualify as a SENCO and update my PGCE. The job starts in September – when, of course, Harry will also be

starting in Year Seven at Eastdene Community
College.

I will take away many happy memories of my time
at Ivy House.

(No longer) Yours,
Gail Prince

Gail re-read this several times before printing it out, adding her elegant flourish of a signature and putting it into
an envelope, and then there was the *ding* of an incoming
text. It was from Eve, who was apparently going to be off
sick today. Gail couldn't remember the last time that had
happened. She texted Eve –

All fine here, don't worry about a thing, get well soon!

– and circulated an internal email to all the staff, saying
Eve was off work.

Two hours later, paperwork sorted and in tray emptied,
Gail slipped discreetly past the staffroom's open door
without making eye contact with any occupants, and
knocked on Tony's door.

'Come in! And it goes without saying that all ye who enter
here should abandon hope!' shouted Tony Salter. 'Ah, Gail.
Smashing! Shut the door behind you, would you, darling?'

Gail shut the door. 'Er, so I just wanted to give you this,
Tony.' And she put the letter on his desk.

Tony stood up and grinned and said, 'Now, before I find out what the hell this is all about, is there any chance you can rustle me up one of your excellent frothy coffees? And what news of Eve?'

'Well, yes, I can do that, but I'd rather you read it first. It won't take a minute. And I think it's a twenty-four-hour noro sort of a thing. I'm sure she'll be back in no time because Eve doesn't really do ill.'

'Good-oh. So, is this letter what I think it is?'

'That depends, obviously.' Gail shook her head in mild exasperation.

'Sit, please, Gail.' Tony opened the envelope, unfolded the paper and scanned it quickly. He glanced up, smiling. Gail was slightly thrown by this. 'Don't know what took you so long. I've been expecting – dreading – this for years, Gail.'

Gail blanched. 'Really?'

Tony exhaled deeply. 'Yes, really. I know why you stopped teaching and I know it was my fault. I know I undermined your confidence. And I know I behaved like a shit after Harry was born. And I know how I had you over a barrel when I said that, if you wanted a year's maternity leave, you could only come back as admin staff. That was pretty despicable of me, but—'

'But, Tony—' Gail attempted to interject but Tony held his hand up, palm outwards.

'If you want the truth, I was irritated by how little help you seemed to need. Overnight, you'd turned into the

Dame Ellen MacArthur of parenting – determined to do it all single-handed, all the way. So I left you to it.' A shrug. 'Which was all I could do, really, seeing as you wouldn't return my calls and I didn't much fancy myself as a stalker. And then, when you came back, it seemed to work out so well between you and Eve – you are a real powerhouse of a team – that I just allowed myself to forget you'd ever even been a teacher, and a good one. For ages, literally years, I figured you'd just moved on.'

Gail shook her head. 'No, Tony, I have never moved on. I love working with Eve, but I've always just been biding my time, busy being a mum and paying the bills. And I've talked to the staff here, of course, and then I read Eve's article and I just saw immediately that she's right. And that made me think again about my own career and my own future, for the first time in years. For ages I thought I might try to go to uni and do a degree in forensics. But then I realized I'd just watched too much TV ...' Gail broke off and shrugged.

'I don't want to lose you, Gail.'

Gail didn't want to think about this – not right now. 'OK, so I'll just go and make you that coffee.'

Tony sighed. 'Gail, I accept your resignation. OK?'

Gail smiled and nodded. 'Thanks, Tony. Sugar?'

Michael Percy unlatched the nursery playground's gate and started to walk home along a route he knew very well. He circumnavigated the car park and the wood-chipped play area, passed the sports hall and the tennis courts and walked along the edge of the cricket pitch towards the furthest corner of the fast-shrinking coppice, where the big diggers were moving backwards and forwards . . . This wasn't the first time that Michael had decided that the actual real tree-house in his own actual garden just over the stile on the other side of the coppice was infinitely preferable to a school called the Tree House, which wasn't a tree-house at all; it was just that, on the couple of previous occasions he'd attempted it, he'd always been caught in the act.

Diggersaurs, thought Michael as he watched their long necks bobbing up and down. Big, yellow diggersaurs!

Just past the diggersaurs stood the stile, which separated his mum and dad's farm from his school. Beyond that was one small pony paddock before the gate to the farm's walled kitchen-garden, which meant that he was almost really home – home to Mummy and something warm and buttery-tasting in the kitchen, and a homely hug instead of a school scolding. Yes, Michael was definitely looking forward to getting home, but first he thought he might stop for a while and watch the big, yellow diggersaurs rolling back and forth across the place where there used to be trees. Back and forth, dipping and bobbing their big, yellow necks, back and forth . . .

And nobody saw that the little boy of not-quite-four, who didn't like 'school' and took his 'blankie' every day in his book bag and missed his mummy each morning and still had lavatory accidents and whose favourite book was *Harry and the Bucketful of Dinosaurs*, was sitting at the edge of the coppice, pretending he was being chased by a digger-saurus . . .

And then the first person who *did* see him was the diggersaurus's unfortunate driver, whose name was Tom and who had a five-year-old lad himself, and who held Michael in his arms as he tried to resuscitate him and, when he failed, howled and swore and dialled 999, screaming into his mobile, 'FUCKING WELL GET HERE *NOW!*'

And by the time the helicopter was making everything windy over by the rugby pitch, an hysterical Tom was being restrained by the site's foreman while another diggersaurus driver had gone to fetch Tony Salter.

From the cricket pitch, meanwhile, a small crowd was starting to descend on the coppice at the same time as the remaining workmen were frantically trying to shoo them away from the sight of Michael Percy, who was alarmingly still and broken-looking, lying within the footprint of one of the dormitory blocks. Tony Salter, shocked into silence as he stood next to the site foreman surveying the chaos, felt tears – of pity? Regret? Shame? *Fear?* – prick at his eyelids. He tried very hard – and failed – to blink them away.

# 41

Having already bunked off work 'sick', it was equally unlike Eve to have a bubble bath rather than a shower in the morning, and to be reading her iPad while she did so, but needs must. It had, after all, been a very exhausting weekend, all things considered.

Eve had continued the logistical chats with Cathy, who had stayed over on both Friday and Saturday night before driving back to town on Sunday morning, after which Eve had gone on a long walk to the stables with Barney and Alice. This was allegedly to see Monty, though in truth she was only really interested in Alice, whom she very much didn't want to neglect. Afterwards, Eve had also finally found time for a talk on the phone with Mike, explaining everything. He had then been invited for Sunday evening's spag bol, and, with the house still reverberating from a weekend's worth of emotional fallout, he had drunk two glasses of wine, dispensed what little wisdom he claimed he could add, and then left by ten p.m. Eve very much hoped he wouldn't tire of all of this domestic clutter getting in the way of the getting-to-know-you phase of their still-impending relationship, but if it did, it did. For what felt like the first time in a long time – since Alice was a toddler, probably – Eve was putting parenting first. She could only hope that Mike, as a non-parent, was sufficiently interested in the novelty of it all to stick around.

And then, after Mike had left, Eve had – nervously – gone upstairs and quietly tapped on Zoe's closed bedroom door. Zoe had been around all weekend, but mostly as a spectral sort of presence, barely speaking, helping herself to cereal, defrosting pizzas, refusing offers of more substantial fare – about which Eve had reluctantly bitten her lip, overcoming the temptation to speak maternal clichés such as, 'But you're far too skinny as it is.'

Eve had quietly congratulated herself for this. However, hovering on the landing, carrying a mug of very likely to be rejected Horlicks and, of all unlikely bedtime offerings, a Tunnock's Teacake, she had been nervous about further rejection from her eldest daughter – the daughter that, since Friday, she barely recognized.

'Come in, Mum,' said Zoe's small voice.

Eve opened the door. 'How did you know it was me?'

'I can hear Alice watching *Secretariat* for, like, the nine hundredth time, next door.'

'*Secretariat*? Isn't that an eighteen?'

'No, Mum – that's *Secretary*. This one's a Disney movie about an American racehorse.'

Eve smiled. 'Right. I knew that.'

Zoe smiled back. 'Thanks for the Horlicks and the Tunnock's.'

'How can you tell it's Horlicks?'

'The smell?'

'Right. Yes.'

'Do you want to talk, or something?' Eve noted that Zoe's tone was neither combative nor submissive – just colourless. 'Cos I'm a bit tired, to be honest.'

'I bet you are. No need to talk, no, if you don't want to. Just checking you're OK.'

'I'm fine. It's all fine. I don't want to talk but, just so you know, Stefan didn't like seduce me. It was totally mutual. Consensual – that's the word.' Zoe shrugged.

'Right, well, whatever, thanks for sharing. But that won't stop your father wanting to punch him, I expect.'

'I'm not sure he'd come out of that on top, to be honest. Stefan's very, um,' Zoe paused, chose her word carefully, 'fit.'

Eve smiled. 'Good night, Zoe. Sleep well.'

'Yeah, you too, Mum.' Zoe's mouth was full of Teacake. 'Luff you.'

'Luff you too, Zo.'

And Eve shut the door, still smiling. It would indeed, she suddenly believed, all be fine, in time. No rush . . .

And now here she was, bunking off work on a Monday morning, and relaxing in the bath while attempting to catch up with an article she'd half heard mentioned two days previously, as she'd lain in bed, still slightly stunned from the events of the previous evening, and therefore only half listening to the Saturday morning edition of *Today*. With her iPad precariously balanced on the rack, it was only now that Eve finally started to read the article in the *Telegraph*..

After announcing she is to leave to run a school in Switzerland, the headmistress of the leading independent girls' school, Wessex Park, has voiced frustration about attitudes to private education in Britain.

Eleanor Hill told the *Courier* that Britain could not celebrate the success and heritage of its independent schools, which are increasingly sought-after among parents across the world. Mrs Hill will leave in the summer to become Director of L'Institut Villa Alpin in Switzerland: 'In the UK, the independent sector has gone through a tough time,' she said.

Eve read on, eagerly.

Mrs Hill predicts more closures and mergers of private schools: 'We probably have too many boarding schools left over from the nineteenth century. There was a boom period when local British people decided that boarding was the best thing, but that is now changing and these days parents want their children at home.' But, according to Mrs Hill, demand from abroad for a British education still booms. 'I cannot say it strongly enough: this is the future.'

With a solar-plexus lurch, Eve realized that, as she had contentedly busied herself for years with her business, which was educating children, Tony had primarily been *running* a business. Why hadn't she realized that all along? Could she really have got quite so far past life's halfway mark and remained so comically naive? Events of the last few days seemed to suggest that this may indeed be the case. Despite a reasonably convincing veneer of sophistication, Eve suddenly felt unprecedentedly gauche. Hadn't she, for example, always simply assumed that Zoe was a Teflon teen, that problems rolled away from her, even as they often clung to Alice like burrs, that Zoe seemed, if not quite blessed, then certainly somehow charmed. And how wrong had that assumption turned out to be? She carried on reading.

Mrs Hill last week criticized schools that increasingly rely on fees from overseas students, making independent schools the preserve of only the very wealthiest. Our survey reveals that a majority of foreign pupils are currently from Hong Kong (almost 6,000 in the UK), followed by China (3,636), Germany (2,281) and Russia (1,695).

We spoke to one head teacher at an independent school where twenty-five per cent of pupils are from overseas. Wishing to remain anonymous, he told us that some schools recruit foreign students in a 'desperate attempt to fill their empty beds'. He said, 'That's not the case here, however, because we recruit successfully from all over the world.'

Finally:

> Many families of foreign pupils are hiring agents or consultants to secure places at good British boarding schools. Some wealthy Russian parents pay £50,000 per child, though commission charges are more usually equivalent to a first term's fees: about £10,000. These agents, currently widely used by British universities, are facing tighter controls in an attempt to squeeze out rogue operators; it also risks creating 'ghettos' of children from the same country at boarding schools, some head teachers have warned.

Fascinating, thought Eve.

Most of the rest of Eve's day passed pleasantly and indulgently – albeit a little guiltily. She'd not quite dared to leave the house in case she was spotted, clearly norovirus-free and footloose, so decided to catch up with the kind of tedious domestic tasks that would assuage any guilt about playing hooky, while leaving her free to think. So it was that Eve had deep-cleaned the oven, tidied the utility room and hand-washed three identical pale grey cashmere sweaters before she picked up Gail's anguished phone message just after three p.m. – she'd been in the garden and hadn't bothered taking her mobile and hadn't heard the landline ringing. She listened in guilty horror – maybe this would never have happened if I'd been there? – before phoning Gail's mobile. She picked up immediately.

'Gail. It's me. My God. I'm going straight to the hospital.'

'But you can't, Eve, not with noro. And, anyway, Tony's there, with the Percys.'

'Fuck noro – I haven't got it. I lied. I –' Eve paused momentarily – 'I bunked off today.' Even as she spoke, Eve was aware that this was a sentence she'd never expected to say. 'Look, I've had a . . . *testing* weekend, but nothing compared to what the Percys are going through, so I'm going right now. Hold the fort at school, Gail, would you? Until further notice?'

'Done. Harry's in After-School Club till six and then he can look after himself. The phones are burning off their hooks. Look, I'd better go. And I can't believe you bunked off.'

'I can explain, Gail. But do we know how Michael is? Is he going to be OK?'

'I have no idea, Eve. No idea at all.'

The following Sunday was, to all intents, a perfect summer's day. Eve was sitting in the garden of the Red Lion, nursing half a lager and lime and popping dry-roasted peanuts as she waited for Simon to arrive. She knew Simon had been surprised when she'd suggested '*Le Lion Rouge*'; it was rare for them to meet anywhere other than on their respective home turfs; however, Eve had chosen the venue with care.

As she waited, she flipped through the *Courier on Sunday* and watched families lingering over their al fresco Sunday lunches – mostly fully loaded roasts, with salad as a seasonal nod. Eve briefly acknowledged people she recognized; *Le Lion* was very much inside the Ivy House catchment, so she'd parked herself in a far corner of the garden in order not to cramp the children's – or, indeed, any of their parents' – style. The children who knew her kept a predictable polite distance; nonetheless, she was sought out by a few parents.

'Hello, Mrs Sturridge – sorry, *Eve*!' said Susie Poe. 'And so sorry to interrupt your, ah, drink, too, but I was just wondering if you'd heard any more news about Michael?'

Eve looked up and smiled. 'No need to apologize at all. My date, that is, my ex-husband, hasn't turned up yet. And I hear that Michael's doing marvellously, all things considered. According to his mother, whom I saw yesterday, he's very chipper and thoroughly enjoying the attention of the nurses, who dote on him. Mrs Percy said that it was, of course, unusual for him to be the centre of attention as a member of such a big family, and that he clearly thrives on it – which made her feel terrible for not giving him enough attention. I told her not to beat herself up; after all, hadn't Michael been heading home when he had the accident? Home to his mum?' Susie Poe nodded keenly. 'Of course, it's too early to know if he'll make a complete recovery. But he is an extraordinarily stoic little man; if his body will let him, I have no doubt in my mind that *his* mind will make it happen.'

It occurred to Eve that perhaps Susie hadn't been expecting quite so much information; however, Eve was becoming used to her role as unofficial mouthpiece for the Percy family. She spoke to them every day and had popped in to the hospital to see Michael three times since Monday. The matron on the children's ward was ex-Ivy House – before Eve's time, of course, but still, old school ties, and whatnot. 'And how are Charlie and Lula getting on at Eastdene? Well and truly settled in, I hope?'

Susie smiled. 'Very well, thank you. They love it. There were a few minor teething problems, of course, which were to be expected, but they came through and now they're just part of that "Eastdene family".' Susie waggled her fingers as air quotes. 'You do know I never would have moved them from Ivy House if it hadn't been a financial issue . . .' Susie paused. 'But, either way, they're very lucky to have had *two* such brilliant head teachers at two such different schools.'

'That's very kind of you, Susie. I'm delighted they're doing well. And they're in very safe hands at any school run by Mr Browning.'

'I suspect you're right. And thanks for the update on Michael – the children know some of his siblings, you see, and have been asking after him every day.'

'No problem; we've all been very concerned. And how are you, Susie?'

'Ah, well, fine. Happily flying solo, no longer single-handedly keeping Kleenex in business, you'll be glad to know –' Eve smiled – 'and enjoying some new challenges. I'm already a parent governor at Eastdene, which is marvellous. And, of course, we're all so thrilled that Gail will be joining the school in September. She'll be such a huge asset.'

Eve raised an eyebrow. 'Yes, I'm sure she will.'

Susie Poe grimaced. 'Oh my god, I'm so sorry! I'd assumed she'd handed in her notice.'

Eve realized she'd done a bad job of disguising the fact that she'd had no idea Gail was leaving. 'Well, I suspect she has, just not to me. I was off on Monday and it's been a very busy week, obviously, as we've all been so distracted by poor little Michael.' Eve paused. What followed came surprisingly easily: 'But, the thing is, Susie, it's not a problem because, strictly *entre nous*, I'll be leaving soon too.'

Susie's eyes widened. 'Well, that is quite a local scoop I've just landed. But, of course, I shan't breathe a word, even though it's what everybody has been expecting, really, ever since your excellent article in the *Courier*. And I heard you on *Today* with Humphrys, too. You did a terrific job – with Humphrys, I mean. You're still doing a terrific job at, uh, everything else.'

It was Eve's turn to be wide-eyed. *It's what everybody has been expecting* . . . Everybody except, apparently, me . . . But, anyway, now I've said it. And to Susie Poe – a journalist – too. So, it's on the record. That's it, then. I'm *off* . . .

'That's very kind of you, Susie. And now here's my ex-husband. Perfect timing! Please, don't let me keep you.'

Eve noted that that particular old headmistressy trick wasn't lost on Susie Poe, who smiled. 'You're not. I'm keeping you. But thanks for the update – and good luck.'

Having just missed being introduced by moments, Simon sat down and watched Susie Poe's retreating back. 'That's a very good-looking woman.'

'Yes. Susie Poe. Down-from-Londoner, journalist, former Ivy-House mother turned Eastdene parent governor, apparently. Oh, and divorced and available – if curvaceous blondes happened to be where your proclivities lay.'

'You know I am very partial to a curvaceous blonde, Mrs Sturridge. Anyway,' Simon raised his glass, 'cheers!'

'Fair enough. In a week when there hasn't really been much to celebrate, I'll raise a glass. Cheers!'

'How is Michael Percy doing?'

Eve repeated what she'd told Susie Poe. 'I believe he's doing very well. Meanwhile, Tony has been worrying himself sick about being sued by the Percys, despite the fact that – the Percys being the Percys – they've told him it will never happen; they are of the opinion, old-fashioned though that may be, that accidents happen, and they therefore have no interest in destroying the school which has done the right thing by all their children. For which we are all very grateful, of course.' Eve sighed. 'But that hasn't stopped Tony shutting down the building works and saying he's having a rethink about, well,' Eve shrugged, '*everything,* apparently.' She paused. 'And that mindset seems to be infectious, because I want to sell the house.'

Simon started; he was clearly thrown. 'But I made that house for *you*. It's a Forever House.'

Eve smiled at the slight tremble in Simon's voice. 'No, Simon. You made it for the person you wanted me to be – or at least the one you hoped I might become – and that's not who I am. And "forever" is a very long time.'

'So who are you?'

'I'm not sure yet, but I'm going to find out.'

Simon sighed. 'So much has changed this year. I can hardly keep up. Do you think you'll move far?'

Eve considered this. 'No, not far physically, I think, maybe just metaphorically.'

Simon smiled. 'Anyone would think you had an A in English at O level.'

Eve rolled her eyes. 'Unlike our youngest daughter.'

'On the subject of which, how are the daughters?'

'Fine, I think. Of course, you know Zo has done her interview with Cath?' Simon nodded. 'And they're doing the photo shoot tomorrow. It'll all be out on Saturday, amazingly. Zoe is very focused.'

'I'll bet. I still fully plan to punch both Stefan Sorensen and the appalling Rob.'

Eve nodded. 'Yup. Good idea. I'm not sure about Sorensen, but, yeah, I think you could probably take out Rob.'

Simon raised his eyes heavenwards. 'Gee, thanks, honey – I'm only twice his size.'

Eve laughed. 'And in all the wrong places, too.'

Simon gasped. 'I cannot believe you just said that, Eve. I am properly shocked and appalled.' But, even as he did his best to disguise it, Eve could see a slight smile playing around Simon's lips.

'Hold that thought, because you ain't heard nothing yet – I'm resigning, too.'

# 42

In the light of recent events, there had been some talk of cancellation; however, the Percy family – enthusiastic upholders of the 'tradition' – would have none of it. Thus, the Wednesday of the last week in June was, indeed, Upside-Down Day at Ivy House, as advertised. Which also meant that Monday and Tuesday, though nominally normal school days, were mostly just the excitable run-up.

At this time of year, post exams, the majority of the school's academic work was done and the focus was on play – sporting play, acting play or just plain old-fashioned playing play. And there was an atmosphere of expectation around this year's Upside Down, a pervasive sense throughout the school that it ought somehow to be made even more fun than usual, for Michael. Thus there was a general feeling of infectious sunniness in the air. The weather helped; it was definitely properly summery. Sports Day – the weekend before Michael's accident, or BMA, as Gail had it – had been a triumph, with more picnic hampers than ever lining the perimeter of the athletics track to witness Dickens winning the House trophy for the third year running, while the cricket pavilion was host to some hard competitive work by the indefatigable Friends of Ivy House, the bunch of closely knit and tireless 'professional parents' (as Eve referred to them, meaning women who made parenting their profession; Gail's preferred description, on the other hand, was 'the sisters of Stepford') whose previous lives as lawyers, PR executives and academics effectively ensured that the cricket tea's Victoria sponge was as unbeatable as the school's first eleven.

It was this atmosphere of fun-by-any-means-necessary that had unexpectedly – to Eve, at least – hastened Eve's decision making. She'd spent quite a bit of time with her boss over the last couple of weeks and had been surprised to discover aspects of him she'd never known: a vulnerability closer to the surface than she could have imagined; a sensitivity around the Percy family that hinted at the possibility of hitherto unprecedented kindness. As emotions had run high in the week after Michael's accident, these discoveries had been baffling to Eve, though not unwelcome.

Even so, it was hard not to break the news she needed to break in as brisk a fashion as possible. So, after tapping on Tony's office door at 9:30 a.m., that's exactly what she did.

'OK, so I shan't beat around the bush; I'm resigning, Tony. I'd like to leave at the end of term, though I appreciate that may be too soon, so, if it's at all helpful to the school, I am happy to work over the summer. But, either way, I'm done. I'm off. And I'm sorry to spring this on you on Upside-Down Day, especially with everything that's happened recently. And what's all this about Gail too, while I'm at it?'

It was rare that Tony's expression gave absolutely nothing away, but, unexpectedly, this was one of those occasions. Tony gave Eve a very long, level sort of stare and then said, 'Actually, I'm not accepting your resignation because I'm sacking you instead. And, as for being any alleged –' he wiggled fingers in the air as quote marks – ' "help", well, that's a bit rich coming from you. So you can sod off right now, today, if you like. Gail's going at the end of term, anyway. She handed in her notice on the day Michael . . . whatever. Anyway. End of an era, onwards and upwards.' He sighed.

Eve hadn't quite expected this. 'You think that that would be good for the school? For the pupils? For staff morale? You really think I should just walk out? What message would that be sending the troops, Tony? Am I going to be escorted from the building carrying my cardboard box of personal effects? Christ, this isn't some steely sort of financial services corporation stuck in a Canary Wharf tower. We're not bloody Enron!'

Tony listened to Eve, cocked his head to one side and said, 'Yeah, I think now is probably as good a time as any. Steve Bryant can be acting head teacher for a fortnight.' He paused and, to Eve's astonishment, suddenly buried his head in his big hands. 'Oh, fuck it, Eve, who am I kidding?

I'm selling Ivy House. I'm done. I can't have little boys being run over by fucking diggers in a school I own. If it was anyone other than the Percys' little boy, I'd be having my arse sued, anyway. Just imagine if it had been a Dershowitz kid, or a Sorensen?'

Eve winced. 'On the subject of which—'

'I know, I *know*. Our last Dershowitz leaves in a fortnight, anyway – I believe they're currently torn between Haileybury and Harrow – and if Sorensen goes down, I expect Anette will move away.'

It was Eve's turn to sigh. 'Who knows, Tony? I shall miss the Dershowitzes; I like them. But the Sorensens I –' she stammered slightly – 'I . . . barely know. Anyway, if you need to sack me for some peculiar control-freaky reason, then go ahead, but please don't mess up Steve's end of term. As Head of Games, he more than delivered with Sports Day – and, anyway, I'm not sure he actually owns any clothing other than tracksuits.' Eve paused, attempted to read Tony's expression. 'Look, Tony, I may as well stay for another couple of weeks, for God's sake.'

Tony pursed his lips and squinted at Eve. 'Up to you. You can either stay for another fortnight, pointlessly, or you can leave right now with six months' salary. Here –' Tony opened a drawer in the Scandi-desk, pulled out a cheque book and scribbled on it with his large, childishly looping handwriting and his illegible flourish of a signature. And, even from where she was standing, Eve could see the noughts . . . Sod it. I'm not too proud to take that! And she surprised herself with how good it felt. Tony handed her the cheque. Eve took it, glanced at it and nodded, folding it carefully and placing it in a pocket. Tony remained standing. 'Uh, the thing is, I have it on very good authority that you bunked off work on the day of Michael's, uh ... We've had the *Battle Observer* sniffing around about that. Perhaps if you'd been around it would never have happened? So, not a fucking word of any of this to anyone in the, uh, media – OK?'

Eve, astonished, couldn't think of a response. Of course, she knew that the only 'very good authority' Tony could possibly mean was Gail. And how extraordinarily unlike Gail it was to whistleblow to Tony against her. Yet that was apparently exactly what had happened. Why?

And then she realized. Of course! It was all so suddenly, completely, comically, staring-you-in-the-face bleeding obvious that she let out an involuntary 'Ha!' Swiftly followed by an 'Omigod!'

Yet, even as all these new and distracting thoughts crowded for her attention, Eve suspected her overriding memory of this moment would be of Tony Salter, standing behind his desk, wearing a tweed skirt suit, American-tan tights, a pair of scuffed brogues and a thin smear of frosted-pink lipstick, with that distinctive messy cowlick protruding from his Margaret Thatcher-style wig. It was all she could do not to explode with laughter.

End of an era, indeed ...

Back outside Tony's office, Eve paused, drew a very deep

breath and then rushed as quickly back to her office as possible, without actually running. Inevitably, Gail was in situ behind her own desk, just outside Eve's office. Eve affected a bright smile that very much belied her true, confused feelings.

'I've just had a quick meeting with Tony and I'm leaving, Gail – right now. So that makes two of us!'

Either Gail hadn't picked up on her last comment or she'd chosen to ignore it. 'What do you mean? Do you have an appointment? Are the girls OK?'

'The girls are fine, but, yes, apparently I have an appointment with the rest of my life. Tony's, um, sacked me, effective immediately. Apparently he's unimpressed with the reasons for my, um, absence on the day of Michael's accident. Talk about Upside-Down Day!' Eve felt that she'd given Gail every opportunity to say *something* . . .

But Gail's jaw went slack. 'What? You're kidding?'

'Nope, not kidding – leaving. And can I ask you a huge favour?' Conscious of being let down – and indeed hurt – by her right-hand woman of the past decade, Eve was now all brisk focus and adrenaline.

'Of course. Jesus, Eve, it goes without saying.'

'Does it? Well, anyway, don't mention this to anybody, if you can avoid it. Say I've gone down with that violently contagious norovirus again, if you absolutely have to.'

Eve paused, met Gail's eye. Gail nodded. 'OK.' And then she carried on nodding. And then her eyes widened: 'Oh no! *Omigod*, Eve! I just let it slip when I was talking to Tony.

I think it was the Tuesday or the Wednesday night, I can't remember. I meant no harm! Tony was, uh, round mine and we were just talking about everything, and – God! Why would he *do* that? Why would he use that against you?'

It was Eve's turn to look bemused. 'I have no idea, Gail. And I had no idea you were so close, you and Tony – until just now, that is, when I did. Anyway, whatever. It would be great if you could pack up my desk a bit. I'm just going to grab my laptop and phone and some correspondence and stuff.'

'Right. OK. But, Eve, this is all mental. Are you OK?'

'Fine. I'm fine. Really. At least, I'm fine at the moment. Tomorrow –' Eve shrugged – 'who knows?'

And as she stuffed random paperwork into her Mulberry first-day-of-the-new-school-year 'satchel' and grabbed her phone and raced through the highly adrenalized final moments before she left, Eve suddenly recognized that she would probably never set foot in this room – her home from home for the past decade – ever again. Of course I won't. This is it. All that work, that passion and dedication, all those hours of worrying and trying to get it right – and for what? To be forced to walk out on children and staff she cared about. The unfairness – the wrongness, frankly – of now leaving *her* school in the hands of the man who actually owned it made Eve, to her surprise and horror, actually cry with fury, fat cheque notwithstanding. A hot tear slid down her cheek – and then very many more as the dam burst. Jesus! I can't let anyone see me leaving like this. I'll have to sneak out, round the back. After ten years, I have to make my exit like a bloody thief.

A knock on the door, swiftly followed by ashen-faced Gail. Her dismay at the sight of Eve in tears was obvious.

'Sorry, Gail, I'm just having a moment – I'll be fine.' Eve sniffed. 'Look, I'm going to leave by the back door, nip down to the sports hall and then round to the bottom car park. That way, nobody will be able to tell that the noro is fake and that what I'm actually suffering from is leaking eyes and –' she glanced at Gail – 'a breaking heart.' Which was all it took to set Gail off, too. 'Stop it,' said Eve. 'One of us has to be the grown-up and, as I've been relying on you to fulfil that role for the past ten years, it would be great if you could carry on for just a few more minutes, thanks.'

Gail smiled wanly. 'I don't know how you retain your sense of humour.'

'Nor do I. But have you actually *seen* Tony all cross-dressed-up in his Joyce Grenfell rig? Just hold on to that mental image. Right, I'm off.'

'Where do you think you'll go?'

'Oh, God, I don't know. It's a bit too soon to think about it, really.'

'No, I mean where will you go *now*?'

'Oh! Yes, of course – er, home?'

'Right. And is anybody there?'

Eve thought for a moment. Alice was probably at the

stables; Zoe was staying at Simon and Ed's this week. Mike was at school, obviously . . .

'Nope, nobody's there. I'll probably be in the pub, slumped over a bottle of Glenmorangie. Anyway, congratulations on your job at Eastdene.'

'I was going to tell you before I told Tony, Eve. But you weren't there, and then everything else happened.'

Eve nodded briskly; she'd been wondering why Mike hadn't told her, too. Then again, she'd hardly seen Mike. 'One day playing hooky off school in a whole decade and I'm certainly paying the price.'

Gail blushed and looked away. 'Eve, if you do end up in the pub, may I suggest you get changed first?'

Eve glanced down at her feet and started to giggle, albeit slightly hysterically. She had, of course, forgotten that she had her hair in bunches and was wearing a short-sleeved buttoned-up white blouse with a red tartan tie, a navy knee-length box-pleated skirt, white ankle socks and a pair of red Mary Janes. She clamped her hand over her mouth and snorted.

'I mean, obviously *we're* all used to the Upside-Down traditions,' continued Gail, deadpanning, 'but, out there in the wider world, a mature woman – never mind a head teacher – wearing school uniform is likely to be interpreted in a very different way. And as for the pub . . .' She broke off, shrugged.

Eve couldn't speak. She thought she would probably either faint or explode with laughter. 'Thank you, Gail –

thank you for being the best. Even if you snitched on me to Tony –' a beat – 'having also withheld the fact that he's Harry's dad for a decade.'

Gail's eyes widened. She looked as though she was going to say something and then thought better of it. Eve continued: 'You know you could have trusted me, Gail? I've always trusted you.' Her tone was definitely more in sorrow than anger.

Gail shook her head, a deep blush already rising up her neck. 'Now is not the time for this.'

'Now was apparently *never* the time!'

Gail turned away so she could avoid Eve's gaze. 'You'd better go before the staff cricket match starts and you're spotted – I can already see Year Seven and the sisters of Stepford making picnic lunches in the sports hall. Go! Can I call you in the morning?'

Eve was already leaving the room. She paused. 'Well, I can't stop you. I might even answer.'

And, with that, Eve walked out of Ivy House for the last time. Buzzing with adrenaline, she stuck her head in the door of the bursar's office en route to the back door. 'Hi, Pat. I'm going out. I may be some time. Like, actually, forever.'

'OK,' said Pat, only half listening and without glancing up from her copy of *Good Housekeeping*, 'but you'll want to be back for the cricket match. Tony's umpiring.'

'That's a shame. I'm sure he'd prefer to be bowling maidens over in his tweed skirt.'

Pat glanced up. 'Sorry, Eve, what was that? Reading a really good article on Emma Thompson. I always liked her more than Ken.'

'Showing your age, Pat. Didn't they split up in, like, the eighties?'

'Nineteen ninety-five, as it happens. But you're right – I do still think the eighties were about ten years ago. I'm not sure where my nineties got to, really.' Pat sighed.

Eve looked at Pat's severely unflattering bob and pastel mother-of-the-bride shift dress and the gilt-chained handbag slung over the back of her chair. 'OK, so, anyway, I'm off.'

But Pat still wasn't really listening. 'Okey-dokey, Eve, see you later. Goodness, that wedding dress of Em's really was an absolute horror.'

# 43

Once she'd reached the Volvo unseen, Eve pulled her hair out of its bunches, rubbed the eyebrow-pencilled freckles off her nose and drove home, deliberately slowly.

As she entered the house, she smelled Zoe's favourite scent – Agent Provocateur, what else? – before she saw her daughter, sitting in the kitchen, wearing pyjamas and eating cereal. Well, it is just about still morning, after all. Zoe waved at Eve and mouthed, 'Just a minute!' as she continued her phone call, so Eve nodded and went to fill the kettle. While she waited for Zoe to finish talking – to Carmen, by the sound of it – her own phone buzzed in her bag. She pulled it out and saw *MIKE* on the screen ID. She swiped the *Slide to answer* icon.

'Mike?'

'Eve! I didn't really expect to get you, but I just wanted to wish you a happy Upside-Down Day.'

'Sweet of you. Couple of things, though – I've just been sacked by Tony, so I'm at home. And, er, why didn't you tell me you'd hired Gail?'

'God, Eve – what with everything else that's been going on, it just didn't occur to me. I assumed Gail would tell you herself, given you're so close. But what the hell do you mean, sacked?'

So Eve explained briskly, editing as she went, conscious that Zoe had now ended her call and was listening, too. She felt suddenly fenced in, claustrophobic. The last few weeks had been . . . exhausting.

'May I come round later?' said Mike. 'I'll take you out for dinner. A proper date dinner that, with a bit of luck, won't be interrupted by any fresh drama.'

And Eve was so tired she simply nodded at the phone.

'Mum, you have to, like, speak!' squeaked Zoe.

'Eve? You still there?' said Mike.

Eve grinned at her daughter. 'Yes; sorry. I'm completely done in. It's all catching up with me. Please, *please* take me out for dinner. I can't think of anything I'd like more, really.'

'Deal. I'll be on your doorstep at seven thirty.'

Eve rang off and shook her head in mock despair at Zoe. 'Crazy days.'

Zoe looked her mother up and down. 'Make sure you get changed before Mike comes, yeah, otherwise he'll think you're a weirdo. And, you know what you need, Mum? A holiday. I think you should go away somewhere lovely, with Alice. I'll stay here and look after Barney and water the garden and be one hundred per cent the kind of daughter you'd like me to be, if only for a week or two – promise!'

Eve narrowed her eyes. 'That's actually not a bad idea. But do I trust you? Won't you just post a party on Facebook and the Barn'll be crashed by a thousand teenagers from all over Sussex – and probably Rihanna and Beyoncé, too, for all I know. Remember, I'm about to try to sell it, so I really don't need it trashed!'

Zoe shrugged. 'No worries. I've come off Facebook for a bit; I'm doing Twitter now. But have you really been sacked, Mum?'

'Depends. It's probably more like "let go". But, yes, I'm gone. Unemployed!'

'But with a nice big cheque. Go on, book a holiday. Then you'll sell the Barn and find us a lovely wonky cottage, hopefully, and—'

'Why do you say, "wonky cottage"?' Eve butted in.

Zoe smiled. 'Because we have the same taste. Don't *you* want to live in a wonky cottage?'

'I totally want to live in a wonky cottage – always have done. But I never dared tell your dad!' Eve smiled sheepishly at her daughter, who had clamped her hand over her mouth and was snorting with suppressed laughter.

'That is the funniest thing I've ever heard. You were married to a modernist architect, so you had to live in a big, shiny *Grand Designs*-y box!'

At which entirely accurate observation, Eve wrapped an arm around her eldest daughter's waist and they leaned into each other, shaking with laughter. 'I know! All I ever wanted was exposed beams and an inglenook fireplace.'

'I'm so telling on you!'

'You're not telling your dad!'

'I so am.'

'I'll kill you!' But Eve was still giggling.

'Do you want me to look after the house while you take your youngest daughter on a lovely mums and daughters spa break, or what?'

'Yes, I do. Very much.'

'So how much is it worth for me not to tell Dad that you want to live in, basically, Ye Olde Curiosity Shoppe?'

Eve giggled. 'Shoes? Is it worth shoes?'

'And . . . ?'

'Um. Maybe more shoes?!'

'Might be!'

Upside-Down Day, indeed . . . thought Eve, suddenly and very unexpectedly enjoying every moment.

After a quick diversion to Tesco Express for milk and something microwaveable, Gail was home later than she'd expected. Harry was out of After-School Club and sitting on the bungalow's garden wall, swinging his legs sulkily and scuffing the backs of his brand-new Nikes. 'Please don't do that, Hazza!' said Gail, feeling a surge of irritation. Fifty quid, even in the sale. Harry was already a size six.

In the kitchen, Gail made herself a cup of tea and picked up the newspaper she'd left folded neatly on the breakfast bar for several days, waiting for the right moment. And

now seemed as good a moment as any other to read the
*Courier*'s interview with Zoe.

## REVENGE PORN – A Victim's Story
### Zoe Sturridge speaks to Cathy Gower

A victim of so-called 'revenge porn', seventeen-year-old
A-level student Zoe Sturridge has opened up to the
*Courier* after sexually intimate filmed footage of her was
put online by an ex-boyfriend. Zoe, of Eastdene, East
Sussex, is also one of six female accusers from around the
world set against American revenge-porn website owners,
Brad Hunter and Chuck Williams, after discovering she
had been featured on their Dontchawish.com website.

In an exclusive interview with us, Zoe spoke out bravely
this week after the two men were indicted in California
for running the site.

'You think that it can't happen to you, but it can,' said
Zoe. 'I was so damaged by it. I just wanted to stay in my
room forever. It just all hit me like a ton of bricks.'

The 'it' she refers to is footage that was uploaded to the
site earlier this year. It took nine days to get the images
removed, but by then it had been mass-texted and
Facebooked to almost everyone she knew. Zoe is now on a
crusade and has been joined by her mother – head teacher
and occasional *Courier* contributor, Eve Sturridge – who
has been dubbed by her daughter 'the Erin Brockovich of
revenge porn'.

'I'm so happy that, finally, something's happening,' Eve told the *Courier*. 'Revenge porn is really just about hurting and humiliating people, trying to ruin their lives. It's a form of domestic abuse, an issue of control and coercion.'

So where does the law currently stand?

'Well, it depends what the image depicts, but, in legal terms, I believe it's more a case of harassment and an issue of protection of privacy,' says Eve. 'There is a Protection From Harassment Act, but it's a breach of privacy if someone posts images of you on the internet, and you could launch a civil case on the basis of that, but not a criminal case.'

'A lot of women are being threatened with just the possibility of revenge porn, too,' says Zoe. 'It's invariably from exes – and usually men, too.' It seems that compassion, respect and empathy are not part of the revenge pornographer's lexicon; Zoe will, according to her mum, have to 'monitor the internet for the rest of her life, because this stuff, once out there, rarely disappears completely. There are all sorts of implications around this, not least for potential employers.'

Zoe, who has been studying for A levels and wants to work in finance, found out about the betrayal from her boyfriend just after they'd split up, and was devastated. 'Those images were private – and I'd trusted my boyfriend to keep them that way, forever. He just said to me, "You are on a website called Dontchawish.com,"' she recalls, '"and you might want to do something about that!" And then he told me he was going on holiday. I haven't seen him since and I don't want to. He's dead to me now.'

Zoe warns others of the potential dangers and hopes that revenge porn – effectively the distribution of a private sexual image of someone without their consent and with the intention of causing them distress – will, in the future, be made an offence. 'Revenge porn knows no borders. When my material first started going viral, straight away I was on a site that was outside of this country. And, while I'm determined that this horrible experience won't ruin my life,' says Zoe, 'I'm just as determined it shouldn't ruin anybody else's, either.'

You can find out more about Zoe's campaign via her YouTube channel and you can follow her on Twitter, @ZoeSSays.

Gail looked at the picture of Zoe, who, she realized with a start, was no longer just long and skinny and leggy, but somehow now properly beautiful, and then she refolded the paper neatly and took a sip of tea, thinking about relationships and their unexpected consequences and then, more specifically, about Zoe's experience. Still, thought Gail, a girl as beautiful and as blessed as Zoe can turn even horrible things like this to her advantage. She'll end up modelling, or on *Big Brother*.

Gail peered out at the garden, distractedly noting that it needed a mow, but also . . . Oh my God! Something very exciting had happened that, what with all the recent chaos, Gail hadn't noticed until now. Had it, in fact, just happened *today*?

Gail unlocked the kitchen door and walked across the lawn to the beds that bordered Mike's boundary. Yes! There were six unfurling buds on the rich pink and yellow 'Bowl of Beauty', the 'Sarah Bernhardt' was coming along too and the extraordinary 'Angel Cheeks' was already in full show-stopping glory.

'Hazza? *Harry!* Come and look at these. Your granddad planted them and they've just come out.' Harry was doing keepy-uppies at the other end of the lawn. He was good at football . . . But still, Gail thought . . . 'Second thoughts, Hazza, you're all right – don't come anywhere near here with your ball.'

She kneeled on the lawn and watched the bloated honey-bees hovering greedily above the bed filled with the feminine, fragile-yet-powerful, late-blooming peonies. 'Peonies from heaven,' as her dad always said; you're beautiful. They'd always been her favourites – flowers that rewarded patience and that, on arrival, announced, 'Your summer is finally here . . .'

## 44

Despite her exhaustion, Eve enjoyed the slightly disorientating feeling that comes of boarding a plane in one climate and disembarking in another. She peered out of the window as the plane taxied to a standstill, heat haze shimmering on the runway's tarmac. Outside, on the steps, just inches away from the air con, the heat hit her like a fat, heavy wave and she had the feeling that even a thirty-second walk to the transit bus would allow the sun to leave its mark on her genetically Celtic skin. Eve didn't really do sun directly, didn't sit in it ever, far less prostrate herself on beaches. She was, by nature and inclination, a lurker-under-parasols, but that didn't mean she didn't like having sun around her – preferably just out of reach.

'What do you think so far?' Eve turned to a smiling Alice. Silence. She tugged off her daughter's headphones. 'I said . . . What. Do. You. Think. So. Far?'

'Cool,' said Alice.

Eve smiled. 'And yet also the exact opposite of that – phew!' She fanned herself.

'Hot flush, Mum?' asked Alice, wide-eyed and faux-innocently.

'Something like that, yes. It is about ninety degrees.'

'Is that in old money?'

'Ha! Yes. Anyway, after we get our bags, we're apparently only about twenty minutes from a pool,' said Eve. 'And I shall this say only once—'

'SUNBLOCK!' said Alice. 'I know. And I also know you'll say it, like, nine hundred and thirty-seven thousand times in the next ten days.'

Eve sighed. Alice was right, but tomorrow, with a bit of luck, she might even start to relax.

Both of them slept deeply that first night: early to bed and early to rise, the better to enjoy their morning foray without the searing heat. It didn't take long to slip into the siesta-orientated swing of things when the alternative was being exhausted and frazzled. Yes, today was definitely the time to strike while the iron was merely warm. Eve was given impressively detailed driving instructions from the hotel's front desk, but apparently the drive in their hired Seat should only take about twenty minutes, door to door, even though the natives habitually did it in well under fifteen.

'We're in no rush,' said Eve. 'Just keen to make it one piece.'

'Well, it's a really gorgeous spot there, just outside Portinatx, which is one of my favourite beaches,' said the boutique B&B's English owner – precisely the kind of deeply tanned, glamorously boho, coolly accessorized Jade Jagger-y kind of thirty-something who made Eve feel like a particularly pale and uninteresting fifty-three-year-old mother-of-two from East Sussex. 'The address you're looking for is one of *the* most amazing new houses on the island – El Paradiso, which everybody slows down to get a peek at when they drive past. Enjoy your morning!'

It took Eve and Alice over half an hour to travel the six or so miles to El Paradiso, mostly because they kept slowing down to look at things and even, at one point, stopped to scrump four large oranges from a branch overhanging their side of the road and which were therefore, according to Eve, 'perfectly nickable'. It was just after nine a.m. and definitely heating up when Alice finally spotted the low-key white gateposts and hand-painted sign.

'El Paradiso! Look, *there!*'

'Well spotted!' said Eve. 'And the gate's open, too.'

As they drove up the shady drive towards the large, low, white single-storey building – relatively modest from this angle, but, Eve guessed, presumably less so once inside – Eve was silently nervous. Alice, on the other hand, was not.

'Wow,' said Alice. 'I mean – *wow.*'

'Yes.' Eve sighed.

'Mum, imagine living here?' Alice's eyes were like a Japanese anime character's.

'I can't, really,' said Eve, 'more's the pity. Right, shall we just see if anybody's in?'

Eve parked in the shade beside a beaten-up white

pick-up with its keys still in the ignition. Alice rapped the knocker against the heavy dark-wood door – the house was virtually windowless, impregnable-looking from this angle – and added a resonant *ting-a-ling* on the proper big bell hanging on the wall beside it. They waited, shifting from foot to foot. Then, finally, muffled, from the other side of the door came the sound of a voice coming closer – an English and, more specifically, male, *London* voice. And then quite distinctly there was an amused-but-resigned sounding, 'All right, all right – whatever, don't put yourself out. I'll get this.'

The door swung open to reveal a tanned, smiling, good-looking man in his late thirties. He was wearing denim shorts, a faded pink Superdry T-shirt and black Birkenstocks.

'Morning! What can I do you for?'

'Oh, er – hi!' said Eve. She held out her hand. 'My name's Eve Sturridge and this is Alice. I think we're expected. Anyway, it's lovely to meet you, Mr . . . ? God, I'm so sorry; I realize I don't actually know your name.'

The man smiled and opened the door wider. 'I'm so sorry, Mrs Sturridge, I didn't recognize you off duty in your summer mufti. I'm Joe Parker; we've not met properly. But I am literally "Parker" to Anette's "Lady Penelope".' Eve grinned. 'I know,' said Joe. 'She's the spit, right? Come in; come in. Everybody else is out the back, by the pool – no surprise, I'm sure. We've been here just over a week, now, and seem to have a routine going.'

'Thanks very much – that's extremely kind of you.'

Eve and Alice stepped into the cool, dark hallway and, as their eyes adjusted, looked around as they followed Joe. The house turned out to be nothing short of astonishing on the inside. Wildly modern with brightly coloured walls, it was a hip interior designer's dream-home-cum-gallery. Perched on the side of a cliff overlooking the sea, the house unfolded over several layers, with a vast glass wall to enjoy the view. Outside, a stone terrace wrapped round the building and led down to a huge infinity pool.

'Oh. My. *God*,' said Alice. 'This is the most amazing house, ever!'

Though modernism was not her thing, in this case, Eve was inclined to agree.

'This is a stunning house, Mr Parker.'

'Call me Joe. "Mr Parker" always makes me feel like I've been stopped for speeding and the Old Bill are inspecting my licence. Not – I hasten to add – that that happens very often.'

Joe led them down a set of sweeping marble stairs and then out through a folding glass wall on to the terrace. At this point, there were more sharp intakes of breath from the Sturridges at the close-up sight of the extraordinary, curvaceous pool, designed to look natural – albeit, thought Eve, natural in the style of, say, Tracy Island. Joe grinned. 'And, yes, you're right, the place *is* very nice. One of the perks of our job, me and the missus, is staying here for six weeks every summer and, instead of *being* the staff, having our *own* staff – though we inevitably end up doing a bit of babysitting for the boss. We're lucky – all the cousins get on. Usually. Well, they are today . . .' Joe broke off and, peering closely at Eve, narrowed his eyes. 'You know that I'm married to Anette's sister?'

Eve shook her head and shrugged. 'I didn't, no.'

But Joe was already moving out of earshot, towards the pool. 'Birgitte! Kids! We have guests.' Five children of various ages and sizes and, apart from one brunette, a similar degree of blondeness climbed out of the pool: three boys and two girls, accompanied by a slim, very attractive, bikini-clad blonde woman in her thirties. The Sturridges, outnumbered, shuffled from foot to foot.

'Hi!' said the woman, smiling and holding out a damp hand. 'You must be Eve? I'm Joe's wife, Birgitte, mother of two of these.' She nodded towards the kids, who, having lined up, now looked like the cast of *The Sound of Music*. 'You could try to guess which were which, but I would forgive you for getting it wrong; from a distance I can't always tell them apart myself. Anyway, from left to right, we have Alvar, Byrge, Petrus, Aija and Chanelle. Joe didn't get a look-in on the baby names, as you can tell.'

Joe shrugged. 'Just as well, or they'd probably have been Kevin and Ron. Anyway, the first two are ours, the second two belong to my sister-in-law and the last one is Aija's best friend, who is here as her guest.'

'Hello, Aija, Petrus, *Chanelle*,' said Eve, smiling at a

lightly tanned and apparently very much at home Chanelle Billings. 'How are you? Having a good time?'

'Totally! It's awesome, Mrs Sturridge!'

'Of course, you all know each other. I am stupid!' said Birgitte, slapping her forehead with her palm. 'D'oh!' The children giggled.

'Don't be silly; no reason why you should remember me at all. But –' Eve waved towards the pool – 'I do feel you ought to know that there's definitely more kids in that pool. Had you not noticed?'

Birgitte smiled and nodded. 'Yup, we have all the Percy kids here too. Anette thought Mr and Mrs Percy – who are her next-door neighbours, of course – would appreciate some time to spend with Michael this summer. And, of course, farming families rarely get to go abroad for holidays, so . . .' She shrugged. 'They all seem to be having a good time, but they do burn very easily, so we are getting through a lot of sunblock. And they're not convinced by the food, but we're working on it.'

'That's so lovely. I'm sure they're having a marvellous time. Which reminds me – Alice?'

Alice rolled her eyes. 'Yup. *Sunblock*. I'm on it – and it's on me. And *I love* the food.'

Birgitte laughed. 'Now, Alice, would you like a swim?' Alice nodded. 'Excellent. We have loads of spare pairs of swimmers in the pool house, if you haven't got any with you right now. Aija and Chanelle, show Alice where to get changed, yeah?'

'Cuppa? Unless you fancy something cooler?' said Joe.

Eve shook her head. 'Actually a cuppa would be perfect.'

'Then I'll stick the kettle on. Sit wherever you like, inside or out, make yourself comfortable. Anette will pop up in a bit. She likes to ride in the early mornings, so she's probably still at our stables.'

As Joe and Birgitte retreated to the kitchen, Eve squinted towards the pool-house cabana, where the kids were hopping in and out, grabbing lilos and noodles and chucking them into the pool. Eve noted with amusement that the fabulously chic pool now resembled an exceptionally well-appointed civic leisure centre. She watched as Alice, who emerged from the cabana in a pretty, *tiny* emerald-green bikini, dived a perfect arc into the deep end and emerged, grinning and spluttering, to applause from the younger kids, and Eve.

As she clapped, she noticed a woman appear through a discreet gate very close to the pool and head towards the terrace. Eve slipped on her shades and squinted some more – the sun was very bright by now – and, though the woman was backlit, Eve could immediately see that it was Anette Sorensen, barefoot, wearing a large white shirt over a black bikini top and denim shorts. Her hair was tied up in a scarf and her sunglasses were pushed up on to her forehead. When she spotted Eve, she smiled and gave a cheerful little wave.

God, thought Eve. Even though this is why I'm here, it's

still potentially pretty awkward. Yet, instinctively, she scrambled to her feet.

Anette was still smiling when she stopped at the table and held out both her hands, taking Eve's and, disconcertingly, squeezing them gently. 'Eve. Thanks so much for coming. And I see Alice is making herself at home in the pool. Marvellous. Ah, tea! Perfect! Thank you so much, Joe.'

Eve noted, not for the first time, how Anette Sorensen's breathily lilting vocal tones had an extraordinarily relaxing effect. She'd make a brilliant hypnotist. Eve felt that, although there might well be some awkward moments to come, things might – just – work out OK.

'You should know – that is, if you don't already – that I removed the children from Ivy House the moment I'd heard you had left.' Anette sighed. The first hint of tiredness Eve had noticed. 'It has been a very busy time, working out what to do next. In so many ways.'

'Yes – yes, it has. And, um,' Eve steeled herself, 'Mr Sorensen? How is his, uh, situation?'

The sun was so bright that Eve could just detect the hint of a frown behind Anette's big and very dark glasses. 'Well, Stefan has been bailed. He is sorting out some business and then he'll be joining us next week.' A pause. Anette pushed the glasses back on top of her head. 'After you've left. The arrest is in error, I can assure you, Eve. Mr Dershowitz is, however, still under arrest.'

'I had heard that, yes.' Eve hoped she was striking the

right tone, but it was almost impossible to judge. 'It must be very difficult for Anna.'

'It will all be resolved very soon, believe me. I think it has been something of a, er, wake-up call for Stefan, but the inconvenience and embarrassment will be temporary; rest assured, he is guilty of no impropriety.' Another pause. 'No *financial* impropriety.'

Eve chose her words carefully. 'Well, I'm glad this is a temporary professional hiccup for Mr Sorensen.' Are we going to dance around this bloody great elephant all day?

At which point, Anette might have read her mind. She gave a polite little cough and took a sip of tea. 'Here is the thing, Eve: I feel very bad for Zoe. For her Odense experience being so, ah –' she broke off, apparently deliberating over her choice of words – 'deeply disappointing and, naturally, very upsetting for you, as a mother. However –' another small cough – 'that's as maybe. We can talk about it; I'm sure we need to. But first, can I tell you a little bit about me, if you don't mind?'

Disarmed, Eve shook her head. She'd meant to nod. 'Please, go ahead.'

So, Anette started at the beginning and told Eve how, as a mysteriously bourgeois child of hippy parents, she had always yearned to live in a shiny executive home with a stay-at-home mother and a father she barely saw, who wore suits to go and do his Important Work. She told Eve she'd dreamed of riding a pink bicycle with handlebar streamers around a cul-de-sac and then returning home to play with a Barbie in an airy bedroom of wall-to-wall carpets, neatly fitted wardrobes and walls covered with posters of ponies. She really hadn't wanted to live in a caravan in a boggy field and have her fringe trimmed with pinking shears or ride to school on a fat little pony with no saddle and spend all day at that school having the mickey taken out of her relentlessly by her fellow students because she was invariably wearing wellingtons indoors, often with no socks, and her jumpers were knitted – badly – by her mum.

And then, Anette told Eve, when her parents had finally left their eco-commune and moved back to Copenhagen, she had begged them to let her try for a scholarship to a posh private school where the girls wore crisp navy uniforms. And so they did, and she won her scholarship and, because her parents weren't at all poor, just slumming, she was therefore able to board – so she did that, too. And then, pretty soon, she'd reinvented herself from the slightly grubby daughter of pothead hippies to the sleekly sophisticated creature who had won Miss Denmark and then, on her first day at university, the heart of Stefan Sorensen – a man who had actually grown up in a shiny executive home in a cul-de-sac. Eve listened, fascinated, as Anette confessed that she had never stopped moving away, very fast, from her quite literally messy childhood ever since.

'And I made myself become that "normal" girl who had grown up in a "normal" home – indeed, almost a parody of that, in fact, when I entered Miss Denmark, which was precisely the kind of thing my parents despised. And nobody knew any different because I never invited them back to my real home. I mean, why would I? By that time, my parents lived "over the shop" – only their "shop" was a notorious hippy hangout, selling bongs and rolling papers and cannabis-leaf bumper stickers. By the time I got to university, I really was my own reinvented woman. It was just incredibly lucky that I met Stefan, too, because I realized not only that, with him, I didn't want to lie anymore, but also that I could probably make the life for myself that I'd never had and always wanted. Because, you see, he *had* had that life, and he knew how it all worked – and, even more importantly, it didn't scare him at all. He didn't want to live in a caravan, either; at eighteen, he wanted to live in a nice neat flat close to the train station. And then, later on, when he'd made his first millions, he wanted to live in a nice big house with a garden – near the airport.'

'Well, it's fair to say he pulled that off,' said Eve.

Anette smiled. 'But, of course, you think the very worst of Stefan – and why wouldn't you?' Eve hoped very much that this was a rhetorical question and that she didn't need to reply. 'In your position, I would too, no doubt of that.'

Eve couldn't help herself. 'But what about *your* position? After all, your husband slept with –' sharp intake of breath – 'my teenage daughter.' And, as she spoke, Eve's eyes followed Alice as she swam a perfect length of the pool at a leisurely crawl. Despite the heat, Eve shivered.

'It's true, and he's an idiot, of course! But both of them admit it was consensual and, as he knows well enough, I have a ban on youngsters. I can only assume he thought Zoe wasn't as young as she is and that, for her part, Zoe did nothing to dispel that belief. Stef and I have an arrangement that works for us. It would not work for everybody.' Anette shrugged. 'Maybe, despite all of *this* –' she waved a hand – 'I am more hippy child than I care to admit. My sister certainly is. She works for me, as does Joe, and they live in a lovely home on the estate, but she'd be just as happy in a tent. I know it. And she's a devoted home-schooler. Me –' she shrugged again – 'I believe in schools. Which brings me neatly to Heatherdown.'

Eve's eyes widened. Anette smiled.

'After a long conversation with your friend, Cathy, who explained very clearly and concisely the terms and conditions surrounding, uh, Stefan and Zoe –' Anette's tone was entirely without animosity – 'well, then I had a conversation with Mr Salter, who had nothing but good things to say about you.' Eve looked baffled, shook her head. 'Yes, Tony Salter. After that conversation and some discussion with my legal team, followed by a call to Adam Vine, I have bought Heatherdown School. So, for every square-peg kid stuck in a nice executive home in a cul-de-sac, dreaming of campfires and climbing trees, woodsmoke and camaraderie – well, there will be a school for them, scholarships on tap.' Anette shrugged. 'But, of course, the real point of this meeting, the reason why I invited you to El Paradiso when Cathy told me you were coming to Ibiza with Alice, was for me to offer you a job, Eve. To, ah, when the deal is done – which I have every confidence it will be, because the terms are attractive to all parties – offer you Heatherdown to run, as head. Adam, meanwhile, is moving to Denmark, where he will help to set up a sister school.'

Still Eve remained silent.

'And this is not just for you, Eve, but for *my* children, too – and indeed for all those other children out there who, whether or not they know it yet, may need a Heatherdown.'

Eve was entirely lost for words. She couldn't quite make sense of what Anette was saying but . . . I must try to sound like a head teacher, at least: 'Well. Of course, I am incredibly flattered – and astonished, frankly, Anette. But—'

Anette interjected. 'Don't "but" me, please, Eve. Don't even bother answering right now. Frankly, you will need time to think, of course. I don't even own the school yet, so there are many things to discuss. The paperwork is underway. I just wanted you to agree in principle. And, while you are thinking about that, I hope you and Alice will relax on the island. And, should you need to talk to me anytime in the next ten days, then I shall be very easy to find. I shall mostly be right here, by the pool, with the kids, or, at sunup and sundown, on a horse. More tea?'

'Thank you, yes.' Eve sat in silence for a moment or two. Then: 'Do you mind me asking you something very personal, Anette?'

'No. If I can answer it, I will. Shoot.'

'Do you think your marriage works because of or despite Stefan's extramarital, uh, behaviour?'

'It's a good question. I think, for most people, it might not work. And I don't say that with any kind of sense of superiority. In truth, a faithful husband would be preferable to an unfaithful one, of course. But the fact is that having a great deal of money can free you up from the pettiness of life. By which I mean that it offers the chance to engage with a bigger, more important picture. Do you see?' Eve nodded. She sort of *did* see. Anette continued. 'By being together, Stefan and I are able to do things we could not so successfully achieve apart. I like to make a difference and if the price I have to pay for that is a husband who sometimes sleeps with other women because he can – and this is, like so many high-achieving men, literally the only thing about which he is lazy – then so be it.' A shrug. 'Hurting people wilfully is entirely unacceptable; hurting people accidentally is also undesirable – which is why there is so much regret with Stefan about Zoe, and for me too – but simply sleeping with people is not unacceptable at all, really. It is a small thing, I think, in the big scheme. There are more important things for us all to worry about, no?'

That's very evolved, thought Eve. I'm not sure I could ever be that evolved, even if I woke up to this view every morning for the rest of my life. 'I think part of me is still angry at Simon, even now, after all these years.' Why am I telling Anette this? 'But I think that might be passing. Finally.'

'I'm glad. Now, can I ask you something?'

'Of course.'

'Are you more angry with your daughter or with my husband?'

Eve considered the question. 'I think I've been angry with both of them for different reasons, but I think that will pass, too – partly because I'm sort of seeing someone and he talks a lot of sense. On your own, it's very easy to lose perspective.'

'That handsome head teacher at Eastdene!' Anette tilted her head to one side.

'Yes, Mike. How on earth do you know?'

'My God – they talk of nothing else at the Bell. I think you need to get out more!' The two women met each other's gaze properly for the first time, and laughed. And carried on laughing. At which point, they were joined by Birgitte. 'Listen, Birgitte, I am telling Eve that everybody knows about her and Mike Browning!'

'The delicious Mike Browning. For ages Anette and I were sure he had to be gay because how else could he not have been snapped up by a sexy single mother – no?'

'Like Susie Poe?' said Anette.

'Exactly!' said Birgitte.

Eve followed the conversation, enjoying the fizz of feminine, sisterly humour. And, apart from banter with the daughters, I really don't get enough of this . . . I must call Sonia.

'So,' said Anette, 'if you turn down Heatherdown, I may just have to offer it to Mike.'

Eve laughed. 'I don't think you'd get very far. He's fairly anti independent education.'

'I'm sure you could talk him round.' More laughter. 'Now, please say you'll both stay for lunch? It would be unfair to drag Alice away from her important new role,' said Anette.

Eve glanced over at Alice, busy throwing a succession of happily shrieking Percys into the deep end of what was almost certainly the loveliest leisure-centre swimming pool in the world. 'Thanks, Anette. We accept.'

Nine days later, Eve and Alice hauled their heavy bags (there had been some shopping during the last few days) down to the 'check-in desk' in the lobby of the boutique B&B – a big, fruit-and-flower-laden table in the hallway, at which 'Jade Jagger' – real name, Anastasia – sat with an iPad, sipping a mug of something fragrantly herbal.

'Hi, Anastasia. We're all good to go, albeit reluctantly. Better settle up.'

Anastasia smiled. 'Nothing to settle. All sorted.' She pointed at the door, through which, right on cue, appeared Joe Parker.

'Hi, Eve. Hi, Alice. We've settled the bill for you – this one's on Anette – and you'll have a nice ride home, too. Mr Sorensen arrived an hour ago – I've just dropped him at the house – and his jet has now refuelled and is waiting to pop you both over to Gatwick.'

'Oh, wow! Awesome!' Alice hopped gleefully from foot to foot.

Eve was not so easily swayed, however. 'Oh, no, I really don't think we can – not after Anette's picked up our tab. And we have perfectly good flights on EasyJet.'

Joe pulled a face. 'I thought you might say that. I've just checked the flight and it's delayed until further notice. Engine failed before take-off on the outbound flight from Gatwick, so it's been grounded. Could be hours.'

Alice was literally hopping. 'Oh, Mum! Come *on*!'

Eve wobbled. The thought of sitting inside Ibiza airport for an indefinite period didn't wildly appeal, so, even though it was terrible self-interest if she caved in, it would still be fun for Alice. 'OK, thanks, Joe. We graciously accept. And do give Anette this, too, when you see her.' She handed Joe an envelope, which he slipped into a shirt pocket. 'No probs, Mrs S. Now, let's go, because, it's a funny thing, but even unscheduled flights like to stick to a schedule.' Alice looked suitably baffled. Joe grinned. 'No, Alice, don't worry, I don't get it either.'

# 45

Just over four hours later, in Eve's kitchen, Mike was at the sink, filling the kettle, brow furrowed, intrigued by conversational shifts that included Alice's detailed description of the idiosyncrasies of travelling by private jet, right through to Eve's thoughts about Heatherdown. He did his best to keep up. 'So you think you want to make a go of it, then?'

Eve looked Mike in the eye and took a deep breath. 'Do you know what? I think I do. And, before you ask, no – I have absolutely no idea exactly how that has happened.'

Mike smiled. 'This is good news.'

But Eve wanted further reassurance, even if it sounded slightly needy. 'Though, you don't really approve of me or the job, do you?'

Mike shrugged. 'I think one of the great things about growing up, generally speaking, is discovering that maintaining an entrenched position can compromise other aspects of one's life far more than one would, uh, like.'

'That's very gnomic!' Eve teased.

'What I mean is—'

'I know exactly what you mean. You mean that ideology is one thing but that people are quite another?'

Mike wasn't the blushing type; though, if he had been, this would have been the perfect moment to indulge. 'Yes, that's exactly what I mean. I'm just hoping that isn't a compromise too far.'

Eve took the proffered tea. 'Yes, me too,' she said, smiling. 'Me too.'

'Surprise!'

As she walked into her father's living room, Zoe dutifully arranged her face into a suitably astonished/delighted/appreciative expression. It had clearly been a very smart move to demand, by force, that Alice fess up – on pain of imminent death – if she heard anything *even hinting* that there conceivably, may, possibly, perhaps be anything even vaguely looking like a surprise party in the offing.

Zoe had barged into Alice's room, which was not a place she felt the need to visit very often, and wrinkled her nose at the acres of rosettes and posters of random horse people doing dressage . . . Weirdo. 'If I find out that there is, and you knew about it, I will . . . I'll . . . um . . .' It was important that she followed through; however, Zoe wished she'd given all of this a bit more thought.

'You'll what? Ban me from borrowing your Big Hair? OMG – my life is totally over! How can I go on?' Alice fell on to her bed, clutching her heart, eyes rolling, dying.

'No, I'll think of something much worse.' An image

flashed into Zoe's head of that old movie, *The Godfather*, that she'd once watched with Rob. 'Something horrible to do with Monty – just leave it with me.'

Alice sighed. 'You weren't always such an utter bitch, Zo. You used to be quite nice.'

Zoe started and then stared at her sister. 'I . . . uh . . .' OMG. She was literally about to cry. Her stupid little sister had made her *cry*, for fuck's sake. She wiped her eyes. 'You know I've had a weird time.' She corrected herself. 'No, I'm still having a weird time.' She flopped on to Alice's bed.

'Want to talk about it?' asked Alice.

Zoe appraised her sister. Oddly, she felt that, yes, actually, she might want to confide in someone. Alice wouldn't have been top of her list, obviously, but she'd sort of started to tell Carmen everything a few weeks ago, and then she'd bottled it. 'OK. So. Tell anyone, especially Mum or Dad, and I will kill you, your horse, your dog, your friends—'

'Stop right there. If you say "family", it's not going to work.'

'Oh, ha ha.' Zoe slapped her sister's leg, but not very hard.

'So, go on, then,' said Alice calmly, moving over on the bed to make room for Zoe.

'OK,' said Zoe.

And she did. She told her that, after her recent fifteen minutes of tabloid infamy, Stefan Sorensen had texted her, telling her he was proud of her – which meant that he did have her number, of course – and she'd not only not replied, she'd *deleted the number.* Alice was very impressed by this – and Zoe had liked that.

Thus, three weeks later, when Alice had tapped on her bedroom door and hissed through the gap, 'Yup, there's something going on. It's at Dad's,' Zoe had been sufficiently forewarned to arm herself.

Hence she was wearing exactly the right sort of face right now, as she scanned the room, smiling. 'Wow! Omigod! How *amazing!*' Necessarily avoiding Alice's wry smile, she practically convinced herself.

Her dad handed her a glass of champagne and the room filled with a chorus of 'Happy Birthday' – loudly from Simon, Eve, Mike, Ed, Jordan, Alice, Carmen, Father Ted and Gramma Grace, slightly quieter from everyone else. After which traditional ritual embarrassment, Zoe started to circulate among her friends and her parents' friends and some slightly unexpected grown-ups whom she liked, such as her Aunt Sonia, and Cathy and Johnny. Zoe watched as Cathy introduced Johnny to her Auntie Sonia, and grinned – she could practically feel the pheromones flying between them. How awesome would that be? Auntie Sonia and Johnny Nicholson? Cathy caught her watching and winked; they both grinned. And *then* Zoe's eyes lit upon the random but madly handsome square-jawed man-boy of about her own age who was standing next to Cathy. Omigod, Abercrombie Model is, like, one of Cathy's sons. My godbrother?!

Zoe moved fast. 'Thanks so much for coming, Cathy!'

'Not only an important godmotherly duty, of course,

but a total pleasure too.' Cathy grinned. 'Do you remember Ethan? Year younger than you? Skate dude?'

'Oh. Uh, yeah – hi.' Seventeen? Too young. Then, as if by magic, Alice appeared by her side. Zoe noted that her sister wasn't exactly panting; however, as she smiled at Ethan, there was a definite golden-retriever puppy look about her. God. Zoe rolled her eyes and couldn't resist: 'Oh, hi, Alice! This is Cathy's son, Ethan. Is that, like, loo paper? Stuck to your shoe?'

Alice looked stricken, Ethan pretended not to hear and Cathy shook her head. 'Don't worry, Alice – no loo paper. Your sister is just being–'

'Just being my sister?' Alice shrugged. 'Used to it.'

Ethan grinned. 'At least you've only got one annoying sibling. I've got two.'

Alice shook her head. 'No, I've got two. That's my brother, Jordan, over there.'

Cathy smiled, turned to Zoe and leaned in to whisper in her ear. 'Many happy returns. Now, you probably don't know this, but Ethan and I are both staying at your mum's this weekend – and I'd really love to spend a bit of time with you, alone, before we leave. How does that sound? Maybe a drink tomorrow night, or, if you're busy, we can grab a few minutes on Sunday?'

Zoe smiled – why not? 'Yeah, that would be really nice.'

Cathy smiled and nodded. 'One of the great things about godmothers, theoretically, is that they have all the good bits of mums, but without having a mum's agenda.'

Zoe nodded. 'Cool.'

'I hope so. Now, go off and enjoy being eighteen. Little Zoe, eighteen! How can that be?'

Zoe grinned. 'And now you sound exactly like my mum.'

Much later, pouring another glass of wine for herself and her sister, Zoe said, 'Sorry about the loo-paper thing. And I probably owe you for alerting me. Think of anything?'

'Yeah, I can,' said Alice, eagerly.

'Shoot.'

So Alice did. And Zoe nodded. 'It's totally impossible, you know that, but I'll see what I can do.' She patted Alice patronizingly on the head. 'Now, stop following Ethan around like a saddo. I'm going off soon to, er . . .'

'Find something you're entitled to vote for? And then get a tattoo?'

'Lunch is served!' shouted Simon.

Zoe laughed — she already had a tattoo, but not one that Alice was ever going to see — and Alice smiled. She liked it when her sister found her funny, which she used to do a lot. 'Exactly,' Zoe said. 'But first, obviously, lunch.'

As they queued for the buffet, laid out under a gazebo in the garden, Zoe found herself standing next to her mother. 'So, have you thought any more about what you'll be doing this academic year?' said her mum, in the new, slightly formal, adult-to-adult sort of tone she'd started using ever since all the *stuff* had happened.

Zoe nodded. 'Yeah, I think I'd like a gap year, after all.

Bit of travelling? I've got my savings, and Father Ted says he'll top me up. Mike says that, if I don't have a gap year now, I never will. He says that they didn't even exist when he was a teenager, but he quite fancies having one when he's fifty.'

'Did he now?' Eve smiled; Mike's fiftieth was in six months' time.

'He also says that I could do modelling in my gap year.' Zoe shrugged. 'Lucrative, but I dunno. Standing around pouting? Boring.'

Eve looked at her daughter, who generally did a very good job of standing around pouting, entirely unpaid. She was currently wearing the very tiniest cut-off denim shorts Eve had ever seen and a barely-there sequinned halter top. On this evidence, there was no doubt in Eve's mind that Zoe could 'do modelling'.

'Well, yes,' she said. 'Though, if high finance is a high-stakes, cut-throat business, I suspect it has nothing on fashion.'

Zoe raised an eyebrow. 'Mum. Can I tell you something about Alice?'

'Of course – as long as it's not telling tales.'

'Look, she knows that five very average GCSEs are never going to be enough to get her a place in the sixth form at Westdene. The thing is, what she really, *really* wants is to do a BTEC in Horse Management.' Zoe waited a beat. 'At Hartsmere.'

Eve raised an eyebrow and nodded slowly. 'Is that so?'

'Yes. She wants a career with horses and she doesn't see any point in wasting anybody's time – not least her own – doing stuff she isn't remotely any good at, and doing it badly.' Zoe shrugged. 'And I kind of see her point, even if you won't. And the other thing – and she won't tell you this herself because she doesn't want to hurt your feelings, but I can – is that she wants to live here, with Dad and Ed, so she can see more of Jordan. Jordan loves horses; a total natural with them, apparently. Alice is teaching him to ride Monty.' Zoe paused. 'Did you even know that?'

Eve raised her eyes and shook her head. 'No, I didn't know that.'

'Well, you do now.'

It was a lot for Eve to take in; however, there was no opportunity to do so at that precise moment because Zoe and Eve were distracted by a small commotion from the direction of the kitchen and, with it, the arrival – accompanied by an excited 'Ta-da!' fanfare from Alice, who announced, 'This just arrived with its very own chauffeur!' – of a vast and glamorously boxed bouquet of flowers.

Eve smiled, fabricating a disingenuous, 'So what's all this, then?' – because she knew what this was – as she watched Zoe park her laden plate on a table in order to inspect the flowers and open the accompanying fat envelope.

Zoe stared at the card inside the envelope for the longest time; Eve and Alice and Simon and Ed stared at her. 'It's from my godmother!' Zoe glanced up. 'It says, *With my very best wishes for a perfect eighteenth birthday! Love Cathy.'* Zoe wiped away a tear and then glanced up in time to catch a fleeting nod and a wink and a smile from Cathy, who mouthed, 'Happy birthday!'

'And that's a very fat envelope for a card,' said Alice. 'What's in it? Like, a million pounds?' Everybody laughed.

'Shut up, Alice,' said Zoe warmly, extracting a pretty, pink leather document-wallet from inside the fat envelope. She opened it. 'Omigod!' said Zoe. *'Omicompletelybloodygod!'*

Alice: 'I was right. It *is* a million pounds!'

'No, no, it's not a million pounds, but –' Zoe's face lit up; it was the first time anybody had seen that proper big, beautiful Zoe smile in a long time – 'it *is* a gap year! It's a cheque for, like, five thousand pounds!'

Alice's eyes widened. 'For, like, real?'

'For like *totally* real!' Zoe looked around for her friend. 'Yay, Carmen! We're *totally* having a gap year!' And then she looked around for Cathy, who, very keen to avoid a fuss, was nonetheless doing a very bad job of trying to hide behind one of the gazebo's spindly legs. Zoe ran towards her godmother and threw her arms around her neck. 'My God, my godmother! Thank you!'

Simon raised an eyebrow and a glass and clinked it against Eve's. 'Well! Let us heartily congratulate ourselves on picking the right godmother. I hope to God Sonia comes through as impressively for Alice in a couple of years' time. Cheers!'

Eve smiled and rolled her eyes. 'Yes, that would be lovely, wouldn't it? I'll flag it up.'

Glancing at her ex-husband, Eve wasn't entirely sure if Simon had picked up on her sarcasm, but realized, to her mild surprise, that in fact she wasn't really bothered either way.

# 47

It was just past nine on the first evening of Ivy House's summer holidays, when the doorbell rang. Gail disliked cold callers generally, even friends, and liked them a great deal less in the evenings, when she was halfway through a fine episode of *Nurse Jackie*. However, she didn't want to be a curtain-twitcher, so she paused the TV reluctantly, took a deep breath and opened the door. At which point she quickly arranged her face into the correct sort of expression while noting that, regrettably, she was wearing an XXXL grey marl onesie and Harry's Christmas present to her: novelty Rudolph slippers, complete with red nose and antlers.

'Hi, Gail, sorry about turning up on your doorstep unannounced like this – I just needed a quick word, if I could?' said Tony Salter, with, Gail liked to think, only the very briefest of glances at her slippers.

She coughed slightly. 'Yes, that's fine, Tony. Um, Harry's in bed – done in after cricket club – and I'm just watching a bit of telly –' Gail could hear herself prattling and willed herself to stop – 'but, yes, come on in. I might even have a beer kicking around somewhere. Or wine? Or tea?' Shut up, Gail!

Tony nodded. 'Yes, any of those – all of them, maybe. Shall I take my shoes off?'

Gail nodded. 'If you wouldn't mind.' In the kitchen, she reached for the kettle, then thought better of it. 'Actually, do you fancy a wine? I've got some in.'

'But is it drinkable?'

'I think so. It's a 2006 white Bordeaux. Mike Browning gave it to me for Christmas.'

'Did he now? Your next-door neighbour, am I right?'

'That's right. Lovely bloke – great head teacher, too. Harry loves him.'

'I bet he does.' Tony heaved himself on to a stool at the breakfast bar. 'But, more to the point, do you?'

Gail blushed; however, because she was facing away from Tony, she could at least attempt to brazen it out. 'Well, I think the whole of Eastdene is a little bit in love with him – even Dave, over at the Bell.'

But Tony had already lost interest in Mike Browning. 'Well, I'm sorry to miss seeing the boy.'

'Yes, it's a shame, but he is usually asleep by now. You should've texted.'

'I always assume they're up till two a.m. these days, surfing porn on the internet.'

'No, Tony, that's just *you*.'

Tony laughed. 'Not totally lost your sense of humour

then, Gail? We don't see too much of it in the office, these days.'

Gail ignored this; Tony might not see much evidence of her sense of humour, but other people certainly did. 'OK. So? What can I do for you, Tony?'

He sighed. 'OK, so I'll never give up asking you to marry me, Gail, but if you won't do that – and I'll assume it's still a no – then at least tell the boy the bloody truth, for Christ's sake. He's eleven. He needs a dad.' A pause. 'Actually, he needs *his* dad – and I need *him*, Gail. I need my son in my life.'

Gail could not entirely ignore the beseeching tone. It wasn't the first time Tony had come begging, but it was the first time he'd sounded quite so . . . desperate. What's brought this on? She felt very calm. 'We get on fine without you, Tony. You know I still haven't touched a penny of the maintenance? It's all still there in a savings account, for when he's eighteen.'

'Lousy rate of interest – I've told you over and over I'd invest it better.'

'It's fine. It's a lot of money – it'll be getting on for two hundred grand by the time he's eighteen, I suppose. And, of course, he'll get this house off me, too, one day. Look, he's a good kid; he won't go bonkers and blow it all down Slots of Fun or end up on *Jeremy Kyle*.'

'Don't change the subject, Gail.'

Oh, for fuck's sake, Tony! thought Gail. 'Why not? You spent years and years changing the subject and, now you've decided you want to have the conversation, I'm just expected to fall in? Well, I'm not.' Gail's voice was somehow louder than she'd realized. She saw Tony frowning and running his fingers through his hair, that messy dark cowlick.

'Mu-um? I can't sleep.' Harry was standing in the doorway wearing pyjama shorts, his still-damp shower-hair all over the shop – that needs a trim – and he was clutching his favourite bear. My man-boy, thought Gail, my Mowgli . . . Her heart lurched with love. 'Hello, Tony,' said Harry.

'Hello, Harry,' said Tony. 'Uh, your mum and I were just talking. How are you?'

And then, quite suddenly, looking at them both standing awkwardly in her kitchen, together but apart, Gail was struck forcefully for the first time by the utter absurdity of the entire situation. Bloody hell, this is mad!

'Hazza? Actually, I'm really glad you're awake, because Tony came round hoping to see, er, you!' Her heartbeat quickened.

'Yeah?' said Harry, now leaning against the breakfast bar, rubbing his eyes with his bear-free hand.

'Yeah –' deep breath, one, two, three – 'and that's because he's your dad, Harry. Tony is your father.'

At which soap-opera-style bombshell, albeit (Gail couldn't help noticing) sadly lacking in EastEnders-style cliffhanger-signalling doof-doof-doofs, Harry simply smiled and yawned and stretched his skinny arms above his head. 'Yeah, I know, Mum.'

Gail turned to Tony, eyes wide in shock. Tony shook his head vigorously, as if to say, *No, I didn't tell him!* She shrugged. They both stared at Harry, baffled.

'Fuck's sake! I've always known, since whenever – because I'm eleven and look at us!' Harry turned to Tony. 'But it would've been better if you'd said –' he affected a deep voice and a truly terrible American accent – 'Harry, I'm ya FADDER!'

'What, like Darth Vader to Luke Skywalker?' said Tony. 'And if I ever hear you say the F-word again, I swear to God, you'll regret it!'

'Yeah, exactly like that –' Harry grinned – '*Dad.*'

At which point Gail didn't know whether to laugh or cry, so, in no particular order, she did both.

# 48

A perfect autumnal morning in late September and Eve threw her bag – last year's bag – into the passenger seat and turned the Volvo out of the Barn's gravel drive, driving past the new *For Sale* sign and on, towards Heatherdown.

Fifteen minutes later, she and Anette were wearing hard hats provided by Simon and half watching numerous topless young men swinging around Heatherdown's scaffolding, like a tribe of depilated primates. Both women stood in front of the building for a minute or two in a companionable sort of silence, which was broken by Eve.

'Please don't let me put you off at this extremely late stage, Anette, but I just want you to know that there really is no such thing as the perfect school.' She paused. 'Mind you, having brilliant staff helps a bit. On the subject of which, I spoke to Ellie just before I left. She's on her way.'

'Good.' Anette smiled. 'And don't worry – I didn't imagine there was such a thing as the perfect school. Not yet. It's probably a lifetime's work.'

'Yes, we'll be learning something new every day,' said

Eve, 'which is OK because, actually, if there's *one* thing I've learned in the past fifty-three years, it's that all of life is school.'

Anette nodded and put her finger to her lips. 'But *shhh* – for God's sake, don't tell the kids. Let them find out themselves, yes?'

Eve smiled. 'Definitely.'

# POSTSCRIPT

OFSTED: RAISING STANDARDS,
IMPROVING LIVES

16th September, 2011

Dear Mr Browning and Students,
This letter is provided for the school, parents and carers to share with their children. It describes Ofsted's main findings from the inspection of their school.

## Inspection of EASTDENE COMMUNITY PRIMARY SCHOOL, EASTDENE, EAST SUSSEX

Thank you for making the inspection team so welcome when we visited your school. We enjoyed having the opportunity to meet you and your teachers. You told us that you enjoy your school and particularly appreciate its family atmosphere.

You are especially well served by an interesting and diverse curriculum and a wide range of extra-curricular activities. Your attendance is excellent and we were extremely impressed by the fact that your teachers know you as individuals and teach you very well. You are also exceptionally well behaved and clearly get on well with each other.

So, in summary, I am delighted to be able to say that you go to an outstanding school. You make outstanding progress in your subject areas and the provision made for your spiritual, moral, social and cultural development is also outstanding.

Congratulations on all your hard work. We wish Eastdene Community Primary School the very best for the future.

Yours sincerely,

Jean Starling
Lead Inspector

# ACKNOWLEDGEMENTS

Many thanks to my editor, Jane Wood, for her great skill and continued patience. This one took a bit longer than either of us had hoped but hey, sometimes life gets in the way.

Above-and-beyond thanks to my wise and witty Special Agent, Jonny Geller. Sorry about all those ranty emails, re 'life getting in the way'.

Thanks are also due to everybody at Curtis Brown and Quercus for all their secret agenty/undercover publishery stuff. You are all very clever and exceptionally kind. And so good-looking, too . . .

Thanks to my delightful not-quite-but-nearly-as-good-as 'stepsons', Archie and Noah, for recognising that 'the X-Box room' is, indeed, also my study.

Thanks to all the teachers in all the schools with which I've ever collided. Mostly for having A Proper Job and (mostly) being brilliant at it, but also for taking the boys off my hands between 9 am–3.30 pm so I can do stuff like this. Grateful.

While it turns out that I am absolutely no fun to be around when I'm writing a book, arguably I am even less fun than that when I'm *not* writing a book. So, very big love and extra special thanks to Julian Anderson for putting up with me (nearly) all the time.

Finally, mega Mum-thanks to my extraordinary sons, Jackson and Rider, who not only inspired this book but are (of course) the very coolest, cleverest and handsomest of 'square pegs'. I love you both far more than you will ever know.

# READING GROUP QUESTIONS

1. When you first met Eve Sturridge at the beginning of the book, did you like her? Did you feel more sympathetic towards her as the action unfolded or less?

2. Were you surprised that Eve had managed to retain a close friendship after she learns that Simon is gay? Do you think she should have been harder on him or did you like her tolerant attitude?

3. Did you think Simon and Ed would make good parents for Jordan?

4. What do you think of Gail? Did you agree with her decision to keep Harry's dad a secret from him?

5. Did you think that Eve gave both of her daughters enough time and attention? Did you think she was a good mother?

6. Eve gives Zoe a lot of freedom: did you think it was too much?

7. Zoe behaves quite badly. Did you feel that Eve was to blame for this at all?

8. Do you agree with Eve's changing attitude towards the education of children?

9. Do you feel that young children's education should be about 'book learning' and the three Rs, or do you believe children learn more by having the freedom to exercise their imaginations through creative play?

10. How did you feel about Eve's daughter, Zoe? Did you like her spirit, or did you think she was a spoiled brat?

11. Were you pleased when Zoe got her comeuppance? Did you feel she deserved it?

12. When a young girl flirts with an older man, do you think she's 'asking for it' or do you believe it's the man's entire responsibility to resist?

13. If men and women share nude photos of each other on their smartphones, would you say that's a good idea, or do you think they're running a dangerous risk?

14. Did you sympathize with Rob's actions at all? Could you write them off as revenge for being cheated on, or did you see them as more serious?

15. At the end of the book, did you feel that everyone got the ending they deserved?